W.J. Burley lived in Newquay in Cornwall, and was a schoolmaster until he retired to concentrate on his writing. He died in 2002.

By W.J. Burley

A Taste of Power
Three Toed Pussy
Death in Willow Pattern
Wycliffe and How to Kill a Cat
Wycliffe and the Guilt Edged Alibi
Death in a Salubrious Place
Death in Stanley Street
Wycliffe and the Pea Green Boat
Wycliffe and the School Bullies
The Schoolmaster
Wycliffe and the Scapegoat
The Sixth Day
Charles and Elizabeth
Wycliffe in Paul's Court
The House of Care
Wycliffe's Wild-Goose Chase
Wycliffe and the Beales
Wycliffe and the Four Jacks
Wycliffe and the Quiet Virgin
Wycliffe and the Winsor Blue
Wycliffe and the Tangled Web
Wycliffe and the Cycle of Death
Wycliffe and the Dead Flautist
Wycliffe and the Last Rites
Wycliffe and the Dunes Mystery
Wycliffe and the Redhead
Wycliffe and the House of Fear
Wycliffe and the Guild of Nine

W.J.BURLEY

WYCLIFFE'S WILD-GOOSE CHASE

WYCLIFFE AND THE QUIET VIRGIN

WYCLIFFE AND THE CYCLE OF DEATH

Wycliffe's Wild-Goose Chase
First published in Great Britain by Victor Gollancz Ltd in 1982

Wycliffe and the Quiet Virgin
First published in Great Britain by Victor Gollancz Ltd in 1986

Wycliffe and the Cycle of Death
First published in Great Britain by Victor Gollancz Ltd in 1990

This omnibus edition published in 2009
by Orion Books Ltd
Orion House, 5 Upper St Martin's Lane
London WC2H 9EA

An Hachette UK company

Copyright © W.J. Burley 1982, 1986, 1990

A CIP catalogue record for this book is available
from the British Library.

ISBN 9781407221137

Printed in Great Britain by Clays Ltd, St Ives plc

www.orionbooks.co.uk

WYCLIFFE'S
WILD-GOOSE CHASE

CHAPTER ONE

Thursday evening. Outside it was raining. The three men sat round the fire in well-worn leather armchairs. Smoke rose from their pipes and drifted along the ceiling between the beams. On the high mantelpiece an alarm clock in a shiny metal case ticked the seconds away, clink-clink, clink-clink . . . Each man had a glass at hand; the major was drinking whisky, the other two, white wine. The room was clean and warm but bare, like a farm kitchen. Apart from the three armchairs there was a large, square kitchen table and four bentwood chairs; there was fibre matting on the floor and a three-legged crock for a coal-scuttle. On the wall opposite the fireplace tiers of shelves were crammed with a tattered collection of books, many of them lacking a spine and therefore anonymous.

Bunny Lane reached for the bottle of white wine which he had placed behind his chair, away from the heat of the fire. 'Can I top you up, Joseph?' Bunny was so called because he had a hare-lip which a black moustache failed to hide and when he spoke his words came with a sibilant whistle.

Joseph, the red-head, held out his glass, 'Thanks.'

Bunny made his own wine, largely from grapes which he grew in the lean-to greenhouse behind the kitchen. 'You all right, Major?'

The major sat back in his chair, his legs stretched to the fire. He was massively built with machine-clipped grey hair which accentuated the Teutonic mould of his skull. He looked at the whisky glass in his hand and said in a gravelly voice, 'I'm well enough.' He had grey eyes which bulged slightly and a steady disconcerting stare.

The fire glowed orange-red with a flicker of flame whenever the coals settled. The major sipped his whisky and sighed; Joseph, the red-head, re-lit his pipe which had gone out. The alarm clock kept up its insistent clink-clink. It was twenty minutes past eight.

Bunny Lane said, 'How are things with you, Joseph?'

Joseph did not answer at once, he smoked his pipe and seemed to be considering. In the end he said, 'I don't know.' Then, after a long pause he added, 'I'm just waiting ...' He made an irritable movement which caused the springs of the old chair to creak. 'I wish to God I'd never agreed to take him in with me!'

The major turned his grey eyes on Joseph. 'Ah!'

Joseph stared into the fire. 'It can't go on much longer ... One way or the other ...'

This was followed by a silence which must have lasted all of five minutes. It was as though they felt the need to atone for such prodigality with words. Bunny rose from his chair and with a pair of tongs took several lumps of coal from the crock and placed them carefully on the fire, then he resumed his seat. The major was the first to speak again.

'What do you say to a game?' He moved round in his chair so that his gaze rested on the box of dominoes which stood ready in the middle of the wooden table.

Without a word the other two got to their feet and, carrying their glasses, moved to the bentwood chairs. The major joined them, towering over the table for a moment before sitting down. Then came the rattle of the dominoes being tipped from their box, the shuffling, the draw, and the silence while they considered their hands. They played with a minimum of words. From time to time Bunny got up to see to the fire or to recharge their glasses. There was a longer interruption while he opened a fresh bottle of wine. The major continued to drink whisky to which he added very little water and as the evening wore on his movements became slower and more deliberate though no less precise and his eyes lost all trace of expression. The only sounds came from the placing of the dominoes, the clink-clink of the alarm clock and occasional crepitations from the fire.

At twenty minutes to eleven, when they had finished a game, the major stood up and, carefully enunciating his words, said, 'I must be going; I wish you both good-night.'

Joseph got up from his chair, 'I'll come with you, Major.'

Bunny saw them to the door. It was still raining. In the tiny front passage the major struggled into his duffle coat but went bareheaded; Joseph put on his fawn raincoat and tweed hat. They muttered good-nights then set off together, Joseph's stocky figure dwarfed by the major's bulk.

Bunny Lane's little house and his workshop formed part of a square of terraced houses. The two men came out of the square and turned down the hill towards Bear Street with the rain driving in their faces. Bear Street, a narrow, ill-lit shopping street was deserted. Joseph stood by his antique shop and let himself in by the side-door.

'Good-night, Major.'

'Good-night! Good-night to you, Joseph.'

The major continued along the street then turned up Dog's Leg Lane towards Garrison Drive.

Hetty Lloyd Parkyn, the major's sister, was in her little sitting-room, sandwiched between the drawing-room and the kitchen. It was a long time since they had used the drawing-room – certainly not since the death of their father. Hetty had her sitting-room on one side of the passage, Gavin's was on the other. Hetty's would have seemed shabby and bleak to a lonely old maid struggling to survive on her pension. The upholstery of the two armchairs was so worn that no pattern was discernible, the carpet was threadbare and the curtains sagged where hooks had come adrift. She sat in one of the armchairs, reading, and placed near her chair was an old-fashioned oil-stove with a red window and a fretted top which gave off a moist, smelly heat.

Hetty was tall and big-boned like her brother, but lean and gaunt; her hair and eyes were grey and her skin seemed to have been bleached of all natural colour. As she read she reached out from time to time to a paper bag of white peppermints.

Somewhere in the house a clock struck eleven and almost at once her sharp ears caught a sound from the back of the house; she heard a door open and shut, a key turn and a bolt shoot home. A moment or two later there were footsteps in the passage, the door of her room opened, and her brother's great bulk almost filled the doorway. His grey hair was darkened by rain, droplets of water stood out on the coarse material of his duffle coat and water dripped from his trousers to the floor.

He stood without speaking, gazing at his sister with expressionless eyes.

Hetty scarcely looked up from her book. 'There's some soup in the saucepan on the stove if you care to heat it up.'

The major turned away, closing the door behind him. She heard him fumbling about in the hall, removing his coat; then heavy slow footsteps on the stairs; he was on his way to bed.

Two nights later – Saturday evening – Joseph Clement sat at his desk by a first-floor window which overlooked the backyard of his house and shop and the backyards of

8

neighbouring houses in Bear Street. Outside, in the leaden dusk, rain fell vertically, unhurried and unremitting. Joseph's room had the unmistakable aura of a cell, a place of refuge from the world. It was a bedsitter, not because of a shortage of rooms in the house, but because Joseph chose to spend as much of his time as possible ensconced with his stamps, his albums and catalogues, his books on English furniture and his notes for a projected history of philately.

The yellow light from a naked bulb fell on his red hair and on a little heap of stamps, each in its polythene envelope: a selection from the early issues of Guatemala, sent to him by a correspondent there. He picked up his forceps and magnifier and bent his head to the task of examining them. But the thrill of the chase was lacking for he had not yet succeeded in shutting out his troubles from the little room, they trailed after him as inexorably as Marley's train of cash-boxes. He persevered because he knew that in the end he would become absorbed; the atmosphere of his burrow would work on him as surely as a sedative drug and he would recapture something of the contentment which, not so long ago, he had accepted as his normal state of being.

He was pleased with two surcharged *quetzal* stamps of 1881, they were not valuable but they filled a gap in his collection; and by three rarer values in the commemoratives for the Central American Exhibition of 1897, one with an unrecorded flaw in the portrait of Barrios.

His breathing settled to a gentle, regular rhythm, his thick fingers which had red hairs on their backs manipulated the stamps with an acquired skill; the slightly humid stuffiness of the room enveloped him and the little clock on his desk ticked the seconds away. It grew darker outside until the window panes were shining black squares. Fifteen minutes to eight.

A buzzer sounded in the passage, someone at the side-door. Joseph got up with a sigh, pushing back his chair. He moved heavily, ponderously, in the manner of an older, bigger man. He was forty-five and though stockily built, by no means fat. He went out into the passage, down the stairs, and opened the side-door. A man in a mackintosh stood there, clutching a leather bag, his shoulders hunched against the rain.

'I'm Waddington, I've come to see Dave Clement; he's expecting me.'

The man made a move to come in and Joseph reluctantly stood aside. 'You'd better come through the shop to the office.' He closed the side-door and opened another which led into the dark cavern of the shop. 'This way!' Without putting on any lights Joseph threaded his way through the stock-in-trade of the antique shop to the office at the back but it was only when he switched on the light there that Waddington was able to follow him.

Waddington came blinking out of the darkness, a weedy specimen, long and lank and sallow as though grown in a poor light. Yet he must have cared for his appearance for the narrow bands of hair which linked sideburns to moustache had been lovingly cultivated. He looked round the office with suspicion. 'Where's Dave?'

'He's out at the moment but I'm expecting him back.'

David Clement stood naked in the shower, sponging himself. He was as unlike his brother as could be imagined, slight of build, very dark, with small bones and delicate features which were almost feminine. He was on the wrong side of thirty while the girl on the bed had several years to go.

'What's the rush tonight?' She put her legs over the side of the bed and sat watching him, scratching her breasts and yawning.

'Waddy is coming at eight.'

'*Waddy*? What does he want?'

Clement reached for a towel. 'I don't know but I can guess.'

'Can he make trouble?'

'Only for himself; he's a stupid bastard.'

'You won't let them talk you out of it?'

'No chance!' He came over and stood by her, rubbing himself down. 'I've told you, Mo, I'm getting out and there's nothing they or anybody else can do to stop me now.'

'How soon?'

'A month? Six weeks? There's no great rush, is there? One or two things I've got to do – flog *Manna* for a start, but I've already put an advert in next week's issue of *Power Boat* and there should be plenty of offers. Boats like *Manna* don't hang about this time of year.'

The girl continued to look worried. 'Is Waddy coming off his own bat or has he been sent?'

Clement shrugged. 'Probably it's Chalky's doing. Chalky is a shit but he knows too well which side his bread is buttered to try anything on.'

Clement pulled on his briefs and reached for his shirt. The girl got off the bed and walked to the shower; she put on a shower cap and tucked in her long, dark hair. 'Shall I see you tomorrow?'

'I thought I'd spend the day on the boat, Mo – get her into shape for a possible buyer.'

'Pick me up, I'll come with you.'

'You're on nights; you need your beauty sleep.'

She paused in the act of reaching for the shower tap. 'It's not the boat is it? It's some bloody girl!'

'Don't be stupid, Mo!'

'Then pick me up like I said.'

'We'll see.'

Clement was dressed, he ran a comb through his hair in front of the dressing-table mirror. 'I must be off; I don't want Waddy opening his big mouth to brother Joseph.'

Clement left the bedroom, passed through the tiny sitting-room to the box-like hall where his wet mackintosh hung on a peg, put it on and let himself out of the flat.

In Godolphin Street the rain fell steadily. Keeping close to the houses he walked the length of the street then turned left into Bear Street where the narrow roadway gleamed in patches under the street lamps and the only sign of life came from a brightly lit restaurant opposite the antique shop.

Through the windows of the antique shop Clement could see a faint glow of light from the office at the back. He let himself in by the side-door and moved soundlessly through the shop so that he was standing in the doorway of the office before either Joseph or Waddington realized that he was there. Joseph was sitting on one side of the big desk, Waddington on the other and between them, laid out on the blotter, were six paperweights which reflected the light of the lamp in a glowing spectrum of colour.

David said, 'Hullo, Waddy! Got something pretty to sell?'

Sunday. After a cold, wet and blustery fortnight it seemed quite possible that spring had arrived; the air was soft and the waters of the estuary dazzled the eyes with scintillating reflections of the low sun. Soon, God and weather permitting, the Wycliffes would be having friends out to admire their camellias, magnolias, azaleas and rhododendrons. Then, in a little while, there would be the occasional meal out-of-doors and they would spend long evenings working in the garden and go to bed dog-tired but with the comfortable feeling that they had in some way put themselves right with the world.

There was no other house in sight on their side of the estuary and so they had a hoard of privacy, the real hard currency of the century. In these days a half-acre of

12

shrubs and trees may give one feelings of guilt or delusions of grandeur, either way the Wycliffes had made up their minds not to be over-run by the lemmings if they could help it. Sometimes he experienced a twinge from his socialist, non-conformist conscience but Helen was made of sterner stuff.

Half-past seven. They were early risers even on Sundays for no day was long enough for Helen. In her dressing-gown she turned the pages of a gardening magazine while she nibbled her toast and marmalade. (A fat-free breakfast with black coffee.)

Wycliffe said, 'I think I'll walk along the shore and collect the newspapers.' He usually did on fine Sunday mornings.

There were more and more things which they usually did, for their domestic life was beginning to gel now that child raising was over. He was forty-nine, an age at which a man must admit that, technically at least, he is over the hill. The twins were gone – flown almost literally from the nest. David jetted about on behalf of some quasi-governmental agency dispensing scientific largesse to the Third World: Nepal, Ecuador, Lesotho . . . not forgetting regular get-togethers in the Eurocaps. Ruth was almost as mobile. As her boss's personal assistant she regularly trailed him around Europe and to the States; she had been twice to Tokyo and once to the Gulf. And the twins were still only in their middle twenties, about the age at which he had first crossed the channel – by car-ferry – feeling a bit like Captain Cook and wondering if he really could drive on the right.

The upshot of it all was that he and Helen were alone again, and liking it, though mildly disturbed by questions. What had it all been about? Where do we go from here? Why did we . . . ? Perhaps understanding for the first time that this is the real thing – not a dress rehearsal. At any rate he was untroubled by professional ambition; he had climbed as high as he wanted to go – higher, he sometimes thought. The arid plateau of pure administration had no allure; not for him the plush office behind the padded door.

People who knew his background thought he had done well. Son of a Hertfordshire tenant farmer, starting as a trainee copper at nineteen, he had become detective chief superintendent and head of C.I.D. for two counties. Yet he was vaguely dissatisfied; secretly he saw himself as a failure. Where did it all lead? To a pension, an up-market bit of silver and, perhaps, an O.B.E. From one day to the next . . .

'See if they've got any white-wine vinegar at the shop, I've run out.'

The village of St Juliot was a mile or so further up the estuary from the Watch House where the Wycliffes lived; nearer the city. Wycliffe let himself out by a little gate at the bottom of the garden, crossed a rarely used public footpath, and dropped a couple of feet to the shingle beach. At this point the opposite shore of the estuary was only a few hundred yards away and through this bottleneck all the shipping of the busy port had to pass.

Half-an-hour since low water. Oyster catchers explored the muddy margins of the tide and further down the estuary a colony of lesser black-backs, uniformly spaced, faced whatever breeze there was and waited, Micawber-like.

Familiarity did not breed contempt but it dulled the edge of perception. He needed to remind himself from time to time how lucky they were to live in such surroundings and still be within twenty or thirty minutes' drive of his headquarters.

He followed the line of high-water where a tangle of drying wrack was mixed with plastic rubbish and an occasional gobbet of black oil. Pollution troubled him but he tried not to think about it; there were a few things he could do something about, better to think of them.

14

Near the village, where the long narrow back-gardens of the cottages reached the shore, there was a row of upturned dinghies, hauled well above the tide line. Off-shore a dozen or more pleasure craft rode at moorings and in a month there would be many more. Beyond St Juliot, still further up the estuary, the city sprawled over its creeks and hills, snug and smug when international squabbles were settled by cannon balls; now, almost entirely rebuilt after a war with aircraft and bombs and asking itself, What next?

At the end of the village there was a quay, once used for shipping stone from a quarry now derelict. A few yards short of the quay something gleamed in the shingle, not far below high-water mark. As he crunched towards it he saw that it was a gun ... a revolver ... service pattern from the last war ... a .38. He picked it up gingerly and sniffed. Recently fired? He thought so, and still loaded in some chambers. The catch was on.

Many times in recent years he had complained that rank cut him off from the early stages of an investigation. 'You come in when the show is half over.' Not in this case; he was in at the start and he could imagine the headline in the local paper: 'C.I.D. Chief Finds Gun On Beach.'

With a bit of string from his pocket he slung the gun from the trigger guard. Although he had found it below the tide-mark the gun had never been in the sea. High tide had been at one in the morning and it would have taken about an hour to fall to where he had found the gun; so, it must have been dropped there at some time after two – within the previous six hours.

Wycliffe took guns very seriously; he did not like them. A man could be blasted out of existence because of some cretin's panic or anger or hatred. Bang! You're dead! And all the King's horses and all the King's men can't put Humpty together again.

He looked around. No sign of any disturbance in the

shingle but that was hardly surprising, he could not pick out his own tracks.

He climbed the granite steps of the quay, steps that were slimy with bottle-green weed at the bottom and encrusted with grey and orange lichens near the top. Except by going through one of the terraced cottages there was no other way off the beach. Grass pushed up between the stonework of the surface of the quay, making its own thin carpet of soil. At the seaward end four broken-off cast-iron pillars were all that remained of a mechanical contraption for loading stone into ships.

Near the pillars he found three places where the grass had been crushed – as it might have been by the wheels of a parked car or van. Where the fourth wheel would have rested there was no grass to take an impression, only smooth stone. The quay was reached by a lane off the St Juliot road; the lane had once been used by trucks and was still passable in a car. At the shoreward end of the quay there was a turning space and a confusion of wheel marks but no obviously identifiable tread.

The church bell tolled for early communion – the tenor bell, slightly cracked. In the lane, after a fortnight of rain, there was a great deal of black mud, too soft to retain any impression. The lane joined a minor road which, coming from the general direction of the city, meandered through St Juliot, on past the Watch House, to the coast.

Outside his shop Tommy Carne, a dark haired, stocky, pre-Celtic Briton, worked with the energy of the self-employed, unpacking his parcels of newspapers.

'Good morning, Mr Wycliffe! You're a bit early but give me a couple of minutes.'

Too busy to notice whether the superintendent carried a gun or a parasol.

The vicar in his cassock crossed from the vicarage to the church as the bell stopped tolling and raised his hands in distant acknowledgement of a lost sheep. The village was coming to life, curtains were drawn back in upstair rooms, dogs were let out to make their morning rounds, the sluggish Sunday routine was getting under way.

There was a telephone box on a triangle of grass in front of the shop. Wycliffe propped the gun on a ledge while he dialled and fed in a coin.

'Police Headquarters.'

'Superintendent Wycliffe. Give me C.I.D., please.'

'Detective Sergeant Kersey.'

Kersey was a recent acquisition from one of the city divisions, a man who had stuck at sergeant because he concerned himself more with the job than with promotion. Wycliffe was nursing him for a belated reward.

'Any shooting during the night?'

'Nothing in the report, sir.'

'Who is with you?'

'Dixon and Potter.'

'Send them out here to me. Dixon can use a camera so get him to bring one. Call Smithy at home and ask him to meet me in my office as soon as possible, then check this hand-gun with Records – a Webley and Scott, service-pattern revolver . . .'

He made a second call, this time to Helen.

'It's me; something's cropped up.'

'In the village?'

'I found a loaded revolver on the beach. I'll ring later.'

He walked back to the corner of the lane to wait for his men.

If the gun had been fired on the beach or the quay it would have been heard in the village. Even a car driven along the lane at night would have attracted attention. St Juliot nights are serenely peaceful and St Juliot people extremely nosy.

A little girl came out of a nearby house and stood staring up at him with unblinking brown eyes; she had a

17

well gnawed rusk in one hand which she seemed to have forgotten about. A milk float rattled by, bottles and crates clinking. The patrol car arrived with a uniformed driver and Dixon and Potter got out, sniffing the air, wondering whether it offered anything more entertaining than playing cards in the duty room. Wycliffe told them what he wanted and left them to it, then he was driven to headquarters in the patrol car.

The building was wrapped in Sunday morning calm. No typewriters tapped, no telephones rang and the desk sergeant was reading the *Sunday Mirror* with a mug of tea at his elbow. An enquiry which breaks on a Sunday gets off to a slow start because policemen like other mortals want to do their Sunday thing; gardening, fishing, sleeping, taking the kids and dogs for walks, even going to church.

Sergeant Smith joined Wycliffe in his office. Smith had been a member of the headquarters crime squad since before the Wycliffe era, first as a general duties officer and part-time photographer; more recently, after an extended Home Office course, as full-time photographer and finger-print expert. Everything about Smith was grey; clothes, skin, hair and personality, but he was good at his job as long as it kept him away from people; people and Smithy did not mix.

He looked at the gun without touching it while Wycliffe explained. 'They're checking with Records.'

'They won't find anything. Too many of these about – souvenirs of the war. People get worried and ditch them in daft places – ought to have another amnesty.'

'Five chambers loaded and, I'd guess, one recently fired.'

Smith's shaggy eyebrows, like miniature horns, went up. 'Any overnight brawls?'

'Nothing reported. I want you to go over it for prints then send it to Melville.'

Melville was a ballistics expert attached to forensic.

18

Smith looked his surprise. He thought Wycliffe was making a mountain out of a molehill but he also thought that it wasn't his place to say so, which was one of the aggravating things about Smith. He went off with the gun which left a faint oily stain on Wycliffe's blotter.

He thought, Nobody would go to St Juliot to dispose of an unwanted, even an incriminating gun; a gun is small enough to be got rid of unobtrusively amost anywhere, by burying it, throwing it in the river or the sea, even down a street drain.

A body is a different matter, especially if one doesn't want to see it again. But contrary to common belief it is not easy to dispose of a body even in the sea. It has to go into deep water at the right state of the tide and for this one needs a pier or quay – often conspicuous places – or a boat. Wycliffe picked up the telephone and asked to be put through to the harbour master.

'I don't suppose he will be in his office on a Sunday morning so try his home.'

It took a couple of minutes.

'Mr Foster? . . . Wycliffe, C.I.D.' The two men had met at several civic bunfights. 'Sorry to bother you on a Sunday morning . . . '

'Think nothing of it.'

'This is my problem: if you wanted to dispose of a body in the estuary and you weren't anxious to see it again, where would you choose?'

'Somewhere without too many coppers about.'

'All right, but where?'

'I'm thinking.' There was a longish pause before he spoke again. 'I can't think of a better place than the bottom of your garden.'

'But that's a shelving beach—'

'And you haven't got a boat, so if I were you I'd do the next best thing and push it off the end of the quay at St Juliot. If you lived the other side of the estuary I'd suggest Potter's Wharf but that's more overlooked.'

'Why those two places?'

'Because they're both near the entrance to the narrows and anything that goes in there at the right state of the ebb is swept out to sea at a rate of knots. You know that as well as I do.'

'You said, the right state of the ebb – when, exactly?'

Foster considered, muttering to himself. 'Beginning from an hour to an hour-and-a-half after high water and lasting for about two hours. The channel is scoured in that time.'

'And last night, for instance?'

The harbour master jibbed. 'Am I going to have to say all this in court?'

'It's possible, I suppose, but if you do I'll give you a chance to think again.'

A brief interval. 'Well, last night high water was at 00.48; there was a stiff breeze – five to six on the Beaufort scale – from the south-east but that wouldn't have affected conditions in the estuary much . . . I'd say the best time was between three and four in the morning.'

'Thanks. One more question: a body put in the water then, from the quay, would you expect to see it again?'

Foster hesitated. 'Not in the estuary, certainly; and nowhere else for quite a time but it would probably turn up further down the coast in the end – might be two or three weeks later, might be only a couple of days. You know what the sea is, everything depends on winds and currents and they're as unpredictable as women.' Foster had three unmarried daughters living at home.

So it made sense for someone with a body on his hands to drive out to St Juliot to get rid of it off the quay. A body . . . His imagination was running away with him. All he had was a gun with five of its six chambers loaded.

The telephone rang; a man from Records. 'You asked about a hand-gun, sir, a revolver—'

'Hold on while I get a pad.'

'The certificate was issued to Lieutenant-General Sir

20

Gavin Lloyd Parkyn of 3 Garrison Drive and it was last renewed three years ago. Shortly after that there was a break-in at the house and the gun was stolen along with certain valuables.'

'Ammunition?'

'None specified, sir. It was a souvenir weapon.'

Wycliffe had a vague recollection of the Garrison Drive case though he had not been involved. A collection of Japaneserie worth several thousand pounds. At the time he had been on secondment to an inquiry in the north of England, an unsavoury affair involving a senior police officer. He would have to dig in the files.

He turned to the bookshelves. In the field of military knights *Who's Who* never lets you down.

'Lloyd Parkyn, Lt-Gen. Sir Gavin . . . ' His date of birth was given as 1893 which would make him eighty-eight but Wycliffe's *Who's Who* was out of date so the old gentleman might have already passed on. A string of decorations and a record of war service in France and Germany during both wars, 'one *s.* one *dau.*' His wife died in 1950.

The next entry concerned the one *s.* 'Lloyd Parkyn, Maj. (R.M.) Gavin, C.B.E. (1970) D.S.O. (1952) and bar (1952); only *s* of Lt-Gen. Sir Gavin Lloyd Parkyn . . . b,1924; educ. Malvern, King's Coll. Cambridge . . . '

A distinguished family, bordering on the eminent.

It occurred to him that Kersey, before joining his headquarters squad, had been with B Division which included Garrison Drive so it was possible that he had worked on the break-in.

He found Kersey in the duty room in Sunday isolation; a cigarette stuck in one corner of his mouth, jabbing away at a typewriter like a hen pecking at corn. Wycliffe sat astride one of the chairs, his arms resting on the back.

'Do you know the Parkyns of Garrison Drive?'

Kersey gave him a wry look. 'The Major – I know him well enough and I've met his sister, Hetty.'

'And father?'

'Father had already passed on when I first came across them a couple of years ago. They had a break-in, lost a lot of Japanese stuff and a gun. Funny business.'

'Why funny?'

'Because it was a one-off job. You usually have a run – a gang working an area. Here there was no repeat performance. We didn't get anywhere, neither did Crime Squad.'

'Was the stuff valuable?'

'Twenty thousand or thereabouts.'

'Insured?'

'As far as I remember – not. Of course, the gun worried us but I don't think it ever turned up.'

'It has now.'

Kersey registered surprise. 'The gun on the beach? Well I'm damned!' He sat back in his chair to digest the news. 'So it could have been local after all; we put it down to a flying visit from the Smoke.'

'I think the gun had been recently fired.'

Kersey crushed his cigarette in a tin lid. 'No dabs I suppose?'

'Smith is checking but I'd be surprised if there were.'

'So would I. In that case there's nowhere to start, is there?'

Although Kersey had been attached to Wycliffe's squad for such a short time there was an easy relationship between the two men. From time to time Kersey threw in the odd 'sir' as a gesture to the hierarchy.

Wycliffe said, 'I suppose the place to start is where you left off – with the Parkyns.'

Kersey agreed. 'I suppose so but I doubt if it will get us far. As I remember we had job enough the first time. I felt like I was talking to myself in a padded cell.'

'We'll try again. At least they're entitled to know that part of their property has been recovered.'

'You want me to come with you, sir?'

'I haven't got a car, we can use yours.'

Kersey said, 'The sister, Hetty, is a recluse; I don't think she ever goes out. But every morning you can see the major bowling along Bear Street in his blue jersey and corduroys, carrying his little string bag. If it's wet or cold he wears an old service duffle coat. His first visit is to collect the paper to see what gee-gees are running, then he looks in on his old pal at the antique shop; after that the betting shop, then it's the butcher, the baker, and for all I know, the candle-stick maker – it wouldn't surprise me; the last time I was in the house on Garrison Drive it was full of smelly oil-stoves. Anyway, Parkyn is a well-known figure in the district – a character, as they say.'

'He bets over the counter?'

'Yes, but as I hear it only on horses with at least one wooden leg a-piece.' Kersey cackled. 'A bookmaker's charity – as though they needed one.'

They drove into the city centre and out in the direction of the old harbour to Bear Street. A quarter past twelve. Although the sun shone there were few people about, just the soberly dressed elect returning from church to their Sunday roast cooked by automatic timer.

Bear Street had been the principal thoroughfare of the Elizabethan town, now it meandered narrowly and aimlessly on the fringe of the modern city to end at the old harbour. Coveted by developers and fiercely defended by conservationists, Bear Street was fought over with no holds barred. Half-way along they turned up Dog's Leg Lane, between houses which were a last remnant of the first Elizabeth. The lane climbed steeply and, after the double twist which gave it its name, came out on the glacis of a great fort. The fort straddled the narrow neck of land which was all that separated the estuary from the sea at this point.

On this former glacis, with an effect of startling

incongruity, Victorian military engineers had built a row of large, detached red-brick houses for the senior officers of the garrison and their families. Architecturally they resembled block-houses but they were surrounded by pleasant gardens which sloped down the glacis, and the view was magnificent; the whole expanse of Porthellin Bay with the great crooked arm of Laira Head on the far side and the little village of Porthellin crouched in its shelter.

In contrast with the others the third house was sadly neglected. The garden was a jungle, the gates were off their hinges and the path up the garden to the front door was made hazardous by pot-holes and crumbling steps.

Kersey said, 'It hasn't changed for the better.'

The door-bell was answered by a very large man in a seaman's jersey, corduroy slacks and slippers.

Wycliffe introduced himself and the sergeant. 'Major Gavin Lloyd Parkyn?'

'Yes, what do you want?' The gravelly voice made Wycliffe want to cough on his behalf.

So this was Major Gavin Lloyd Parkyn, Royal Marines, C.B.E., D.S.O. and bar. Middle fifties, hair machine clipped, large features and grey eyes which bulged slightly.

'You'd better come in.'

The drawing-room was dustily, shabbily elegant and never used. It had a cold, damp, neglected feel and smelled of dry rot. But there was a magnificent Turkish carpet with a Tree of Life design, deep leather armchairs, a grand piano – now almost certainly untuneable – and two massive cabinets displaying blue-and-white porcelain.

Parkyn offered them chairs but he remained standing by the window so that his bulk was silhouetted against the light. Kersey did not sit down either.

'A little over two years ago you had a break-in and, among other things, your father's service revolver was stolen.'

24

Parkyn let out a short guttural bark which could have been a laugh. ' "Among other things" is right! My father's Japanese collections which the old man had not thought it worth while to insure.'

'I came to tell you that the gun has been recovered – by chance. I found it on the beach this morning at St. Juliot. It was loaded and I think it had been recently fired.'

The grey eyes stared at him unblinking. 'What was it doing on the beach?'

'I've no idea but we shall have to try to find out and that means taking another look at the original theft.'

The massive shoulders lifted in a slow shrug. 'Yes. Well, I've no objection but I can't see you getting far. After all, you didn't the first time.'

Wycliffe said, 'You may remember that Sergeant Kersey was concerned in the original inquiry.'

Parkyn glanced at the sergeant without interest.

'Of course, I shall turn up the files on the case but I should like you to tell me what you can of the circumstances and I would like to see where the gun and the other missing objects were kept.'

Parkyn seemed about to make some objection but changed his mind. 'If you like. Come with me.'

His manner was neither patronizing nor condescending, merely indifferent. As a little boy before the war Wycliffe had known someone very like Parkyn – 'The Colonel' – the big landowner in the district where the Wycliffes had been tenant farmers. The Colonel had the same monumental presence, the same gravelly voice matured on whisky and cigars, the same protruding grey eyes, and, above all, the same air of unconscious, effortless superiority.

They followed Parkyn out of the room and down a long passage to the back of the house; a thin haze of blue smoke from over-heated fat came from the kitchen. Parkyn pushed open the door of a large room. 'My father's den.'

The outmoded word aptly described the room which had grown comfortably shabby round the personality of the old general; tailored to fit, like a snail's shell. It was dominated by his portrait in oils over the mantelpiece, full-length, in dress uniform. He resembled Parkyn but was leaner, more finely drawn, with an aesthetic cast of countenance and thinner lips below the close-clipped moustache. Under the portrait the general's medals and decorations were displayed in a glass case.

The top of a large mahogany desk was laid out with his morocco leather blotter, scuffed at the edges; his address book and engagement diary; a perpetual calendar on a lignum-vitae stand; a cut-glass pen-tray; a stand with headed paper and envelopes and a little travelling clock which ticked away as though its owner had only just left the room. Photographs of army occasions jostled for position on the walls and there were shelves of well-thumbed books – memoirs, biographies, works on oriental art – real reference books ante-dating the era of coffe-table glossies. A row of fat exercise books could have been the general's journal.

The place was a shrine. But what astonished Wycliffe was that it had been kept spotlessly clean; every surface shone.

Parkyn said, 'He kept his Japanese stuff in that cabinet which he had specially made.'

It was a tall rosewood cabinet with drawers, some very shallow, others up to four inches deep.

'In the shallow drawers he kept his *netsuke* – little toggles from Japanese traditional dress, most of 'em carved from ivory or wood or bone . . . '.

Words came from the major in short bursts with intervals as though a certain internal pressure had to build up before they could be discharged.

'Then there were the sword furnishings – mainly guards, and in the deeper drawers he kept his collection

26

of *inro* – lacquered boxes which used to be worn on the girdle . . . '

Parkyn opened a couple of felt-lined drawers – now empty. 'There wasn't enough stuff to fill all the drawers so in one of them he kept his service revolver along with other odds and ends. Everything went . . . '

'The thief got in through the window?'

Parkyn was mocking. 'As we found the window open and a pane of glass missing that seems probable.'

'At night?'

'Evening. I was out; my sister was in her room with the radio on.'

'This was shortly after your father's death?'

'Two or three months, I suppose. The stuff had been valued for probate along with everything else.'

The door opened and a tall, grey, bony woman came in to stand just inside the door. The family resemblance was unmistakable, even to the lustreless, slightly bulging eyes.

'What is it, Gavin? What are you doing in father's room?' Her manner was that of an irritable parent to a child.

Parkyn took his sister's arrival and her revealing question in his stride. 'My sister: Chief Superintendent Wycliffe and Sergeant Kersey . . . ' He added, 'The superintendent found father's gun on the beach at St Juliot and he thinks it had been recently fired.'

'Indeed!' Unimpressed. 'I do not like people in this room.'

Wycliffe said, 'I intend to re-open the inquiry into the theft. I can't hold out much hope but we shall do our best. Your brother has been good enough to answer a few questions.'

'Questions! We had enough questions last time with no result.'

Hetty was a few years older than her brother; her grey

hair was thin and wispy, her skin dry and wrinkled and whatever reserves of human warmth and emotion she may have had seemed to have seeped away with her femininity.

'How well known was your father's collection?'

Parkyn said, 'He built it up over a great number of years mainly through his contacts in Japan though occasionally he bought through London salerooms . . . He corresponded with a few collectors but I doubt if many people knew of the collection.'

Hetty spoke as though her brother had not opened his mouth. 'I think it must have been very well known. The man who came to value it for probate said that it was a celebrated collection – those were his words – "a celebrated collection".' Dogmatic emphasis.

'Who was that?'

It was Parkyn who answered. 'A chap called Clement . . . The younger of two brothers who run an antique business in Bear Street. He's a specialist in that sort of thing.'

'I suppose there is an inventory or catalogue giving technical descriptions of the items in the collection?'

Kersey said, 'There was one in the file of the case, sir.'

'Then we can circulate the dealers. By this time the chances are that a few of the things may have found their way back into the legitimate market and we may be able to get a lead from there.'

Parkyn came with them down the garden to where the car was parked. They stood for a moment by the car. Wycliffe said, 'You realize that I am most concerned about the gun.'

Once more he had the impression that the major was faintly amused. He said, 'I wish you luck, Superintendent . . . And good-day.'

As Wycliffe was being driven away he looked back at the major, standing on the pavement, motionless. It was hard to imagine the life he and his sister must lead in that gloomy house. Did they ever carry on a normal conversation? Did they ever laugh together? Or even quarrel?

Wycliffe said, 'Didn't you say something about Parkyn calling each morning at the antique shop?'

'Yes, I did, sir. He seems quite matey with the elder brother, not the one who did the valuation.' Kersey broke off while he negotiated the awkward double twist which gave the lane its name. 'At the time I had an idea along those lines but I got rapped for it.'

'What lines?'

'Well, as I understand it, the major didn't figure in his father's will; everything went to the delectable Hetty. God knows why.'

'So?'

'About the time of his father's death he sold his boat which he'd kept at St Juliot for a couple of years before that. Backing horses – especially his sort – can be an expensive pastime.'

'So you thought he might have engineered the break-in with the help of his friends in the antique shop?'

'It occurred to me as a possibility but the notion wasn't popular with my D.I. at the time and I got rapped for slanting the inquiry in that direction.'

'Why?'

'I've no idea, sir.'

'Are the Clement brothers crooks, in your opinion?'

'I've no reason to think so, it just seemed to me a line worth following up.'

As they reached the bottom of the lane where it joined Bear Street, Kersey said, 'Where to, sir?'

'Drop me at home.'

In Bear Street Kersey slowed almost to a stop as they passed the antique shop. The frontage dated from before the first war and the paintwork was neglected and peeling. The shop was double-fronted with tall narrow panes of glass, arched at the top, and the fascia was decorated with elaborate cast-iron ornament. In

29

one of the windows a card on an easel read: 'We buy and sell fine antiques of every description and we are specialists in oriental *objets d'art*. Collections purchased. Qualified valuers.'

'So you're here.'

'Sorry I couldn't let you know.'

Helen was making a white sauce. In the living-room a record player made sweet music.

'Recognize it?'

He listened and thought furiously. He was being tested as part of his musical education. 'It's one of the Mahler symphonies.'

'Good! Which?'

'Well, we've only got four of them and it's not the one with the soprano soloist – I'll say it's number six.'

'Wrong! It is the one with the soprano soloist – number four.'

'Anyway, I'm improving. What's for lunch?'

'Chicken casserole. I thought if you didn't come home I could put it in the oven again this evening.' She poured the sauce into a sauce-boat.

'What's all this about a gun?'

'I found it on the beach by the quay – loaded and recently fired. I've found since that it belonged to the late Lieutenant-General Sir Gavin Lloyd Parkyn, if that means anything to you.'

'Hetty's father.'

Wycliffe was impressed. 'You know them?'

Helen was full of surprises; she was not one of those women who exhaust themselves and their families with good works, neither was she a member of the coffee-morning fraternity, but her contacts, such as they were, seemed to provide her with a great deal of information about life in the city at all levels.

'I don't know them but Joan Langford who comes to the art classes lives next door to them in Garrison Drive.

Hetty is something of a cross; she's taken a dislike to Joan and she shows it by dumping her more unpleasant garbage over the hedge. When Joan complains she says it must be the sea-gulls.'

'What about Hetty's brother? What does she say about him?'

'Very little except that he must have a lot to put up with. Do you have to go out again?'

'I'm afraid so.'

After lunch he drove to headquarters in his own car – a Rover, chosen not because he knew anything about the relative merits of cars but because it was British and he refused to 'go foreign' even if the thing broke down twice a month – which it didn't.

Dixon, one of the young hopefuls he had let loose at St Juliot, was in the duty room typing his report.

'We didn't find anything, sir. Two of the cottagers reckoned they'd heard a car in the small hours. A Mrs Clara Barton—'

'From the corner house?'

'That's right. She says she was woken by a car engine whining, then it was quiet for a moment, after that the car seemed to drive off normally.'

'I suppose she heard the car being reversed off the jetty.'

'That's what I thought and so did she. She says couples sometimes spend half the night down there but they don't usually drive out on to the quay.' Dixon paused. 'I questioned her husband but he hadn't heard anything. Sleeping it off, by the look of him.'

'That's more than likely.'

'A Mrs Pascoe from the third cottage tells the same story except that she heard a shout which seemed to come from the beach not long before she heard the car. She didn't take a lot of notice because some of the local lads often go out for a night's fishing on Saturdays if the tide is right.'

'Was anybody out last night?'

'Yes, sir. Two brothers – Nicky and Charlie Byrd, but we haven't seem them yet. By the time we heard about them they'd gone off to town and they're not expected back until the pubs shut.'

Dixon glanced at his notes. 'We measured the tracks and took a few photographs and I've sent the results to the Vehicle Department for their opinion.'

Wycliffe had the file concerned with the original break-in sent up from the basement and sat at his desk turning over the papers which were neatly clipped together in sets. The work had been done thoroughly and as far as he could see there was no line of inquiry which had not been followed up.

In bed that night, in the small hours when self-criticism is at its most coldly clinical and its probes are sharpest, he concluded that he was making a fool of himself over a gun; building up a case out of nothing more than unlawful possession and disposal.

CHAPTER TWO

Monday. Another fine day. The sun had come round to shine through the window of Wycliffe's office revealing smears on his desk-top and dust on his bookcase. It was the weather to start thinking of holidays, not the two or three weeks of expensive frustration in some strange place, but the holiday idea – the holiday ideal.

His personal assistant, Diane, came in, smelling of eau-de-Cologne, immaculate, efficient and off-putting. His younger colleagues, frustrated in their licentious desires, called her the Ice Maiden. Maiden she certainly was. She brought a bundle of memoranda slips – bits of different coloured papers, the colours denoting their department of origin. Wycliffe recalled and regretted the days when, if you had something to say to somebody, you walked down the corridor, kicked open his door and said it. Now multi-coloured flimsies descended like leaves in autumn and because people had to write down their messages they said more and meant less.

'Put them there, Diane.'

She arranged the bits of paper in neat rows. One of them (pink for Vehicles) was headed, *Report on the Wheel Tracks at St Juliot Quay.* It made a typescript page out of the fact that an expert believed the tracks to be those of a B.L. Maxi but wasn't sure.

Kersey rang to say that Dixon had spoken to the Byrd brothers about their fishing trip. 'They arrived back at their moorings at about half-past two on Sunday morning and they saw a car reversing off the quay. They didn't take a lot of notice and I gather they were pretty far gone;

these trips seem to be more for boozing than fishing.' Kersey paused, then went on, 'I wondered if you'd thought any more about the Clement Brothers, sir?'

Kersey was dogged. Wycliffe had thought about them and decided that grounds for connecting them with the robbery and the gun were too slender. Was it likely that a local dealer, an accredited valuer, would connive with a householder in theft? He thought not. In any case he couldn't see Major Parkyn as the other party. But when Diane's appetite for paperwork was finally satisfied he said, 'I'm going down to Bear Street, if anybody wants me they can try the car radio.'

He collected his car from the park and drove through the heavy morning traffic. He was not a good driver; he enjoyed no rapport with the internal combustion engine nor, indeed, with the age which had deified it. He often told himself that he had been born out of due time, that he should have muscled in on the age of steam and grown old while, among other things, it was still possible to be a Fabian Socialist and believe in the perfectibility of man.

He left his car in front of the old custom-house which brought back memories of another case* and entered Bear Street from that end. In the morning sunshine it looked like a street scene by Pissarro; the light seemed to vibrate, softening outlines, dazzling the eyes. It was all a great deal more animated than it had been on Sunday morning. The street was noted for its specialist shops: a high-class grocery, a well-stocked delicatessen, a good wine shop, a home bakery and a discriminating butcher ... Young and middle-aged women, golf-club wives, subscribers to *House and Garden*, parked their Mini Metros, their Fiats and their Fiestas and worked their systematic ways through the street with exotic shopping lists. In all this the neglected paintwork and murky

* Death in Stanley Street

windows of the antique shop stood out like a poor relation at a wedding.

Wycliffe spotted Parkyn some way ahead; he still wore his sailor's jersey and corduroys, but with canvas shoes, and he carried a string bag full of groceries. At the antique shop he paused and peered in, shielding his eyes from the light with one hand; then he was on his way again, covering the ground rapidly with his curious gait which seemed to involve scarcely any movement of the body above the knees. He glided as though on wheels.

The antique shop was closed. Wycliffe rang the side-door bell but there was no reply. He was aware of being watched by a woman in the café-restaurant opposite. The morning coffee trade was over and lunch had not yet started so she had no customers. He crossed the street and sat at one of the tables which was covered with a red and white checked cloth. The woman was fat with almost black hair and attractive amiable features; she spoke in a soft Devonshire brogue, rich and thick as clotted cream.

'Coffee?'

'Black, please.'

She went to the coffee machine.

'I can't get any answer opposite.'

'No, they're closed.' She moved slowly, shifting her weight from one foot to the other with deliberation. She was eyeing him, sizing him up in a way that all policemen know well.

'Police?'

'Yes.'

'I thought so. What's happening over there?'

'Nothing that I know of.'

She was looking across at the shop with a thoughtful air. 'There's something, and I'm a bit worried.' She twisted a gold wedding ring on her finger. 'They're a couple of bachelors. Joseph, the elder brother, comes in

35

here most days for his mid-day meal, and David comes sometimes when he's home. The shop was open as usual on Saturday and Joseph was in at lunch-time. Sunday, I didn't see them all day and they didn't draw back the curtains in their sitting-room; this morning, they haven't opened the shop. I said about it to my husband. Of course they're never very fussy about opening hours, they'll put up a notice, "Back in ten minutes" and stay away all morning . . . All the same . . . '

'Don't they sometimes go away together?'

'Never. Joseph never goes away and David is away at least half his time.'

She moved back to her customary place behind the counter. An appetising smell came from the kitchen and it seemed a good idea to lunch there.

'Your husband does the cooking?'

She nodded. 'Do you like pot roast?'

'It smells good.'

She laughed, a rich attractive laugh. 'We cater mainly for regulars at lunch times but if you want to stay . . . '

A girl in a blue trouser-suit came down the street on the opposite side. She had dark shoulder-length hair and a good figure but her features were a little too sharp. She tried the door of the antique shop, rattled it, then tried the side-door and ended up by ringing the bell, keeping her finger on the button for some time.

'There you are! If they'd gone away or anything, she would know.'

'Who is she?'

'She's called Stokes and she's David's girl-friend.'

'She looks young.'

'I don't know about that; she must be twenty-four or five.'

It dawned on him that he was assuming the Clement brothers to be at least middle-aged; two ageing bachelors cultivating their grey hairs and their paunches and indulging their whims. 'So they're young men?'

'Don't you know them?'

'We've never met.'

She considered, pouting her lips like a schoolgirl with a problem. 'They're not exactly young. Joseph must be in the middle forties and David is thirty-one or two. They're not a bit alike. Joseph is stocky like his father and a red-head; David is slight and very dark, like his mother. Joseph took over the business when his father died. He lost both of them – mother and father, inside a fortnight – influenza followed by pneumonia.' She sighed. 'That must be ten or twelve years ago.

'Ever since then Joseph has taken his mid-day meal here. Of course, David has only been in the business about three years. I remember him as a schoolboy, then he went away to college and after that he got a job in London with a big insurance company. We didn't see much of him for years; then, apparently, he got tired of life in London, chucked up his job and came back here.'

'Do the two brothers get on together?'

She hesitated. 'They seem to but I'm not sure. David does a lot of travelling and they say he's got the right connections among collectors and such like. It suits him to be always on the move, just as it suits Joseph to be a stay-at-home. All the same, I've had a feeling lately that Joseph isn't happy with the way things are going.'

The restaurant began to fill and the fat woman was kept going, to and fro between the hatch and the tables. Although she moved with such deliberation and never allowed herself to be hurried, she kept pace with the orders and found time to exchange gossip and wise-cracks with her customers.

'Do you want a drink?'

'I'd like a lager with this.'

The pot roast was delicious but not the sort of meal to go back to work on. The lunch-time customers included a surprising number of young people from neighbouring offices but some of them were content with a bowl of

37

soup and a bread-roll. From time to time a little man in a chef's hat supported on his ears, looked in; he stood in the doorway of the kitchen and exchanged greetings with the customers in English that was resourceful if inaccurate.

The fat woman smiled affectionately. 'Czech, from Prague. He came over in the '68 uprising.'

Wycliffe kept an eye on the antique shop. One or two people stopped to look in the window but nobody tried to enter the shop and nobody rang the bell.

He left the restaurant after his meal and walked down the street on the same side as the antique shop until he came to a narrow alley, a mere passage between two shops. It led to a back lane where grass grew through the cracks in the tarmacadam. Each of the buildings on that side of Bear Street had a backyard and a door opening into the lane. The Clement brothers had a garage as well. The yard door opened easily.

The yard, paved with moss-covered bricks, was scarcely big enough to turn round in. There was no car in the garage. Two ground-floor windows faced the yard, they had not been opened in years and were covered with a wire-mesh, but through one of them he could see the glow of a lamp – a desk or table lamp to judge from the level. The house door was solid and there was no bell or knocker but to his surprise, when he put his hand to the knob, it opened easily. He rapped on it with his knuckles and when this brought no response he pushed it wide and called out. No-one came so he went in. The room, previously the kitchen of the house, was now a cloakroom with a washbasin and a cubicle housing a W.C. To his right was another door which led into the room from which the light came.

It was an office with a large desk, a swivel chair, a filing cabinet and a massive, old-fashioned safe, painted black, with brass fittings. On the desk was a telephone and an adjustable lamp which was switched on; a sale catalogue lay open on the blotter, a ball-point pen beside it. There was a perpetual calendar and an ashtray almost full of stubs and an empty cigarette pack. Wycliffe's first impression was that someone had just slipped out. Except that the room had a chilly, unused feel and the calendar, for what it was worth, showed Saturday 9th instead of Monday 11th.

He crossed the room to another door which led to the shop, a dimly lit cavern with a musty resinous smell. At the back of the shop, screened from the street by the furniture display, there were tables and a showcase laid out with porcelain and glass, a few bits of ivory and silver and a collection of coins. Apart from a monumental lacquered cabinet there was nothing to suggest an interest in oriental antiques.

In one corner an iron spiral staircase led to the floor above. He climbed the steps and came to a landing from which conventional stairs went down to the side-door and a corridor led off to the first-floor rooms.

'Is anybody home?'

He pushed open the first door he came to; a sitting room. A conventional three-piece, the worse for wear; a television set, a moth-eaten carpet ... The window overlooked Bear Street and the restaurant opposite. The next room along the passage was a bedroom with a double bed, wardrobe and chest-of-drawers, Edwardian style. On a bedside table there was a studio photograph of the girl in the blue trouser-suit. She was pretty but her sharp features, rather pinched, suggested the acute aggressive awareness of certain small animals.

On the other side of the passage, at the back of the house, there was a kitchen and bathroom which had been modern fifty years ago, then a room furnished as a bed-sitter. There was a desk placed under the window and it was a moment before he saw the body of a man lying on the floor by the desk, a man with red hair.

He bent over the man; he was dead, shot through the

right side of the skull, behind the ear. Round the wound of entry he thought he could see the faint impression of a gun muzzle. The body lay in a twisted position, the left side of the face in contact with the floor, obscuring the exit wound which must have been extensive to judge from the blood and tissue on the carpet.

Suicide? No sign of the gun but it could be hidden under the body. Murder was a possibility.

The man had been working on his stamp collection; there was a loose-leaf album on the desk, a few stamps in polythene envelopes, a magnifier and a pair of forceps. There was a pipe too, and other pipes in a rack on the wall by the desk, an ashtray and a tobacco jar.

Shelves over a single bed held books about stamps, catalogues, albums, and a collection of works on English furniture. Wycliffe liked the look of it all; he had a soft spot for collectors, most of whom were amiable even when slightly dotty.

He left the room and went down the spiral staircase which vibrated with his every step. Back in the office behind the shop he telephoned headquarters and spoke to Kersey.

The gun on the beach had led him to this but was there really a link? He would only know when the bullet which killed the red-head had been found and a comparison test made by a ballistics expert.

While waiting for his men he looked over the things on the desk. The catalogue referred to a London auction, held several months earlier, and it was open at a page which listed a collection of glass paperweights. A sum of money had been pencilled against each item – presumably the price fetched at auction, and the amounts varied from three hundred to well over three thousand pounds. Six of the more costly weights had heavily scored lines against them in the margin of the page.

Standing between the desk and the safe he noticed for

the first time a broken statuette, it was a Parian figure of a nude girl and it looked as though it might have been knocked off the desk. A struggle? If so, there seemed to be no other signs.

Kersey was the first to arrive. Wycliffe had told them to use the back lane to avoid turning their activities into a spectator sport. Kersey had an I-told-you-so look. 'Dr Franks was at the hospital – some committee meeting – but they've been in touch and he's on his way.'

Franks was the pathologist.

'Who's dead?'

'Presumably the eldest brother, Joseph, I gather he was a red-head.'

'Murder?'

'I'm going to treat it as murder for the moment but it could turn out to be suicide?'

'How did he die?'

'Shot but there was no gun to be seen. It could be under the body.'

'Or it could be with old Melville at Ballistics.'

No need to answer that.

'Did either of the Clement brothers have a car?'

'David, the younger one, did – a blue Maxi, I think.'

'It's not in the garage and David doesn't seem to be around.'

Smith arrived with two more detectives but until the pathologist had examined the body there was little they could do. Wycliffe left them in the office and went upstairs to get the feel of the place. As before he was struck by its threadbare shabbiness. Two bachelors, neither of them houseproud; tobacco-ash in saucers, mouldy scraps of food forgotten in kitchen cupboards, grubby linen and a faint but pervasive smell of sweaty socks. He started in the sitting-room. Apart from the worn and dusty suite there was a bookcase with books mostly on antiques, and on the floor, stacks of trade journals and sale catalogues in no sort of order. The

41

pictures on the walls were dreary over-varnished landscapes which looked as though they had failed to draw a bid at some sale. Apart from them there was a framed photograph, presumably of the brothers, taken years ago.

The one Wycliffe identified as Joseph was a stocky young man in his twenties; he looked at the camera with a dutiful if tentative smile on his heavy face. His brother, a schoolboy, had made no such concession, his expression was one of bored indifference. He was cast in a different mould from his brother, a thin, intelligent face and a look which, despite the disparity in their ages, suggested that it was he rather than Joseph who had sized up the business of living and come to terms with it.

The spiral staircase vibrated under at least two pairs of feet and Wycliffe heard Franks in the passage. It would not be long now. After a few minutes he went out into the passage and joined Smith who was taking photographs from the doorway of the dead man's room as the pathologist turned the body over for examination. Franks glanced up and saw Wycliffe.

'Hullo, Charles! If this is suicide then somebody nicked the gun, it isn't here. He was shot through the temporal bone just above and slightly behind the mastoid process – an unusual spot for murder or suicide. *If* he shot himself he may have read about bullets passing through the frontal lobes and not doing their job. It's surprising the things people know these days. When I started in the business not many knew their palate from their patella. I suppose they learn in the hope of defending themselves against bloody doctors . . . The wound of exit is a fair sized hole as you probably gathered from the mess on the carpet. The left side of the skull is completely shattered. I'd guess the bullet lost most of its momentum and is probably lying on the floor somewhere.'

Franks dribbled a continuous flow of words. He

reminded one of a baby, pink, bald and shining. He shifted the body to a fresh position and Smith's camera clicked again.

'Seems he was keen on stamps. People with a hobby don't often do themselves in unless things get badly screwed up.' He straightened, brushing the knees of his trousers, and turned to Wycliffe. 'Well, you can have him shifted when you like – give your chaps a chance to start work.'

'Time of death?'

Franks passed a plump hand over his bald head. 'He's been dead quite a while.'

'How would Saturday night fit? Say, sometime between the shop closing and Sunday morning?'

Franks considered. 'Forty-odd hours. That might do. Look at the extruded muck – the way its's congealed. Anyway, I'll do what I can and ring later.'

Two men carried the body away on a stretcher. There was no question of taking it down the spiral staircase and so it had to go by way of the side-door and out into Bear Street where it attracted plenty of attention.

The body gone, Franks looked round the little room. 'Perhaps you'll get someone to send me that little square of carpet – it will have to be cut out. Who's attending?'

A police officer attends a post-mortem whenever it is likely that a court case will follow.

Wycliffe said, 'Scales will be here directly, I'll send him along.'

With the body and the pathologist out of the way work could begin.

Clement must have been sitting at his desk when he was shot (or shot himself). His body had slipped between desk and chair, pushing the chair aside as he collapsed to the floor. If he had been bending over his stamps and someone had come into the room he might not have looked up. Absorbed in his work he could have acknowledged the visitor with a muttered word. A

43

moment later he would have felt the cold contact of the gun against his skin then the fleeting but final trauma before oblivion.

That would account for the unusual position of the wound of entry and it would be murder. Wycliffe tried to convince himself. Why would anyone remove the weapon from the scene of a suicide? And the weapon itself? Surely Joseph must have been shot by the gun on the beach, one chamber fired, wiped clean of prints? But if so, why had it been ditched, and ditched so ineffectually at St Juliot?

Guessing games. But one thing seemed certain, his idea that a body had been disposed of at the quay was a non-starter.

John Scales, his deputy, arrived and Wycliffe sent him to join Franks at the post-mortem. Three more men turned up from headquarters, drafted to the new case as they reported back from other jobs. He briefed them.

'House-to-house in Bear Street and the immediate neighbourhood. Get a move on before the shops shut. Get what you can on the Clement brothers and don't turn your noses up at gossip. The critical period seems to have been from the time the shops closed on Saturday until the small hours of Sunday morning. The younger brother is missing; so is his car – probably a blue Maxi but get details from Vehicle Records and have them circulated.'

He followed the men out into the back lane where a constable in a patrol car was maintaining radio watch and gave instructions for an incident caravan to be parked in front of the old custom-house by the harbour. These vans are self-contained incident posts with radio-telephone links and accommodation for limited office work and interviews. A handy base for men working on the case and somewhere convenient for locals to go with information if they have any.

Back in the house Joseph Clement's room was being systematically and minutely investigated.

The sight of large men moving about a small room, solemnly and ponderously circumspect, engaged in the most zany tasks, always struck Wycliffe as bizarre and slightly ludicrous. Dixon was on his knees cutting out the square of carpet where Joseph's head had rested; the middle-aged D.C. Fowler was crawling about, examining the floor inch by inch in search of the missing bullet; Sergeant Smith was testing likely surfaces for prints and pausing now and then to photograph what he found.

A room is immortalized by having someone killed in it. The most prosaic little room has only to become the scene of a murder to be dissected, studied and recorded with at least as much skill and care as would be expended on an important archaeological site. The anatomy of the room goes on file in the form of inventories, plans and photographs, which are preserved with as much care as the site records of an Arthur Evans or a Mortimer Wheeler.

He left them to it and crossed the street to the restaurant where he had lunched. It was closed, but there was a card in the window saying that it would re-open at seven for dinner. He tapped on the glass door and after a moment or two the fat woman came through from the back premises. She recognized him and opened the door.

'I thought you might be back.'

'The girl in the blue trouser-suit – Stokes, I think you said – do you know where she lives?'

'I saw them coming out with a stretcher; who was it?'

'Joseph.'

Her eyes glistened on the verge of tears. 'I was afraid so. Poor man! He never did anybody any harm. How did it happen?'

'He died of a bullet wound but that's all I know at the moment. About this girl . . . '

'She lives in Godolphin Street, just round the corner. It's a house which has been converted into flats; I think it's number 15 but you can't miss it.'

'Thanks.'

'I don't know if you'll find her home; she's a nurse at the Horton Radford so it depends what shift she's on.'

The Horton Radford was a private hospital, expensive and exclusive.

'What about David?' The fat woman wanted as much as possible.

'I haven't seen him; that's why I want to talk to the girl.'

It was four o'clock and the children were going home from a nearby junior school. The sky had clouded over and great drops of rain made circular patches on the pavements. It looked like the start of a thunder shower but Godolphin Street was not so far.

Number 15 was a Georgian town house which had been converted into flats while preserving the frontage. Once inside there was little evidence of Georgian elegance. The name board gave M.K. Stokes as the occupant of flat three on the first floor. Wycliffe climbed the stairs and rang the door-bell.

He had almost given up when the door was opened on a chain and he saw the face of the girl in the trouser-suit but her eyes were puffy and her hair was confined in a net. He showed her his warrant card.

She hesitated but did not ask what he wanted. 'Wait a minute.'

The door was closed again but after a full two minutes she opened it wide. 'You'd better come in.'

She had run a comb through her hair and put on a dressing-gown. Perhaps she had used cleansing tissues for her skin looked less shiny.

The room was small, just big enough for a couple of

armchairs, a table, a bookcase and a televison set. The tall, rectangular window with its many panes, part of the original house, seemed incongruous. The place had a woman's smell, a woman who was not fastidious.

'I was in bed; I'm a nurse at the Horton Radford and I'm on nights.' She lit a cigarette and drew on it with the single-minded concentration of an addict, then she perched herself on the arm of one of the chairs and drew her dressing-gown about her legs; her feet were bare. She looked at him and her manner was more speculative than apprehensive. 'Is it about David Clement?'

'Why do you ask that?'

'David Clement at the antique shop – I'm beginning to be a bit worried. I haven't heard from him since Saturday and now the shop is shut.'

Wycliffe was stolidly unforthcoming. 'I want to get in touch with the Clement brothers and I thought you might be able to help.'

'Has something happened?'

'It's possible that there has been a break-in at the shop; the back door was unsecured and we've no way of knowing whether there has been an intruder on the premises until we get in touch with one of the brothers.'

She seemed to accept this. 'I don't know where they are; I can't understand it. David and I had a loose arrangement for Sunday morning but he didn't show up. I rang the shop a couple of times but there was no answer and this morning they were shut.' She swept her hair back from her eyes in a nervous gesture. 'David is pretty casual and it wouldn't be the first time he's gone off somewhere without letting me know but Joseph should be there.'

She had the professional self-assurance of most nurses and she had cultivated a manner of speech appropriate to the Horton Radford where patients arrived and left in chaffeur-driven limousines but

47

neither was more than skin-deep and underneath she was probably a very ordinary young woman.

'Were you expecting bad news?'

'No – not at all!' She crossed her legs in a vigorous movement. 'I'm a bit bothered, that's all. It's natural, isn't it?'

The room had two doors apart from the one by which he had come in; one stood open to the kitchen in which it would hardly have been possible to take more than a couple of steps, the other was shut and led, presumably, to the bedroom.

'How well do you know him?'

'Well enough but what's that got to do with it?' She paused then went on, 'We've been seeing each other for more than a year and sleeping together when the occasion offered. Will that do?'

He told her about Joseph and she was clearly shocked. 'You mean that Joseph is dead – murdered?'

'It looks like murder but in any case it's important to get hold of his brother.'

She hesitated as though trying to come to grips with what she had heard. 'You're not suggesting that David killed him?'

Wycliffe was non-committal. 'I've told you all I know; Joseph is dead and David is missing.'

She looked at him, trying to make up her mind. 'I hope you're being straight with me because you can forget the idea of David killing his brother or anybody else.'

'You seem very sure.'

'I am. Like a lot of small men David can be aggressive but there's no violence in him. When you've slept with a man you know these things.' She stood up with nervous vigour and crushed out her cigarette in an ashtray on the mantelpiece. 'What do you want from me?'

'Information. When did you last see David?'

He had to wait while she lit another cigarette, fumbling

with her lighter. 'Saturday evening. As a matter of fact, Saturday was my day off and we spent the afternoon together until half-past seven or a bit later. He left then because he had an appointment at the shop.'

'Did he say who the appointment was with?'

From the sudden change in her expression it was obvious that an idea had occurred to her but all she said was, 'No, just that it was some chap who wanted to sell something. It was nothing unusual; a lot of their business is done after hours – buying and selling.'

'When you were with him on Saturday did he seem his usual self?'

'Quite!' She frowned as though trying to recollect the day. 'He came over just after lunch and we drove out to Hembury where an old girl had some family heirlooms she wanted to sell. They were mainly bits of silver and not of much account so David wasn't interested. We came back here, I cooked a meal, and sometime before eight he left.'

'And you haven't heard from him or seen him since?'

'No, I told you. We had a tentative date for Sunday morning – I was half expecting him to come over for me but he didn't turn up.'

'How did the brothers get on?'

'All right, I think; probably better than most brothers who work in the same business. Joe is – was a good deal older and a bit of a drag where anything new was concerned but David usually managed to edge him along without having rows.'

'Did Joseph have a woman friend?'

She laughed. 'I shouldn't think so; women scared him.'

'Did he go out much?'

'I don't know. If I went to the flat of an evening he was sometimes there, sometimes not. It didn't make any difference, if he was there he would be shut up in his room with his precious stamps.'

'Is the business prosperous?'

'I suppose so. David never seems to be short.'

'Have they any relatives?'

'Their parents are both dead, I do know that. As to aunts, uncles and the rest I've no idea. I've never heard David speak of any.'

Her room gave little away; it was as impersonal as a room in a boarding house. No pictures, no photographs, no books; just one or two ornaments which could have come from a fairground.

'When David was here on Saturday, did he have his car?'

'No, we went to Hembury in my Mini; I like driving.'

'Have they got many friends?'

'I shouldn't think so. David doesn't make friends easily and Joe . . . I suppose Joe must go out with somebody when he isn't home but I've no idea who.'

'Major Parkyn?'

She grinned. 'Popeye! Could be, I suppose.'

Wycliffe was asking questions at random – fishing, and prepared for anything he might catch. There was something odd about the girl's attitude but he couldn't put his finger on it. She was surprised and shocked by Joseph's death and concerned about her boy-friend but . . .

'Do you think they had any enemies?'

'Enemies? I shouldn't think so, they weren't the sort to go around upsetting people.'

Rain beat against the window and he could glimpse a leaden sky above the houses opposite.

'Have you a photograph of David?'

'A photograph? Not a proper one; I've probably got a few snapshots.' She looked at him accusingly. 'You *do* think he shot Joe!'

'I think nothing of the sort but if he really is missing then we have to find him.'

She got up and went into the bedroom to return in a few minutes with three snapshots. 'That's the best I can do.'

One of them showed David Clement in swimming trunks on the foredeck of a cabin cruiser and the girl, in a bikini, at his side. She had her hand on his shoulder and she was an inch or two taller.

'Who does the boat belong to?'

'To David.'

'You didn't tell me he had a boat.'

'You didn't ask me.'

'Where does he keep it?'

'At the moment it's moored off St Juliot but all winter she's been laid up in Morcom's yard.'

'When did he put her off to moorings?'

She frowned. 'A week or ten days ago. He's keen on cruising and he likes to make the season last as long as possible.'

'Is it a big boat?'

'Depends what you call big; she's got a four berth cabin and the usual offices.'

'What's she called?'

'He re-christened her *Manna* when he bought her. It was a joke because he bought her with an unexpected windfall.'

This opened up possibilities which looked bad for David Clement. Wycliffe put the photographs in his pocket. 'I'll take these and I'd like a brief description of him.'

'If you must. He's about five-feet-five, thin, with almost black hair and rather pale skin . . . '

'What was he wearing when you last saw him?'

'A fawn denim bush-jacket and slacks with fawn suede shoes. I think he had on a sort of grey-green shirt.'

Wycliffe stared at the girl with dreamy eyes, wondering how much she knew that she was not prepared to say; a profitless speculation.

'In the office behind the shop there's a little Parian figure of a naked girl lying, smashed, on the floor.'

'Smashed?' She looked surprised. 'That's Monica.

David kept her on the desk to tease Joseph who's very straight-laced. Actually Monica is a bit naughty. David says she's one of a set of six designs made by a Victorian potter for a rich customer to give as presents to his friends . . . Joseph wasn't killed in the office, was he?'

'No, in his room.'

It seemed that there was nothing to be gained by staying so he left. Outside the streets were wet but it had stopped raining; thunder rumbled around with the occasional flash of lightning. He felt like a juggler who is trying to keep too many balls in the air at once; more accurately, like someone trying to make a jig-saw puzzle with pieces which don't all belong. The revolver on the beach, the break-in at Parkyn's, Joseph's body in his room, the Saturday-night caller at the shop, the open door of the house, the light left burning, David's disappearance, the car, the boat . . .

David had left the flat in Godolphin Street before eight on Saturday night to keep an appointment with his client, an appointment which might or might not have involved Joseph. Now Joseph was dead and David had disappeared. A car had been heard and seen on the quay at St Juliot early on Sunday morning and Parkyn's revolver had been dropped on the beach at about the same time.

The boat added a new dimension and it was almost certainly the link between St Juliot and the rest.

A police Range Rover was edging its way along Bear Street with one of the blue incident vans in tow. News of trouble at the antique shop had spread and a single uniformed copper was having his work cut out keeping people on the move.

A reporter from one local paper recognized Wycliffe. 'What's happened to the other brother, Mr Wycliffe?'

He said, 'We are trying to make contact,' and escaped into the shop. He found Kersey in the office at the back. 'How are they getting on?'

'Dixon has finished his bit of carpet surgery and the piece has gone to Franks. Fowler found the bullet under Joseph's bed in a pile of fluff which must have been there since Adam; I've sent it to Melville. It's a bit flattened but I've seen worse used in comparison tests. Smith is still working on the bedroom and the others are going over the rest of the flat.'

'You haven't touched anything down here?'

'Not yet.'

'Good! The Clements had a client due at eight on Saturday evening. He wanted to sell something and the chances are they did their business here. When Smith has finished upstairs he'd better start on this.'

'Anything else?'

'Yes; observation on Molly Stokes. She lives in a flat round the corner in Godolphin Street. Twenty-four hour obo but no interference. She's a nurse at the Horton Radford and I want her tailed going and coming. It's important she shouldn't know she's being watched . . . Oh, yes, if possible I'd like a photograph of her in her street clothes.'

'David's girl-friend?' Kersey's ugly, intelligent face was alive with curiosity.

'Yes, I had the impression that while she was shocked to hear of Joseph's death, her boy-friend's disappearance was less of a surprise. I'm not saying she expected it, only that she didn't seem as concerned as she might have been.'

'You think she knows where he is?'

'It's possible. Anyway, it's worth keeping an eye on her for a day or two.'

He went back through the shop and up the spiral staircase. Dixon and Fowler were working in the sitting room, searching and sorting with the curtains drawn and the lights on though it was still daylight outside. What they were doing was probably a waste of time but one can never tell. Detection is a labour-intensive industry.

He looked in on Smith and handed over the snapshots he had got from the girl. 'Suitable enlargements for circulation when you can.'

The wheels were beginning to turn.

He went downstairs and let himself out by the side-door. It was raining again and this had cleared the street more effectively than the lone policeman who was sheltering in a doorway. The fat woman in the restaurant was setting the tables for dinner. Each table now had an ornamental candlestick in the middle of the check cloth. He turned down Bear Street to the harbour where the incident van was in position outside the old custom-house. In the little duty-room a young detective constable was filing house-to-house reports and the silence was broken only by occasional exchanges on the police radio.

'Telephone working?'

'Yes, sir.'

He looked up a number and dialled.

'Mrs Williams? . . . Is Toby about?'

Toby Williams was a St Juliot man. Retired, he supplemented his pension by keeping an eye on the craft moored off the village. His garden ran down to the shore and he had a shed where owners kept some of their gear.

'Mr Wycliffe?' Toby's bellow vibrated in the receiver. 'Is it about that little craft you thought of buying? . . . *Manna*? Mr Clement's boat – Yes, I look after 'er but she ain't 'ere now; 'e took 'er off sometime Saturday night – anyways she was 'ere Saturday night and she was gone Sunday morning . . . No, I weren't worried because 'e left a note in my shed like they all do.'

Wycliffe said, 'I'll look in for a word on my way home if it's not too late. See if you can find that note.'

So *Manna* was missing. At least that made sense of the St Juliot angle. On the face of it David Clement had cleared off in his launch. After murdering his brother?

54

And what about his car? If he had driven himself to St Juliot alone, the car should still be there. But were there two men involved? Two men of whom one had gone off in the launch and the other in the car. And the gun – had there been a scuffle in which the gun had been dropped and lost? One of the witnesses had mentioned a shout which seemed to come from the beach.

He needed to know more about the Clement brothers. The men on house-to-house would come back with the usual mix of fact and fiction but aside from that he had only the Stokes girl and the major. The fact that Parkyn regularly called at the antique shop on his daily round must mean something.

CHAPTER THREE

It was dark by the time he set out for Garrison Drive to talk to Parkyn. He climbed the steep slope of Dog's Leg Lane and came out on to the glacis where a cold, moist, salty wind off the sea took him by surprise. It was very dark and no feature of the coast was discernible except the clustered lights of Porthellin; the sea was a black void with a pin-point of light here and there marking the position of some ship. At precise intervals the beam of a distant lighthouse swept its arc across the sky. Three inadequate street lamps marked the line of the drive but all the houses seemed to be in darkness. He stumbled up the steep path of Number 3 and had to feel for the bell-push when he arrived at the front door. Having found it he kept his finger pressed and listened with satisfaction to a subdued but insistent buzzing somewhere in the house. Even so it was a long time before a light came on in the hall and he saw Hetty's gaunt form through the hammered glass panels of the door.

'Who is it?'

He was suddenly ashamed. If the woman was on her own in the house she had every right to be nervous in this lonely place.

'Superintendent Wycliffe.'

She seemed to hesitate and for a moment it was on the cards that she might turn back into the house and leave him standing, but finally she drew back two bolts and opened the door.

'Do you have to come at this time of night? Anyway, my brother is out.'

They were standing in the hall with a damp breeze blowing through the open door.

'May I come in and wait?'

'I've no idea how long he will be.'

He persisted; there was a chance he might learn something from Hetty though he was not optimistic. She gave in with a bad grace and he followed her down the passage to a little room between the drawing-room and the kitchen. It was furnished with a couple of armchairs, a bureau and a few bookshelves. An old oil-heater with a fretted top and a red window gave off a stuffy, smelly heat. An open book and a pair of glasses lay on one of the chairs.

Hetty's boudoir.

'You'd better sit down.'

He was still wearing his wet mackintosh and in a few minutes it would begin to steam. Hetty picked up her glasses and her book, sat down and resumed reading, holding the book high and close to her eyes. Of all things it was Vincent's *Defence of India*. The Parkyns were full of little surprises.

Hetty was well into her sixties, an age at which most women are grandmothers, aunts or both, and they have photographs on their walls to prove it. Hetty had her photographs but, as far as Wycliffe could tell, they were all of her father, the general. There were studio portraits of him in uniform at different ages and ranks but the greater number were of army occasions in which he was the central figure. Three, larger than the others and more elaborately framed, showed him in attendance on royalty and one of these bore an illustrious signature.

'I want to talk to your brother about the Clements.'

'What about them?' She did not look away from her book.

'Joseph, the elder brother, has been shot and David is missing.'

She turned her head. 'Indeed? I am sorry to hear it but how does it concern my brother?'

'I understand that he was a friend of the dead man.'

'Really? I know nothing of his friends.' And she resumed her reading as though there were no more to be said.

He had rarely met anyone so blankly unresponsive. Curiosity, nervousness, a desire for self-justification, even a simple dislike of silence, will usually prompt people to talk but now there was silence in the dreary little room without even the ticking of a clock to relieve it. Hetty must spend her evenings like this. Well, he had no justification for putting pressure on the woman and no desire to do so.

But after a while he became aware that she was eyeing him with quick, appraising glances. For a time it was almost a game between them. Evidently she was not as detached as she appeared; she wanted to say something but could not make up her mind. At last it came, dry and categorical.

'I see that you are interested in my photographs.'

He was non-committal. 'They seem to be an interesting record of your father's army career.'

'Only some of the highlights . . .' She looked at her book once more as though about to resume reading but it was obvious that having broken the ice she had more to say.

'We are an army family, Mr Wycliffe; my father, grandfather and great-grandfather on the Parkyn side were all generals and my mother came from a family with an army background.' She closed the book she had been reading and held it up with a bleak smile, 'I suppose my reading is not what you would expect of a woman . . .'

Probably Hetty had had few opportunities to talk to anyone since her father's death and here was a quiet, serious man who seemed to be receptive. What difference did it make that he was a policeman? She studied him, her prominent grey eyes intent and searching.

'It was natural that my father should want his only son to follow in the family tradition but Gavin was rather foolishly obstructive and difficult. Of course he was spoiled by my mother as a child. Anyhow, when father assumed that he would enter the army after Cambridge he deliberately enlisted in the navy.' She laughed without humour. 'But even they recognized that he was cut out for a soldier and persuaded him into the marines.'

Wycliffe listened with a bland expression on his face but said nothing.

'I am afraid my father and brother never *got on*.' Like Queen Victoria, Hetty had a habit of emphasizing certain words. She turned to look at the photographs of her father. 'He was a profoundly *religious* man in the tradition of many of our most distinguished generals. In his younger days they called him Pi-Parkyn but such cheap jibes never bothered him . . .'

Hetty's pale expressionless face was coming alive as though fresh blood had been injected into her veins. She launched with enthusiasm into a eulogy of the general in which he appeared as a bowdlerized version of Gordon, bible in one hand, sword of righteousness in the other and never a brandy bottle in sight.

Wycliffe listened with solemn attention and when she finished he said, 'Your father must have been a remarkable man.'

For the first time he saw her really smile. 'He was! A *most* remarkable man. As I have told you, he was a teetotaller and he hated – *hated* gambling.' She hesitated, then went on, lowering her voice, 'In that as in so many things, Gavin deliberately disregarded his wishes.' She paused, then added, 'And there were debts!'

She allowed time for her confidences to sink in.

'Of course, Gavin did well in the Korean affair.' Hetty

dismissed the whole Korean war as she might have done a frontier skirmish in the days of the Raj. 'It looked as though he was settling down and we were quite hopeful; then, shortly after the armistice in Korea, he allowed himself to be seconded to some quite absurd quasi-civilian appointment . . .' Her contempt was withering. 'It was a fresh blow to father's hopes for him and they drifted further and further apart . . . Then, when he finally came home for good, he adopted the extraordinay way of life which he now follows. I am *sure* that it contributed to father's death, *quite* sure.'

After a little while she added, 'So, as you see, my brother and I lead seperate lives.'

There was no answer to that so he said nothing.

'We have nothing in common and we have never been close. We live together only because it was my father's wish that I should provide a home for my brother.'

Another interval, then the final dénouement: 'You see, Mr Wycliffe, this is my house; father left everything to me.'

There was a sound from the back of the house, a door opened and closed and there were footsteps in the passage.

Hetty was alert. 'That will be my brother. If you want to talk to him hadn't you better go to him?'

'I assumed that he would come here.'

'Why should he?'

Why, indeed?

He found Parkyn in the dimly-lit hall taking off his duffle coat. The major greeted him with neither interest nor surprise. 'So you're here.' He hung up his wet coat on the hallstand and wiped his face and head with a red-spotted handkerchief. 'You'd better come to my room.' He pushed open the door of a room on the other side of the hall from his sister's. It was even more spartan; the carpet scarcely covered the floorboards. There was a roll-topped desk, a table littered with old newspapers, and a couple of armchairs. A paraffin heater similar to Hetty's was already burning.

Long ago, as a child, Wycliffe had gone with his mother on some forgotten business, to visit their landlord, The Colonel, and been received by the great man in his study. That too had seemed, even to a little boy, untidy, dirty, and even smelly but when he had mentioned it to his mother afterwards she had said in a voice that was almost reverential, 'Those people are different, Charlie; not like us.' A line had been drawn which, in all the years since, he had found it difficult to cross. It accounted for his tentative attitude now.

'Pull up a chair and sit down.' Parkyn sat down himself and stretched his legs to the heater. 'I've just come from the antique shop. I rang the bell and a young copper answered it. "Who are you? What do you want? Answer at dictation speed so that I can write it in my bloody notebook" – sort of thing. Then he wouldn't tell me what it was all about.' Parkyn brought out his pipe and started to fill it. 'What's happened down there?'

'You've no idea?'

'If I had I wouldn't be asking.' He held out his pouch. 'Smoke?'

'Not just now.' Wycliffe told him what had happened and he listened without interruption.

'So Joseph is dead.'

'Yes. Was he a friend of yours?'

He gave Wycliffe a curious look. 'Friend? I've never thought about it.' He hesitated, choosing his words, 'He was a companion; we met fairly regularly. Joseph was a good fellow; one of nature's innocents. Good men often are – I expect you've noticed that in your job.' He glanced sideways at the superintendent. 'You haven't said that he was murdered but I suppose he was otherwise there wouldn't be all this flap.'

'We are treating it as a case of murder at the moment.'

61

So far, if this was an interrogation there was no doubt who was asking most of the questions.

Parkyn got up from his chair, went to his desk and returned with a bottle of whisky, two glasses and a carafe of rather murky looking water. 'Drink?'

'No, thanks.'

He glanced at Wycliffe with a half smile which could have been contemptuous, then he poured himself a drink, took a good swallow, wiped his lips and sighed. 'Of course you'll have no trouble catching him.'

'Who is it that we are supposed to catch?'

'The brother – David. You say his boat is missing but he won't get far; he's not very bright.'

Wycliffe stretched his legs to the heater and relaxed in his chair. He said, dryly, 'You seem rather better acquainted with the Clement brothers today than you were yesterday.'

Parkyn did not rise to that. He said, 'Indeed?' Then he added, as though making a simple statement of fact, 'David is a rat.'

He sipped his whisky then balanced the glass on the arm of his chair.

Wycliffe said, 'Perhaps you'd better tell me about your relationships with the brothers.'

'If you like, but there isn't much to tell—' He broke off as a board creaked in the passage and looked sharply towards the door, but after a moment he resumed speaking without lowering his voice. 'I've known Joseph for years, long before he made the mistake of letting his brother into the business. I see him a couple of times a week in the evening and I often call in at the shop in passing.'

'To collect his bets.'

'As you say.' No animosity, no embarrassment. The man was unassailable.

'And David?'

'I see as little of him as possible. It's not difficult to

avoid him as he seems to be away most of the time on his so-called business. I guessed a long time ago that he was lining his pocket at Joe's expense and that one day he would probably clear out and leave Joe stranded. Joe is no business man and lately, from things he's let drop, I'm sure that David has been disposing of stolen goods through the firm – what you people call fencing.'

Parkyn puffed at his pipe, sipped his whisky and sighed. 'Not that I would trouble myself about that but Joe's life centred on that shop and he was an honest man.'

'Has it occurred to you that the younger brother might have been involved in your break-in?'

Parkyn turned to face him briefly then looked away again. Wycliffe decided that he was not to be answered but after a moment Parkyn said, 'I've thought so for some time.'

'But done nothing about it.'

The major raised his huge shoulders in a slow shrug.

The man's detached omniscience was beginning to irritate. Wycliffe said, 'Well, it looks as though David has cleared out as you expected but Joe has been shot; did you expect that too?'

Parkyn did not bother to reply. He struck a match to re-light his pipe and held it poised. 'I think that Joe must have threatened him with the police. The last time I saw Joe he was a very worried man.'

'When was that?'

'Thursday evening, I think – yes, he was with me that evening and on Friday morning I looked in at the shop but he had a customer so I picked up his slip and left. I expected to see him again last night but he didn't turn up.'

The match burned down to his fingers; he threw it away and struck another. 'There was nothing unusual about that, our arrangements were always loose. However, when the shop didn't open this morning I began to wonder a bit and this evening I went along there. You know the rest.'

He put the match to his pipe at last and puffed it into life. Wycliffe wondered what the two men could have had in common. He had not met Joseph but from what he had heard and from the photograph in the sitting-room he had the impression of a timid, introspective individual, the sort who might be relied upon to follow in father's footsteps without protest, even with grati-tude. His whole existence had been bounded by the antique shop while Parkyn, despite Hetty's scorn, had played his part on a larger stage.

Another swig of whisky, another sigh. 'About my father's gun – is there any evidence that it was the gun which killed Joseph?'

'I'm waiting for a report from ballistics.'

It was odd. Wycliffe had an uncomfortable feeling that behind these exchanges it was he, Wycliffe, who was being shrewdly assessed and marked down. It annoyed him the more because he suspected that the feeling arose from his own absurd sense of inferiority. He told himself that by this time of night the man was seeing the world through an alcoholic haze. His movements were studied and slow and his eyes had acquired that glazed look which usually precedes sleep or the stupor that passes for sleep.

There was another loud creak from the passage and this time the door opened and Hetty stood there like a headmistress, ready to tear strips off an unruly class.

'Your supper is ready.'

Wycliffe stood up. 'I won't keep you.'

Parkyn saw him out and stood on the doorstep while he made his way down through the sodden garden to the road. It was still raining and the collar of his mackintosh felt clammily cold against his neck. He hurried down Dog's Leg Lane to the comparative cosiness of Bear Street. The old people knew how to build their streets so that they weren't wind tunnels. The fat woman's restaurant cast a pool of orange light over the road but the steamy windows made it impossible to see inside. He walked the length of the street to the harbour.

The lights of the police caravan were the only sign of habitation though navigation lights burned on the quay and at the mastheads of some of the moored craft. Reflections shimmered over the water.

The duty constable was reading a paperback.

'Anybody else in?'

'No, sir. Mr Scales is still with Dr Franks. Vanstone is keeping obo in Godolphin Street—'

A car drew up outside and Inspector Scales came in. 'I thought I might catch you.'

John Scales had been with Wycliffe for years, he was the backbone of the squad. He specialized in business and law but he was a first-class all-rounder as well.

'Anything from Franks?'

'Nothing helpful. He's fairly sure that Clement died on Saturday evening or during the night, he won't go further than that. The path of the bullet through the skull suggests that the gun was held with a considerable upward inclination – as it probably would have been if he shot himself.'

'Or if he was bending over his stamps when somebody shot him. I'd like to believe it was suicide, but the removal of the gun ... Did he say anything about the man's general health?'

'Good for a man of his age leading a rather too sedentary life. No sign of organic disease, no serious disabilities.'

They chatted for a few minutes and it was agreed that Scales should concentrate on the business side of the antique shop, through the accounts and by contacts with their bank manager and solicitor.

Wycliffe turned to the duty constable. 'I'm on my way home.'

But before going home he wanted another word with the woman in the restaurant and he walked down the street in the drizzling rain.

She was alone, clearing the tables. Gutted candles stood in a row on the counter with salt and pepper pots. He tried the door; it was locked but she saw him and let him in.

'You're all I need!'

'I won't keep you – just a couple of questions. Have you had a visit from my lads?'

She was grim. 'I have. One of them arrived while I was in the thick of it, following me round with his questions. I'm afraid I gave him short change. I know he's got his job to do but I've got my living to get . . .'

'I suppose you opened as usual on Saturday night?'

'It's our best night.'

'I wondered if you happened to notice anybody visiting opposite, say between seven-thirty and eight o'clock?'

She lowered her bulk on to one of the straw botto-med van Gogh chairs. 'If I don't take the weight off my feet I shall fall down.' She stooped to massage her ankles. 'Saturday evening . . . We had veal – veal cutlets done in white wine. We don't offer any choice of the main dish – one dish, but good, that's been our policy from the start. It was slack to begin with . . .' She studied the rings on her soft, plump fingers. 'There *was* somebody, a bit before eight, I'd say. He came in a taxi and it was pouring with rain. After he'd paid off the taxi he couldn't get any answer at first, ringing at the side-door, then somebody came and let him in. I couldn't see who it was.'

A sound of whistling came from the kitchen and she grinned. 'My man, clearing up. He's only little but he's got go in him – more than I have. Anyway, about this chap, he was let in and that was the last I saw of him.'

'Can you tell me what he looked like?'

She frowned and pouted. 'I didn't see him all that well because he had his back to me most of the time but he was tall, and on the thin side.'

'Young?'

'Not exactly young – thirty-fivish, I'd say.'

'How was he dressed?'

'A dark mack – made of the stuff policemen wear, I think.'

'Hat?'

'No hat; he had dark hair – oh, and he was carrying a leather bag, like a large brief-case.'

'Were there any lights on in the shop?'

'No, I don't think so.'

'Did you see his face at all?'

'Well, I must have seen it but not clearly – he had a moustache.'

'And you didn't see this man leave?'

She shook her head. 'I didn't see him or anybody else after that except customers. We started to get busy and I didn't have time to look out of the window. Anyway, once this place fills up on a wet night you can't see because the windows get steamed over.'

'You've been a great help – thanks.'

'Is it true that they've both been murdered?'

'I told you, Joseph was found shot in his room upstairs.'

'And David?'

'I wish I knew. By the way, what's your name?'

'Blazek – Annie Blazek. I was a Drew before I married. My people are farmers over to Bere Alston.'

Taxis are a policeman's best friend. It was a simple matter to telephone headquarters and get them to put out a call for any driver who dropped a fare in Bear Street just before eight on Saturday evening. He used Annie's phone and that done he went back to his car and took the road for St Juliot and home.

If Joseph Clement had been shot on Saturday evening

then the visitor who, according to Molly Stokes, had come to sell something, was very much in the picture along with brother David.

Toby Williams, the boatman, lived in one of the row of cottages whose long, narrow gardens reached down to the shore. It was almost eleven but there was a light in his downstair room and Wycliffe picked his way down three or four steps to the front door. When he knocked it was opened almost at once by Toby himself.

Toby was a little barrel of a man. As always he wore a sailor's blue jersey but Wycliffe now saw him for the first time without his cap which had left a red line just below the line of his sparse grey hair. He had a splendidly lush moustache and a small tuft of hair on his chin.

'The wife's gone to bed; she can't keep 'er eyes open after ten and that's just when I begins to wake up.'

'Give the man a drink, Toby!' A West African grey parrot in his cage watched Wycliffe with a beady eye, standing first on one leg then on the other.

Toby laughed. 'Beer, Mr Wycliffe?' There were two glasses on the table ready with a quart jug of beer. 'I brews me own an' I can say 'tis better than the cat's piss they sell in pubs.'

The parlour was small and Wycliffe's head scarcely cleared the ceiling beams but it was cosy. A fire burned in the tiny grate.

'I want to get in touch with David Clement so if he's gone off in the *Manna*, we need to find her.'

Toby took a gulp of beer. 'Your health, Mr Wycliffe.'

'Bottoms up!' The parrot said.

'Clement left a note?'

Toby reached for a crumpled sheet of paper which had been wedged between two ornaments on the mantelpiece. 'This is it; I searched through the rubbish after you rung.'

It was a sheet of paper with the firm's printed heading

and a scribbled note written with a ball-point. 'I've taken *Manna* from her moorings – D.C.'

'I suppose it *is* his writing?'

Toby scratched his head. 'God knows, Mr Wycliffe! You can't expect me to know how they all write.'

'Has he taken the boat out before at night?'

'Not as I remember. Some of 'em do though.'

'What sort of trip would she be capable of? Could she cross the channel, for instance?'

'Oh, yes. No problem. You could take 'er almost anywhere in reason. She's a good sea boat and Clement knows 'ow to 'andle 'er. I'll say that for 'n.'

'What about fuel?'

'Well, 'e wouldn't cross the channel with what she was carrying, that's for sure. Without filling up 'e might make forty mile – no more.'

'She was moored off; how did he get out to her?'

'The dinghy was kept upturned on the shingle at the bottom of my garden an' rowlocks and oars was in my shed. Each one of my owners 'as got 'is own sort of rack in the shed.'

'Can you give me a description of *Manna*?'

Toby got up from his chair and went to the sideboard where he rummaged in one of the drawers and came up with a snapshot. 'That's *Manna*, Mr Wycliffe, my gran'son took that.'

It showed the boat clearly enough with Toby's bulk poised in the act of climbing over the side into the dinghy.

'The young devil said 'e thought I was going to fall in an' 'e wanted something to remember me by.' He added, 'You can see 'er lines an' I can tell 'e anything else you want to know.'

Wycliffe took down a detailed description of *Manna* and by that time the banjo-clock on the wall was showing ten minutes to twelve. Toby saw him to the door and the parrot said, 'Don't 'e bother to come back.'

Toby apologized. ''Tis only a bird, Mr Wycliffe, 'e don't understand.'

Helen was in their living-room, reading. 'Have you had a meal this evening?'

'No, but I had a good lunch. You go to bed, you shouldn't have waited up.'

'There's some cold chicken.'

'A little chicken with a slice of bread and a cup of tea would do me very well.'

The man in the taxi was certainly the man who had come to sell the Clement brothers something and the marked catalogue, open on the desk, suggested that the something might be glass paperweights. High quality bijouterie; small, easily portable and reasonably negotiable; a man could carry a fortune in his briefcase.

But what had gone wrong? Whatever it was, Joseph was dead and his brother had cleared off in *Manna*. That left the visitor and David's car unaccounted for. It was tempting to link the two. Was it credible that the visitor had dropped David off at the quay then driven away in David's car? It covered the broad facts.

Glass paperweights.

He remembered having seen something about them recently but could not recall the context.

Baccarat, Millefiori, Clichy, St Louis ... Beautiful things, beautiful names ... The sounds had a soothing, soporific effect ...

'Charles!'

For a moment he had no idea where he was then he saw Helen bending over him. He was lolling on the settee and there was a trolley at his elbow with supper.

'You dropped off; you must be exhausted.'

CHAPTER FOUR

Tuesday morning was fine with blue skies and fleecy white clouds but there was a nip in the air, a reminder that spring had not yet truly arrived. Even so police headquarters was unusually cheerful, everybody greeted everybody else with a complacent grin as though claiming some part in the improvement.

The local paper was on his desk. 'City Antique Dealer found Shot – Murder say Police.' The police had said no such thing but some oracle in the chief's office had announced in the usual bland gobbledygook: 'The possibility of foul play cannot be excluded at this stage.' But Clement's disappearance and the absence of *Manna* from her moorings would keep the press busy for a while; they might even help to find them both.

Among reports was one from Melville of Ballistics. Melville had done a thorough job at the cost of a night's sleep. There were photographs taken with a comparison microscope showing, side by side, different views of the bullet recovered from Joseph's room and one newly fired from the gun Wycliffe had found on the beach. In Melville's opinion both had been fired from the same gun; in other words, Joseph had been killed with the general's gun.

A bit of firm ground.

And it seemed that the watch on Molly Stokes might be about to pay off. Molly had returned to the flats at seven that morning off night-duty and at eight a taxi had arrived. A minute or two later Molly came out, smartly dressed, and carrying a week-end case. Crowther was keeping observation from a parked van and he followed her taxi to the railway station where she took a ticket to Bournemouth.

The duty C.I.D. officer immediately asked Bournemouth police to tail her on arrival and a description given over the telephone was followed by a picture by wire.

Of course it was possible that the girl was going to spend a day or two with friends but it seemed unlikely that she would leave home at this time unless her trip were in some way connected with Clement's disappearance. If Clement was operating on the wrong side of the law it was possible that they had arranged a rendezvous – not specifically for this occasion but in case things went badly wrong at any time.

Wycliffe telephoned the Horton Radford. 'Is it possible to speak to Nurse Molly Stokes?'

A plummy voice, accustomed to soothing the jangled nerves of top people, said, 'Staff-nurse Stokes went off duty at six-thirty this morning and she is not due back until mid-day on Thursday.'

So she had not thrown up her job and it looked as though she would be back in a couple of days; by which time he hoped to be in a position to call any bluff she chose to try.

He spent a few minutes editing Toby's description of *Manna*, then handed it over for circulation to port authorities and coast-guards on both sides of the Channel. That done, he called Sergeant Bourne, his administrative officer, on the internal telephone.

'These so-called "art-robberies" in the stockbroker belt round London – I suppose you've got copies of the missing-property lists put out by the Met?'

'Yes, sir. They've been circulated to all dealers in our area.'

'Bring the copies to my office, please.'

Bourne was an extremely efficient young man; his soul yearned for administrative perfection. No doubt he prayed daily in the computer room: 'Thy Kingdom come; Thy Will be done.' No doubt either he would one day rise to the top of the hierarchy where such qualities were increasingly valued. But Wycliffe could not learn to love him any more than he loved foam-plastic bread or reconstituted, hydrated ham. Wycliffe was not in harmony with his time, neither was he enamoured of those who were.

Bourne came in, correct and assured, a fine pinstripe; hairstyle, a perfect compromise between short-back-and-sides and the trendy; two copies of the lists in his hand.

'Sit down, Bourne.'

Wycliffe leafed through one of the lists. 'In total it makes a tidy haul, doesn't it?'

'Fourteen break-ins over the past two years with a total insurance loss of more than three hundred and eighty thousand pounds.'

'Thank God it isn't on our patch! All small stuff?'

'Small but valuable. Snuff boxes, vinaigrettes, miniatures, medallions . . . '

'Glass paperweights?'

'The very last list, sir. A collection of glass paperweights valued at nearly twenty thousand pounds, most of them purchased by the owner at a London auction only a few months earlier.'

Wycliffe turned the pages to the appropriate list. Twenty-six weights in all. He usually looked through the missing property lists when they arrived from another force and a glance now left him in no doubt that this was where he had first seen the evocative descriptions: 'A Baccarat patterned concentric millefiori primrose weight . . . A St Louis faceted mushroom weight . . . A St Louis concentric millefiori shamrock weight . . .' He picked up the internal telephone and dialled.

'D.C. Trice?'

D.C. Trice was a blonde enlisted under the sex-equality

banner with some misgiving but she was good at her job.

'. . . The stuff brought back from the antique shop . . . The sale catalogue that was open on the desk – will you read out the marked items on the page at which it was open? . . . Slowly! I want to check them against a list . . .'

Bourne listened to Wycliffe's side of the conversation with interest. When it was over Bourne said, 'The Clement brothers were fencing the stuff, is that it?'

'All six items marked in the catalogue were on the Met's stolen property list. It seems that the Saturday night visitor had come to fence part of the haul and in order to come to terms they were checking against the sale prices.'

Bourne was delighted. 'In that case he must have been in on the robberies and that will be news for the Met.'

News which Bourne would be anxious to pass on himself, laying up treasure in heaven.

'If we get a reasonable description from the taxi driver you can put it on the telex then get hold of whoever is in charge of the case at the Met and put him wise personally.'

Bourne was eager. 'We've already got the taxi driver's statement, he was in an hour ago. I brought a copy with me.' He handed over a typewritten slip.

The description tallied with what Annie Blazek had told him as far as that went. Tall, slight of build, dark with moustache and sideburns. Aged about thirty-five. He carried a brown leather case and the driver had picked him up at West Hill station among the passengers off the London train at 19.25 and taken him direct to the antique shop.

'Well, that's it, Bourne. Good hunting!'

Bourne paused for a moment at the door with a backward glance. He was never quite sure when the mickey was being taken.

The case was on the move. Either the motor cruiser

had taken fuel aboard or she had not gone far. They were now looking for the motor cruiser, a car and two men – David Clement and his visitor. The more the merrier; time to worry when there were no leads.

Wycliffe glanced through the reports of house-to-house enquiries in Bear Street which were still in progress. So far they were not encouraging; the shops on either side of the antique shop were lock-ups with no-one living over and this applied to most of the premises in the street which was essentially a business area. Joseph had probably shot himself or been shot at some time between eight o'clock when Annie saw the visitor being admitted and, say, one in the morning. The gun had been dropped on the beach at St Juliot at some time after two and the fishermen had seen a car backing off the quay at about half-past.

He settled to a morning's desk work and was interrupted by John Scales.

'I've talked to the bank manager. A bit sticky at first but he came round. The affairs of Clement Brothers Antiques don't look too rosy. Turnover and profits have been falling and Perrins – the bank manager – thinks that in a year or so they would have been finished. He blames David. Under the elder brother the business made steady though not handsome profits. Incidentally, there is no sign of all the business David is supposed to have done on his travels. Cash transactions I imagine – no records, no tax, no questions.

'Anyway, I asked about a solicitor and the bank manager referred me to Lambert Parkes and Davis. He remembered that they had acted for Joseph's father. I saw Mr Davis, a smug individual who was reluctant to say more than "Good morning!" When I pointed out that we were probably dealing with a murder case he condescended to tell me that they had received no instructions from Joseph since the proving of his father's will. Presumably there was a deed of partnership when he took David into the business but if there was Mr Davis did not draw it up.'

They chatted for a while then Scales said, 'It looks as though Clement and his visitor drove to St Juliot early Sunday morning. Clement went aboard his boat leaving the other chap with the car. When the fishermen saw the car backing off the quay, Clement must have been on his boat, waiting for the coast to clear before putting to sea.'

Wycliffe sighed. 'I suppose that makes sense but still there's the problem of the gun.' He shifted irritably in his chair. 'I don't think we've got it right, John – not yet.'

The scene-of-crime reports arrived – a file in themselves. They included a scale plan of the dead man's room, a score of photographs, an inventory and a detailed account of the examination that had been made. Most of this was for the courts if it ever got that far but the section on fingerprints interested him.

The telephone and the door handles of the office doors carried no prints – they had been wiped clean. The door to the yard carried one set. Some joker (surely not Smith?) had made the most of these; 'they were those of a known person, viz: Chief Detective Superintendent Wycliffe.' Two sets of prints had turned up in profusion all over the building, the dead man's and, presumably, his brother's.

Wycliffe could think of no reason why David Clement should have wiped his prints off the telephone and the door knobs so, presumably, the wiping had been done for, and perhaps by, somebody else. The Saturday night visitor? It was an attractive idea.

On the brass handle of the old safe there were blurred prints – quite unidentifiable. In another part of the report the contents of the safe were listed and these came as a surprise. They included two gold snuff boxes and a couple of ivory figurines – not on any lists of stolen property, as well as fifteen hundred pounds in cash. If

Clement cleared out voluntarily was it likely that he would have left all that behind? The answer seemed to be an emphatic No! But the inference – where did that lead?

Wycliffe had lunch in the Bear Street restaurant for no better reason than a need to establish a routine appropriate to the case. This was his way; every new case found him trying to fit his actions as far as possible into a routine. Only then did he feel free to devote his whole energy to the problems on hand. He could not have explained it any more than he could explain why he always walked on the cracks in the pavement or invariably put on the right before the left leg of his trousers when dressing. Yet he had never hated his father or despised his mother.

He was early and the fat woman had not started to serve.

'What is it today?'

'Beef casserole with boiled potatoes and carrots.'

'Good!' But not for weight watching.

'I'll bring you your lager.'

Afterwards he looked in at the incident van by the harbour and glanced through three or four reports which had just come in. D.C. Dixon was duty officer.

'Anything in these?'

'Two things, sir. A woman who lives over the shop next but one to the antique shop says she was awakened on Saturday night by a car being started and driven down the back lane. She sleeps in the back of the house, sir.'

'Has she any idea of the time?'

'All she can say is that it was after one because she'd been reading in bed and she didn't put the light out until a few minutes to one. She thinks she went to sleep almost at once and that she was awakened not long afterwards.'

'And the other report?'

'From the landlord of the *Seven Stars*, sir. He says that David Clement came into his bar just before nine on Saturday evening. He bought a packet of cigarettes, had a beer, and stayed about twenty minutes.'

'Is he a regular there?'

'No. The landlord says he comes in occasionally when he's run out of cigarettes after the shops have shut; then he has a drink to make it look right.'

'Is he sure of the time?'

'Apparently. They have a TV in the bar and Clement came in while they were waiting for *Dallas* to start.' Dixon, uncertain of his chief's acquaintance with the classics of TV, added, 'It's a show about Texas, sir.'

So far this was the last occasion on which anyone had admitted having seen Clement.

He drove back to headquarters through the chaotic traffic of the city centre and arrived at his office just in time to take a call from Kersey. Kersey had gone to St Juliot in response to a report that David's car had been found at the bottom of the disused quarry, about three hundred yards off the road through the village.

'Driven over the edge deliberately, sir – a drop of forty feet . . . Yes, I've been down, there's nobody in it . . . Smith is with me . . . No, it won't be too difficult to get it up, I've sent for the recovery truck . . .'

So much for the idea that Clement had gone off in his boat and the visitor in his car.

Wycliffe said, 'So it's possible that the two of them went off in the cruiser.'

Kersey seemed doubtful. 'I suppose so, but why go to the trouble of ditching the car?'

'It was hidden. Left on the quay or in the village it would soon have raised questions. As it is, if it wasn't for the gun on the beach we might still not be in on the act. Somebody was buying time.'

It occurred to Wycliffe as he dropped the phone that Clement might, after all, have gone to St Juliot alone, driven the car on to the quay, unloaded his baggage, ditched the car and then boarded his boat.

Leaving a small fortune, easily portable, in the safe? It hardly seemed likely. Perhaps he panicked? But he was calm enough to write a note which made sure that Toby Williams would not raise the alarm when he saw that *Manna* was missing from her moorings.

Wycliffe turned to the little pile of documents on his desk awaiting signature but almost immediately he was interrupted by Sergeant Bourne.

'I passed on the news to the Met, sir. The officer in charge of the case is Chief Inspector Worth and he's quite chuffed. It's the first promising lead they've had and he's sending down a Sergeant Minns by train with a special mug book – cons not at present in gaol but with the right kind of form for these jobs. Minns is due in at three.'

'You'd better get hold of the taxi driver and Annie Blazek. Bring them here with Minns when he arrives.'

Bourne went off, tail high.

Wycliffe thought, 'Too much happening – the storm before the lull.' If the case ran true to form they would be biting their nails for days after this.

Bourne collected Sergeant Minns from the station and picked up the taxi driver and Annie on his way.

The taxi driver had first go with the mug book, seated at the table in Bourne's office, watched by Bourne and the Met sergeant. After a while they were joined by Wycliffe. It was routine, but routine which often carried with it a measure of suspense. The driver, a plump, comfortable man, reading glasses half-way down his nose, took his time, turning the pages slowly, studying the photographs with care and occasionally going back for a second look. Finally, about two-thirds of the way through the book he stopped and said, 'I think that's the man.'

Bourne told him there was no hurry, that he could go

through the whole book again, but the man was firm in his choice. 'No, that's him all right. I know it was raining and dark but I saw him plain enough in the lights under the station canopy.'

Minns was delighted and when the taxi driver had left the room with Bourne to sign a formal statement he said, 'George Alfred Waddington, sir. Two-year suspended sentence for burglary in '68 and a five year stretch in '71 – both country-house jobs badly bungled. Now Alfie seems to have lined up with a brainier mob. He's a wizard with alarm systems and that's the only reason why they would use him. Outside of that he must be a pain in the neck.'

Annie came in and took her place at the table with the mug book. She cast a shy, rather nervous glance at Wycliffe, intimidated by her surroundings. But she soon settled down and spent a long time turning the pages of the album with her plump, ringed fingers. In the end she couldn't make up her mind between two men. 'I think it's one of them, Mr Wycliffe, but I can't honestly be sure.'

Waddington was one of the two she had chosen and that was enough for Minns.

'I'd better get back as soon as possible, sir. We shouldn't have any trouble picking him up. We know his haunts and he can't know we're after him.'

Wycliffe was by no means so confident but he said nothing.

Annie had continued to turn the pages of the mug book and suddenly she said, 'That's David Clement!'

It was not a mug-shot but one of a number of shots in the back of the album, apparently taken in bars. It showed four men seated round a table in front of them.

Minns turned to Wycliffe, 'What on earth is she talking about?'

Wycliffe explained and Minns went on, 'Those shots were taken by our undercover boys of meetings between known criminals with the right M.O. for these art jobs. Just in case something might click.' He grinned. 'Naturally, we don't ask their permission or let them catch us at it if we can help it. Even the landlords of the pubs aren't too keen if they find out what we're up to.'

Annie was looking at Wycliffe with eyes that were almost pleading. 'I really ought to get back . . .'

'Yes, of course.' He took her to Bourne and arranged for her to make her statement. 'Mr Bourne will see that you are taken home and thank you for your help.'

Back in the office he asked Minns if the three men with Clement were known.

'I'll say! That's the point. One is Waddington and the other two have form for housebreaking; their mug-shots are in the album too. The man you say is Clement isn't known to us but if he's not a villain himself then he's picked some dandy playmates.' Minns could scarcely conceal his satisfaction. 'With a bit of luck this should wrap the whole thing up.'

'We shall want first call on this man Waddington.'

Minns nodded but without conviction. 'Waddington is no killer, Mr Wycliffe, you can take that from me; all the same, I'll mention it to my guv'nor.'

'So will I, Sergeant. So will I.' Wycliffe was looking at the photograph which included David Clement. 'When and where was this taken?'

Minns turned to an index sheet. 'It was taken last January in the lounge bar of a pub in St John's Wood; quite a respectable place. These chaps fancy themselves; they reckon they've got class; no third-rate boozers for them. Waddington, for instance, has taught himself to speak proper and he plays golf at the weekends.'

Wycliffe smiled. 'It looks as though we've got interests in common, Sergeant.'

Minns closed his album. 'You can say that again, sir. So if that's all, I'll be getting back. If I put my skates on I could make the 17.52. The sooner we get moving the better.'

'I agree. Mr Bourne will arrange for you to be taken to the station. Thank you for your help and my compliments to Chief Inspector Worth.'

Inter-force co-operation; everybody agrees that it is a splendid thing – absolutely essential. And everybody goes about it tongue-in-cheek or at least with fingers crossed, especially when it involves the Met.

Alone, he went back to his office with the photographs Minns had left so that copies could be made – the shot of Clement with his cronies in the pub and the mug-shot of Waddington.

David Clement had joined his brother in the business about three years since. Before that he had worked in a London insurance office, now he was consorting with known criminals and handling nice little portable antiques which, if not worth their weight in gold were moving in that direction. It could be made to hang together.

From what he had heard of Waddington he was even less inclined to believe that Clement had cleared out in his company and he had not even suggested the possibility to Minns.

Five o'clock. Diane came in with a neat folder of letters to be signed.

Sometimes he envied people with jobs where they knew exactly what they had to do. Their days had a beginning, a middle and an end. One might take a pride in doing such a job well. He seemed to spend his time floundering in a welter of activity which might come to something or nothing. Only rarely was it possible to go home at the end of the day with any feeling of completion, there was always the carry-over to tomorrow. But when he confided such thoughts to Helen he got little sympathy. 'It's what you live for. Goodness knows what will happen when you eventually retire.'

The telephone rang and Diane answered it. She put

her hand over the mouthpiece. 'Superintendent Redfern from Bournemouth on the line.'

'Tell them to put him through.' He took the receiver. 'Hullo, Jimmy! Any news for me?' They were old friends, having survived several courses and conferences together.

'About your girl, Charles. She arrived on schedule and our chap tailed her. She walked to Canning Terrace in the area behind Central Station where there are three or four blocks of flats. She went to one of these – Gort House – and took the lift to the fourth floor. My chap took a chance and went up with her, pretending to be calling on someone on the same floor. She had a key to Flat C on that floor and she went in. After about fifteen minutes she was out again but without her weekend case. She then took a leisurely stroll to the town centre and had a late lunch in a restaurant. Since then she's done a bit of window shopping and bought some food in a supermarket.'

Wycliffe's thanks were sincere. Having done his share of foot-slogging surveillance he knew the amount of patience and skill needed to gain that amount of information without being spotted.

'Do you want to keep it up, Charles?'

'I'd be grateful.'

'No problem. We're fairly quiet at the moment, holding our breath until the season starts. Incidentally, I made a few inquiries about Flat C on the fourth. It's leased to one Alan Page, said to be some sort of salesman or commercial rep. It's small, just a bedroom, living-room, kitchen and usual offices.'

'Thanks again.'

He finished with the paperwork to Diane's satisfaction and she whisked it away. An empty desk.

He was pleased with what Redfern had told him. The flat in Bournemouth was just the bolt-hole he had hoped to find. All that was needed now was for Clement to turn up there.

And what if he did?

Did he really believe that David Clement had murdered his brother? If not – if Joseph had committed suicide, what was all the fuss about? The art robberies were not his business. He had found a loaded gun on the beach and from that a case had mushroomed, but what was the case?

He stood at the window of his office which overlooked one of the main highways out of the city. The evening exodus was beginning. Suddenly he felt depressed.

There was a tap at the door and it opened. 'Oh, there you are, Charles!' Hugh Annesley Bellings, the deputy chief constable. As though it was a surprise to find him in his own office. Bellings was tall, lean, handsome and suave. He was, as Wycliffe thought of him, 'the other kind of copper' – really an administrator like Bourne, but Bourne with Winchester and Balliol behind him. He sat in his office reading and annotating reports, studying statistics and musing on trends. His greatest concern was the public image of the force.

'I've read your reports, Charles. Odd case, isn't it?'

Bellings never discussed a case as such, only in terms of its possible political, social or personal implications. Wycliffe wondered which it would be this time.

'I met the elder Clement once – rather an uncouth sort of chap I thought, but he knew about furniture. I was offered a little Carlton House table at what seemed a reasonable price but a friend advised me to let Clement have a look at it before buying. Luckily I did. The thing had been cannibalised and he picked it up at once.' Bellings smiled in gracious acknowledgement of his own fallibility. 'Of course, that was years ago, before this brother came into the business.'

Wycliffe contented himself with looking bland and saying nothing.

84

'I've noticed that Gavin Parkyn's name keeps crop-ping up in the reports.'

They had arrived; this was the reason for the visit.

'You know him?'

A foolish question. Just as Wycliffe and his colleagues studied to know every villain on their patch, so Bellings made a similar effort to acquaint himself with everyone of rank, wealth or of any kind of distinction, from the patrician vice-chancellor of the university, to the scaffolding-to-boardroom chairman of Purvis Construc-tions; from the Lord Mayor of the city to the little chit of a girl who was spoken of as a possible for the athletics team in the next Olympics.

Bellings drew in his lips. 'I can't say that I *know* him; I doubt if anyone does and in any case I have had very little contact with him since we were young men serving together in Korea.'

It was the first time Wycliffe had heard of the deputy's active service experience. 'In the marines?'

'A marine commando unit, yes. We were together for just a few months and since then I have only met him a couple of times though, of course, I have heard quite a lot about him.' Bellings studied his long thin hands in reflective mood. 'He was a strange character. We called him Moggy Parkyn because he seemed to have at least as many lives as a cat. He was totally regardless of his own safety – but totally! One supposed that he either believed in a charmed existence or cared nothing for his life. But it was after the Korean affair, when he resigned his commission, that his career really began. He transfer-red to Intelligence and worked in Europe. The work he did in that field in the late fifties and through the sixties and seventies is still very little talked about but he was, I understand, a key figure in Western counter-espionage.'

'You surprise me.'

Bellings laughed and was gratified. 'I can see that. My dear fellow! You musn't be misled by what he seems to be now. Do you know that he speaks five langauges with impeccable fluency – including Russian?'

Wycliffe said nothing and Bellings went on, 'I'm glad I came to see you, Charles – glad that I was able to put you in the picture. Now that you know . . . '

It was part of the Bellings technique to leave sentences in the air so that he did not have to make points with vulgar directness or commit himself further than was necessary.

Wycliffe straightened the objects on his desk, a sure sign to those who knew him that he was about to be obstinate. 'I have no reason to think that Parkyn is criminally involved in this business but his association with the Clement brothers means that he must be questioned like anybody else and, after all, Joseph was shot with the general's gun.'

'Stolen by the younger brother.'

'Possibly, but Parkyn himself acknowledges that he was a regular caller at the shop; he went there each morning to collect Joseph's betting slip, and the two met in the evenings at least twice a week.' He paused, then went on, 'Whatever Parkyn may have been in the past his present interests seem to be gambling on horses and stupefying himself with alcohol.' Even as he spoke Wycliffe experienced a twinge of conscience in thus describing the major.

Bellings shifted in his chair and Wycliffe knew that he was needled. 'I've heard something of the sort; he seems to have taken to an eccentric way of life, but I expect the sudden break – the abrupt transition from stress and even danger, to the humdrum existence of a man on pension – has been difficult to cope with. However, what I am saying, Charles, is that despite his idiosyncracies it is unthinkable that a man like Parkyn could be involved in a sordid little crime. And what is more, anything that looked in the least like harassment on our part could have serious repercussions at the highest level. However he lives, Parkyn still has sufficient influence—'

'To be immune from the ordinary processes of police investigation?'

For once Bellings lost his cool. 'Don't be ridiculous, Charles! You seem to have a grudge against the man!'

The interview ended as most exchanges between the two men did with irritation on both sides. Bellings was annoyed because he had been forced to spell out his message to no apparent purpose; Wycliffe was annoyed for more complex reasons which included the fact that Bellings always manoeuvred him into betraying a strain of priggishness in his nature.

Bellings stood up. 'Well, it's your case, Charles.'

'Yes, it is.'

Wycliffe could imagine him muttering under his breath, 'Uncouth fellow!'

But he was more troubled by the remark he had actually heard: 'You seem to have a grudge against the man!' It annoyed him that he had so far shown his feelings that Bellings was able to read something special in his attitude to Parkyn. Of course it was absurd to suggest that he bore the major any grudge; the truth was more subtle and more complex. His attitude owed something to recollections of childhood, something to his sense of inferiority which put him on the defensive but much more to the fact that Parkyn's way of life seemed to express that particular brand of disillusionment which sometimes threatened his own peace of mind. 'There, but for the grace of God . . . ' And he was by no means sure of that. 'I'm feeling my age,' he told himself.

He had planned an early night, an evening by the fire with Helen; a book or the television. But he knew that if he went home now he would spend the evening moping, a menace to Helen's peace of mind as well as his own. He reached for the telephone and asked for his home number.

'Is that you? . . . I'm afraid I shall be late . . . I've got nothing done today and there's a stack of stuff . . . No, don't save food for me, I'll get something . . .'

It was true; there was always a stack of paperwork waiting to be done but if Bellings . . .

He took a bulky file from a drawer of his desk: *Proposals for a new Command Structure with Observations on Staffing.*

The headquarters building was emptying and the familiar background noises gave way to an unnatural stillness. Odd that police headquarters should maintain only a skeleton staff during the hours when sixty percent of crimes are committed. Outside the flow of traffic dropped to a trickle and soon only single cars disturbed the silence. At a little after seven he switched on his desk lamp. He had waded through about a fifth of the file and annotated a good deal of it. A pall of grey smoke hung over his desk, rising slowly until it was caught and whisked away by the erratic air-conditioning. He was beginning to feel at peace with himself once more, fit to mix with other human beings. He had told Helen not to keep a meal so he telephoned the restaurant in Bear Street and spoke to Annie.

'I expect we can manage one extra; what time are you coming?'

'Say, eight o'clock.'

At a quarter to eight he stopped work, cleared his desk and fetched his coat from the cloakroom. He was leaving his office when the telephone rang.

'A woman from the restaurant in Bear Street, sir. She says she was speaking to you earlier—'

'Put her through.'

'Oh, it's you at last!' Annie was almost inarticulate with excitement. 'He's here again – outside the antique shop. The man who came on Saturday evening – he's ringing the bell at the side-door . . .'

'Can you see him now?'

88

'Yes, he's—'

'Don't ring off.' He got Information Room on the inter-com and gave instructions for cars in the neighbourhood of Bear Street to intercept. 'Detain for questioning suspect at present outside Clement's antique shop in Bear Street. Description . . . ' He recited the description which was now firmly fixed in his mind. 'Stop me if I go wrong, Annie . . . Have you go that? . . . All right, get on with it but keep this line open. Can you still see him, Annie? . . . Good! They shouldn't be long . . . '

He looked at the wall clock; the seconds hand seemed to race round the dial. Annie reported that her man had moved from the side-door to the door of the shop and was tapping on the glass. How long would he keep trying?

'What?'

Annie told him that a police car had arrived. Another interval. 'What did you say? . . . Good! Any trouble? . . . That's fine, and thank you. You've saved us a great deal of bother.'

He spoke to Information Room again. 'Tell them to take the suspect to Mallet Street.' Mallet Street police station was only an estate agent's stone-throw from the antique shop.

Five minutes to eight. Sergeant Minns would still be in the train on his way back to London. Childish to laugh. He picked up his car and drove to Mallet Street. Kersey was already there.

'I heard the kerfuffle on the car radio.'

Every living creature has an environment to which it is best suited, in which it looks and feels most at home; from the koala bear in its gum tree to the virtuoso conductor on his rostrum. For George Alfred Wadding-ton that optimum was a bar stool with a double whisky in front of him and a busty barmaid to chat up. In the aseptic bleakness of a police interview room he was lost.

'Mr Waddington? George Alfred Waddington?'

'Yes, but I should like to know—'

Seen in a good light Waddington was a poor specimen; round shouldered, skin and bone. Not so long ago he would have been written off as 'consumptive.' Yet he was a dandy with his trendy moustache, his sideburns and his well-cut grey pinstripe.

'Where have you been since Saturday evening?'

The pale brown eyes were evasive. 'Since Saturday?'

'Isn't that when you arrived here? On the train from town which got in at seven twenty-five in the evening – isn't that right?'

'Well—'

Whatever his skill with security devices Waddington wasn't bright.

'Simple, straightforward question – where have you been since then?'

'At my hotel, the *Unicorn* in Duke Street.'

'Evidently you haven't been keeping up with the local news, Mr Waddington.'

'I don't know what you're talking about.'

Wycliffe was more than half convinced that he didn't. There had been nothing about the case on the radio or television and nothing in the national press.

'Joseph Clement has been shot and his brother has disappeared.'

Waddington was shaken but he mustered all his intelligence and put on a bold front, 'Who are they?'

'Strange!' Wycliffe made a strategic pause to fill his pipe, a leisurely business, watched by the poor devil as though it were some sort of sacrament. 'You went straight from the railway station to their shop on Saturday night and you were ringing their door-bell again this evening but you don't know who they are.'

'I've nothing to say.' He'd made it at last but far too late.

It was Kersey's turn. 'A bit of business involving glass paper-weights. You see! We don't need you to talk, we *know*. You've got form, Waddington, two convictions, and it looks as though you were the last person to see Joseph Clement alive.'

'Christ! You're not saying I killed him?'

'Didn't you? Anyway, let's get back to what you were doing at the shop on Saturday evening.'

Wycliffe said, 'Mr Waddington won't mind if we take a look in his bag.'

Kersey picked up the bag and snapped it open then he began lifting out the contents on to the table. 'Pyjamas, sponge-bag, electric razor, tissues . . . brush and comb . . . What's this, then?'

A pair of socks turned inside out over some hard and heavy object which, unwrapped, proved to be a glass paperweight in its chamois-leather pouch. And there were three more in Waddington's laundry.

Kersey said, 'It beats me how you've managed to stay out of gaol so long.'

Waddington looked at the four weights, gleaming in the light, and said nothing.

'And there's still the shooting.'

'But I swear—'

'I shouldn't bother to swear, just tell us what happened when you went to the antique shop on Saturday evening.'

Waddington looked bleakly round the bare little room, knowing that he was destined to see a good many more like it in the future.

Time for the famous caution, part of the British legal handicapping system. 'You are not obliged to say anything but anything you do say may be taken down and given in evidence.'

Waddington sighed. 'What's the use? The long and short of it is, Clement wanted out and the others didn't see it that way. If he went, we were washed up.'

'Because he was the brains.'

'Not altogether. He had inside information on these

91

houses and he was in the trade with the right connections for fencing the stuff but that was all.'

'Clement set up the jobs and fenced the proceeds – but that was all. What more did you want? Anyway, what *I* want is to know exactly what happened at the antique shop on Saturday evening.'

Waddington had given up. 'Well, Clement had set up the paperweight job before backing out so we had the stuff on our hands.'

'Go on.'

'Well, the others – my associates – fixed for me to bring the weights down here and ask him to find a buyer.'

'And if he refused?'

Waddington hesitated. 'I was to hint that he might find himself in trouble with you lot.'

Kersey said, 'I can see why they picked on you. So, there you were, standing out in the rain with fifteen thousand quid's worth of glass burning a hole in your little bag. What happened?'

'I didn't know the chap who let me in but he said he was Clement's brother. He took me to an office at the back and asked me a lot of questions but I wasn't sure where he stood in the business so I played dumb. Then Dave turned up and the brother pushed off without another word.'

'What was David Clement's attitude when you'd said your little piece?'

'Oh, he didn't seem bothered. He said he thought he might have a customer but that it would take a day or two and that I was to come back on Tuesday – that's tonight.'

'I asked him what he thought I was going to do meanwhile and he said he'd fix me up in a quiet pub where I could lie low and keep out of the way.'

Waddington ran a hand through his dark hair. 'In the end I had to go along with that but it was when he said,

"You'll have to leave the weights, nobody's going to buy that sort of thing blind," I said that wasn't on and he just waved his hands and said, "Piss off then and catch your train."

'I didn't know what to do so I rang . . . I rang one of my associates and he spoke to Clement. After a bit of arguing they agreed that I should leave two of the weights and hold on to four.'

Wycliffe said, 'Did you see anybody while you were in the shop except the two brothers?'

'Nobody.'

'What time did you leave?'

'Coming up for a quarter to nine. David fixed me up at the *Unicorn* by phone.'

'Why did you wipe your dabs off the telephone and the door knobs?'

He looked blank. 'I don't know what you're on about; I never wiped off any dabs. I didn't know somebody was going to get done there, did I?'

So much for the Saturday night visitor. What Waddington had said turned a certain amount of speculation into fact and some of his statements could be checked. At least, David Clement's role was now clear. With knowledge gained from his work in insurance he had set up a number of robberies and used the cover of the antique business to sell stolen goods. But there are limits to the value of such inside information, however valuable in the first place. Clement had banked on a short but profitable career in crime and it seemed that the time had come for him to retire. But had he done so on his own terms?

CHAPTER FIVE

April is a fickle month and on Wednesday morning a southerly gale blew up the estuary bringing frequent rain squalls with intervals when the sun shone down on a turbulent sea flecked with white foam.

'Take your heavy mackintosh, not your raincoat.'

'I'm not going trekking across country.'

'No, but take it all the same.'

He was tired and not in the best of tempers. The headquarters building looked blatantly bleak. The glass and concrete pile, brain-child of a distinguished architect of the sixties, triumphed over the landscape in mindless assertiveness. He spurned the lift and ran up the stairs three at a time, an example of what the psychologists call displacement activity.

Before taking off his coat he called Bourne on the internal phone.

'Bourne? . . . Yes, that's what I'm ringing about. Any word from the Met? . . . Oh, Minns again; you'd better tell him to get a season ticket . . . No, I leave him to you . . . I don't care a damn about Waddington except in so far as our case is concerned . . . '

The truth was that he felt disappointed and frustrated. When Annie Blazek had telephoned to say that the Saturday night caller was back it had seemed for a moment that all might be over bar the paperwork but half-an-hour with Waddington had brought disillusionment. Everything pointed to Waddington being a small-time crook who had been taken up by a few of the bigger boys because of his skill with alarm systems. It had been Waddington's bad luck to get caught up in the drama of the Clement brothers which, almost certainly, had nothing to do with him.

The drama of the Clement brothers; here he was back to the beginning: one dead, the other missing, the gun on the beach, the car, the boat, the girl . . . At any rate, Minns was right, Waddington was no killer, and if he had been he would hardly have been daft enough to go back for a second look three days later. But suppose David had shot his brother in a quarrel over the Waddington business then panicked and bolted?

Could it have been like that? Hardly. If Joseph was murdered he was shot while sitting at his desk with the gun held to his head. In other words, if he was murdered, it was in cold blood. Far more likely that Joseph shot himself. But his suicide would focus attention on the affairs of the antique shop and that would be unhealthy for David. But David had just had five thousand pounds' worth of coloured glass dropped in his lap. Had this been sufficient inducement for him to bring forward his plan to clear out?

What plan? With an elaborately prepared cover ready to move into he hadn't turned up there. Apparently he had not got that far. Add to that the cash and valuables left in the safe and the gun on the beach and it began to look more like panic flight than planned retreat. 'Which,' Wycliffe muttered to himself, 'is more or less where we came in.'

Yet against that shambles there was the car, astutely hidden, the note to set Toby Williams's mind at rest about *Manna* and the prints which had been removed in the downstairs office. Judicious foresight and panic bungling in about equal measure.

Quod est absurdum! as they used to say in the geometry books.

The telephone rang. 'Wycliffe.'

It was the harbour master, Sam Foster. 'It's possible we've got something for you, Mr Wycliffe.'

'About *Manna*?'

'Indirectly. Ron Bryce, the harbour master at Porthellin, rang me this morning about a dinghy they found holed and floating gunnel-down on Sunday morning. She was brought in and pulled up on the slipway there. This sort of thing happens all too often early in the season when the weather is dicey; dinghies break loose from their moorings or they may be washed off the beaches. Anyway, Ron didn't think much about it till this morning when he noticed a baling tin wedged under one of the thwarts and he saw the name, *Manna* sort of scratched on it. There are dozens of these little two metre dinghies about and one is much like another but the baling tin clinches it.'

Wycliffe thanked him. 'I'll get hold of Toby Williams and we'll go down together and take a look.'

But before leaving the office he telephoned Superintendent Redfern at Bournemouth.

'You seem very edgy about this one, Charles!' (Did it show even on the telephone?) 'Anyway, the girl spent the night at the flat and an hour ago she was still there; no sign of any man but she's been questioning the caretaker about Page. When did he last see Page? How long did he stay? The caretaker told our chap that Page had been there for a couple of nights a fortnight ago. That's all for now, but we'll keep in touch.'

Porthellin village lay three miles down the coast in a bay of the same name. Sheltered from the west and south by the crook of Laira Head, it lies more or less open to the south-east. Once the village lived off fish, now it is a tourist trap but April is too early for them.

Wycliffe picked up Toby Williams at St Juliot and drove over the hump of the peninsula through a maze of lanes which were becoming lush with spring growth. Toby sat immobile in the front passenger seat, staring straight ahead, smoking his pipe which had an incredibly short stem.

'Did you ever come across Major Parkyn when he had a boat at St Juliot?'

'The major? Yes, I looked after his boat for a couple of seasons. Nice little craft; cutter-rigged with auxiliary motor . . . The *Clarissa* – that's what she was called. Never forget the name of a boat . . . 'E sold 'er a couple of years back to a chap over to Brixham.'

'How did you get on with him?'

'All right. Never said much but never grumbled neither.'

'A good man with a boat?'

'Oh, the major knew 'ow to handle a boat. No doubt about that; he could take 'er out in most any weather and come back with a dry arse as they say.'

On the outskirts of Porthellin a sprawl of ugly bungalows gave way to the old stone cottages of the original village, then they were in the single main street which was so narrow that it was impossible for two vehicles to pass and traffic was regulated by lights. Now the village seemed deserted, the gift shops were closed and shuttered, cafés were boarded up and only a couple of food shops remained open to cope with the slender winter trade. The traffic lights flicked pointlessly through their routine. Ron Bryce, lanky and one-eyed, was waiting for them. His other eye was permanently closed on an empty socket. The tide was just beginning to make and there were patches of slimy mud still showing in the basin. The holed dinghy was drawn up on the slipway. Toby Williams looked her over.

'That's Mr Clement's dinghy all right. I can tell from the little split in the stern thwart.'

She was carvel built and the planking had been stove in amidships below the waterline.

Wycliffe said, 'Where was she picked up?'

Bryce pointed to a stretch of sandy beach beyond the village. 'Off Hucket's Cove there. She was riding gunnel under. Bert Simms spotted her and brought her in.

Sunday morning about twelve when the tide was three-parts in.'

Wycliffe picked up the end of the painter which was neatly whipped, there was no question of its having frayed through or having been cut.

Toby said. 'Mr Clement weren't the sort to lose 'is dinghy.'

The three men stood on the slipway contemplating the little craft, watched by several locals who were waiting outside the pub for the doors to open.

Wycliffe said, 'If he deliberately cast the dinghy adrift would he have gained much in either speed or the distance she would travel?'

Ron Bryce studied Wycliffe with his single eye. 'There could be something in that. Towing a dinghy even with a short line can be a drag though it don't usually signify much.'

Toby, better informed about the problem on Wycliffe's mind, came straight to the point. 'It wouldn't 've made five miles difference to 'er range and not 'alf a knot to 'er speed.' He lifted his yachtsman's cap and scratched his head. 'She must 've put in somewhere if only for fuel but why ain't we 'eard?'

The sky was clouding over as the wind rose off the sea in preparation for another squall.

'Where did *Manna* carry her name?'

Toby considered. 'On 'er transom an' on the front of the wheel-'ouse.'

'Easily changed?'

'If you 'ad new boards ready to put in place or if you 'ad time to re-paint 'em, but changing 'er name wouldn' account for the dinghy.'

'No, it wouldn't; I was trying to think of possibilities.'

The rain came hissing down, driven before the wind, and the three men hurried across to the pub which had just opened.

'Let's try again . . . ' Wycliffe had ordered drinks and

they were sitting round one of the painted metal tables at some distance from the bar. 'Say that Clement put out from St Juliot between two or three on Sunday morning, a couple of hours or less into the ebb. I understand that it was calm—'

Toby interrupted. 'Not all that calm – not outside Laira; there was a fresh breeze from the south-east, enough to bring up quite a chop – nothing to worry a boat like *Manna* but she would lose a bit if she was 'eading into it.'

'All right, it was choppy. Now, say that somewhere off here he abandoned *Manna* and took to the dinghy—'

The two men looked at him in amazement. 'Why would 'e do a damn fool thing like that?'

Excursions into lateral thinking are all very well until they run up against a wall of common sense. Why, indeed? 'But *if* he did, could he have made it ashore?'

Both men shook their heads. 'Not in the dinghy, not if he was outside. Not with the ebb and a choppy sea, he'd never have brought her in. Of course, if he was in the bay and inside the shelter of Laira, it would be different. He could've rowed himself ashore all right then.' It was Bryce speaking and he turned to Toby for confirmation.

Toby nodded. 'Yes, but it's a damn fool notion, Mr Wycliffe. I mean, if 'e brought the launch in under Laira then abandoned 'er, where is she?' He looked out of the window at the grey waste of sea, still lashed by rain, and said with heavy sarcasm, 'I don't see *Manna* out there, do you?'

Bryce grinned. 'Toby's right, Mr Wycliffe, she'd have gone ashore on the rocks next tide and probably ended up like the dinghy.'

But Wycliffe was not giving up. 'Just one more question. If the dinghy broke adrift or was cast adrift from her tow, outside the bay on an ebbing tide, would you expect her to end up in the bay the next morning?'

Bryce paused with his beer half-way to his lips. 'No, I

wouldn't. You got a point there, Mr Wycliffe. Almost for sure she'd have drifted further down the coast.'

Toby emptied his glass, looking troubled. 'Yes I go along with that.'

Wycliffe thought, Mr de Bono rides again! 'So it looks as though the launch probably did come into the bay and that the dinghy was set adrift in the bay – perhaps after someone came ashore in her.'

'And the *Manna*?' The question came from Toby.

'If there were two men, one might have gone ashore while the other put to sea again.'

Toby nodded. 'That could be, it's the only way to make sense of it all.'

Sense for Toby Williams but did it make sense for the case? Two men again. He arranged for Bryce to get the dinghy under cover in an old fish loft and for a search to be made along the shore for the oars, then the three of them had a meal in a little room behind the bar – grilled mackerel with boiled potatoes.

It was two o'clock when Wycliffe arrived back at his office. The morning's work had served to confuse him rather than otherwise. Two men, one of whom had gone ashore at Hucket's Cove. If one of the men was David Clement who was the other? And which of them had gone ashore?

While he was out there had been a call from a lawyer with offices in Bear Street; a lawyer he had never heard of, a certain Everett Friend. Friend had said that he had information about Joseph Clement's will and that he wanted to talk to someone concerned in the investigation of his death.

Plain speaking from any lawyer. Wycliffe decided to go himself.

Everett Friend was not prosperous, he had an office over the Bear Street bakery; two dingy little rooms and a landing cluttered with wooden filing cabinets like stacked coffins. In one of the rooms a middle-aged woman sat at a table with a pre-war Remington and a telephone; in the other Mr Friend brooded over a desk littered with dusty pocket files and bundles of paper tied with pink tape.

Friend belonged to Joseph's generation and he was a man of the same stamp; one could guess that they shared other characteristics including an innate gentleness which unsuited them for business. He greeted Wycliffe with a sad smile; wheezy-voiced, watery-eyed and smelling of menthol.

'I've been away from the office for a couple of days with a bad cold. I heard of poor Joseph's death yesterday but there was nothing I could do . . . My Clerk . . . ' He gestured vaguely towards the other room but did not finish his sentence.

'You said something about a will.'

Mr Friend stirred himself as far as to remove the tape from one of the pocket files. 'Yes, we have custody of his will. His father employed another solicitor but when Joseph took over he came to me. We were at school together . . . Do you really think that he was murdered, Superintendent?'

The lawyer's contribution was circumlocutory and lugubrious; fragments of information emerged unpredictably like droplets of moisture condensing out of a fog. Wycliffe sat back in his chair, put on his most bland expression and resigned himself. He was seated by a low window which overlooked the bakery yard and from time to time a stout lad in grey overalls crossed between the buildings carrying a sheath of cakes or rolls on his head – for all the world like a figure in a Brueghel painting.

Under the partnership agreement David received forty percent of the net profits and secured a similar interest in all other assets *except* the building. Friend leaned forward on his desk to emphasize the point. 'Except the building. It was as though Joe had some uneasiness about the partnership even then for he kept the building in his own name.'

'The partnership was not a success?'

The lawyer took time off to blow his nose. 'Joe never confided in me but I certainly had the impression that it had been a great mistake and this was confirmed when he gave me instructions to prepare a new will . . . '

'About the will . . . '

But it was another five minutes before he succeeded in bringing Friend to the point. At last the lawyer took a single sheet of paper from the pocket file and read it through as though seeing it for the first time.

'Yes, this supersedes an earlier will made in favour of his brother, David. In this will, made less than a year ago, he leaves everything to his friend, Michael John Lane of St John's Court, and I am appointed executor.'

'Do you know this man Lane?'

'By sight. He's a cabinet maker and he has a workshop next to his house—'

'Married?'

'I think I'm right in saying that he is a bachelor as Joseph was.'

'Has he been notified?'

'I telephoned him this morning and I have an appointment with him tomorrow.'

'What about the funeral?'

Friend became even more solemn. 'Under the will I am required to make arrangements for the interment. It seems that Joseph had a horror of cremation. I have been in touch with the coroner's office and I should receive a disposal order this afternoon. As you know, the inquest stands adjourned. I have provisionally arranged for the funeral to take place at Mount Charles cemetery at three o'clock on Friday afternoon.'

Friend came with him to the top of the stairs where they were enveloped by the warm, yeasty smell of fresh bread.

102

'If Joseph was murdered, Superintendent, I hope that you will succeed in finding his killer. Joseph was an honest man and there are not too many of them left.'

Wycliffe walked the few yards to Annie's restaurant. She was at work with a vacuum cleaner and chairs were stacked on the tables. She switched off the cleaner and turned to him with a surprisingly girlish smile.

'I hope I did right yesterday.'

He was warm in his thanks. 'You shall have a personal letter from the chief constable to hang on the wall.'

She laughed, 'It would scare my customers away.'

'Do you know a friend of Joseph called Michael Lane?'

'Lane? The only Lane I know round here is Bunny Lane, the cabinet maker. Everybody calls him Bunny because he's got a hare-lip. I didn't know he was a friend of Joseph but he could have been.'

'Married?'

'No, he's a bachelor and he's lived alone since his mother died. Come to think of it he and Joseph would have a lot in common.'

St John's Court was tucked away behind Bear Street at the harbour end; a little square of houses. Bunny Lane's was like all the others except for the workshop attached, a sensible arrangement which, remarkably, had survived the planners. The door of the workshop was open and Wycliffe went in, his nostrils assailed by the scent of freshly worked timber and glue. It was a shed, long and dimly lit by windows of overlapping panes of glass. There was a central bench on which a number of hardwood drawers were held in clamps to allow the glue to set; pieces of reproduction period furniture stood about at random and in all stages of completion and there were sophisticated machines for drilling, planing and sawing.

'Anybody home?'

A short, stocky man with dark curly hair came out of a sort of glass cage where an electric lamp burned. He had a generous moustache which just failed to cover his hare-lip and when he spoke his words came with a sibilant whistle.

'Superintendent Wycliffe.'

'I suppose you've come about Joe; you'd better come into the house.'

Wycliffe followed him out to a back-yard, through a lean-to greenhouse with a giant vine, through a workman-like kitchen and into a plain but clean and comfortable living-room. There was an open grate, a cast-iron crock for coal, three leather armchairs, fibre matting on the floor, a big square table and a number of kitchen chairs. On the mantelpiece an alarm clock ticked loudly. No sign of period furniture either genuine or reproduction. On the walls were tiers of shelves crammed with books, many of them without spines and therefore anonymous.

Lane said, 'I've got a little parlour but I never use it – not since my mother died.'

'Obviously you've heard what happened to your friend Joseph.'

Lane nodded. He was very dark with rather sombre eyes and a heavy set to his jaw which gave an impression of strength.

'You didn't think to contact us?'

'What good would it have done?' He was not aggressive, merely objective.

'You were close friends?'

'I suppose you could say that, I've never thought about it. Joe's been coming here two or three times a week for several years.'

Wycliffe was looking round, wondering how the two men spent their time, then it dawned on him that this was where Parkyn and Joseph met, not two men but three gathered round the fire in this room which reminded him of the farm kitchen of his childhood; one of the three armchairs was the major's.

'You haven't mentioned Parkyn.'

'You didn't ask about him.'

'But the three of you met here regularly?'

'There's no secret about it.'

No secret, certainly, but Wycliffe was beginning to understand; in meeting as they did the three men retained their own individuality, their own privacy. There was no commitment, nothing was surrendered, and none felt free to speak of the others. Parkyn had not mentioned Lane and Lane had not referred to Parkyn.

'Just the three of you?'

Lane smiled briefly, revealing more of his hare-lip, 'Just the three of us.'

'How did you spend your time?'

The question arose from curiosity more than anything else and Lane did not resent it.

'It depends; sometimes we sit and talk, sometimes we just sit. There's always a glass and a smoke, and sometimes we play dominoes.' He glanced across at the big square table covered with oilcloth.

Wycliffe could see the attraction of this way of going on. If he was ever alone it was the kind of relationship he might seek. He asked, knowing the answer in advance, 'Did Clement confide in you at all?'

Lane shook his head, 'It wasn't like that.'

'I imagine you are as anxious to find out who killed him – if he didn't die by his own hand – as we are.'

'There shouldn't be much difficulty about that; David has cleared out, hasn't he?'

Exactly Parkyn's response if not his actual words.

'Was there friction between the brothers?'

Lane looked at him appraisingly and seemed to reach a decision. 'I won't be a minute.' He disappeared into the kitchen and came back with a bottle of white wine and two glasses.

'Will you try it? It's three years old and made from my

105

own grapes mostly.' He drew the cork and poured a little of the wine into a glass. 'Try it – see if you like it.'

It was good – light and flowery. Lane filled the glasses.

'Your good health!' A moment or two for appreciation then, 'Does Parkyn drink wine when he's here?'

Lane was curt. 'The major drinks whatever he feels like drinking at the time. But you were asking about Joseph and his brother.' He sipped his wine then wiped his moustache with a khaki-coloured handkerchief. 'Joseph was a simple sort of chap really – not stupid by any means, but straightforward. When his father died he was quite capable of carrying on the business as it always had been and that is what he did. It was only when the prodigal son returned that Joe got into difficulties. He wasn't up to his brother's tricks, he just didn't understand that sort and almost before he knew it he was up to his eyes in all sorts of funny business.'

Lane lifted his glass to the light, admiring the clarity and colour of his wine. 'Nice, isn't it? Makes you feel good to look at it.' Then he sighed. 'It's hard to believe that they were brothers, they were as different as chalk and cheese.'

'Did Joseph know what his brother was up to?'

'I don't know what he knew; all I can say is that he was a very worried man. For more than a year he hasn't been himself.'

'But he never discussed his troubles with you?'

'No. He would make the odd remark like, "I don't know where it will all end," or "One of these days he will land us both in trouble." Things like that but no details.' Lane fingered his glass. 'We didn't pry into each other's affairs, we didn't ask questions or offer advice.'

It wasn't difficult to imagine the three of them, sitting round the fire in the leather armchairs, a bottle of wine and a bottle of whisky close at hand; saying little, making no demands and so able to relax in each other's company. Had one of them wanted a closer relationship no doubt he would have married.

'Did you know that he was leaving everything to you?'

'Not until the lawyer phoned; it was very thoughtful of him.'

'You say that the three of you met here two or three times a week; did you never go to Parkyn's place or to the shop?'

Lane's reproachful look seemed to suggest that he thought Wycliffe had understood the situation better but he contented himself with a simple, 'No.'

'You never visted the shop?'

'Sometimes on business. I did small repair jobs and a certain amount of restoration work for them. That's how I first met Joseph – back in his father's time. They made a big thing of furniture then, and when they had a nice piece that needed a bit of attention they sent for me.'

'And recently?'

He shrugged. 'I've probably been in the shop five or six times in the past two years.'

'And when was the last time?'

'Saturday night – I didn't actually go in but I called there.'

Wycliffe felt a little tremor of excitement. 'Last Saturday night – at what time?'

'A bit before ten, a quarter to, maybe. I don't know exactly. It was pure chance. When Joe was here on Thursday evening I offered to lend him Anthony Coleridge's book on Chippendale but he forgot to take it. On Saturday I'd been cooped up in the workshop all day so in the evening, when the rain stopped, I thought I'd take a stroll and it occurred to me to drop the book in.'

'You went to the side-door?'

'I intended to but I saw a light in the back of the shop so I just tapped on the glass and David came out.'

'Did you see Joseph?'

'No, David said that he was a bit seedy and that he'd gone to bed so I gave David the book and asked him to pass it on.'

'You realize that must have been somewhere near the time Joseph died?'

'I don't know when Joseph died. I only know what I read in the newspaper.'

'In any case, you were the last person we know of to see David Clement. How did he seem? Normal? Excited? Edgy?'

Lane laughed briefly. 'Much as usual – not exactly welcoming and I had the impression that he was expecting someone else but I could be wrong about that.'

Wycliffe stood up. 'Thanks for the wine.'

Lane saw him out by the front door into a deserted square which looked like a film set waiting for the action to begin. He collected his car and drove back to his office feeling subdued. The visit had left a vivid impression on his mind; he could see the three men seated round the hearth in Lane's living-room, each with a glass in his hand, staring at the fire. For long periods the silence would be broken only by the ticking of the clock on the mantelpiece and the occasional sounds of coals settling in the grate. The atmosphere would be close with a thin pall of smoke drifting near the ceiling and the fruity smell of the wine blending with the more astringent odour of the major's whisky.

'Shall I top you up, Joe?'

'No, thanks; I'm well enough.'

Lane would pour a little of the clear pale wine into his own glass then place the bottle well away from the fire to keep it cool. The clock would tick away another five, ten – perhaps fifteen minutes . . . The major would say, 'Do you think a game . . . ?' And they would move to the square table taking their glasses with them. The rattle of dominoes, the draw, the play . . .

'Your glass is empty, Major. Try a drop of this for a change . . .'

Did they call the major Gavin? It was unlikely.

A sort of refuge. For the major from his sister, her house, and possibly from disillusionment. For Clement, from his brother and from the business which had been his standby and was now only a source of worry and foreboding. For Lane – perhaps from his hare-lip and all that it had meant to him since infancy when he had first realized that he was different.

Kersey was waiting for Wycliffe.

'Mr Redfern telephoned. Molly Stokes caught the eleven o'clock train and she arrived at three. I've put Fowler to keep an eye on her. According to Mr Redfern she made no contacts that could mean anything and he thinks she's as anxious to find Clement as we are.'

'What about the Waddington saga?'

'Bourne is looking after Sergeant Minns. Minns has had two sessions with Waddington, with a lawyer, and he's spoken to his chief on the phone. They want him back in London.'

Wycliffe's mind was still on Lane and the meetings of the three men in his living-room. To Kersey he must have seemed heavy and inattentive.

'What do you think?'

Kersey said, 'I can't see Waddington as a killer.'

'Neither can I and if we want him we shall know where to find him. Tell Bourne to make sure he gets the paperwork right and when it's done they can have him.'

Wycliffe always found it difficult to sustain a logical train of thought for long. His mind didn't work that way. Ideas seemed to surface, link together in some sort of pattern and break up again as in a kaleidoscope which is gently shaken. Now and then a particular pattern appealed to him and he would try to look at it more closely.

'Perhaps we are meant to think that David Clement has cleared out.'

'You mean that he hasn't?'

'That's the other side of the coin and it scarcely makes sense, does it?'

Kersey tried again. 'You mean that he might still be here in the city?'

'That doesn't seem very likely.'

'No, I don't think it does.'

Wycliffe had arrived at a decision. 'Are you doing anything special this evening?'

Kersey grinned. His family didn't go in for much social life. 'I think we might have a free evening.'

'I want you to go to Bournemouth – clear it with Mr Redfern first – and see what you can find out about this Alan Page, the chap who holds the lease on the flat in Canning Terrace. We must be sure that he is Clement, otherwise we shall be caught with egg on our faces. If he is, then we want to know everything about him as Page.'

'Anything else, sir?'

'No. I'm going to talk to Molly Stokes.'

But before he could get away he had to cope with Diane at her most efficient.

'Mr Bellings is wondering if you've overlooked his memo 395/TC.'

'What's it about?'

'Your views on the possibility of cutting fuel costs by re-planning the rosters of crime and traffic mobiles.'

'The answer is yes.'

'Yes, what?'

'I have overlooked it.'

Diane would have liked to push a little harder but thought better of it. 'Then there's the crime prevention advertising campaign on TV. The agency have the specimen runs ready and the chief would like to see them with you.'

'When?'

'Tomorrow at ten.'

'That's another day.'

It was childish. He was childish; but there was more to it than that. Sometimes he felt the need to cut himself off from everything that was not connected with the case on hand, otherwise he would lose touch; ideas would not surface and patterns would refuse to form.

It was gone six when he eventually arrived in Bear Street and parked by the police caravan. The wind had dropped but the sky was still heavy with rain clouds. The shops were shut and the street was empty. He did not go into the van but walked along the wharf looking down at the still, sombre waters of the harbour.

If Clement had really bolted, surely he would have gone to Bournemouth, to the flat. But *Manna* had been taken from her moorings and her dinghy had turned up, damaged, off Hucket's Cove. Somebody had gone ashore there, of that he felt certain. But had there been one man on the launch or two? David Clement alone, or David Clement and another? If two, then one had remained on board the launch and taken her – where? But if Clement was alone, what had happened to *Manna*? Had he scuttled her? The idea came to mind only to be dismissed. He was muttering to himself. Drops of rain made tremulous expanding circles on the surface of the water; a gull, perched on the roof of the police van, fixed him with a sardonic eye.

And where did Lane come in? And Parkyn? Did they come in at all? The major, Bunny and Joe. Like a circus act. The three musketeers. All for each and each for all. Lane admitted being at the shop at shortly before ten; the major knew all about boats and it was his gun though probably stolen. And Joe was dead.

Joe was dead. And David was missing.

Time to stop this nonsense! Wycliffe rebuked himself. It was starting to rain much harder and he pulled up the collar of his mackintosh and set off to call on Molly Stokes. Fowler was on duty in Godolphin Street in the not very original cover of a television repair van. It faced away from the house but, presumably, he could see what went on through his wing mirror.

He rang the bell of the girl's flat and after a short wait the door was opened on a chain.

'Oh, it's you! What do you want now?'

She released the chain and opened the door wide. She wore a housecoat of dark, silky material with an oriental design which, with her almost black hair, was in startling contrast with the pallor of her face. She looked ill and it was obvious that she was a very worried young woman.

'You'd better come in, I suppose.'

The little flat was filled with a not very appetizing smell of cooking; the kitchen door was open and he could see saucepans on the stove.

'Will you be long? If so I'd better turn that off.'

'It depends on you.'

She whisked into the kitchen, turned off the stove, and came back, closing the door behind her. 'Sit down if you want to.'

But he continued to stand while she perched on the arm of one of the chairs and lit a cigarette. He was in no hurry to begin.

'Well?'

'You've been away.'

'Have I?'

'Bournemouth, wasn't it?'

'Is that illegal?'

'Why did you go?'

She was watching him closely; no fool, she knew better than to lie outright. 'I do sometimes on my change-over break at the hospital.'

'Did you stay with friends?'

She hesitated. 'Not exactly.'

'Flat C on the fourth floor of Gort House.'

She was shaken but she made an effort to come back

112

fighting. 'I don't suppose I can stop you spying on me but I don't know what good it will do you.'

'Is Alan Page your friend?'

She did not answer. The gas fire was burning and to Wycliffe, in his heavy mackintosh, it seemed uncomfortably hot but she was wearing little or nothing under her housecoat.

'Did you meet Page?'

'No.' She fetched an ornament from the mantelpiece to use as an ashtray.

'Where is he?

'I've no idea at the moment; he sells jewellery and fancy goods to the shops and he travels a lot.'

'But you have a key to his flat.'

'Yes.'

'What does Clement think about that?'

'That is none of your business.'

'At this moment one of my officers is on his way to Bournemouth to investigate the myth of Page.'

It was not in his nature to bully a witness but, without realizing it, he had been standing over the girl and his manner probably seemed menacing. At any rate there was a flicker of alarm in her eyes.

He went on, less dramatically. 'He will confirm that Alan Page and David Clement are the same and then we shall know that the flat and the alias were intended to help Clement get out from under whenever things got too rough for him. I'm not really very concerned with Clement the thief, but I am very concerned with Clement, the possible murderer.'

She held her ground and said in a level voice. 'I've no more idea than you have where David is; you can believe that or not – as you wish, but, as I've told you before, he is no killer.'

'But you went to Bournemouth expecting – at least hoping, to meet him?'

She did not answer but he had no need of an answer. He took off his mackintosh and laid it across one of the chairs then he sat down. It was a gesture, an acknowledgement that in some sense they had come to terms.

'For two years at least David Clement had been mixed up with a London mob. He's been responsible for organizing break-ins and for disposing of stolen property through his business connections in the antiques trade. In that time he must have accumulated a considerable sum of money; do you imagine for one moment that this money has gone into Clement Brothers Antiques Limited?'

She tapped the ash from her cigarette. 'Is this some sort of quiz? I've told you, I know nothing of David's business affairs.'

'It's an old trick to prepare for retirement from a venture in crime by establishing another identity – someone to hold the purse while the fight is on. It's less common than it was because professional snoopers and the computer make it more difficult but it can still be done. It's one of the freedoms we can still enjoy if we're smart enough.'

She swept back her dark hair with a careless movement of her arm. She really was an attractive girl, and a shrewd one. 'Why are you saying all this to me?'

'Would you have known about Clement's other life if you weren't intended to share it one day? Would you have agreed to share it unless it offered you something a good deal better than you have at the moment? You are no starry-eyed young girl, head-over-heels in love and blind to the grocery bills.'

She stubbed out her cigarette. 'Thanks for the testimonial but where does it all lead?'

'Simply to this: if Clement hasn't turned up in his new role he must have been prevented by something important. I want to know what that something is and so do you.'

She said nothing though he sensed that she was tempted.

'*Manna*'s dinghy has been found off Hucket's Cove in Porthellin Bay.'

That startled her. 'Wrecked?'

'Damaged; it looks as though someone came ashore in her then set her adrift. She was found on Sunday morning but I've only just heard of it.'

She was caught off guard. 'You think that he might—' But whatever it was she had been going to say she changed her mind.

It seemed the moment to go.

He went downstairs and out into the street. Fowler had turned the van round to get better vision as the light faded. At least he had something to put in his report to show that he had stayed awake. The rain was falling vertically and Wycliffe quickened his pace along Godolphin Street and through Bear Street to the old harbour and the police van.

D.C. Richards was duty officer and Dixon was there typing house-to-house reports. Poor old Richards suffered from premature hardening of the intellectual arteries. He was morbidly conscientious and totally lacking in imagination.

'Anything new?'

Richards shook his head. 'It's dead, sir; in my opinion we're wasting our time here.'

'Is the house-to-house complete?'

Richards nodded towards Dixon. 'Dixon is typing his last report.'

'All right, we'll move the van tomorrow and you can tell them to cancel the roster from then.'

This upset Richards who liked to grumble but did not really want to be taken notice of because that involved responsibility. 'I didn't want to speak out of turn, sir.'

'No question of that. You said what you thought and you are probably right.'

He looked round the little compartment, reluctant to tear himself away and go home. Last Sunday he had never heard of the Clement brothers, of Major Parkyn or of Bunny Lane; now it seemed that his life was bound up with theirs and it was a wrench to walk out on them and return to his own domestic circle. He stood over Dixon, fingering the sheets and putting the young man off so that he fumbled the keys.

'These are the last four, sir. We managed most of the street yesterday but there are always a few out, or away. I think the second one might be worth following up.'

Dixon made one more desperate attempt to finish and then drew out the sheets with a flourish. 'I'll just separate the carbons . . . ' He did so, then handed a sheet from the pile over to Wycliffe.

Wycliffe glanced at the report. 'Who's Marilyn Ford?'

There was a dry cackle from Richards and Dixon said, 'She's a pro, sir. She and another girl have rooms over the fish shop which is next to Annie Blazek's place and almost opposite the antique shop. There is a little passage beside the fish shop and the girls have their own entrance up a flight of steps. They both went off to what they call, "an engagement in the country" and they didn't get back until this morning. That's why we haven't been in touch with this girl before.'

'All right. Let's have it.'

'Well, Marilyn says that she was in her room alone; a client had just left, and she heard a sort of bang – like a car backfiring but she hadn't heard any cars in the street. She looked out of her window but she couldn't see anything and she forgot about it.'

'This, I take it, was Saturday evening?'

'Yes, shortly after nine. She remembered the bang when I started talking about a shot.'

'You think she's reliable?'

Dixon frowned. 'You know what these girls are, sir. When they've got no reason to lie they make good witnesses; they've got to have their wits about them or they wouldn't last long. More than that, they don't want to upset our lot if they can help it.'

If the girl really had heard a shot shortly after nine o'clock then that seemed to let brother David out, for at that time he was at the *Seven Stars* buying his cigarettes.

There was another report from the man who had interviewed the landlady of the *Unicorn* where Waddington had stayed. According to her, Waddington had arrived there between half-past eight and nine which provided him with an alibi if he needed one.

Enough hinged on the prostitute's evidence to warrant checking. It might be necessary to arrange an action replay with someone firing the gun in Joseph's room to find out what could be heard in the girl's flat.

He walked up Bear Street as far as the fish shop. It was still raining and there were few people about. The windows of Annie's restaurant were steamed over so that it was impossible to see inside. The narrow passage by the fish shop led to a yard and from the yard there was a flight of steps to the first floor. At the top of the steps there was a covered landing, a light and a front door with two bells, one of which was labelled M. Ford. Wycliffe pressed the bell and hoped that the girl was free.

The door was opened almost at once by a plump brunette.

'Miss Ford.'

'That's me.'

The Monro legend had persuaded him that all Marilyns were blonde but here was proof to the contrary. She wore a pale pink wrap-over-dress and she had dark, laughing eyes. Over the years he had had dealings with many prostitutes but he had known very few who really laughed. This girl seemed to be on the point of laughing all the time.

'Police. Superintendent Wycliffe.'

'You'd better come in.'

Her room, which overlooked the street, gave one the impression that a candy-floss machine had got the bit between its teeth and bolted. It was dimly lit and there were cushions and draperies in pastel shades everywhere. The smell was like a close encounter with the cosmetics department of a big store and he felt that he was being enmeshed in scented cotton wool. He stood in the middle of the room like the proverbial bull in a china shop with his mackintosh dripping on the carpet.

'I suppose it's about the shot.' She was a little unsure how to treat him. 'There isn't any more I can tell you. I had a visitor who left a few minutes before nine and this bang came not long afterwards. I remember it was after the church clock struck.'

'So you would be prepared to swear if necessary that it was after nine o'clock?'

She nodded vigorously. 'Oh, yes. Definitely.'

He asked her one or two more questions for form's sake, standing by the window, looking down into the street. The street was empty and the streaming road surface shone in the light of the street lamps. A couple, sharing an umbrella, came into sight and made for Annie's next door. Opposite, the antique shop already had that derelict look which buildings have when they are waiting for the 'For Sale' notices to go up.

'I don't suppose you saw anyone entering or leaving the antique shop that evening?'

'No – no, I didn't . . .' She paused. 'Wait a minute, I've been in the country for a couple of days and it puts things out of your head – there was somebody, I remember now. I should think it was a bit before ten. I went to the window to look down into the street like you do sometimes if you're a bit bored. There was nobody about, then I saw a man coming up the street from the harbour end. He was on the same side as the

118

antique shop and when he got there he went to the shop door and I think he must have tapped on the glass or something because somebody came and let him in.'

'You're quite sure about this?'

'Yes, I am. I'd forgotten but you know how things come back to you.'

'You know the Clement brothers, I suppose?'

'By sight, yes.'

'So it wasn't one of them you saw?'

'Oh, no. Definitely not. I couldn't see this man all that well but well enough for that. He wasn't very tall but broad and he wore a cloth cap – not many men do these days so I noticed.'

As Wycliffe's eyes became accustomed to the dim light he saw the bed which seemed to be a mound of pink silk. Marilyn must have a good class clientele; no short-time customers for her.

'Could you see who it was let the man in?'

'No, they didn't switch the lights on.'

'Do you know a man called Bunny Lane – a man with a hare-lip?'

She shook her head. 'I can't say I do. Is he from round here?'

She was beginning to show signs of edginess, once or twice she glanced at her watch; evidently she was expecting a client and wanted him to go. Finally she took her courage in both hands: 'Look, I'm sorry . . . I'm expecting a friend . . . '

As he reached the bottom of the stairs he heard footsteps coming, not from Bear Street but from the back of the premises. A man emerged from the darkness and hesitated when he saw Wycliffe. Some of Marilyn's friends preferred the back way in.

The girl's description fitted Bunny Lane as far as it went and it seemed likely he might wear a cloth cap. Bunny had said that he had called at the shop with a book for Joseph but he was quite definite that he had not gone in.

Wycliffe drove home. Helen heard the car and was standing in the doorway of the house from which light streamed out across the gravel. It was still raining hard.

'Aren't you glad you took your heavy raincoat?'

CHAPTER SIX

The alarm buzzed insistently and he reached out to stifle it. He was aggressively disposed to alarms of all sorts but most of all to the modern buzzers, hooters, sirens and other banshee devices. What was wrong with bells?

'Was that the alarm?'

'Yes.'

Helen sighed. 'Pity! I was hoping I'd dreamt it.' She turned over on her back and wriggled luxuriously. 'You haven't forgotten that Ruth is coming home today?'

He had but he wasn't going to admit it. Ruth was their daughter, aged twenty-three.

'She's due around lunchtime. I suppose there's no chance of you taking the afternoon off?'

'None I'm afraid.'

'But you'll make it in time for a meal at a reasonable hour this evening?'

'I'll try.'

'If you don't I'll file for divorce. Do you know we haven't seen her for six months?'

'She's happy in her job.'

'She seems to be but sometimes I think there's more to it than that.'

'Such as?'

'That it's more her boss than her job.'

'Ah well, he's rich.'

'Charles! When you say things like that you worry me. I'm not altogether sure that you're joking.'

'Neither am I. After all you wouldn't want her to start married life scraping the bottom of the barrel every month as we did.'

'I don't know. I never complained, did I?'

'No, but you had me.'

Another wet day; white horses in the estuary which meant that the wind had freshened again from the south or south-west. He arrived at the office by eight-thirty and already there were two reports on his desk. One was the forensic report on David Clement's car and told him nothing he did not already know except that they had found very small quantities of hardwood dust – probably oak – on the floor of the car by the driver's seat. It was tempting to think of Bunny Lane's workshop which was carpeted with the stuff but that would be too easy.

No news of *Manna* which was odd and getting odder day by day. A thirty-foot cabin cruiser doesn't just vanish off the face of the sea and such boats are largely port-bound. When they put into shore they need a berth, they can't be dragged up on some secluded beach; they need fuel, they need water . . .

He picked up the telephone and asked to be put through to the harbour master.

'Mr Foster? . . . Wycliffe . . . Are you likely to be available in your office during the next hour? . . . Will it be convenient if I come along for a chat? . . . Thanks, I'll be there in fifteen minutes . . .'

It was an over-optimistic estimate; the traffic through the city centre on a wet morning seemed always on the point of coming to a permanent halt. He swore like anybody else and asked, 'Don't we have traffic policemen any more?'

Foster's office stood on the wharf by the 'new' harbour, next to the 'new' custom-house built in 1875. Wycliffe was ten minutes late but Foster, like most men of the sea, was leisurely and relaxed. He was a small man with a very red face which shone as though it had been polished.

'I suppose you have charts of the waters round here?'

'Of the estuary and the approaches.'

'Porthellin Bay?'

For answer Foster opened a long drawer and drew out an Admiralty chart which he laid on the desk. Wycliffe put his finger on a shallow indentation in the outline of Laira Head, a little to the south-west of the village.

'Hucket's Cove?'

Foster nodded. 'I gather the dinghy was found drifting just off there.'

'Yes. Now, perhaps you will treat what I'm going to ask you as confidential. It's a shot in the dark and will probably lead to nothing.'

'I'm not a great talker, Mr Wycliffe.'

'Good! Then my question is this; if I was in Porthellin Bay on the night of Saturday/Sunday in a motor cruiser which I wanted to scuttle then row myself ashore in the dinghy, how would I set about it? You can assume that I am a knowledgeable yachtsman, familiar with the coast.'

Foster's face registered amazement. 'Good God! You can't think – No, I won't ask questions, I'll see if it's possible to answer yours.' He took off his uniform cap and laid it aside, revealing a bald head which shone to match his face, then he settled to a careful study of the chart. At one point he consulted a little book with ruled columns in which entries had been made in ink. After a full ten minutes he turned to Wycliffe with a half-smile.

'It's an interesting problem. At first I thought there wasn't much prospect of giving you anything like a helpful answer; now I'm not so sure. I take it you want to scuttle several thousand pounds' worth of boat where it would be unlikely to be found in a hurry and then get ashore in the dinghy without too much risk of having to swim for it.'

Wycliffe nodded. 'That's about it.'

'Well, it happens that there are a number of factors limiting your choice – more than I thought. First, on the night in question, the wind was from the south-east –

123

force five to six on the Beaufort Scale, and that would be blowing straight into the bay. It would raise a bit of a sea and there would be some white water. While that wouldn't worry the launch, it would the dinghy – unless he took advantage of the shelter of Laira.'

With a soft pencil he ruled a faint line on the chart from the tip of Laira Head to the jetty at Porthellin. 'If I wanted to put myself ashore in the dinghy with an ebbing tide and a twenty-knot wind I'd want to be inside that line, for a start.'

Wycliffe looked at the roughly triangular area enclosed by the crooked headland and Foster's pencilled line. 'That leaves quite a lot of water.'

'Yes it does, but we can do better than that. If you didn't want your boat sticking up like a sore thumb at the first low-tide she would have to be well outside the low-water mark of the springs.' He sketched another pencil line. 'I don't think she could afford to be closer in than that. And there's another thing which should occur to anybody who knows the bay well, all this here . . . ' He shaded a substantial area extending out from the shore across the angle of Laira. 'All that is deep enough to cover your boat at any tide but the bottom is rocky and she might well break up in the first real easterly or south-easterly blow that coincided with a low tide. Then you'd have flotsam coming ashore in no time.'

He paused, smoothing his bald head and staring at the chart. 'It comes to this, then . . . ' He pencilled in an oval area lying off the cove. 'Here you have a pebbly bottom covered by four or five fathom at the average ebb – more at the neaps, less at the springs. If you were as knowledgeable as you say, and wanted to do such a damn-fool thing, you'd have done it inside that oval.'

'Roughly, how big an area is that?'

Foster laid a scale across the chart. 'Say four hundred yards long and about half that across.'

'Possible to search?'

He shrugged. 'I should think so; it would be a slow job. You'd need to quarter it with a boat towing a grapnel or a special trawl. That way you would pin-point the boat if she was there. After that it would be up to the divers.'

Foster replaced his cap with a pleased grin on his face. 'Only one thing, Mr Wycliffe, if you're going to use that I'd like a chance to check my facts first.'

Wycliffe drove back to headquarters not at all sure that he wasn't about to make a fool of himself but determined to go ahead unless they had news of *Manna* or of Clement. He was acting on a hunch but there was a kind of logic to support him. He could not believe that David Clement had gone off voluntarily leaving money and valuables in the safe. The alternative seemed to be that he had been kidnapped or even killed. If Clement had been killed then there was a body to dispose of and the scuttling of *Manna* would then appear in a new light.

'The chief wants to see you, Mr Wycliffe.' Something had occurred to disturb Diane's customary serenity, she looked almost distressed.

'Is he free now?'

'He said, whenever you came in.'

The chief constable and the deputy had their offices at the end of a carpeted corridor approached through a heavy panelled and padded door which closed with a swish of displaced air. The chief's personal assistant, a grey-haired lady of impressive dignity, known irreverently as Queenie said, 'I'll see if Mr Oldroyd is free.'

She pressed a button on the intercom. 'Mr Wycliffe is here, Mr Oldroyd.'

'Ask him to come in.'

Unlike Bellings, Oldroyd was, in Wycliffe's opinion, a real policeman, deeply concerned about crime and not merely about the statistics of crime. Wycliffe sometimes differed from his chief but with mutual understanding and that was more than could be said of his relations with the deputy.

Oldroyd was standing, looking out of the window at the rain-swept car park. 'Come in, Charles! Sit you down. Busy?'

'Yes.'

'The Clement affair. I've been reading the reports. Odd business, isn't it?'

Oldroyd was a spare figure, always casually dressed; like a country gentleman who has looked in at the estate office on his way to something more interesting. It was a deceptive impression; he was a professional to his fingertips. He turned from the window and sat in an armchair opposite Wycliffe.

'Too busy for crime prevention, I gather.'

'Frankly, sir, too busy for publicity stunts.'

Oldroyd sighed. 'I wish I was, but these things have to be done. In the long run we work with public approval or we don't work at all.'

'I suppose so.'

'You don't suppose anything of the sort.' Oldroyd laughed. 'You're arrogant, Charles, beneath that veneer of modesty. As long as you know you're right, what the hell does it matter what anybody else thinks?'

Wycliffe said nothing. The chief brought out a box of cigars. 'I don't suppose I can tempt you? All right, smoke that pipe of yours if you must.' He nipped off the end of a cigar and lit it. 'I don't suppose Bellings has told you his news?'

'News?'

'He's leaving us – off to Oxford, a lectureship in criminology. Don't talk about it until he tells you himself. A surprise, isn't it? I shall miss him. He helps to keep me on the administrative rails – you too, I shouldn't wonder.'

'He's a good adminstrator.'

Oldroyd smiled. 'We have to find someone to take his place. Of course there will be a Board but I shall have to work with the new man so I expect they will listen to me.'

Wycliffe was at sea, and looked it.

'I'm asking you, Charles, whether you would like to put yourself up for the job?'

'*Me?*'

'Why not? You've got the rank and the experience and God knows you've been critical enough of those of us who are in the hotter seats. It seems only fair that you should have a go.'

'It's not my line of country.'

Oldroyd drew on his cigar and released a thin spiral of blue-grey smoke. 'I know you want to keep the mud on your boots but you can't expect the top jobs to be done as you want them done unless your kind of people have the doing of them.'

'It's good of you to have me in mind and I appreciate it but—'

'Think it over, Charles; talk to Helen about it. It's Thursday – let's say next Wednesday evening. Come and have a meal with us – both of you and we can talk over what you decide.'

'Yes, of course. Thank you.'

He stood up to go.

'Don't be in such a hurry, Charles! This case – the Clement affair – Bellings is afraid you might get your fingers burnt dealing with Parkyn.'

'I'm not sure that it's my fingers he's worried about.'

A disapproving frown from the chief who liked his version of the proprieties to be observed. 'Your fingers, his fingers, my fingers – we are in it together, Charles! This is no one-man band.' Acid.

'Sorry.'

'Have you any reason to think that Parkyn might be involved – criminally involved, I mean?'

Wycliffe considered. 'He was on fairly intimate terms

with the dead man and he thinks that the younger brother was involved in the break-in at the house in Garrison Drive. A gun was stolen at that time and a bullet from that gun killed Joseph Clement.'

'Put like that it sounds pretty damning.'

'Yes, but there are other ways of putting it. The real answer is that I've got an open mind.'

'You've questioned him – how many times?'

'Twice, and I intend to see him again tonight.'

'Has he shown any resentment?'

'Not a bit. I get the impression that it amuses him.'

'Good! I just want to know where we stand. Go ahead. If there is any attempt at tail twisting you can rely on me to see 'em off.'

Wycliffe was at the door.

'Don't forget, Charles. Next Wednesday.'

Back in his office he felt slightly dazed. Diane put a fresh cup of coffee on his desk.

'You missed your coffee. I made some more.'

It dawned on him that he was being fussed over because he was supposed to have been on the carpet.

'Nothing from Mr Kersey?'

'No, Mr Wycliffe.'

He asked for the keys of the antique shop to be sent up to him. He could not have explained why he wanted to go there again; there was nothing he wanted to see, no new idea to be tried out. All he knew was that he must keep in touch. That was why he found it impossible to conduct an investigation from a desk, sending people here and there, issuing instructions and receiving reports. A little time away from the place where it happened, from the people most closely concerned, and he would begin to lose contact, to see people and places, not as they really were but as his mind had made them.

'Will you be back before lunch?'

'No, I shouldn't think so.'

He walked down the stairs and out of the building, ignoring the man at the desk, preoccupied, but not with thoughts of promotion. He was trying to justify to himself an expensive operation which might turn out to be a mare's nest. The hire of the launch . . . divers . . . two or three days, perhaps a week if the weather was bad. He drove through the city centre to Bear Street and parked outside the old custom-house. The police van had gone.

He walked along the street which was as busy as he had ever seen it; the pavements crowded and the traffic trying to edge its way through. One of the current Bear Street wrangles concerned the pros and cons of making it a pedestrian precinct. The rain had stopped and there was a blue sky just visible through a rift in the clouds.

He let himself into the antique shop by the side-door and climbed the stairs to the flat above. The rooms had already acquired a musty smell. He drew back the red velvet curtains in the living-room, letting in the light of day, and stood for a while looking down into the street.

Annie was having her quiet spell between coffee and lunch. He could see her putting pepper and salt pots on the tables and straightening the straw-bottomed chairs. Next door was the fishmongers with a colourful display of lobsters and crabs holding pride of place on the marble slab. On the floor above, Marilyn Ford's room was discreetly curtained. It was from that room with its candy-floss decor that she had looked down the rain-washed street and seen a man coming from the direction of the harbour – 'not very tall, but broad', and he wore a cloth cap. According to Marilyn it was a little before ten.

Bunny Lane had said, 'I'd been cooped up in the workshop all day so in the evening, when the rain had stopped, I thought I'd take a stroll and it occurred to me to drop the book in . . . I gave David the book and asked him to pass it on . . . '

The girl's story was different: ' . . . he went to the shop

door and I think he must have tapped on the glass or something because somebody came and opened the door and let him in.'

He turned back to the room and ran his eyes over the bookshelves and the piles of magazines and catalogues which littered the floor beneath the shelves. They were not all concerned with antiques, there were several yachting and power-boat magazines and in the shelves, books on navigation and seamanship. Evidently David took his cruising seriously. No sign of Joseph's interests; he seemed to have withdrawn almost completely into his own room. Over the years he had built up a life for himself, following well-trodden paths, asking little except to be left alone. Then David had wanted to come into the firm. Well, that was reasonable, no doubt he was entitled to his share and he had modern ideas. Together they would prosper and Joseph must have thought that he would be relieved of some of the drudgery and responsibility.

But it hadn't worked out like that; in less than three years David had destroyed the basis of his security and contentment and involved him in activities which threatened bankruptcy and worse. Not surprising if Joseph saw no point in carrying on; the man with his paperweights could have been the last straw. Not surprising then if Joseph had committed suicide. But if he had, why had the gun been removed? Why had fingerprints been wiped off in the office behind the shop? And where was David?

He crossed the passage to Joseph's room and pushed open the door. The room looked undisturbed. Joseph could have walked in, taken his seat at the desk and carried on where he had left off. Wycliffe felt pleased with his men; there was scarcely a sign of the meticulous examination to which the room had been subjected. A little square of carpet missing – that was all.

Out of curiosity he looked through Joseph's bookshelves for Coleridge's book on Chippendale – the book Bunny Lane said he had handed to David during his stroll on Saturday evening. There it was. He took down the book and opened it; the fly-leaf was inscribed in an old-fashioned copy-book hand, 'Michael Lane'. At first this seemed to be confirmation of Lane's story but then it struck him as odd that a book, casually handed in three-quarters of an hour after Joseph's death, should find its way into his shelves. Was it likely that David would have taken the book upstairs to the dead man's room and put it in the shelves? It was odd. Very odd indeed.

He went down the spiral staircase which seemed to vibrate even more noisily in the deserted building, and into the office. Here too everything looked much the same as when he had first seen it. He checked the safe door to make sure that it was locked; they had found the keys in Joseph's pocket. Then the telephone made him jump.

He picked it up and gave the number.

A man's voice said, 'Is that Mr Clement?'

He explained that Mr Clement was not available but offered to take a message.

'Ah! That will do. I've been trying to get hold of him since yesterday but there's been no reply. My name is Vincent – James Vincent of Porton House, Manningtree, Essex. I saw his advertisement in yesterday's issue of *Power Boat* and I'm interested in making an offer for *Manna*. I shall be free to come down at the weekend. If he could ring me . . . '

So David had planned to sell *Manna*; that made sense. It would have been too tricky to take her with him into his new life and he was not the sort to leave several thousand pounds' worth of boat as a memento to St Juliot. It meant that he was winding up his affairs preparatory to bowing out; it also meant that he hadn't intended to go when he did.

Wycliffe made his way through the shop, dodging the pieces of furniture, to the front door where several envelopes lay on the mat below the letter-box. He picked them up and sorted them on the nearest table. Bills and circulars. Nothing there.

He let himself out by the side-door and walked down the street to the newsagent on the corner where he bought a copy of *Power Boat*. He was among the first of Annie's lunch-time customers.

'Fricassee of chicken – how will that suit you?'

'Very well.'

'Shall I bring you a lager?'

Hesitation. 'No, I'll have a half-bottle of white Bordeaux.'

'Celebrating?'

'More like getting into training.'

While he waited he turned the pages of *Power Boat* and found Clement's advertisement: 'Motor cruiser, *Manna*. 4 berth OAL 30ft . . .'

He was back at the office by two o'clock feeling sleepy due to the wine. Kersey had left word for him to ring the Bournemouth police.

'It's extension 57, sir.'

'Get him for me, will you?'

The office seemed stuffy. Air conditioning! As if a man needed to be cultured like plants in a greenhouse! He often recalled with nostalgia his early days in the west country, before this present glass-and-concrete horror was built. He had his office in a Queen Anne building. It had an ornamental plaster ceiling, a wainscot and a marble fireplace which burned coal. When you felt cold or disgruntled you threw on another lump and imagined that you were burning your troubles. Most changes in the past twenty years had been, in his opinion, for the worse. Now they wanted to shut him up in a padded cell for the rest of his working life.

'Kersey?'

'Ah, thanks for ringing back, sir. I've got some news. There's no doubt that Clement and Page are the same – the caretaker of the flats and two or three of the tenants identified Page when I showed them Clement's photograph. The story is that he's a traveller for some firm dealing in cheap jewellery and fancy goods. He spends a few days a month in the flat, he has next to no mail and few visitors. Several times a girl has stayed there for a night or two, sometimes with Page, sometimes alone. One of the tenants and the caretaker identified Molly Stokes.

'Next, by visiting the local banks and being a bit devious I found that Page kept an account at the London and Counties in Gervis Place. My reception there was a bit frosty but when I'd explained that Page was an impostor the manager was more co-operative. Page opened his account two-and-a-half years ago on a reference from a firm of jewellers. The account has been fairly active but never overdrawn. Page has been buying securities in a straight forward way and depositing them with his bank. That was as far as I could get.'

It was far enough and the picture held no surprises but the crucial question remained. What had happened to Clement/Page?

That afternoon Wycliffe met reporters in the briefing room at headquarters. The case had attracted little attention at first, now it was beginning to interest the national press, radio and TV. For some reason antique dealers and the sea, like children and animals, are always newsworthy. With a bonus link to the London art robberies the combination was irresistable. He put his cards on the table in the hope that publicity might help rather than hinder.

'Do you think Clement came ashore in the dinghy, Mr Wycliffe?'

'I wish I knew.'

'Are you continuing to look for him in this area?'

'In this area and elsewhere; we are anxious to find both the boat and the man.'

'If Clement is found will he be arrested?'

'If Mr Clement is found he will be asked to help with our enquiries.'

'There are rumours that he took a large sum of money with him.'

'I know nothing about that.'

'Why was his car driven into the quarry?'

'Presumably it was intended to hide the car for as long as possible to delay an investigation.'

'Are you satisfied that Waddington was not concerned in Joseph Clement's death?'

'We don't expect to bring any charge against Waddington.'

'But what about the art robberies?'

'They are not our concern. Waddington is now in the custody of the Metropolitan police.'

'Isn't it a boost for West Country police in general and for you in particular that these robberies should have been solved down here after two years of work by Scotland Yard?'

'It would be quite wrong to think in those terms; a great many investigations involve co-operation between forces and success or failure is a joint responsibility. Often, as in this case, it is largely a matter of luck.'

Afterwards he had to say much the same thing to the TV cameras outside.

Back in his office he grumbled about a wasted afternoon but he was not very clear about what else he would have done. It was five o'clock.

'I'm going home.'

'But—'

'No buts, Diane! I'll see you in the morning.'

They were surprised to see him so early and he was surprised by the elegant and sophisticated young woman his daughter had become. Her new job and her new boss had changed her. He felt absurdly shy until she put her arms round his neck and kissed him in the old way.

'I'm afraid I have to go out again later.'

'How much later?'

He muttered, shamefaced, 'Half-past seven to eight.'

'Then we must eat early.' Helen's response was a good deal milder than he had feared.

While they were eating he said, 'The Oldroyds want us to come to their place on Wednesday.'

'But we were there less than three weeks ago and we haven't had them back.'

'I know, but I think we'd better go.'

'Is there something on?'

'It's confidential at the moment but Bellings is going and Oldroyd wants me to apply.'

Ruth said, 'But that's marvellous! With Mr Oldroyd's backing there wouldn't be much doubt, would there?'

'Probably not, if I applied.'

'If? Surely . . .'

Helen came to his rescue. 'It's not as simple as that; the work is quite different and your father may not feel that he wants to make a change.'

'But won't it have a big effect on your salary and on your pension? In these days it's income you have to think of – not capital . . .'

Wycliffe was constantly surprised by his children. At one moment you were feeding them on purée and rusks, the next they are telling you how to plan for your old age.

'Don't you think your brother ought to be in on this?'

Ruth looked at him, her face blank. 'David?'

'If we are going to make the decision in family committee.'

It took a moment to sink in then she blushed and laughed at the same time.

'I'm sorry. Richard is always telling me that I'm too ready to offer advice.'

'Richard?'

'Richard Locksley, my boss.'

He left the house at a little before eight and drove to Bear Street to park in front of the old custom-house. This was part of his ritual for the case. It was a dry night and the air was still. He walked the short distance to St John's Court and knocked on the door of Lane's cottage. Footsteps in the stone passage, a key turned and the door opened. Lane stood, his stocky figure silhouetted against the light from the open door of the living-room.

'Mr Wycliffe! I wasn't expecting you. You'd better come in . . . ' Not a gushing welcome. Lane helped the superintendent off with his coat and hung it on one of several pegs in the passage. The major's duffle coat was there and two or three cloth caps.

'I've got company tonight, but you know Major Parkyn.' Wycliffe made no bones about it. 'Yes, being a Thursday, I guessed that I might find you together.'

It was as he had imagined it. Parkyn was relaxed in one of the three armchairs, his long legs stretched out to the fire; comfort beyond anything Garrison Drive could offer. He was in the act of lighting his pipe. Lane's pipe smouldered in a large ashtray placed on a low stool between the two chairs.

Lane pulled forward the third chair. 'Sit there, Mr Wycliffe. I believe you are a pipe smoker so carry on if you want to.'

The major acknowledged him with a nod which, if not cordial, was not disagreeable either. The room was over-warm but cosy. Lane drew a curtain across the door to exclude possible draughts. The box of dominoes was already in place on the square kitchen table. Wycliffe couldn't help thinking, 'If I were Joseph Clement . . . ' He filled his pipe, taking plenty of time as it was proper to do. The alarm clock on the mantelpiece showed half-past eight. It had a shiny metal case which gave the tick a metallic echo, clink-clink, clink-clink . . .

Bunny Lane sat down and reached for his pipe.

Wycliffe said, 'I came for information and advice.' He turned to Lane. 'You told me that you went for a stroll at some time before ten on Saturday night and that you dropped in a book which you had promised to lend Joseph.'

'That's true.' Lane puffed away at his pipe.

'You saw a light at the back of the shop, tapped on the glass door, and David came out – is that right?'

'That is so.'

'Did you go into the shop?'

'No, I told you; I handed in the book and left.'

So as not to disturb the tempo of the proceedings he allowed a long pause. 'I am asking you this because a new witness has told us two things; first, that she heard what was probably the shot which killed Joseph at a little after nine; second, that she saw a stocky, oldish man wearing a cloth cap, come up the street from the direction of the harbour at a little before ten. This man appeared to tap on the shop door which was opened to him and he went in.'

Lane smiled, briefly exposing his teeth and his hare-lip. 'She must have seen me but she's got it a bit wrong.'

'I see. But you understand how important it is. David must have answered the door to you less than an hour after the shot.'

Lane nodded. 'It looks that way if your witness is reliable but it's difficult to believe.'

Lane was being either completely honest or he was clever enough not to protest too much.

'Just one more question, do you have a car?'

Lane looked surprised. 'Not a car; I have a little van which I use to deliver things I've made or worked on.'

Parkyn shifted heavily in his chair, causing the springs to creak. Lane glanced at the clock. He said, 'About this time, Mr Wycliffe, we usually have a drink. If you would like to join us . . .'

137

'I wouldn't say no to a glass of your wine.'

Lane got up and went through to the back kitchen. Parkyn continued to smoke, staring into the fire which had a glowing orange-red centre. The clock ticked a couple of minutes away then Lane came back with a tin tray on which he had a bottle of wine, a bottle of whisky, three glasses polished so that the light glistened on them, and an earthenware pitcher of water. He removed the ashtray and put the tray on the stool.

'Help yourself, Mr Wycliffe. Whisky if you prefer it.'

'No thanks, I'll stick to wine.'

Parkyn put his pipe in his pocket, leaned forward and poured himself a generous whisky to which he added a spoonful of water.

'Your very good health!' He took a gulp of the spirit and sighed deeply.

'Cheers!' Wycliffe sipped his wine. 'I believe that at one time you used to do some sailing round this coast, Major?'

The grey, slightly bulging eyes regarded him with an expressionless stare which might have intimidated the less hardened, and it was some time before he answered, 'I had a boat for a while when I first retired.'

'A sail or power boat?'

'Sail with auxiliary diesel.'

'So you know the coast pretty well.'

Parkyn took another gulp of whisky and wiped his lips before replying, 'I don't recall getting lost.'

'Are you a boating man, Mr Lane?'

Lane got up and placed fresh lumps of coal on the fire, arranging them strategically. 'Not me; I like dry land under my feet.'

Wycliffe said, 'I expect you know that David Clement seems to have cleared off in his motor cruiser and that her dinghy was found adrift off Hucket's Cove on Sunday morning, rowlocks in place, planks stove in.'

He waited for some acknowledgement but hardly

expected to get one. However, after the mandatory interval, Parkyn said, 'Hucket's is in Porthellin Bay; what was he doing in there?'

'Our first idea was that he had lost his dinghy.'

'Anything is possible with the fools who take to the water these days.' The major emptied his glass and leaned forward to replenish it; this time he added no water.

'The boatmen at St Juliot say that he was very competent.'

'Ah!'

'I would be obliged by your opinion. It seems to me possible that Clement rowed ashore at Hucket's. You see, *Manna* had only enough fuel for forty miles yet, despite the fact that we have alerted every port up and down the channel, there has been no news of her.'

Parkyn brought out his pipe again, knocked it out on the fender and turned to Wycliffe. 'Are you suggesting that he left her adrift and that she's bobbing about out there in the channel?'

'No, I'm suggesting that he scuttled her.'

Parkyn raised his great shoulders in a slow shrug indicating that there was no more to be said.

'And I'm considering the best way of finding her.'

Parkyn was filling his pipe from an old oil-skin pouch, his large, freckled hands seemed capable of remarkable precision of movement, there was nothing clumsy about his broad, square-tipped fingers. At Wycliffe's remark he stopped what he was doing and once more stared at the superintendent, then he laughed. 'I wish you joy, Mr Wycliffe! There's a hell of a lot of water within rowing distance of Hucket's.'

Lane sipped her wine and smoked his pipe which made little bubbling sounds but he said nothing.

'I understand that there was quite a strong breeze from the south-east on Saturday night and in these circumstances, with an ebbing tide, they tell me that

139

there wouldn't be much chance for a small dinghy unless she was sheltered by the crook of Laira.'

Parkyn, having filled his pipe, proceeded to light it. Only when he had finished and it was drawing nicely did he make any comment. 'I gather you've taken professional advice.'

'From Sam Foster the harbour master.'

'I see.'

'Would you agree with his assessment?'

'I wouldn't disagree; I don't know enough about it.'

'It seems that when one takes into account the shallow areas and the nature of the bottom there is a relatively small area in which *Manna* could have been scuttled without the possibility of her showing up again on the next ebb.'

Parkyn nodded. 'That's very interesting, but why would Clement put to sea at St Juliot only to scuttle his boat and go ashore in Porthellin Bay?'

'Perhaps on the principle that it's safest to hide near home?'

Parkyn shook his head. 'It doesn't seem very likely to me.'

The fresh coals took fire in little spurts of blue and yellow flame and the clock sustained its monotonous metallic tick. It was twenty minutes past nine. Parkyn was becoming restless again, shifting his position so that the springs of the old chair constantly protested. In the end, almost shamefaced, he said, 'I don't suppose you play dominoes, Mr Wycliffe?'

'I did at one time but it's a long time ago.'

'But you do know the rules?'

'More or less.'

Parkyn's face brightened. 'It will soon come back.' He took another great gulp of spirit. 'I expect Mr Wycliffe could do with topping-up, Bunny.'

They played in silence, sitting on the bent-wood chairs at the big square table which was covered with oil-cloth. Two or three times Bunny replenished their glasses and once he got up to put fresh coal on the fire. When the little shiny clock showed twenty minutes to twelve the major stood up. 'I must be going; I've already overstayed my time. Thank you for a pleasant evening.' The only effect of all that he had drunk was to make him rather slower in his movements, rather more precise in his speech.

Wycliffe said, 'I'll come part of the way with you, Major.'

Was he consciously doing what he supposed Joseph would have done?

Bunny saw them to the door. Outside it was a quiet clear night; so quiet that they could have been in the country. Their footsteps echoed through the deserted square and as they turned down into Bear Street they caught the fresh, salty tang of the sea.

'A pleasant evening, Wycliffe.' Wycliffe noted that he had been received into the major's orbit and was none too pleased though he realized that he had only himself to blame. Again, as they separated, it was 'Good-night to you, Wycliffe. Perhaps we shall be able to do that again.'

'Good-night, Major.'

CHAPTER SEVEN

A myth with a long pedigree would have us believe that scientific research consists in being open-minded and doing experiments until some inescapable conclusion is forced on the experimenter by the logic of his results. Of course, nobody ever has worked like that or ever could. A researcher starts with a notional conclusion (hunch) and devises experiments to find out whether it will stand up. A detective works in the same way and for the detective, as for the scientist, his work is as good as his hunches. But policemen and scientists and other people too, prefer to believe that their actions are guided by the pure light of impeccable logic.

Wycliffe was no exception, he was ashamed of his hunches and he had to wrestle with his conscience over them especially when, as now, playing a hunch was likely to cost the taxpayer money. It troubled him over his toast and marmalade.

'I shouldn't worry about it; after all, the main thing is to do what you are happiest doing.' Ruth, making a long arm for the marmalade.

He looked at her, puzzled. 'What on earth are you talking about?'

Helen laughed. 'You see! I wouldn't mind betting that it hasn't entered his head since we were talking about it last night.'

Which wasn't entirely true. In the lazy interval between sleeps at about four in the morning, he had tried to think himself behind the padded door without much success.

142

He was in his office by twenty minutes past eight, beating Kersey by a short head.

'I came back last night, sir. What's on the menu?'

'Trawling in Porthellin Bay. I'm going to have an area trawled for *Manna*.'

Kersey's bushy eyebrows went up. 'Something new?'

'No. It's just that the longer we go without news of either *Manna* or Clement, the more convinced I am that he didn't leave the antique shop of his own accord. He wasn't the sort to walk out and leave a small fortune behind. I'm beginning to wonder if he left the place alive.'

Kersey looked solemn. 'You think he might be down there with his boat?'

'It's a possibility.'

'If so we shall be all the more interested in the guy who went ashore.'

'Exactly. And this is what I want you to do: inquiries at Porthellin and at any houses along the coast. It's my guess that our man landed at Hucket's where he stood little chance of being seen but he might have had the nerve to come ashore at the slip-way or even the jetty. After all it must have been dark or only just beginning to get light. You may come across an insomniac or it's possible that there were boats out long-lining; I gather they still do it in a small way.'

When Kersey had gone Wycliffe telephoned Foster. 'I've decided to go ahead with the search and I'm wondering whether you can advise me about the hire of a suitable boat and crew?'

Foster was obviously pleased. 'I'll set it up for you if you like. I must confess I shall get a bit of a kick out of it. Of course I shall have to do it through Ron Bryce at Porthellin but that's no problem.'

'Good! That would certainly be a weight off my mind.'

'When do you want to start?'

'Yesterday.'

Foster chuckled. 'I'll see what I can do; I suppose you want it kept as quiet as possible?'

'On the contrary, the more publicity the better.'

So that was that.

He lunched at Annie's and in the afternoon there was Joseph's funeral.

It was a surprise to see the little chapel full and it was not until the mourners gathered round the grave that he was able to sort them out. Molly Stokes was there and she seemed to share the role of chief mourner with Bunny Lane; an incongruous pair. Molly wore a dark green winter coat and carried an umbrella. Wycliffe was surprised to see how pale she was and once when their eyes met across the open grave he fancied that she looked at him less as a threat than as someone to turn to.

Head and shoulders above the rest, in a heavy service-mackintosh which had seen better days, the major looked neither to the right nor the left. His bulging eyes seemed to be focused on the far distance. Annie Blazek was there and Friend, the lawyer. Friend's eyes were moist and he was flushed; from time to time he turned aside to blow his nose in a grubby handkerchief. A couple of journalists and a photographer hovered on the fringe and the rest were almost certainly tradespeople from the street, members of the Bear Street Traders' Association, a significant lobby in city affairs.

When the service was over Wycliffe drove straight back to his office. A fallow day. At five o'clock he picked up the telephone and asked for his home number.

'Ruth? . . . How would you and your mother like to eat out tonight?'

There was a brief consultation followed by agreement.

'I'll book a table.'

He telephoned the restaurant in Bear Street and booked a table for three at eight-thirty.

At nine o'clock the Wycliffe's were starting their main course: *Porc dijonnaise*. The restaurant was full and Annie had an assistant, a girl Wycliffe had not seen before. There was a hum of conversation, a rattle of knives and forks, and the windows were steamed over. Wycliffe looked surreptitiously at his watch and as he did so he heard a sound like a firework going off, muffled and distant. He glanced round the room; no-one else seemed to have noticed.

Kersey had fired the general's revolver in Joseph Clement's room and Marilyn Ford was co-operating to the extent that she had agreed to remain in her room though she had not been told for what purpose. By chance the conditions were almost identical with what they had been on the night Joseph died; it had rained for most of the day and Bear Street was deserted.

On Saturday morning it was a relief to look out of the window and see the estuary sparkling under a watery sun; it made him realize how much he was counting on the operation in Porthellin Bay.

'Six days shalt thou labour and do all thy work . . . ' For most of us the divine ordinance has been cut to five and though he commonly worked six and sometimes seven, Wycliffe enjoyed a greater sense of freedom at weekends and felt more at liberty to follow his nose. He would not let his anxiety about the trawling get the better of him and he took a leisurely breakfast so that when Ruth came down in her dressing gown at nine o'clock he was still at the table.

'Not going in today?'

'Later.'

'That was a good meal last night, dad. Is she a friend of yours?'

'The way things are, you might say that we are colleagues.'

At half-past nine he drove to Bear Street, walked to

Godolphin Street and rang the bell of Molly Stokes's flat.

She opened the door wearing an old pair of slacks, a cotton top and with her hair caught back by a piece of ribbon; she had no make-up on.

'Have you heard something?'

He followed her into the living-room where the remains of her breakfast were still on the table.

'I wanted to tell you that I was in the antique shop yesterday when a man telephoned to say that he'd seen David's advertisement in *Power Boat* and wanted to make a bid for *Manna*.'

'So?'

'Isn't it obvious that David was planning to get out but that he went before he intended?'

She was tense, very near to tears but she was not the crying sort and her emotion exploded in anger. 'All right! All bloody right! He's gone, but where? You're the policeman, so find him!' Driven to some sort of activity, she started to clear the breakfast things away, carrying them through to her little kitchen.

He watched her for a moment then he said, 'I'm having part of Porthellin Bay trawled, starting this morning.'

She stopped in her tracks. 'Trawled. What for?'

'For *Manna*.'

She put the flat of her hand to her forehead in a helpless gesture. 'Oh, God!'

'Don't think I know anything which you don't. I've no idea what they will find, if anything. You and I are asking the same questions.'

She looked as though she wanted to believe him and he added, 'The point is, the longer we go on with no news the less likely it seems that David left of his own accord.'

She took out a cigarette with a trembling hand, and lit it. 'That's where I'd got when I came back from Bournemouth. But who would force him to leave and why?' She stood with one hand resting on the back of his chair, smoking nervously. 'His whole future depended on the Bournemouth set-up; even if he wanted to ditch me, he couldn't afford to let that go.' After a pause she said, 'It doesn't look too good, does it?'

Wycliffe stood up. 'Try not to worry too much. I'll let you know as soon as I have anything fresh to tell you.'

She came with him to the door, reluctant to let him go.

As he turned the corner into Bear Street he saw the major coming out of the betting shop and he began to feel, in some strange way, that things were coming right. He was not sitting at a desk reading reports about people, he was out, meeting them. He waited and watched Parkyn trundle down the street to his next port of call, the mini-market.

A man's barber, his doctor, his priest, his children, his mistress and his wife have all been considered by different authorities as best placed to form a true estimate of his character. Nobody, it seems, has suggested his bookmaker – yet, for a betting man, the bookie is as likely to get it right as any of the others.

Wycliffe crossed the street to the betting office.

'Mr Lacey, please.'

The clerk recognized him and raised the counter flap. Wycliffe passed through a room where two more clerks were talking on telephones and knocked on a glass-panelled door.

Lacey looked more like a trendy parson than a bookie in his pepper-and-salt suiting, his quiet tie and discreetly striped shirt.

'Trouble, Mr Wycliffe?'

'Not for you. I want to pick your brains about Major Parkyn.'

Lacey took off his gold-rims and laid them in the middle of a huge form on which he had been working. 'Professional ethics, Mr Wycliffe.'

'I know all about that but I'd still like your opinion of Parkyn.'

'As a man or as a punter?'

'Doesn't it come to the same thing?'

Lacey grinned. 'You could be right. Anyway, it's a tall order; all I can say is that he isn't what he seems. I mean, if I didn't know him I'd say he was the sort who if he bet at all would put his money each-way on the favourite with an occasional flutter on a double.'

'But it's not like that?'

'No way! He'll go for two or three weeks, betting sensibly, even cleverly, until he's got a fair sum then, when his pension comes or whatever, he'll come in here and put the lot on some crazy accumulator which is sudden death – I know it and he knows it. In the early days, once or twice, I gave him a friendly warning but all I got for thanks was that cold, fishy look which makes you wonder if you've left your flies undone or something.' Lacey looked at Wycliffe and spoke with deliberation. 'I'm quite sure that these crazy gambles are the only ones which give him a kick – the rest are build up.'

'And when he loses?'

'No effect.' Lacey picked up his glasses. 'No apparent effect, anyway.'

'Has he ever come up.'

'Once in the five or six years he's been with me. I can't remember the amount but it was several thousand and he'd lost it again in weeks rather than months.'

'Was he thrilled at winning?'

'Not so's you'd notice. Underneath, he's some sort of wild man, Mr Wycliffe. I can't explain it but it seems to me he's one of those chaps who's always got to be on a tightrope.'

Wycliffe did not go back to his car, instead he walked along the street and up Dog's Leg Lane to Garrison Drive. The sun was shining through a thin mist making the air luminescent, and somewhere someone was

148

mowing grass. The Parkyn house stood out like a sore thumb among its pampered neighbours but he had not come to visit the Parkyns. He walked the length of Garrison Drive which ended in a wooden fence with a stile and a notice which read, 'Footpath only to Porthellin.' From the top of the stile he could see the whole of the bay with the village in the far corner. Between the village and the crook of Laira the little shingle beach which was Hucket's Cove stood out white against the sombre cliffs. He could just make out a small boat which seemed to be cruising parallel with the shore. It was ten minutes past eleven.

He followed the footpath which soon joined the road and the road pursued a devious course round the margins of the bay to the village. The walk took him about forty-five minutes and must have been close on three miles. To Hucket's Cove would be another mile-and-a-half. He walked through the almost deserted village to the quay. There was little sign of activity, just a knot of men on the eastern jetty looking out to sea; one of them was Foster, the others were villagers.

'Well, we've made a start, Mr Wycliffe,' Foster said. 'We're using Bert Cundy's *Blue Boy*, she's more manoeuvrable than the bigger boats. Ron Bryce is out there with Bert.'

The blue launch looked insignificant in the great expanse of water and the crooked headland seemed far away. Wycliffe was shaken, the operation which had seemed reasonable on the chart now looked absurd. A needle in a haystack!

'You see those four dan buoys, Mr Wycliffe? They mark the four corners of our pitch, so to speak.'

After a moment of looking Wycliffe could see four little flags sticking up out of the water.

'It's like ploughing a field, but when you're ploughing the hedges stay still unless you've had a few. Here they don't; although each of the dan buoys is anchored with a grapnel on the bottom and won't shift, the buoys themselves move with the tide and wind. We've got to allow for that.'

'Yes, I see.'

'Good! Now look at the two nearer buoys. Can you see a line of floats between them?'

'Yes.'

'Well there's a similar line of floats between the two outer buoys which you probably can't see from here. The floats are ten yards apart and they help Bert to keep a line. On this game you can't look back and see the furrow.'

Wycliffe did not want to ask the question but he felt driven to it. 'How long do you think it will take?'

Foster pursed his lips and frowned. 'Well, I reckon he's got to do the length of the course at least a hundred and twenty times, which mean's he's got to cover forty miles. Towing the trawl he's not making more than three knots so that makes thirteen hours to cover the ground and that's not allowing for a certain amount of double-tracking which is bound to happen.' Foster lifted his uniform cap and smoothed his bald head. 'He got started about eight so he's unlikely to finish today unless he finds something. You can't work in the dark on this game and he'll have to have a break now and then.'

Wycliffe watched the launch traverse a length, turn, and come back down the course. It was exceedingly boring. He had to admit that he had arrived with a certain excitement, now he felt let down.

'What about divers, Mr Wycliffe?'

'Divers?'

'You're going to need 'em if we strike something.'

'But not today?'

'No, if we're lucky enough to pick her up today we shall put out a marker buoy but then you would need them tomorrow. I think we should contact the navy because tomorrow's Sunday and it might not be easy unless we give them notice. They'll insist on using their own boats. You know what they are; any boat that doesn't carry the white ensign must have a hole in her bottom and they don't like getting their feet wet.'

Wycliffe did not answer at once; he had to admit to himself that he had lost confidence in the whole operation.

'I'll get on to them if you like, Mr Wycliffe. We speak the same lingo.'

'I'd be glad if you would.' Wycliffe felt ashamed of himself.

Foster looked at him with a faint smile. 'We'll find her if she's there. There's no point in you hanging about though. It's sure to be a long job.'

Wycliffe returned home and tried to put *Manna* out of his mind. It was a glorious April day and Helen and Ruth were working in the garden. After lunch Foster telephoned to say that the navy had agreed 'In principle' to provide divers once the boat had been located but they wanted Wycliffe to attend at the Admiral Superintendent's office to deal with documentation.

Two hours of exquisitely polite Arab-tea-party chit-chat confirmed him in his total ignorance of salvage law and worried him the more about the documents he had to sign. But at the finish, the officer, a lieutenant-commander, said, 'Not to worry old chap. On these salvage larks you can't go wrong; either you get your money back with interest from the owner or you flog the thing and make a bomb. I've often thought of taking it up as a business when they put me out to grass.'

At six o'clock he drove to Porthellin, feeling distinctly edgy. The village lay serene in the evening sun. *Blue Boy*, Bert Cundy's launch, was moored in the basin, riding high with the tide which was only an hour past the flood. Out in the bay, three of the dan buoys and the floats had gone and a single buoy remained as a marker, hopefully, indicating the position of *Manna*.

He found Bert Cundy and Ron Bryce in the bar.

'We got her in less than seven hours, Mr Wycliffe,' Bryce said.

'You think it's the *Manna*?'

'If it isn't it's something very like her.'

'We tried 'er from all ways,' Bert said. 'O' course it was coming up to 'igh water so we couldn't see nothing.'

'What are you drinking?'

'Pints will do us, Mr Wycliffe.'

The atmosphere in the pub was intimate and friendly; all the regulars seemed to take satisfaction in a job well done. 'When you come to the sea, Mr Wycliffe, there's nobody on these coasts to touch a Porthellin man.'

'What happens now?'

Ron Bryce ran his hand through his curly black thatch. 'That depends on the navy but if they'll only get their fingers out they could lift her tomorrow morning. It's low water at half-eleven. If they go down and get their hawsers attached by then, that's all we shall want 'em for. We then stand by until about a quarter to six in the evening for high water and tow her into the basin.'

Wycliffe had seen this sort of thing done once before *

'Then we shall have to wait for the tide to go down again and leave her high and dry. Is that it?'

'In a nutshell, Mr Wycliffe. You'd be able to go aboard her sometime before midnight tomorrow night. After that, it depends.'

'What depends?'

Bryce sank the best part of half-a-pint in one swallow. 'Well, if she was scuttled by opening her sea-cock all we got to do is shut it and she'll rise like a bird on the next tide, but if she's got any planks stove in then they'll have to be botched up before she'll ride.'

It all sounded simple and reassuring.

He arrived home again just before nine. There was a

---

* *Wycliffe and the Pea-Green Boat*.

message from Foster to say that the navy would be on the job in the morning – weather permitting. He listened to the forecast. 'Continuing fine at first tomorrow, with long sunny periods, but rain will reach the south-west later in the day with strengthening winds.'

Was it too much to ask that for once a poor, struggling policeman might be favourably noticed by Providence?

CHAPTER EIGHT

Sunday morning, exactly a week since he had found the gun on the beach at St Juliot, and another Oh-to-be-in-England day, but no leisurely stroll along the shore to collect his newspaper.

'Will you be home for lunch?'

'I expect so but I shall have to go out again.'

He would probably spend the day waiting around. On the assumption that all would go well he had arranged for Kersey and three men to be available with an emergency vehicle and floodlamps for work after dark.

He drove to Porthellin and arrived there shortly after eight to find the navy already in possession. Two un-naval looking craft, like grey tubs, were anchored near the remaining dan-buoy and several men were moving about in them. One of the boats carried a number of white cylinders which Wycliffe supposed to be the floats which (fingers crossed) would, with the help of the tide, eventually lift *Manna* clear of the bottom.

Ron Bryce and Bert Cundy were on the quay, grumbling. 'A toffee-nosed sub-lieut as good as told us to keep out of the way.'

Foster arrived and joined the group. He glanced at his watch. 'Eight forty-five; I don't think they'll start diving until half-past nine at the earliest, that would give them more than two hours to low water and they'd be working in under five fathom.'

In fact, it was a little after nine-thirty when the first wet-suited diver went over the side. He was down for a minute or two and when he came up two others went down to surface again after a couple of minutes.

Ron Bryce said, 'You'd think the bastards would signal or something.'

As though Bryce had been overheard, one of the divers raised his hand in the thumbs-up sign.

Wycliffe breathed a sigh of relief.

There was a lull, then the divers went down again and each appeared to be carrying a line. The church clock chimed and struck ten. The watchers on the quay were joined by others, including a contingent of children. The sun was shining and the bay sparkled under an almost cloudless sky.

'The weather looks good.'

Bert Cundy grimaced and squinted at the sky. 'All right for a few hours but there's rain and wind on the way.'

'That's what they said in the weather forecast.'

'Then they'm right for once.'

One of the navy vessels had shifted her position and eight of the floats were now bobbing about in the water between the two boats. The church bell tolled for the morning service. There had been several more dives and now the divers were swimming about on the surface, manoeuvring the floats.

The ebb was running out now and in the basin boats were lying over on their beam ends or resting on their legs. The water was running away in rivulets and streams leaving the muddy, weedy bottom exposed. Bert Cundy spat down into the mud.

'It's going to be a bit tight, Mr Wycliffe. I was out there this morning on top of the tide – at 'alf past five. I took a few soundings with a lead line and I reckon she was lying in six fathom – that's thirty-six feet of water. We'll get about a nineteen or twenty foot tide, so, when they lift 'er she'll still be sixteen or seventeen feet down – do you follow me?'

'Yes. You mean that when the tide has lifted her she'll still be under sixteen or seventeen feet of water.'

'Exactly. And we shall 'ave about eighteen foot of water in the basin so there's going to be little enough to spare but I reckon we'll manage.'

Foster said, 'Look! They're taking up the slack on the hawsers.'

Wycliffe could see the floats coming into line, two lines of four. He glanced at his watch, it was eleven-thirty – eight minutes to low water.

'You got to 'and it to 'em; they're doing a fair job,' Cundy conceded.

Foster said, 'There's nothing we can do now except keep an eye on her until high water this evening. No point in you hanging about, Mr Wycliffe.'

He was not unwilling to escape. He drove to Bear Street, up Dog's Leg Lane and out to Garrison Drive. It was a week to the hour since he had first made acquaintance with the major. He rang the door-bell and in a little while the door was opened by the major himself.

'Ah! Wycliffe. You come most carefully upon your hour.' He stood aside to let Wycliffe through. 'Second door on your right.'

It was the little room in which they had talked the previous Monday evening. Although it was warm outside the paraffin heater was on and the room seemed oppressively stuffy. He waved to a chair and sat down himself. His pipe and a box of matches rested on the arm of his chair and there was a glass of whisky on the floor at his feet.

'Smoke if you want to . . . Will you have a drink?'

'Not just now, thanks.'

How much time did Parkyn spend in this bare little room, curled up like a dog in its kennel?

'Have you a telephone in the house?'

'Telephone? No, I've no use for the thing.'

'How about Lane?'

156

Parkyn turned slowly in his chair to look at Wycliffe before saying, 'He's got a telephone. I suppose he needs it for his business; I don't have any business.'

'We think we have located Clement's boat.'

'Ah!'

'On the bottom, off Hucket's Cove.'

'So you were right.'

'Someone must have scuttled the launch, rowed ashore in the dinghy and walked from the cove, probably before daylight on Sunday morning, but there's quite a chance he might have been seen.'

Parkyn, in the middle of lighting his pipe, gave him a sideways glance. 'You think so? Are you going to get her up – the launch, I mean?'

'Navy divers were out there this morning; they've attached floats and we are hoping that she will lift with tonight's tide and that we shall be able to tow her into the basin.'

Surely Parkyn must have seen something of the activity in the bay?

'She can't be very deep if you can lift her with the tide alone.'

'No, she's lying in about six fathoms at high water.'

'You are fortunate.'

There was a prolonged silence during which Parkyn smoked contentedly and there was no atmosphere of tension. When Wycliffe spoke again it was in the manner he might have adopted in discussing a troublesome case with a colleague.

'It's a complicated story and there are too many gaps but I'm hoping that we shall be able to close some of them when we've raised *Manna*. There's no doubt that David Clement was a crook, involved with a gang of London thieves, and that he fenced their stolen property through the firm. One of his associates called by appointment on Saturday evening at eight o'clock.

David was out and Joseph admitted the visitor but David arrived shortly afterwards and Joseph left them to their business in the office behind the shop.'

The feeling of the little room was not the same as in Bunny Lane's kitchen. This was the refuge of a solitary man. Parkyn stooped for his glass, 'Sure you won't join me?'

'Not just now.'

Parkyn drank some whisky and sighed.

'The visitor left at about eight-forty and at nine o'clock David was in the *Seven Stars*. At about this time a neighbour heard a bang which was probably the shot which killed Joseph. Less than an hour later the same neighbour saw a stocky, oldish man, wearing a peaked cap, go to the shop door. The witness says that the shop was in darkness but that someone came to the door and let him in.'

Wycliffe paused. 'I'm not boring you?'

'By no means.'

'At some time after one o'clock another neighbour was awakened by a car being driven down the back lane behind the shops. Between two and three in the morning, witnesses at St Juliot heard a car reversing off the jetty. On Sunday morning I found your father's revolver within a few feet of the jetty, lying on the shingle not far below high-water mark.'

Parkyn shifted heavily in his chair but said nothing.

'On Monday Joseph Clement's body was found in his room, according to the pathologist he had died some time on Saturday of a bullet wound in the head. The ballistics expert says that he was shot with your father's gun.' Wycliffe broke off and moved his chair back a little further from the heater. 'If it hadn't been for the absence of a weapon we should have treated the case as suicide and I am still inclined to think that is what it was. However, we found afterwards that *Manna* had been moved from her moorings, David Clement's car was discovered in St Juliot's quarry, *Manna*'s dinghy turned up damaged and adrift off Hucket's Cove and now we have *Manna* herself sunk in the bay. With all this there has been no news of David Clement since he was seen by Bunny Lane on Saturday evening.'

In the silence which followed the only sound was Parkyn's deep, almost laboured breathing. In the end Parkyn said, 'It's a strange tale – difficult to see how it can all be made to hang together.'

'You have no suggestions to make?'

'Me? Good God, no! I'm not good at that sort of thing. Not my line at all.'

The two men looked at each other for some time and it would have been hard to say which had out-stared the other, but finally Wycliffe got to his feet.

'Are you going?'

'I won't keep you from your lunch and I must get home to mine.'

Parkyn followed him into the hall. Hetty was standing near the bottom of the stairs and she came forward. In a harsh voice she said, 'You are becoming a regular visitor, Mr Wycliffe.'

Wycliffe thought that she looked less composed than he had yet seen her; her grey hair was untidy and there was a wild look in her eyes. He said, 'I shall trouble you as little as possible, Miss Parkyn.'

Parkyn watched him down the slope to the road.

Back in his car he sat at the wheel for a while, indecisive, then he started the engine and drove home.

Helen and Ruth were drinking sherry in the kitchen, marking time before serving the meal. 'We had almost given you up.'

After lunch he sat in an armchair with a book and promptly fell asleep. When he woke he thought for a moment that he must have slept through the afternoon for the room was almost dark, then he saw the inky-black clouds which had crept up over the estuary and

159

the white flecks on the sea whipped up by a freshening wind. As he watched the rain came sweeping in beating down on the water and on the shrubs in the garden which seemed to cower under its force. A quarter past four; in an hour or thereabouts they would begin towing *Manna* into the basin and he wondered how much the weather would interfere.

He found the two women in Helen's workroom, cutting out a dress. 'I have to go out. Expect me when you see me.'

He put on his heavy mackintosh and a fly-fisherman's hat of which he was secretly proud. He stowed a pair of wellingtons in the boot of the car. It rained heavily all the way to Porthellin and when he came in sight of the bay he was shocked by the grey turbulent waste which a few hours before had looked like a tourist poster. Bert Cundy's launch was in position, tossing up and down by the marker flag which rocked madly. He thought he could see two figures in the launch, one crouched over the tiller, the other by the decked-in fo'c'sle. Even in the shelter of the basin the swell was rocking the moored boats and slapping against the quay. He found Foster in the boatman's shelter with four or five other men.

'So Bert's out there already.'

'Oh, he's been out there since the tide began to make – him and Ron Bryce. You see, once she lifts, there's nothing to hold her but the kedge the navy put down and with this bit of sea we don't want accidents now. Bert's got a tow-line on her and in another half-hour or so he'll start bringing her in.'

At the entrance to the basin the swell was causing a rise and fall of two or three feet; it looked ominous but Foster was reassuring. 'There between the heads is the worst bit, there's a sort of bar, but if Bert plays his cards right the swell could help him. Caught right, it could lift *Manna* over.'

Wycliffe was given a cup of strong, scalding tea with scarcely any milk. The rain eased but the wind strengthened. One of the men said, 'I'll bet ol' Ron is as sick as a shag; 'e never could abide being moored up in a swell.'

They all laughed. Evidently the thought added spice to what was an enthralling spectator sport. At twenty minutes past five one of them said, 'He's drawing up on the kedge – there, she's free.'

'Won't be long now, Mr Wycliffe.'

It was a minute or two before he could detect any movement then he realized that the launch was creeping slowly nearer the shore. It was a slow business because the drag of the submerged *Manna* was considerable; however, the distance steadily diminished and at eighteen minutes to six the launch was between the heads, rising and falling with the swell and as she rose the men in her were level with their companions on the quay.

Foster said, 'He's towing on a short line so there's no risk of the tow fouling the heads.'

Cundy was at the tiller and Bryce, grey-faced, at the engine. Cundy was looking back over his shoulder, watching the floats and the progress of each swell. Suddenly he shouted, 'Now!' Bryce opened the throttle and the launch surged forward just as the swell lifted the white floats behind her. Foster said, 'Oopsa daisy!' and they saw the dim outline of the submerged *Manna*, like a giant fish, glide through into the basin. Foster heaved a great sigh of relief.

There was a certain amount of manoeuvring to get the cruiser into the most sheltered position, a mooring rope was thrown ashore, then Cundy dropped his tow and brought *Blue Boy* round to the steps. He came up, grinning, closely followed by Bryce who looked sorry for himself.

'She'll do nicely there, Mr Wycliffe. The twin-keels will keep 'er trim when the tide leaves 'er.'

Wycliffe realized that any particular show of appreciation would not be in order and he contented himself with a nod. 'Good!'

At ten-thirty that evening Wycliffe was back on the quay again, looking down at *Manna* whose super structure was already uncovered by the ebbing tide. The wind was still strong, there was white water in the bay and rain came in frequent and sudden squalls out of the darkness. But *Manna* lay snug in the shelter of the basin.

Sergeant Kersey arrived, closely followed by a police emergency vehicle carrying flood-lamps and a generator. The lights were switched on and directed down into the basin; their ghostly brilliance cast strange shadows and made the surrounding darkness seem even more impenetrable.

Kersey said, 'She's safe enough there, sir. There'll be another low at mid-day tomorrow and it will be a lot easier—'

Wycliffe cut him short. 'We are doing this tonight.'

The deck of the *Manna* was only a yard from one of the iron ladders clamped to the quay wall and Ron Bryce laid a plank across the gap but it was too early to go down, the well-deck was still awash. The whole forepart of the boat was decked over to form the accommodation and there was a raised wheel-house with engine controls.

Wycliffe stood with the collar of his mackintosh turned up and his hat pulled well down, apparently oblivious of the driving rain. Kersey said, 'There's no point in getting soaked. Come into the car.' Kersey's Ford Escort was parked close by.

They sat in the little car in silence and a few minutes later they were joined by Sergeant Smith with his cameras and his pipe so that they had to lower the window for ventilation. At eleven o'clock the pub closed and its customers split into two parties – one for home and bed, the other for the seamen's shelter and whatever excitement the night might bring. A quarter of an hour later Ron Bryce tapped on the car window and the policemen joined him on the quay.

'The water must be clear of the sea-cock by now, Mr Wycliffe; if you like, I'll go down and see what the damage is.'

He climbed down the ladder and sloshed about in the basin where there were still several inches of muddy water. With the help of a hand-torch he made an inspection of the hull which occupied him for three or four minutes then he called up, 'Sound as a bell, as far as I can see, Mr Wycliffe. It must be the sea-cock; shall I go aboard and shut it?'

'Is it possible to plug the drain from outside?'

'If you say so but it's easier to go aboard and shut the valve.'

'I'd rather you plugged it from outside.'

Wycliffe climbed down the ladder and stepped across the plank to stand for a moment, poised on the gunnel, then he stepped down into the well. Everything had a coat of slime; other than that and the seaweedy smell it was all surprisingly normal.

The door of the wheel-house had a brass lever-catch which shifted easily under the pressure of his finger-tip. He wanted to avoid confusing any prints which might have survived immersion. The wheel and engine controls were set on the port side and on the starboard side a couple of steps led down to the cabin-saloon.

This was it. Another door, another lever-catch which moved as easily as the first and he was looking into the saloon. The light from the flood-lamps was filtered by the glass portholes and skylight but he could see well enough. Cushions and blankets were lying in a tumbled, sodden heap on and under the long, narrow table. The locker doors had burst open, spilling their contents so that broken crockery, glasses, cans of beer, life-jackets and paperbacked books were scattered all over the heap.

What did he expect? His hunch had proved right; the salvage operation had justified itself. He had reasoned correctly from the holed and drifting dinghy that someone had rowed ashore from *Manna* and that *Manna* herself had either been scuttled or she had put to sea again and gone – gone where? With only forty miles of cruising in her tanks she had vanished without trace. Well, he had the answer to that one; now the question was, who had gone ashore in the dinghy? David Clement? He had never taken that possibility seriously; it made no sort of sense. So, if Clement had been aboard *Manna* on Saturday night the chances were that he still was.

All he could see for the moment was the jumble of gear. He started to move the cushions – foam rubber, and absurdly light despite the soaking – and almost at once he saw a fawn suede shoe and the leg of a pair of fawn denim slacks . . . He moved enough of the stuff to finally satisfy himself. David Clement was aboard. David Clement was dead.

So it was on the cards that *Manna* had been scuttled to dispose of a body.

The clothing removed from the body was laid out in polythene bags on a bench in Dr Frank's laboratory. Apart from the clothing there were the contents of the pockets: loose change, a handkerchief, a ball-point pen, a disintegrating cigarette pack, a cheque-book and card, fifteen pounds in notes and two glass paperweights in their chamois leather pouches.

The naked body lay under the white light; a slight figure of a man, under five feet six inches tall, less than one hundred and thirty pounds weight. Franks, in a green surgical gown, made his examination of externals and dictated notes to his secretary, a sleepy-eyed girl, called from her bed.

The wall clock showed twenty minutes to four, the time at which human vitality seems to be at its lowest ebb. Wycliffe felt cold in the pit of his stomach and the stink of formalin nauseated him.

The features of the dead man were unrecognizable due to distortion and there were patches of greenish lividity, but where the body had been protected by clothing the changes were less marked. Mercifully the fish had been unable to reach it.

'Three or four fillings and a couple of extractions, Charles. Taken with an appendix scar about fifteen years old you should have no trouble in settling any question of identity . . . '

'What about the cause of death?' Wycliffe was impatient.

Franks was silent for some time then he said, 'There's a pretty extensive skull fracture; I'm not sure yet whether it was the actual cause of death . . . He didn't drown, if that's any help to you . . . '

Three hours later the message was the same or very nearly. 'Well, Charles, the skull fracture in the left temporal region certainly killed him; the skull was shattered with a massive internal haemorrhage.'

'A heavy blow?'

'You'd think so but you'd be wrong in this case; this chap's skull is of very uneven thickness and in this area, bordering the left squamous suture, it's thinner than any I've come across in twenty-five years of this job.'

'An egg-shell skull.'

'In that area, yes.'

'So a fall or a blow?'

Franks shook his head. 'It wouldn't have taken much of a knock but I can't answer the crunch question, fall or blow.'

'Is he healthy – *was* he healthy in other respects?'

'As far as I can tell he was a fit young man. Unfortunately he suffered a bump on the head which to anyone else would probably have caused little more than temporary discomfort, perhaps mild concussion. It could have happened to him at any time had he the ill-luck to knock himself in that particular place.'

Wycliffe was thinking of the smashed Parian figure of the naked girl lying between desk and safe in the office behind the antique shop. He said, more to himself than Franks, 'But if it was an accident there would have been no reason for all this rigmarole in disposing of the body.'

Franks grinned. 'Your side of the fence, Charles. But I agree – no more reason than to remove the weapon from the scene of a suicide.'

Wycliffe growled. 'You've got a point there.'

Franks was stripping off his gown in preparation for scrubbing himself. His secretary came in with coffee in pottery mugs.

'Sugar, Mr Wycliffe?'

'No thanks.' But he sipped the coffee and changed his mind. 'Everything in this place tastes and smells of formalin.'

He left the laboratory at a little before seven and on his way home stopped at the flat in Godolphin Street. A police watcher was in position but whether he was awake was another question. Anyway, there was no point in watching the Stokes girl now.

She came to the door in her dressing gown. 'Come in.' She led him into the little sitting-room where the curtains were still drawn. She stooped and switched on the fire then hugged her body and shivered. 'It's cold!' and then, 'I know you've got bad news.'

'We've raised *Manna*.'

'And?'

'David was aboard . . . I'm afraid he's dead.'

She sat down. 'Drowned?'

'No, the pathologist attributes death to a head injury.' He added after a moment, '*Manna* was scuttled; somebody opened the sea-cock.'

She looked up, wide-eyed, incredulous. 'You mean that David was murdered?'

'Apparently he had a very thin skull.'

'What's that got to do with it?'

'It's possible that his death was an accident – at least that he was not deliberately murdered.'

She put her hands over her face and remained still for a long time. In the end she said, 'I would like to see him.'

Wycliffe hesitated. 'There will have to be a formal identification but whether—'

She cut him short. 'I know; he's been in the water a week, but I'm a nurse.'

'I'll give you a telephone number and you can arrange it.'

She shivered again. 'We were going to live together, perhaps get married. I don't know what he really thought of me but he was the nearest I've ever come to—' She broke off, her features distorted by emotion.

Wycliffe said, 'I'm very sorry. You still can suggest no way in which all this might have come about?'

Her emotion discharged itself in a flare of temper. 'God! Don't you think I want to? There's no point in beating about the bush now. David was going to sell his boat and in a few weeks he would have pulled out. I was to join him in Bournemouth after an interval . . . I don't know what went wrong.'

They were silent for a while then he said, 'Will you be all right here on your own?'

'What? Oh, yes. You don't have to worry about me.'

It was a fine morning though mist on the horizon promised showers to come. It occurred to him that there was something wrong with the light over the estuary, then he realized that it was his internal clock that was wrong, insisting that it was evening after a night without sleep.

He felt depressed. As he saw it he had made little real

progress. Despite the fact that they had unearthed Waddington, located the motor cruiser and found David Clement he was no nearer an explanation for what had happened. And though both the Clement brothers were dead by violence he was not in a position to say that either of them had been murdered. In fact, he was becoming increasingly convinced that Joseph had shot himself. The only reason for doubt was the absence of a weapon but the idea of a double murder was scarcely credible; the brothers had died in quite different ways, and why dispose of one body and not the other?

This sort of logic left him with questions: Why had the gun been removed? How and why had David Clement died? And who was responsible? Despite his mood he grinned wryly, 'Write your answers clearly in the spaces provided.'

Helen said, 'You look all in; you're going to bed now, surely?'

'For a couple of hours.'

'I'll get lunch for one o'clock.'

'Make it twelve.'

He set the alarm because he did not altogether trust Helen to wake him. At ten minutes past twelve he telephoned his headquarters and spoke to Bourne.

'Kersey and Smith have been down at Porthellin since early this morning, sir. Mr Scales is deputizing in your office.'

He had a prickly sensation in his eyelids and a dull ache at the base of his skull but after a bath and a light lunch he felt better. At half past one he set out for Porthellin. The mist which had earlier veiled the horizon now enveloped land and sea alike, translucent and luminous. Colours were muted like soft washes in a water-colour painting and as he approached the village it seemed possessed of an air of transience and unreality. The tide was coming in, lapping round the twin keels of *Manna*; a uniformed policeman stood near the top of

168

the iron ladder looking bored. When he spotted Wycliffe he smartened up and saluted. It was difficult to take it all seriously, the little blue and green and white boats, the pub with its lobster-pot sign, the fish-lofts which had been converted into gift shops and the cafés with their winter shutters still in place.

'No pressmen?'

The constable grinned. 'Not since the pub opened, sir.'

Kersey was in the wheel-house-chartroom of the cruiser with pub sandwiches and cans of beer. 'We've about finished here, sir. Smith has gone back to work on his stuff.'

'Has he got anything?'

'Nothing that will get us anywhere. The wheel and the engine controls have been wiped clean. This chap isn't making the kind of mistakes Smith can put on film.'

Somebody had mopped up the wheel-house and made it habitable.

'Have a beer, sir; glasses by courtesy of the owners whoever they may now be.' Kersey looked round at the white paintwork and tarnished brass. 'She's a nice craft and very well fitted out; when I come up on the pools I shall buy one like this. Esther and the girls would be over the moon.'

Wycliffe opened a can of beer and poured himself a glass. 'Any cash or valuables?'

'Not a thing.'

A gull perched on the gunnel and edged crabwise along it to peer in at the food; two more circled overhead, squawking and waking echoes in the village.

Kersey asked, 'What did Franks say?'

'Death was due to a skull injury but he had an egg-shell skull.'

'That's a fat lot of help! But however Clement died somebody thought it worth organizing that elaborate cover-up. In my opinion Lane knows something about it; I don't go for that book yarn of his. Lane went into the shop as the Ford girl says he did and, on his own showing, he was the last person we know to have seen David Clement alive.'

Wycliffe got out his pipe and started to fill it. He was still affected by a sense of unreality and found it difficult to focus his thoughts. After a little while he said, 'Who would want to kill Joseph? Conceivably his brother, though I see David as a rogue rather than a killer and, in any case, he had an alibi. In my opinion Joseph shot himself while his brother was out buying cigarettes.'

Kersey agreed. 'It looks that way, and I suppose it's possible that David didn't even know his brother was lying dead upstairs when Lane arrived.'

But Wycliffe's thoughts were following a different line; he said, 'The three of them were very close.'

Kersey looked at him, 'Sir?'

'The major, Bunny and Joe.' Wycliffe recited the three names with a half smile on his lips which puzzled Kersey. 'If Joe shot himself the other two would have blamed David.'

Kersey frowned. 'Are you saying that Lane might have roughed him up and gone further than he meant to – or something on those lines?' He broke off. 'It's an idea! And if I had my way it's an idea that would be put to Master Lane before he's much older.'

Wycliffe shook his head. 'You wouldn't get anywhere with Lane.' He added after a moment, 'I was wondering who telephoned who.'

'Telephoned?'

'Somebody wiped the prints off the telephone and they must have had a reason. Clement would have had no reason to remove his own prints . . . ' He broke off to put a match to his pipe.

Kersey gathered up the remains of his sandwiches and threw them overboard to the waiting gulls who

170

swooped and squawked and quarrelled out of all proportion to the prize.

Wycliffe said, 'Parkyn isn't on the phone.'

'Parkyn?' Kersey laughed. 'Plenty of people are.'

The sun broke through the mist striking answering gleams from the tarnished brasswork of the wheel-house. The tide was making rapidly now and already several of the smaller craft in the basin were afloat. The two men sat in silence for a long time; Wycliffe seemed to be absorbed in watching the shimmering reflections in the green water while Kersey sat still, holding his peace and waiting.

Wycliffe said quietly, as though continuing a train of thought, 'I've talked to Parkyn four times and he's never put a foot wrong.'

Kersey looked at him in surprise. 'You think that Parkyn—'

Wycliffe cut him off sharply. 'I think that Parkyn is playing a game with us; his whole attitude is a silent challenge. If a policeman came to see you four times on a case with which you were only marginally connected wouldn't you want to know what the hell he was after?' Wycliffe did not expect an answer and none came; he went on, 'Not Parkyn. He sits and smokes and drinks his whisky and laughs up his sleeve.'

It was rare enough for Wycliffe to air his thoughts in this way but what astonished Kersey was the uncharacter-istic vein of bitterness which informed the words. He realized that Wycliffe was talking to himself rather than to him and said nothing.

'We've got to pin him down and the way to do that is to go back to the beginning. We must carry out another house-to-house in Bear Street and neighbourhood but this time we are only interested in the movements of three men: Parkyn, Lane and David Clement.' He looked straight at Kersey as though challenging him to protest, 'We'll bring this out into the open and see how the major reacts then.'

Kersey was still silent but there was a shout from the quay, 'Mr Wycliffe! What about a word?' The reporters were back.

Wycliffe sighed. 'I thought I had something then but it's gone . . .'

CHAPTER NINE

Tuesday morning, with a gale from the south-west bringing squalls of rain. During the squalls the sky and sea were blue-black but the sea was flecked with crests of startling whiteness. Wycliffe breakfasted with scarcely a word to Helen and he was in his office by eight o'clock. At the cost of a restless night he had recalled what it was that had escaped him in talking over the case with Kersey – Bunny Lane had arrived at the antique shop that Saturday night *in response to a telephone call*. Although it was by no means a blinding illumination it fitted in to a more or less coherent theory which was forming in his mind, a theory which could only be put to the test by inviting confrontation. But even that might achieve no more than 'I warned you!' from Bellings and a ton of bricks from on high. However, the time had come to risk it.

Through Kersey he had arranged a special briefing session for nine o'clock.

'We are going to carry out another house-to-house inquiry in Bear Street and neighbourhood, to include Dog's Leg Lane, Garrison Drive, St John's Court and the harbour frontage. But this time we are interested in only three men – all of them well known in the district – Major Gavin Lloyd Parkyn, Michael John "Bunny" Lane, and David Clement. Your job will be to find anyone who saw these men after, say, six o'clock on Saturday evening.

'Unfortunately people's recollections are now ten days old so help them by recalling that night – the fact that it was a Saturday will mean something to most people, and remember that it was pouring with rain until late evening.'

The atmosphere in the briefing room was tense, quite unlike Wycliffe's usual sessions in which he encouraged a relaxed, conversational approach. His manner was terse and mandatory, creating a gulf between him and his listeners which could be measured by their silence.

'Any questions?'

There were none.

Back in the office Diane said, 'You know that the new duty schedules are due out on Friday—'

'Later, Diane! Get Sergeant Smith to come to my office, please.'

When Smith came a few minutes later Wycliffe's manner was equally curt.

'I want you to go back to Bear Street and look for prints or other traces which you might have missed first time round. I want that place put under a microscope. Take somebody reliable with you.'

Smith, scenting his mood, was cautious. 'You know it isn't possible to treat every surface, sir, can you suggest—'

Wycliffe cut him short. 'If I'm right, our man was waiting around, killing time, probably in the office behind the shop. Try to think what he might have done and the traces he might have left *before he had any reason to be on his guard*. Remember the exchange principle; nobody goes anywhere without leaving a trace and taking away some memento of the visit.'

Smith was nettled at being treated like a greenhorn, 'I know all about the theory, sir, but—'

Wycliffe cut him short again. 'Just try, that's what I'm asking you to do. During the morning I hope to send you a fresh set of prints for comparison purposes.'

'Is that all, sir?' Very formal.

'That's all.'

The odd thing was that he didn't feel bad tempered, only deeply preoccupied.

When Smith had gone he left the building and drove through the city, down Bear Street and up Dog's Leg Lane to Garrison Drive where the row of red-brick houses was dwarfed by the grey walls of the fort, by the great plain of the open sea, and by the menacing sky. The wind blew in tremendous gusts and his car steered uneasily. The whole place had an air of desolation, even the houses on either side of Number 3, ostentatiously cared for, looked as though their occupants had deserted them and left them to the elements.

On his way up the steep path to the house he had to brace himself against the wind in his back. Hetty opened the door, holding it with her body, and he edged his way round her into the hall. She shut the door and shot one of the bolts to stop it blowing open again. The dimly-lit hall seemed unnaturally still after the tumult outside.

'My brother is out.'

'I would like to wait for him if I may.'

She hesitated and for a moment he thought that she would make difficulties but instead she said in a voice which sounded oddly conspiratorial, 'Come with me!'

He followed her down the passage to the general's study where she opened the door and stood aside for him to enter. 'There!' She pointed to a worn leather chair by the window. 'You may wait for him in here.' She said this in the manner of one conferring a notable favour.

Hetty had changed; her movements were jerky, her eyes, which never met his, were restless, and her hair had escaped from almost all restraint so that it hung in ragged wisps about her head and even over her eyes. But the room looked much as he had first seen it – spotlessly clean and polished though now an oil-stove, less odorous than others in the house, was alight and brightened the dimly-lit room with its orange glow so that it was almost cosy. And there was another change: in a corner by the fireplace a dressmaker's model was draped with the general's dress uniform. Draped was the word, for the general's bulk bore little relationship to the dimensions of the dummy which was enveloped rather than clothed, like a children's guy on firework night. But Hetty had done her best and the figure carried the general's sword and displayed his medals together with the badge and star of his Order.

'You see!' she said. 'Isn't it just like the portrait?'

She came and stood over him, hands clasped together, knuckles showing white, and he wondered what was coming next.

'Would you like a cup of coffee?'

A reflex refusal was stifled just in time. 'Thank you, I would.'

She went out, leaving the door wide open.

Presumably, despite the weather, the major was doing his daily round – the newsagent, the betting shop, the butcher . . . The roar of the wind was subdued by the stout walls and the back of the house was to some extent sheltered, but now and then a more powerful gust made the whole building shudder and fragments of plaster rattled down the chimney into the empty grate.

He could hear Hetty moving about in the kitchen and ten minutes later she came in with a tray, two chipped pottery mugs, a jug of coffee, milk and a bowl of sugar.

'Black or white? . . . Do you take sugar?'

It was incredible.

When the coffee had been poured and she was holding her mug in both hands as though to warm them, she said, 'Have you come to arrest Gavin?'

'Arrest him? Of course not! Why do you ask that?'

She smiled a bleak little smile. 'I am not a fool, Mr Wycliffe. I listened to what you told him on Sunday. I have to listen at keyholes or I should hear nothing.' She sipped her coffee, her eyes on him. 'You told him what happened in that antique shop and how the boat was taken round to Porthellin and sunk in the bay and how somebody rowed ashore in the little dinghy . . . ' She paused for a while then added, 'It was obvious you suspected Gavin and now, since then, you've got the boat up and found another dead man. I heard that on the wireless.'

Wycliffe said nothing.

Hetty, taking her coffee mug with her, walked over to the fireplace where she stood with her back to Wycliffe looking up at her father's portrait. 'When you arrest someone do they have to be put on trial?'

'Anyone charged with a crime has to appear in court—'

'Even if they confess?'

'Confession to the police is not accepted as proof of guilt, but you really must not jump to—'

She turned to face him abruptly and put her finger to her lips enjoining silence in a childish gesture. 'Sh!'

There were sounds of a door opening and closing, a man's cough . . .

'Here he is!' She hurried out of the room with the tray.

Parkyn came to the door. 'Ah, Wycliffe! A wild day!' His face was flushed by the wind. 'Come to my room.'

'No! Let him say what he has to say here.' Hetty was standing behind her brother, hidden by his bulk.

The major turned slowly to face her and looked at her for several seconds without a word, then he said, 'This way, Wycliffe.'

It was the first time he had been a witness to open hostility between them and the first time he had seen Hetty quelled.

In Parkyn's little room the inevitable heater was already burning, giving off its clammy warmth. Parkyn stooped to the cupboard and came up with his tray – whisky, carafe, glasses . . .

177

'Will you join me?'

'Not just now.'

Wycliffe's visits were already acquiring a ritual character and the fact was not lost on the major who greeted his reply with a sardonic smile. He poured himself a half-tumbler of whisky and added a little water.

'Sit down, Wycliffe.'

Parkyn lowered himself into his own chair in which the worn upholstery, devoid of all pattern and texture, had moulded itself to his form. He stretched out his legs to the heater; his trousers were soaked to the knees. A gulp of whisky was followed by the ritual sigh. 'Well, what is it this time?'

'I suppose you've heard that Clement's boat has been raised and that we found his body in the cabin?'

'Yes, I heard that. How did he die? Was he drowned?'

'No, he died of a fractured skull which caused a severe brain haemorrhage.'

Parkyn was holding his glass to the light, apparently studying the clarity of the whisky. 'A blow?'

'Possibly. The pathologist tells me that he had what is known as an "egg-shell" skull.'

Parkyn balanced his glass on the arm of his chair. 'Ah! I've known such a case; a man in our unit knocked his head against the vaulting-horse during a training session and his skull seemed to collapse. Of course, that was an accident.'

'So might this have been, but it could have been manslaughter or even murder.'

Parkyn shook his head. 'A murderer could hardly be expected to have knowledge of the thickness of his victim's skull.' He got out his pipe and pouch. 'Smoke?'

'I won't smoke now, thank you.'

The major's back was to the door but Wycliffe was sitting side-on and he could see that the door was very slightly ajar though he felt sure that Parkyn had closed it. No doubt Hetty was listening.

Wycliffe said, 'I wonder if you telephoned Bunny Lane before or after David Clement died?'

Parkyn was filling his pipe but he looked up with one of those faint smiles which was no more than a twitch of the lip.

An unmistakable creak came from the passage and Wycliffe was surprised that Parkyn either had not heard it or chose to ignore it. He had filled his pipe and was going through the ritual of lighting it. Between puffs he said, 'Why did you come here this morning, Wycliffe?' His manner was unconcerned, casually curious.

More than once in the past few days Wycliffe had thought that he was allowing himself to be intimidated by this larger-than-life character whose peace of mind, according to Bellings, was still of concern in high places. Would he have behaved to any other suspect as he had behaved – was behaving, with Parkyn? In any case he had decided on confrontation.

'I want you to be quite clear about where you stand.'

The prominent eyes widened. 'Ah!'

Wycliffe followed up with a request which he had intended to put with greater subtlety. 'There is something else; you are under no obligation at this stage but I would like you to have your fingerprints taken for purposes of comparison.'

'Isn't it usual to say for purposes of elimination?'

Wycliffe said, 'If you will come with me to Mallet Street police station it will only take a few minutes and I will bring you straight back.'

Parkyn removed his pipe from his mouth. 'No, Wycliffe. I am not going to any police station and I will have no truck with your little inky pads, but if you want my prints you can have them.' He lifted up the whisky bottle which was almost empty and drained it into his glass, then he offered it to Wycliffe. 'There, that should do you . . . Wait a minute . . .'

He heaved himself out of his chair and went to his

179

desk where he found a crumpled carrier-bag. He dropped the bottle in the bag. 'There! That will keep the rain off.'

Parkyn came with him to the door and stood on the steps, in front of the closed door, while Wycliffe fought his way down the garden in the very teeth of the gale, clutching his carrier-bag.

Seated at the wheel of his car, he swore. He was in no doubt about who had come off best in that round. But the defeat was moral, not professional. He was not disappointed. With Parkyn's temperament and experience it was unlikely that he would make the mistake of saying too much and, in fact, he had said almost nothing. But Hetty had talked; so much so that he was uneasy. Hetty was convinced that it was only a matter of time before her brother's arrest. 'When you arrest someone do they have to be put on trial? . . . Even if they confess?'

It was the threat of disgrace to the saintly and gallant general's memory which troubled Hetty.

Wycliffe parked his car by the old custom-house and walked up Bear Street to the antique shop. There were few people about and in one place a swirling mass of brown water extended half-way across the road where a drain had become blocked. He handed over the major's whisky bottle to Smith whose manner was even more withdrawn and morose than usual.

'Anything fresh?'

'No, sir.'

Annie was serving lunches so he crossed the street and took his seat at one of the tables. While he was eating he realized that he was being pointed out by the knowing regulars to others not so knowing.

Afterwards he returned to headquarters and to his office. It was still raining and even through the hermetically sealed double-glazing he could hear it lashing against the glass.

Diane came in. 'Mr Bellings has been asking to see

you; he would like you to go along to his office when it is convenient.'

Diane was stiff and formal, still responding to his manner of the morning.

'I'll go now.'

She looked at him in surprise at his ready compliance. The truth was that he felt himself to be in some sort of limbo – waiting and hoping that something decisive would turn up before a fresh wave of publicity caught up with the case and the press started handing out cod about a possible security angle. It would come. Sooner or later a bright reporter would spot his interest in Parkyn, do his homework, and then the gentlemen from Millbank really would get interested.

He walked down the main corridor, through the sacred door and into the carpeted precincts. Bellings's personal assistant said, 'Go straight in, Mr Wycliffe. Mr Bellings is expecting you.'

'Oh, Charles! Nice of you to find the time.' A hint of sarcasm? Who could tell?

The reason for the interview was soon apparent; Bellings had chosen this moment to tell him of his impending departure.

'A chance I can't afford to miss, Charles! A lectureship in criminology is the sort of pipe-dream one has but never expects to realize ... You and the chief have always looked on me as a too academic policeman and, here I am, proving you right.'

Bellings's words were, as always, accompanied by restrained though expressive gestures with his long, aesthetic hands. He punctuated what he had to say with precisely calculated pauses and, at the right moment, he would catch the eye of his listener with a deprecatory smile. Wycliffe thought, He can't fail to be a hit with his students; especially the women.

Bellings went on to indulge in elegant nostalgia with a discreet measure of self-denigration, rounded off with a few well-turned phrases expressing thanks and appreciation of 'your unfailing support and co-operation . . . '

Wycliffe put it down as a well-rehearsed performance and acknowledged it as graciously as he was able. At the same time he had been taking stock of the deputy's office which, if he said 'Yes' on Wednesday evening, might be his. The office was little different from his own, a little more plush, and it looked out over the car-park instead of the highway; but beyond the car-park there were real fields with cows and trees. True, the developers and planners had their beady eyes on that land but the conservationist lobby was learning the tricks of the trade and becoming almost as devious as the opposition. Not that he would be influenced by the view, it was that padded door which swished shut behind one – a symbol.

Bellings was looking at him as though he expected something. 'Well, that's it, Charles; the end of a chapter for me! I start afresh with the Michaelmas Term in October.'

'Yes, yes, I see . . . ' Wycliffe's thoughts had wandered and he was a little at a loss so that he changed the subject with unflattering abruptness. 'You were telling me the other day about Parkyn's career and his reputation; I wonder if you could tell me a bit more about him as a man?'

Belling's expression froze. He would have liked to refuse but he hesitated to put himself in the position of withholding information from a colleague on police business. He spread his pale hands in a helpless gesture. 'What, exactly, do you want to know?'

'His temperament; the kind of man he is?'

Bellings answered tight-lipped, 'I've already told you that my direct knowledge of Parkyn comes from a brief spell of service with him in Korea – a few months only, when we were both very young men . . . ' He paused to allow the point to sink in and give himself time to think.

'I have told you that he was the sort of man who seemed to put himself at risk as a matter of deliberate choice – he didn't wait until he found himself in a tight corner, he sought out such situations. He trailed his coat, as the Irish say. Or so it seemed to me and to others who knew him at the time.

'There was no question of going hunting or histrionics, he was always extremely taciturn about his exploits, often aggressively so, and it sometimes seemed to me that he was ashamed of this wild streak in his nature.'

Bellings picked up a slim, expensive ball-point and played with it. (Wycliffe had been given a similar one for Christmas but preferred a Staedtler Stick).

'He seemed to be driven, as I believe some men are, constantly to challenge fate – to hazard himself.' Bellings added, with more insight than Wycliffe would have given him credit for, 'I have thought since that such men may feel menaced by fear – the fear of being afraid and so they put themselves to endless tests . . . '

'And socially? How did he get on with his companions?'

Another frown and a caustic aside. 'The conditions were hardly conducive to an elaborate social life. However, Parkyn was as self-effacing as a man of his bulk could be but the truth is that he didn't fit in terribly well. At that time he didn't drink or smoke and he detested sport . . . Of course, nobody had any idea then of his potential . . . '

Bellings would not have been flattered had he realized that Wycliffe was matching this assessment with that of Parkyn's bookie and finding, on the whole, that they made a good marriage.

Wycliffe was going though the case-file. At a certain stage in an investigation he would spend time browsing through the records which, for the most part, were as exciting as last week's news, but there was a chance that something, passed over at the time as trivial, might now have importance.

The telephone rang – Smith, his manner a mixture of satisfaction and lingering resentment, 'I've found a set of prints which seem to match those you brought me. I'm speaking from the antique shop but I propose coming back to do a proper comparison. The prints – index, second and third fingers of the right hand – were on the underside of the lavatory seat in the downstairs cloak-room.'

Wycliffe heaved a sigh. It was no absolute break-through, there was nothing to say how long the prints had been there – but it was a sign, like Noah's dove returning with an olive leaf in her beak.

He turned again to his file, in particular to a packet of photographs labelled with a series of index numbers; photographs taken by Smith of Joseph's room after the removal of the body but before it was disturbed by the searchers. Smith was a good photographer; every detail stood out clearly and, taken together, the photographs made an almost complete record of the room without need of written report. Wycliffe spread them on his desk.

Joseph's bed – a single bed with a crumpled beds-pread; even in the photograph it looked grubby. Over the bed Joseph kept his books on makeshift shelving; books on furniture and on stamps. It was possible to read the titles on many of them. Another photograph showed the top of the desk; a loose-leafed album with quadrille rulings open at a page labelled, *Guatemala: Quetzal Design of 1879*, in careful italic script. The tools of his hobby were there: forceps, magnifier, perforation gauge . . . a few stamps in polythene envelopes. Then there was a large china ashtray, a willow-patterned tobacco jar and the pipe he had, presumably, been smoking was laid down by the album. There was a glass pen-tray with ball-points and pencils and an old-fashioned

184

stub-nibbed pen for writing the headings in his albums.

Wycliffe turned to another of Smith's studies – for that is what they were – showing the wall to the right of the desk where there was a picture, a dim oil-painting in a gilt frame, and below it a rack of Joseph's pipes, more than a dozen of them, all of similar pattern with small, squat bowls and long, slender stems. Interesting, a man's choice of pipes; what did these tell one about Joseph? That despite his apparent sturdy stolidity there was a finer, aesthetic side to his nature? Parkyn, too, went in for long-stemmed pipes but preferred a bigger, deeper bowl giving a longer smoke. Parkyn's pipes were similar to Wycliffe's own. And Bunny Lane? Bunny stuck to the relatively short stem and stout bowl of the honest tradesman, ignoring the fact that the species had all but disappeared with Stanley Baldwin.

The internal telephone buzzed and he depressed a key. 'Sergeant Kersey to see you, Mr Wycliffe.'

'Send him in.'

Kersey came in, glanced at the photographs spread on the desk, and said with a grin, 'English interiors of the late twentieth-century Smith school. I recognize the technique.'

'You've got something?'

'Something. D.C. Edwards, on house-to-house, has just reported in. I don't know if you remember, but in Dog's Leg Lane, on the right-hand side, just below the bend there's a house with a little window low down, almost level with the street. An old couple called Poat have lived there since way back and on Saturday evening, when it was raining like a flood, the drain choked outside and they had water coming into their kitchen. Old Poat had to go out and clear it and while he was at it Parkyn went by.'

'What time was this?'

'A bit before eight.' Kersey went on. 'The odd thing is,

the major didn't go down the hill towards Bear Street but turned off along the alley which runs behind the houses.'

Wycliffe said, 'The Ford girl!'

Kersey nodded. 'It's the only answer. My mother used to say God puts at least one surprise in every packet and she was dead right.'

Wycliffe said, 'Go and talk to her.'

When Kersey rang the bell he could hear a vacuum cleaner at work and when Marilyn opened the door she was wearing an overall with a scarf round her head.

'Afternoon, Marilyn. Cleaning up?'

She looked at him with a suspicious air. 'I thought we'd lost you. Didn't you get promoted or something?'

'Or something. Can I come in?'

She stood aside. 'You will anyway. Have you come for my statement?'

Kersey went into the candy-floss room, lifted a satin doll off one of the armchairs and sat down. The vacuum cleaner stood in the middle of the floor. It was like seeing a night-club in the cold light of day.

'Make yourself at home.'

'Thanks.' Kersey was manipulating the limbs of the doll into grotesque attitudes which made the plump girl laugh.

'I thought I knew all your regulars, Marilyn.'

She stopped laughing. 'You cops think you know everything.'

'Major Gavin Lloyd Parkyn, R.M., C.B.E., D.S.O. etc., etc . . . '

'I don't know what you're talking about.'

'Not what, who. His father was a "Sir" and a general and he's been quite a nob in his day. You're moving up in the world, love.'

'What do you want?'

'A week ago last Saturday, at a little before nine, you

186

heard a shot; later, you saw a man come up the street and go into the antique shop. That's what you told my boss.'

'It's true.'

'Yes, but what you didn't tell him was that Parkyn was with you until a few minutes before you heard the shot. How long, exactly?'

'If he wasn't here, I can't tell you how long it was before he left, can I?' She pulled off the scarf from round her head and released a great bouncy mass of dark curls as though in defiance.

Kersey wagged his finger at her. 'Naughty! We know he was here; you won't do yourself any good by lying about it. How long before the shot did he leave?'

She turned to the vacuum cleaner and seemed about to switch it on. 'You're hindering me in my work.' It was a half-hearted tactic; she had had too many dealings with the police to believe that she could get away with it.

Kersey remained good humoured. 'And you know that I shall hinder you a hell of a lot more if you don't tell me what I want to know.'

'You can't make me answer questions; I don't do anything against the law.'

'Who said you did? But one of my lads spending the odd evening now and again lounging about in your alley would scare your clients away for weeks.'

'You're a real bastard!' But she said it without heat. 'Less than five minutes.'

'Five minutes or less after Parkyn left you heard the shot; is that it?'

'About that. Of course, as I told your boss I didn't realize it was a shot then.' She looked at him, suddenly wide-eyed. 'You're not saying that he—'

'How long has Parkyn been coming here?'

'A long time; probably a couple of years, perhaps more, but it's ridiculous for you—'

'How often?'

'Usually Wednesdays and Saturdays.'

'How do you get on with him?'

'That's what I'm trying to tell you. He's real nice; I only wish there was more like him; he wouldn't hurt a fly.'

'One of those who come mainly for the chat, is that it?'

'What's that got to do with you?'

'All right, was he his usual cheery, chatty self on Saturday evening?'

'I didn't see any difference; he's always pleasant which is more than I can say for some.'

'Has he been here since?'

'As usual.'

Kersey tried again. 'Has he mentioned the Clement brothers or what happened over there?'

'He never talks about other people; he's no gossip.'

'You should write him a testimonial. Which way did he leave?'

'There's only one way out of here – down the stairs.'

Kersey's manner hardened. 'Don't be funny with me, girl! I'm not joking about queering your pitch. Which way?'

'You know most of 'em go and come the back way.'

'And Parkyn that Saturday night?'

She hesitated. 'I think he went out the front way, I thought I heard his footsteps in the street but I couldn't say for sure.'

'Come off it! You went to the window, didn't you?'

She gave up. 'All right, I saw him. When I looked out he was on the opposite pavement talking to the younger brother from the antique shop.'

'You mean he'd knocked at the door or something?'

'I don't think so. I think they'd just happened to meet there; that's what it looked like.'

'And?'

'And nothing. My telephone rang and I went out into the passage to answer it. I wasn't on the phone more than a couple of minutes and it was when I came back in here that I heard the bang.'

Kersey stood up and replaced the doll on the chair. She watched him, apprehensive, 'I hope he's not going to be in trouble.'

Kersey said, 'You want to watch out, my girl! When you start worrying about other people it's a bad sign.'

'Bastard!'

Before he had closed the door behind him he heard the vacuum cleaner start up again.

Wycliffe went back to his photographs and wondered what he had been thinking about before Kersey interrupted. Pipes – that was it; nothing worth remembering. He was about to gather up the photographs and return them to their envelope when his eye was caught again by the one of Joseph's desk. It showed the album with his stamp gear, the tobacco jar and ashtray – and the pipe. The pipe lay beside the stamp album as though it had been one of Joseph's last acts to place it there before . . . But the pipe was not like the others in the rack on the wall. It had a long stem like them but a heavier, deeper bowl.

It must have been the estimable Poirot who said, '*Mon ami*, a clue two feet long is every bit as valuable as one measuring two millimetres.' One up to the little Belgian's grey cells. Criminal investigation is apt to get bogged down by minutiae. Well, the pipe on the desk was not two feet long but it was big enough to have been overlooked.

He spoke to D.C. Trice on the telephone. In addition to being responsible for scene-of-crime inventories she was also custodian of the stuff recorded. When the police handed back premises to the owners it was her job to deal with suspicious relatives wanting to know what had happened to aunty's butterfly-wing brooch or granny's silver bracelet.

189

'Yes, sir. There was a pipe in the pocket of the jacket Joseph was wearing – half smoked ... I'm not an authority on pipes but this one had a small, squat bowl, a long stem and a broad mouth-piece ...'

'Listen! I want you to go to the flat, to Joseph's room, and collect the pipe you will find lying on his desk next to the open stamp album. Hand it over to Sergeant Smith for prints. If he doesn't find any identifiable prints there is still the "bite" which is nearly as distinctive ...'

Kersey came in looking moderately pleased with himself. 'I think we've pretty well nailed him this time, sir. We've got a witness prepared to say that he was outside the antique shop, talking to David Clement, within a minute or two of nine o'clock.' He told his story. 'Parkyn must have run into David as he was leaving the house to buy his cigarettes.'

Wycliffe said, 'I think we may have another witness to say that he went inside.' He held out Smith's photograph and pointed to the pipe lying beside the open album.

Kersey frowned. 'I don't get it.'

'That pipe is not like the ones in the rack on the wall but it *is* like the pipes Parkyn smokes.'

Kersey, a non pipe smoker, looked dubious. 'You think he left it behind?'

Wycliffe was sitting back in his chair looking dreamily at the litter of photographs on his desk. 'It's not difficult to imagine. You've just said that Parkyn ran into David as he was leaving the house. Presumably Parkyn said he'd come to see Joseph and David told him that Joseph was up in his room. "You can go on up." On the stairs, or in the corridor upstairs, Parkyn heard the shot and rushed into Joe's room to find him collapsed on the floor by the desk. Parkyn was carrying a pipe in his hand – I often do when I go into someone else's house – he dropped it on the desk while he knelt down to see what could be done for Joe ...'

190

Kersey screwed up his features into one of his famous grimaces. 'And forgot about it! I wonder if he remembered it afterwards. Is it still there?'

'I've sent Liz Trice to collect it and take it to Smithy.'

Kersey scratched his chin. 'To think that it's been there under our noses from the start . . .'

CHAPTER TEN

The telephone rang. 'Wycliffe.'

Information Room with a report of a fire at Number 3, Garrison Drive. 'Knowing your interest in the premises, sir . . . '

Wycliffe swore. 'I'm going to Garrison Drive, Diane. Find Kersey and tell him to join me there.'

The rain had stopped but he drove through the streets which were still streaming with water and every vehicle carried with it a plume of spray. In Bear Street men in orange jackets languidly organized chaos round the blocked drain but he got through to the turn-off for Dog's Leg Lane. As he topped the rise and came out into the open, there was the bay a vast cauldron of white foam, and the air was misty with driven spray. Helen would be worried about salt-burn on her camellias.

From the house in Garrison Drive a ragged plume of dense black smoke like a fox's brush was being whipped inland.

There was a fire tender, two ambulances and a police car parked in the road; hoses snaked up through the garden of Number 3. He could see smoky orange flames flicking upwards from the back of the house, possibly from the general's study or the room above. Luckily the Victorians had not been miserly with space, there was a thirty-foot gap between the houses.

A young fire officer was talking on the radio in the cab of the tender; he recognized Wycliffe and came down. 'I've got another appliance round the back but the fire has a strong hold.'

'The occupants – a man and his sister – what happened to them?'

'Both have burns – the woman quite bad burns it seems. The brother got his fishing her out of the room where the fire started, downstairs at the back. I gather there was an oil-stove overturned.' The young man treated Wycliffe to a canny look. 'Is there something I should know about all this?'

Wycliffe said, 'I'm interested in these people; it's possible there may be a forensic angle.'

There was a sound of splintering wood and myriads of sparks shot up above the house and tore off on the wind.

'That'll be the floor of the room above, now it won't be long before the roof timbers are alight. I'd better get back up there.'

The ambulance men were coming down the garden of the next-door house carrying a stretcher between them. A uniformed constable walked beside them. The stretcher was put into the first ambulance and Wycliffe had a glimpse of Hetty's face, unnaturally pale but composed. Was she unconscious? A man got in beside her and the ambulance moved off.

'How is she?'

The constable answered. 'Quite badly burned about the legs, sir, but they seem to think she'll make it.'

'And the brother?'

'They're seeing to him now. His hands and arms caught it, dragging her out. He'll go in the other ambulance; they didn't want to keep his sister waiting.'

A few minutes later two other ambulance men came down the garden, one of them carrying a folded stretcher. Parkyn walked with them, evidently refusing to be a stretcher case; his arms and hands were smothered with bandages and he wore his old duffle coat draped over his shoulders and held there by a loop of string. His eyes lighted on Wycliffe and he grinned briefly. 'I've heard it said that there's no show without Punch.'

He steadied himself against the corner of the ambulance. 'It was the heater in the old man's room; she must have knocked the damn thing over.' With a sigh of resignation he allowed himself to be guided into the ambulance.

'Where are they being taken?'

'Casualty at County General. The woman may be transferred to a burns unit.'

'Will the man be kept in?'

'At his age with second-degree burns and shock they won't let him go for a day or two.'

Kersey arrived and found Wycliffe at the back of the house surveying a random collection of furniture and other belongings which had been rescued from the house and now lay half-buried in the wilderness of the garden.

'You'd better stay here. Get hold of the social services people and ask them to make arrangements for this stuff to be stored. I want a police watch on the place until forensic have had a look at it; not that what they say will make any difference but we must go by the book.'

Half the house had been destroyed and the fire was still not out though more or less under control. There was a great gap in the roof and flames still licked round the carbonized rafters.

Kersey said, 'You think it was an accident?'

Wycliffe snapped. 'Of course it wasn't! If I'd had any sense I should have expected something of the sort.' He looked up at the still burning house. 'The woman is obsessed; this is a belated funeral pyre for the old general, a sort of time-lapse suttee . . . ' He smiled with a certain bitterness. 'But Gavin fished her out and spoiled it.' He looked round him in a vague way then braced himself, 'Anyway, I'm off!'

194

He drove back to his office. The streets were no longer like rivers and the wind was dropping. He put in half-an-hour at his desk on the day's paperwork.

People were going home, the bulding was emptying. He stood by his window watching the homeward traffic. Everything had been washed clean and overhead the clouds were parting leaving a great rift of blue. He was tempted to call on Bunny Lane but he wanted to talk to the major first. At six-fifteen he went down to the canteen where he was an infrequent visitor. Sausages, bacon and fried bread – the kind of meal likely to benefit only the police pension fund; afterwards he drank two cups of canteen coffee. He smoked a pipe while chatting to a colleague from Traffic and it was seven o'clock when he returned to his office.

He picked up the telephone and asked for the casualty department at County General. Hospitals are not fond of policemen, they suspect them of having designs on their patients, which they often have.

'Casualty Sister . . . Yes, we have had a Gavin Lloyd Parkyn in casualty . . . We applied dressings and administered a sedative . . . He was not admitted to any ward . . . Certainly he should have been but he refused admission and took himself off . . . Of course it was stupid – an oldish man suffering from second-degree burns and shock needs professional attention but there was nothing we could do about it. I have enough problems looking after the people who want what we have to offer them . . . Our receptionist called a taxi and one of my nurses saw him into it . . . I've no idea; you'd better speak to the receptionist. I'll have this call transferred.'

The receptionist told him that she had phoned Radio Taxis who had an office just round the corner from the hospital and that Parkyn had left in one of their taxis at just before six-thirty.

Wycliffe had no doubt where the major would have made for and phoned Bunny Lane.

Lane said, 'I haven't seen him, Mr Wycliffe. Is there something wrong?'

Wycliffe told him. Bunny had heard nothing of the fire.

Wycliffe then spoke to the taxi firm: 'One of your chaps picked up a fare from casualty at County General at a little before six-thirty this evening . . .'

They agreed to trace the cab and ring back.

Kersey telephoned. The fire at Garrison Drive was out but a fire appliance was standing by. Kersey had arranged for a police guard and no examination of the ruin would be possible until mid-day tomorrow.

He had no sooner finished with Kersey than the taxi people were back on the line. 'Our driver has just delivered the fare to a house in St John's Court. The delay was due to the fact that your man stopped at three public houses on the way, telling the driver to wait. He came out of the last one carrying a bottle of whisky.'

Wycliffe drove through the city; the streets were quiet and so were the elements after a tempestuous day. Cotton wool clouds drifted across the sky. He parked, probably for the last time in this routine, outside the old custom-house and walked to St John's Court.

Never in twenty-five years of C.I.D. work had he found himself nearing the end of a case with so little idea of how it would turn out. It had been not so much a case as a battle of wits. He had very little doubt now about what had happened but much depended on interpretation and, in particular, on the framing of the charges. For the two men concerned that could make the difference between a longish spell in prison and a suspended sentence. The prudent course for Wycliffe would be to steer clear – prefer a holding charge and leave the rest to the police lawyers, but he was rarely prudent in his own interest.

His feelings must not enter into it but they inevitably would. The major and Bunny had taken the law into

196

their own hands – a heinous crime. Far safer to bash an old lady over the head and run off with her handbag. British justice abhors private enterprise but Wycliffe did not always share that view. And at the back of his mind was the uncomfortable feeling that in pursuing the case he had also pursued a personal end though he would have had difficulty in saying what that end was.

There was a light showing through the fanlight over Bunny Lane's front door. Wycliffe knocked and almost at once there were footsteps in the stone passage and Bunny opened the door. He seemed relieved.

'Mr Wycliffe! Come in, let me take your coat.' He added in a lower tone, 'He's here and I'm very worried about him.'

The room looked just as it had done when, a few nights earlier, he had played dominoes with the major and Bunny; the box of dominoes still stood in the middle of the big square table. A fire burned in the grate and the major was seated in his usual chair, a bottle of whisky and a jug of water at his elbow. His arms were bandaged and the left was in a sling but his right arm was free and in that hand he held a glass of whisky, half-full. His cheeks were unnaturally flushed, his eyes seemed more prominent and his breathing was loud and laboured. But he greeted Wycliffe with his customary sardonic smile.

'You didn't waste much time, Wycliffe!'

Bunny said, 'The major arrived here twenty minutes ago.'

Wycliffe turned to the major. 'You should be in hospital.'

Parkyn took a mouthful of whisky, swallowed it, and clumsily wiped his mouth with the side of his hand. 'I prefer it here.' He added after a moment, 'Bunny telephoned to ask about Hetty. They say she's as well as can be expected, whatever that means.' He turned in his chair to face Wycliffe and winced at an unexpected aggravation of his pain. 'I suppose you realize that she tried to burn herself alive in there with the old man's bits and pieces?' He sighed. 'I never knew she felt that deeply about it all . . . Think of it!' He turned away. 'No right to push her that far . . . '

Wycliffe thought, 'Poor Hetty! Now she owes him her life and she'll never forgive him for that.'

Once more the room seemed to dictate its own pace, its own silences, as the clink-clink of the little clock chased the seconds away. The major's breathing maintained an uncertain rhythm with breaks which caused the two men to look anxiously at his flushed features.

The gravelly voice resumed. 'Hetty was always a strange girl. She should have been a man; that's been her trouble all along. She's never forgiven me for being one and not making a better job of it.' He grinned unexpectedly, 'My God, if she had been, the army would have had to look out!'

He turned again to Wycliffe with a sheepish expression. 'If she gets over this, let her tell her own story – eh? Give her own version. No need to put words into her mouth . . . I mean, she might not want to admit . . . ' He broke off once more and when he spoke again he was on another tack. 'She couldn't bear the thought of me coming up before the courts over this affair and letting the old man down.' He laughed briefly. 'That's what I've been doing for most of my life according to her – letting the old man down.'

Another mouthful of whisky, another sigh. 'Well, I don't think she need worry now.'

Bunny Lane was watching him with the concern of a mother for her child. 'He shouldn't be drinking like that . . . His heart—'

The major cut him short. 'Don't be such an old woman, Bunny!'

Lane said, 'I think we should call MacDonald.

198

MacDonald is his doctor – he's under treatment for heart trouble.'

'You can call MacDonald or you can call the bloody undertaker when I've said what I want to say to Wycliffe but not before!' He made an effort to ease himself into a more comfortable position. 'You realize, Wycliffe, that Joe shot himself because of the antics of that bastard brother of his?'

Wycliffe nodded.

'I was on the stairs ... I heard the shot. Another minute and I could have saved him ... The brother was out, I'd just left him in the street.' His voice failed him and he breathed heavily for a while, then he took another drink.

'Am I the only one drinking? What are you thinking about, Bunny? Is Wycliffe a teetotaller?'

Bunny looked at Wycliffe, anxious, questioning, and Wycliffe nodded. Bunny got up and left the room.

The major followed him with his eyes. 'Good chap ... Salt of the earth. Try and make it easy for him ... My fault; imposed on his loyalty ... Never been able to resist the chance to cock a snook.'

Wycliffe said quietly, 'At what?'

The major frowned. 'Fate, I suppose. What else?'

'You are a fatalist?'

'Dyed in the wool. I've always taken a fatalistic view of life and that means that I was bound to see myself as impotent.' He laughed then winced at the pain. 'My reason tells me that, but the rest of me resents it like hell.'

'And so?'

An irritable gesture. 'And so me! A contradiction – isn't that what we all are? Nothing at all, pretending to be something.'

Bunny came back with the inevitable tin tray, the bottle of white wine and the highly polished glasses. He put the tray on a low stool, removed the cork which had already been drawn and looked at Wycliffe.

'Thanks.'

As well be hung for a sheep as a lamb. Wycliffe's proper course was to insist on a medical opinion but he needed no doctor to tell him that the major was a very sick man.

Bunny poured two glasses of wine and passed one to Wycliffe, then before sitting down, he put several lumps of coal on the fire. With an effort the major poured himself some more whisky and added a dash of water.

'Your very good health, gentlemen!' He drank deeply. A long-drawn-out sigh and the heavy, more or less regular breathing resumed. The major was gazing into the fire, motionless except for the heaving movements of his chest. The other two waited for him to speak and when he did his voice and manner were set in the low key of reminiscence.

'There was nothing to be done for Joe – half of one side of his face .. I went down to the office and telephoned Bunny then I waited for the brother to come back. When he did I showed him what he was responsible for – *what he had done.*'

The major's manner was grim and Wycliffe had never been more conscious of the power of the man.

'He didn't say much but his attitude was callous – indifferent. I said my piece and he became offensive. By that time we were back downstairs with the intention of phoning the police.' The major's voice strengthened, 'It was then that he made a remark which angered me and I hit him . . .'

The silence which followed lasted so long that Wycliffe wondered if Parkyn had said all he intended or was able to say. His breathing had become shallower and his cheeks seemed to have lost something of their unnatural colour. He raised his glass to his lips but changed his mind and did not drink. When he spoke again he made a couple of false starts before his voice found its usual register.

'I hit him only once and he went down. On the way he struck his head against the corner of the desk and knocked over the little figure of a naked woman which stood there . . . Somehow he cracked his skull. You tell me he had a thin place; anyway, he never moved again.'

The major drew a deep breath, raised his glass to his lips once more and this time he drank deeply. The whisky must have entered his air passages for he began to cough; a great spasm of coughing shook his whole body. Lane took the glass from his hand but he and Wycliffe could only look on helplessly while the major's body was racked convulsively. The fit lasted a couple of minutes then subsided, leaving him red-faced and gasping, but after a little while he recovered.

'Sorry! . . . Went the wrong way . . . ' He reached for the glass which Lane had taken from his hand and sipped slowly. 'Ah! that's better! . . . Much better! . . . As I was saying, he was dead. I hadn't intended to do him an injury, merely to chastise him, but there it was . . . I can't pretend that I felt greatly distressed; I've seen too many better men die for no reason at all in war and he was a rat!'

Once more silence took possession of the room broken only by the ticking of the clock and the major's laborious breathing. It might have been expected that Wycliffe would have questioned the two men but he sat as they did, staring into the fire without a word.

After a time the major's breathing became easier and he resumed where he had left off. 'It was about then that Bunny arrived. I let him in through the shop. Of course he didn't know about the younger brother and it came as a shock . . . ' The major was speaking in short phrases separated by long intervals, partly because of difficulties with his breathing but also because his manner was once more reflective and he seemed to be speaking as much

201

to himself as to Wycliffe. Then his voice strengthened and became more incisive, 'I decided not to call the police.' He turned painfully until he was facing Wycliffe. 'If the bastard had lived I would have made it my business to expose him as a cheap crook; now that he was dead he should be known for what, in my view, he was – a murderer.'

Another long period of silence during which the little clock chivvied the seconds away.

'He had killed Joe as surely as if he had pulled the trigger ... The scheme was simple enough; David Clement would disappear with his boat and it would seem that he had cleared out after killing his brother. All that was necessary was to remove the weapon and dispose of the boat and the body. I saw no injustice in that – neither do I now ... ' His voice faltered and he added, 'But it was irresponsible, and in terms of its effect on Hetty it was damnable.'

Perhaps it was ironic to hear a man who had so recently affirmed his fatalism talking of motives and laying claim to guilt but that was not how it seemed to Wycliffe at the time.

The major took a gulp of whisky and once more started to cough. This time the glass slid out of his hand and rolled off his lap to the floor before anyone could catch it. The paroxysms were worse and they followed each other more quickly so that he had no time for more than an occasional wheezing inhalation before he was seized with another spasm. Then, quite suddenly, the coughing stopped, the major's body ceased to heave, and he was still.

Bunny said in a hushed voice, 'He's gone!'

Wycliffe bent over the motionless body.

Bunny said, 'I'll phone MacDonald.'

After he had telephoned the two men sat waiting. Outwardly nothing had changed. Daylight had faded imperceptibly so that the only light in the room now came from the fire. Bunny got up, switched on the light, then, like a prudent housekeeper, drew the curtains.

Bunny's voice was uncertain as he said, 'When he arrived he'd already had quite a few and he brought a full bottle with him. He just sat there and drank and there was nothing I could do . . . ' His eyes were glistening with tears. 'He told me how he got his burns and he said, "Our friend Wycliffe was nearly cheated of his prize."'

'Is that what he said?'

MacDonald arrived, a large, red-headed Scot. He looked at the major. 'What the hell has he been doing to himself now?'

Lane explained and the doctor made a brief examination. 'No surprises there. Usquebaugh – the water of life. Sadly you can have too much of it, especially with a dicky heart and after a set-to with an oil-stove.' The doctor was looking down at the major's body. 'Well, nobody can say he wasn't single-minded about killing himself one way or another.' He turned to Bunny Lane. 'If his house is burnt down it's no good taking him there so what do you suggest?'

Bunny said, 'I'd like him to stay here.' He looked doubtfully from the doctor to Wycliffe and back again. 'I don't suppose the three of us could get him into my little parlour? There's a bed there where my mother died. Towards the end she couldn't get up the stairs.'

MacDonald shrugged. 'You'll have to square it with that sister of his afterwards.'

'Give me a couple of minutes to get the bed ready.'

Bunny busied himself like an anxious housewife and ten minutes later when they carried the major into the parlour the brass bedstead had been made up with clean linen which smelt of lavender.

Bunny said, 'I'll ring Marty Jewel, the undertaker; he'll see to everything.' He gave Wycliffe a wry look. 'I'll leave him a key so that he can get in when I'm not here.'

After the doctor had gone and Bunny had spoken to the undertaker the two men sat in front of the fire in the living-room, smoking. The little clock on the mantel-piece showed half-past nine and Wycliffe checked with his watch before he could believe that only a couple of hours earlier he had been in his office.

Once or twice Lane opened his mouth to speak but thought better of it and said nothing. Then Wycliffe added casually, 'Did the major tell you what it was David Clement said which provoked him?'

Bunny shifted in his chair, 'It was what you'd expect; he referred to his brother, the major and me as "three addled old poufs".'

'I see.'

Another long interval of silence with Lane becoming increasingly uneasy at Wycliffe's passive attitude; no doubt he had expected that events having reached a crisis, the action would move swiftly to a climax. But Wycliffe sat and smoked, holding his pipe so that his hand covered the bowl.

His next question when it came seemed absurdly trivial. 'What about the Chippendale book? It was in Joseph's room.'

'I lent it to him earlier; I used it for an excuse . . . '

'I suppose it was you who drove the car and after-wards ditched it in the quarry?'

'Yes, then—'

'And you walked home?'

'Yes, I—'

'Just answer my questions; you will be asked to make a statement later.' Wycliffe's manner was curt, distant, authoritative.

The next question was a long time coming. 'You wanted it to appear that Clement had killed his brother and cleared out; wouldn't it have been more convincing if you had emptied the safe of money and valuables? You had the key.'

'I thought of that but the major wouldn't hear of it; he said we had no idea who the contents belonged to.'

A nice sense of morality, the major's.

'There were two paperweights worth about five thousand pounds in the pockets of Clement's bush-jacket.'

'They must have been there all along; we didn't put them there.'

Clement had probably slipped them into his pocket to keep them out of his brother's sight.

The little clock ticked away another couple of minutes. 'Did the major tell you that he intended to scuttle *Manna* in Porthellin Bay?'

'No, he simply said he knew a place where he could scuttle her without much risk of her being found and from where he could row ashore.'

'How did the gun come to be left on the beach?'

Bunny shook his head. 'I don't know; it happened while I was ditching the car. The major told me afterwards he'd dropped it while dragging the dinghy down the beach and couldn't find it again.'

'Did you believe him?'

'I'm not sure. The major was a strange man, never content unless the odds were against him.'

'Did he know it was his father's gun?'

'I don't know.'

At a quarter past ten by the little clock Wycliffe got up from his chair. 'I'm not taking you into custody. I want you to go to Mallet Street police station at nine o'clock in the morning and make a voluntary statement. You will be charged with being an accessory to the unlawful disposal of a body and brought before the magistrates. The police will not oppose bail. There could be other charges later . . . We shall have to see.'

Bunny stood up, incredulous. 'You mean I don't have to go with you?'

Wycliffe did not answer; he put on his mackintosh in

the little passage. Bunny opened the front door on the deserted square; it was a fine, clear night.

'Get yourself a good lawyer and tell him the truth.'

Helen was watching *Newsnight* on television and she switched off as he came in. She looked at him in a special way. 'Is the case over?'

His manner was surly. 'There was no case, only a wild-goose chase.'

Helen said, 'The paper says it was very clever of you to find the boat.'

'Too damned clever; it would have been better to have left her where she was.' He was on the point of adding, 'The major is dead, Hetty is in hospital and Bunny Lane . . . ' but there would have been too much to explain.

'I'll get you some supper. What about a bit of cold lamb with salad?'

'Anything.'

A quarter of an hour later when she came back with his tray he was sitting staring into the fire. 'Tomorrow night we are due at the Oldroyds' and we haven't made up our minds.'

Helen put the tray on a low table near his chair. 'I think we have.'

THE END

WYCLIFFE AND
THE QUIET VIRGIN

Mulfra is a tiny hamlet in Penwith, known
for its chamber tomb or 'quoit'. I have taken the
liberty of using the name for a village on the coast
road between Zennor and Morvah, a village which
only exists between the pages of this book.
W.J.B.

CHAPTER ONE

Marsden opened his eyes; the plaster between the rafters was greyish white, the rafters themselves cobalt blue, painted by Emma; spiders' webs in the corners. The light from the little window was grey and cold, the air damp; even the sheets felt clammy. He could hear Emma downstairs in the kitchen, running water, the only place in the house where there was water and that came from an overhead tank, pumped from a well.

Marsden scratched himself.

Twenty-five minutes to nine by the alarm clock on the little cast-iron mantelpiece which was also cobalt blue. Marsden raised himself on his elbow so that he could see out of the window. Fine rain out of a leaden sky.

'Bloody hell!'

The front door slammed, then the car door; the starter of Emma's M-registered Mini whined a couple of times, seemed to give up, then in its last gasp, set the little engine puttering. An uncertain cough or two, a spluttering in the exhaust, and Emma was away.

Marsden got out of bed; a large man, fleshy without being fat, powerful; built like a gorilla. A mop of black hair, and a generous moustache; good features, eyes wide apart, and a broad, high forehead. He thought he looked like Balzac and cultivated the resemblance. The locals said that he had Romany blood and that pleased him too. He was forty-six.

He stood by the window, stooping to clear the sloping roof. Down the narrow valley mist blotted out the sea. Brown smoke came from the Lemarques' chimney, the only house he could see, perched some way up the opposite hill, white against the sludge-green heather. A mail van picked a cautious way along the old mine track which led there. He pulled on a paint-stained dressing-gown, fished his slippers from under the bed with his toes, and wriggled his feet into them without stooping. He slouched across the room to the landing, the floorboards creaked under his weight and the jars and bottles on Emma's dressing table clinked together. He negotiated the narrow, twisted stairs down to the living-room.

A large, square table covered with a plastic cloth and on it, a battered blue enamelled coffee pot and a mug inscribed 'Hugh' (from the days when Emma still believed that he could be domesticated). There was a note in Emma's writing propped against the milk jug: 'I've shut that blasted cat out because he messed in the kitchen again. If it's still there when I come home this evening you'll be doing the cooking, not me.'

'Bitch!' Mechanical, without venom.

Marsden opened the front door; the cat, a complacent tabby, was asleep in the shelter of the porch. Marsden picked him up, made soothing noises, and carried him indoors. He poured milk into a saucer and put it on the floor. 'There, Percy, old boy! She's gone now.' The cat lapped up the milk, purring away like a Rolls Royce.

Marsden felt the coffee pot then went to the kitchen to warm it on the stove. While he was in the kitchen he splashed cold water over his face and groped for the towel. The flow from the tap was a mere trickle. 'The bloody tank's empty again!'

With his mug full of black coffee he came back through the living-room and into his studio, followed by the cat. The studio was a lean-to built on to the end of the house in times past, as stabling for mules. With his own hands he had removed the roof and replaced it with corrugated perspex which gave a diffused north light when it was not covered with moss and gull shit.

6

He ferreted about, looking for matches, and when he found them he lit the paraffin stove. There was an electric heater but he used that only when he had a model. A canvas stood on one of the two easels: a landscape, blocked in. Although Marsden was best known for his landscapes and marines he was a studio painter. 'None of that muffler and hot-water bottle crap for me; I find my *plein air* in the studio next to the oil-stove; "Emotion recollected in tranquility" – in comfort anyway.' He reached for a brush from the pot, changed his mind and drank his coffee instead, in two or three great gulps. Then he lit a cigarette. Marsden was coming to life, the skin round his eyes seemed less taut and his mouth had lost its sour taste. He moved to the second easel where there was another canvas, this one covered by a cloth; he removed the cloth and stood looking at the painting: Portrait of a Young Girl. She wore a flowered wrap which had slipped to expose one breast, and she regarded herself in a large mirror with an ornately carved frame; her expression intent, frowning. Red-gold hair reached to her shoulders, her cheeks were lightly flushed. Marsden had caught the fine delicacy of the girl's brows, of her lashes, of her lips but mostly he had captured her total self-absorption.

He stood back. 'Marsden, my boy, you're a painter!'

The mirror and the padded seat were still set up in one corner of the studio.

He had told Emma nothing of the sittings which had taken place while she was at work and his studio was sacrosanct, but yesterday he had shown her the painting. He could have written the script in advance:

'That's the Lemarque girl.'

'Full marks for observation.'

'She's jail-bait in any language. How did you manage it? At that age they want more than sweeties. Really, Hugh, you must be out of your mind!'

'I painted the girl, I didn't screw her.'

'Even if I believed you it wouldn't make any difference; she's quite capable of saying that you did.'

'If it came to that I'd prefer her mother; there's a dark little mystery package that needs working on! Unfortunately, now that her husband's out of clink, there's a sitting tenant.'

'You're vile!'

His palette for the painting, covered with cling-film, stood on a table by the easel. He couldn't make up his mind whether or not he had finished with it. He replaced the cloth and started to sing in a croaking baritone: 'The rich get richer and the poor get children'.

The cat, couchant by the oil-stove, tucked in his paws and prepared for sleep.

Marsden said: 'I wonder what she would do if somebody locked her in without a loo,' and chuckled at the thought. 'I tell you what, Percy, I'll make you a cat-flap. I know I've said it before but this time I really will!'

The letter-box in the front door rattled and he went back to the living-room.

A small shower of mail on the mat. Marsden gathered it up and shuffled through the envelopes with a certain urgency, then he seemed to relax: Christmas cards for Emma, a couple of circulars, an electricity bill, a letter from a West End gallery: ' . . . We regret that we cannot offer you a one-man show in the coming year but if you will consider joining with—' Marsden screwed up the letter and aimed it at the fireplace. 'No, sir! Not with that bloody ponce. We haven't got quite there yet.'

The final envelope was also for Emma. He recognized brother Tim's prissy italic script and he knew those letters by heart as Emma always left them lying about. There would be the usual news of successful-accountant brother Tim, of his pasty-faced wife, and of their two brats – with snapshots thrown in to highlight the attractions of conjugal felicity. Then the brotherly advice: variations on a theme – 'I've heard from mum and dad again. Really, Em, I can't understand why you

8

throw yourself away on that man. Apart from being an absolute scoundrel, he's nearly old enough to be your father . . .'

'I am old enough to be her bloody father,' Marsden had said. 'I started early.' He propped Emma's mail on the mantelpiece, against a vase in the form of a fish standing on its tail.

'He's right though, Marsden, you scum! Give the gentleman his sister back.'

The time had come to allow her family to entice Emma away. She was taking over and, in any case, life had grown too complicated.

He opened the front door to stand in his little porch, looking up at the sky. Fine rain still drizzled out of low cloud. *'Gloom!* Damp, grey, dreary, bloodless gloom!' Eight hours between sunrise and sunset, the twenty-third of December, two days to Christmas, the very nadir of the year.

Jane Lemarque was in her living-room; a smoky fire burned in the grate, the room was furnished with unmatched and incongruous pieces which looked what they were, random discards from a more affluent home. She stood by the window, looking out on a familiar scene; mist hid the sea and inland she could just distinguish the grey rectangular bulk of the church tower. This, and the hill opposite, scarred by old mine-workings and capped by a great cairn of boulders, set the limits of her world for days at a time.

Jane had dark hair and deep blue eyes, an oval face, rather pale; and an expression of madonna-like serenity. Only people who knew her well (and few did) realized that though she might seem passive she was anything but serene. Even now as she stood gazing out of the window her lips moved and she murmured a barely articulate form of words, half prayer, half incantation: 'Please God make it all come right . . . Oh, Lord, don't let it happen . . . Dear Lord I promise . . . Don't let Francine . . . Don't let Alain . . . '

She looked across at the painter's cottage, crouched at the foot of the hill, last of the struggling outliers of the village. Marsden, in his dressing-gown, was standing in his porch, staring up at the sky. The sight of the man increased her disquiet. Recently she had tried to avoid coming face to face with him but sometimes on her way to or from the village they would meet. He was always polite but he looked at her in such an intimate and knowing way that she felt vulnerable, naked, so that her flesh trembled and her face burned.

Now he was taking an interest in Francine, encouraging and helping her with her painting; he had given her colours and brushes which she believed were expensive to buy. 'Please don't let . . . '

Her attention was distracted from the painter by a figure in an anorak trudging along the narrow road which led from the cove, past the painter's cottage and on to the village. Paul Bateman, youngest of the Bishop clan. The Bishops, Penzance lawyers for generations, lived at Mynhager House down by the cove. Paul was seventeen and for the past six months he had pursued Francine with earnest solicitude. Either he was on his way to the village or he was coming to see her now and she was still in bed. Jane watched the boy. He had reached the painter's cottage and he would continue along the road or he would turn off down a steep footpath to the bridge over the stream. Jane watched him. 'Please God he doesn't come here . . . Please God . . . ' But God wasn't listening, the boy turned down the footpath to the bridge.

Agitated, Jane went to the bottom of the stairs and called to her daughter. She could hear the radio playing, the eternal Radio One.

'Francine!' She called twice before she was answered by a voice that sounded petulant rather than sleepy.

'What is it?'

10

'Paul is on his way here.'

Silence.

'It's nearly half-past nine, don't you think it's time you got up?' Pleading.

'Tell him I'm sick.'

'I can't tell him a deliberate lie.'

'Why not? You want to stop me seeing him.'

'I didn't say that, Francine! I said it wouldn't be a good idea to let your friendship with Paul grow into something more. That doesn't mean—'

'I wish you'd make up your mind what you do mean.' But the radio was switched off. 'All right, I'm coming down.'

Jane felt tears of misery and frustration smarting in her eyes. She returned to the window. Paul was climbing the flight of steps which led up to the front door. She opened the door before he knocked but did not invite him in. The boy stood there, long and lean, droplets of moisture dripping from his hair and running down his face.

'I wondered if Francine would come with me to St Ives this afternoon. John Falls is putting on an exhibition of those crazy models of his. He thinks he might sell one or two as Christmas presents and I said I would come.'

'I can't. I've got the play at the church this evening.' Francine had come downstairs silently; she was wearing a track suit, her hair uncombed about her shoulders.

'I know, but we shall go in the car and be back long before then.' Paul had just passed his driving test.

'I've got to finish learning my lines.'

Jane said, 'So Paul has wasted his trip over here. Why didn't you phone, Paul?'

The boy looked embarrassed. 'I didn't mind the walk.' He lingered. 'If Francine can't come this afternoon perhaps I could pick you both up this evening and take you to the church – unless Mr Lemarque is going . . .'

11

Jane felt trapped, she didn't dare refuse. 'That is kind of you, Paul. I don't think he will be going.'

'Half-past seven, then . . . Will that do? Earlier if you want.'

'Half-past seven will be all right,' Francine said.

Paul smiled uncertainly and took himself off.

Jane looked sorrowfully at her daughter. 'Really, Francine!'

'What have I done now?'

At Mynhager House, down by the cove, Virginia Bishop was perched on a tall step-ladder in a corner of the big drawing-room, pinning up the last of the Christmas decorations. Elaborate though faded paper-chains festooned from the central chandelier and there was a Christmas tree, draped with tinsel and hung with shiny balls and coloured lights. Seen from this unfamiliar angle the room seemed more shabby than ever; the colours of wallpaper, upholstery, carpet and curtains had merged to the same drab fawn; the gilt-framed oil paintings might have been hanging in a saleroom and the sprigs of holly tucked behind their frames seemed absurdly incongruous. Even the grand piano, Carrie's pride and joy, had a bluish bloom on its polished lid.

Virginia looked down at her sister, kneeling on the floor, putting away unwanted decorations for another year, putting them back into a box which had held them for a lifetime. Virginia thought: Caroline is putting on weight, and slacks do nothing for her figure. At least I've kept slim. Of course, she drinks too much. There was a time when people used to take us for twins. They couldn't now.

She came down the steps and brushed her hands together. 'That cornice is thick with dust.'

'You say that every year, Vee.'

Virginia stood by the window. 'This damned mist, you can't see a thing.'

'What do you expect in December? If it's not fog it's

wind.' Caroline got to her feet and stooped to massage her knees. 'Well, that's done for another year, thank God! Why do we bother? Christmas! I feel worn out already and it hasn't even started.'

'We've got Ernest's friend, Wycliffe, coming this afternoon.'

'I can do without reminding. I wish Ernest wouldn't invite people here to stay. Poor old Ada is getting beyond it and the extra work falls on us.'

'Mother used to cope with a houseful.'

'Mother was a marvel but don't let's start getting all sentimental or I shall howl. I need a drink.'

'Where's Paul?'

'I'm not sure but I think he's gone to see Francine.'

'He's been seeing a lot of her recently.'

'Yes, I'd rather he wasn't.'

'Why?'

'For one thing I think she's got all the makings of a little whore.'

'And?'

'Isn't that enough?'

'Yes, but I don't think it's true. I think we see the worst side of Francine. Jenny Eggerton is her form mistress and she was saying Francine's main trouble is that she keeps herself too much to herself. She holds everybody at arm's length – other girls, staff, and boys. Incidentally, Jenny was at a rehearsal for the vicar's nativity play and she was really impressed by Francine's performance as the Virgin.'

'I don't doubt she puts on a good act but she would need to in that role.'

'She's got a wonderful voice for a girl of her age.'

'I know, but that doesn't stop me wishing she would keep away from Paul. Not that what I think will make any difference; I'm only his mother.' Caroline moved towards the door. 'I'm going to fetch that drink; are you sure you won't have something?'

'All right, a small sherry, just to celebrate.'

Virginia was left alone. Thirty-five, a spinster, a teacher of biology in a comprehensive school; at nineteen it would have seemed a fate worse than death, now she thought there were compensations. The mist had thinned and through the mullioned window she could see the lichen-covered balustrade at the end of the terrace and the grey sea beyond. To her left she glimpsed the hump of Gurnard's Head only to lose it again almost at once. Mynhager House, built on the rock platform of an ancient landslip, facing four-square to the Atlantic and backing on a steep boulder-strewn slope.

'Here we are, then!' Caroline with a whisky and a dry sherry on a tray.

They sat on one of the massive settees.

Virginia said: 'Are you meeting Gerald off the train this evening?'

'No, he's driving down, thank goodness!'

'How long is he down for?'

Caroline sipped her whisky. 'I've no idea. The House reassembles on the seventh or eighth but with luck he should have gone back before then. There's a cabinet reshuffle in the wind and they're all running round in circles with their little pink tongues hanging out. It seems Sir James is almost certain to be kicked upstairs to the Lords and if that happens, Stafford will step into his shoes and Stafford has more than hinted to Gerald that he would be very much in the running as his P.P.S.'

'Gerald will end up in the cabinet himself one of these days.'

Caroline pouted. 'If he doesn't it won't be for the want of keeping in with the right people.'

'You're hard on that husband of yours.'

'You think so?'

'You won't even live in his constituency.'

'I told him when we were married, "This is my home".'

'He wasn't an MP then.'

'That's his affair.' Caroline rolled the whisky tumbler

14

between her plump hands. 'Incidentally, I shall be out this afternoon.'

'Isn't your car in dock? Of course you can borrow mine if you want it.'

'Thanks all the same, but I can walk where I'm going.' Caroline said this with a certain smugness.

Virginia looked at her sister, perplexed at first, then accusing: 'You're going to see Marsden!'

'How did you guess?'

Virginia was shocked; she got up and crossed to the window. 'Really, Carrie! You told me that was all over . . . It's like going to a brothel.'

'Why not? Women's lib and all that. But perhaps you'd prefer it if he came here?' Caroline yawned. 'There's no point in turning pi on me, Vee. For Christ's sake try living in the real world for once!'

'With your son here and your husband coming home tonight . . . I just don't know what to say!'

'Then don't say anything, dear. I need a man now and then, a real man, it's as simple as that. Sleeping with Gerald is like bedding down with a wet fish – and that's all I've got to look forward to for the next week at least. I don't know how you manage and I don't ask; perhaps we're different.'

'My God, I hope so! It's obscene!'

Caroline sounded bored. 'Don't be so damned self-righteous, Vee!'

Two o'clock. Joseph Bishop's glasses had slipped to the end of his nose and his eyes were closed; a long, thin hand rested on the open book in his lap. At seventy-four Joseph remained physically active and mentally alert but in the hour after lunch he was often overtaken by drowsiness which he resented and did his best to combat. He usually took his exercise in the mornings, walking on the cliffs or over the moor, and in the afternoons he read, though now his reading was increasingly restricted to books he had read before.

15

When he drowsed he seemed to be half remembering, half dreaming of the days when his father was alive and Mynhager House was still part of the cultural gilt on the Cornish gingerbread.

There were photographs on the walls: D.H. Lawrence with Frieda, Middleton Murry with Katherine Mansfield, Maynard Keynes, Lytton Strachey, Duncan Grant, the Woolfs – all taken on the balcony outside the very room where he now sat. Virginia Woolf's genuine original lighthouse, setting aside all Hebridean substitutes, was just a few miles up the coast. And cheek-by-jowl with the photographs were paintings given to his father or to him by notables of the St Ives and Newlyn schools. There was a single portrait, the head and shoulders of a young woman with auburn hair coiled on the top of her head like a coronet. The frame carried a little plaque: Ursula 1929.

A knock at the door. Joseph roused himself, adjusted his glasses and closed the book on his finger. 'Come in!'

His son, Ernest.

The old man said, 'You're home early!'

'Charlie Wycliffe is arriving this afternoon and I thought I'd better be here to welcome him.'

At forty-five Ernest had only to look at his father to see what he would himself become in another thirty years – if he lived that long. The Bishop line must have accumulated a hoard of dominant genes; their men were tall, thin, and long-boned, with a tendency to early baldness. And so far, through several generations, they had shown a marked aptitude for survival in a changing world.

'Do you mind if I help myself to a sherry?' Ernest went to a little cupboard and lifted out a tray with a bottle of Tio Pepe and glasses. 'Will you join me, father?'

'I've just had my lunch. Have you got something on your mind?'

Ernest poured himself a glass of sherry. 'I had a visitor in the office this morning. Who do you think?'

16

His father made an irritable movement. 'I've never been any good at guessing games, Ernest. Get on with it!'

'Lemarque.'

He had the satisfaction of seeing the old man surprised. 'Lemarque? What did he want?'

'He came about the cottage.'

'They're moving out.'

'On the contrary. He gave me a cheque to cover the rent for the two years during which, as he put it, "I was detained elsewhere". Of course I said there was no need but he insisted.'

'And?'

'He said he wanted to continue the tenancy for at least a year and he suggested an agreement. He said he would understand if we wanted to raise the rent and that he would pay what was reasonable.'

Joseph stroked his silky moustache. 'Extraordinary! What's behind it? Why didn't he come here?'

'I suppose he wasn't too sure of his welcome and he wanted to keep it business-like.'

'I haven't seen him since he came out, how does he look?'

'I don't think he's suffered unduly from the slings and arrows but he's drinking; he's got that look. Apart from anything else it was just before one when he came to see me and he was smelling of whisky then.'

The old man shook his head. 'I don't understand what he's up to. What did you say to him?'

'That they are more than welcome to stay on in the cottage for as long as it suits them but that we would prefer not to enter into any formal agreement.'

'All you could say. This scheme he's supposed to be involved with, do you know anything about it?'

'Only that it's in some way connected with Rosemergy Minerals.'

'That's Tim Trewhella; you should talk to Tim.'

'I have, and I'm no wiser.'

Joseph sighed. 'Curiouser and curiouser! Have you mentioned this to Caroline?'

'Not yet.'

'Then don't. Have a quiet word with Gerald when he comes; we don't want any upset over Christmas.'

Ernest drained his glass. 'I'm wondering if this is in some way to do with Gerald.'

'Why should it be?'

'At the time, Lemarque said he had enough evidence to take Gerald to jail with him.'

A dry laugh. 'Just talk! You've always had a tendency to believe what people say, Ernest. Fatal in our profession. But even if Lemarque was speaking the truth he's missed the boat. He's left it too late.'

'Too late to put Gerry in jail, perhaps, but not too late to throw a spanner in his political works, or at least to threaten to.'

'Blackmail?' The old man dismissed the idea. 'You're dramatizing the situation! All the same I'd be interested to know what Rosemergy Minerals can do for Lemarque and even more in what they think he can do for them.'

Ernest said: 'I don't like the idea of him settling here. Whatever we say in the interests of the family, you and I know that Lemarque is a very clever rogue though not quite clever enough. Gerald was mixed up in his shady business and he was lucky to get out of it without a major scandal. All I'm saying is that I hope we're not going to get the scandal now.'

Joseph brushed the notion aside. 'You worry too much, Ernest! Relax!'

Ernest stood up, still holding his empty glass. 'I'll take this down. Don't forget we've got Wycliffe with us for dinner this evening.'

'I'm not yet totally senile, Ernest. As a matter of fact, I'm looking forward to meeting the man. What's he like? Will he get on with Carrie and Vee?'

'If he doesn't, it won't be his fault.'

18

A broad grin. 'You'll have to keep Gerald out of his hair.'

'I think Charles can take care of himself.'

Joseph, now thoroughly roused from his lethargy, said: 'Good! I feel I'm going to have a nice Christmas. Tell Ada I intend to be hungry tonight.'

CHAPTER TWO

'Turn left here unless you're going through St Ives.'
Wycliffe muttered the words. It was what Helen would
have said had she been with him. But Helen was far
away in Kenya, staying with their newly married son
who had a job there. In a year or two they would be
grandparents. Salutary thought! As a couple they were
post-reproductive, being gently but surely edged aside
by the mainstream of existence. Perhaps the slippered
pantaloon bit was still some way off but one saw it
coming. He found wry consolation in the thought that
he must be in Shakespeare's fifth stage: 'the justice, In
fair round belly with good capon lined . . . full of wise
saws and modern instances.' Not so wide of the mark for
he was on his way to spend Christmas with Ernest
Bishop, a lawyer with a practice in Penzance.

Wycliffe did not even know him very well; they had
met in the courts and on various committees. During
a three-day conference Bishop had stayed with the
Wycliffes, now he was repaying the hospitality debt.
Quiet, reserved, with a wicked wit, his comments on the
law and its practitioners were trenchant and amusing.
He had a curious hobby which was characteristic of him:
he collected and studied flies.

But Wycliffe was not at all keen on the prospect.
Ernest was a bachelor and the house was run by his two
sisters, one of whom was married to Gerald Bateman,
M.P., so that the position of Ernest's guest might be
uncomfortably peripheral.

Three o'clock and raining out of a sombre sky; hardly
any traffic, but when another car did pass, the bow

20

waves sprayed both vehicles. Dipped headlights and the screen-wipers rocking. He climbed the slope outflanking Trencrom Hill and came out at last on the coast road. Another three or four miles.

The sea on his right, the granite moorland on his left, a bleak landscape where the men of Bronze built strange megaliths for their dead and the men of Iron had seemed content to live in their thatched huts and cultivate their little fields. The dimly shining strip of road rose and fell like a miniature switchback, complicated by meanders orginally plotted by medieval cattle. An early nineteenth-century traveller got it about right: 'the moorstone or granite lies dispersed in detached blocks, many of them huge enough for another Stonehenge. Scarcely a shrub appears to diversify the prospect; and the only living beings that inhabit the mountainous parts are goats . . .' Wycliffe saw no goats.

Suddenly he was there; houses on both sides of the road – the village of Mulfra, a mining village when there were mines. The houses, mostly small, were strung out along the coast road and clustered round the church; black soil, granite walls, and slate roofs covered with grey lichen. The church tower, four-square, no nonsense, and forty feet high, to remind hardened hearts of the all-seeing eye. Some of the villagers had tried to ameliorate this stark severity with gaily painted front doors and bits of scrolled ironwork but they would have had more success with paper chains in a morgue.

Ernest's letter had said that he must turn down by the pub. He spotted a narrow gap between pub and cottage and a blue and white wall sign which read: 'To Mulfra Headland and Cove.' The pub was The Tributers and Wycliffe prided himself (a foreigner) on knowing that tributers were 'free' miners working under contract for the adventurers. Cornishmen avoided being wage slaves whenever they could.

A few more cottages and the road degenerated to a dirt track between low granite walls. Another cottage, standing alone, and the track became even rougher with a rising boulder-strewn slope on one side and a shallow reedy valley on the other. A sudden twist in the track and he had arrived. Mynhager House was perched on a ledge above the sea, stark against a darkening sky, but there were lights in several of the windows.

He pulled into a paved courtyard, muttering to himself: 'I'm not looking forward to this.'

A door from the house opened and Ernest Bishop in a shabby waterproof and a cap came across to him. 'Charles! So very pleasant to see you again! No use apologizing for the weather, it's what we expect here at this time of the year.'

Ernest insisted on carrying his suitcase and led him through a short passage into the front hall. He dropped the suitcase and pulled a grubby white handkerchief from the pocket of his raincoat to wipe his glasses. With the handkerchief came a little shower of glass specimen tubes. Ernest picked them up, smiling. 'For my flies. I'm never without them.'

Wycliffe was introduced to a dark haired woman in her late thirties. 'My sister, Mrs Bateman.' Ernest smiled. 'Caroline to you, I think.'

Caroline was running to fat and she had that pouting, slightly sullen expression of the spoiled self-indulgent woman. Her greeting was polite but without warmth. 'I expect you would like to go to your room and freshen up . . . I hope you will be comfortable.'

He was given a front bedroom overlooking the sea and the cove. A huge Victorian wardrobe, a dressing table, a chest of drawers, a monumental brass bedstead and a couple of armchairs, still left plenty of room on the well-worn Wilton.

Caroline said, 'There's only a shared bathroom, through that door.' She laughed. 'As long as you secure yourself from the other side you'll be all right. If there's anything you want don't hesitate to say.'

At the door she turned back. 'Oh, do come down to

the dining-room when you're ready. Make yourself at home. This evening we shall have our meal early because some of the family go to the Song Play at the church, a thing the vicar does every Christmas. I know it sounds awful but they do it quite well and you might even enjoy it.'

So far so good!

He put his hand on a massive old-fashioned radiator which looked as though it had been built for the Albert Hall. It was hot. There was a washbasin and two rough turkish towels on a heated towel rail. Things could have been a lot worse. He walked over to the window; almost dark. He could see a paved terrace below the window, then a steep slope of forty or fifty feet to the sea. It was calm and the gentle surge of the dark water could be detected only in the changing pattern of reflections from its surface. To his left he could just make out the cove which seemed to be choked with leg-trapping boulders.

Half-an-hour later he went downstairs, hair combed, hands clean, and washed behind the ears. Ernest was hovering in the hall, a nervous host.

'There you are, Charles! Come into the drawing-room, you must be longing for a cup of tea.'

In the large, time-worn drawing-room Caroline was standing by the fire talking to her husband who was seated in one of the armchairs and Wycliffe had the impression that their conversation had not been amicable. Gerald Bateman M.P., known to everyone for his TV appearances, always ready with concise, dogmatic pronouncements on any issue from genetic engineering to the decline of flax growing on St Helena: 'My dear Robin (or Brian, or John), I fully appreciate the complexity of the problem but . . .' His real hobby horse was Law and Order: the Supremacy of the Law, Individual Responsibility, Justice, and Punishment.

In the corridors of power they called him The Sheriff, but behind the political façade there was a thin-lipped intelligence which had enabled him to keep head and shoulders well above water through the recession.

Ernest said: 'You've already met Caroline; this is her husband. No introduction necessary, I'm sure.'

Bateman sprang to his feet with instant charm: 'My dear Mr Wycliffe! This is a real pleasure. I'm quite sure we shall have some interesting talks while you are here; interesting and instructive for me at any rate.'

Ernest said: 'Gerald is anxious to brief himself for a debate on the crime statistics when the House re-assembles. Remember, Charles, you do not have to say anything but whatever you do say may be taken down and used in his speech.'

Bateman smiled. 'Ernest must have his little joke; it is a family idiosyncrasy.'

Bateman was forty-six, tall, with a youthful figure, and good looking in the clean-limbed, manly virtues fashion: dark hair well cut, carefully trimmed guards' moustache, and perfectly shaved.

Ernest turned to his sister: 'See if you can hurry up Virginia with the tea, dear.'

A tall, elderly woman made an entrance. No question that she was a Bishop: big boned, spare, with angular features and deep-set eyes. She wore a mauve satin frock, badly creased, an orange silk scarf loosely knotted, and her grey hair had a wispy wildness. The White Queen straight out of Alice.

Ernest hastened to introduce her. 'Mrs Burnett-Price, my Aunt Stella: Chief Superintendent Wycliffe.'

The old lady acknowledged the introduction with gravity then went on: 'I'm so glad you are here though it surprises me that they should send a chief superintendent to deal with a few instances of pilfering. However, as my husband used to say: "The army has its own way of doing things" and I suppose it is the same with the police.' She laughed, still a musical sound; she must have been a charmer in her day.

An imploring look from Ernest. Wycliffe merely

24

nodded and looked amiable. Ernest conducted his aunt to a straight backed chair near the fire.

Tea arrived on a trolley, with Virginia, a younger, slimmer version of her sister.

'Two more members of the family still to meet,' Ernest said. 'Father, who doesn't put in an appearance until we sit down to our evening meal, and my nephew Paul, of whom the same can usually be said.'

Tea and little rock cakes which had spent too long in the oven. Ernest said: 'I don't know if Caroline mentioned the vicar's play which is on this evening ... I usually go, so do Virginia and Paul. I wondered if you might be interested?'

Wycliffe protested that he was looking forward to it.

In what promised to be a stilted conversation with Caroline he happened to mention the piano, by far the most elegant piece of furniture in the room, and she warmed to him at once.

'It's a Steinway, and it's mine; father indulged me terribly when I showed some talent for music. It wasn't literature, which would have pleased him more, but it was something to have a daughter who would make a name for herself in music. Of course, I never did. All the same, it's my one claim to any sort of culture.' She laughed. 'Pictures, sculpture, literature, and even gourmet eating, leave me cold, but music ... Music to me is like sex; with the advantage that it lasts longer and they tell me you can still enjoy it in old age.'

Wycliffe realized that he had been received into that circle of acquaintances with whom Caroline found it amusing to flirt.

Bateman, left out, stood alone looking patient, like a well-mannered Doberman waiting to be noticed and patted. Obviously the distinguished politician cut little ice at Mynhager.

When Caroline was called to the kitchen she was replaced by Virginia; the Bishops were not neglecting their guest. He was briefed on the family and the house.

25

'The house was built by my great-great-grandfather. The Bishops have always been slightly crazy. They made money out of tin and banking, and building Mynhager was their bizarre way of proving that they had it. Then my grandfather imported culture; he was a Cambridge Apostle and this place became a sort of Cornish outpost for the Bloomsbury Set.'

Virginia talked with animation and from time to time she glanced up at him with a disarming grin as though apologizing for her chatter. 'I even owe my name to Virginia Woolf of blessed memory who delighted grandfather by sending him pre-publication copies of her novels.'

Unexpectedly Aunt Stella weighed in from her chair by the fire: 'My husband used to call them "a pack of left-wing intellectuals, ready to bite the hands that fed them." He couldn't bear to stay in the house when any of them were here. And that included poor Arnold Forster who was such a nice man and, although he was a socialist, really quite civilized. He wrote a book about gardening in this part of the world and he lived at Eagle's Nest, just up the coast from here.'

Virginia said, as though in total explanation: 'Uncle George was in the army.'

'Your uncle was a major general, my dear,' Aunt Stella amended.

They had their meal at six and Wycliffe met Joseph, head of the family, and young Paul, for the first time. The old man was an earlier edition of Ernest: tall, spare, amiable, and with a caustic wit. By the same token the seventeen-year-old Paul was every inch another Bishop. Wycliffe wondered how Bateman came to terms with the fact that his paternal contribution had been so effectively swamped.

During the meal Joseph, in a relaxed mood, told stories of village feuds in the Cornwall of sixty years ago and wound up: 'I tell you, Wycliffe, they were a sombre lot around here and they still are. Wesley spread a veneer of religion over 'em but he didn't change the nature of the beast.'

Afterwards, Ernest said, 'Virginia and Paul are going to pick up Jane Lemarque and her daughter, Francine. The Lemarques live in a little house on the other side of the valley, and Francine is playing the Virgin in tonight's play.'

So Wycliffe went with Ernest in his ancient, 3-litre Rover which the family called 'The Hearse'. Ernest drove through the darkness and the mist with the caution appropriate to an acrobat balancing a pretty girl in a wheelbarrow on the high wire.

'I must apologize, Charles, for not warning you about Aunt Stella. Since George died she's been a bit queer in the head. She hides things, forgets where she's put them, then imagines they've been stolen. But it isn't all genuine. She's not above putting on an act for the fun of it, as she did this evening.' Ernest laughed: 'You may have gathered that some of the family have a peculiar sense of humour.'

They reached the church well before eight when the play was due to begin; the bells were ringing a peal. The leafless sycamores in the churchyard made weird shapes and shadows and there was a misty halo around the lamp over the church porch. People were arriving in a thin but steady stream. Virginia and Paul were already in their seats with another woman, an attractive brunette. As they filed into the same pew, Ernest murmured introductions: 'Mrs Jane Lemarque, Mr Wycliffe ... Francine, Jane's daughter, is the star this evening.'

The dark woman smiled, the closed smile of a nun.

Wycliffe found himself between Ernest and his sister. A large man with a mass of curly black hair came in and sat a couple of seats in front of them.

Ernest said: 'That chap who's just come in – the big fellow who looks like a gipsy, that's Marsden, our local

27

painter – I wonder why he's here; I wouldn't have said this was his sort of thing, would you, Vee?'

'I've no idea!'

Wycliffe thought she had snubbed her brother and wondered why.

The bells stopped ringing, the hushed conversations died away, the organ played a melancholy little tune of single notes, like a pipe; the lights dimmed and went out. For a long moment the church was in total darkness then a light in the form of a star came on over the chancel. A large suspended backdrop hid the altar and was illuminated from behind by slowly changing coloured lights: green to blue, to mauve to violet . . . There was no one to be seen, but a girl's voice sang, sweet and true and unaccompanied:

'I cannot rest beloved, fear steals away my sleep;
    Why should a humble maiden have such a trust
        to keep?
    Did I but dream of the Angel, did I but think
        him there?
    How can I hope that my body the infant Christ
        will bear?'

A baritone voice answered:

'Be not afraid, sweet Mary; queen among women,
        blest;
    God and His Holy Angels shall set your fears at
        rest.
    High in the heaven above us the natal star doth
        shine,
    Token that God in His mercy will grant the gift
        divine.'

Came the inevitable duet. A trite little song, simply and honestly sung, but in the old parish church with no

28

performers in view, and no set, only the empty chancel and the discreetly changing hues of the backdrop, the audience was caught and held.

Darkness once more, then the star.

Mary, seen now, in a simple blue dress with her baby on her lap. She had red-gold hair, like the Renaissance madonnas, coiled loosely on the top of her head. As she bent over the child it caught the light and there was the suggestion of a halo. She sang a plaintive cradle song and an invisible choir brought the glad news to the shepherds. 'Glory to God in the highest and on earth peace, good will toward men.'

The shepherds, first seen as shadows on the backdrop growing in size, came into view singing lustily like Disney's dwarfs. The clowns of the piece, three folklore rustics, they became silent and subdued in the presence of the girl with her baby. Shyly, they handed her their tributes – three posies of wild flowers, and gravely she took them, one at a time, and said: 'White flowers for Innocence . . . red for Majesty . . . ' And after a long pause, and in a low voice, 'and purple for Death.'

In that moment Wycliffe felt that he had glimpsed the forgotten magic of Christmas.

Solemn organ music heralded the approach of the kings as their shadows grew larger. They introduced themselves with courtly manners and in elegant language spoke of the star they had seen in the east. They foretold the greatness of the child and presented their gifts.

Mary received them, saying: 'From Melchior, Gold for Royalty . . . From Caspar, Frankincense for Divinity . . . ' And in a low voice which seemed to falter: 'From Balthazar, Myrrh for Death.'

She thanked them and the kings departed. Joseph had his dream in which he was warned by an angel of Herod's intent and the play ended with the Holy Family setting out on the flight into Egypt. Mary sang her final song which was a prayer for their safety.

Wycliffe was moved and deeply impressed, in particular by the girl. She had seemed quite unaware of her audience. With scarcely any movement and with an expression of grave wonder, she had allowed the action to take place about her but leaving no one in any doubt that she was the still centre and focus of it all.

It had lasted an hour and when the vicar gave his benediction the audience sat on for a while as though reluctant to come back into the real world. Wycliffe turned to congratulate Jane on her daughter's performance but she had already left the pew.

Paul said: 'Mrs Lemarque has gone to the vestry to help Francine. If you will excuse me . . .'

Ernest laughed. 'Poor lad! After tonight he'll be in deeper than ever. Anyway, there are refreshments in the church room; if we go along we shall be able to meet the vicar and his cast. What about it?'

'I'd like to meet that girl,' Wycliffe said.

Ernest was pleased. 'Better than all the tinsel and shiny balls, don't you think? A little magic now and then for thy soul's sake.' He sighed. 'Francine is a very talented girl, but difficult.'

Outside the rain had stopped, it was very dark and still and the air was fresh with the tang of salt.

The church hall was a converted barn, clean but spartan; dedicated women stood behind trestle tables selling tea, coffee, and sausage rolls in aid of the church restoration fund. Within a remarkably short space of time seventy or eightly people were clustered in groups, each with a cup and saucer in one hand and a sausage roll in the other. The vicar, at the centre of the largest group, towered head and shoulders above them, lean, blond and saintly.

'He's not liked by everyone,' Virginia said. 'For one thing he's a bachelor and that doesn't suit, then he's too "high" for some: confession, incense, and all that sort of thing, but he's a clever man, and a kind one.'

'Ah, Miss Bishop!' The vicar ploughed through to speak to Virginia. 'Mrs Lemarque asked me to pass on her apology. Francine is being difficult again. It seems that as soon as our play ended she changed back into her ordinary clothes and walked out.'

'Walked out? But where has she gone?'

'Home, presumably. Her mother is very upset and insisted on going home herself. I begged her to wait, then Paul wanted to drive her home but she wouldn't hear of it.' The vicar smiled. 'I think there will be some straight talking in the Lemarque household tonight. A pity!'

'But what was the matter with Francine?'

The vicar raised his hands. 'What is ever the matter with Francine? I suppose we must allow for temperament but really I think she should have stayed. Everyone wants to congratulate her, we have two reporters here, and I know that the Women's Guild have a very nice present for her.'

Somebody said: 'Was she holding a real baby? Once I thought I heard it whimper.'

The vicar smiled. 'No, not a real baby; that was Francine's black doll. It seems to be her mascot.'

'A black doll?'

'Why not? Apart from any other consideration they tell us that our Lord probably had a dusky skin.'

Wycliffe was introduced to the vicar and he met the rest of the cast, all a little flustered by success: Joseph, a local farmer's son; the shepherds, members of an amateur pop group; the three kings, the choir . . .

As the church clock was striking ten Wycliffe and Ernest were walking back to the car and in The Tributers they were singing "Good King Wenceslas" with variations.

The drawing-room at Mynhager looked as festive as it was ever likely to. A good fire burned in the large open

31

grate which Ernest called 'The Miners' Friend', though tonight it was burning logs.

Joseph had stayed up later than usual in deference to their guest and everyone was drinking. Joseph nursed a glass of port which he frequently replenished. Wycliffe, Gerald Bateman and Caroline drank whisky; Virginia, Paul and the elusive Ada drank white wine. Ernest had lime juice. It was the first time Wycliffe had seen Ada: a plump, energetic little woman of sixty-five with remarkably clear skin, and grey hair gathered into a bun on the top of her head.

Between sips of gin and tonic, Aunt Stella knitted. A long, scarf-like strip depended from her needles, overflowed her lap and reached for the floor. Wycliffe was reminded of Madame Defarge at the foot of the guillotine.

Caroline, watched by her husband, sprawled in one of the armchairs, showing a great deal of thigh; she had put away several whiskies and Wycliffe judged that she was drunk enough to cause a scene if Bateman attempted to interfere.

They talked about the 'festive season' and the inability of the English to celebrate; the Anglo Saxon's failure to overcome his inhibitions and let his hair down.

'Except in outbursts of drunken violence' – Virginia.

'Imagine Mardi Gras in Malvern' – Ernest.

Aunt Stella began: 'When George and I were in Madras . . .' But the memory, whatever it was, faded, and she lapsed into silence.

Paul said: 'At least we have Notting Hill.'

His father was derisive. 'The West Indians are responsible for that, it's their show. As far as Europeans are concerned it's only in those countries with a Catholic tradition that you get the true spirit of carnival.'

'Nonsense!' Joseph obviously welcomed a chance to challenge his son-in-law. 'Catholic, Protestant, Jew or atheist, it makes no difference: celebration and self-denial or deprivation are two sides of the same coin. Ash Wednesday follows Shrove Tuesday; Easter Day follows Good Friday; there's no satisfaction – no joy, in the one without the other. Of course we can deceive ourselves. As a nation we've become pathologically self-indulgent but we pay the price in a joyless existence of boredom and frustration.'

The old man's eyes sparkled from the port he had drunk. 'Look at us now, preparing to celebrate the birth of our Lord; each one of us with a quiet determination to take aboard enough alcohol to enable us to endure the boredom until bedtime!' He turned to Wycliffe, 'Isn't that so?'

Wycliffe smiled. 'I'm certainly not bored.'

The old man laughed. 'No, I can believe that. For an observer of human nature a family like ours is better than a whole load of case-books.'

In an uncomfortable silence Paul said: 'I think I'll go to bed. Good night everybody.'

A chorus of good nights. A welcome signal for the party to break up.

Wycliffe climbed into the great bed and snuggled down under the blankets. A strange family! But aren't all families a bit odd seen from the inside?

He thought of Helen, living it up somewhere in the Kenyan highlands and wondered what the weather was like. Anyway she would be in bed; it would be three o'clock in the morning. Silently he wished her good night.

He lay there listening to the tide surging and chuckling between the boulders in the cove, then sucking back. As he listened the sounds seemed to get louder. He tried to imagine what it would be like in a Force 10 nor' westerly when those boulders must grind together like the mills of God.

'White flowers for Innocence . . .' The words came back to him and with them a vivid mind-picture of the

33

girl. There was something about her ... How old was she? Seventeen? Eighteen, perhaps? – not more ... Lemarque; they must be of French extraction ... No mention of a father ... He hoped there would be a chance to meet her ...

' ... and purple for Death.' How absurd! He could not get the girl or the play out of his mind.

He fell asleep still thinking of Francine.

CHAPTER THREE

Christmas Eve Morning. Wycliffe went out on to the
terrace and stood, arms resting on the balustrade.
Further along a herring-gull perched on one leg,
motionless. The weather was sunny and still. He was
missing his after-breakfast pipe; a fortnight of absti-
nence had convinced him that this was the time of day
when resistance was at its lowest ebb. Virginia came out
of the house and the gull launched itself into the air with
an angry squawk.

'Good morning! Lovely day!'

She wore a fluffy woollen jumper and a matching
skirt. Wycliffe thought she looked young, fresh, and
wholesome; sorting through his stock of adjectives he
might have conceded pretty. She joined him, arms
resting on the balustrade.

'Wonderfully mild for the time of year, isn't it?'

She was dark, with freckles which stopped short of
her eyes and reminded him that this was the first time
he had seen her without her glasses. They stood,
looking down into the water, so clear they could see the
yellow sandy bottom with a school of small fish darting
and wheeling above it like a flock of starlings in the air.

'Is the sand uncovered at low tide?'

'No, thank goodness! If it was we should be overrun
with trippers in the season.'

A fishing boat rounded Gurnard's Head and cruised
parallel with the shore.

'Half-decked St Ives gig,' Virginia said, showing off.
'That'll be the *Jennifer*, Bert Gundry's boat; he takes us
out now and then.'

A figure at the tiller raised a hand in salute and she waved back.

'Fishing, another dying industry in these parts.' She pointed across to the ruins of a mine stack and engine house jutting up like a broken tooth from one of the smaller promontories. 'Tin, copper and fish, the three-legged Cornish stool. The first two have dropped off and the third is suffering from Common Market disease; so we sit back and watch our county being destroyed by tourism.'

Wycliffe chuckled. 'A sombre diagnosis.'

'A plain statement of fact.'

'Isn't that Ernest over there?' Wycliffe pointed across the inlet to a rocky beach strewn with kelp washed up by the tide. A crouching man in a khaki waterproof seemed totally absorbed in turning over the weed.

'He's looking for flies.'

'At this time of year?'

Virginia laughed. 'I don't know much about the group but I think quite a few species are about in winter, especially in a mild spell like this. In any case there are larvae which live between the tide lines.'

Wycliffe said: 'Interesting, don't you think? The things people choose to do as opposed to the things they have to do to get a living.'

'Yes. But the lucky ones make a livelihood out of their interest. Ernest became a lawyer because it was expected of him, but he's a good naturalist and might have made a good biologist. Did you choose to be a policeman?'

'I'm afraid I did.'

'Why? Not because you enjoy ordering people about; you obviously don't.'

Even his wife had never asked him such a direct question and he was embarrassed, but he had raised the subject. 'When I was young I didn't quite know why, but as I've got older I've realized that I have a horror of disorder; the prospect of anarchy appals me and I suppose I feel I'm helping to stave it off.'

She looked at him in surprise. 'You see anarchy as an immediate threat?'

'Sometimes I feel that we live in a house of cards and the thought gives me nightmares.'

At that moment Paul came out of the house and, with a brief apology to Wycliffe, approached his aunt. He looked worried.

'I tried to ring Francine, but she isn't there and her mother says it seems she didn't come home last night.'

Virginia was incisive. 'Seems? Doesn't she know?'

'Apparently Mr Lemarque was in bed when Mrs Lemarque got home from the church and she thought Francine must have gone to bed too. It wasn't until half-an-hour ago, when they called Francine and she didn't answer, that they realized she wasn't in her room. Her bed hadn't been slept in.'

'Haven't they any idea where she might be?'

'Mrs Lemarque thinks she's gone to stay with a school friend; she says she's done it before.'

'Without a word to her parents?'

'I think so, yes.'

'Are they making enquiries among her friends?'

Helplessness and frustration got the better of the boy. 'I don't know what they're doing. Nothing, I expect!'

Virginia took pity on her nephew. 'Would you like me to look in and try to be helpful?'

'Would you, Vee?' Aunt and nephew were clearly on good terms.

'Tell your mother that Mr Wycliffe and I are going for a walk but I shall be back in plenty of time to help with the lunch.'

'I don't suppose I can do anything?'

She grinned up at him. 'No, you just stay here and worry.'

She watched the boy return to the house. 'Poor lad! He's in a bad way.'

Wycliffe said: 'You can't want me with you.'

'Why not? I'd like you to meet the Lemarques. I'll get a coat and you could probably do with one.'

As they walked along the track away from Mynhager she pointed out the Lemarques' cottage on the other side of the valley.

'It belongs to us and originally we let it to Alain only as a weekend place. At that time he and Gerald were partners in a London company with a chain of antique shops and picture galleries, doing very well; then things went badly wrong. Alain was a good businessman but it seems he didn't know when he was beaten. Gerald got out, but Lemarque dug himself in deeper and deeper until he finished up in jail for fraud. He came out a few weeks ago.'

'Are they French?'

'Alain's father came over with de Gaulle and stayed. Jane is English and Francine was born in Richmond where they lived when they had money. They lost everything and now the cottage is the only home they have.'

'Hard on the wife and child.'

'It is, very.'

'How old is Francine?'

'Just sixteen; she had a birthday last month.'

'Sixteen! Surely her parents should be taking this more seriously?'

'Yes, you would think so but Jane may be right. Francine is a talented girl but difficult. Like a lot of young people these days she's got a keen sense of justice and if she thought she had a real grievance I wouldn't put it past her to walk out like this.' She laughed. 'Young Paul will have his problems if their friendship ever comes to anything but I don't think it will. Francine gives him very little encouragement.'

Wycliffe was intrigued by Virginia's uninhibited but amiable gossip. There is an appealing innocence about the virgin schoolgirl turned virgin teacher.

38

They were approaching another cottage, standing alone, just a yard or two back from the dirt road. Music came from inside: old-style jazz played very loud.

'That's Marsden's place, the painter; you saw him in church last night.'

'Does he live alone?'

'With a succession of different women; the present one's been there several months, longer than most; usually they come and go in a matter of weeks. He's our scapegoat for scandal; very convenient, I suppose, but we could well do without him. There's been talk recently of Francine going to the cottage when the woman is away at work.' Virginia made a little gesture of distaste. 'I doubt if there's any more substance in that than there is in most of the gossip round here. You know what villages are. All the same it's very unpleasant.'

The sunshine heightened colours in the landscape, the drab green of heather and gorse, the red-brown splashes of dead bracken, and the grey-white boulders. But out to sea black clouds were creeping up the sky.

'Of course, a lot of Francine's trouble is that she reacts against her mother.'

'Why against her mother?'

Virginia considered. 'Jane is a difficult woman to live with; she seems to carry about her an aura of sadness, as though she were in perpetual mourning for somebody or something.'

'Is this because of her husband going to jail?'

'No. She's been like that for years. Odd, really, she used to be such a cheerful girl when we first knew her. She's never been the same since Francine was born.'

They turned off down the steep slope which led to the footbridge and because it was narrow they had to walk in single file.

On the other side she went on: 'It's hard to explain. Jane is the most passive of women, if passive is the right word, but if I had to live with her I'd probably end up by

39

doing something dramatic and stupid like Francine, just to provoke a response.'

So Francine was barely sixteen, he had thought her older.

The Lemarques' cottage, weathered and grey, seemed to have grown out of the hillside, a larger version of the granite boulders which littered the slope. Parked at the bottom of the steps which led up to the front door was a small grey van, several years old, with patches of red paint on the grey to cope with rust.

'Poor Alain used to drive a Jaguar,' Virginia said. 'A new one every couple of years.'

Jane Lemarque must have seen them from the window for as they reached the other side of the footbridge the front door opened and she was standing at the top of the steps. Dark hair and blue eyes, a pale oval face with high cheek bones. Beauty without artifice, perhaps without awareness.

'Compliments of the season, Jane!' Virginia could hardly wish her a merry Christmas. 'Paul told us about Francine and as we were out for a walk I thought we might look in and see if we could be of any help.'

'You're a stranger, Vee! Do come in.'

The words were welcoming but the voice was flat and indifferent; the beautiful face was not exactly vacant but unresponsive.

They were shown into the living-room, characterless and uncared for. A coal fire burned half-heartedly in the grate. No Christmas decorations, no tree; the only sign of Christmas, a number of cards arranged on the mantelpiece. In the adjoining kitchen something simmering on the stove gave off little jets of steam and an unappetizing smell.

'I'll call Alain.' She called him, standing at the bottom of the stairs. 'Virginia is here, Alain. With a friend.'

Alain came down the stairs; a small man, very dark, swarthy. At first sight Wycliffe thought that he must have seen the man before, then he realized that he was recognizing a type, a genus. Lemarque had the sad, deeply furrowed yet mobile face of a clown. His manner was uneasy, a man not at home in his own house.

'Hullo, Vee!' Sheepish.

Wycliffe was introduced. At close quarters he noticed a slight reddening around the mouth and nose. A whisky flush? If so it had been acquired in a few weeks.

'You haven't come about my daughter?' Suspicious.

It struck Wycliffe as odd that this strange little man could claim Francine as his daughter. He said: 'No, I happened to be staying at Mynhager and we were out for a walk.'

Virginia, insensitive to the pitfalls of social contact between an ex-con and an officer of the C.I.D., ploughed in: 'But Mr Wycliffe could be very helpful if you decided to call in the police.'

Lemarque looked at his wife. 'Jane says she's done this before, while I've been away.'

Jane said nothing now. She sat bolt upright and quite still, her gaze fixed on the fireplace. Her hands were clasped so tightly together in her lap that her arms seemed to tremble. Safety valve screwed right down.

But she was beautiful. Watching her, Wycliffe had unchaste thoughts, though it might be like sleeping with a sphinx. Probably only Lemarque had had the chance to find out. But agile little men, simian types, are often proud of their sexual prowess. Would Lemarque have been content with a frigid wife? Anyhow the hazards of sexual selection and the genetic lottery had produced Francine. Irrelevant thoughts of a chief superintendent.

Virginia was saying: 'Why does she do it – go off without a word?'

Jane said: 'To punish me.' The words seemed to escape almost against her will.

'To punish you, Jane? Surely not!' Virginia.

Lemarque glanced quickly at Wycliffe and away again.

Silence.

Virginia tried to bridge the gap with words. 'I'm sure Francine is quite safe but, if you don't hear today, think how worried you'll be; and all that time lost!'

Wycliffe felt that the tension had little to do with the missing girl. They were like actors playing a part while preoccupied with their real lives. There was no rapport between man and wife or between them and their drab surroundings. More than once Wycliffe saw the woman's lips moving as though in prayer.

The room was a collection of odds and ends; nothing chosen or valued or cared for. The little window looked out across the valley and from where Wycliffe sat there was no sky to be seen, only the dun-coloured and barren hillside opposite. A dismal, lonely prospect. What did the woman do all day when her husband was away? No books, magazines or newspapers; no sewing or knitting; not even a television set or a radio.

The silence seemed to challenge someone to break it; even Virginia was subdued. Lemarque said: 'What do you think, Jane?'

'It's up to you.'

They seemed to exist in a limbo of inaction and yet under almost insupportable tension. Lemarque turned to Wycliffe. 'What do we have to do?'

'Nothing at the moment. I'll arrange for someone to come and talk to you about Francine, and the routine enquiries will go ahead.'

With any other parents he would have felt the need to reassure them: 'The police are quite good at this sort of thing; it happens more often than you think so don't worry too much . . . '

He could have telephoned from the cottage; the telephone was there in the living-room but he preferred to wait until he was back at Mynhager. One reason was that he did not want to appear too directly involved.

Jane seemed greatly relieved to see them go; she even came out on to the steps and wished them a happy Christmas.

It was a relief to be once more out in the sunshine. As they were crossing the bridge Wycliffe said: 'An extraordinary couple! It's hard to imagine what life must be like in that . . . that vacuum. And the girl . . . Is Jane Lemarque frightened of something?'

Virginia said: 'She certainly seems worse than she was. I'm really glad you came, they wouldn't have done anything otherwise. What do you think about Francine?'

'What can one think? I very much doubt if she's staying with a school friend. Can you imagine any parent collecting a young girl, late in the evening, without previous contact with her parents?'

'You think something has happened to her?'

'That's what we've got to find out, but her parents know more than they've told us. Do you teach Francine?'

'No, she goes to a different school.'

Unconsciously he was adopting his professional role. He was disturbed.

Back at Mynhager he telephoned Chief Inspector Clarke of Divisional C.I.D. When the conversation was over Clarke put down the telephone, crushed out his half-smoked cigarette and cursed. 'Right on his bloody doorstep, and over Christmas. That's all we needed!'

He picked up the telephone again and called Detective Inspector Wills. 'I've just had the chief super on the line, Jim. He's spending Christmas in Mulfra village with Bishop, the lawyer. Some kid, a girl of sixteen, has gone missing right under his nose. Here are the details, such as they are . . . Ready?' He passed on the information he had. 'It's your patch, Jim, so watch your step. You're to send somebody to talk to the parents pronto, and the governor must be kept informed . . . Didn't Curtis work under him on some case? . . . The undertaker, that's it! Then Curtis is the man for this job. Not that it will amount to much. The kid will be back with mamma, wet and weepy by tonight. But if there's any cock-up, for God's sake let me know and put your head on the block, ready. And a very merry Christmas to you and yours!'

So the file which was not yet a file ended up on the desk of Detective Sergeant Curtis.

'That damned girl is going to spoil your Christmas, Wycliffe. Don't let her! She's only trying to make some impression on her mother. Not that I blame her for that. Lemarque spent years trying to do the same thing and look where it landed him!' The old man chuckled. 'Jane is like Everest, an enduring provocation simply by being there.' He turned to his son-in-law, 'Isn't that so, Gerald?'

They were at lunch and Gerald Bateman was trying to retrieve a small pat of butter from the table cloth without being noticed. He snapped: 'I'm quite sure Jane had nothing whatever to do with Lemarque's troubles.'

Caroline said: 'It wouldn't surprise me if she had gone off with some man, and I mean, man.'

Paul was staring at his plate without eating.

Aunt Stella, appetite unimpaired by age, consumed cheese and biscuits with the concentration and delicacy of a chimpanzee grooming for lice. She broke a water biscuit into four and placed a modicum of cheese on each section. 'If she's gone away then at least she is showing more discretion than most of them do these days.'

There was a noticeable silence then Ernest said with quiet emphasis: 'We are talking about Francine, aunt – Jane's daughter.'

Stella looked surprised. 'Francine? But she's only a child! It's hardly—'

'Francine is sixteen, aunt.'

Stella took into her mouth a portion of biscuit and cheese, patted her lips with a napkin and said: 'Isn't that what I was saying? These days they behave at sixteen as we wouldn't have dared to do at twenty-five!'

44

After the meal Wycliffe said to Ernest: 'I hope you don't mind; I've asked my people to keep me informed here.'

'My dear chap! You're doing us a favour.'

Wycliffe felt drowsy; the unaccustomed combination of whisky before and white wine during lunch was having its effect. He went into the drawing-room where there was a fire in the grate and the presents were laid out like votive offerings round the Christmas tree ready for distribution that night. The room was empty. He settled in one of the easy chairs with a magazine and was slightly embarrassed to wake up and find Ada standing over him.

'Sergeant Curtis wants to see you; I've put him in the dining-room.'

It was half-past three and almost dark. In the gloomy panelled dining-room Ada had switched on the dusty chandelier with its crystal drops.

Wycliffe knew Curtis of old and was pleased to renew the acquaintance. Curtis had the build of a heavyweight wrestler, with a great moon-like face in which eyes, nose and mouth were grouped together like palm trees in a desert oasis. A man of few words, he supplemented speech with gesture which sometimes reached the level of mime. He took a notebook from his pocket and placed it on the table but Wycliffe knew that he would not refer to it.

'I talked to madame; monsieur was out.' The huge hands seemed to pluck little manikins from the air and present them for inspection. 'They've no idea where or why the girl might have gone. Extraordinary! The woman seems to know nothing about her own daughter, about her school, her teachers or her friends . . . '

Curtis stared at the ceiling. 'I tried to find out what could have made the girl go off. Something must have. Had there been a row? "We don't have rows" madame informed me.' Curtis looked wide-eyed. 'Funny family in that case! Of course I suppose it's possible the girl was abducted but that hardly seems likely to me.

45

'I asked about friends visiting the house, letters . . . Friends don't visit, madame told me, but Francine does have letters occasionally. Big deal! Who from? Where from? . . . The silly woman doesn't have a clue. "We don't spy on our daughter." ' Curtis heaved a profound sigh. 'Neither did we on ours but we made damn sure we had some idea of what she was up to. I looked at the cards on the mantelpiece – most of 'em were for Francine, all signed with pet names. Unisex. Madame could only tell me about one which came from the Bateman boy and you'll know about him, sir.'

'Did you ask about relatives that she might have gone to?'

'It seems that Lemarque has no relatives in this country that he is in contact with.'

'And Jane?'

'She has a sister in Bristol and an aunt in Oxford; they keep in touch more or less, but she says Francine scarcely knows them.'

'Did you see the girl's room?'

'No problem. When I asked, madame said: "Upstairs; the door in front of you". Liberty Hall! Didn't tell me much though.' Curtis sketched a box in the air. 'Poky little room; the usual posters of pop stars on the walls; the usual collection of teenage clobber in the wardrobe and drawers – all looking as though it had been thrown out by Oxfam. When I was young, girls wanted to look pretty. I asked madame if she had taken any clothes with her other than what she wore. Madame (would you believe?) wasn't sure. All she was sure of was that the girl had taken her doll.'

'Her doll?'

'A black-faced doll she's had since she was an infant. She always slept with it in her bed. Our Gwen had a teddy bear which she put on her pillow every night right up to the time she got married. Afterwards too, for all I know.'

'Go on.'

Curtis recovered his narrative: 'About her bedroom: there were a few books, all school issue except one on adolescent sex. (I suppose that could be school issue too, these days.) A few tubes of paint, some brushes, and a blank sketch-pad. No pictures of hers or anybody else's. I had the impression she was thumbing her nose at me and at any other snoopers that happened along: "Make something out of this, Buster!"'

Curtis grinned. 'I couldn't and didn't.'

'Did you ask about what money she might have had?'

'I did, sir, but not to much purpose. It seems she had a job as a waitress in St Ives during the last summer holidays but what she earned or what she did with it her mother has no idea. Otherwise mother gave her money as she wanted it for some specific thing.'

'So what is your general impression?'

Curtis closed the notebook to which he had not once referred. 'A planned flit with a deliberate touch of the old melodrama. The day before Christmas Eve, and after playing the star role in the vicar's play, Bingo! the lady vanishes.' A deep sigh. 'Is that how you see it, sir?'

Wycliffe wasn't sure. Curtis's diagnosis seemed reasonable; a gesture of defiance, an expression of frustration, an assertion of independence. Take it out of that.

'You've got a photograph?'

Curtis looked sour. 'Two years out of date.'

'What else have you put in hand?'

'I've got a couple of chaps trying to make contact with her teachers and, through them, with her school friends. The chances are she talked to somebody. A teenage girl who doesn't tell at least some of it to her best friend would be a very rare bird. Of course, she may be just that.' Curtis shook his great head. 'Having Christmas round the corner doesn't make it easier. I found that in the village; characters who would be glad to talk their heads off normally have something better to do.'

'Did you get anything?'

'Not much. Of course you never know what the Cornish think, only what they say, and that's often the family or the village line. In this case they're saying that Francine is no better than she ought to be and that her mother and father are not liked.' Curtis lowered his voice. 'I'm afraid that's true of the Bishops too.'

'Nothing specific on the girl?'

'Just two things. The other members of the cast who were in the vestry when the play ended say she came in, went behind the curtain, changed into her outdoor clothes and left without a word to anybody.'

'And the other thing?'

'A little old woman, living alone . . . ' Curtis's hands somehow conveyed five-feet nothing of skin and bone. 'A real tartar with a tongue like a serpent's tooth. After telling me that a chap called Marsden, a painter, is having it off with half the female population of the district including the girl, she said she saw him talking to Francine last night after the play. They were just beyond the church.'

Marsden: Virginia had mentioned the gossip. Wycliffe said: 'It may not mean much but if he was the last person to be seen with her we'd better talk to him.'

He went into the drawing-room to leave word that he was going out but there was no one there. In the end he found Caroline in the kitchen. She was topping a trifle with little blobs of whipped cream and there was a strong smell of brandy. Ernest was with her, licking his fingers like a guilty schoolboy.

'I'm afraid I have to go out in connection with the Francine business.' He felt like a schoolboy himself, asking permission to leave the room, but Caroline was cheerfully indifferent.

'It's every man for himself until we eat at seven. Don't be late then.'

Wycliffe had to admit to a more than professional interest in this painter who looked like a gipsy, had a

48

reputation as a seducer, and listened to jazz blasted out in megabels.

Curtis was waiting in his car. It was quite dark now with a thin rain which smelled and tasted of the sea. Still no wind. They drove along the track, Curtis hunched over the wheel of his little Fiesta like some giant animal brooding its young. There was light in the painter's window and as soon as the engine cut they could hear the inevitable jazz. Not for the first time, Curtis surprised Wycliffe.

'Benny Goodman's "One o'clock jump"; that takes me back!'

They knocked, then banged on the door until the music was shut off. Heavy footsteps, then the door opened and there was Marsden; monumental against the light, like a Graham Sutherland portrait in 3-D. They introduced themselves.

'You'd better come in.'

The room was spartan. Apart from the record-player in one corner it was little different from how it must have been a century earlier when a Cornish mining family lived there. A floor of blue slate slabs with mats; a large deal table now littered with dirty dishes; and a couple of Windsor armchairs, one on each side of the fire. In one, a tabby cat was asleep, in the other there was an open book, and on the floor by the chair, a bottle of wine and a glass.

Marsden placed two kitchen chairs for his visitors. 'What's this about, then? I suppose I should apologize for the mess but it's the servants' night out. You know how it is with the lower classes these days.'

He spoke in a guttural voice and the words seemed to surface with some difficulty from a great depth.

Wycliffe said: 'I suppose you know that Francine Lemarque is missing?'

Marsden's expression froze. 'Missing? How long since?'

49

It was Curtis who said: 'Since last night.'

Marsden turned to Curtis. A confrontation between heavyweights; they were summing each other up. Wycliffe was amused, but though the two men had something in common, they were very different. Curtis was shrewd and subtle but essentially gentle, whereas in Marsden one sensed a potentiality for violence.

Marsden's attention came back to Wycliffe. 'You must think this is serious; a chief super on the job already.'

'Not necessarily. I happen to be involved because I'm staying with the Bishops over Christmas.'

Marsden grinned. 'Ah, the Bishops! God bless their little grey souls.' He took a cigarette pack from his pocket and lit one. Despite his bulk there was no clumsiness; he was as delicate and precise in his movements as a fastidious girl. 'I spoke to Fran after the church do last night. But the village K.G.B. will have told you that; it's probably why you're here.'

'Did she say why she didn't stay for the vicar's little party?'

'She said she couldn't face the vicar's sausage rolls.'

'How did you come to be talking to her?'

'Well, I saw her standing on the pavement like she was waiting for somebody. I told her I'd enjoyed the play and we chatted for a minute or two. I thought she was probably waiting for the Bateman boy to take her home the long way round. I believe that sort of thing is still done.'

Curtis said: 'Was she carrying anything?'

Marsden looked at Curtis with a speculative gaze. 'Ah! The monkey as well as the organ grinder. Yes, she was; a little holdall. "What did she have in it?" you say. And I say: "I do not know. I did not ask." '

Wycliffe said: 'I believe Francine sometimes comes here to your cottage.'

'True!'

'You are on friendly terms with her?'

'I am. She's a very intelligent girl, bored to the

50

eyeballs most of the time by the people she has to cope with. Me too, when I was a boy.'

'She comes here regularly?'

'She does, but I don't screw her if that's what you're asking.'

'Was the young woman who lives with you here last night?'

'No, the young woman who lives with me was not here last night; she went home to mother for Christmas.'

Curtis asked: 'Is she coming back?'

'I never ask women if they're coming back; it makes 'em think they're important. But she left her clobber here so I suppose she will.'

With an irritable movement Marsden threw the remains of his cigarette into the fire and got to his feet. 'I'll show you something. Come with me.'

He crossed the room, led them through a curtained doorway in the end wall, and switched on a strip-light which flickered into life. A large, bare room with a sloping roof on which the rain was pattering.

'My studio.'

It was very cold.

A couple of easels, a trolley painting-table, canvases stacked against the walls, a random assemblage of possible props, and the all-pervading smell of oil paint.

'Over here!'

Another strip-light. 'These things are supposed to give a north light, so that I can paint at night. No good! They're all wrong in the bloody yellows. Still, they're the best you can buy.

'Now look at this.' He lifted a cloth from a canvas on the second easel. 'There's our Fran for you. Stand back! You're not looking for the sodding signature.'

Wycliffe stood back and was impressed. A study in blues and greys and greens and purples with just a flush of pink in the flesh tones. The girl wore a flowered wrap, one breast exposed, and she looked at herself in a mirror.

51

Marsden said: 'She's not seeing herself; she's catching a glimpse of the promised land and she's not sure that she's going to like it. She's on the threshold. In another week, another month, perhaps a little longer, she'll have crossed over, she'll be a woman, then nobody will ever see that look again. But there it is on canvas; caught like a butterfly pinned out in a box. For good!' Marsden sighed. 'To do that you have to be a painter, and a bloody good one!'

Curtis said: 'It's a nice picture.'

Marsden turned to Wycliffe. 'Now you've seen that, do you think I screwed her – or, for that matter, that anybody else did? I could have; she's ready for it, and I'd have been a damn sight better for her than some sweaty youth, all elbows and acne who doesn't know what he's about. But I didn't.'

He continued to look at his picture. 'She'd hold that pose, with rests, for two hours without moving a muscle, and do you know what she'd say at the end of it?'

'I've no idea.'

'She'd say: "That's eight quid you owe me." '

'You paid her?'

'Of course I paid her; well above the going rate. She wouldn't have sat for me otherwise. She's not stupid.'

'How many times did she sit for you?'

'God knows! Seven or eight; you'll have to ask my secretary.'

He shepherded them back to the living-room, sat in his chair, and lit another cigarette. 'Now we know where we stand I've made up my mind to pass on one or two things I gathered from Fran.' He looked at Wycliffe. 'Of course, you know about papa Lemarque?'

'What about him?'

'That he's been in jug and only recently come out.'

'Go on.'

'It seems that Francine was very much looking forward to him coming home. You know how girls can get a fix on father; well, I won't say it went as far as that but,

52

after the best part of two years living with mother, I think she was counting on it all coming right when dad came back. It hasn't.'

'What was wrong, living with mother?'

Marsden pouted his thick lips. 'I'm not her confessor. She talks sometimes while I'm working and mostly I don't even answer, let alone ask questions, so I've no more than an impression.'

'And that is?'

'You've met the lady?'

'Mrs Lemarque? Briefly.'

'Then you can't fail to have noticed the Mona Lisa façade; the beautiful constipated nun look. One's natural reaction to that is: "Get behind it, mate, and you'll be all right." But what if there's no getting behind it? I know the score with her sort, it goes on and on until she gets clobbered and some poor bastard is carried away screaming: "There's nothing there! It was only a bloody record!"'

'Is that an expert assessment of why Francine has gone away?'

Marsden laughed. 'It's what you like to make it, mate. Now, if you don't mind, I was listening to some music and getting pissed ready for Christmas.'

'Benny Goodman,' Curtis said.

Marsden gave him a sour look. 'Who's a clever boy, then? I'll tell you something: when you pass this cottage you're just as likely to hear Bach or boogie-woogie.'

Outside, Curtis said: 'That gorilla isn't altogether stupid; I'll give him that.'

Wycliffe grumbled, 'Everybody seems anxious to talk about the mother rather than the girl. But it looks as though you were right. A planned get-away and she probably isn't short of money. It seems that somebody was due to pick her up in a car, so before we enlist the media with the "Have you seen?" bit we ought to really get down to finding who it was. There must have been quite a few people about, collecting their cars after the play. Only a fraction of the audience stayed for the sausage rolls but, according to the vicar, people came from all over this part of the county so you need to rope in other sections and get more men on the job. I'll speak to Division.'

Curtis said: 'I'll run you back to Mynhager, sir.'

'No need; I'll walk. I can do with the fresh air.'

'It's dark and it's damp, sir.'

'I'll survive.'

When Curtis drove off in the direction of the village the intensity of the darkness took Wycliffe by surprise. He set out with the fine rain in his face, picking his way with care, but soon the vague outlines of the landscape materialized out of the night and he walked with more confidence. The only light he could see came from across the valley, a dimly glowing orange rectangle, the window of the Lemarques' living-room. It happened that as he watched, their front door opened, illuminating a second rectangle; a figure appeared briefly in the light then the door closed again. Someone had come out of the house, someone with a torch; he could see the wavering pin-point of light as, whoever it was, descended the steps.

A few minutes later he rounded the bend which brought him in sight of the lights of Mynhager. Suddenly the sea sounded much louder and at intervals the low cloud was lit by diffused flashes from the lighthouse down the coast.

The meal over, they moved into the drawing-room. The wind had risen and despite the thick walls and heavy velvet curtains they could hear the waves breaking over the rocks and surging into the cove.

Joseph said: 'It's going to blow tonight.'

Time for party games.

Wycliffe sat in one of the big armchairs and his gaze ranged over the assembled Bishops and their distaff

54

branch, the Batemans. He was bored and he amused himself by trying to sum them up. Joseph, head of the clan, naturally domineering, presumed on the privileges of old-age to be caustic and sometimes cruel. A widower. Presumably the young woman in the only portrait amongst the pictures had been his wife. Ernest, over-dutiful son, suffered like his prototype in the parable. No fatted calf for Ernest. And the sisters? Virginia: unmarried, but still eligible if she got a move on: intelligent, good to look at, though spoiled at the moment by a too fussy hair-do and spectacles with shiny rims that were too large for her. Prim, in her royal-blue Jaeger frock, and probably in her panties, too. A hint of suppressed tension? Perhaps.

He wished that he could smoke but pride forbade it. Helen had said: 'Give it up in the New Year; you'll never hold out over Christmas.'

Then Caroline: plump but by no means cosy; her trouble was drink; more accurately, drink was the symptom of her trouble. Twenty-four hours at Mynhager was enough to convince anybody that her relationship with Gerald was not based on connubial felicity. Caroline, blatantly sexy, had opted to be separated from her husband for most of the year. There must be a story there. Wycliffe ruefully decided that he had missed his role in life; he should have been a housewife, peering through lace curtains. Are there any left?

Bateman was the odd man out. He lounged elegantly in one of the big chairs, smoking a cigarette, and staring at the ceiling but very far from being relaxed. No one could fail to be aware of his isolation, even from his son. It occurred to Wycliffe that Gerald had not yet subjected him to the threatened interrogation and he wondered why. They had scarcely exchanged half-a-dozen words.

Virginia, anxious to promote the party spirit, asked: 'What shall we play?'

Paul said: 'Let's play Who Am I?' The boy looked very

55

pale but he was behaving normally; keeping a stiff upper lip.

Who Am I? turned out to be a version of Twenty Questions in which one of them assumed the identify of a famous personage, living or dead, and the others had to discover that identity in not more than twenty questions.

Ernest, the first victim, was unmasked as Oscar Wilde by the sixteenth question. Virginia followed, and beat the field as Lady Astor.

Aunt Stella said: 'I knew Nancy Astor; we were invited to Cliveden several times. I always felt sorry for poor Waldorf, he was such a kindly man and Nancy was a dragon!'

Then it was Gerald's turn.

Joseph had been taking a lively part in the questioning; now he said: 'I'm enjoying this! Psychological striptease! Who would have thought poor old Ernest had tendencies or that Vee's frustrations were political? Your turn now, Gerry, and you'd better watch your step, you're treading on eggs! What about Churchill, or Ramsey Mac? Or go the whole hog with Talleyrand, he turned his coat so often that nobody knew for certain whose side he was on.'

Some years earlier Gerald had crossed the floor of the House and kept his seat.

Virginia and Ernest ignored their father but Gerald became very tense. In a manner far from his usual self-assured benevolence he said: 'I thought this was a game; but if you intend to use it as an occasion to work off some of your mischievous witticisms I am sure that you will manage just as well without me!' With that, Gerald got up and walked out, closing the door carefully behind him.

Joseph had cut too deep and he felt foolish. In the silence he said: 'What's the matter with him?'

Caroline muttered: 'Stupid bastard!'

Very slowly the party recovered its equanimity and its momentum. At ten o'clock Wycliffe was called to the telephone.

Curtis reporting: 'Some progress, sir. A witness says she saw the girl who took the part of the Virgin, getting into a car near the church at about nine-fifteen. She couldn't say what make the car was and she couldn't see its colour because the light was poor, but she thought it could have been red. She thought it looked a bit like a sports car, but old. She couldn't see who was driving.'

'Anything else?'

'Yes, and it ties up. One of my chaps unearthed the girl's form teacher. She says that at least twice in the last few days of term Francine didn't catch the school bus home; she was picked up by somebody in a red car. She only saw the car from a distance and couldn't see who was driving, but she had heard that Francine's father was back home and assumed that he was calling for her but didn't like to come too near the school.'

'You may have a good lead there.'

Back in the drawing-room they were passing round refreshments, little morsels on sticks and balanced on biscuits. Surely Christmas must be the feast of gluttony. Then more games, more drinks. At a little before midnight Gerald came back and resumed his seat as though nothing had happened. Glasses were filled with Joseph's '55 port then, with the radio switched on, they waited for the time signal. At midnight precisely they drank a toast 'To Christmas, friends and family!'

Even then Joseph had the last word: '"And God bless us all! said Tiny Tim."'

Came the presents; distributed by Paul, the youngest member of the party; the great business of unwrapping, the floor littered with pretty Christmas paper; the cries of surprise and delight; the somewhat effusive expressions of gratitude; and the moments of secret misgiving when one wonders whether one's own contributions have matched the general level, appearing neither ostentatious nor mean.

And finally, at about one o'clock, up the stairs to bed. By this time the gale was blowing in mighty gusts so that the old house shuddered. A single gust might last for fifteen or twenty seconds, followed by an abrupt and uneasy calm, an interval while the wind seemed to gather force for its next assault. Occasionally the electric lights flickered and Wycliffe wondered what it must have been like when the only lighting came from candles and oil lamps.

In his bedroom Wycliffe drew back the curtains but dared not open the windows. The roar of the sea and wind merged in a fury and it was impossible to decide whether the water streaming down the window panes came from rain or from spray. Through the watery curtain he looked down on the seething whiteness of breakers racing into the cove. He listened, and thought he could hear the great boulders grinding together, underscoring the rest of the wild orchestration.

In 120 years the house must have come through worse.

He thought about the Bishops. They had been pleasant enough, almost embarrassingly attentive, thoughtful and generous with their presents. Leaving aside the old man's mischievous wit, their hospitality could hardly be faulted. But he felt uncomfortable; there was an atmosphere: they all seemed edgy and preoccupied. They were going ahead with the business of entertaining him and with the rituals of Christmas but he had the impression that their thoughts were on something quite different.

Francine Lemarque?

Perhaps. It was natural that they should be concerned about the girl but there seemed to be more to it than that.

His thinking was muzzy; he had had rather too much to drink. He prepared for bed and got between the sheets.

Despite the pandemonium outside he could hear a woman's voice in the next room: Caroline, quarrelling with her husband. A happy Christmas.

He switched off the bedside lamp and snuggled down, thinking vaguely of Helen and tropical nights.

CHAPTER FOUR

He slept well considering the violence of the storm. Now and then, when rain or spray lashed against the windows with malevolent force he would mutter sleepily to himself, but he had gone to bed slightly tipsy, enough to feel superior to the elements.

He was up by eight-thirty; the worst seemed to be over though the wind blew at storm force and from time to time squalls of drenching rain swept in from the sea. The sky was a low canopy of driven clouds and the sea was lashed to foam for as far as the eye could see. The terrace was drenched by every wave and spume slid down the window panes.

Breakfast was a scratch affair, with Virginia and Ada in the kitchen handing out coffee and toast to anyone who turned up. Ernest was there, eating toast with so much butter on it that his moustache dripped and made Wycliffe feel slightly embarrassed. Joseph, Gerald, and Paul did not appear but to Wycliffe's astonishment, Caroline was in the drawing-room playing Rachmaninov with tremendous zest in the fortissimo passages. The morning after? A release from frustration? Or a celebration of victory? Strange woman!

Ernest said: 'Carrie is good, don't you think? She was at the Royal College and she did a year in Paris. She could have made a career but she said she'd been away from home long enough, so that was that. A real Cornish girl, our Carrie!'

Wycliffe asked: 'Have you heard from the Lemarques this morning?'

'No, I haven't. I'll telephone presently if the lines aren't down.'

A few minutes later Curtis came through. 'Not too early for you, I hope, sir? A happy Christmas! I'm speaking from home, as you can probably hear.'

Thumps, squeals and shrieks in the background from Curtis's grandchildren.

'Anything fresh?'

'We've traced the red car, sir, a 1975 Triumph belonging to a young layabout called Pellowe – Timothy Pellowe. His father is a builder in a small way in St Buryan.'

'How young is young?'

'Oh, he's not exactly a boy, he's nineteen, rising twenty. The perpetual student type who never studies anything. He got chucked out of university last July for failing his exams and he's been bumming around ever since, coming home to mum and dad when times are hard but taking off into the wide blue yonder when it suits him. Like now. This time he's been home since early December.'

'Anything known?'

'No, he hasn't got form but, from what I hear, he's not the sort I'd want a daughter of mine running off with.'

'His parents haven't any idea where he might be?'

'Not a clue; nor has anybody else we've talked to so far. All he said was that he'd probably be back in a few days.'

'Of course you must do this through Division, but I want all you've got on the couple and the car put on the telex. At the same time they might try to find somebody in the TV and radio newsrooms who stays awake over Christmas and see if we can get a mention.'

Ernest could not get through to the Lemarques. 'Their line is dead; it's usually like this after a blow; a toss-up who gets cut off and who doesn't. I'll take a walk over there directly.'

Wycliffe said: 'I thought of going over myself.' He contrived without being offensive to convey the message that he wanted to go alone.

'Oh! In that case . . . ' After a pause Ernest went on: 'This young fellow she's gone off with; they must have planned it.'

'Of course.'

'Then wouldn't you have expected her to leave a note of some sort?'

'Perhaps she did.' Wycliffe went on quickly: 'I don't know if you would care to give Paul the latest news — such as it is.'

Perversity decided him to walk, despite the weather. He put on his heavy waterproof and a matching peaked cap which, according to Helen, made him look like Our Man in Berlin. It was not actually raining but mist and spray mingled in the rampageous air and he was driven along the dirt road by the force of the wind. He reached the painter's cottage where there was no sign of life. Marsden was probably sleeping it off. He turned down the footpath to the bridge, but the bridge, a ramshackle affair at best, had collapsed and been swept away by the stream, now a miniature torrent of brown water. He would have to walk to the village and down the old mine track on the other side.

He was out of humour with himself, low on Christmas spirit, and disgruntled with his job. Why was he getting into this anyway? A missing girl, a juvenile who had run away with a boy three or four years older. Teenagers went missing every day; and every day a few more took to glue sniffing; smoking pot; swallowing, sniffing or injecting themselves with daydreams which turned into nightmares. And the police were all but helpless. Every day young people (older ones too) robbed or mugged or raped or murdered, and many chief constables would be over the moon if their detection rate came within shouting distance of 50 per cent. Add to this strikes, violence on the picket lines, violence at football matches, violence at demonstrations for and against almost everything.

He was Canute, striving to halt the tide; Quixote, tilting at windmills; better still, that Greek chap, Sisyphus, condemned through all eternity to roll a stone uphill so that it could roll down again.

Sensible people raised the drawbridge, kept their fingers crossed, and learned Russian. But here he was, getting wet to bring to the Lemarques news of their daughter's stupidity. Curtis could and would have done all that was needed. The truth was that he felt uneasy. During the night he had recalled an incident that had occurred on his way back from the painter's cottage in the dark. The orange rectangle of the Lemarques' window, the opening and closing of their door, and the erratic movements of a flashlight held in someone's hand. It was absurd, but that trivial sequence of events had acquired a dramatic significance in his mind.

In the village street a little boy was pedalling furiously around on a brand new 'Chopper' bicycle, oblivious of the weather, imagining himself on a Yamaha or a Honda. Outside two or three of the houses cars were unloading guests laden with parcels; there were Christmas trees with lights in several windows and through some he could see the flickering glow of a television set. The Tributers was not yet open but there were a few cars parked by the church and he could hear the sound of the organ.

He had trouble finding the alley which led to the mine track but came upon it at last between the Mechanics' Institute (1853), and a terrace of cottages. In places it was rough going with puddles of peaty water which could only be avoided by taking to the heather, and now the wind was in his face. Head down, he fought against it and reached the cottage at last. There was no van parked at the bottom of the steps and he was wondering if they had gone out when he saw that the front door was open. From that moment he had no doubt that his instinct had been right.

He climbed the steps. The door was wide open and the drab carpet and mats in the little passage were sodden with blown rain. A flimsy plant-stand had been overturned, perhaps by the wind, so that plant and pot had parted company and there was soil strewn over the floor.

He was picking his way through to the living-room when he heard a sound and he called out: 'Is anyone there?'

Heavy footsteps, and Marsden appeared in the doorway of the living-room. He looked at Wycliffe in a bemused, uncomprehending way and for a moment Wycliffe thought he was drunk. He was wearing slacks that were wet below the knees and a roll-neck pullover stained with paint and grime; his black curls had been flattened by the rain and there were droplets of moisture caught in his moustache.

Wycliffe said: 'What are you doing here?'

The painter supported himself against the doorpost and spoke as though he were short of breath. 'I saw from my place that the door was open when I got up this morning . . . Half-an-hour later it was still open and I wondered if there was something wrong. Lemarque's van wasn't there and I thought they might have gone off and not shut the door properly . . . The bridge was down so I had to walk round.' He gestured weakly. 'There seemed to be nobody here and it was obvious the door had been open for a long time. I couldn't understand it so I came in to look round . . . Of course, I found her.'

'Francine?' Wycliffe's voice was sharp.

'Not Francine, Jane. She's up in the bedroom, and she's dead.'

'Stay where you are!'

Wycliffe went up the stairs. At the top was a landing

with three doors opening off. The room in front of him was Francine's, he could see the single bed and the pop-star posters on the wall. Another door opened into a tiny bathroom with a loo. He turned to the third door; it was almost closed and he pushed it open. There were yellow curtains drawn over the tiny window and a pale, jaundiced light reached into the room from the grey world outside. It was a moment before his eyes became adjusted to the gloom. A double bed took up most of the space and the bed was made up, though untidily, as if someone had been lying across it.

Then he saw her, on the floor, her body was wedged between the bed and the dressing table. She was wear-ing the drab woollen two-piece he had seen her in the day before. He bent over her. In order to do so he had to sprawl across the bed. She was lying on her side but her head was twisted so that he could see her face. The pale, serene features had been grossly mutilated by a bullet leaving her skull; a bullet which must have made its entry through the back of the head or the neck. He reached down and tried to raise her hand. Jane Lemarque was dead and she had been dead for several hours.

He got to his feet and looked at his watch. Ten thirty-five.

'At ten thirty-five on the morning of December 25th I entered the larger of the two bedrooms and found the deceased lying on the floor between the bed and dressing table. She appeared to be fully clothed. She was in such a position that I was able to see the injury to the upper part of her face which I took to be the wound of exit of a bullet fired from behind. I satisfied myself that life was extinct . . . '

Accustomed to such scenes, his reactions were profes-sional, but he had never become hardened. He was still deeply shocked by violent death; by the senseless destruction of a web of consciousness which reached back to the womb.

Marsden mustn't be left downstairs alone. What the

hell had he been doing in the living-room anyway? And he was not wearing a coat or mackintosh, only a pullover and slacks . . . But Jane Lemarque had been dead for many hours.

Downstairs, Marsden was still standing in the doorway of the living-room as though dazed.

'You saw her?'

He couldn't keep the man standing there, he was liable to fall down but if he let him go back into the living-room the scene-of-crime chaps would go berserk.

'You can sit on the stairs.'

Marsden lowered his bulk on to the second stair and sat with his hands on his knees. His pullover was quite dry.

'Where's your coat?'

Marsden pointed to the living-room. 'In there.' He passed a hand over his forehead. 'Christ! I hardly know what I'm doing. I went in there to telephone but the bloody wires had been cut . . . I was going to call your lot and I thought the quickest way would be to twist the ends together.' He held out his right hand and opened it. He had been gripping a small penknife with an open blade which had cut into the flesh and brought blood.

'I was stripping the wires when you came.'

'And your coat?'

He shifted irritably. 'I slipped the bloody thing off because it was in the way. Why keep on about it?'

It sounded feasible.

'You stay where you are.'

Wycliffe went into the living-room and to the telephone. The wires had been cut near the instrument and the ends were bared. Marsden's coat — stained and worn suede with lambswool facings — lay in a heap on the floor.

He twisted the wires together as best he could and it worked. He made the routine calls. To Division: Locate Detective Sergeant Curtis; send a patrol car, a couple of uniformed men, and a police surgeon; notify the

66

coroner. Then he spoke to his own office. That Christmas morning the duty strength at C.I.D. headquarters was a detective sergeant and two constables, all three engaged in the perilous cut and thrust of gin rummy. Along with a lot of other people they were about to have their simple pleasures brutally cut short.

Wycliffe's deputy, Chief Inspector John Scales, was located at the home of a friend and from now on the wheels would begin to turn. The pathologist would be notified, a mobile incident post would be sent to Mulfra and preparations put in hand to get a team on the road. The leader of the team: Detective Inspector Kersey. In the interests of promotion Kersey had served his time in the wilderness, now he was returning to the fold and no one was more pleased than Wycliffe.

He rejoined Marsden.

Marsden had a cigarette going and he had recovered something of his usual poise. 'So that's how it's done.'

Wycliffe said: 'You will be required to make a statement later but I am going to ask you a few questions.'

'Ask away.'

'Yesterday morning I saw an old grey Escort van parked outside here. Is it theirs?'

'I suppose so; it turned up shortly after he came out of jail.'

'You knew Lemarque before he went to prison?'

Marsden looked around for somewhere to dispose of the butt-end of his cigarette then pitched it through the open doorway. 'I knew him by sight and to pass the time of day. They came down quite often and stayed at the cottage for a weekend; longer, sometimes. He had money and a Jag then.' Marsden grinned in something like his old style. 'But no particular interest in impoverished genius, women, or booze, so our paths didn't cross.'

'While Lemarque was in jail, did his wife associate with other men?'

'How the hell should I know?'

67

'You were recommended to me as an expert on such matters.'

A short laugh. 'I'm flattered. But I'm no expert where that lady is concerned. She strikes me as the sort who needs a man about as much as I need a hole in the head but you never can tell; impressions can be deceptive.' He broke off. 'Christ! It's hard to remember that she's up there, poor little cow! Was that a shotgun wound?'

'No. What time did you get up this morning?'

Marsden passed a hand over his hair and looked at it foolishly when he realized that it was wet. 'I shall catch my death over this, I've got a weak chest. My mother used to say, "Keep your head, your feet and your bum dry and you'll be all right." It must've been about nine.'

'And the van was already gone?'

'Yes.'

'When did you last see Lemarque?'

The painter grimaced. 'I haven't a clue.'

'His van?'

'You'll think I spend my time looking out of the bloody window like the old bags in the village, but it happens I did see the van yesterday afternoon, at about half-two, perhaps earlier, being driven along the track towards the village. I suppose Lemarque was driving. I don't think Jane can – could.' He hesitated. 'You think he killed her?'

Wycliffe said, 'Do you? Or do you have good reason to know that he didn't?'

The painter shook his head. 'My God! This should teach me not to play the good Samaritan. In future, Marsden, you'll keep your head down, and your eyes shut. I don't know whether Lemarque killed his wife but it wouldn't surprise me; not that I know anything about Lemarque but some women are born victims and she was one.'

On the face of it the shooting had taken place sometime the previous evening or early in the night. It had the marks of a domestic crime; no evidence of burglary (was there anything to take?), apparently no sexual overtones; and no husband available for comment. Unless he had a cast-iron alibi it looked as though the case would be as good as over when Lemarque was brought in. And that shouldn't be difficult.

It would be simple to put Lemarque and his van on the telex. As an ex-con Lemarque would be on record and details of the van should be available through Vehicle Registration. But he needed to get Marsden off his hands first. He didn't want an audience.

The sound of a car grinding along the track. Wycliffe went to the door. Two coppers in a patrol car, their meditations on the Nativity in some quiet lay-by rudely interrupted. Curtis came hard on their heels. Wycliffe put him in the picture.

Curtis's button-eyes looked at Wycliffe with concern. 'Do you think this has anything to do with the girl?'

'How do I know? But it makes it all the more important to find her.' He gave Curtis detailed instructions to put Lemarque and his van on the telex, then he called Marsden over. 'Mr Marsden will go with you to make his statement.'

Marsden gave him a sour look. 'And when will Mr Marsden get back to feed his cat and perform other necessary domestic chores?'

'That depends on Mr Marsden.'

'I suppose I can take my coat?'

'Not for the moment; anyway, there's central heating in the nick.'

As Curtis was leaving with Marsden, two uniformed men arrived in a Panda Car with a detective sergeant from Division.

It would be the better part of two hours before the pathologist or the headquarters circus could arrive so he left the detective sergeant in charge and got one of the patrolmen to drive him back to Mynhager. The car jolted over the bumpy track and splashed through the pools while the uniformed driver sat beside him, stiff and silent as though stuffed. It was raining hard again; the village street streamed with water, gleaming darkly, and was utterly deserted. There were cars outside The Tributers, the bar was brightly lit, and they caught a snatch of song as they passed. Turning off down the road to Mynhager they met the full force of the wind with the rain driving straight off the sea.

'Are you due off at two?'

'With a bit of luck, sir, I'll be able to spend some time with the kids.'

'Have a good day, what's left of it.'

Wycliffe was thinking of Francine's disappearance and of her mother's murder. A connection? He believed in coincidence as he believed in Sants Claus but coincidences do happen. Arthur Koestler wrote a book about them. A girl goes missing on the night before Christmas Eve, and on Christmas morning her mother is found, shot dead. And her father? Wycliffe was relieved that Francine had been seen getting into the red car, otherwise the prospect might have seemed even more sinister.

But his immediate problem was with the Bishops. The Bishops, the Batemans and the Lemarques had been closely associated for years and the Lemarques had been almost members of the family. Not any more. After Bateman pulled out of the partnership and Lemarque got the bit between his teeth to end up in jail, the situation had changed.

Policemen are fated to be an embarrassment to their friends and to themselves. Accept a lift in a friend's car and he thinks you are checking his tax disc, his speed and his braking. Jane Lemarque had been murdered and now questions would be asked, some of them relevant, others not. But the people questioned would feel disturbed and possibly threatened, and the Bishops and Batemans were bound to be in the forefront. Even if it turned out that Lemarque had killed his wife, the police would need to know why, and they would look to Mynhager for at least part of the answer.

Ergo: it was impossible for him to continue as a guest in the house.

Ernest, his glasses pushed up on to his forehead, was sitting at a table looking down a binocular microscope at a minute insect impaled on a pin. On the table was a shallow, cork-lined drawer with its glass cover lying beside it. In the drawer, other flies, similarly impaled, were lined up like guardsmen, each with a tiny cardboard label. A cabinet under the window held at least a score of such drawers.

'I hope I'm not disturbing you.'

Ernest swivelled his chair away from the table. 'My dear Charles! I'm merely filling in time until lunch looking at a few flies I took yesterday.'

His 'den' was a little room sandwiched between dining-room and drawing-room. The window, covered with a grubby net curtain, looked out on the courtyard at the back of the house.

'Any news of Francine?'

'Not of Francine but I'm afraid there's very bad news of the Lemarques.'

'Indeed?' A look of concern.

'Jane has been shot; when I saw her earlier this morning she had been dead for several hours at least.'

Ernest's features expressed total incredulity. 'Shot? You mean she's killed herself?'

Wycliffe shook his head. 'It wasn't suicide, it was murder.'

'And Alain?' The question seemed to be forced from him.

'Lemarque and his van are missing.'

'Oh God!' He got up from his chair and went to the window. 'Are you suggesting that he killed his wife — murdered her?'

71

'All I can say is that Jane Lemarque has been murdered and that her husband is missing. You know them better than I do. Is it credible that he murdered her? Is he a violent man? Do you know of any motive he may have had or thought he had?'

An electric clock on the wall above the table flicked the seconds away. Ernest had his back to the room; he was wearing a woolly cardigan which hung limply from his thin shoulders and his whole body seemed to droop. He looked like an old man. At last he turned away from the window. 'Alain is not a violent man, Charles, quite the contrary, and I'm sure that he was fond of Jane.' But he spoke without conviction. 'I don't know what to say. Is this anything to do with Francine running away?'

'I've no idea.'

Ernest said: 'I suppose you will be taking charge of the investigation? You don't need me to tell you that you are welcome to stay on here.'

'I'm very grateful but it wouldn't do at all. You must see that.'

Ernest looked at him in pained surprise. 'Surely, this isn't going to affect us — our relationship, I mean?'

'I'm afraid it's bound to do until the case is over. I have to go back to being a policeman. You're a lawyer, you know the score. How can I possibly conduct an investigation while remaining on intimate terms with a family so closely connected with the dead woman?'

Ernest slumped into his chair and swivelled listlessly to and fro. 'No, I suppose you are right, but I have to admit that it's a blow . . . What a Christmas Day this has turned out to be!'

Wycliffe was aware of the curious museum-like smell of the room, a blend of cork, naphthalene, old books, and preserving spirit. He had the odd notion that it was Ernest's main concern to arrest the passage of time, to hold on to the moment and preserve the status quo . . .

'So you are leaving us . . . You'll stay to lunch — you won't just walk out?' It was a plea.

'Of course I'll stay; and thank you.'

'Good! Just give me a few minutes to break the news to the others.'

In the dining-room everyone was subdued and Wycliffe felt like a leper though they seemed anxious to make it clear that his position was understood. Only Joseph and Aunt Stella were seated, Paul wasn't there, and the others stood about going through the motions of helping themselves to bits of chicken, slices of ham, and a variety of salads, all laid out on the table.

Virginia said: 'It's hardly credible! In less than forty-eight hours, the whole family . . . Just gone!'

Caroline picked at the chicken with her fork. 'I can't believe that Alain killed her. Jane was difficult, God knows, but she was the only one for him. I doubt if he ever looked at another woman.'

Joseph was helping himself from a bottle of hock. 'If I'd been married to Jane I can imagine a situation in which I might have strangled her, but shooting, that's another thing altogether. You have to have a gun, you have to load it, aim it, and pull the trigger. Premeditation.' The old man shook his head. 'But who else is there?'

Aunt Stella had seemed unaware of or indifferent to what had happened and what was being said; she had a plate of food and she was working through it. Then, abruptly, with perfect enunciation, she recited:

' "Lizzie Borden with an axe,
Hit her father forty whacks.
When she saw what she had done,
She hit her mother forty-one." '

A shocked silence, but the old lady was in no way subdued. She looked round at the family. 'What's the matter? All I'm saying is I would be more willing to believe it of the girl than of her father. We all know that

73

Alain Lemarque is a rogue but nothing will convince me that he is a murderer.'

Virginia was outraged. 'But that's monstrous, Aunt Stella! A terrible thing to say!'

Caroline turned on her sister. 'You've always defended Francine but there's something in what Aunt Stella says. I don't know whether Francine could or would have done it but I don't forget what she was like when she was here. Don't you remember when she smashed her mother's gold watch just because she was stopped from going on some trip? How old was she then . . . five? . . . six? No tears, no show of temper but straight up the stairs to her mother's dressing table. And that's not the only—'

'Stop it, Carrie!' Ernest's voice raised in real anger. 'There may be some excuse for Aunt Stella but there is none for the rest of us. We are turning a tragedy affecting our friends into poisonous gossip!'

Wycliffe noted the effect of this outburst on the others. Bateman nodded agreement. Old Joseph looked at his son with a faint smile on his lips. Caroline's expression was one of unbelief like a cat who has been bitten by a mouse. Stella remained unperturbed.

Lunch was over at last and Wycliffe went upstairs to do his packing. There was a knock on his bedroom door and Gerald Bateman came in, a diffident and confiding Bateman.

'I hope I'm not intruding but I felt that I must speak to you before you cease to be a guest and become a policeman.' A thin smile. 'You can imagine how I feel. I've known Alain and Jane for twenty years. Alain and I not only worked together but we shared a good deal of our social life both here and in London. The differences I had with Alain which ended our partnership and led eventually to his trouble with the law in no way diminished my affection and respect for them both. We continued friends.'

'Have you seen anything of him since you've been home this time?'

'I called there; it was my first chance following his release.'

'How did you find him?'

The great man considered. 'I found him changed but what could one expect?'

'Depressed?'

'Not depressed, subdued.' He lowered his voice. 'As a matter of fact he was sounding me out about putting up capital for a scheme he had in mind. He wasn't ready to discuss it in any detail but I gathered that it was local and concerned with tourism. More than that he was not prepared to say at this stage.'

'Were you able to give him any encouragement?'

'Yes, I was, and not only out of a desire to help an old friend. Alain is a first-rate businessman and, with certain safeguards, I would be fully prepared to back a scheme he believed to be sound. Of course, a partnership would hardly be practicable in the new circumstances but I think he has it in mind that I should provide the capital and he would run the business for a share in the profits.'

Wycliffe stooped to fasten his suitcase. Politicians are by nature devious and he was wondering about the real purpose of Bateman's confidences. However, he rarely tried to meet guile with subtlety. The suitcase secured, he straightened up, put on his ruminating-cow look, and asked: 'Why are you telling me all this?'

By the same token Bateman was far too old a hand to be disconcerted. 'Because I want you to know that whatever precipitated this tragedy it was not, I think, a feeling of hopelessness about the future.'

Wycliffe thought, he wants me to believe that Lemarque murdered his wife and he may well be right. He said: 'Paul wasn't at lunch; if he's around I would like a word with him before I leave.'

No doubt Bateman had survived many more devastating snubs and he took this one in his stride. 'There is just one other matter: I hope you won't be influenced by the talk during lunch. I'm afraid my wife is in the habit of making outrageous remarks, just to shock. The family take no notice, but to a stranger . . . ' A bleak smile. 'As for Aunt Stella's nonsense! . . . '

Wycliffe said: 'I expect I shall hear a great deal of nonsense during the next few days.'

Bateman nodded. 'You reassure me. If you want Paul you will almost certainly find him in his workshop. It's his refuge in time of trouble. The old wash-house, I'll show you.'

They had to go through the kitchen where Ada was washing dishes, then through an empty cavernous room with whitewashed walls and a slate floor.

'Here we are!' Bateman pushed open another door and they were in a businesslike workshop. There was a carpenter's bench, woodworking tools neatly arranged in racks, and the delectable blended smells of resin and sawdust. Paul was there, bending over what looked like a bench-end, supported on trestles.

'Paul is carving new ends for some of the pews in the church . . . I'll leave you to it.' Bateman, being discreet.

Paul straightened. He was holding a gouge and he was engaged in carving a new bench-end which had already been shaped. The motif was a herring-gull, about to touch down on the water. It was simple and incisive, fitting the rectangular space. There were three more ends lying against one of the walls, carved with a crab, a lobster, and a St Ives gig.

'I came here because I couldn't think of anything else to do.' He stood, taller than Wycliffe, pale-faced, diffident, and slightly embarrassed. 'It's only a hobby for the holidays.'

'But they will be used, surely?'

'Well, yes. The Vicar thinks the Victorian bench-ends are dull; there are only two survivors of the original sixteenth-century ones and he feels that we could liven some of the rest up a bit. Uncle Ernest said he would pay for the wood and the fitting if I carved them.' He paused awkwardly. 'I don't suppose there's any news of Francine?'

76

'I'm sorry, no. I came here because I thought you might help me. I'm trying to find out what things were like in the Lemarque household before and after Mr Lemarque came out of prison . . . You realize, Paul, that the time has gone for any kind of reticence.'

The boy nodded. 'I see that, but there's very little I can tell you. Francine never talks much about her home. I don't think she got on very well with her mother and sometimes she seemed quite rude to her, but I think Mrs Lemarque used to exasperate Francine by always being . . .'

'Being what?'

'I don't know; sort of miserable, I suppose, and resigned to being miserable. I think that is what upset Francine.'

'What was Francine's attitude to her father?'

'She seemed to look forward to him coming home.'

'And was she disappointed?'

He hesitated. 'I think she was.'

'Have you any idea why?'

He looked worried. 'It's very difficult to say, but Mr Lemarque had changed; I could see that. He was very quiet and he seemed depressed. He didn't have a lot to say before, but he used to be cheerful, he would tease people, especially Francine, and they used to laugh together.'

'Have there been quarrels since he came home?'

'I don't know; I only know that Francine was even more unhappy. Just a couple of days before she went away she said: "There's one thing you learn from parents – never get married." '

Wycliffe said: 'You are obviously very fond of Francine and you will not want to betray her confidences but in the new circumstances you must realize that you can help best by being completely frank. Has Francine said anything to you recently which, with hindsight, might throw any light on what has happened?'

Paul stood, testing the edge of the gouge with his thumb. 'I can't think of anything. I mean, she doesn't confide in me much . . . The only thing she said recently which I didn't understand was something about me knowing more about her . . .'

'What exactly did she say?'

'It was something like: "When you know more about me you won't want me".'

'There's more, isn't there?'

He coloured. 'I said that I wanted to spend my life getting to know her and she laughed. She said that it wouldn't take that long; that I might find out more than I wanted to know very soon.'

Why did Wycliffe at that moment feel that Paul would follow in his uncle's footsteps? A confirmed bachelor, never taking a firm grip, making the best of a life divided between his work and his hobbies: the legal practice, Mynhager, wood carving, the aunts . . .

Wycliffe said: 'Thanks; you've straightened out my ideas a bit. I'll let you know as soon as we hear any news of Francine.'

Paul turned to put the gouge he was holding back in the rack so that Wycliffe could not see his face. 'Did my father . . . ?'

'Yes?'

He shook his head. 'Sorry! It doesn't matter.'

'You missed lunch. See if Ada has any food left in the kitchen.'

The boy smiled. 'I might do that.'

Wycliffe's case was in the hall; someone had brought it down. Ernest and Virginia came out to see him off. Ernest said: 'I hope you'll come again, bring Helen, and stay longer.'

Ernest walked with him to the car. 'Carrie's tongue runs away with her. She really doesn't mean what she says. Alain, Jane and Francine were like members of the family and what has happened is a tragedy for all of us.'

78

CHAPTER FIVE

He drove back to the Lemarques' cottage. Still raining, and in an hour or so the gloom would merge with the dusk. In the village, at the turn-off to the mine track, a uniformed copper was poised to direct new arrivals and divert the inquisitive. When he saw Wycliffe's indicators flash he raised a minatory hand and came to the car window.

'Do you have business down there, sir?' Water dribbled off his flower-pot helmet as he stooped to speak.

'Chief Superintendent Wycliffe.'

'Sorry, sir! I didn't recognize you. You know where it is?'

'I don't think I shall miss it. Has anybody arrived?'

'The police surgeon has been and gone, sir; a headquarters party is there, and Dr Franks, the pathologist, went down a couple of minutes ago.'

So far none of the locals seemed to have realized that anything was happening, but that would change; with more police activity than the village had seen since D.H. Lawrence and Frieda were chased out as suspected German spies during the First War.

Lined up along the track beyond the cottage were two police cars, a police Range Rover, and a lethal-looking James Bond vehicle which could only belong to Dr Franks, the pathologist.

Franks himself was standing just inside the front door of the cottage, spick and span in herring-bone tweed with a striped shirt and club tie.

'Hullo, Charles! Is this your idea of Christmas? Apparently the lady most concerned in all this is upstairs and Fox is up there with the photographer taking pictures while she's *in situ,* so to speak. Fox is a keen lad; he doesn't want me prodding her about until they've finished. What's it all about?'

'A shooting.'

'I know that, but why was she shot? A domestic tiff?'

'I've no idea.' Although they had worked together for years, Franks still irritated Wycliffe by his frivolous attitude in the face of death, with the effect that Wycliffe became morose and taciturn.

'I hear that you are staying down here.'

Wycliffe pointed across the valley. 'With the Bishops; he's a lawyer, you may know him.'

Franks grimaced. 'I do. Christmas with him must be as exciting as a Jewish funeral. And this place — fine in summer but now! You're a masochist, Charles! I hear Helen is in Kenya. Nights of tropical splendour and all that. Well, I suppose that's how you want it.'

'Ready for you, doctor.' Sergeant Fox, in charge of the scene-of-crime investigation and successor to the misanthropic Smith, now retired. This was Fox's first murder case since joining the squad. Seeing Wycliffe, he came downstairs and Franks went up. Fox was twenty-eight, thin with sandy-coloured hair and freckles; he had a prominent nose and a receding chin but contrived to look intelligent despite everything.

'I didn't know you were here, sir.' Fox was preoccupied, watching Franks as he climbed the stairs; he said wistfully: 'I wish Dr Franks would wear the correct gear.' Fox, himself, looked like a one-man decontamination squad. The idea was to minimize 'exchange' at the scene of crime, to ensure that traces left by the criminal were neither confused nor destroyed by the investigator. Wycliffe remembered a pathologist who scattered cigar ash over the scene of crime as a priest sprinkles holy water.

He was depressed by changes, they made him feel

old; like the reading glasses, tucked neatly in their case in his right-hand jacket pocket. He would bring them out only when absolutely necessary, and put them on with the surreptitious air of a man who is forced to zip up his flies in public.

The doldrums: a period after the discovery of a major crime during which resources are mobilized and the preliminary technical data are established. No point in rushing around in ever diminishing circles while this is going on.

Dr Franks came down the stairs. 'She's on the bed now, Charles. Move her when you like.'

'The van is on the way. What have you got for me?'

'Not much. She was shot with a large calibre bullet which your chaps will dig out of the walls or the woodwork. It must have played merry hell inside her head and neck. She's been dead between sixteen and twenty hours so she was shot between four and eight yesterday. No sign of other injuries that I can see; no indications of assault, sexual or otherwise, apart from the shooting. If there's any more to tell you, after I've had a chance to take a real look, I'll be in touch later today. Who's attending?'

'Inspector Trevena from Division is coming with the van.'

Franks stood at the top of the steps. It was quite dark now, every light in the little cottage was switched on and a weak orange glow reached out into the pit-like darkness of the valley. It had stopped raining but the air was full of moisture and tangy with salt. The gale had blown itself out but the continuous muffled roar of the sea seemed sometimes very close, sometimes distant.

He held out his hand. 'I'll be off then. What a way to spend Christmas!'

A moment or two later, the roar of his car engine, two great shafts of light cleaving the valley, a skidding of tyres, and he was away.

Not robbery, not a sex crime; just a housewife shot

with a heavy calibre gun. Probably she had been threatened downstairs and, terrified, she had retreated up the stairs with some idea of protecting herself, only to be ruthlessly cornered and shot. Like an execution.

By her husband? Caroline Bateman hadn't thought so. 'She was the only one for him. I doubt if he ever looked at another woman.' And Wycliffe suspected that Caroline understood these things. But a passionate quarrel, perhaps over Francine running away? A quarrel which suddenly flared into uncontrollable violence? Joseph had pointed out the snags there. 'You have to have the gun . . . load it, aim it, and pull the trigger.' It becomes in some degree a premeditated act. But what other possibilities were there? Francine? There were cases on record of young girls murdering their parents, but he couldn't take the possibility seriously here. Anyway, what had happened to Lemarque? There remained the ubiquitous outsider . . .

His instinct was to wander around the little house, soaking up the atmosphere, getting the feel of how it had been lived in, but if he did this before the scene-of-crime boys had finished he would be unpopular with Fox. Criminal investigation, like other social studies, was struggling to qualify as a science, to join the other sacred cows and become a private stamping ground for experts. Wycliffe sympathized to some extent with the ineffable Poirot and his little grey cells. 'It is the psychology, *mon ami!*' In particular he agreed with the Belgian that a clue two-foot long is in no way inferior to one that must be sought under a microscope.

He growled like an irritated grizzly, giving vent to a vague and disquieting awareness that he was becoming increasingly out of step with the way things were going in his profession. He climbed the stairs. Fox, as though activated by a spring, came out from the main bedroom. 'You wanted me, sir?'

'No.'

'We've got the bullet and cartridge-case. It's a nine-millimetre.' Good dog, waiting to be patted.

A cold look. 'You know what to do, I suppose?' Wycliffe, like Talleyrand, distrusted enthusiasm: Above all, gentlemen, not the slightest zeal.

He followed Fox into the bedroom. The room looked as though it had been got ready for the removal men; the bed was dismantled, the bedding neatly folded; drawers were removed and the furniture pulled as far as possible away from the walls.

'Found anything?'

Fox pointed to the dressing table. Laid out on the top were a number of documents and papers beside an old-fashioned cash box with a brass handle. 'The papers were in the box and the box was in one of the drawers, locked.'

Wycliffe looked through the haul: passports for the family, none of the stamps less than three years old; birth certificates, marriage lines; a couple of policies, one for the van; a few bank statements, and an envelope boldly marked with a date: 15·4·79.

Fox said: 'One of the other drawers is stuffed full of letters but I haven't had a chance to go through them yet.'

Wycliffe was intrigued by the dated envelope but all it held 'was a press cutting:

Professional Men's Annual Dinner

Nearly a hundred members of the West Cornwall Association of Professional Men, with their guests, attended their annual dinner at The Royal Hotel on Easter Saturday. Mr Ernest Bishop, retiring chairman, presided, and the guest speaker was Mr Gerald Bateman MP. The theme of Mr Bateman's address was the need to maintain high standards of integrity and independence in the face of growing domination of the professions by central and local government . . .

And three bags full! Why had Lemarque kept this cutting along with things which he obviously regarded as important?

Wycliffe said: 'I'll take this and give you a receipt.'

He left Fox to his work and crossed the landing to Francine's room. He stood in the small space between bed and chest of drawers, looking about him. Francine's school books were on two shelves above the chest of drawers. In addition to her textbooks there was a pile of exercise books, neatly arranged: Mathematics, English, Chemistry, French, Biology, History . . . Wycliffe flicked through some of them. The handwriting was more sophisticated than he would have expected from a girl of her age; the marks were average, the comments often acid. On the chest itself there was a swing mirror, a sketch pad and a box of watercolours, along with a few cosmetic jars and bottles. He tried the drawers, the top left-hand one, the only one fitted with a lock, was quite empty. The other top drawer held a jumble of underclothes and a box of cheap jewellery – beads, bracelets, rings and earrings. The other drawers were given over to clothes.

The empty drawer was where she had kept those things without which the little room became anonymous. Her letters, cards, snapshots, sketches, and all the other trifles she had thought worth keeping. She had taken them with her – or she had destroyed them.

Jane Lemarque had been murdered and her husband was missing, yet Wycliffe's thoughts still centred on their runaway daughter. He could not rid himself of the memory of the girl in the blue dress who, in that little grey church, had evoked the Madonna; remote, mysterious, and deeply moving in her sad presentiment: ' . . . and purple for Death.' Twenty minutes later she had been picked up by the youth in the red car.

'Francine is a very talented girl but she can be difficult . . . if she thought she had a real grievance . . . Young Paul will have his problems if their friendship ever comes to anything.' Virginia.

'It wouldn't surprise me if she had gone off with some man, and I mean, man.' Caroline.

Then there was the story of Francine and her mother's watch.

The Lizzie Borden fantasy was bizarre but he felt in his bones that the runaway girl held the key to her mother's murder.

He returned his attention to the rest of the room. No desk, no table, not even a chair. Probably she had done her homework sitting up in bed, scribbling away with a ball-point while pop music kept the silence at bay. Her radio was on the floor within reach of her hand. The bed was a divan with a narrow gap underneath to accommodate the castors. He knelt down, felt underneath, and came out with a little paper-covered notebook and a ball-point pen. One up on Curtis! But no real score. Most of the pages had been torn from the notebook and the remaining five or six had been used for notes on biology. There were headings: Eye Colour, Hair Colour, Skin Pigmentation, Blood . . . with brief notes under each and, in one case, a diagram.

Heredity. Wycliffe had only vague notions on the subject, derived from elementary lessons at school on the breeding prospects of peas and little red-eyed flies. He put the notebook back where he had found it.

Curtis was right, the girl had made sure that nobody would learn much from her room. In fact, he could get no feeling anywhere in the house that it had been really lived in, only that people had camped out there.

A voice at the bottom of the stairs said: 'Mr Wycliffe! Mr Kersey is here, sir.'

The return of the prodigal. Warmth on both sides.

'Good to be back, sir! Like old times.' The difference being that Kersey was now an inspector instead of a sergeant. 'The van is parked by the church and D.C. Dixon is duty officer, so we are in business.'

Now they had a base linked in to the police communication network as well as the public telephone service.

85

The two men had always worked well together though physically and temperamentally they were very different. Wycliffe, spare, thin-featured, thin-lipped, and sandy-haired, nick-named The Monk. Kersey, stocky of build, full of face, very dark, with features which looked as though they had been roughly moulded out of plasticene and carelessly stuck on. By the same token, Wycliffe was taciturn and inclined to be prudish in speech and attitude, while Kersey often thought aloud and was not averse to what he called basic English. Together, they drove back to the village.

At Mynhager the family would be sitting down to their Christmas meal: turkey with all the trimmings, pudding with clotted cream, (cholesterol by the spoonful), plenty of wine; crackers to pull, and flushed faces afterwards. In the village people were beginning to take an interest in what was going on. Although it was quite dark people were standing in their doorways, others had the curtains drawn back in their front-rooms. Not that there was much to see.

The van was parked near the wall of the churchyard and opposite the village's two shops, now closed for the holiday. Inside the van the radio crackled in staccato outbursts: 'Alpha one-four to Alpha Victor. I am attending an R.T.A. at . . .' 'Alpha Victor to Alpha three. A householder at Nance Cottage, Sancreed, reports an intruder in her garden . . .'

A disturbance by youths on motorcycles in a car-park, a Ford Escort saloon apparently abandoned . . . The bread and butter of police work.

D.C. Dixon had a mug of tea at his elbow, already somebody was pecking away at a typewriter in the next cubicle, the van was an old model and had the authentic smell of a nick. The blinds were down and there was an atmosphere of stuffy cosiness; some wag had suspended a sprig of mistletoe from one of the roof struts. Home from home.

Dixon had news: 'Message from D.S. Curtis, sir. He's

on his way here with Timothy Pellowe. He said you would understand.'

So Pellowe and his red car had, presumably, been picked up on their doorstep. And Francine?

While they were waiting Wycliffe put Kersey in the picture.

Timothy Pellowe was lean and lank and pale, a weed grown in poor soil and a bad light. At nineteen he retained an adolescent spottiness, and the inability to cope with his legs and arms. He sprawled over a chair and on to the small table which separated him from Wycliffe. They were in the interview cubicle of the van; Kersey sat by the door, just out of the boy's line of sight.

'I was staying with a friend in Exeter; we had a party last night and it was lunch time before I was up. Then, on the news, I heard about Mrs Lemarque. They said the police wanted to contact her husband and daughter; then they said the police wanted to interview the driver of a red Triumph and they gave my number . . . ' His voice faltered. 'It was as if they thought . . . ' Words failed him.

'You were asked to go to the nearest police station; why didn't you?'

The muscles round his right eye twitched in a nervous tic. 'I was scared; I mean, once the police get hold of you . . .' He realized that he was not being diplomatic and dried up.

'So what did you do?'

'I drove home and told father; he said I should talk to Mr Curtis and explain to him.'

'Now Mr Curtis has brought you here, so you can explain to me. Where is Francine?'

The pale blue eyes sought Wycliffe's in pathetic appeal. 'I don't know – honest to God I don't. I—'

'When did you last see her?'

'The night before last when I dropped her off outside Exeter railway station; she said she was catching a train and that the lift would save her a good chunk of the fare.'

'What time was it?'

He frowned: 'I picked her up just down the road here at a bit before half-nine, so it must've been about half-eleven when I dropped her.' His manner became petulant, as with a child coming near to tears. 'Like I said, I just gave her a lift . . . I haven't done anything!'

'Obviously you picked her up by arrangment; when was the arrangment made?'

'She rang me up that morning. She knew I was going to Exeter for Christmas and that I was driving up that evening. She asked me to pick her up in the village between a quarter and half after nine. It just meant going a bit later than I intended to; no bother.'

Pellowe turned his uneasy gaze on Kersey who looked about as reassuring as a lion working up an appetite for his next Christian.

Wycliffe persisted: 'Did she say why she wanted the lift – where she was going?'

'She said she was going to spend Christmas with relatives, that was all. Fran never says much, I mean, she never really tells you anything.'

'Did you know that her parents had no idea that she was going away?'

'Of course I didn't! How could I? She said she was going to stay with relatives.'

'How did you meet her?'

'At a disco in St Ives. She goes there most Friday nights and she would let me take her home.' Naive in his humility.

'And after school? You picked her up from school sometimes?'

Pellowe nodded. 'A couple of times.'

Kersey said: 'Did you have it off with her?'

The boy jumped. 'By God! She's not that sort!'

'No? What sort is she, then?'

He hesitated. 'It's hard to say. I mean, I don't think any other girl could get away with it.'

'With what?'

He searched for words. 'Well, you have to make all the running; she never sort of meets you half-way, but she can still take her pick.'

'And she picked you?'

The boy was not stupid; he saw the point. 'Yes, well, I never try anything on, I mean nothing much. I know she won't stand for it.' He grinned for the first time. 'Only last week a bloke got a bit randy with her; she poured a whole glass of iced coke down his jeans and said: "Better if chilled before serving".'

'According to you she doesn't say a lot, but you must have been with her for a couple of hours in the car on your way to Exeter. What did you talk about?'

He shook his head. 'We didn't. When I tried she just said, "Oh, shut up, Timmy! I'm trying to think." Of course it isn't always like that; she can be very sort of friendly and nice.'

More questions, but no more revealing answers. In the end Wycliffe left him with a D.C. to make his statement.

Kersey said: 'A made-to-measure Wet!'

Wycliffe was thoughtful. 'I wonder if she's with her father.'

'It's a possibility.'

The investigation was getting off the ground. Four men, working in pairs, had started house-to-house enquiries. Wycliffe had small hope of picking up any direct leads and the questions were largely camouflage for gossip which he hoped might be a worthwhile harvest.

Sergeant Fox and his team were still at the cottage.

End of a day. Christmas Day.

CHAPTER SIX

Wycliffe opened his eyes and wondered where he was. Light from a street lamp filtered through orange curtains drawn over a small square window. There was a sloping ceiling with beams exposed. Then he remembered: he was staying at The Tributers, and Kersey was in the next room. The rest of the headquarters people were at a boarding house in St Ives. He switched on the bedside lamp to look at his watch: five minutes past seven. Boxing Day. A funny Christmas!

He listened; the silence seemed absolute, then he began to hear the ticking of the grandfather clock at the bottom of the stairs. He felt relaxed. An accommodating landlady had taken them in on Christmas night and fed them on cold turkey with a salad. She had promised them breakfast at eight, earlier than they could reasonably expect over the holiday.

'Think nothing of it, my lovers! If you can find out who 'twas that put a bullet in that poor soul's head then you'll be doing us all a big favour. I can't say I exactly liked the little woman, nor him neither, but I wouldn' wish that on my worst enemy, an' tha's a fact!'

The Tributers had been in the hands of the Tregidgo (second g, soft) family since the early 1800s and Phyllis was first cousin as well as wife to the present owner. 'We've always tried to keep it in close family, sort of,' she said. ''Tis the best way.'

At ten minutes to eight he joined Kersey in the dining-room. Kersey looked like the morning after; dark people are rarely at their best in the morning. 'She asked me if we wanted the full treatment and I said we

90

did.' A delicious smell of frying bacon came from the kitchen next door. 'I don't know about you but I'm not allowed to have it at home; Joan says she wants me to live long enough to draw my pension and that means two rounds of wholemeal toast with margarine scrape, or a bowl of some bloody cereal with bran in it, and black coffee. Sometimes I wonder if it's worth it.'

Phyllis came in with heaped plates: bacon, egg, sausage and tomato. 'Now then! Get that inside of you an' you'll feel better. 'Tis a mucky ol' morning.' Phyllis, at fifty, was plump, clear-skinned and rosy-cheeked, low in polyunsaturates, high in cholesterol.

On the radio, the weather forecast: 'The mild weather over south-west England will continue. Winds will be light and variable and in the extreme south-west mist and fog now affecting coasts and hills will persist for most of the day.'

As the light strengthened they could see that the dining-room looked out on a small patch of garden but the boundary hedge remained insubstantial as a shadow. At intervals the foghorn on Pendeen Watch moaned piteously.

They listened to the eight o'clock News which, in deference to Christmas, tried to mitigate its intrinsic gloom. At the end there was a brief item on the Cornish murder, followed by: 'The police are anxious to contact the husband and daughter of the murdered woman, Alain and Francine Lemarque. Anyone with information which may help to trace them should telephone 0736 212121 or contact their nearest police station.'

At half-past nine, someone did. Wycliffe and Kersey were in the Incident Van. D.C. Potter was duty officer, a man not made to fit into cubicles so that he had difficulty in accommodating himself between desk and partition. He had a bottled gas heater going which made the air steamy instead of merely moist.

In the next cubicle Wycliffe and Kersey heard him take the call.

'Yes, Miss . . . That is correct. Can I have your name, please? . . . No, it isn't essential . . . Yes, I'll put you through to the officer in charge.' Potter being diplomatic for once.

Wycliffe picked up his telephone and switched on the desk amplifier. The girl's voice was harsh and brittle; her manner aggressive. Wycliffe imagined her, thin, angular, mousey-coloured hair, pinched nose, tiny mouth.

'Are you the man in charge?'

'Chief Superintendent Wycliffe.'

'They said on the radio you want to know where Francine Lemarque is. She's at Flat 4, 14, Burbage Street, Camden.'

'Thank you. Is she with her father?'

'I don't know anything about her father; I'm telling you about her. You got the address? 14, Burbage Street, Flat 4.' And she put the phone down.

Potter stood in the doorway. 'That was a pay-phone call, sir.'

Wycliffe said to Kersey. 'More than a bit of spite behind that but it didn't sound like a hoax. We'll check with the Met and get them to make contact. We want her here but if she doesn't want to come it will be difficult; I doubt if we have grounds for compulsion so it will have to be persuasion.'

'She must know about her mother.'

'I shall be surprised if she doesn't but that must be the Met's initial approach, to break the news. Boxing Day: no trains and no coaches. Potter! Find out if there is an afternoon or evening flight from Heathrow to St Mawgan, or even Plymouth. If there is, and the Met can get her on it . . . '

Kersey said, 'We'd better warn them in case her father is with her, we don't want him to slip through our fingers.'

Wycliffe agreed, but casually.

Across the square from the church there were two

shops, and one of them, Mulfra General Stores, was open, a phenomenon unknown in most places on Boxing Day. A constant trickle of customers kept the doorbell jangling. Kersey stood up. 'I want to slip over to the shop.' He had sufficient tact not to mention cigarettes.

Kersey's attempts to kick the habit were regular and only briefly sustained; this was an interregnum but he was resolved to try again in the New Year. Wycliffe watched him cross the square. No doubt the shop also sold pipe tobacco. He sucked the end of his ball-point and reflected that human existence was a long sad story of self-denial. Then he saw Marsden making for the shop, carrying a shopping bag, and ploughing along like an old Thames barge under full sail.

Kersey returned with a question: 'Did you see the chap who came into the shop after me?'

'A big fellow with dark curly hair?'

'Yes.'

'That's Marsden, the painter who found the body. His statement came in this morning. What about him?'

'I've seen him before somewhere.'

'He's not the sort you'd be likely to forget.'

Kersey brooded. 'It was a good while ago and he didn't have the trim on his upper lip, but I'm damned if I can remember when it was or in what connection.'

'You think you've come across him professionally?'

'I'm sure of it.'

'Then you'd better try to remember.'

'It's no good forcing it.' Kersey was thoughtful. 'What's he like, apart from his looks?'

'I think he could cut up rough if provoked. He's fond of women, very much in the plural. For what it's worth I'd say he's a good painter. He plays jazz music very loud . . . Oh, yes, and he's got a cat called Percy.' Kersey looked at his chief, puzzled. Even after years of working together there were still quirks of character which he could never understand. 'They took his prints yesterday

93

for elimination purposes so if you have any suspicion we can check with C.R.O.'

On Wycliffe's table little heaps of typescript had begun to grow and in yet another cubicle a D.C. was going full-hammer to maintain the supply. Wycliffe put on his spectacles. Franks had dictated a memo over the telephone, his preliminary report. No revelations. Jane Lemarque had died of 'injuries to her head and neck inflicted by a heavy calibre bullet which had entered in the region of the axis vertebra and pursued a complex course through the skull to exit anteriorly through the face, destroying a large area around the bridge of the nose, and affecting the eyes and the orbits on both sides. The trajectory suggests that the deceased might have been in a crouching position at the time the shot was fired. This would be consistent with her position when the body was found, between the bed and the dressing table.'

Regarding the time of death, Franks showed his usual caution: 'Death probably occurred at some time between four in the afternoon and eight in the evening of the 24th.'

'The poor woman was cornered and trying to shield herself by squeezing under the bed,' Wycliffe said. 'It looks more and more like cold-blooded murder.'

Kersey agreed. 'But cut out passion and you have to look for a rational motive.'

Wycliffe doodled on a scrap pad. 'We've got to know more about what went on in that house before and after Lemarque came out of jail.'

'The girl should be a help there.'

The girl — Francine, the Virgin in the blue gown. Once more Wycliffe recalled the deep impression she had made on him with her air of total detachment. Marsden, in his painting, had interpreted it as self absorption. Perhaps he was right. Anyway, what did it matter? Irritably, he pushed his doodle aside — a thing of triangles and squares. 'I think that we shall get from the girl only what she chooses to tell us, but I'm hoping for another angle from the chaps on house-to-house. The woman can't have lived in complete isolation while her husband was in jail, there must be someone who can claim to know her.'

Kersey was turning over a slim bundle of question-naires already completed in house-to-house enquiries. 'There's not a lot here. The locals seem generally anti-Lemarque but on no specific grounds. I get the impression that outsiders are simply unwelcome and if you happen to be one you have to keep running to stay where you are.' He flipped through the pages. 'There is something though: Two people say they saw Lemarque's van being driven through the village on Saturday afternoon – Christmas Eve. It was travelling in the direction of Pendeen. One of them says Lemarque was driving.'

'At least that ties up with what Marsden told us.' Wycliffe sounded bored.

Kersey took the hint and stood up. 'I'll get on to the Met and ask them to check that address. We should have something from them during the morning.'

'One more thing: we need to know something about Lemarque. I want H.Q. to go to work on the story of the Lemarque/Bateman partnership. What were they up to? What went wrong? And what precisely landed Lemarque in jail? Anything which helps to put the man in focus.'

'I'll pass the word.'

Left alone, Wycliffe tried to take stock. Of the Lemarque family, Jane Lemarque had been murdered, and her husband and daughter were missing. He now had a line on the girl but none on her father. Passports for all three had been found in a drawer of the dressing table and among a few letters in a sideboard drawer downstairs, there was an address for Jane's sister in Bristol. She was being contacted through her local police. Fox had reported that most of the clothes in the main bedroom wardrobe belonged to Lemarque: three good suits, a couple of raincoats, and an overcoat, as well as a good range of casual clothes; relics of past prosperity. Impossible to say what he might have taken with him, but Fox's guess was, very little. Not, apparently, a planned exit.

Wycliffe was staring out of the window of his cubicle. A few yards away in a bay-window of one of the larger houses, a little old man in a tartan dressing gown was seated in some sort of wheelchair and he seemed to be returning Wycliffe's stare but his old eyes were probably too weak to focus at the distance. Behind him the light caught the shiny balls on a Christmas tree.

The scene-of-crime people had now finished at the cottage; some material had gone to the forensic laboratories for the boffins to brood over, including the fatal bullet and a nine-millimetre cartridge case, but the fingerprint and photographic evidence was at headquarters for processing. No joy yet, and forensic eggs are sometimes addled before they have the chance to hatch.

Which left the house-to-house enquiries, and they had produced little so far. But he had not yet tackled the most promising of the houses.

He could hear Kersey's voice in the next cubicle, talking to somebody at the Met. Time to stir himself. *Courage mon brave!* He said to Potter: 'I shall be at Mynhager.'

He got into his car and drove past the pub along the track to Mynhager and the sea. Mist enveloped the moors and rolled down the slopes, dissolving and condensing by turns, so that the near landscape was at one moment clearly seen and at the next, entirely hidden. He felt blinkered, and lowered the car window in the hope of better vision. Although there was no breath of wind a sea swell, aftermath of the storm, continued to break along the shore with a booming sound which reverberated up the valley, through the fog.

He parked in the courtyard of Mynhager and went round the house to the front door. The terrace was drenched in spray from the last tide. Caroline answered his ring.

She seemed surprised and pleased to see him. 'Charles!' She looked behind her into the hall and lowered her voice. 'Come in.' Her manner was almost conspiratorial. 'In here! Ernest has gone out.' She led him into Ernest's little office and closed the door. 'I wanted to talk to you, Charles, but I didn't want to be seen going to your caravan thing by the church. Do sit down.'

Caroline in slacks and a woolly jumper. A different and diffident Caroline, uneasy, perhaps in search of reassurance. She looked pale, her eyes were puffy with tiredness and she had been drinking. 'I'm worried, Charles. I suppose I can talk to you? I mean, if what I tell you isn't directly relevant to . . . to Jane's death, it won't go any further, will it?'

'If it really isn't relevant, no.'

She was sitting in Ernest's swivel chair, swinging from side to side like a nervous child. 'Hugh Marsden was taken to the police station to make a statement, because he found her. At least I suppose that was the reason. You see, I can't find out anything; I mean, Hugh isn't on the phone, and as things are I daren't go there . . .' She paused, apparently in the hope of getting some encouragement, but Wycliffe merely looked at her, benevolently non-committal, and she went on: 'You must have guessed if you haven't already been told, that Gerald and I are not the ideal married couple. We keep going for Paul's sake and for appearances generally.' Another pause, then: 'He's my cousin, you know – mother's twin sister's child. He used to spend a lot of time here when mother was alive. I don't know why I married him – he was handy, I suppose.'

'Why are you telling me this?'

She wriggled in her chair, easing her slacks round her

thighs like a man. 'Because I've been having an affair with Marsden off and on for the past two years.'

'So?'

'My God! You don't make it easy! I'm trying to tell you that I know Hugh Marsden very well; he confides in me; we are good friends, quite apart from the other thing.' She was staring out of the window though there was nothing to see but the grubby net curtain and the mist beyond. 'There are no strings; I don't care a damn about his reputation.'

'You mean that your relationship with him is different – special.'

She turned on him angrily then decided against aggression. 'All right, damn you! – yes. As a matter of fact he's getting rid of the girl who lives with him; she's never been much more than a housekeeper anyway.'

Wycliffe wondered where all this was leading but he asked no questions.

She came out with it abruptly: 'Is Hugh under suspicion?'

'He wasn't detained after making his statement.'

She made a derogatory gesture. 'That's a big help!' She hesitated, then went on: 'Of course I know he's had other women, everybody knows it; what they don't know is that one of those women was Jane Lemarque – just the once, while Alain was in jail.'

'So?'

A look of intense exasperation. 'Jane, being the fool she is – was, might have told Alain when he came out.'

Wycliffe was beginning to see light through the fog. 'Presumably Marsden told you.'

'Only because I made him tell me about his other women.'

'Are you suggesting that the incident between Jane Lemarque and Marsden gave her husband a motive for murdering her?'

She looked at him quickly and away again. 'I don't know about that. I've told you this because I'm pretty

98

sure Hugh won't. You mightn't think so but he has scruples about things and they could land him in trouble.'

'I see. You think that when we find Lemarque all this could come out anyway.'

No answer. He imagined that as far as Caroline was concerned their *tête à tête* was now over but she had more to say: 'There's something else. I shouldn't have said what I did about Francine yesterday. About her going off with a man and the idea that she might . . . Well, what Aunt Stella said was obvious nonsense and I shouldn't have encouraged her.'

'You've seen her portrait?'

She had been staring out of the window and she turned on him, ready to spit fire, but once more she changed her mind and managed a sheepish grin instead. 'You're a clever bastard in some ways. I suppose when it comes down to it I'm like any other woman where a man is concerned, I can cope with competition from my own age group but if it comes to teenagers . . . '

Wycliffe said: 'In this case I don't think it has.'

She looked at him, surprised. 'No? Well, thanks for that anyway.' She got up. 'I suppose you came to see Ernest but, as I told you, he's out. He should be back in time for lunch.'

Wycliffe remained seated. 'I came to talk to your husband.'

She seemed surprised. 'Gerald? Gerald has gone to lunch with one of his party cronies in Penzance. God knows when he'll be back. Late this afternoon, probably.'

'Is Paul about?'

'Paul? He's gone out walking with his uncle.' She saw Wycliffe glance out of the window at the fog. 'I know; they're both mad.'

'Perhaps you will tell Paul that we have some news of Francine. An anonymous telephone caller said that she was staying at an address in Camden. That was all; but we are arranging for someone to go to that address and, if she is there, they will try to persuade her to come home.'

A mocking grin; something of the old Caroline. 'My, my! There is, after all, someone in this house who's managed to kindle a spark. Anyway, I'll tell him!'

Wycliffe got up to go. 'Just two more questions: How long has Marsden lived down here?'

'About four years, perhaps a bit more.'

'Have you any idea where he came from?'

'Why don't you ask him?' Aggressive.

'Perhaps I will. I wonder if I am allowed to ask if he rents or owns the cottage?'

She relented. 'Sorry! People have it in for Hugh just because he doesn't fit into any of their mean little pigeon holes. Before he came here he lived in London – Bayswater, I think. The cottage belongs to us. Believe it or not there is a Bishop Estates Limited in which we all have shares. It's some sort of tax wangle, I think. When my great-great-grandfather built the place he bought the whole valley and the farms on both sides.'

'Thank you.'

'You said there were two questions.'

'So I did! I wonder if you remember whether the Lemarques were down here for Easter '79?'

She frowned. 'I can't remember '79 especially but they never missed being here for Easter. Why?'

'Just routine.'

Poor Caroline! A real home-loving Cornish girl but unable to do without sex and preferably sex without a husband cluttering up the place.

As she was seeing him off in the hall, Joseph came down the stairs. 'Wycliffe!' The old man descended the remaining three or four steps. 'No news of Lemarque?'

'Not so far.'

'And Francine?'

'It seems she's staying at a flat in Camden; we've had an anonymous call and we're following it up.'

Joseph laughed. 'She'll give you a run for your

100

money, that one! She's one of the new breed, Wycliffe. The future, if there is one, belongs to the women. Do you realize that? They're flexing their muscles, testing their strength; come the sexual revolution, Francine and her kind will be the brains behind it. Have you heard the latest R.C. joke? At the next Vatican conference bishops will bring their wives. At the one after that the Pope will bring her husband. Thank God I shall be dead by then! Anyway, don't let me detain you; I'm off for my walk.'

'Not in this fog, father!'

Joseph looked at his daughter. 'Your time is not yet, my child. A man can still make some decisions for himself.'

CHAPTER SEVEN

Without much conviction Wycliffe supposed that he must be making progress. Seemingly unrelated events were falling into an intelligible pattern and what more could he ask? Lemarque, having been home for a matter of weeks, learns from his wife that she has been to bed with the painter. Surely more than enough to raise the tension in the Lemarque household. Francine, caught in the middle, decides to get out, presumably until the worst is over. Then, on Christmas Eve night, with matters made worse by Francine running away, Lemarque, in a blazing row, loses all control and shoots his wife. Exit Lemarque.

Tidy. Tidy and simple. Most homicides turn out that way when you are lucky enough to pick up the right lead. Now they were on the track of the girl and the next step was to find Lemarque and charge him.

In his mind's eye Wycliffe saw the little man: the solemn features of a clown, the long-limbed, agile frame of a monkey. He recalled Lemarque sitting in the dismal living-room of the cottage, trying to play second fiddle to his wife who refused to play at all. A killer? Well, there must be a great deal more to him than appeared that morning. He had helped to build a very successful business and he had shown sufficient resolution to stay with it against the odds. Foolish, perhaps, but neither stupid nor weak.

He parked his car by the police van and went in. The clock over Potter's table showed twenty minutes to twelve. The lights were on in the van, fighting the gloom of the morning.

Potter said: 'A nice mug of coffee? Keep the fog out.'

But Wycliffe was irritable. 'You missed your calling, Potter: a white coat and a coffee bar in Cornwall Street. Is Mr Kersey in?'

'Next door, sir.'

Kersey was waiting for him. 'The Met really got their skates on. I had their report a few minutes ago. The Burbage Street flat is occupied by three girls and a boy, students at the Poly. Oh, to be eighteen again! In my day you had to make do with the shop doorway furthest from the street lamp. But I'll bet they've got that poor stupe doing the cooking and the washing-up. Anyway, two of the girls went home to mummy for the Christmas hols, leaving a cosy *ménage à deux* until Francine turned up. Unexpected, according to Cuthbert. Believe it or not, that's his name. It seems she had a school-kid thing going with him when they both lived in Richmond, ring-a-roses in the park, and they've kept in touch. He's a couple of years older, of course, and is a bit coy about it now. One gathers his flatmate wasn't enthusiastic about Francine's arrival but they let her stay.'

'How did she explain, turning up there like that?'

'The universal password: getting away from the family.'

'At some stage they must have heard about the shooting.'

'Not until this morning. It seems that the young miss who phoned us got up early. That means any time up to eleven, and she heard our bit on the radio. Instead of telling the others she went out to a public box and phoned us. When she got back she woke her boyfriend and they decided to confront Francine.'

'Well?'

'They couldn't. The bird had flown.'

'When?'

'They reckon she must have gone during the night or early morning. She had a radio in her room and she probably heard the news before they did.'

103

'So we are back to square one.'

'Except that we know she isn't with papa.'

'Wasn't with papa, you mean.' Wycliffe was not pleased; he had counted on making contact with the girl, even if it had to be at second-hand.

Kersey said: 'She may be trying to get home but with no public transport she's likely to have problems.'

'Anything else?'

'The Bristol aunt telephoned – Jane Lemarque's sister, a Mrs Devlin; she's on her way down by car. Sounds prosperous and capable.'

'I'm glad somebody is.'

Kersey said: 'It's still Christmas. What about a drink before lunch? Phyllis told me she serves a genuine home-brew in the bar. They get it from a brother in Helston or some place.'

'Nobody cares a damn! It's Christmas. No newspapers, no trains, no buses, no mail; the television squeezing out strawberry mousse with whipped cream topping. This week has been cancelled; the whole country is in a coma.'

Kersey grinned, mellowed by the Tregidgo home-brew: 'Scrooge!'

But Wycliffe was not to be diverted. 'At any other time Lemarque's van would have been spotted and we should be getting reports of him having been seen anywhere and everywhere between the Isle of Mull and Oxford Street.'

'Don't tell me you miss our friends of the press?'

'Perverted as it may be, I do.'

It was half-past two, they were back in the Incident Van; Dixon had replaced Potter on the desk. There was a tap at the door and D.C. Curnow came in, one of the house-to-house team. A young giant, he had to stoop to clear the lintel.

'I've just come from 6, Wesley Terrace, sir, a Mrs Evadne Penrose, a widow. She says she was a close friend of the dead woman and that they were in touch on Christmas Eve, the day of the murder.'

'And she's just remembered it?'

'No, sir. She spent Christmas with her mother in Padstow and didn't hear about the murder until she got back this morning.'

'Well?'

'She won't talk to me; it has to be "the officer in charge" and she won't come here, though God knows why not.'

'What's she like?'

An amused grin. 'Very forthright and she talks a lot about astrology.'

'Kinky?'

'I wouldn't say kinky, sir, eccentric.' D.C. Curnow had a nice feeling for words. 'I think she's probably reliable.'

Wesley Terrace was a row of sizeable cottages near the Mechanics' Institute and number six was double-fronted. The front door was provided with a cast-iron knocker in the shape of a lion's head. Wycliffe knocked and the door was answered by a small, thin woman with sharp features and frizzy, greying hair cut short.

'Mrs Penrose?'

'Evadne Penrose. You must be the chief superintend-ent.' Almost an accusation.

Wycliffe was shown into an over-furnished little room which reminded him of the parlour of the farmhouse in which he had been born. There was a three-piece suite, an upright piano, a chiffonier, a fireplace with brass fire-irons, and framed coloured prints on the walls.

'I'm sorry to get you here but when I have something to say I believe in saying it to the man in charge but I didn't fancy going along to that hut on wheels in the square.' Her brown eyes darted fierce glances, like a firecracker giving off sparks, and her bony little paw gripped like a pincers. 'Do sit down.'

'You knew Mrs Lemarque?'

A vigorous nod. 'I was Jane's friend, perhaps her only

friend. After that terrible business with Alain going to prison I could see that she needed someone. Apart from anything else there was the dramatic change in their circumstances. She lost everything! Of course, the people round here are terribly clannish; they've no room for outsiders, and they tolerate me only because my husband was one of them . . . You don't mind if I smoke?' She brought out a cigarette pack from the pocket of her woollen frock, lit one and inhaled like a deprived addict.

Wycliffe made a bid for the initiative. 'We need to know more about Mrs Lemarque, about the family and their connections. As a friend, you may be able to help if you are ready to be quite frank.'

She had perched herself on the arm of the settee. 'But that's why I've asked you to come here, so that I can be frank! That's why I'm talking to you instead of to your young men who are making the rounds like Kleeneeze salesmen.'

Wycliffe tried again. 'You became friendly with Jane Lemarque after her husband went to prison?'

'I knew her long before that; they were down here quite a lot, either staying with the Bishops or at their cottage, but it was only after the calamity that I really got to know Jane. I made a point of it, because I could see that she was a woman at the end of her tether, and when I see something that needs doing, I do it.' A pause for this to sink in. 'I'm a Sagittarian, you know. Poor Jane was a Piscean; emotionally dependent, incapable of any decisive action. I spotted her at once, I wonder if you've noticed that Pisceans can sometimes be recognized by their slightly protruding eyes and vacant expressions?

'No wonder there was stress in their marriage. Alain is an Arien.' Evadne looked around for an ashtray.

Wycliffe said: 'So the Lemarque marriage was not a success?'

Evadne snorted irritably. 'My dear man! I've just told you it was a disaster! They were incompatibles. Alain is

106

vigorous, aggressive, demanding, while Jane was merely passive. I can assure you that Ariens expect more from a woman than passivity; I was married to one. Aries is the sign of the Ram.'

Wycliffe felt a pang of sorrow for the late Mr Penrose who, Arien or not, must have lived out his married life under a constant threat of being eaten.

'I understand that Lemarque was fond of his wife.'

'In the same way as you might be fond of a cat. All is well as long as the cat purrs, rubs round your legs, and jumps on to your lap. Alain's fondness demanded continuous recognition, a constant response, but Pisceans are incapable of any sort of constancy or, indeed, of any deep emotion. And when they find themselves in double harness with an Arien . . . ' She left the prospect to his imagination.

'The point is that after Alain came out of prison they found it even more difficult to live together.' She lowered her voice. 'Neither of them was the sort to clear the air with a row, so they each suffered in their own way and in silence.' Through the haze of tobacco smoke she fixed Wycliffe with an unblinking stare, and spoke slowly, emphasizing her words: 'Jane was afraid that Alain would commit suicide. I told her there was no risk of that with an Arien but she was convinced that she had let him down so badly that he would kill himself. Apparently he had a gun.'

'He had a gun?' Wycliffe did his best not to seem unduly interested.

'So she said; it seems he got it when they were living in Richmond and had all sorts of valuable antiques and pictures in the house.'

'You were in touch with Jane on the day she died?'

'Indeed I was. She telephoned; she often did when she was depressed and alone.'

'At what time did you speak to her?'

'At half-past four.'

'You are sure of that?'

'Quite sure. I was on the point of leaving to spend Christmas with my mother and sister when the phone rang. I said to myself: "Half-past four! I'm late already!" Of course it was Jane. The usual thing: she was depressed and she was sure that Alain was going to kill himself and that if he did it would be her fault. She said that he had gone out soon after lunch and that she was alone when the policeman came about Francine. She'd just been to the drawer of the dressing table where he kept his gun, the drawer was locked but she found a key that fitted, and there was no gun there; it had gone.' Evadne sighed. 'I didn't think Alain was likely to kill himself so I didn't take it very seriously. Of course, I wish I had now. But I did ask her how long it was since she had last seen the gun and she couldn't remember. When it came to the point, she wasn't even sure if she'd seen it since they left Richmond.'

For the first time she looked at Wycliffe with a certain diffidence. 'I suppose he shot her? I don't think that possibility had ever occurred to her, or me . . . '

Wycliffe went off at a tangent: 'I suppose it was the strain between her parents that induced Francine to go away?'

'Of course! Why else would she walk out like that? I admit that she's a difficult girl and sometimes I've felt like giving her a good slap but she's had a hard time in many ways and, of course, she's a Scorpio. You know what that means.'

Wycliffe didn't and didn't want to. He got up from his chair. 'You've been very helpful, Mrs Penrose. I'll send someone along to take your formal statement.'

She came with him to the door and watched while he walked along the street towards the van.

Kersey said: 'Any joy, sir?'

'Lemarque had a gun, at least he had when he was living in Richmond, and Jane Lemarque was speaking to our widow on the telephone at four-thirty on Christmas Eve afternoon.'

'Is the woman sure?'

'There is nothing of which Evadne Penrose is not sure including, as far as I could tell, that Lemarque shot his wife because she didn't purr when she was stroked. But to be fair, I think she's probably reliable in matters of fact.'

A girl's voice in the next cubicle, talking to Dixon. A tap on the door and Dixon came in. 'Francine Lemarque, sir.'

She stood in the doorway. She wore jeans and an anorak, both darkened by rain and obviously soaked through. Her dripping hair hung round her shoulders in rat's tails and her face was wet. She looked pale and very tired.

For a long moment Wycliffe just stared at her; he found it hard to accept that this was the girl he had last seen as the Virgin in the blue gown.

'Are you the man in charge?'

'Chief Superintendent Wycliffe.' Absurdly, he felt uncomfortable under the girl's steady gaze.

'I remember you were staying with the Bishops.' She spoke as though recalling something which had happened a long time ago.

Wycliffe, recovering his poise, said: 'How did you get here? You were in London last night.'

'I hitched. I was lucky; I did it in two hops as far as Truro. Last night I heard on the radio what had happened to my mother. They said on the radio that she was shot; is that true?'

'I'm afraid so.'

'And you think he did it?'

'We don't know who did it; we are trying to find out. Naturally we want to speak to your father but so far we haven't been able to find him.'

He was puzzled by her manner; she was certainly distressed, but her strongest emotion was incredulity. 'Don't you think you should get into some dry clothes? We can talk afterwards.'

109

She ignored him. 'Whoever did it must have had a gun.'

'Some time ago your mother told Mrs Penrose that your father had a gun which he got when you lived in Richmond.'

A momentary hesitation. 'Yes he did, a revolver. I remember him showing me how it worked and explaining how dangerous it was. He was always afraid of being burgled in those days. Are you saying that my mother was shot with that gun?'

'You said it was a revolver?'

'Yes, it had a cylinder thing where you put the bullets. I asked you if you thought my mother was shot with that gun?'

'She wasn't shot with a revolver.'

'Well, then!'

Wycliffe saw trouble ahead. In the Children and Young Persons' Act, 1969, a child is defined as someone under the age of fourteen; a young person is someone over the age of fourteen but under eighteen. So here was a young person. He was vague about the provisions of the Act affecting young persons in need of care but his heart sank at the thought of becoming the meat in the sandwich between Francine and some dragon of a social worker. Then he remembered and thanked God for the Bristol aunt.

'Your aunt is on her way down from Bristol; she should be here shortly.'

'Aunt Alice. I hardly know her.'

'When she comes we can make some arrangements: where you will stay and who will look after you. At the moment we don't know where your father is.'

'Why can't I stay at the house and look after myself?'

'That isn't possible, certainly not while the police investigation lasts.'

He had not said one word of sympathy nor offered any consolation. He felt as though he had been justifying himself. Absurd!

110

She stood for a moment as though making up her mind then she said: 'All right! But if I can't stay at the house I need to collect some things from my room.'

'I'll take you down there.'

He picked up her holdall and took her out to the car. She got in, fastened her seat belt and sat there perfectly composed.

The old mine track to the cottage was even more rutted and pot-holed than the one to Mynhager and the mists were going to outlive the day. It must have been a desperately sad and depressing homecoming, but she gave no sign.

'Have you had anything to eat?'

'I had a snack in Truro.'

'This must have been a very great shock to you.'

'Yes.'

He could think of nothing more to say.

He parked the car and they climbed the steps to the front door. He fumbled with the key in the lock and she said: 'Give it to me; there's a knack.' Then, inside: 'I want to collect a few things from my room.'

He almost told her to go ahead but thought better of it. He did not want her in her parents' room. 'I'll come up with you.'

He followed her up the stairs on to the landing. 'Why don't you go into the bathroom and dry yourself?'

'Where shall I be staying?'

'At The Tributers I suppose, until your aunt comes at least.'

She went into the bathroom, taking her bag with her, and ten minutes later, came out with her hair in a frizzy mass, wearing a dry pair of jeans and a woolly top. She spent some time in front of the little swing mirror in her bedroom, brushing her hair until it looked like a TV shampoo advertisement.

Although Wycliffe was watching her from the landing, she behaved exactly as though he wasn't there and he began to wonder why he was. It had been one of

111

those spot decisions which, if they turn out to be justified, are credited to a good copper's instinct.

She was going through her drawers, putting selected items into a travelling case which she brought from the landing cupboard. Finally she snapped the catches shut and straightened up. 'All right.'

He was on the landing and she was in the doorway with her hand on the electric light switch when she suddenly darted back into her room, stooped by the bed, and picked up the little red notebook he had found there. She looked at him with a hint of uncertainty in her manner.

'I might need this; something to write on.'

It was not; for the few pages which remained had already been used. Her uncertainty and the need she had felt to explain were so out of character that he reacted: 'Let me have it, please.'

She held out the little book without hesitation, he took it and slipped it into his pocket. 'You won't mind if I hold on to it for a day or two?'

She looked at him briefly, then turned away.

Alice Devlin was a year or two older than her sister but more animated, more responsive, and Wycliffe liked her on sight. Fortune had dealt with her more kindly. A sporty Sierra, current year; a suede coat, and underneath, a simple frock of some luscious Liberty fabric, definitely not by D.I.Y. out of Pattern Book.

'I knew nothing about it until the police came, I suppose we hadn't been listening to the news over Christmas. It was a shock.' She was clearly upset, grieved, but by no means prostrated. 'Jane and I had gone our separate ways but we had kept loosely in touch; you know the sort of thing: birthday and Christmas cards with the occasional note.'

Her attitude to Francine was warm and sympathetic without being cloying or intrusive. 'You're living through a nightmare, my dear, but it will pass. Try to feel that you are not alone. I don't want to press you but you can come back with me and stay until things are sorted out – or as long as you want. Philip and I would like that.'

They took rooms at The Tributers and Phyllis laid on an early meal. Wycliffe sat in on the meal without taking part and through it all Francine remained quietly aloof. Had she been persuaded out of her eternal jeans? At any rate she wore her woolly jumper with a tartan skirt. Her hair, dry now and shining in the light, was caught back with a clasp. She still looked very tired; her eyes dark, her face pale, her features a trifle pinched. When their meal was over Wycliffe said, 'Now we have to talk.'

Francine's response was immediate; she turned to her aunt. 'I want to talk to him alone.'

'Of course! That's natural.' Understanding woman.

In the Incident Van Wycliffe said: 'Before we start, why don't you ring Paul?'

'Paul? What for?'

'He's been worried about you.'

She hesitated, then: 'All right, if you like.'

Wycliffe said to Dixon: 'Get Paul Bateman on the telephone for me, please.'

When the boy was on the line Wycliffe handed over to Francine.

'Is that Paul? . . . It's me – Francine . . .' He could hear the boy's elated response but Francine remained casually matter-of-fact. ' . . . No, I'm with the police in their van thing . . . Yes, in the village . . . No, I shouldn't think so . . . I'm all right. My aunt is down . . . I can't talk any more now.' And she put down the telephone.

She and Wycliffe faced each other across the table in the little interview cubicle. Kersey sat by the door. It would have been politic to have a W.P.C. sitting in on the interview but the girl had committed no offence; on the contrary.

'You ran away – why?' Wycliffe's manner was sympathetic, not accusing.

113

'I didn't run away, I left home.'

'For good?'

'That depended.'

'On what?'

'On whether I could get a job and on what happened at home.'

'Getting a job was bound to take time; how did you intend to live meanwhile?'

'I had money. I've been working in the holidays and saving for a long time.'

'With the idea of leaving home?'

'Perhaps.'

'Why did you make up your mind to go?'

She smoothed her hair away from her eyes with a slow movement of her hand but said nothing.

'Weren't you happy at home?'

'Happy? No, I wasn't.'

'Were your parents unkind to you?'

'No.' She sounded mildly impatient. 'I can't explain; you wouldn't understand. It was like being smothered in cotton wool.'

'Over protective?'

'I told you you wouldn't understand.'

'And things got worse when your father came home?'

'Yes.'

'You blame your mother?'

'I don't blame anybody; mother had to make herself suffer.'

'I don't understand.'

'There's no reason why you should!' With tired indifference.

'As a policeman, I'm afraid there is. Why was the situation worse when your father came home?'

The atmosphere in the little cubicle was claustrophobic. An electric lamp in the low ceiling gave a yellow light which shone on the girl's hair and was reflected dimly off the scuffed and worn plastic surfaces of the walls and fittings. Outside it was quite dark and a blind was

114

drawn over the tiny window. The three of them seemed as isolated as if they had been in a space capsule; the only sound came from sporadic chatter on the radio in the adjoining cubicle.

Kersey said: 'You don't seem to realize, Francine, that we are trying to find out who killed your mother and why.'

She turned to face Kersey then back to Wycliffe. 'When there was just the two of us mother was always explaining how she had failed as a wife or failed me. If it wasn't that, it was how everyone despised her for being such a failure.' She had been looking down at the table top, now she raised her eyes to meet Wycliffe's. 'I think she really believed what she said but she didn't do anything about it. It was so hopeless!' Her voice softened and he thought that she might weep but the moment passed. 'And that Penrose woman with her nonsense about the stars didn't help. "My dear Jane, you are a Piscean! You can't change that!"' For an instant the indomitable Evadne was in the room with them.

Wycliffe persisted: 'But how did your father coming home make things worse?'

'Does it matter?'

'I think you should tell us.'

With a small helpless gesture, still with her eyes on Wycliffe, she said: 'While he was in prison mother let the painter come to the cottage.'

'What do you mean, she let him come to the cottage?'

'All right! She let him go to bed with her.'

'More than once?'

'Not as far as I know.' Indifferent.

'And your father found out?'

'She told him.'

'What happened?'

'Nothing happened.'

'Didn't your father become angry?'

'He was never angry, and that made mother worse. She wanted to be punished.'

115

Not a trace of emotion; she spoke of her mother, her father, and even of herself, as though none of them had any more significance than the characters in a novel. Once more Wycliffe was aware of the stillness which seemed to envelop this girl like an aura; never once did she fidget, and all her movements were deliberate and controlled. He reminded himself that she was just sixteen, a schoolgirl; he had seen her room with its posters of pop stars, and her school books; in six months time she should be taking her O-levels. She had lost her mother, and her father was missing in suspicious circumstances, yet she fended off any attempt at sympathy or understanding as a boxer parries a blow.

'Did you know about your mother and Marsden when you sat for your portrait with him?'

'She told me.' After a pause: 'Mother had to tell everything. When she couldn't get me to listen she would go and confess to the vicar.'

'The Marsden business didn't upset you?'

She looked at him blankly. 'What difference did it make?'

Was she truly indifferent? Or was she maintaining a profound reserve, refusing to allow him any insight into her mind or her emotions?

He tried another approach. 'You must have planned to go away at least a day or two before you left. Why didn't you leave a note?'

'I did.'

'Both your father and your mother said there was no note.'

'Perhaps they didn't want you to see what was in it.'

'Did you say in the note where you were going?'

'No.'

'What did you say? The kind of things you've told me now?'

'More or less.'

'Have you any idea where your father might be? With a relative, or a friend?'

116

'I've no idea.'

'Who do you think killed your mother?' Gently.

'I don't know. I've sometimes thought that she might take her own life; are you sure that she didn't?'

Wycliffe changed the subject. 'Your father had some idea of going back into business; do you know anything about that?'

'I've heard them talking; something about a tourist park on some waste ground where there used to be mine workings. He was expecting somebody to put up money for it.'

'Did your parents have many outside contacts? I mean, did people visit them, ring them up, or did they go out a lot?'

She shook her head. 'Only the Penrose woman came to our house and sometimes mother would ring her up.'

'And your father?'

'Nobody came to see him but he went out a lot with the van.'

'Did he get phone calls?'

'I think he made his phone calls when I wasn't there.'

'What makes you think so?'

'Because sometimes when I came in he would be on the phone to someone and he would ring off as soon as he could.'

'You realize that anything you can tell us may help to solve the mystery of your mother's death and your father's disappearance. Is there anything you can tell us that you overheard on the phone?'

'No, I didn't take much notice.'

'Did you gather what his phone conversations were about?'

'Oh, about money and business.'

'Were they friendly conversations?'

'Just ordinary. One day last week he seemed to be annoyed. He was almost shouting until he saw me.'

'What was he saying?'

She frowned. 'It didn't make much sense. Something

117

like: "Five years ago we were all in the same boat – or perhaps I should say the same car. Not any more! I no longer belong to the club." Then he turned round and saw me and I realized that I had put him off.'

What more could he ask? He walked back with her to The Tributers. The misty rain had stopped and the weather seemed to be clearing; stars twinkled through rifts in the clouds.

'Good night, Francine.'

'Good night.' Casual.

He was moved by her isolation. Rarely in the thousands of interviews he had conducted had he learned so little of the personality of the other party. Businessmen, lawyers, even the Mr Bigs of the crime world, all gave something of themselves away, but not this girl of sixteen. Although she had answered his questions, at no time had he been allowed a glimpse of her private world; he still had no idea of what she thought or felt, no clue to suggest what she might do. Talking to her was like playing chess with a computer, yet everything about her pointed to an intense emotional life behind the façade.

Kersey said: 'It adds up to Alain Lemarque. When a man murders his wife we look for the instant of passion but Lemarque wasn't that kind of man. The girl says he never got angry; what she means is he didn't show it. In other words, he's the type who's capable of nursing a sense of outrage, coming to a decision and carrying it out. Now we know he had a gun.'

'A revolver according to Francine.'

'Surely she was mistaken!'

'From her description, that seems unlikely. What did you make of her?'

Kersey, although he looked like Red Riding Hood's surrogate grandmother, had two lovely daughters and could be considered something of an authority. 'My guess would be that she's putting up a smoke screen, but why?'

Wycliffe had no answer for that. 'According to Evadne Penrose, Jane Lemarque thought her husband intended to kill himself and Francine seemed to believe that her mother might commit suicide. A suicide pact isn't out of the question, I suppose, though there's every sign that the woman was trying to escape being shot. We just don't know what's happened to Lemarque, whether he's alive or dead.'

They were having their evening meal, waited on by a village girl called Lorna; dark, freckled, and pretty. In the bar next door things were warming up, with the occasional shout and outbursts of laughter, punctuating the general level of chatter. They had spoken quietly with an eye on Lorna's comings and goings but she must have heard something. 'I saw Mr Lemarque's van out to Mennear Bal Saturday afternoon.'

Kersey said: 'That was Christmas Eve.'

'Right first time.'

'The day his wife was shot. You haven't said anything about this before; why not?'

'Well, I wasn't asked, was I? They came and talked to mum and dad but nobody said a word to me. In any case, as I heard it, she was shot in the evening in her own home, and this was in the afternoon between three and four.'

'Where is Mennear Bal?'

'Just a bit down the coast; it's where there used to be mine workings; now 'tis no more 'n a lot of old ruins and heaps of spoil. There's plenty of tracks though and his old van was going slow along the one out near the cliff. My Aunt Flo lives near the workings and she says she seen him down there once before since he was let out of prison. There's a rumour that he's after renting the ground from the mine company though like my dad says, God knows what he thinks he'll do with it.'

'Did you see Lemarque?'

'I didn't see anybody, just the van; I was a good way off. I recognized it because it's the only one around like that.'

119

'And this was definitely at three o'clock?'

She pouted. 'I can't say to the minute but I was home by half-past so it must have been close. I had to walk home and when I got there mother was just leaving to catch the half-past three bus.'

When they were dawdling over their coffee, Wycliffe said: 'It ties up nicely; Marsden saw Lemarque's van being driven towards the village at about three or a bit earlier; it was seen passing through the village in the direction of Pendeen; now we have it among the mine dumps where, apparently, he hoped to build his tourist park. Curtis arrived at the cottage at about 2.45 and Lemarque had already gone. It ties up, without meaning a damn thing as far as we are concerned because, like the girl said, Jane Lemarque wasn't shot at Mennear Bal but in her own home, at some time between four and eight.'

'It looks as though he drove home, shot his wife, then took off.'

Wycliffe was thoughtful. 'Perhaps I saw him leaving.' He told Kersey what he had seen on his way back to Mynhager from the painter's cottage. 'But I don't believe it.'

Lorna came back into the dining-room: 'You're wanted on the telephone.'

He took the call, standing in the passage between the cloakroom and the bar. It was Helen, calling from Kenya.

'I rang Mynhager and spoke to Ernest. He told me you were on a case and gave me another number . . . '

He explained, but contending with the racket from the bar probably meant that his explanation lacked lucidity.

'Anyway, there's nothing wrong with you?' Helen getting down to the things that mattered.

'No, I'm fine. And you?'

'It's nearly midnight here and we've been sitting out

120

of doors with iced drinks; me in a sleeveless dress. Wish you were here . . .'

'Me too.'

'If I bring home all I've bought, our place is going to look like the Museum of Mankind . . . Well dear, I mustn't run up their bill. Dave and Elsa send their love. Look after yourself, darling. Night . . .'

'I will; and you . . . Night.'

It took him a minute or two to bring himself back.

Jane Lemarque was shot 'with a nine-millimetre automatic, using a parabellum cartridge with a Neonite propellant. The markings on the bullet and the cartridge case strongly suggest that it was fired from a Walther P-38.' A dribble of technical jargon from the ballistics expert. Useful, if they had found a gun or the person who had used one. There was also a sheaf of scene-of-crime photographs with a report from Fox, necessary documentation when and if it came to preparing a case; not much use now. He had reported on prints found at the cottage: family only, except for Marsden's prints on the telephone and those of 'one of the investigating officers'. Fox had tact as well as zeal.

But it hardly looked as though the boffins would make a great contribution to the case.

Wycliffe and Kersey were in the Incident Van and the village had a different, more cheerful aspect this morning, a fine morning after yesterday's gloom: blue skies, sunshine, and not a breath of wind. An interlude between fronts, the weathermen said. Both the village shops were open today and the second one turned out to be a butcher's.

Already, a green bus had lumbered into the square, lingered for a minute or two, then moved off without picking up a single passenger. But, like Noah's olive leaf, it was a token from an awakening world outside. Kersey collected a selection of newspapers but the Cornish murder rated only a few lines on an inside page of one of them.

The Chief Constable telephoned: Bertram Oldroyd,

a good policeman and a sensitive man, keenly aware of the need to strike a balance between protection and repression. He had a horror of political manipulation. As he grew older in the professional tooth he devoted more of his time to public relations and left the general administration of the force to his departmental heads. He fended off interfering politicians and reserved his most scathing rebukes for those of his staff who lost their footing on the tightrope between Left and Right, Black and White, Pro and Anti.

'Nasty business, Charles! A domestic, I gather.'

'Probably.'

'The girl is safe and sound so that's something. I believe this chap Lemarque was in partnership with Bateman at one time. Any complications from that direction?'

'He seems content to be a spectator at the moment.'

'Good! But you'll need to watch him; he can be a pest.'

'I thought he was on our side.' Wycliffe being naughty.

But Oldroyd only laughed. 'Well, you know what they say: Who needs enemies while we've got friends like him? What about the media?'

'Sleeping off Christmas.'

'Let's hope it stays that way. Heard from Helen?'

'She telephoned last night: David and Elsa are doing her proud.'

'We had a card from her a couple of days before Christmas; give her our love when you're next in touch. But you should be out there, Charles! You take too much on your own shoulders instead of delegating. We're a team — remember?' The big chief chuckled. 'Wasn't it Kant's dove who thought he might fly better in a vacuum?'

The only Chief Constable in captivity to read philosophy.

Kersey was looking out of the window. 'You spoke too soon; we've got visitors: Ella with a cameraman in tow.'

Ella Bunt: freelance crime reporter, thirty-five, a redhead and a militant feminist. ('We're not equal we're better! I've proved it in bed and out.') Ella owed her husky voice to cigarettes and her complexion to whisky but she rarely missed out on a story and few editors could afford to ignore her. Wycliffe knew her of old and between them there was a love-hate relationship.

Kersey met her at the door. 'No pets! Leave him outside, Ella.'

The cameraman said: 'I'll be about.'

Ella sat opposite Wycliffe. 'Had a good Christmas with your lawyer friend? You won't mind if I smoke?'

'Make yourself at home, Ella.'

She blew smoke across the table. 'Awkward for you finding yourself a house guest with the principal suspects, but I gather you moved out. Sensible! Warm in here.' She stood up and slipped off a fleece-lined leather jacket which smelt of goat. 'It looks dicey for The Sheriff. I wouldn't be surprised if this started a whole lot of rumours. And him all set for office. I've been doing my homework on the Lemarque/Bateman set-up. It's a wonder he survived that and kept his seat; he may not be so lucky this time. Of course he must have friends. Lemarque probably felt he'd been left holding the shitty end and maybe he was intending to get his own back.'

Wycliffe said: 'Don't let me spoil things for you, Ella but it was Mrs Lemarque who was shot.'

'I know. Odd that. Something went wrong somewhere. So you've found the girl; what does she have to say?'

'Very little.'

'Can I talk to her?'

'It's not up to me; her aunt is down.'

'Where's her papa?'

'I was hoping you might help me to find him. I expect you've had the hand-outs about him and his van.'

'And that's all you've got on him?'

'Scout's honour.'

'No reported sightings?'

124

'Not one.'

'There you are then! It would make more sense than killing her, don't you think?'

'I try not to. Look, Ella, if you haven't got any questions I can answer, why not let us get on with it in our own bumbling fashion?'

'I want background.'

Wycliffe made a broad gesture. 'It's all out there. Take what you want.'

'Very funny! How about a couple of shots inside the Lemarque house?'

'Not a chance, but you can take all you want outside.'

'Thank you for nothing. What about the gun?'

'A .38 automatic.'

'Have you found it?'

'No.' Wycliffe stood up. 'You want the human interest angle, Ella. Go and talk to Evadne Penrose, 6, Wesley Terrace, but don't say I sent you. Friend of the dead woman, astrologer extraordinaire, and probably glad of somebody to talk to.'

'Are you fobbing me off?'

'I wouldn't dare.'

She got up and struggled into her jacket. 'I hope not. Anyway, I'll be around for a bit.'

When she had gone Wycliffe said: 'Ella's nobody's fool but she and Evadne deserve each other, don't you think?'

Among other memoranda that morning there was one from C.R.O. in response to Kersey's enquiry about Marsden. Their reply was succinct: 'This subject has no criminal record.'

Kersey stared at the memo. 'I know I've come across that great baboon somewhere, in a nick and on the wrong side of the counter, but I'm damned if I can remember—' He broke off in a triumphant *eureka* moment of recall: 'I've got it! I was a wooden top in Paddington on a six-month stint as part of an exchange programme; finding out about the other half. Marsden was nicked by the art forgery boys. I wasn't on the case but a mate of mine in C.I.D. was roped in to help with the leg work and it opened his eyes to what goes on in the art racket.'

'Did it come to court?'

'I can't remember; I may not have heard because it was towards the end of my time. He can't have been convicted otherwise he'd have form.'

Wycliffe was putting on his overcoat. 'Follow it up I'm going prospecting.'

'Around Mennear Bal; I thought you might.'

Wycliffe drove out of the village in the direction of Pendeen. Beyond the Mechanics' Institute the cottages petered out, and the road ran between dry-stone hedges with an occasional dwarf hawthorn, sculptured like a fox's brush by the salt winds. After half-a-mile the hedge on the right gave way to an open space with a few cottages and ramshackle bungalows scattered at random among patches of rough grass. Several tracks led off in the general direction of the sea. He pulled off the road and got out. Three or four old bangers were dotted about, parked or dumped, and a stocky young man with curly black hair was working on one of them. He did not look up though Wycliffe came to stand within a couple of feet of him. The genuine Cornish article, unadulterated by foreign genes. He and his kind were already established in the county when the upstart Celts arrived and ever since they've been plagued by strangers.

'Good morning! Is this Mennear Bal?'

'Used to be.' Still without looking up.

'Which of these tracks leads to the cliff?'

'They all do.'

'Can I drive out there?'

'Tha's up to you; whether yer bothered about yer suspension.'

Wycliffe was and decided to walk; he chose the first of the tracks he came to. The ground was flat (an elevated plain of marine denudation, geologists said) and dotted with ruined buildings, heaps of rubble, and the occasional inhabited cottage. Between St Ives and Cape Cornwall copper and tin mines were once strung out along the coast like beads on a string, now only one is working; the others are in ruins, or have disappeared altogether or, like the quoits, graves, standing stones, and courtyard houses of prehistory, are being preserved because of their archaeological interest.

Mennear Bal was a ruin, rather a collection of ruins; a chimney stack or two, crumbling engine houses, roofless sheds, and intimations of what once had been a maze of arsenic flues. In the sunshine and the silence it was hard to imagine scores of bal maidens and buddle boys thronging the site, smashing ore, feeding the stamps, and doing homage to their employer for fivepence a day. Even harder to imagine bands of happy campers paying their dues to Bateman and Lemarque. Wycliffe had heard the expression, 'cheerful as a knacked bal', now he knew what it meant.

But a quarter-of-a-mile ahead the sea sparkled under the sun, an enduring backdrop. Wycliffe's track joined others and eventually he was walking along a broad path, parallel with the sea; on his left the grass curved smoothly and swiftly away to the cliff edge and a drop of more feet than he cared to think about. At a short distance off-shore a St Ives boat was cruising, perhaps her first chance to put out following the storm and the fog. Far out a container ship forged her way up-channel.

The track, made up of coarse mineral waste from the spoil heaps, was peppered with pot-holes and there were broad puddles, but scarcely any mud. He had hoped to find traces of Lemarque's van but he was disappointed. The man had probably stopped somewhere along the track to brood like Moses on the promised land; though, again like Moses, he would have needed all his entrepreneurial optimism to see milk and honey in the prospect. Which did not mean that he would be in a mood to go home and shoot his wife.

Wycliffe continued walking until he was leaving the mine workings behind. At this point, just before the track narrowed to a footpath, he noticed furrows in the grass bordering the track on the sea side, and the furrows were of a kind that might have been made by the wheels of a car or van. The slope to the cliff edge was steep, too steep and slippery for a man to risk climbing down, and the furrows were cut into the mounded grass where it met the path; he could distinguish three of them clearly with the hint of a fourth. Once over that mound nothing could have stopped any vehicle hurtling down.

As he examined the surface of the track he could see that the ballast had been disturbed by a swirling movement of the kind made by skidding back wheels. He worked back along the way he had come for about two hundred yards, examining the ground carefully as he went, and found what he had missed before: two wheel-ruts where the back wheels of the vehicle had dug in as a consequence of rapid acceleration. The story seemed to tell itself. Someone in a vehicle which was either stationary or moving very slowly, suddenly accelerated, steered for the end of the track where it narrowed, swerved off down the grassy slope and over the cliff.

An accident? An improbable one.

Was it Lemarque's van which had left those tell-tale signs? More than likely. It would explain why the van had not been spotted, or Lemarque either. But he had to bear in mind the possibility that one of the inhabitants of Mennear Bal had finally tired of his vintage jalopy and hoisted it over the cliff. The authorities might frown on such practices but there was a maverick strain in these people who shared their ancestry with Bishop Trelawny.

He looked around for any position where he might

128

get a view of the cliff face but there was none, then he spotted a place where the grassy slope to the cliff edge looked less steep and less slippery, where the grass grew in hummocks which offered some sort of foothold. He stepped gingerly off the track, wedging his foot against one of the hummocks; it felt precarious and immediately the edge seemed much nearer and the sea a very long way down. He decided to sacrifice dignity to relative stability and got down on all fours. Working backwards, groping with his feet, and clutching at the mounds of grass with his hands, he moved crabwise down the slope feeling like a fly on the wall.

'Police Chief Killed in Fall from Cliff. Foul Play Not Excluded', nor idiocy neither. He was as near the edge as he dared go; now he had to wriggle round so that he could look over. The grass was short near the edge where soil was almost non-existent and his knees suffered painful encounters with protruding rocks, but he managed it. He peered over the edge and received a dizzy impression of dark blue water and a lacy edge of foam; he was never at ease when his feet were higher than his head but he collected his wits and realized that the cliff was not sheer to the sea. Half-way down, perhaps eighty feet or so, there was a substantial abutment, presumably the result of a landslip, and lodged on this broad ledge was a vehicle of some sort. It was lying on its side and all he could see of it was a front wheel and part of the bonnet in profile. He felt sure that it was Lemarque's Escort van but he could not be certain.

He crawled back with less difficulty than he had experienced getting down but when he stood once more on the old track he was trembling; his trousers were covered in greenish slime and his right hand was bleeding from a graze. He tidied himself as best he could and found his way through the maze of tracks to where he had left his car.

*

They studied the map, identified the tiny inlet where Lemarque's car might be, and agreed on a map reference. Wycliffe arranged for the cliff track to be sealed off and for a scene-of-crime team under Fox to make a meticulous search of the whole stretch. Prospects were poor after the storm on Christmas Eve but it had to be done.

Then a telephone call to the Naval Air Station and an accommodating Lieutenant Commander. Yes, they had an Air Sea Rescue helicopter in the neighbourhood on a training flight; no problem to have a look-see. Call you back. That simple.

Kersey said: 'If Lemarque is at the bottom of that cliff he must have shot his wife before he went joy-riding among the mine dumps.'

'If he shot his wife, what you say seems reasonable.'

Outside a car engine cut, a door slammed, and they heard Alice Devlin's voice talking to Potter. She came in, crisp and fresh and smelling expensive.

'I hope I've done the right thing; I've allowed myself to be persuaded or bulldozed. That young lady knows her own mind and I had little option. I've left her with the Bishops.' She slipped off a suede shoulder bag and put it on the table.

'Do sit down. This is Detective Inspector Kersey. I don't suppose you want to risk police coffee? . . . I don't blame you.'

'She asked me to take her there. I suppose it was only natural she should want to see them and they her, the two families were very close before Alain got into trouble. But I must admit I was surprised when they asked her to stay at Mynhager and she agreed – just like that; no argument, no discussion. Of course I don't know her very well but it seemed out of character. I think they were a bit surprised too.'

'Who did you see?'

'Ernest, is it? And his two sisters; the old man, and a lad called Paul. Early on we were joined by Gerald

Bateman M.P.' She smiled. 'I hadn't realized we were moving in the corridors of power; the name didn't click at first.'

'Did she give you any idea why she is so anxious to stay with the Bishops?'

'Only that she knew them well and that she had spent a good deal of time in the house. She feels closer to them than to me, so I suppose it's all right for the time being.'

She sat back in her chair. 'No news of Alain?'

'I'm afraid not. I assume you are doing the necessary to put other members of the family on your side in the picture, but we are concerned about the Lemarques. We've no contact. I don't suppose you can help?'

She shook her head. 'All I know is that Alain's father came over with the Free French during the war.'

Wycliffe tested the water. 'I suppose you realize that one possibility is that your sister was killed by her husband?'

'Of course I've thought of that.'

'You think it credible?'

A lengthy pause. 'I simply don't know. I've see Alain three or four times and then only briefly. He struck me as being very fond of Jane and perhaps over anxious to please her.'

'I don't want to put any pressure on Francine but I suspect she could tell us more than she has.'

Pursed lips. 'You could be right but if she's keeping anything from you, she hasn't confided in me. I've been kept very much in my place as a visiting aunt of slender acquaintance. Not that I blame her, poor child.'

She picked up her bag. 'I suppose it might be useful if I was around for a day or two?'

'I'm sure it would be.'

'Good! Apart from anything else, Francine may need a shoulder to weep on, though I doubt it.'

They talked briefly of the inquest, of the need for a disposal certificate and of the funeral which must come sometime.

Sensible woman!

On cue, as the Sierra was driven off, the Lieutenant Commander called: 'I think we've located your motor; the chaps have just radioed in. Something the worse for wear I gather. Ford Escort van, grey; registration number: Oscar Foxtrot Quebec One Three Four Papa. Snap?'

'Snap.'

'They couldn't get close enough to read the engine number. Sorry!' Funny man. 'No sign of any occupant; one door missing, the other hanging, three wheels adrift and the bodywork suffering from multiple contusions.'

'Any ideas on accessibility?'

'I enquired. Our chaps say the vehicle is caught on a sort of abutment, a land slip, about eighty feet above the tide line. They reckon the base of the cliff is uncovered at low water but it sounds as though you'll need a lift if you want to recover.'

'Any chance of your people taking it on?'

'Why not? It would be a useful exercise. I'd have to get clearance but I think that could be arranged if your lot are prepared to pay the piper.'

'Just one more thing: we want the driver of the van. He may or may not have gone over with it but we have to start looking.'

'Did all this happen before or after the force 10 on Saturday?'

'Shortly before. I wondered if you could manage a low-level sweep or two while your chaps are in the air?'

'Can do, but I don't hold out much hope of finding anything. The van didn't go all the way, but he probably did and it's unlikely that he's still in one piece.'

'Thanks. I'm notifying Coastguard and I'll keep in touch.'

Kersey said: 'I agree that we want the van and having the fly-boys lift it is probably the best way. But we want Lemarque more. If we don't find him the case folds.'

Wycliffe glanced at his watch: 'Eleven-fifteen. Jus

over five hours of something like daylight. If the tide is right and there's a boat available we could take a look.'

'That "we" – is it the royal, the editorial, or does it just mean you and me?'

'In this instance it means you.'

'I was afraid of that. Marine exploration is not my thing.'

'It broadens the mind.'

'And empties the stomach.'

'If Lemarque did go overboard with the van, the longer the delay the less chance we have of finding him in identifiable pieces if at all. Get on to Coastguard and see if you can arrange for the inshore lifeboat. Take one of our chaps along who's grasped the rudiments of being able to stand upright on a slippery rock. I don't want any mountaineering; if it comes to that we'll bring in the professionals. And don't be defeatist; it's like a millpond out there.'

'Until you're on it.'

Kersey reached for the telephone.

'Do it next door.'

Alone, Wycliffe pared his nails, brooded, and tried to order his thoughts. Whether they admitted it or not, all concerned seemed to assume that Lemarque had killed his wife. And it was a reasonable assumption, given support by the finding of the van. Lemarque had taken his van to Mennear Bal and committed suicide by driving over the cliff. A believable reaction to a crime of passion. Remorse, promptly followed by a dramatic and final expiation. But Wycliffe had already questioned the passion, and all but settled for premeditation. So, a different sequel: After shooting his wife, Lemarque had ditched the van at Mennear Bal to create the impression that he had killed himself, and was now on the run.

But there were flaws, possibly fatal to both notions: Franks believed that Jane Lemarque had died between four and eight, and it now seemed that the dead woman had been talking to the ineffable Evadne at four-thirty.

A fat boy sitting on the low wall of the churchyard was watching him solemnly and intently through the window. Wycliffe winked at him and immediately felt guilty when he saw the shocked look on the lad's face. One more recruit to the ranks of disillusioned youth.

Where was he? A third alternative — was there such a thing? Anyway, a third possibility: Lemarque had ditched his van before killing his wife. Improbable but not impossible. It would mean that he had really planned the killing in cold blood.

At least he had clarified his own thoughts. The thing now was to recover the van and find Lemarque, alive or dead.

By dint of persuasion, warnings, even threats, he obtained authority from the mandarins in Accounts to employ an R.N.A.S. helicopter for the recovery of Lemarque's van.

'Is it absolutely essential to the chain of evidence? Is there no other way in which recovery could be effected? By boat, for example? Have you considered recovery by sea? Surely there is a well known climbing school and cliff rescue centre in that neighbourhood — couldn't they do what is necessary? You do realize that helicopters are fiendishly expensive to hire? I mean even more expensive than fixed-wing aircraft.'

'I suppose a fixed-wing aircraft might scoop the thing up at a hundred and twenty knots provided it didn't hit the cliff face.'

'You are being facetious, Chief Superintendent. I am only trying to do my job.'

'Aren't we all?'

Probably the Lieutenant Commander would have complementary difficulties with his administration, but at last the financial and logistical problems would be solved and arrangements made. Too late for that day.

Wycliffe arranged for the house-to-house to be extended to the cottages at Mennear Bal. Others might have heard or seen as much or more than the girl at The Tributers.

He had a snack lunch alone in the bar. Ella Bunt was there, sharing a table with Marsden. They seemed to be getting on well together.

As Wycliffe passed their table on his way out, Ella looked up. 'Thanks for the tip; you did me proud. I'll remember it.'

Thanks from a reporter must sound ominous in the ears of any policeman. Wycliffe wondered what she had cooked up with Evadne Penrose and the painter.

It was not Kersey with his inshore lifeboat who found Lemarque but a St Ives boatman, catching up on the wind and fog. Lemarque's body, drifting just below the surface of the water, nuzzled his bows, slid silently along the port side and would have cleared his stern had he not seen it, cut his engine and grabbed it with a boathook. He secured a rope round the legs and towed it back because it was difficult to get aboard without assistance. In any case he didn't fancy the job.

Arrived in harbour, he telephoned the police, and Sergeant Curtis came down to inspect his catch. Curtis recognized Lemarque, the proportions rather than the features, and reported to Wycliffe.

'The left side of his neck and the right side of his face are badly damaged, sir. The fish have been busy but there's more to it than that. He was shot, or he shot himself.'

Wycliffe left the duty officer to make the routine notifications and drove to St Ives.

St Ives: 'a pretty good town and grown rich by the fishing trade' – Daniel Defoe, a one-man K.G.B., reporting to Speaker Harley in 1702. Now it has grown richer, not on fish but on tourists and the reputations of dead painters. But, despite its prosperity, for seven or eight months of the twelve its streets are empty and many of its shops, cafés and restaurants are closed. Wycliffe arrived in the after-glow of sunset, the town in shadow, the bay lambent and still. A few figures on the quay, motionless in silhouette, standing near a little mound of plastic sheeting.

Curtis was there. 'This is Jack Martin; he brought him in. Found him floating in the lee of Clodgy Point.'

A short stout man in a sailor's cap and a duffel coat held out a firm plump hand.

The plastic sheet was lifted. Lemarque wore an anorak, zipped to the neck, brownish trousers, no shoes. The shoes belonging to Lemarque at the cottage were all non lace-ups, so it was likely that those he had been wearing had fallen off. His socks had been nibbled at in several places revealing sometimes pallid skin, sometimes abraded flesh. But Wycliffe's attention focused on the face and neck. No doubt that Lemarque had shot himself or been shot; a bullet had entered the neck just below the jaw-bone and made its exit high up the face on the other side. The wound of entry had been enlarged and made more ragged after death, presumably by the fish. It would be up to the pathologist and the ballistics experts to decide, but there seemed no obvious reason why the original bullet wound could not have been self-inflicted.

He was wearing a wrist watch, and the metal bracelet had cut into the swollen flesh. The glass of the watch, badly cracked, must have let in water but the hands were undamaged and showed twelve minutes past three. There was a day/date inset but Wycliffe could not read the display; the experts would have no difficulty.

'All right, you can cover him up.'

The police surgeon arrived, a man of few words, he made a cursory examination and left. A van brought the plastic shell in which the body would be conveyed to the mortuary, there to await the arrival of Dr Franks for the post mortem. Wycliffe spent a few minutes with Curtis in the local station then drove up the long steep hill out of the town on his way back to Mulfra.

It was almost dark but far out the sea gleamed in the last remnants of the day, and the sky was faintly flushed with red; the promise of a fine tomorrow.

So Lemarque was dead; shot through the neck and head, as his wife had been. Suicide or murder? The positions of the wounds of entry and exit were consistent with either. Lemarque could have driven his van over the grassy hump which bordered the cliff track and in those seconds while it was hurtling to the cliff edge, he could have shot himself. It was not especially uncommon for determined suicides to do a belt-and-braces job: shooting themselves in the instant of jumping off a bridge; taking poison, then drowning themselves. There was even a case on record of a man who hanged himself and cut his throat.

The van had landed on a projecting platform of rock well down the cliff face and the shock of impact would almost certainly have burst open the doors so that a man in the driving seat might well have been thrown clear and continued on down to the water. Memo: check on tides. Was Lemarque left-handed?

But now came the crunch: was it likely that Lemarque had carefully planned and executed his wife's murder, then committed suicide? More than that, if the time by Lemarque's watch was an indication of the time of his death then there was no way in which he could have been his wife's killer.

Adding it all up, Wycliffe was being forced to face the possibility of a double murder and if that was the case he was literally without a clue where to begin; they were up the creek without a paddle.

When he arrived back at the van Kersey was plaintive. 'Have you ever been out in one of those inflatables? It's like putting to sea on a couple of salami sausages; the damn thing keeps bobbing up and down like a cork.

Under the cliff you catch the swell going in and bouncing back. My stomach feels like an overworked yo-yo. And all for nothing! Some other guy a mile or two up the coast beats us to it.'

Joseph had spent most of the day in his room, a good deal of it looking out of the window. He had watched an Air Sea Rescue helicopter fluttering up and down, following the configuration of the coastline, at or below cliff-top height. Then, later, the inshore lifeboat had taken over, nosing into the coves and inlets, lost to sight for long periods but always emerging to round the next promontory. It was not a novel routine, it happened in the tourist season when a too confident swimmer or some idiot on an air-bed got swept out to sea, and something similar occurred in the winter when they were searching for drums of toxic chemicals washed overboard from a freighter, or for bodies from a wrecked ship. But today's activity had worried Joseph because he could not get it out of his head that they were looking for Lemarque.

Now it was dark and the search had either ended or been postponed.

He could not focus the reason for his unease. Jane Lemarque had been murdered, apparently by her husband; a tragedy in any circumstances but the more stark because it concerned people one knew, people with whom there had been intimacy and friendship. But Joseph had never been a sentimentalist and now he had reached an age when, like any sensible man, he had cultivated a nodding acquaintance with death and the habit of distancing himself from grief.

His disquiet stemmed from an illogical conviction that the tragedy was not yet played out, that it would move nearer home. He looked round at his books, at his photographs and paintings, at the room which sustained him in his old age and for the first time felt

138

insecure. Absurdly, he associated this foreboding with the arrival of the girl. That morning she had moved in . . .

He got up from his chair and in a single irritable movement swept the curtains over the window so that the wooden rings rattled together. 'God! I'm going soft in the head!'

A tap on the door and Ernest came in. 'Are you all right?' Concerned.

The old man snapped at him. 'Of course I'm all right! Why shouldn't I be?'

Ernest, not reassured, knew better than to argue. 'Wycliffe has been on the phone.'

'They've found Lemarque.'

'How on earth do you know?'

'Dead?'

'Yes.'

'Drowned?'

'Shot, but Wycliffe didn't give details. All I know is that his van was found half-way down the cliff at Mennear Bal and his body was picked up floating in the sea. He wanted to know if Lemarque was left-handed.'

'He wasn't, was he?'

'No. I suppose they're thinking of suicide, presumably after killing Jane.'

The old man made an irritable movement. 'All nice and tidy! So it's as good as over; soon everybody can pack up and go home.'

Ernest's astonishment was obvious. 'I don't understand.'

'You wouldn't! Has anybody told the girl?'

'Vee is with her now.'

'Yes, well, we shall see.'

Caroline came into the room from the kitchen, Virginia from the hall. The family, apart from the two sisters, was already seated round the table which was set with nine places.

Joseph sat at the head of the table, waiting.

Somebody said: 'Is she coming down, Vee?'

'I think so; she wants to change first.'

Joseph thought: Vee's pleasure in life consists in persuading people to do what they don't want to. The born schoolteacher.

The high, gloomy room, panelled by its nineteenth-century architect, was dimly lit by electric bracket lamps in the form of fake candles. Family portraits by indifferent Victorian and Edwardian painters were flattered by the poor lighting.

Paul was staring at his empty plate and fiddling with his soup spoon. 'She won't let me talk to her.'

'You must give her time, Paul.'

Too easily hurt. Paul had the Bishop looks, something of the Bishop temperament, but not the Bishop hide.

Joseph's feelings of unease increased, he sensed that they were moving towards a crisis. A premonition? He did not believe in such things. Or did he? At seventy-five he realized that all his life he had adopted postures to defend himself against a corroding sense of insecurity. These postures had fathered his beliefs. Was this true of others? Of Bateman, for instance? If it was, did he know it?

All Joseph knew at this moment was that he was listening to meaningless verbal exchanges between members of his family while underneath . . .

Virginia took her place beside Paul; something more than aunty affection there. She was explaining: 'When I went to her door I could hear her voice and I thought someone must be with her but she was alone. She was sitting in the dark by the window with the curtains drawn back. I said: "I thought you were talking to someone", and she said: "I was, I was talking to Blackie."'

Joseph was impelled to question. 'Blackie?'

'The black-faced doll she's had since she was a baby.'

Caroline amended: 'I gave her that doll on her third birthday.'

Stella reached for a bread roll and started to crumble it on her side plate. Joseph thought: Stella can't wait for her food. At least I haven't become greedy in my old age. Not for food, anyway. Stella was saying something: 'I used to talk to my dolls when George was away. I had thirty of them from every part of India.'

Bateman made his contribution: 'She's had a terrible shock, poor girl. How is she taking it, Vee?'

'I really don't know. She seemed strange rather than grieved but you can't . . . ' She broke off as Francine entered the room.

Joseph drew in his breath. Francine wore a blue dress that was almost a gown; her red-gold hair was gathered into a coil on the top of her head displaying her long youthful neck. Beautiful! Necks and ankles are the erogenous zones for a young woman. The eighteenth century understood this: display the neck, titillate with the ankles. Women have lost the art of titillation.

Joseph felt compelled to pay homage. 'I'm very glad you've come down, my dear.'

'Thank you, daddy Jo.' It was the name she had called him from the time she had learned to talk. God alone knew why.

Caroline said: 'I'll tell Ada we're ready.' She came back a minute or two later, with Ada carrying a large tureen of soup. When it had been served, they settled down to their meal. No one could think of anything to say and as the silence lengthened so the tension seemed to rise. Several times Ernest cleared his throat as though to speak but changed his mind.

Joseph thought: He's on edge. He keeps looking at the girl. Covert glances, as though he's anxious not to be seen to look at her. If I didn't know him I'd think it was lust. What's the matter with him? There is a streak of weakness, a flaw, which makes him unpredictable. Even as a child . . .

Then there was Gerald, nephew and son-in-law, yet Joseph had always found it difficult to think of him as

141

one of the family. He sat bolt upright, staring straight ahead, going through the motions of drinking the soup like an automaton. He was good at it, never spilling a drop. Joseph thought: He knows; his politician's antennae are signalling trouble ahead.

Caroline was uneasy too. She was of coarser stuff than her sister but more perceptive. Vee lived on the surface of things, responsive to every wind that blew, but Carrie was aware of the undertow of life, which was probably why she needed to drink. Neither of the girls had turned out like their mother.

Joseph felt a warmth behind the eyes, remembering his wife. Ursula. Her name still had the power to move him. He was trying to recall how she had looked when they first met. Ursula at seventeen . . . 1927; talkies and the slow fox-trot; Rex Whistler at the Tate, Aldous Huxley, Evelyn Waugh, Virginia Woolf . . .

His gaze rested once more on Francine and he was startled. Why had he never realized it before? Or was he imagining it now? He had never seen the girl with her hair up until tonight . . .

Vee was helping Ada to serve the main course. Spare ribs of beef in a marinade: one of his favourite dishes but his appetite had gone. He was watching Francine. She had small helpings but she ate with prim and delicate efficiency. Apart from Stella she seemed to be the only one untroubled by the silence.

After the meal they went into the drawing-room for coffee. Conversation, which began around the percolator, continued when they sat down; the spell of silence had been broken. They talked about the weather; the mild spell, the prospect of January frosts and, inevitably, someone quoted: 'As the days begin to lengthen, the cold begins to strengthen.'

Francine sat in one of the smaller armchairs and Virginia squatted on the floor at her side. Virginia was a great floor squatter. Joseph could see her lips moving almost continuously, provoking only occasional responses from the girl then, abruptly, during a lull in other conversation, Francine's voice became clearly audible to all: 'The man they found this afternoon was not my father!' Her voice was taut and brittle. She got to her feet, looked about her uncertainly, then hurried from the room. Virginia went after her and Paul, very pale, followed them.

Bateman said: 'Poor child!'

Caroline looked round at the others. 'Do you think I should go up?' And when no one answered decided to stay where she was.

Ernest sat in his chair, staring with absorbed attention at his empty coffee cup.

Stella went on with her knitting as though nothing had happened and the ultimate platitude was left to Ada. 'She'll be better after a good cry.'

CHAPTER NINE

Wednesday morning; Christmas Day plus three. A second fine day in a row, an achievement for late December. When it happens a Cornishman begins to wonder if something has gone wrong with the Divine Order. Wycliffe and Kersey arrived at the Incident Van at half-past eight after breakfasting with Alice Devlin. Alice had decided to stay on until after the joint funeral of her sister and brother-in-law. 'But I must slip up to Bristol for one or two nights to deal with things. My husband is in Brussels.'

The newspapers were on Wycliffe's table and Ella Bunt had made the front page of one of the tabloids under an 'exclusive' tag.

Former Partner of Law and Order M.P. Missing
Alain Lemarque, recently released from prison after serving a sentence for fraud, is wanted for questioning in connection with the murder of his wife, Jane, at their Cornish cottage on Christmas Eve.

Gerald Bateman M.P., known to his colleagues as 'The Sheriff', and tipped for office in the forthcoming government re-shuffle, was a partner in the Lemarque enterprises before they ran into trouble; trouble which culminated in Lemarque being sentenced to two years for fraud. Mr Bateman, when he is not at Westminster or in his constituency, lives across the valley from the Lemarques with his in-laws, the Bishop family who, for generations, have been lawyers in the neighbouring town of Penzance.

By coincidence, the head of the area C.I.D. Chief Superintendent Charles Wycliffe, now in charge of the inquiry, was staying with the Bishops at the time of the tragedy. It is understood that he has since removed himself to the local inn . . .

Wycliffe muttered: 'It could have been worse I suppose.'

At nine o'clock Dr Franks telephoned his preliminary report on the autopsy.

'Obviously the man was shot not drowned but his body must have got into the sea very shortly after death . . . He was shot through the left side of his neck with an upward inclination of the weapon and the bullet emerged higher up on the other side. A repeat performance of his wife's killing except that the gun was probably held close to the skin if not actually touching . . . Difficult to be quite sure about that because the wound of entry was enlarged through being nibbled by fish. On the evidence of the body alone I'd say it could have been either suicide or murder.'

'He wasn't left-handed.'

'Ah! I was coming to that, but it doesn't make much difference. If he was steering the van to the edge of the cliff when he fired he would have had his right hand on the wheel. If he didn't steer the van Sod's Law would see to it that the thing tipped over and stuck half-way down the slope without reaching the edge. Very frustrating for a chap all set to make a dramatic exit. And you must know that it isn't difficult to fire a gun with your left hand if you don't have to aim it.'

Wycliffe was watching Kersey light a cigarette. Automatically he reached into his right-hand jacket pocket where for twenty-five years he had kept his pipe; it was no longer there. Frustration, and an empty feeling akin to hunger. He muttered angrily to himself: 'I'm like an infant deprived of its dummy!' Absurdly, his manner towards Franks became noticeably sharper: 'The real question is whether Lemarque was in the van when the shot was fired. For all we know it was pushed empty over the cliff.'

Franks was amused. 'Fascinating! The idea of this bloke pushing his van over the cliff, then taking a running jump after it, shooting himself on the way. A bit whimsical, don't you think?'

A rueful laugh. 'Go to hell! What I'm really saying is that the evidence of his watch makes it less likely that he killed himself. Why should he if he hadn't killed his wife?'

'Search me! Motive is not my problem, Charles. I can tell you though that if he was shot in the van, whether he did it himself or not, I'd expect a fair old mess of spattered blood and soft tissue. At least you'll be able to check on that when they hoist the van aboard. And one more thing you can chew over in the silent watches: when we were undressing him we came across plant fragments caught between his anorak and his shirt. They included two dried up, papery little bladder-like objects. My assistant, who knows about such things, says they are the calyces of the sea campion. It seems those often survive on the flower stalk through the winter; and the sea campion, according to her, is found on the grassy slopes of the cliffs. So it looks as though our friend might have had a roll in the grass before finally taking off. How's that for service beyond the call of duty?'

Wycliffe had to admit that Franks had given him more than he could reasonably expect in a preliminary report. And on balance it seemed to strengthen the case for believing that Lemarque had been murdered. A double murder.

With any luck they would have the wrecked van available for examination later in the morning. The weather was calm, the sea placid, visibility excellent. Ideal flying weather, and there might not be another such day for weeks. The van would be lifted by the helicopter on to a truck parked on the cliff-top, then taken to a police garage for forensic examination.

Detailed arrangements had been made and it was all systems go.

Kersey said: 'This case, like Topsy, jes growed! From a silly girl going a.w.o.l. to a couple of homicides.'

'And we've next to nothing to go on. I want you to get in touch with Rosemergy Minerals and find out the state of play between them and Lemarque over the Mennear Bal site, also how far Bateman is known to be involved.'

Kersey had been turning over the latest reports.

'Anything new?'

'What there is comes from Mennear Bal. Two more sightings of the grey Escort van being driven in the direction of the cliff at around three o'clock on Christmas Eve. More interesting: there's a statement from a man out walking his dog . . . ' Kersey searched for the page. 'Alamein Montgomery Choak, aged forty-two; he would be with a name like that, poor bastard! He was walking along the track at the cliff edge when he came across the van, parked unattended. He actually passed it.'

'Interesting! What time was that?'

'He says about half-past three.'

'Say, an hour before Jane Lemarque telephoned Evadne Penrose. Was Lemarque alive or dead at that time?'

Kersey put the report back in its file. 'Good question. If we go by his watch he was already dead.'

Wycliffe got up from his seat. 'I shall be at Mynhager for the next hour or so.'

'Anything particular in mind?'

'Just a fishing expedition.'

Outside in the sunshine he decided to walk to Mynhager. It was part of the folk-lore of headquarters that the chief never drove if he could walk because walking was quicker. The truth was that he disliked being driven, and when he drove he rarely clocked

147

much over 50. Anyway it was a nice day, almost like summer, though tomorrow or the day after could bring a tempest or a frost. At the moment women stood in their doorways, and little knots of people were gossiping outside the shops and on the sunny side of the street.

Wycliffe turned down by the pub, preoccupied. If there had in fact been a double murder, why had anyone wanted to kill Lemarque and his wife? Bateman and the Bishops had been on more or less intimate terms with them for nearly twenty years so Mynhager was the obvious place to start. But there was more to it than that.

An ancient Mini passed him and came to a stop a little way ahead, by the painter's cottage. A blonde young woman got out, came round to the back, opened the boot and lifted out a large travelling case, obviously empty. Marsden's woman friend come to collect her belongings? She slammed the boot shut and went into the cottage. As he drew level Wycliffe could see the two of them through the window of the living-room.

He plodded on along the track until he rounded the bend and came in sight of Mynhager. Even in the sunshine the house stood out starkly against the sky. He went round to the front and rang the bell. To his surprise it was answered by Francine. She look strained, hollow-eyed and pale, but her manner was not unwelcoming. She even managed a smile.

'You'd better come into the drawing-room; I don't know who you want to see . . . '

Sunshine flooded through the big window so that the fire in the grate was dimmed by its brilliance but the room itself appeared more tatty than ever, the holly looked sad, the paper chains, pathetic.

She picked up a large photograph album from one of the settees. 'Shall I tell them you're here?'

'Family photographs?'

'I was looking at them.'

'Do you mind if I look?'

He sat on the settee, took the book from her hands, and turned the pages while she stood over him. He had the impression that she was not displeased.

The usual family snapshots, mainly of groups of people either posed formally on the terrace or snapped casually on picnics or boating trips. None of them was recent.

'Most of them were taken before I was born.'

He stopped at a lively group taken in a sandy cove. It was dated 1967. She said: 'Mamma Bishop took most of these. I used to call her that; she died when I was five.' The men, Joseph among them, wore trunks or shorts, the girls, bikinis.

'That's my mother, a year before I was born.' Even in the snapshot the girl stood out as a quite exceptional beauty; she was laughing and seemed to be putting up token resistance to an attempt by a boisterous Bateman to place a garland of seaweed round her neck. All the others wore crowns and garlands of seaweed while Ernest had contrived a kilt for himself and stood in regal pose holding a paddle in place of a trident. Lemarque crouched frog-like on the sand beside a slimmer, almost lithe Caroline, who was adding something to his crown. Virginia watched her sister with obvious disapproval.

In later snapshots Francine was there, first as a baby in the arms of one or the other, later as a toddler, then as a trim, self-possessed little girl.

Wycliffe was puzzled, not by the snapshots but by Francine's satisfaction in his interest. It was as though she was saying: 'I want you to see how things were.'

Then the door opened and Bateman came in. His astonishment was obvious. 'Charles! I had no idea you were here. I've been wondering if we might be in touch. Of course I heard from Ernest . . . '

Francine said: 'If you want to talk I'll go somewhere else.' She went out, taking the album with her.

Bateman went on: 'I was greatly tempted to ring you

but I knew you wouldn't wish to be pestered until you were ready.'

What was it about this man which made Wycliffe bristle? Paleface speak with forked tongue but what politician does not? Nearer the truth, he had a barely conscious prejudice against those who swim where others sink; against chronic survivors. Totally irrational! Where would we be without them? But Wycliffe's sympathies were with the dinosaurs.

'Francine should have told me you were here but the poor child has had such a terrible shock.'

Bateman was casually elegant in corduroy slacks, checked Viyella shirt, cashmere cardigan, and custom-made house shoes. His broad dark moustache bristled in a perfect symmetry of graded lengths, and he was meticulously shaved. 'May I offer you something, Charles?'

'Thank you, no. It seems that Francine is taking an interest in times past.'

'Oh, the album . . . It belonged to my mother-in-law who never failed to record every family occasion. I don't know how Francine got hold of it.' Bateman dismissed the irrelevance and went on smoothly: 'I suppose we all knew in our hearts that this was the outcome to be expected but it still comes as a great shock.'

Wycliffe looked blank. 'What outcome? I don't understand.'

Bateman sat in an armchair, entirely relaxed. 'I merely meant that for a man like Alain there could be no other way. He must have been devastated by what he had done in a moment of madness.'

'You are assuming that he committed suicide after killing his wife?'

'What other explanation can there be?'

'We've reason to think that Lemarque predeceased his wife.'

Bateman's expression was one of total incredulity.

'Forgive me, but there must be some mistake! Who, other than Alain, could possibly have murdered Jane? Who had a motive? And why, if Jane was not dead at the time, did Alain kill himself? I can understand that a man facing the rebuilding of his life in middle age might feel intensely depressed but I have already told you that he was absorbed in a new venture which, knowing him, would certainly have restored his zest for life.'

Unconsciously Bateman was adopting his House of Commons tactics: beginning with an assertion and embroidering it with rhetorical questions.

By contrast, Wycliffe sounded casual. 'It's more than likely that Lemarque did not commit suicide.'

'I don't understand.'

'It's probable that he too was murdered.'

Bateman's hazel eyes studied Wycliffe intently for several seconds before he said: 'I find that quite incredible!'

At that moment there was a roar overhead and a helicopter appeared from over the house, flying low and following the line of the coast. At a distance of about half-a-mile it hovered, lost more height and vanished, hidden by the intervening headlands.

Both men were gazing out of the window. The sea stretched to the horizon, filling the framed picture except for a succession of headlands sheering away to the south-west. They could hear the pulsing of the helicopter's rotor blades but could not see it.

Wycliffe said: 'They're going to pick up Lemarque's van, what's left of it.'

He sensed a tremor of disquiet affecting them both. Was it that the tragedy seemed suddenly more real? But for Wycliffe at least the moment soon passed. Policemen, like doctors, deal in cases not tragedies.

He said: 'If this is a case of double murder, and I feel sure that it is, then we have to look outside the Lemarque family for a motive and for the killer. So far

151

we know almost nothing about them, while you and the Bishops have known them since before their marriage; naturally, we come to you for information.'

Bateman sat, finger tips matched; he spoke with careful deliberation: 'I can't believe that you are right but I will cooperate in any way I can and I'm sure the same goes for the rest of the family.'

Wycliffe's poker face would not have shamed Andrei Gromyko. 'For the moment I have only two or three questions: the first is probably the most important. From your knowledge of the Lemarques can you think of anyone with a grudge against them—against either or both?'

'No, I cannot.'

'I would like you to keep that question in mind; give yourself time to think about it. I suggest that you go back over the past few years which saw the break-up of your partnership and Lemarque's conviction for fraud. Later I may have to ask you for an account of your relations with Lemarque over those years and of his other contacts so far as they are known to you.'

'And your second question?' Bateman's cordiality had vanished.

'I need to know if Lemarque had any relatives in this country and whether he was in touch with them.'

'There, I'm afraid, I can't help you. Alain was always reticent about his family. To the best of my knowledge he came over here with his parents as a very young child, at the time of Dunkirk.'

'My next question is a simple matter of fact: when did you last see Lemarque or his wife?'

'I saw them both briefly on Christmas Eve.'

'At what time?'

Bateman was accustomed to being interrogated by TV interviewers about his politics, not by policemen about his private life; his distaste was obvious and his answer curt. 'At about two o'clock or perhaps a little later.'

'After your lunch here.'

'Certainly! You were our guest if you recollect.' Acid. 'I went for a walk and it occurred to me that it would be a friendly gesture to call on the Lemarques and try to cheer them up. At the same time I hoped to hear something more of the type of investment Alain had in mind.'

'And did you?'

'No. I had chosen a bad moment; how bad I've since realized. I could see that they were both under considerable strain and though they were perfectly civil it was obvious that I was anything but welcome at that particular time. Of course, as soon as I could decently extricate myself, I left. I wasn't in the house above five minutes.'

'Had you offered or been persuaded to back Lemarque's project with a large sum of money?'

Bateman looked startled. 'Certainly not! I didn't even know what he had in mind. All I did was to indicate a sympathetic interest.'

'What did you do when you left the cottage?'

A long slow look. 'I continued my walk.'

'Where did you go?'

This was too much for Bateman. 'Really! This begins to look like an interrogation.'

Wycliffe was coldly objective. 'I am asking you questions which seem proper in the circumstances but you don't have to answer them at this stage. As far as I know you were the last person to see Jane Lemarque alive apart from her husband and her killer. For that reason your evidence is important and you will be asked to make a written statement later.'

Bateman realized that he had made a tactical error, and acknowledged it with a thin smile. 'You are quite right. One has to get used to the idea of being a suspect but it is not something which comes easily.'

Wycliffe declined the bait. 'So where did you go?'

'I walked as far as Busullow and back through Morvah. I need plenty of exercise as I spend too much time at a desk.'

'Did you meet anyone?'

This was bloody-mindedness, but Bateman was not going to make the same mistake twice; he answered mildly: 'I suppose I must have done, especially walking back along the road but I don't remember anyone in particular.'

It was a reasonable answer.

Wycliffe had been watching Bateman, trying to sum him up, not because he had any real suspicion of the man but because he found the Bateman phenomenon interesting. A perceptive doctor, merely by looking at his patient, may spot the constitutional weakness which could mean future trouble in one or other of the organ systems of the body. Wycliffe tried to do something similar in his professional encounters though he was looking for moral weakness, for the heel of Achilles which made them vulnerable. In Bateman's case he thought he had found it. Bateman was a strong man but a vain one and his vanity laid him open on all fronts. He had to succeed or learn to despise the object of his failures.

Wycliffe wondered how he had come to terms with his marriage and his situation in the Bishop household.

'Just one more point.' Wycliffe drew from his pocket the envelope containing the newscutting, found amongst Lemarque's papers.

Bateman took it, read it, and handed it back. 'I don't understand. Where did you find that?'

Bateman had done his best to sound casual but Wycliffe was in no doubt that he was disturbed. 'You remember the occasion?'

'Of course I remember it. As you see I was guest speaker at the dinner.'

'Was Lemarque there?'

'As a guest, yes. Ernest invited him. The Lemarques were staying with us and it was an evening out for Alain.'

'Not for Jane?'

Bateman laughed. 'I'm afraid not; it was a stag party occasion. But why the interest?'

154

'These things crop up.'

Abruptly, the sound of the helicopter rotors, a muffled beat, increased in volume and the helicopter appeared, hovering clear of the headlands. Suspended from it by an invisible cord was a box-like contraption which could only have been the wreck of Lemarque's van. The helicopter moved a small distance inland, hovered, and again lost height. The transfer of its load to the waiting truck took place out of their sight, hidden by intervening higher ground. The truck would take the wreckage to the vehicle department at headquarters where Fox would examine it with an expert from Forensic.

Wycliffe got to his feet. He had learned something from Bateman, enough to be going on with. There would be time for more questions when he had more ammunition. 'Well, thank you for your co-operation; I'll arrange for someone to take your statement. Now, is your father-in-law at home?'

Bateman seemed surprised but made no comment. 'I think so. I'll take you to his room if you like.'

But in the hall they were waylaid by Aunt Stella who seemed to be doing sentry-go at the foot of the stairs. Aunt Stella in a blue silk blouse and a red skirt with the inevitable orange scarf.

'Ah, there you are, Mr Wycliffe! I've been waiting for you, but we can talk better in my room . . . '

Bateman shrugged and made his escape.

Aunt Stella had one of the bedrooms as a sitting-room. It was like a cave; the windows were draped with heavily patterned net; the decor, from the Bukhara carpet to the flock wallpaper and the upholstery of the Edwardian suite, was predominantly red. There were wall-cabinets chock full of bric-à-brac: ivory and ebony elephants of all sizes, multi-limbed Shivas in brass and bronze, various Buddhas cheek by jowl with Hindu gods and goddesses. Two massive radiators maintained a hothouse temperature.

'Do sit down, Chief Superintendent.' Stella's manner was confiding, even conspiratorial. 'Coffee to begin with I think.'

A coffee percolator on the hearth emitted jets of steam accompanied by vulgar noises and there was a tray with cups, a bowl of sugar, and a jug of cream on a low table near the window.

'As you can see, I have my own rooms.' She pointed to a door which broke the line of wall cabinets. 'My bedroom and bathroom are through there.'

The little red light on the percolator glowed, and its flatulence subsided. 'Ah, there we are! Black or white? . . . An oatmeal biscuit, Chief Superintendent?'

She had style, Wycliffe could imagine her, the pukka memsahib, presiding at tea parties, entertaining Indian big-wigs and high ranking civil servants to dinner. Always serene, always amusing and ready with that morsel of gossip, delicately spiced, which would titillate without vulgarity.

The preliminaries over, Aunt Stella said: 'I suppose keeping a gun without a permit is a serious offence?' She went on without waiting for an answer: 'They've probably told you that I'm weak in the head and that my memory is not what it was; that may be true, but I'm not bonkers, you understand.'

She looked at him, her little grey eyes alert for his reaction but he gave no sign. He sat in his chair, bolt upright, looking blank but not bored; his listening role. Over the years he had found that most people will talk more freely to a neutral listener, one who gives little indication of being either for or against, believing or unconvinced.

'They say I hide things then accuse people of having taken them; I assure you that I don't hide things – or not very often. I put them away and forget where I put them . . . ' A girlish laugh. 'Of course I sometimes say things just to shock them – silly things, I suppose, but even at my age one has to get some fun out of life. Now and then I'm quite wicked and I embarrass them in front of their friends, then they have to explain that I'm not quite right in the head.' She chuckled. 'But Ernest is so stuffy, worse than his father! And the two girls irritate me with their patronizing attitudes. I suppose it comes of having lived such sheltered lives.'

He felt sure that she was preparing the way for an admission which she regarded as more serious than possession of an unregistered firearm.

The room was so hot that he could feel the little beads of sweat forming on his forehead.

'About your gun, Mrs Burnett-Price . . . '

'I don't have a gun, Chief Superintendent! I was thinking of my husband's. He was a major general, you know. As an officer he had a service revolver but I am speaking of a rather special pistol which was given him by a maharajah. The butt was inlaid with silver and it carried an inscription. "Given in friendship to Major General George Burnett-Price, C.B.E., M.C., September 1947." George was very proud of it.'

'Where is it now?' Wycliffe's manner was such that he could have been a doctor enquiring about a patient's symptoms rather than a policeman conducting a case.

She patted her hair in a vain attempt to control the wispy escapes. 'I don't know: it's gone.'

'When did you last see it?'

She looked at him, frowning. 'Months ago, it could be a year. I'd forgotten all about it.'

'What reminded you?'

'Why, the Lemarques, what else? Both of them were shot were they not?' Her voice faltered and suddenly all trace of her rather coy silliness vanished, leaving her a sad and very worried old woman. She smoothed her skirt then clasped her bony misshapen hands in her lap. 'It was late last night; I was sitting here brooding on the Lemarques when it occurred to me that if they had been shot . . . ' She hesitated and stopped speaking as though she wished to rephrase what she was about to say; then

157

she went on: 'I thought I ought to see if George's pistol was in its proper place, in the cupboard where I kept it.'

'Why connect your husband's pistol with what happened to Jane and Alain Lemarque?'

She was silent for a time. Somewhere in the house somebody was using a vacuum cleaner while outside the window gulls were screeching. When she spoke her manner was petulant.

'Do you think this is Chicago, Chief Superintendent? How many guns would you expect to find in Mulfra?' Whatever the shortcomings of her memory, she was shrewd.

'Go on.'

'Well, I looked for the gun and it wasn't there.'

Wycliffe said: 'Just now you spoke of your husband's service revolver, but you called the gun given him by the maharajah, a pistol – do you know the difference between a pistol and a revolver?'

She was contemptuous. 'I wasn't married to an army officer for nearly fifty years without learning something about firearms. In fact, when we were in India I did a certain amount of target shooting myself.'

'Show me where the gun was kept.'

She went to one of the cupboards below the glass-fronted display cases and brought out a sandalwood box. He saw a look of astonishment on her old face as she lifted the box but she said nothing. She placed it on a low table and raised the lid.

Inside were gun-cleaning materials and a chamois leather pouch in the shape of a holster. The butt of an automatic pistol, inlaid with silver, protruded from the pouch.

The old lady looked at the contents of the box in bewilderment, then at him. 'I don't understand! It wasn't there last night.' She repeated with emphasis: 'It really was not there!'

She put out her hand to pick up the pistol.

'Don't touch it!' He went on: 'So you are quite sure the gun was not in its place last night?'

She nodded. 'I wish to God I wasn't.'

'Can you tell me what sort of gun this is?'

She went back to her chair and sat down, obviously distressed. In a tired voice she said: 'It's a Walther P-38. German – that was the one thing which disappointed George. Of course they are wonderful pistols but he hadn't got over the war . . .'

Wycliffe murmured: 'Jane Lemarque was killed with a .38 automatic, almost certainly a Walther.'

She said nothing but he saw her hands tighten on the arms of her chair.

He spoke gently: 'I shall have to take this away with me for tests – box and all. Were there any cartridges?'

She made a feeble gesture with her hand. 'That little cardboard box in with the gun: there were a few single cartridges in that. I don't know how many . . . or how many are left.' She went on as though speaking to herself: 'To think that someone took the pistol . . . and put it back. They must have put it back in the night . . . they must have!'

'Who knew that you had this gun?'

'Who knew? Why, everybody must have known about it when it was presented to George – all the family, I mean.'

'But that was thirty-seven years ago. Most of the people in this house now were either very young or they had not been born.'

This brought her up short. 'I hadn't thought of that. One forgets how time passes . . .'

'When did you come to Mynhager to live?'

'Three years ago; after poor George died. Before that we lived in Dorset.'

'Did you speak to anyone about the gun then or have you mentioned it since?'

She shook her head. 'I don't think so. I can't remember.' She was becoming agitated. 'I just don't know!'

He was sorry for her. 'I know this is very distressing for you but I want you to say nothing about it to anyone for the time being. Will you agree to that?'

'If you say so.'

'I'll give you a receipt for the box and its contents.' He wrote out a receipt and handed it to her. 'Just one question: Who, in your opinion, could have come into your room during the night or this morning to put the gun back?'

She looked at him, frowning. 'Anyone! Anyone at all. I close my bedroom door at night so I wouldn't have heard anyone in this room.'

'And this morning?'

'This morning?' She looked troubled and a certain vagueness returned to her manner. He mustn't push her too far.

But she went on: 'This morning I got up at seven as I usually do and my breakfast was brought to me here at eight-thirty. I was here until just before you arrived.'

He left, carrying the sandalwood box in a Marks and Spencer bag she had given him. In the hall he encountered Bateman who was obviously intrigued by the bag but did not refer to it.

'Did you speak to my father-in-law?'

'No. I'm afraid that wasn't possible; I spent some time with Mrs Burnett-Price.'

A suave smile.

Bateman saw him off.

His thoughts were sombre. Two guns, one a revolver belonging to Lemarque, the other, an automatic, belonging to Stella Burnett-Price but accessible to the whole household at Mynhager.

It now seemed that the Lemarques had both been murdered by the same hand and that he was in possession of the weapon. Jane Lemarque had died at some time after four-thirty on Christmas Eve, her husband probably earlier, at about three o'clock.

Wycliffe's thoughts went back to that day. In the

morning he had been at the Lemarques' cottage with Virginia; he had lunched with the family at Mynhager and afterwards, feeling drowsy from too much drink, he had dozed in an armchair in the drawing-room until Curtis arrived. He recalled that he had joined Curtis in the dining-room at half-past three, by which time Lemarque must have been already dead . . .

Had he seen any of the others after lunch? Caroline and Ernest in the kitchen; she was making a brandy trifle and he was dipping his fingers in the cream . . . Then he and Curtis had gone to see Marsden. He was back at Mynhager in good time for dinner at seven . . . He had gone to his room and by that time Jane Lemarque was almost certainly dead.

Was it possible that he had sat at table that evening with a double murderer?

He was walking back along the track to the village; the Mini was still parked outside Marsden's cottage but now the back was packed, almost to the roof, with cardboard boxes and bulging polythene bags. As he reached the cottage the young woman he had seen before came out of the front door carrying yet another bag. She looked at him with a hint of aggression. A handsome blonde, in peevish mood.

'Is Mr Marsden at home?'

'No.'

'I am Chief Superintendent Wycliffe.'

'I know. If you want him you'll find him at The Tributers.' She bundled her latest bag in on top of the rest and slammed the car door. As she turned away she seemed surprised to find him still standing there.

'Perhaps you will give me a few minutes of your time.'

She was about to refuse but thought better of it. 'All right, but you'd better come inside.'

In the living-room he was not asked to sit down. The fire in the grate had gone out and Marsden's cat was sleeping in the fender. The table was littered with an even greater accumulation of dirty dishes and empty tins. The girl stood by the table, hands thrust deep into the pockets of her bush jacket, waiting.

'You are Miss . . . '

'Call me Emma.'

He realized that this was not a concession, rather a refusal to tell him her surname. 'Your name, please?'

'Emma Gregory.'

'You've lived here for how long?'

'Nearly a year.'

'And now you are moving out.'

'As you see.' Her jaw set in a hard line.

'You know that Mr and Mrs Lemarque are both dead?'

'I knew about Mrs Lemarque; he told me about the husband this morning.'

'You mean that Mr Marsden told you?'

'Yes.'

'Since you have lived here have either of the Lemarques called on Mr Marsden?'

'I work in St Ives; I've no idea what happens when I'm away, but I've never seen her here.'

'What about Mr Lemarque?'

'He's only been out of jail a few weeks but in that time he's called twice in the evenings – that is to say when I've been here.'

'Did he stay long?'

An impatient movement. 'I wasn't watching the clock. About an hour each time, I suppose. They went into the studio to talk, presumably because they didn't want me to hear what was said.'

'Perhaps they were discussing pictures.'

'Perhaps.'

'Did they seem friendly to each other?'

'Not especially.'

'What does that mean?'

'That they didn't seem particularly friendly.'

Wycliffe snapped: 'Don't play games, Miss Gregory! In what way did they seem unfriendly?'

162

She had flushed at his change of tone. She was not as hard as she pretended. 'Well, Hugh didn't seem pleased to see him and when they were in the studio I heard Hugh's voice raised several times. Of course it doesn't take much to make him shout.'

'On Lemarque's first visit did Marsden seem surprised to see him?'

'That wasn't my impression.' She glanced at her watch. 'If there's nothing more I've got a lot to do.'

'I won't keep you but I would like your address in case we need to get in touch.'

She hesitated, realized that it was pointless to refuse and said: 'Emma Gregory, 14, Seaview Road, Penzance. But I hope you won't want me, my parents have had more than enough to put up with as it is.'

He continued on his way back to the village. Clouds which had been building over the hills were spreading seawards, obscuring the sun, and as he reached the van the first drops of rain began to fall. It was one o'clock and Kersey was waiting.

Wycliffe put his carrier bag on the table.

'Been shopping, sir?'

'I want this properly packed and sent by special messenger for ballistic tests.'

Kersey was made to feel that his humour was ill-timed but he wasn't easily repressed. 'Is one allowed to enquire where it came from?'

Wycliffe brought him up to date then he put through a call to a friend in Ballistics asking for most urgent treatment.

'One more thing before we eat.' Once more Wycliffe produced his envelope with the newscutting. 'I want someone to go through the Incident Records for anything of note occurring in this area on the 15th and 16th of April 1979.'

'I'll see to it, sir.'

They walked across to The Tributers with the rain gathering purpose, and went up to their rooms to wash.

'See you in the bar later.'

Wycliffe was the first down; he had to pass the open door of the kitchen to reach the bar. Phyllis was in the kitchen, wearing a white apron, cutting up meat on a floury board. There were several little heaps on the board.

'Do you like pasties – real Cornish pasties, I mean?'

'What? Yes, I think so . . . '

She laughed. 'Bless the man! He's miles away. Pasties – that's what you'll get this evening unless you say different now.'

'Yes, pasties – very nice.'

In the bar less than half the tables were occupied but Marsden was there reading a newspaper, a glass of ale, an empty soup bowl and a spread of crumbs in front of him. He acknowledged Wycliffe with a lift of the hand.

Lorna was behind the bar, archly familiar: 'So what can we do for you today?'

'A half of home-brew.'

'Nothing to eat?'

'I'll wait for Mr Kersey.'

He took his drink to a table by the window. It was raining hard now, vertical silvery cords blotted out the view and the gloom inside made it difficult to see across the bar. Lorna switched on the lights. 'Let the dog see the rabbit.'

Kersey arrived and they ordered bowls of soup and bread rolls with garlic butter.

Kersey spoke in a low voice: 'I had a bit of news this morning about our friend. My mate called. He's station officer now. He remembered the case but he's been digging around for details. Of course it was four years ago.'

Wycliffe was staring across at the painter who seemed absorbed in his newspaper. Kersey wasn't sure whether to go on or not. In the end he said: 'He can't hear us.'

Wycliffe seemed indifferent.

'Marsden was charged with selling a painting of his

own, executed in the style of and purporting to be the work of another – in English, flogging a fake. They could have brought half-a-dozen similar charges but the one they chose referred to an alleged Gauguin. He sold it through a go-between to a seemingly reputable dealer. The case didn't hold up in court because the jury couldn't make up their minds at what stage the picture was provided with its forged documentation or who added a spidery little "P Gauguin" in one corner of the picture.'

Kersey waited but Wycliffe went on with his meal.

'Don't you want to know the name of this reputable dealer?'

Wycliffe muttered something.

'Lemarque Galleries Limited; a subsidiary of Lemarque Holdings.'

Wycliffe emptied his soup bowl and patted his lips with a paper napkin. 'You may be right. Lemarque's organization may have had dealings on the shady side of the street and it's possible that Marsden worked for him. The fact that the two of them have been in contact since Lemarque came out of jail seems to support the idea and we should know more when we get a report on the Lemarque/Bateman partnership. But we are looking for a motive for the murder of Lemarque and his wife by someone who had access to the pistol kept in Stella Burnett-Price's room. That limits the range of motives as it limits the number of suspects.'

'But it leaves Bateman in with a chance.'

Wycliffe got to his feet. 'If you've finished your meal let's go.'

Kersey said: 'What meal?'

CHAPTER TEN

As they left Marsden once more raised his hand in casual salutation.

Wycliffe was worried – afraid, yet he could think of no particular reason for fear. The killer had done his work (her work?) so all that remained for him to do was to 'identify and apprehend' as they used to say in the days when quite ordinary people spoke English. And if he was right about the pistol he had only to look among that small circle which formed the household at Mynhager. The process would be painful but the outcome certain.

They crossed the square to the van in drenching rain which was coming down faster than the drains could carry it away. As they were hanging up their waterproofs Kersey said: 'Something wrong?'

'The girl. I'd feel happier if we could get her away from Mynhager.'

Wycliffe went into the cubicle he had adopted as his temporary office and slid himself on to the bench between table and wall.

'How did you get on with Rosemergy Minerals?'

Kersey stood in the doorway. 'I've got an appointment in Penzance at 2.30 with a chap called Trewhella, their estate manager.' He glanced at his watch. 'I'd better get started.'

Wycliffe was left to brood on his in-tray. Away from headquarters he missed the guiding hand and steely resolve of his personal assistant, Diane. Diane, the immaculate, would never have permitted such an accumulation. The mound consisted of reports and memoranda, each one with an attached tag on which he was expected to indicate how the item should be dealt with.

He picked up the first document, glanced through it, and slipped it to the bottom of the pile; the next he initialled for filing, and the next. The fourth item was the little page-depleted notebook which he had found under Francine's bed and stopped her from taking away. Why? Now his action seemed insensitive and officious. But there had been something odd about the way she had darted back into the room at the last moment, something self-consciously deceitful in her manner which seemed out of character. At the same time he was prepared to believe that retrieving the notebook had been her main purpose in going upstairs.

He turned over a few pages. Francine's writing had character, a mature hand, bold and decisive. But her style was cryptic. He was reminded of his rough notebook at school where barely comprehensible statements were interspersed with doodles and unflattering sketches of the teacher. No sketches here.

'Blue-eyed people homozygous for recessive but more to it than that: Modifiers. Possible for blue-eyed parents to have brown-eyed child but only a 1:50 chance.' The figures were ringed.

'Dark hair dominant to blond but dark-haired parents can have redheads or auburn-haired offspring.'

There was a page on blood grouping on the ABO system with two heavily underlined sentences: 'Not possible for parents both lacking agglutinogen B to have a child of group B or AB.' And: 'For a mother of group A to have a child AB the father would have to be group B or AB.'

The last page was blank except for the query: 'Body form?'

The telephone rang. 'Records for you, sir.'

A list of incidents in the area on 15/16 April 1979, covering the night of the professional men's dinner in

Penzance. The clerk gabbled through them. A routine lot: a couple of break-ins; a spate of minor R.T.A.s; vandalism on the promenade at Penzance, youths tearing up flower beds . . . The only major incident, a hit-and-run with a young girl killed and her body left in the ditch. This, at some time after midnight in, of all places, a country lane between Badger's Cross and New Mill.

'Was the driver traced?'

'No, sir. The file remains open. There was strong suspicion but insufficient evidence.'

Wycliffe vaguely recalled the case through reports. 'Send the file on to me here.'

He spread an Ordnance map on his table and identified the lane in which the girl had been killed then he called in D.C. Curnow. 'I believe you come from these parts?'

'Born and brought up in Penzance, sir.'

'You know this lane?'

'Very well. It runs past the site of the iron-age village at Chysauster.'

'You wouldn't go that way if you were driving from Penzance here, I imagine?'

'Certainly I wouldn't, sir. You can see it puts a good distance on the trip and the road is poor – no more than a country lane.'

'Is it much used?'

'There's a fair amount of traffic in the summer with visitors to the site but otherwise, next to nothing.'

Well, he would give the file an airing. Curnow returned to his cubby-hole and a minute or two later there was another telephone call. Pigeons returning to roost, bread which had been cast upon the waters . . . This time, Sergeant Fox with a preliminary report on the recovered van:

'I've been over the vehicle with Alan Taylor from Forensic. Of course, there's all the detailed work still to be done but we've got identifiable prints. In the driving compartment Lemarque's dabs are all over the place;

with two or three of hers in the passenger seat area. No strangers in the front of the van. The same applies to the exterior bodywork, but in the load compartment, apart from Lemarque's we found three sets all from male subjects; two belonging to the same man and fairly old, the third recent and fresh.

'We've collected dust and other detritus samples and Taylor is taking them back for examination.'

'Any sign of blood or other body tissue?'

'None, sir. Of course the door on the driver's side was not recovered but Taylor thinks it virtually impossible that the man could have shot himself while in the driving seat, causing the wound of exit described, without contamination of the interior.'

So Lemarque had not shot himself in the act of driving over the cliff; neither had he shot himself nor been shot in the van. Was it conceivable that he had pushed his van over, then shot himself as he jumped? Fantasy! Lemarque had been murdered as his wife had been murdered.

He drew geometrical designs on his scratch pad but his thoughts were far from forming any rational sequence. He sometimes said that he was incapable of real thought because his mind was preoccupied with recollected pictures, with snatches of conversation, and incidents of dubious relevance, which presented themselves with compelling clarity but in random sequence. He would play with his recollections, fitting them together, discarding and rearranging, until he made a credible pattern. 'Like a child playing with bricks,' he told himself. Did they still play with bricks? Or with computer graphics?

Francine with the shepherds' posies . . . 'and purple for Death'.

The Lemarque's living-room where the two of them played out their mysterious charade for his benefit and for Virginia's. Why had they suppressed the note which Francine said she had written?

Jane Lemarque wedged between dressing table and bed with half her face blown away.

Alain Lemarque, his little simian body distended, lying on the quay in a puddle of seawater which had drained from his clothing.

'She's never been the same since Francine was born . . .'

'Why does she do it – go off like that?' . . . 'To punish me.'

'She's only trying to make an impression on her mother . . . Lemarque spent years trying to do the same thing and look where it landed him . . .'

'She let him go to bed with her.'

'Mother has to tell everything.'

And mother had told Evadne Penrose: ' . . . he must have taken the gun!'

Of another gun Aunt Stella had said: 'It wasn't there last night . . . They must have put it back . . .'

So many fragments of memory. They crowded in, taking possession of his mind and seeming to jockey for position. Now there was this damned notebook.

'Not possible for parents both lacking agglutinogen B . . .'

He brought his fist down on the table and probably woke D.S. Shaw in the next cubicle. He picked up the telephone. 'Try to get Dr Franks on the line.'

For once Franks was in his room at the hospital. 'Not another body for me, Charles?'

'I suppose you did blood grouping tests on the Lemarques?'

'As a matter of routine. I don't put the results in my preliminary report unless they seem relevant. If you hold on I'll look them up.'

Franks didn't keep him long. 'Jane Lemarque was Group A Rhesus positive, and her husband, also Rhesus positive, was Group O.'

'So they could not have had an AB child?'

'You know the answer to that as well as I do, Charles.'

So Francine was not Alain Lemarque's daughter. Not

170

difficult to believe, but hardly a motive for double murder, though it might explain a good deal about Francine.

Four-thirty, and already it was dark. The lights were on in the van and he pulled down the blind. Deprived of his pipe, he played with matches from a box Kersey had left behind. By slotting the ends with his penknife he contrived a creature which suggested a cross between a donkey and a kangaroo and when Kersey arrived back from his appointment in Penzance he found his chief putting the finishing touches to this chimera.

'Make another and we could race 'em.'

Kersey inserted himself into the bench seat and Wycliffe brought him up to date but he was unimpressed.

'So the girl was conceived on the wrong side of the duvet. Who was her real father? One of the Mynhager lot? If so, sexual limitations being what they are, there aren't many candidates. There's Ernest, Bateman, and the old man. But really, sir, who is likely to worry unduly about it after nearly seventeen years?'

Wycliffe said: 'The girl, perhaps.' But he agreed with Kersey. 'Anyway, how did you get on in Penzance?'

'Tim Trewhella, their estate manager, is a decent chap. He was helpful once he'd grasped the situation. It seems Lemarque approached him about a month ago with a scheme for leasing and developing the Mennear Bal site. He'd worked it out, presumably during his long idle hours in the nick. The idea was to clear the site to within 200 metres of the cliff and lay it out for chalets and touring caravans with a swimming pool, restaurant, shop and the rest.

'Trewhella asked about capital and Lemarque said he had one backer for £50,000 and, once the scheme was launched, he had no doubt he could raise the rest.'

'Was the backer's name mentioned?'

'Apparently not.'

'What about planning?'

'Lemarque reckoned that the authorities would play

along because the scheme would reclaim an industrial wasteland in an area of great natural beauty.'

Wycliffe, a conservationist, said: 'Of the two, I'd prefer the mine dumps. Sounds like a pipe dream to me.'

'Me too. Trewhella said businessmen are liable to these flights of fancy and that reality only moves in with the accountants.'

Wycliffe adjusted the hind-legs of his creature so that it stood properly. 'You think it likely that Bateman committed himself to put £50,000 into that?'

'Perhaps Lemarque was in a position to squeeze; in which case we have a man with a motive.'

'For a double murder? Anyway we shan't get much further along those lines until we hear from John Scales what he's been able to find out about the Lemarque/ Bateman partnership.' He picked up the telephone and asked to be put through to D.C.I. Scales at police headquarters.

'Is that you, John? . . . About the Lemarque/Bateman partnership . . . It's the information I want, John, not bits of paper to stick in a file . . .'

Kersey thought: Temper! He's missing his pipe.

Wycliffe wedged the phone against his neck while he went through the clumsy ritual of putting on his spectacles, then he began to scribble notes. It was five minutes before he put down the phone and turned back to Kersey.

'Lemarque was a bigger rogue than we've taken him for. The Bishops gave the impression that he was a victim of circumstance but according to this he was operating several profitable rackets in the art trade: fencing choice items of stolen property, arranging illicit export deals, and handling fakes . . . He had a high powered organization with two or three recognized experts on his pay-roll. The Met, using a softly-softly approach, were building up a nice dossier when there was a leak, somebody pressed the self-destruct button

172

and the organization just melted away. At the finish the Met boys were left with red faces and Lemarque on a comparatively minor charge.'

'What about Bateman?'

'According to this he was responsible for the antiques side of the business – a separate company which seems to have been more or less above board. Bateman's main source of embarrassment came from an alleged statement by Lemarque, quoted in a coat-trailing Sunday paper, to the effect that if he went to jail he could take Bateman with him. There was a libel action against the paper, settled out of court, but there were awkward questions and for a time it looked bleak for Bateman politically, then it all blew over.'

'So where do we go from here?'

'We talk to Marsden. If he can't do anything else he may be able to throw a bit more light on the Bateman/Lemarque set-up.'

'Now?'

'Why not?'

Outside, the rain had stopped and the air was clear and fresh. 'We'll walk.'

As they turned down the track by the pub they could hear the slow ripping sound of waves breaking along the shoreline. There was a light in Marsden's cottage and the music this time was neither jazz nor Bach but Tchaikovsky's *1812*, blasting hell out of the French and everyone else within range.

They had to bang on the door before Marsden heard them above the racket but their reception was not unfriendly. 'I suppose it's no use telling you I'm busy? You'd better come in.'

He switched off the record player and the instant silence assaulted the ears. With a certain reverence he slid the record back into its sleeve. 'Poor Peter Ilyich died from drinking water; a warning to us all.'

To Wycliffe's surprise the table had been cleared of dirty dishes and was now covered by a chenille cloth; the floor, too, looked reasonably free of debris. The painter read his thoughts: 'Yes, well, when you don't have a dog you have to do your own barking.'

A fire burned in the grate and Percy lay at full stretch on the hearth-rug.

Marsden looked at Kersey: 'What's this then, a new stooge?'

'Detective Inspector Kersey.'

Kersey said: 'We've met before.'

Marsden looked him over. 'The occasion escapes me.'

'Paddington Green nick, 1980.'

'I was acquitted.'

Wycliffe lifted a bundle of newspapers off a chair and sat down. 'All the same, whether you signed them or not, whether you provided the authentication or not, you painted fakes for Lemarque Galleries.'

Marsden pushed a low stool in Kersey's direction and sat in his own armchair. 'Correction on two counts: I did not paint fakes; I painted pictures "in the style of" and I did not deal with Lemarque Galleries but, believe it or not, with The Stylov Gallery – Stylov – get it? You need to be six years old to really appreciate the subtlety of these guys. They had a shop in Kensington where they sold pictures in the style of almost any painter you fancied. Nothing illegal about it; all open and above board except for the mark-up they put on a poor bastard's blood and sweat. A couple of us did the grind and they collected.

'Say you wanted a picture in the style of that celebrated French Impressionist, Le Merde; if they hadn't got one in the racks, they would provide me with a suitable stretcher, I would refresh my memory of the gentleman's palette, style and technique and get cracking.

'It worked well enough until Lemarque Galleries bought out Stylov as a front to get hold of suitable canvases for "upgrading".' A throaty chuckle.

'And you expect us to believe that you didn't know what was going on?'

174

'All that matters to me is that the jury believed it.'

'Or had their doubts.'

'As you say, but their doubts were good enough for me. By the way, that was a damn fine Gauguin. The old rogue would have liked it and it would have taken me in if I hadn't painted it.'

Wycliffe said: 'But not, apparently, the experts.'

Marsden was contemptuous. 'Experts my arse! The clowns slipped up on the paperwork.'

Kersey lit a cigarette and threw the dead match in the direction of the fireplace. 'How come you end up down here within spitting distance of Lemarque and his former partner?'

Marsden picked up Kersey's match and put it in the fire. 'A gesture on the part of the old firm when the balloon was about to go up.'

'To encourage you to keep your mouth shut.'

'A reward for services rendered to art.'

'Not as a suitable base to start a spot of blackmail?'

Marsden coughed bronchially and spat in the fire. 'You'll find that horse won't run. Not my line.'

The room was utterly silent. Perhaps that was why Marsden felt the need from time to time to drench himself in sound. He settled back in his chair; a cigarette placed centrally between his lips seemed in imminent danger of setting his moustache alight.

Wycliffe said: 'These visits you've been receiving from Lemarque since he came out of prison: what was he after?'

Marsden looked mildly put out. 'Emma's been talking. Why are women so spiteful? Lemarque wanted to revive the Stylov caper; he's been scratching about looking for a new launch pad. He'd given himself twelve months. "In a year, one way or another, I'll be back up there – or I'll shoot myself." That sort of talk. I told him he'd have to manage without me. I've gone soft since I've been down here and I've got used to crowing on my own dung heap. What's more I've come to prefer genuine Marsdens to Stylov versions of museum fodder.'

'You told me that you had no contact with Lemarque.'

'A tiny fib in an ocean of truth.'

'In your position you can't afford such luxuries.'

Wycliffe tried another approach. 'Lemarque is supposed to have said that he could have taken Bateman to jail with him. What did you make of that?'

'A shot across the bows.'

'You mean he could have done it?'

A moment for consideration: 'I doubt it, but the threat would have made Bateman think twice about joining the hounds.'

'In your opinion was Bateman involved in fraud?'

Marsden chuckled. 'My God! What a question! Let's say that in copper's terms he was probably in the clear.'

Some clarification; no enlightenment. They walked back to The Tributers and to Phyllis's pasties which spanned ten-inch dinner plates.

Afterwards Wycliffe said, 'Well, we're as fully briefed as we are ever likely to be. By the morning we should have official confirmation that it was the old lady's pistol which killed Jane Lemarque and that gives us the necessary cover if anyone wants to get legalistic.'

'So?'

'So tomorrow we move in. Formal interviews and statements from every member of the household. I want you to do it with whatever assistance you need. Pick your own men. I shall hold a watching brief.'

'I'll fix it from the duty roster.' Kersey hesitated. 'I take it you want this done by the book – uniformed men outside?'

'By the book.'

Wycliffe walked across to the Incident Van where D.C. Curnow was duty officer until shut-down at ten o'clock.

Curnow, an earnest young man, put down an improving book. 'This arrived by messenger, sir.'

The file on the hit-and-run, a formidable bundle.

Wycliffe skimmed through it. A nineteen-year-old

girl was walking home after visiting a friend. Less than a mile separated their two houses. She was in one of the widest sections of the lane when, according to the pathologist, she was hit from behind by a vehicle travelling at a fair speed. In the off-season the lane was little used except by a few people who lived along it, and even during the day traffic was minimal.

Again, according to the pathologist, after the accident the girl's body had been dragged off the road into the ditch. The scene of the incident, worked over by experts, yielded nothing, mainly because of torrential rain later that night. The inquiry had been thorough: over 200 people questioned; publicans within a range of fifteen miles interviewed, and garage owners quizzed about damaged vehicles. Suspicion rested on a local character who at the time was under a ban for a drunken driving offence. But there was no real evidence and his alibi, though it offended police nostrils, could not be broken. The only possible material clue was a few fragments of glass recovered from the scene. According to the experts they were not from the fittings of any vehicle and probably had nothing to do with the incident.

Wycliffe put the documents back in the file. Almost certainly an irrelevance. But why had Lemarque kept that press cutting?

Anyway, tomorrow they would move into Mynhager with all the ammunition they could hope to have in order to ask the right questions and be able to judge the answers. But tonight?

He was uneasy.

Curnow was ready to shut up shop for the night. With the rest of the headquarters team he was lodging in Penzance. Wycliffe signed the book and by the time he had reached the door of The Tributers the church clock was striking ten and the lights had gone out in the caravan.

He spent an hour with Kersey, working out the strategy for the morning.

*

177

Sleep would not come; he resigned himself and tried to resolve the confusion of his thoughts with one more review of the facts and their interpretation.

The Lemarques had been murdered and the sequence of events seemed clear. The killer made an appointment to meet Lemarque at the site of his proposed tourist park, ostensibly to discuss plans; in fact, to kill him. Lemarque was shot and his body pushed over the cliff. Later the van was driven erratically along the track and pushed over, to convey the impression of a suicidal act.

The van disposed of, the killer went to the cottage and in what must have been a horrifying scene, shot Jane Lemarque. He then left the cottage and Wycliffe believed that he had seen the light of the man's hand torch from the other side of the valley.

The crux of the problem was motive. Jane Lemarque was killed because she might have been able to point to her husband's killer; more than that, the strategy of the crime was to suggest that Lemarque had committed suicide after killing his wife. But why was Lemarque killed?

There was no evidence that Bateman was being blackmailed for his part in the Lemarque frauds; in fact there was no indication that he had been criminally involved. The question of Francine's parentage provided no grounds for murder. There is no longer any blackmail in bastardy.

Wycliffe sat up in bed and pounded his pillow. The room was cold and the light from the street lamp coming through the curtains had a frosty brightness. Enough light to see the time by his travelling clock: a quarter past one. His thoughts had been going round in circles for two hours and he had indigestion. He had eaten Phyllis's pasty too greedily. He got out of bed, padded across to the washbasin, and drank half-a-glass of water from his tooth mug.

Back in bed, chilled, he still could not settle down. The pistol, the Walther P.38 with its inscribed silver plate, seemed to pin the crime down to Mynhager. Would he be in the absurd position of knowing the criminal without having discovered the motive? And what had happened to Lemarque's revolver?

Lemarque. From the day of his release he had set about promoting the new enterprises he had dreamed up in jail. 'In a year, one way or another, I'll be back up there, or I'll shoot myself!' All his activity seemed to be directed to this single end: his contacts with Rosemergy Minerals, with Bateman, with Marsden, his trips in the van and his surreptitious telephone calls sometimes cut short by the arrival of Francine.

Those telephone calls. What was it Francine had overheard him say? Something about five years ago and being in the same boat . . . 'Five years ago we were all three in the same boat, or should I say car? Not any more!' Something like that anyway.

Suddenly the words acquired a new and threatening significance. It was five years since the girl's death in a hit-and-run. 'All in the same boat, or should I say car?'

Wycliffe turned over violently, sweeping the bedclothes along with him. Was it possible . . . ?

CHAPTER ELEVEN

A clear and almost windless morning. Hoar-frost on the slopes.

'Just coffee and toast for me, Phyllis.'

'And me.'

A buttery laugh. 'Indigestion, I'll be bound! Didn't I say you had to work or walk down a pasty? Instead you spend your time sitting around, the pair of you. What you need after a pasty, apart from a bit of exercise, is a drink of tea – about an hour after, for preference, and with a bit of sugar in it. I don't hold with sugar in tea as a rule but after a pasty 'tis the best thing if you don't want to be going for the bicarbonate later.'

When they were alone Kersey said: 'Did I hear you go downstairs some time in the early morning?'

'I went for a drive.'

'Good God! Are you going to tell me about it?'

'Later, in the van.'

They were at the van well before nine but just in time to take a call from Forbes, the ballistics expert. Forbes was one of those fortunate people who are paid for work which they find totally absorbing. He functioned in a sound-proof basement and the succession of day and night meant as much to him as to a mole.

'I've only done the preliminary work on this one, Charles, but I can tell you that the bullet and cartridge case found at the scene of the crime were from the Walther P.38 you sent me yesterday. The rifling and striation marks on the bullet, and the extraction marks and head scratches on the case correspond precisely with those on the test-fired specimens. No doubt at all.

Incidentally the Walther wasn't properly cleaned after firing and it hadn't been looked after before that. It's had very little use – probably fired less than half-a-dozen rounds since it was new in the mid-forties. The mechanism is stiff and the clown who used it was lucky it didn't jam.' Forbes felt about firearms as others feel about pets and children. 'Criminal to neglect such a nice mechanism!'

Wycliffe spent a few minutes looking over the newspapers. Ella Bunt's story had been taken up by the rest of Fleet Street to be re-run with variations and given extra punch by the discovery of Lemarque's body. The Cornish murders were news.

Kersey said: 'I'm more interested in your night driving. What made you go off in the small hours?'

Wycliffe explained.

Then the moment he had been waiting for and dreading. The evidence of the pistol made it certain that the killer of Jane Lemarque and, by extension, of her husband, was a member of the household at Mynhager.

He turned to Kersey. 'Are we ready?'

'All lined up, sir.'

Wycliffe, Kersey, D.S. Shaw, and a female clerk-typist, a blonde with a pretty little snub nose and a portable typewriter, went in Wycliffe's car. Two uniformed men followed in a Panda. At shortly after eleven o'clock they set out. Two cars one behind the other on a deserted track make a procession and so it must have seemed when they arrived in the courtyard at Mynhager. Even against the background of a glittering sea the house looked grim. Wycliffe had discovered that Mynhager could be translated from the Cornish as 'edge parlous'. It was apt; it had a sinister Arthurian ring.

One of the uniformed men remained in the courtyard; the other took up his post on the terrace. Anyone wishing to enter or leave the house would have to account for themselves. Kersey was aware of Wycliffe's intense distaste for what had to be done, and sympathized.

Ernest answered their ring. 'Ah, Charles! I suppose this is an official visit? You'd better come in.'

In the dim, cave-like hall the silence was punctuated by the majestic ticking of the grandfather clock. Wycliffe introduced his men. 'Inspector Kersey and Sergeant Shaw will be conducting the interviews . . . It would be helpful if they could have a room where they can be private and undisturbed.'

'The dining-room, perhaps . . . '

It would have been obvious to Ernest that something of the sort was bound to happen, he must have been expecting it. He escorted them to the dining-room. The heavy velvet curtains were almost meeting across the window allowing only a strip of light to enter. But it was warm; there were two of the Albert Hall type radiators.

'I hope this will suit you.'

Kersey said that it would, very well.

Ernest was pale and he looked as though he had lost a lot of sleep. His manner was dry, distant, and correct. They could hardly expect anything else.

Sergeant Shaw settled himself with his notebook and papers at one end of the long table. Unlike some of his colleagues, Shaw was always formally dressed and he might have been taken for the family solicitor on a business visit. The typist found a small table for her machine near the window.

Kersey said: 'I wonder if you can tell me, sir, whether any members of the household are out at the moment?'

Ernest went to the window and drew back the curtains so that light off the sea flooded into the room to combat its drabness. He said: 'I don't keep a register of comings and goings, Mr Kersey, but we are all here as far as I know.'

Shaw made an entry on one of his sheets of paper.

Kersey said: 'Thank you, sir. Could we start with Miss Bishop?'

Ernest looked surprised. Perhaps he had expected to head the list.

To Wycliffe the proceedings, although familiar enough in other settings, seemed unreal. Virginia arrived looking apprehensive. She took the seat Kersey offered, looking up at Wycliffe as though in some hope that he might be taking over, but he joined Ernest in the hall.

'I would like to talk to your father if that is convenient.'

'I'll take you to him.'

Up the stairs and along the corridor, past the room where he had slept as a guest. Joseph's room was at the end of the passage. Ernest tapped on the door and opened it.

'A visitor for you, father.'

The old man was sitting by the window, a book on his lap. He dropped a half-smoked cheroot in the ashtray and got up. 'Ah, Wycliffe! Come in, my dear fellow, sit down . . .'

'Charles is here officially, father.'

'So? What difference does that make? He can still sit down, I suppose?'

'I'll leave you with father, Charles.'

As the door closed the old man said: 'He's never learned to be objective; always tripping over his own emotional bootlaces. So you're getting down to business and you've come to tell me about it.'

It was the first time Wycliffe had been in Joseph's room. The bow window opened up a tremendous panoramic sweep and the old man made an expansive gesture. 'This window faces due west, nothing between me and White Bay Newfoundland except, and thank God for it, the Gulf Stream.'

Wycliffe stayed on course: 'I had confirmation this morning that Jane Lemarque was shot with the pistol presented to your late brother-in-law Major General Burnett-Price. It seems likely that Alain Lemarque was shot with the same weapon but because of the circumstances we have no proof.'

Joseph picked up his cheroot which had gone out and threw it away. 'Go on.'

'Your sister looked for the pistol on Tueday night and she was distressed to find that it was not in its usual place. Yesterday, Wednesday, she called me in to tell me it was missing but when she showed me where it was usually kept, there it was.'

The old man stroked his moustache with the back of his hand. 'And your boffins were able to show that the gun had been recently fired?'

'More than that, they are able to prove that the bullet and cartridge case recovered at the scene of the crime came from that pistol.'

It was impossible to say how much of this was already known to him or guessed at but the old man had not batted an eyelid. 'So you concluded that someone in this house was responsible, certainly for the first crime.'

'I concluded that I had grounds for doing what is now being done.'

A shrewd glance. 'Of course! I wouldn't quarrel with that. You think you've established the means, that leaves opportunity and motive. I'm afraid I can't help you with either. I spent the whole of Christmas Eve afternoon here, conserving my energy for the festivities. I don't think I saw anyone – yes I did! At about four Ernest brought me my tea and biscuits; one of the women usually brings it but I gathered they were otherwise engaged.'

Wycliffe looked about him. It was obvious that the room and the man had grown together to such a point that separation would destroy them both. The paintings, the photographs, the books and the furniture were as much part of him as his memories, and together they constituted his life. Did he see them as threatened? If so, how far would he go in their defence?

'My wife, Ursula.'

Wycliffe happened at that moment to be looking at the only portrait in the room, a head-and-shoulders painting of a very beautiful young woman. Her light-auburn hair was coiled on top of her head; her attention seemed to be directed at something far away and one had the rather absurd impression that the painter had taken her unawares.

'She was nineteen when that was done. She had an identical twin sister, Gerald's mother. We are an inbred family.' The old man chuckled. 'Perhaps in danger of becoming incestuous.'

It was a fine performance. He was being offered a recipe for the investigation but whether with the intention of leading or misleading, it was impossible to say. He was not deceived by Joseph's apparent calm or by his almost bantering manner. The old man had suffered sleepless hours; the skin was drawn more tightly over the bones of his skull, his eyes seemed more deeply set and he was even paler than when Wycliffe had first seen him.

Joseph lit a fresh cheroot. 'I gather you've given up smoking. I shall soon be old fashioned in that respect as in most others. Ernest gave it up four or five years back – drinking too in his case, except for the occasional sherry, but at seventy-five I feel that self denial is likely to prove an unrewarding investment.'

A marble mantel-clock which looked like a graveyard ornament chimed prettily. A quarter to twelve. Joseph waited for the sounds to die away. 'I should imagine your principal difficulty will be motive. It's hard to see how anyone in this house would have gained through the deaths of Jane and Alain Lemarque.'

The pale grey eyes watched him with speculative detachment but Wycliffe, bland, attentive, almost deferential, gave nothing away.

'Alain and Jane looked upon this as a second home while my wife was alive; they, with our three and Gerald, were like brothers and sisters. As you know, Gerald had a business relationship with Lemarque which, for a number of years, strengthened the bond. Of course things went very wrong there. Alain's business methods ran foul of the law and he ended up in jail.

185

Gerald had already broken with him but his political career was certainly not helped by the partnership. Even now it is a sensitive area.'

Joseph tapped the ash from his cheroot. 'Despite all that, it seems that Gerald was still prepared to put money into some scheme of Alain's. That shows how deeply they were attached. With Gerald's political prospects being what they are I think he was running a very considerable, perhaps a foolish risk of reviving old accusations and suspicions.'

Wycliffe thought: End of lesson. The old man had said his say; he would not embroider. He had made up his mind about Wycliffe's intelligence, its scope and limitations, and calculated the dose he judged to be sufficient. If the family had to suffer there was an obvious sacrificial candidate.

Well! Two could play at that game. Wycliffe got to his feet. 'Thank you for talking to me, Mr Bishop. Inspector Kersey will be asking you certain questions and inviting you to make a formal statement later.'

It was not what the old man had expected and he was immediately uneasy. He glanced at the mantel-clock. 'I usually allow myself a glass of sherry at about this time; why not stay and join me?'

But Wycliffe excused himself and went downstairs.

The house was silent except for the muffled tapping of the typewriter. Yet the impression of calm was an illusion. They were all there, bottled up: Joseph and his three offspring, his grandson, and Bateman. Bateman who was in the family but not of it. And the pearl in the oyster – the Lemarque girl. Six days ago Wycliffe had arrived, wondering about his reception, now they were all watching him with apprehension. Not that the fact gave him any satisfaction.

He pushed open the door of the dining-room. Kersey was seated on one side of the big table with Caroline opposite him. So Virginia had had her turn. Shaw, at one end, was filling that most ancient role of scribe as,

186

with slightly different materials, he might have done at the court of Sargon of Akkad, four millennia ago. Wycliffe wondered how long it would be before even low tech found its way into the legal labyrinth. By the window the typist was rattling out Virginia's statement which, later, she would be asked to sign.

Caroline glanced up as Wycliffe entered. She sat in one of the 'carvers' belonging to the dining suite, apparently relaxed, and somewhat slovenly in a woollen suit which seemed to cling in the wrong places.

'Did you see your husband shortly after lunch on Christmas Eve?'

'Yes, briefly, I was in the kitchen with my sister, washing up, when Gerald came in and said he was going for a walk. He had missed his morning walk and he likes to get in some exercise each day.'

'Do you happen to know at what time he returned from his walk?'

'No. The next time I saw him was between six and half-past when I went upstairs to put on a decent frock for the evening and he was in our bedroom changing into a suit.'

'You spent most of the afternoon in the kitchen?'

'Yes; getting ready for the evening.'

'Alone?'

'Most of the time. After we had finished washing up my sister went upstairs to do some cleaning but she came down again later.' Caroline glanced across at Wycliffe. 'The superintendent looked in at about half-past three to say that he was going out with Sergeant Curtis who had called to see him. My brother, Ernest, turned up shortly afterwards. We usually have a cup of tea around four. Ernest and I drank ours together in the kitchen then he took one up to father with a few biscuits . . .'

Wycliffe went over to the window and picked up the statement forms which had already been typed and were awaiting signature.

187

Virginia had said: 'Our housekeeper has the afternoons free and over Christmas there is a lot to do so my sister was working in the kitchen and I was upstairs doing some cleaning. I didn't come down again until nearly five, then I stayed with my sister in the kitchen getting things ready for the evening meal.'

Kersey was asking Caroline about the pistol.

'Of course I knew that my uncle had been presented with a pistol by the Maharajah of somewhere or other; it was part of the family lore, but it never occurred to me to wonder what had happened to it when he died and Aunt Stella moved in with us.'

'So you didn't know there was a pistol in the house?'

She made an impatient movement. 'I didn't know it or not know it; I simply never thought about it.'

Virginia had said: 'I knew the story about my uncle's pistol but I had no idea it was in the house.'

Kersey had finished with Caroline. 'Thank you Mrs Bateman.'

'Is that all?'

'For the present. We shall ask you to sign a statement later.'

She got up from her chair. Kersey looked after her as the door closed. 'She's a cool one. I wonder if she realizes how far she's helped to put her old man on the spot.'

Wycliffe was unsettled; he had an itch to be doing something but no clear idea what it should be. The interviews going on in the dining-room were an inquest into what had already happened; he was more concerned with what was likely to happen, what might be happening at this very moment. Where were the others? What was going on? What really troubled him was the possibility that the action might not be over.

If only he could smoke his pipe . . .

He left the dining-room and prowled about the hall like a suspicious dog sniffing out the corners. He found himself in the dark little passage behind the stairs which led to the kitchen. The kitchen door was ajar and he could hear voices. Ada was saying something in her sing-song brogue; then a man's voice. He pushed the door open.

Ada and Paul. Ada was at the sink, washing dishes, Paul was standing by her, listless, depressed. He must have come to her like that many times before, from infancy upwards. He looked around, startled, as Wycliffe came in; his eyes were red.

'Do you know where Francine is?'

The boy turned away. 'She's in her room, I think.' He was struggling to control his voice.

'Where is her room?'

Ada answered for him. 'Turn right at the top of the stairs and it's the last door on your left.'

'When did you begin to think that he might not be your natural father?'

She was sitting in a cane chair by the window of her room, looking out at the hillside swept by a curtain of rain. She wore jeans and a jumper of washed-out blue which suited her colouring. Her hair hung about her shoulders.

'At school last term we did a bit about human inheritance: blood groups, eye colour, hair colour, that sort of thing. I suppose that made me think. I brought home one of those do-it-yourself blood group cards and tried it on mother just out of curiosity. That was while he was still in prison.'

'And?' Like any good interviewer he tried to confine his questions to prompting.

'Well, when he came home I asked him if he knew what his blood group was and he said that when we lived in Richmond he'd been a donor. He was group O. Of course I knew then.'

'Did you say anything?'

'To mother, not to him.'

'What did she say?'

'She admitted it. She'd had a thing with Paul's father.' A helpless gesture. 'You saw the photographs in the album. Of course that was why she's been so concerned about Paul and me. Poor mother! She needn't have worried.'

She spoke slowly, in a low monotonous voice without emphasis or inflexion but it was the first time he had heard her give expression to any sentiment or admit to any sympathy.

'You've told Paul?'

'Only last night.'

'He seems very upset.'

A slight movement of the shoulders. 'He'll get over it. It will suit him better to be a brother when he gets used to it.'

'And your true father; have you said anything to him?'

'This morning. I only told him that I knew. He wanted to talk about it but I wouldn't.'

'You'll have to, sooner or later.'

'Perhaps.'

They were silent for a time; the only sounds came from water gurgling in a downpipe outside the window. It was raining harder and although it was still short of one o'clock the light was so poor that the girl was hardly more than a silhouette against the greyness outside.

She was the first to speak. 'What happens if you find out who killed my mother but you can't prove it?'

'I don't think that is very likely.'

'But it can happen?'

'Sometimes we think we know the identity of a criminal but we are unable to prove it to the satisfaction of a jury.'

'What then?'

'Either there is no prosecution or the prosecution fails.'

'And the criminal goes free?'

'A suspect is not a criminal until he is found guilty of a

190

crime.' Arid words but what else could he say? He was a policeman.

'I see.' After a pause she said: 'I suppose it depends on getting a good lawyer.'

He was concerned. 'I shouldn't think too much about it if I were you.'

She turned on him fiercely. 'You are talking about the man who killed my mother!'

He had never seen her so deeply moved and he was worried, but he hardly knew what to say. 'Your aunt will be back tomorrow.'

'I know.'

At shortly after one o'clock the interrogations were suspended and the police contingent went, in a body, to The Tributers. Afterwards Wycliffe and Kersey crossed over to the Incident Van where Fox was due with his photographs and a report on Lemarque's van.

One of the cubicles had been laid out with a display which could have been mistaken for a photographic exhibition and Fox was ready to expatiate but Wycliffe cut him short.

'At the moment we are only interested in the prints found inside the load compartment of the van.'

'Apart from Lemarque's, there were three sets, sir; two were several months old and probably belonged to the former owner, but the third set, on the inside door-handle, was quite fresh.'

Fox pointed to a blow-up of part of a thumb and three fingers of a right hand and there were still larger versions of the individual digits.

'No problem about identification if we get hold of a comparison set, sir.'

Kersey said: 'The man out walking his dog went past the van, our chap hiding inside was scared and got careless — is that the idea?'

Wycliffe was dour. 'That is the idea; let's hope it's the right one.'

CHAPTER TWELVE

It was after four o'clock and already almost dark when the interviews were resumed in the dining-room at Mynhager. Ada was first. Asked where she was on Christmas Eve afternoon, she said she had spent it in her room.

'What time did you leave your room?'

'I don't really know. Oh, yes I do, it must have been about four because I saw Ernest taking in Mr Joseph's tea.'

Bateman was next.

The cashmere cardigan had given place to a Harris tweed jacket. Looking slightly pale but otherwise as usual he sat opposite Kersey in the dining-room. Wycliffe watched and wondered whether they would achieve more than a fat file of statements.

'You gave an account of your movements on Christmas Eve to the chief superintendent.' Kersey turned to Shaw: 'Read it please.'

Sergeant Shaw referred to his papers. 'Mr Bateman said that he had visited the Lemarques at about 2.0 pm on Christmas Eve afternoon and stayed only five minutes. Afterwards he went for a walk which took him to the hamlet of Busullow; he then returned to the main road and came back through Morvah without meeting anyone who remained in his memory.'

Kersey said: 'Would you like to amend that in any way, sir?'

'No, that is what I did.'

'Can you say at what time you arrived back here?'

192

'Not exactly, but it would have been between half-past five and six.'

'So it was dark.'

'Oh, yes. Quite dark.'

'You know that Jane Lemarque was shot with a pistol which belonged to the late Major General Burnett-Price?'

'I have heard that, yes.'

'You knew about the pistol?'

'I knew that my uncle was given a pistol by a maharajah.'

'And that it was in the possession of your aunt?'

'I suppose I would have known that had I thought of it, but I didn't.'

Surprising the number of people who denied ever having thought about the pistol.

Bateman was gaining confidence; perhaps he was having an easier passage than he expected.

Kersey broached the possibility of blackmail but Bateman remained apparently unconcerned.

'You told Mr Wycliffe that you had not committed yourself to putting money into Lemarque's project. Is that correct?'

'Of course! How could I commit myself? I had no real idea what the project was.'

'Lemarque is supposed to have said that he could have taken you to jail with him; does that mean he was able to put pressure on you to support his scheme?'

A thin smile. 'To blackmail me, you mean. No, it does not. I've been the victim of gossip but I have never been vulnerable to blackmail by Lemarque or anyone else.'

Wycliffe was sitting at the end of the table furthest from the window, being as unobtrusive as possible but well aware that they were getting nowhere. Kersey, through no fault of his own, was fishing in dead water. What was needed was confrontation but a confrontation that achieves nothing is a self-inflicted wound.

However, it was a risk he had to take. He got up quietly and went out. In the hall, he knocked on the door of Ernest's study and went in.

Ernest was sitting at his table, the binocular microscope had been moved to one side and in front of him was an open book, the text interspersed with drawings of the wings of flies. But he was not working.

'I hope I'm not disturbing you.' The banal courtesy was ironic in the circumstances.

'Not at all.' In a tired voice. 'Is it my turn for the black chair?'

Wycliffe seemed at a loss. He stood by the table looking vaguely about him. He picked up a glass jar which held a number of specimen tubes in which maggots were stored in spirit.

'Are these the little tubes you carry about with you?'

'Yes, I use them for bringing back adult specimens as well as for storing larvae, but I don't suppose you came here to talk about flies.' Ernest's manner was subdued, almost resigned.

Wycliffe put the jar down. 'You must drive into Penzance almost every day, which way do you go?'

'There isn't much choice. I go from here to Treen then across the county through New Mill; it's only six or seven miles.'

Wycliffe was looking over the bookcase, packed with literature on entomology, from massive Victorian volumes to paper covered transactions and proceedings of the societies. Not a legal tome in sight.

'I suppose it's further if you go by way of Chysauster?'

'Chysauster?' Ernest's voice had suddenly sharpened but immediately he resumed a conversational tone. 'Yes, it's further and not a very good road. Why do you ask?'

'Will you drive me to Penzance?'

Ernest closed the book in front of him with slow deliberation. 'If you wish. In the morning, perhaps?'

'Now.'

'If you say so.' Ernest displayed the absorbed concentration of a man picking his way through a minefield.

Wycliffe led the way out into the hall. He opened the door of the dining-room and spoke to Kersey. 'Mr Bishop is going to drive me to Penzance and I would like you and Mr Bateman to come with us.'

Bateman turned in his chair. 'May I ask the purpose of this excursion?'

'I want to clear up certain points which may have a bearing on this investigation.' Deliberately meaningless and as pompous. Bateman, about to protest, thought better of it.

A few minutes later the four men, wearing raincoats, trooped out into the courtyard. It was quite dark except for the light from the house, and rain blew in from the sea. The watcher in the Panda car got out and approached Kersey.

Wycliffe said: 'Borrow his torch.'

Ernest reversed his car out of the old coach house and the three of them climbed in. Wycliffe insisted on Bateman travelling in front with Ernest.

At a sedate speed they covered the seven miles to Penzance almost in silence. Once Bateman said: 'This strikes me as some kind of charade! I hope it has some purpose.'

There was no response. As they reached the railway station on the outskirts of the town Ernest asked where he should take them.

'Drive along the waterfront and the promenade and stop by the Royal Hotel.'

There were few people about; Mounts Bay was a void, with the lights of Newlyn and Mousehole twinkling through the rain. Ernest drove the length of the promenade, negotiated the roundabout, and returned to pull up outside the Royal Hotel. When he cut the engine they could hear the waves breaking along the shore.

'Well, do we get out?' From Bateman.

'No, we go back by a different route.'

In a voice that was scarcely recognizable as his own, Ernest asked: 'What route is that?'

Wycliffe said: 'On Easter Saturday 1979 you both attended a dinner at this hotel. Lemarque was a guest. Do you remember the occasion?'

A barely audible affirmative from Ernest.

Bateman said: 'I told you I was the guest speaker.'

'You drove home together?'

'Naturally, but I can't see how it can have any possible connection with the crimes you are supposed to be investigating and I protest most strongly against this . . . this melodrama!'

'You are under no obligation to co-operate; perhaps you would prefer more formal questioning at the police station?'

'You are threatening me, Chief Superintendent.'

'No sir. I am offering you an alternative. So the three of you drove home together. In this car?'

'Yes.'

'Mr Bishop, were you driving on that occasion?'

A police prowl car cruised along the promenade, slowed suspiciously as it drew level with them, then continued on its way.

Ernest said: 'I can't remember who was driving.'

'Mr Bateman?'

'To the best of my recollection, it was Lemarque.'

'And Lemarque is dead. At any rate you set out from here at about midnight. It was raining, as it is tonight. All I am asking is that we reconstruct your journey home. Shall we start?'

Ernest switched on the engine and they moved off, back along the promenade and the wharf, past the railway station, then they left the coast road and began the steady climb to the central moorland. As they were approaching the first fork Wycliffe said: 'Instead of turning off left, keep on this road.'

Ernest obeyed without comment but Bateman was

truculent: 'You realize, I suppose, that we are now on our way to St Ives?'

The road climbed steeply between rows of cottages which soon gave place to hedges. Phantom streaks of rain gleamed in the headlights and the screen wipers beat with the regularity of a metronome. Wycliffe tried to convince himself that he was not organizing a fiasco. The greenish light from the dashboard lit up the faces of the two men in front, obliquely and in profile. Kersey sat, hunched in his corner, so still that he could have been asleep.

'Turn left at Badger's Cross and that will bring us back eventually to the road home.'

'Which we need not have left as far as I can see.' Bateman again.

At Badger's Cross Ernest turned off into a lane which ran between high hedges; it was undulating and sinuous. From time to time the headlights picked out a farm gate, or a stile, and once or twice they saw the lights of a house. Wycliffe had in his mind an accurate picture of the area for, apart from studying the map, he had driven along the road in the small hours of the morning.

'On the night of your dinner, at about midnight, a girl was walking home along this road. She had been visiting a friend in the house now coming up on our right and she lived about a mile further on. She was nineteen, home on vacation from a teacher training college.'

Ernest was driving even more slowly now; the old Rover revved away, mostly in second gear and the hedges crept by with majestic slowness.

A road sign, caught and held in the headlights, read: 'Chysauster: Ancient Village'. The remnants of a cluster of iron-age huts lay two or three fields away, up on their right; a bleak place.

'The girl was killed in a hit-and-run and the police were convinced they were looking for a drunken driver but they never found him; torrential rain later that night had washed away any clues there might have been.

197

'The girl's father searched the road between the two houses but failed to find her and called in the police. By that time it was raining heavily and they were working under difficulties but they found her at last, dead. She had been dragged off the road into a ditch. It was then half-past three in the morning.'

Wycliffe was talking into a wall of silence. Once Bateman turned abruptly in his seat as though to say something but he did not speak.

The headlights shone on a house straight ahead which seemed to block the way. Ernest negotiated a ninety-degree turn at snail's pace then stalled the engine as he tried to accelerate. 'I'm not going on with this!' But there was more of despair than defiance in his voice.

'Will you drive, Mr Bateman?'

'Certainly not!'

'Then Mr Kersey . . . '

Without a word Kersey got out and went round the car to take Ernest's place at the wheel. Ernest climbed into the back with Wycliffe. 'I'm sorry . . . '

Wycliffe said to Kersey: 'About a quarter-of-a-mile; I'll tell you when to stop.'

Kersey restarted the engine and they cruised down a gentle slope, past another little house with outbuildings.

'At the bottom.'

Kersey pulled off the road on to a patch of rough grass and brought the car to a halt. When he cut the engine the silence was complete.

'The pathologist reported that the girl had suffered a compound fracture of the left femur along with other less serious injuries, none of them likely to prove fatal in ordinary circumstances. The compound fracture was complicated by her being moved off the road into the ditch but the immediate cause of death was loss of blood. She bled to death and, according to the pathologist, it would have taken about three hours.'

The windows were beginning to steam up and Wycliffe wound down the one on his side, letting in the moist night air and the fresh but slightly acrid smell of the moor.

'This is the place where it happened. The girl lived in a little house at the top of the next slope. You can see the light.'

Although the evening was not cold Wycliffe shivered. Suddenly in a harsh voice he said: 'Get out and see for yourselves where she died!'

They trooped out like tourists on their way to inspect some curiosity *en route*. They crossed the road, Kersey played his torch on the ground and lit up the ditch which was overhung by gorse and brambles.

Wycliffe's voice came, dry and unrelenting. 'She was walking on the right hand side of the road. There was plenty of room for any vehicle to pass.'

They stood there, a disconsolate group with the quiet rain sifting out of the darkness.

'All they found here was a few fragments of broken glass – very thin glass, perhaps a broken specimen tube. It meant nothing to the police at the time.'

Bateman had been silent for a while, now in a more conciliatory tone, he said: 'Of course we knew of this tragedy, Mr Wycliffe, everyone did in this part of the county at least, but I cannot see—'

'Shut up!' Wycliffe's voice, vicious with suppressed anger, silenced the politician as if a switch had been thrown. They stood there a little longer in the moist darkness then, wearily, Wycliffe said: 'Let's get back.'

Kersey took the wheel and they drove up the slope, past the house where the girl had lived, then down the other side to join their road back just beyond New Mill. Another fifteen minutes and they were pulling into the courtyard at Mynhager. Not a word had been spoken on the way.

Caroline was in the hall where a uniformed constable tried hard to be invisible. She tackled her husband: 'What the hell is happening?'

Bateman snapped: 'I've no idea!'

199

'Those cretins in there wouldn't tell me anything.'

Wycliffe ignored her and turned to the two men. 'I want to talk to you in the dining-room, one at a time; you first, Mr Bishop. Mr Bateman will remain with the constable.'

In the dining-room Ernest occupied the chair. Shaw was in his place at the end of the big table and the typist had moved away from the window into a better light. Wycliffe did not sit down but stood near Ernest's chair. His voice was hard, his manner abrasive.

'Jane Lemarque was shot with a pistol taken from your aunt's room and returned there without her knowledge. So the killer is a member of this household; one of the family.'

Ernest said nothing; he sat, his soft white hands clasped tightly together, on the table in front of him.

'Lemarque was also shot but we have no evidence concerning the weapon though I think defence counsel would have difficulty in separating the two crimes.'

Ernest removed his spectacles and began to polish them.

'The problem was motive; neither Bateman's possible involvement in the Lemarque frauds nor the question of Francine's parentage, both hinted at by your father, seemed to stand up. It was only in following up the curious matter of Lemarque's press cutting, reporting your dinner, that I came upon the hit-and-run affair and finally linked the two. Three professional men on their way home after a night out. The driver was so drunk that he missed his way on a familiar road, and a girl was knocked down, injured, and pushed into a ditch to die.'

There was a long silence. Wycliffe was oppressed by the contemptible shabbiness he had uncovered, by a spectacle of self-interest carried to the length of murder so that three lives were sacrificed to secure the personal ambition of a politician and the comfortable humdrum existence of a small-town lawyer.

Ernest broke the silence at last; in a low voice he said: 'We thought she was dead. Lemarque was quite positive.' He coughed, then spoke more strongly. 'He said he was absolutely certain and he was the only one who touched her. Otherwise . . . '

Wycliffe drew a deep breath like a sigh, then in a voice that was almost coaxing he said: 'Lemarque was not driving that night, was he?'

There was an interval. Shaw and the typist, roused out of their professional apathy, were hanging on Ernest's words. 'I was.'

Wycliffe turned to Shaw. 'Ask Mr Bateman to join us please.'

Ernest sat motionless, staring straight in front of him, his features devoid of any expression.

Bateman came in, alert, suspicious, metaphorically sniffing the air. Wycliffe pointed to a chair next to Ernest. 'Please sit down,' and went on at once: 'We now know that Mr Bishop was driving his car when the accident involving the girl occurred.'

Bateman looked at Ernest, then at Wycliffe, hoping for a lead but found none. 'Is this some kind of trap?'

'Ask Mr Bishop.'

In a flat voice Ernest said: 'I told him. I've lived with this for five years and, God knows, that is long enough.'

It was impossible to interpret Bateman's expression but he must have been struggling desperately to adjust and adapt, finally he seemed to resign himself: 'Then we shall have to pay for our folly. All I can say is that if I had suspected for a moment that the girl was not dead I would have summoned assistance whatever the consequences. As it was, I allowed myself to be persuaded. Believing that nothing could be done for her I admit that I did consider the possible consequences of making a report. Ernest's whole career and way of life would have been irreparably damaged and, though I was only a passenger in the car, I should have suffered politically.

201

My decision was highly improper but, in the circumstances, I think understandable.'

A worthy extempore performance.

Wycliffe was staring intently at Bateman. His face gave nothing away but under his gaze Bateman became increasingly restless. He began to tap on the table with the fingers of his right hand, a tension reflex which had often irritated his colleagues in the House.

'I can well understand: a country-town lawyer and an ambitious politician. I doubt if even clergymen are so vulnerable.' Wycliffe was scathing. 'After you had failed to call assistance at the time of the accident and even more so when it became known that the girl had not died until three hours after she had been dragged into a ditch, you both knew without a shadow of a doubt that the truth would ruin you. As a businessman and an entrepreneur Lemarque might have scraped by, but a lawyer, and a politician with a taste for office . . . ' He spoke directly to Bateman: 'You must have realized too that the business was so unsavoury that even those people who will sometimes provide a niche for a discredited politician would have found you untouchable.'

Bateman's fingers were working overtime, tapping out a monotonous rhythm. 'Will you tell me where all this is leading?'

'To the point that you were wide open to blackmail and Lemarque was quick to take advantage of the fact when he came out of jail. "Five years ago", he said, "we were all three of us in the same boat or should I say car? Not any more! I no longer belong to the club." You remember Lemarque on the telephone? I can see that you do. From that point onwards your political career was going to be expensive. No doubt Ernest's turn would come but you were to be first in line.'

Ernest sat quite motionless, staring down at the table top.

'But Lemarque had underestimated you and that mistake cost him and his wife their lives.

'You weren't your brother-in-law, he would have bought his peace of mind. Or tried to.'

Bateman had come to a decision. 'I have nothing more to say. I am in your hands for the moment, but I warn you that I shall exercise all my rights under the law.'

'What you say is noted. The constable in the hall will go with you to your room and you will point out to him the clothing you were wearing on Christmas Eve afternoon. This will be checked and sent for forensic examination. Later you will be escorted to the Divisional police station where your fingerprints will be taken for comparison with prints found inside Lemarque's van. You will be given the opportunity to make statements in respect of the hit-and-run accident and the unlawful killings of Alain and Jane Lemarque.'

To his surprise Bateman raised no objection; he would make no more difficulties and answer no more questions until he was in the hands of his lawyer. Wycliffe signed to Kersey who escorted him into the hall.

Wycliffe was left in the dining-room with Ernest, Sergeant Shaw, and the young typist. They heard voices, footsteps on the stairs, then nothing.

Ernest had scarcely moved, he sat staring at his hands, clasped together on the table top. In a tired voice he asked: 'What happens to me?'

'You will be taken to the police station and given the opportunity of making a statement in connection with the hit-and-run accident. You will be asked further questions in connection with the deaths of Lemarque and his wife.'

The minutes dragged by, the silence broken only by the sporadic rattle of the typewriter. Wycliffe wondered what was happening to the others. Were they gathered together, speculating on the turn things had taken or were they each hiding in their separate cells? And of the future: what would happen to Francine? Would she go

203

back with her aunt to a new and different world? Wycliffe felt sure she would not; far more likely that she would join the Mynhager ménage where life would go on much as before free of intrusions by the alien Bateman.

In rapid succession three shots echoed through the old house as through a cavern. Wycliffe made for the door, crossed the hall, and bounded up the stairs. On the first landing Kersey was bending over Bateman who lay in a great pool of blood; the uniformed constable was standing by, dazed, still holding a plastic bag full of clothing.

In a voice scarcely recognizable, Kersey said: 'Dead! Shot through the neck and chest. I saw her standing on the landing when they went up to his room but the gun was hidden ... Then, as they came back along the corridor to the top of the stairs, she fired ...'

Wycliffe heard Shaw preventing the family from coming up; mercifully it seemed that they were all downstairs. Francine was standing just a few feet from the dead man, the gun still in her hand, held limply at her side.

'Give it to me.'

She did so without a word.

Wycliffe was in the Incident Van; rain drummed on the roof. Potter was at the duty desk; it was almost midnight. A car drew up outside, a door slammed and a minute or so later Kersey came in.

'Well?'

'I've handed her over. A W.P.C. is looking after her and she seems perfectly calm. She insisted on taking her black doll with her.'

For a long time the two men sat opposite each other in silence. Wycliffe was the first to speak.

'I feel responsible. It never occurred to me that she had taken Lemarque's gun with her when she left home, yet from her point of view it was an obvious precaution.'

'On the principle of keeping matches away from children.'

'Yes, you could put it like that. She cross questioned me about what would happen if we couldn't prove our case and I still didn't see . . .'

Kersey said: 'She wasn't prepared to leave anything to chance.'

THE END

WYCLIFFE AND THE CYCLE OF DEATH

Chapter One

Charles Wycliffe, Detective Chief Superintendent, and Matthew Glynn, bookseller and district councillor, were spending their Saturday eighty miles apart with no idea that their paths would cross; in fact, in ignorance of each other's existence.

Wycliffe had a free weekend and intended to enjoy it at home with his wife in their house on the Tamar estuary. Matthew Glynn expected to spend most of his day in the shop: Glynn's of Penzance, one of the most prestigious bookshops in the county.

It was a remarkably warm April morning and the Wycliffes ate their breakfast toast and drank their coffee out of doors on the paved terrace in front of the house. A blackbird asserted its territorial claims from a maple tree; in the pond, three or four goldfish chased a gravid female, churning the water into turmoil; and the Wycliffe cat, pretending that food did not come in tins, stalked invisible mice in the herbaceous border.

At about the same time Matthew Glynn was in the bathroom, shaving; he had not taken to electric razors, preferring the ritual of soaping his face and cleaving a path through to the smooth skin in a minimum number of strokes. But this was becoming more of a challenge as the furrows deepened year by year. Now when he looked in the mirror he saw his father's face as he most clearly remembered it, lean and gaunt, grey and lined — the Glynn face.

But there was a difference: he carried the mark. He could not have described the mark or explained exactly what he meant, but it was there and sometimes he wondered why others could not see it.

He was fifty-two; not yet old, but over the hill, definitely.

Wycliffe was not brooding upon his age but counting his blessings from a comfortable cane chair. The rhododendrons and azaleas were coming into their own, the magnolias and camellias were at their best, and through a screen of trees at the bottom of the garden he could glimpse the shining waters of the estuary. Altogether, at that moment, there was little to remind him that all is vanity under the sun.

He settled more comfortably in his chair. If he had been a cat he would have purred.

Helen poured a second cup of coffee. 'It's going to be a good weekend!'

Matthew Glynn, back in his bedroom, knotted his tie and put on the woolly cardigan he wore in the shop. His father had worn a tailor-made three-piece, summer and winter, and a white shirt with gold cuff-links. 'Mr Glynn is always immaculate,' the women used to say.

Matthew combed the remnants of his hair. In the mirror, behind his own image, he could see his bed — an old-fashioned and massive double bed, made up for one. 'I'm a lonely man,' he told himself.

A morning for reflections.

Outside the sun was shining and from the window of his bedroom Matthew could see Mount's Bay, level and serene. Once he had imagined that middle age might be like that, a plateau, a period of equipoise before the final descent. Instead he found himself, like Alice's Red Queen, having to run faster and faster to stay where he was.

The Red Queen reminded him of chess, chess reminded him of Ronnie Swayne, and Ronnie Swayne reminded him of money.

A bell rang somewhere in the house and Wycliffe said: 'The postman.'

Helen got up from her chair. 'I'll go.'

She was soon back with a little sheaf of letters and a wad of junk mail by courtesy of reluctant trees.

8

An air mail envelope received priority notice. 'It's from David'—their son, who was working in Kenya. Helen slit open the envelope with a buttery knife, spread the pages, and scanned her son's scrawling script. She was excited. 'They're coming home! In July . . .'

'For good?'

'Two months, then they expect to go back to Nairobi on a new contract.'

'They'll be pleased about that.'

'Jonathan has two teeth . . .'

Matthew Glynn went downstairs. He could hear his son's voice coming from the dining-room. As he pushed open the door it would cease as though a switch had been thrown.

His son, Gerald, and his elder daughter, Gina, were already at table. They acknowledged him as he sat down. Gerald was twenty-seven, a couple of years older than Gina. Gina fished in the muesli packet for extra raisins; Gerald cut a sausage in two, speared one portion on his fork, then popped it in his mouth followed by a piece of toast. Matthew poured himself a cup of coffee.

The Glynn dining-room faced the yard, which caught the morning sun, but the room itself was gloomy: faded wallpaper, brown-painted woodwork, dark oak furniture and drab fabrics. Cobwebs hid in the corners of the dusty cornice.

For the sake of saying something Matthew asked: 'Where's Barry?' Barry was his son-in-law, Gina's husband.

'Jogging — it's Saturday.'

An accountant, Barry did not work on Saturdays.

Gerald cleared his mouth of food and looked at his father, about to speak. Matthew, knowing what was coming, forestalled him: 'You said your piece yesterday, Gerald. Give it a rest.'

Father and son, out of the same mould, confronted one another. Gerald dropped his gaze and said nothing.

Sara, Matthew's sister, came in from the kitchen wearing the sombre grey overall she used for work. Every inch a Glynn, Sara was dark, big boned, and gaunt; her clothes hung from her shoulders as though from a coat-hanger. She brought with her a fresh supply of toast and a boiled egg.

9

'Oh, you're down, Matthew. Do you want an egg?'

'No — no, thank you.' Matthew buttered some toast. He watched his sister eating, her every movement was precise and economical; she ate without pleasure, as though each mouthful was a self-inflicted penance. She was three or four years younger than he and though they had been brought up together, living in the same house, they had never had any real contact. Yet if ever anyone saw and recognized the mark, it would be Sara.

Years ago, when his wife left, Sara had taken over the running of the house and the bringing up of his children. His parents were alive then but living the life of a retired couple. Nobody had asked Sara to step into the gap, the matter was never discussed. Sara was there, and she did what was necessary without apparent enthusiasm or resentment.

Matthew sighed and three pairs of eyes turned on him.

The long-case clock cleared its throat in preparation for striking. Matthew got up and switched on the radio which stood on the sideboard. The 'pips' coincided with the first strokes of the clock and were echoed by the church clock close by. The News.

Wycliffe went into the house through the french window to switch on the News and stayed to listen to the usual litany of disaster, wars, famine, and crime.

'And now a summary of the weather: a complex area of low pressure is expected to reach the extreme south-west by early evening, bringing with it squally showers, mist and drizzle . . .'

He refused to be bludgeoned out of his euphoria and rejoined Helen on the terrace. 'I think I'll cut the grass.'

'It's still wet, we've had a heavy dew; you'll have to wait for it to dry out.'

He stood, hands thrust into his trouser pockets, surveying the garden.

Helen said: 'That shirt, Charles! It's filthy; you can't be seen in that.'

'I don't intend to be seen.' But the pristine brightness of the day was already tarnished.

Matthew Glynn switched off the radio and returned to his place; he poured himself another cup of coffee. He saw Gerald and Gina exchange glances; something had passed between them: a signal? Recently he had become convinced that there was something going on behind his back; he read disturbing meanings into the looks they exchanged; even into their silences. Was it his imagination?

Christine, his younger daughter came in, still in her dressing-gown, her eyes puffed with sleep. She looked very young and vulnerable. Christine was a student nurse in the local hospital and this was her free weekend.

'Isn't there any Shredded Wheat?' No one answered and she stood for a moment, looking over the table. She met her father's eyes. 'Anyway, I don't think I'll bother with breakfast.'

Sometimes he thought that what went on around him might be entirely comprehensible if only he could crack the code.

He got up from his chair. 'I shall be in the shop.'

The shop, which adjoined the house, was reached by a communicating door on the ground floor. Glynn and Son: New, Second-hand, and Rare Books: Established 1886. It was a large shop, double fronted, with bays after a fashion that was current in bookshops before shop-lifting became a national sport. Second-hand and rare books were housed on the floor above.

Matthew went to the switchboard and lights flicked on in the bays, then he made his way to the back of the shop where there were two offices, his own, and a smaller one for his typist. His office had a window and a door to the sunlit backyard which it shared with the house.

Gerald came in, tight-lipped, and held out his hand for the keys to open up. Gerald was responsible for the new book trade; Gina would be upstairs with the second-hand and rare books. A family concern. Paula James, his typist, arrived by the back door.

'Good morning, Mr Glynn!'

'Good morning, Paula.'

Paula was eighteen and plump; addicted to short, tight skirts and plunging necklines. She disappeared into the toilet.

A day like any other.

Matthew dictated two or three letters about delayed orders and queried accounts; a local author came in, trying to arrange a signing session for his new book but anxious to have it understood that he was conferring a favour.

At half-past ten Paula made coffee.

Hours of idleness vanish like salt in water and by lunchtime Wycliffe had done nothing but moon about the garden, digging out the odd weed. At half-past twelve they had lunch on the terrace and the sun still shone. Afterwards he read the newspaper and dozed in his chair. Helen looked at him with affection.

That Saturday afternoon trade at the bookshop was brisk and Matthew Glynn found himself serving in the shop for most of it. At five-thirty they closed, cashed up, and Gerald went to put the takings in the night safe at the bank.

At six-thirty they sat down to their evening meal, the whole family. For some reason there was more talk than usual. Barry, his son-in-law, was musical and was off to a choir practice; Christine was going to an amateur dramatics thing at St John's Hall; Gerald was playing in a snooker tournament in St Ives . . . They talked to each other, even involving Sara, but not to him. When the meal was over he stood up, looked around at his family, and said: 'I think I shall go over to Ronnie Swayne's for an hour or two.' For some odd reason it seemed that he was making a declaration.

Later they would say that this was the last time any of them had seen him alive.

The Wycliffes had their evening meal at a table by the window, enjoying the misty twilight, watching the colours fade and the emergence of twinkling lights in the estuary.

'Anything on television?'

'No.'

'Do you feel like a walk to the village?'

12

So they walked to the village and had a drink in the pub where the landlord collected ships in bottles and there was a Saturday-night sing-along. Walking home, they could see the distant lights of the city flaring in the night sky.

Wycliffe said: 'Tomorrow I'll do something.'

Matthew Glynn held his remaining bishop poised and muttered under his breath: 'Bishop to R5.'

Ronnie Swayne raised his head in order to see the board through his half-glasses, then the little freckled hand swooped. 'Rook to Kt7.'

When a game was approaching its climax the two were in the habit of announcing their moves as though to lend them increased significance, and because they were both past middle age they used the old notation.

Glynn pondered, kneading his rather prominent nose between finger and thumb. 'Knight to R4.'

'Queen takes pawn.'

'Queen takes queen.'

With a thin smile Swayne administered the *coup de grâce*. 'Bishop takes queen.'

Glynn sat back, meditative and rueful. 'No point in playing it out. Wasn't it Bardelebden, in a similar plight, who put on his hat and walked quietly home?'

Swayne chuckled. 'That's the story.'

They were in Ronnie Swayne's sitting-room. A heavily shaded standard lamp illuminated a small area around the fireplace: the mantelpiece with its marble clock and matching vases, the chessboard on a low table, the two armchairs . . . On one arm of Swayne's chair a huge tabby cat lay couchant, paws and tail tucked in. The pool of light failed to reach most of the room but, with the curtains undrawn, a streetlamp cast crooked shadows on the ceiling.

Glynn brooded on the chessboard and the evidence of his defeat. The marble clock chimed and struck nine.

Swayne, a neighbour of the Glynns, lived over his tiny shop where he traded in stamps, coins and medals. Over the years he had carved out for himself a notable place in the strange world of dealers and collectors. He was a fierce-looking little man with strands of red hair combed across the freckled desert of his skull.

'Don't take it to heart, Matt; we all have our off-days.'

Glynn grimaced. 'I don't mind being beaten but I don't like being crucified.'

'Then set 'em up again and have your revenge; the night is young.'

'No, Ronnie, I'd like to but not tonight. I've work to do in the office. I'll chalk this one up to experience.' Glynn was replacing the ivory chessmen in their box where each had its velvet-lined recess.

Swayne picked up a whisky bottle from the floor by his chair. 'All right, if you won't stay, just a small one before you go.' He poured a generous tot and passed over the glass followed by the water jug. 'You were off form tonight, Matt, and no wonder — other things on your mind.'

Glynn sipped his whisky. 'You can say that again!' He went on, very tentative now: 'I don't suppose you've any news for me yet?'

Swayne spread his hands, his manner apologetic. 'It's early days, Matt, but my contact tells me he's been in touch with an interested party.'

'Any figure mentioned?'

A reluctant smile. 'You know already we shan't be talking about value at auction or anything like it. At this stage $50,000 US has been mentioned but that's only a basis for bargaining.'

Glynn did some mental arithmetic. 'About £31,000; perhaps a quarter of their true value.'

Swayne stiffened. 'True value! From your experience in the rare book trade, Matt, you must know there's no such thing. It's the same in my business, value depends on the market you sell in.'

Glynn was embarrassed. 'Yes, yes of course! I'm not being ungrateful, Ronnie, just working things out.'

Swayne leaned forward in his chair. 'Look, Matt! I shall be in London next week and I'll have a word — see if I can't stir up a bit of competition.'

Glynn was doubtful. 'I can't afford to risk starting any gossip.'

'Neither can I, so don't worry.'

Glynn finished his whisky and stood up. 'You're being very good about this, Ron, and I shan't forget it.'

'Nonsense!'

The clock chimed the half-hour as Glynn was leaving. Swayne went with him and the cat padded after them down the stairs and out into the yard.

Glynn laughed. 'Clarence, off on his nightly prowl — he comes in to see me sometimes . . . Well, good night, Ronnie, and thanks.'

He walked the few steps up the back lane to his own yard and entered by the plank door. He was about to shoot the bolt but changed his mind and left it unsecured. The wind was blowing in gusts bringing flurries of rain, but overhead the cloud was still broken.

In the drawing-room Gina had fallen asleep watching a film on television. Images flickered across the screen and a gas fire burned on the hearth but there was no other light. The drawing-room was in the front of the house, the window overlooking the street where traffic was sporadic.

The front door opened and closed and a moment or two later her sister, Christine, came in looking slightly flushed; raindrops glistened on the collar of her anorak and in her hair.

Gina opened her eyes. 'Hullo! Is it raining?'

'Showers.'

Gina yawned. 'I must have dropped off. What time is it?'

'Half-past ten. I'm going to make a hot drink. Would you like anything?'

'I wouldn't mind a cup of Horlicks or cocoa or something — whatever you're making. Be a dear! Switch off the TV and put the lights on. I'm not watching whatever it is.'

'Is everybody else out?'

'Aunt Sara's up in her room, Gerald and Barry are still out, and father is next door playing chess with Ronnie Swayne.'

Ths sisters had the dark hair and eyes of the Glynns but

their pale, oval faces with a tendency to freckles must have come from their absent mother or they were the outcome of a genetic compromise. Gina was well covered; Christine, an inch or two taller, had the slim, rather bony physique of the Glynns.

Christine took off her anorak and went through to the kitchen. A few minutes later she was back with a tray: milky drinks and biscuits.

'Father must be in his office, I could see the light from the kitchen.'

'Where did you go this evening?'

'I told you; the amateur dramatics thing at St John's Hall.'

'Oh yes, *A Doll's House*. Any good?'

'I thought so: Stella Gibbs as Nora was really good. Didn't you do Ibsen for your special paper in Finals?'

'For my sins.'

Christine was pensive. 'Tonight I thought I might have got some idea of why mother walked out on us.'

'Because father was another Helmer and mother, another Nora — is that it?' Gina was derisive.

Christine flushed. 'All right! I don't remember mother; I just thought, knowing father, it could have been like that.'

Gina took a second biscuit, dunked it in her drink and avoided the implied question. 'One thing's certain, Ibsen understood women and he's one of the few playwrights who did. Shakespeare didn't — all that stuff with the Lear sisters. And Desdemona! Every time I think of that woman I want to spit!'

Christine chuckled. 'I wish I'd tried your line on old Ellis when I was at school.'

'You'd have ended up with a delta. Who did you go with — David?'

'Yes.' Defensive.

'So it's getting serious. Father won't be keen on you getting mixed up with Uncle Maurice and David with things as they are.'

Christine fiddled with her bracelet then, abruptly, she looked up: 'Gina, I'm not going on with nursing.'

Her sister paused in the act of nibbling a biscuit. 'Not going on? What the hell are you talking about?'

'I'm going in with them at the pottery; they need more help, I've enjoyed working there in my off-time, and they say I've got the makings of a potter . . .'

The words which had been tumbling out suddenly dried up. 'And?'

'Well, it's different from here — the atmosphere. I mean, we always seem so tense and nobody . . .'

'Nobody what?'

'I don't know.'

'So when are you planning to make this change? I suppose you'll give yourself time to think, time to talk it over at the hospital and with father?'

She became sullen. 'I've done all the thinking and talking I intend to do and I've handed in my notice at the hospital. As a matter of fact it expired yesterday.'

Gina was shaken. 'God! Father will have a stroke! Are you going to marry David?'

'Perhaps. I shall be living there anyway.'

'You do realize that father and Uncle Maurice may go to law over Trebyan?'

Christine's eyes had reddened. 'I can't help it, Gina. I can't see it father's way. I'm on their side — it would be criminal to build houses out there. With father it's money — always money!'

Gina reached out to put her mug on the tray. 'You can't get far without it but I don't suppose what I say will make any difference. What is it about David that gets you? Is it sex?'

'No, it damn well isn't!' Christine paused. 'Well, sex comes into it, but it isn't everything, not even the main thing. Dave believes in something — a way of life that doesn't destroy things or people and he's prepared to work for it. Surely you can see that there must be people who are ready to . . . to . . .'

'Stand up and be counted?'

'You're laughing at me!'

Gina shook her head. 'No, I'm not laughing at you, Chris, not really. Perhaps I'm a tiny bit envious.'

17

They heard the front door open.

'There's Barry now.'

Barry came in and stood, blinking in the light, aware that once more he had blundered into a situation.

Barry Morse was fair and too delicately made so that his good looks were almost feminine. He was short sighted and he wore gold-rimmed spectacles which enlarged his dark blue eyes in a way that could be disquieting.

'Is Gerald in?'

'Not yet.'

Barry looked at Christine, then at his wife. 'Yes, well . . . I think I'll go straight up.'

'Don't you want anything?'

He hesitated, pondering the question. 'No, I don't think so, thank you.' He turned to Christine: 'I'll say good-night, then.' At the door, he looked back at his wife. 'See you later.'

Suddenly it seemed to Christine very odd that in a little while her sister would be getting into bed with this man.

Gina picked up the tray. There was a commotion at the front door, the door slammed and there were heavy footsteps in the passage.

'Gerald.'

Gerald was big-boned and lean like his father, but nurturing an embryonic beer belly. His dark hair was wet and there were raindrops on his cheeks.

'The old man locked me out! I put the car away and tried to come in by the back door as usual but he's slipped the bloody bolt. I had to walk round the block and it's raining. I'm bloody wet!'

Gina said: 'Poor you, but I don't suppose it will be fatal.'

'He did it on bloody purpose! Spite, because I spoke my mind yesterday.'

'You upset him.'

'It's time somebody did; if we go on as we're going we shall end up in queer street.'

Sara crossed the yard, running blindly. By the kitchen door she stopped, holding on to the door latch to steady herself.

Her heart was racing and she had difficulty in breathing. She made a determined effort to take slow, deep breaths. It made her feel giddy at first and she was afraid she might faint but after a little while she began to feel better.

She tried to see into the kitchen through a slit in the curtains; the light was on but there was no one there. With great care she opened the kitchen door, stopping short of the position where she knew it would squeak. A moment later she was inside; a few steps and she had reached the passage. The light was on there also but that was usual. She could hear voices coming from the sitting-room — Gerald's and Gina's.

Six paces to the stairs. They were carpeted but they creaked. She reached the landing, trembling but immensely relieved. At that moment someone flushed the lavatory at the end of the corridor and in panic she ran the few steps to the door of her room and went in, shutting and locking the door behind her regardless of noise.

She was in her sitting-room. For a long time she stood leaning against the door in the dark. Slowly her heart and her breathing returned to something like normal but the trembling had turned to shivering. She was cold. She switched on a light and lit the gas fire; she huddled in an armchair, pulling her wet raincoat about her, then she kicked off her shoes and held her stockinged feet to the warmth. She tried to think but her brain was numb. Then she noticed her shoes lying on the hearthrug and snatched them up. She examined them minutely, uppers, soles and heels before dropping them once more on the floor.

Chapter Two

Sunday morning

It was shortly before seven on Sunday morning when Wycliffe first heard of Matthew Glynn. He was still in bed when the call came through from the duty officer at CID headquarters.

'Sorry to disturb you, sir, so early on a Sunday morning, but we have a report of a homicide: Matthew Glynn, a bookseller, fiftyish, with a shop and house in Lady Street, Penzance, found dead in his office by his sister at 06.05 this morning . . . The local DI says it looks as though he was strangled. This message timed at 06.58 . . .'

Sunday. Usually rousing policemen or anybody else to a sense of urgency on a Sunday is like trying to stir cold treacle. Somebody must have done pretty well.

'All right; leave it with me.'

Helen raised herself on her elbow. 'You have to go out?'

'Penzance.'

She put her feet over the side of the bed, reaching for her dressing gown. 'I'll make some coffee.'

He telephoned John Scales, his deputy. 'I want a team, John: Kersey in charge, Shaw, Lucy Lane if she's available . . . I don't want an army; say three DCs in the first instance and see where we go from there . . . I'm driving down . . .'

Matthew Glynn, bookseller of Lady Street, Penzance; fiftyish . . . The first shreds of information about a man he would probably come to know in death better than most of his friends and acquaintances knew him in life.

More telephoning; coffee and toast at his elbow while he

20

was at it; a quick shower, shave, dress — a sombre suit and tie . . .

Penzance was about eighty miles west, almost at the toe-end of a county which vaguely resembles a foot jutting out into the Atlantic. America next stop. He recalled with affection a rosary of place names: Newlyn, Peñlee, Mouse-hole (pronounced like tousle), Lamorna, Tater-du, Nanjizal . . . and that was only the coastal fringe to Land's End.

The weathermen had got it right: blustery showers out of a turbulent grey sky. When Wycliffe arrived in the town shortly after ten the godly were thinking about church and the rest were either still in bed, or meditating on what to do with a wet Sunday, or both.

He drove along the waterfront, open to the great expanse of Mount's Bay. There was the grey-green Mount of St Michael, a tide-island, topped by its castle; the island of Ictis, where Celtic entrepreneurs were trading Cornish tin to the Greeks when Alexander was a boy. Later to become the site of a medieval monastery, now the home of an English lord.

Wycliffe drove past a toy-town dry-dock and a Trinity House repair yard where great steel buoys looked absurdly self-conscious out of the water like fat ladies indecently exposed. Before reaching the promenade he turned off in search of Lady Street which is close by but cunningly concealed. He found the church, and the narrow street snaked uphill from there. A few doors up, police vehicles were parked on one side and on the other, despite the rain, a small crowd waited, perhaps for Godot, perhaps for the second coming. An alert copper watching them saw Wycliffe's car about to park and advanced with intent, but changed his mind.

He saluted. 'Through the shop, sir.'

Lady Street is in the older part of the town; both the Glynn house and their shop next door were built while Napoleon was teaching Europe how to make war; brick with granite dressings. Most of the other houses in the street are either of naked granite or hidden under stucco, some of which is ennobled by a Regency label. Altogether a mixed bag, a pleasant jumble, two, three and four storeys high, they make interesting roof profiles and, along with shops, offices, cafés and pubs, there is still sufficient residential usage to maintain an agreeable balance.

The Glynn bookshop was double-fronted, painted olive-green with gilded motifs. A hanging sign in the form of an open book was inscribed: 'Glynn & Son. New, Second-hand and Rare Books. Estab: 1886.'

Detective Inspector Trice, the local DI, met him at the door. 'He's in his office at the back, sir. The scenes-of-crime chaps are there.'

Trice, like many western so-called Celts, was stocky of build with a large flat face, small features, and hazel eyes. The steady gaze from those eyes was a professional asset.

The shop belonged to another time; there was a cash desk near the door but beyond that it was divided into bays. Wycliffe was conducted down an aisle between the bays, past stairs leading up to the second-hand and rare books department.

Trice pointed to a door under the stairs. 'Leads into the house, sir; it's the only communicating door.'

At the back another door opened into a small office with a window to a yard which seemed to be shared with the house.

'A girl, a sort of secretary, works here,' Trice said.

Glynn's office was next door, it was larger and had a door to the yard. Sergeant Fox, the scenes-of-crime officer, and his assistants were putting the room on film, preparing a scale plan, and beginning a thorough examination of everything in it. One man was going over the main surfaces with a miniature vacuum cleaner, collecting the dust into plastic bags according to its source. Another was crawling over the floor making a meticulous study of the carpet and marking his finds with little white circles. An unbiased observer might have found difficulty in distinguishing between those scientific techniques and the rituals of an African witch doctor.

Scenes-of-crime procedures rest mainly on the assumption of Locard's Exchange Principle which asserts that a criminal will always leave traces of his presence at the scene of his crime and that he will, inadvertently, take away evidence of his visit.

'There he is, sir.'

Matthew Glynn was sprawled on the floor by his mahogany desk; on the desk: a telephone, an open file, a scribbling pad, an engagement diary, a whisky bottle and a couple of glasses. Wycliffe noted these things sub-consciously. He stooped over the body: the odour of stale whisky lingered. Glynn was a big man but he carried no surplus flesh; he was bald except for an exiguous fringe of greying hair; his face was long and deeply furrowed; a distinguished-looking man, a man to be reckoned with. He wore a striped shirt, a cardigan, corded trousers, matching socks and brogue shoes.

Someone had hit him on the back of the head, a blow which had given rise to bleeding; a small area of the carpet where the head rested was encrusted with coagulated blood. The blow had not been fatal and the killer had finished his work by strangulation. The ear which could be seen was blue, so were the lips, and the tongue protruded. There were marks on the sinewy neck left by a plaited ligature. Bell-flex?

Trice said: 'Odd, isn't it?'

Odd for a man to be strangled. Strangulation is a common crime, usually committed in a moment of intense passion arising from anger or sexual frenzy. Otherwise it is the work of a sadist. In either case the victim is usually a child or a woman. A strangler needs to be significantly stronger than his victim, but in this case any possibility of resistance had been ruled out by the knock on the head.

'What did the surgeon say?'

'Not much; death probably occurred late yesterday evening or early in the night: a single, stunning blow which must have caused severe concussion but wasn't fatal, followed by strangulation with a plaited ligature.'

Wycliffe felt at a loss, like an actor who has anticipated his entrance by many lines in the script. It was unusual for him to arrive before his headquarters team. Now Trice was looking at him expecting action, but what he wanted was time to take

23

in the setting then, slowly, to learn about the man, his family, his friends . . .

He said, in order to say something: 'Premeditated murder.'

'That's for sure, sir. You don't pay a social call with a cudgel and a length of bell-flex in your pocket.'

'Is there anybody with the family?'

'No, sir. My sergeant took a brief formal statement from Sara Glynn, the dead man's sister, she found the body; but I thought it better to leave the rest to your people — not to muddy the water. The family have been asked not to leave the house for the time being.'

'How have they taken it — Glynn's death, I mean?'

Pouted lips. 'Hard to say, sir. They're shocked; who wouldn't be? But I haven't seen any red eyes.'

Fox, the scenes-of-crime officer, felt that he was being left out. 'Look at these, sir.'

He pointed to certain of the little circles which his colleague had drawn on the carpet. Wycliffe stooped, and saw that each circle enclosed a faint paw mark, the marks led away from the area round the dead man's head for several feet in the direction of the door to the yard.

'A cat,' Wycliffe said, obligingly perceptive.

'Exactly, sir.' Fox was an oddity: very thin, with a profile like Mr Punch. Half-glasses, habitually worn well down his nose, added to the bizarre effect. 'It looks as though the creature sniffed around the dead man, stepped in the blood, then went for the door.'

A question was required and Wycliffe asked it: 'Was the door open or shut when the body was found?'

'It was shut, according to Sara Glynn; shut, but not locked. On the mat near the door there are cat hairs and further traces of blood. It looks as though the cat sat there for some time, waiting for someone to let it out.'

'Is there a cat belonging to the house?'

'Not as far as I have been able to ascertain, sir.' Sometimes Fox sounded like Jeeves.

Odd about the cat though; wherever it had come from it must have been shut in for a time. Either the killer had stayed on for some reason, ignoring the cat, or someone had opened the door, after the killer had gone, and let it out.

'The cat wasn't here when our chaps arrived this morning?'

'No, sir; I enquired.'

He stood by the dead man's chair. A little more than twelve hours earlier Matthew Glynn had sat in that chair, involved in the convoluted patterns of his existence. The file on his desk containing minutes of a council committee was heavily annotated; the engagement diary was sprinkled with appointments, some of which he had kept, others he would never keep. Matthew Glynn was dead, an inanimate object which in a short time would be at the mercy of the pathologist's scalpel . . .

There must have been a visitor, possibly a member of his family; in any case someone sufficiently at home to move freely about the office, to take up a position behind the seated man so that he could strike a vicious blow. No struggle; Glynn had slipped to the floor, pushing his chair away as he fell. The murderer must have knelt beside him, taken a plaited flex from his pocket and slipped it round the neck of the unconscious man. A knot, a thin rod, even a pencil inserted in the knot, and there was a tourniquet. Simple! No strength required; a woman could have done it; a child. Wide open.

Wycliffe looked about him.

The office dated from early in the century: the mahogany desk, the wooden filing cabinet, the massive green-painted safe with its brass handle and a design in gold on the front. The desk chair swivelled on four sinuously curved wooden legs. On the wall there were framed photographs of three earlier Glynns with the dates during which they had done their stint for the firm. They impressed Wycliffe. The Glynns of today are living fossils; in this brave new world only institutions are capable of such feats of survival, and few enough of them.

Wycliffe turned to Fox: 'No sign of any break-in?'

'None, sir. The exterior doors of the whole premises are provided with mortice locks and the windows are wired to an alarm system. *If* the killer did not come through from the house then Glynn must have left this door to the yard *and* the door into the back lane unsecured. *Or* he admitted the killer himself.' Like Queen Victoria, Fox tended to speak in italics.

Wycliffe returned to the smaller office and Trice joined him. 'Tell me about the Glynns.'

Trice considered his words. 'On the face of it they're a typical business family of the old school — not many of their sort left; they make their money quietly, no show, and they do their best to keep family skeletons decently locked up. Discreet — that's the word.' Trice smiled, pleased with himself.

'What sort of man was Matthew? Well known? Well liked?'

'Well known anyway: a local businessman and a district councillor. As to being liked, I've never heard much against him. He's made a bit of a reputation for sniffing out backstairs deals in local government and I suppose that's more likely to make him enemies than friends.'

'What about the rest of the family? Is there a widow?'

Trice smoothed his double chin. 'Good question, sir. The lady walked out seventeen years ago and she hasn't been seen since.'

'She walked out and was untraced?'

'So it seems.'

'There must have been a missing persons inquiry?'

'There was. It was before my time but I know they picked up her car, abandoned, somewhere in Exeter.'

'Apart from the hypothetical widow, what about the rest of the family?'

'They had three children and all three are still living at home: Gerald, a bachelor in his late twenties, works in the business; Gina, a bit younger, also works in the shop. She's married to a chap called Morse — Barry Morse, an accountant with Mitchell and Slade. Morse is a retiring sort of chap, very musical, but they say he's a wizard with accounts. Then there's the youngest: Christine, she's a student nurse at the local hospital.'

'The Morses live next to the shop with the others?'

'Oh, yes; that's a biggish house next door so I don't imagine they are falling over each other. Then there's Sara, Matthew's unmarried sister, she lives there too. She seems to have taken over when Matthew's wife walked out; she's younger than Matthew — late forties — and what you might call a worthy virgin.

'Until a few months ago there was Granny Glynn — she died around Christmas, nearly ninety. Big funeral, everybody there who was anybody or wanted to be.'

At the start of any case there is a flood of fact and fiction; the job is to find out which is which and whether the facts are relevant. In the present case Wycliffe would only gradually come to realize the full significance of what he had just been told, that Granny Glynn — a very old lady — had recently died.

'Are they still one big happy family?'

Trice grinned. 'They live together anyway.'

Wycliffe was juggling with names, names which, with one exception, were not yet attached to faces; the exception was the dead man. In the next few hours he would have to acquaint himself with the whole family, with their relationships in terms of both kinship and sentiment, but experience had taught him to take information in small doses.

'Let's take a look outside.'

The yard was common to shop and house, paved for the most part but with a couple of flower beds and shrubs in tubs.

They went out into a narrow lane where the back doors of Lady Street confronted those of a row of houses in the next street. The lane was a track just wide enough for the refuse truck. Uniformed coppers were, as they say, 'combing the area' in and out of the yards, poking about in the weedy margins of the track and turning out the contents of dustbins.

Trice said: 'They're searching for the weapon — I suppose we ought to say weapons: there's the bell-wire as well as the blunt instrument. It's just possible he tossed them over a wall.'

Possible, but unlikely; all the same the police had to search; no stone unturned. Soured policemen know that truth lies under the unturned stone.

'Hullo, Dippy! What do you want?'

A scrawny little man had appeared in a doorway almost opposite the Glynns'. He looked at Trice without enthusiasm. 'I was out here last night and I thought maybe this gentleman would want to know what I saw.'

Trice turned to Wycliffe: 'Dippy Martin, sir. Dippy used to be a regular customer at our nick — specialized in ladies' handbags, but he's a reformed character now. Isn't that right, Dippy?'

'If you say so, Mr Trice.'

'Anyway, what did you see last night?'

Dippy threw away the butt of the cigarette he had been smoking. 'I saw young Glynn — Gerald; he'd just put his car away in one of the lock-ups at the top of the lane and he come down to go in through the yard door but it was bolted and he couldn't. It was raining, he'd had one or two, and he was cursing fit to blister the paintwork, but in the end he give up and off he goes round the block. I s'pose he got in the front way.'

'What time was this?'

'After eleven; p'raps ten or quarter past.'

'Is that all?'

'No.' Dippy, now sure of his ground, stopped to light another cigarette. 'After that I strolled up to the corner and I hung about there for a bit. When I was coming back I saw a woman just going in.'

'Into the Glynns' yard?'

'Into their yard. It was dark and she was a fair bit away so I couldn't see who it was.'

'But you're sure it was a woman?'

'Unless it was a pansy in drag. No, it was a woman all right.'

'What time was this?'

'Half-eleven, give or take a few minutes, sir.'

'You know the Glynn women, could it have been one of them?'

'Could've bin, sir. I jest couldn't say one way or t'other.'

'Did you see or hear any more after that?'

'No, sir. I was there till past midnight and I didn' see nothing more.'

When they were back in the yard Wycliffe said: 'I notice you didn't ask him what he was doing, hanging about in the rain.'

'He was looking for his daughter. Poor old Dippy, he's not a bad sort and he's got his troubles. Cissie is feeble minded and whenever she gets loose she's off after men.'

Wycliffe said: 'Getting back to the Glynns: are there any other relatives living locally?'

'Two brothers: Alfred, who's older than Matthew, has the chemist's shop down the street. He's a queer one; he's unmarried and lives over his shop. As far as I know he never sees anybody but his customers and there can't be many of them. Maurice, the younger brother, has a pottery over at Trebyan, near St Hilary — five or six miles from here. He's a widower, with a grown-up son.'

'Do the brothers get on?'

Trice spread expressive hands. 'I believe there's been a long-standing quarrel between Matthew and Alfred — the chemist. Until their mother died Alfred used to visit but I gather he hasn't been near the place since. And recently I've heard talk of a row between Matthew and the other brother, Maurice. It seems Matthew wanted to build houses close to his brother's pottery and, according to gossip, they nearly came to blows about it in the bookshop.'

Wycliffe was used to it; lift any stone and there is life underneath and life is tension; if family quarrels were motive for murder there would be no problem of over-population.

Trice said: 'Will you let me give you a bit of advice, sir?'

'Why not?'

'You haven't had much experience in this part of the world.'

'I've been in the south-west long enough — you know that.'

'I'm not talking about the south-west or even about Cornwall, I'm talking about Penwith; in Cornish penwyth means "the extreme end". The people here feel different — they *are* different.'

Wycliffe sensed the unspoken 'Thank God!'

'It's not that long since Penzance had its own schools, its

own library, its own fire brigade, its own police.' Spoken with nostalgic regret.

'So?'

'The real locals are suspicious of outsiders; it's been that way since the Saxons arrived — before that.'

'So what should I do?'

Trice laughed. 'Bear in mind that they're not just being bloody-minded.'

Wycliffe heard voices coming from the shop; his team was beginning to arrive. Now he would be able to retire from centre stage and feel free to prowl at will. He went to meet Kersey: for many years the two men had worked together on most of the major cases in the police area.

Kersey said: 'I've got Lucy Lane, Shaw, and Curnow with me, sir. There are three more DCs on the way. Shaw has gone along to the nick to see about organizing an Incident Room but I gather they're pushed for space so we may have to look elsewhere. I take it we shall use local talent for the house-to-house and Lucy, with Curnow, can start on the family . . .'

They discussed organization and tactics.

Premeditated murder is not usually committed by a stranger so Glynn's acquaintances, his intimates, and his family would be investigated in ascending order of importance. As always it would be a time-consuming, tedious, and delicate undertaking.

Wycliffe said: 'Any news of Franks?' Franks, the pathologist.

Kersey grinned. 'He expects to be here about lunchtime. He isn't pleased; he was all set to go sailing.'

Wycliffe and Kersey worked well together, partly because their manners and attitudes complemented each other. On the surface Kersey was the typical cop: perhaps the type specimen of the genus Cop: hard faced and hard headed, cynical and born to the job. On the other hand Wycliffe gave the impression of a studious, mild-mannered man who had somehow — and surprisingly — found himself in the police force. Both assessments had an element of truth, no more.

*

Christine stood by the window of her attic room, surrounded by familiar things yet totally at a loss; her mind in turmoil. Her father was dead — murdered. She was shocked, grieved, incredulous; all that was quite genuine, but the sources of her distress went even deeper. She was trying to rid her mind of a possibility, a nagging suspicion, which she could neither face nor totally reject. Her whole world seemed to have fallen apart, yet out there, on the other side of the window panes, nothing had changed. The church tower, the bay, Newlyn, Penlee Point, looked as they had always looked, and the church bells were ringing for morning service.

When it seemed that she might remain indefinitely standing there she found herself creeping down the stairs to her father's room where there was an extension telephone, the only one where she could hope for privacy. She tried not to see the bed with its honeycomb quilt or the heavy walnut furniture, she tried to ignore the unique blend of smells which identified the room more precisely than any visual image. She went to the bureau, picked up the telephone and dialled her uncle's number. She waited until someone answered: David, thank God! If it had been her uncle she would have put the telephone down.

'It's me.'

'Yes.'

'You know what's happened?'

'Aunt Sara phoned father early this morning. I'm very sorry, Chris. God! that sounds so stupid! I don't know what to say . . . I've been mooning about the house wondering if I ought to come over. I want to see you so much —'

'I don't think the police would let you in.'

'Are you . . . well, are you all right?'

'I suppose so. I can't think.' Her voice trembled.

'Darling!'

She was not getting to the point and at any moment somebody might pick up one of the other phones — or worse, find her in her father's bedroom. She was resolute. 'How is Uncle, Dave?' And she added: 'How did he take it?'

There was a pause then the boy said: 'I don't know. After Aunt Sara called he just told me what had happened and shut himself up in the stock-room. I can see him in there — not doing anything, just standing around with his hands in his pockets.'

She said: 'I'm coming over.'

'Will they let you?'

'I shan't ask. I'll be at the hut in about an hour.'

Alfred Glynn walked down Church Street oblivious of the drizzle, nearing the end of his Sunday morning constitutional which was almost as much a part of him as his pharmacy and the rooms above it where he had lived for thirty years. He walked with his eyes focused on the middle distance, a tall, shabby figure; his long black raincoat sagged at the hem and his homburg hat was frayed at the brim. He looked like a rabbi who had seen better days but he covered the ground in measured strides and with a magisterial dignity. No one who saw him pass would have guessed that his mind was in turmoil or that he doubted whether he could sustain himself until he reached his own door.

He was aware of the police cars outside his brother's house and he had to walk in the road to avoid people gathered on the pavement opposite, but his awareness had a dream-like quality, related to but not central to his inner concerns: his physical illness and mental distress.

His pharmacy was only five or six doors below the bookshop and he inserted the key in the lock of his own shop door with a sense of incredulous relief. The uniquely familiar smell of the shop enveloped and soothed him.

As a young man Alfred would have nothing to do with the family bookshop, he had wanted to be a doctor but, failing to make the grade, he trained as a pharmacist and his father had bought him an established business. The shop had changed little in the intervening years: it was shabby, congested, and stocked with remedies and palliatives, cosmetics and toiletries rarely seen elsewhere.

Alfred's clientele had dwindled, though to a few — mainly

32

women — he was still half apothecary, half confessor: a confidant to whom they could whisper their most intimate secrets, as to a priest. The brown eyes never wavered; words, when they came, were few and lacking in any emotion. Perhaps a question or two, then: 'You should see a doctor, but if you have made up your mind not to . . .' Occasionally he would say with finality: 'I can do nothing for you; see a doctor or take the consequences.'

He passed through the shop to the dispensary where, after much fumbling, he dosed himself with ouabain on his own prescription. He sat on a stool and felt his strength slowly returning; he breathed more freely, his muscles no longer seemed on the point of failing him and, after a few minutes, he felt equal to climbing the stairs to his living quarters.

In the little hall at the top of the stairs he removed his hat and coat. He called out: 'It's me, darling! I'm back.' There was no reply but he seemed content. He changed his shoes for slippers and slouched into the living-room muttering to himself.

For years he had repeated the formula: 'I'll do nothing while mother is alive . . .' This declaration alternated with another: 'When mother is gone, I'll kill him!' With the passage of years the words had lost their literal meaning and become no more than a soothing incantation, part of the ritual by which he cut himself off from the need to act for the future or think of the past. But his mother had been dead for four months.

Alfred was bemused, adrift; sometimes he felt that he could no longer distinguish between reality and illusion.

There were four main rooms above the shop: kitchen, living-room, and two bedrooms. The living-room looked down on the backyard and out over the grey-roofed houses, across the grey, misty sea to Newlyn and Mousehole. It was some time since the room had been cleaned; much longer since any attempt had been made at repairs or decoration: there was a damp patch on the chimney breast, paint peeled from the walls, and there was a film of grey dust on every ledge and surface. Crudely made shelves occupied much of the wall space and these were crowded with books, books which were largely anonymous because their spines had faded or were missing altogether.

For a while Alfred looked about him in vague, unfocused despair, then he went to a record player on a table by the window. From a box of records he selected one and put it on: an old Mantovani recording dominated by syrupy strings. Then, leaving the door open, he went out to the landing. He inserted a key into the lock of one of the bedroom doors and opened the door a little way. No light came from the room where the curtains must have been drawn. With his head in the gap he said in a low voice: 'Are you awake, dear? . . . I've put on a record and I'll leave the doors open so that we can both listen . . . I'm going to warm a can of soup—leek and potato—and we'll have it with some of that nice crusty bread . . .'

His every movement was slow and hesitant, he was aware of a disturbing hiatus between the decision and the act; his thoughts came sluggishly and refused to follow a rational sequence. He was aware of all this but seemed powerless to change it. He went into the kitchen but almost immediately a bell rang downstairs. Someone was at the back door. He stood with a can of soup in his hand, distracted by the bell, uncertain what it was he had set out to do. The bell sounded again but he made no move. Then he heard the door being opened.

'It's me, Alfred — Sara.'

Sara. He could not remember how long it was since his sister had last visited him, whether it was days, or weeks, or even months. He did not speak but went to stand at the top of the stairs, the soup can still in his hand. Sara was already half-way up. He showed no readiness to move and she had to push past him.

He had always been scared of Sara. While still in her teens she had been able to subdue him at will merely by hinting at things he preferred to forget. On an instant little humiliations and embarrassments of the past could be dredged up and given fresh currency. Without raising her voice or losing her temper she could bring him to heel.

She went through to the living-room where the record was still playing at full volume. She lifted the pick-up and the ensuing silence was dramatic.

'Do sit down, Alfred!'

Obediently he sat in his old wing-back chair with the broken springs.

'Have the police been?'

He did not answer at once, then he said: 'The police . . . I've been out.'

'I know, I've been trying to get you on the telephone.'

'I've been out.'

'But have you seen the police?' She spoke slowly and distinctly.

He shook his head.

Sara pulled up a chair and sat opposite her brother. 'You've heard about Matthew?'

He passed a thin hand over his face and said in a tired voice: 'He's dead; I heard that.'

'How did you hear?'

No answer. His eyes, surprisingly brown in contrast with his bleached skin, were restless and refused to meet her gaze.

'You know that he was murdered?'

A nod. It was only then that he seemed to realize he was still clutching the can of soup. Very deliberately he reached over the arm of his chair and placed it on the floor.

As though speaking to a child, Sara said: 'Look, Alfred, this is important. The police will come, asking a lot of questions, and not only about what happened last night. You understand?'

Alfred's pale hands caressed the arm of his chair. 'I suppose so.' He seemed indifferent but, suddenly, he became animated and made as though to get up. 'I must tell . . .' The words died on his lips as he caught Sara's eye and he subsided into his chair.

Sara was watching him; her brother; he was fifty-five yet he looked like an old man and his mind was wandering. Her big brother; her clearest memory of him went back to her early teens when he was a young man of twenty-one or two.

She said: 'You are a sick man, Alfred; perhaps you should have someone to look after you —'

35

He became agitated, leaning forward in his chair. 'No, Sara! No! Please! There is nothing wrong with me and I don't want anyone in the house — anyone!' He was pleading.

'All right! All right, Alfred; we won't talk about it now but do try to compose yourself. Sit quietly for a moment.'

For some time they faced each other in silence; the only sounds came from outside, from the maze of little alleys at the back. A car door slammed, a woman's voice called to her child, milk bottles rattled in a crate.

Abruptly, Alfred said: 'Have you told Maurice?'

'I phoned Trebyan first thing this morning.'

Another interval. Alfred seemed lost in thought, eventually he muttered to himself: 'Trebyan.'

'What about it?'

He looked up as though surprised to see her there. 'Trebyan — you remember the little hut?'

'Of course I remember it.'

'Is it still there?'

'I've no idea. Does it matter? It was all a long time ago, Alfred; when we were young.'

He nodded, and repeated, softly: 'When we were young — yes. Matthew wanted to build houses there, he would have pulled it down . . . That little hut was where my wife —'

In a level voice Sara interrupted him: 'Don't be absurd, Alfred! You know very well that you never had a wife. All this brooding on the past is turning your mind. The past is gone — finished! Forget it!'

Alfred looked at her with the eyes of a frightened child.

But she went on, speaking harshly though without raising her voice. 'You never had a wife, Alfred, and you were lucky; the woman you would have married was a bitch and a whore, and you know it. You've made yourself ill with self-indulgent fantasies and now this has happened. If you don't pull yourself together we shall have it all over again.'

Alfred was cowering in his chair as though he was being whipped, his face covered with his hands. From time to time he made little whimpering sounds but Sara's voice continued, unemphatic but relentless . . .

Chapter Three

Sunday (continued)

They found the weapon used to stun the bookseller: a piece of half-inch iron pipe about ten inches long. It was the ideal court exhibit, complete with bloodstain and a fragment of adherent skin. It had been tossed into a bed of nettles against the wall of the churchyard. Even its provenance had been established: a whole heap of such material — mostly in longer pieces — had been ripped out of a nearby house and lay, awaiting removal. Now the piece had been put into a polythene bag and given a label pending its despatch for forensic examination. Needless to say it carried no prints.

Wycliffe went in search of Sara and was received in the drawing-room.

'A worthy virgin' Trice had called her and Wycliffe saw at once what he meant. There was something essentially virginal about Sara Glynn, not the virginity of naïvety or innocence, but the soured virginity which arises from resentment of the female role. She might have been the headmistress of a certain type of girls' school, now almost extinct, or a Mother Superior in an enclosed order. At any rate there could be no doubt that she had found the temptations of the flesh resistible.

She wore a dove-grey Jaeger frock, discreet and asexual, but off an expensive peg. She was hollow eyed, drawn, and seemed very close to exhaustion but she had herself well in hand.

'I understand that it was you who found your brother's body?'

37

'Yes, and it was I who informed the police.' Prompt and explicit.

'You found him in his office at shortly after six this morning?'

'That is so.'

Wycliffe was gentle but persistent. 'You had a reason for going there at that time?'

'I did. I woke feeling unwell and I decided to go downstairs and make myself a cup of tea. In the kitchen I noticed that there was a light in my brother's office. It was possible that he had forgotten to switch it off last night or that he was at work early, but it was also possible that there had been an intruder. I went there to find out.'

'You couldn't see into the office from the kitchen?'

'No, the curtains were drawn.'

Sara Glynn sat opposite Wycliffe in the big, rather gloomy room with its dark wallpaper, over-varnished oil paintings in gilt frames, and leather-upholstered chairs.

There was something about the woman which brought out the official streak in Wycliffe and with it the pompous, well-rounded phrases: 'I'm afraid that we shall have to look into your brother's affairs and into his relationships both inside and outside the family. Some of the questions that are asked may seem impertinent, but you may be assured . . .' The official blend of stimulant and tranquilliser.

She shifted her position and adjusted the fine wool of her skirt over her bony knees. Despite her tiredness her movements were deliberate, unhurried, and self-absorbed; like a cat. When her attention returned to Wycliffe it was almost as though she found it an effort to recall what they were talking about. She said: 'Of course it goes without saying that you will receive full co-operation from the family.'

Wycliffe was well aware that it did not 'go', with or without saying. As far as Sara was concerned he would hear only what she considered fit for him to know.

'Perhaps you will tell me something about last night, how you spent the evening, whether you noticed anything unusual. You have an evening meal?'

'At 6.30.'

'So we will start there. Everybody was present at the meal?'

'Yes.'

'What happened afterwards?'

She pursed her lips and considered. 'My niece, Gina, helped me with the washing-up. The woman who comes in goes at five. Afterwards I went to my room and spent the evening reading and writing letters.'

'You spent the evening in your bedroom?'

'No, Chief Superintendent; I have a sitting-room as well as a bedroom upstairs.'

Every word seemed to have been crafted and polished before it was allowed to escape through her discriminating lips.

'You saw or heard nothing unusual?'

'Nothing.'

'Does your room overlook the back or front of the house?'

'The front.'

'You are quite sure that you did not go out at all last evening?'

'Quite sure.'

'When you went to your brother's office this morning was there a cat in the room?'

'A cat? No.'

'You are saying that you did not see your brother alive again after the meal you had together yesterday evening. Is that so?'

She lowered her eyes and her voice. 'That is correct.'

It was like filling in the blank spaces on a form and equally unprofitable. More than that, she was lying; somewhere along the line, and perhaps more than once, she had found it necessary to lie. He was sure of it but there was no point in putting on pressure until he had more to go on. He changed the subject.

'You had three brothers, Miss Glynn: Alfred, Matthew, and Maurice. One would have expected that Alfred, as the eldest, would have taken over the family firm or that it would have been left to the four of you jointly.'

39

'Alfred very much wanted to be a doctor and father encouraged him. When it became obvious that he would not be successful he decided to train as a pharmacist and father set him up in business.'

There was an answer for everything. Clearly all things worked together for good in this family where friction was as rare as in a well-oiled machine.

'And Maurice?'

'Maurice, as a young man, had a strong antipathy for business; he went to an art college and after . . .' She hesitated, searching for the acceptable phrase. 'After some false starts he set up as a potter at Trebyan in St Hilary — a property which belongs to the family. His work is becoming well known and he is able to live comfortably.'

'Your father financed him?'

Did Sara allow a slight irritation to show? At any rate she did not answer at once and Wycliffe had to insist. 'I'm afraid that such questions will have to be answered, Miss Glynn; if not by you, then by others.'

'All right; I will tell you. My father provided Maurice with a capital sum and leased him the property he now occupies at a nominal rental.' Her look clearly said: 'That must surely satisfy you!'

It did not. 'When your father died — how many years ago?'

'My father died in 1977.'

'So at that time the freehold of the property leased to your brother must have passed to someone else.'

'Under my father's will that part of his property went to my brother Matthew.'

'Your mother died quite recently, was she not involved in any of these dispositions?'

A downturn of the lips: 'Glynn women have never figured in wills; it has always been assumed that the men would look after them along with their other properties.'

Interesting. The first intimation of discord, even of bitterness.

The room was depressing: the single window looked out on the narrow street; there were net curtains as well as heavy, red velvet drapes drawn half-way across. Yet one was aware of everything that went on outside, of voices, of footsteps, of whatever traffic there might be.

She waited unruffled for his next question; a woman distressed but confident in her ability to handle any situation.

'Are either of your brothers married, Miss Glynn?'

'Alfred is not; he lives alone, over his shop. Maurice is a widower and has a son, David, who is twenty.'

'Presumably they know what has happened?'

'I have just come back from talking to Alfred and I telephoned Maurice.' A moment of hesitation, then: 'I think you should know that Alfred is a sick man; he has a heart condition . . .' It was clear that she had not yet made her point. 'He is also a little eccentric, sometimes very odd, probably through living so much alone . . . I hope that you will not think it necessary to harass him.'

'I'll remember what you say, Miss Glynn. There is just one other matter on which I shall be grateful for information. I understand that about seventeen years ago your sister-in-law walked out of her home and did not return.'

'So?'

'At that time your younger niece must have been still an infant.'

'Christine was two years old: Gina was eight, Gerald eleven.'

'It seems very remarkable that a woman would walk out, leaving her children like that.'

'Inez, my sister-in-law, was a very remarkable woman.'

'Was there another man?'

'I presume so.'

'You don't know?'

A slight lift of the shoulders.

'Was there a crisis in the marriage before she left?'

'No, there was no crisis.' A small smile. 'Nothing disturbed the even tenor of our days. Inez left, ostensibly to spend Sunday with a woman friend, and she did not come back. They found her car abandoned in Exeter.'

'Your parents were alive then; what was their attitude?'

41

She considered her answer. 'My father was entirely pragmatic in his response to all situations, even the most distressing. He believed, as I do, that people cannot be changed, that one must learn to cope with them as they are.'

'And your mother?'

'Mother was naturally very distressed.'

Sara straightened her skirt once more. 'That is all I can tell you, Mr Wycliffe, because it is all there is to tell. I have been frank because there is no purpose in your people hunting for family skeletons which do not exist.'

He went out into the passage and through the communicating door into the shop. Voices came from the direction of the offices and he found Fox expostulating with a tall youngish man, a Glynn without doubt and the heir apparent.

'I want to see my father and your man here won't let me. I've a right —'

Fox said: 'Mr Gerald Glynn, sir. I wouldn't let him through without your authority.'

Wycliffe was soothing. 'Well, now I'm here, you can come in with me, Mr Glynn.'

There was likely to be more interest in a member of the family who seemed to have come to the boil than in Sara who would cost time and patience to bring to blood heat. Wycliffe led the way into Glynn's office where one of the scenes-of-crime team was still at work. Wycliffe stooped and lifted the sheet which covered the body.

Gerald stood, looking down at his father, his face expressionless. After a moment or two he asked: 'Did that knock on the head kill him?' He added with a hint of apology: 'I don't understand about this sort of thing.'

'No, your father was strangled.'

'It must've been a pretty powerful bloke who did that; father was no weakling.'

'We think that he was first stunned by the blow on the head.'

'Ah! So anybody could've done it?'

'So it seems.'

42

'A woman?'

'Yes, but why do you ask?'

Gerald said nothing but his gaze shifted to the desk, to the whisky bottle and glasses. 'Somebody got him pissed, I expect; it wasn't difficult.' He sounded tolerant, almost affectionate.

Back in the outer office Wycliffe said: 'A few questions while you are here, Mr Glynn . . .'

They sat down. Gerald was subdued. He said: 'I could have seen him this morning before your lot arrived but I funked it.'

Wycliffe nodded. 'That is understandable. Now for my questions: It seems that your father willingly admitted his killer. Can you suggest any visitor who might have arrived, late in the evening, and been admitted like that?'

'Anybody.'

'Anybody?'

'That's what I said. If you're in politics you have to cope with two sorts of people, the ones you can use, and the ones who want to use you. Father made sure he was well acquainted with both sorts. He kept his ear to the ground and he spent a lot of time in his office after hours. All sorts would turn up for a little chat.' Gerald smiled. 'The old man was a damn good listener when it suited him and he knew the right questions. I can speak from experience.'

'Presumably he would be alone with his visitor during these sessions?'

'Of course! People likely to provide him with ammunition for his little campaigns wouldn't appreciate an audience any more than they'd want to be seen tripping up the steps of the council offices to some bloody committee room.'

'Wasn't it unwise of him to keep open house like that, with direct access to his office from a back lane?'

'Probably, but he's been doing it for years.'

'Is it possible, in your view, that he might have been killed because of his "little campaigns" as you call them?'

Gerald was contemptuous. 'These things are only shadow boxing, overgrown schoolboys sparring; they never come to much. The alternatives are bowls, golf, or chasing widow women.'

'There was a cat in your father's office last night.'

'That doesn't surprise me; the old man was fond of cats so Sara decided to be allergic to cat's fur and father encouraged the neighbourhood moggies into his office with kitchen scraps. Ronnie Swayne's — from next door — a monstrous beast, is one of the regulars.'

Gerald pulled out a crushed packet of cigarettes from a trouser pocket and lit one. He took a brief draw then fingered tobacco grains from his lips.

Wycliffe changed the subject. 'Your father must have had many acquaintances in business and in his council work, but did he have any close friends?'

'Old ferret-face next door — Ronnie Swayne; he deals in stamps, medals and coins. Then there's Mike Doble who keeps the wine shop farther up. They meet fairly often to play chess.'

'Here?'

'Swayne's place; he lives over his shop. Father was there last night.'

'Three of them play chess?'

'Don't ask me; I never mastered Snakes and Ladders. Anyway Mike is ill in hospital at the moment and unlikely to play chess for a bit.'

'How did you spend yesterday evening, Mr Glynn?'

'At the Grantham in St Ives playing snooker.'

'At what time did you get home?'

'About 11.15, give or take a few minutes.'

'You were driving?'

'I was.'

'What did you do with your car?'

'I keep it in one of the lock-ups at the top of the back lane.'

'And did you come into the house by the back or the front door?'

'The front. I didn't have any choice; the yard door was bolted. I had to walk round the bloody block.'

'Is that usual?'

'No, of course it isn't! I thought father had done it out of spite. We haven't been getting on too well lately.'

Wycliffe spoke to the scenes-of-crime officer: 'When you arrived this morning was the yard door bolted?'

'Yes, sir.'

'Check to see if that was the position when our chaps first came on the scene.'

Gerald said: 'I suppose somebody could have been in there doing the old man while I was trying to get in. But if the door was bolted this morning . . .'

'You were seen trying to get in last night, Mr Glynn.'

'I know; Dippy Martin was out looking for Cissie.'

'And some time after you went round to the front of the house a woman was seen to go in.'

'A woman? I don't get it.'

'That is what Martin says; he was some distance away at the time and wasn't able to see who it was.'

'You've lost me.'

'Is there anybody who might have had a serious grudge against your father?'

Gerald shrugged. 'Sounds a bit hyped up put like that but he and Uncle Alfred had a long-running feud.'

'What about?'

Suddenly Gerald became vague. 'A quarrel about some girl, I think. It's been that way ever since I can remember. Something from the hot, heady days of youth when the sap was rising. There were never any dramatic confrontations; they just didn't have anything to do with each other.'

'Your uncle is the pharmacist, down the street?'

'Yes, but you can't seriously think . . . He's a sick man and he's . . . I mean you only have to look at him. He couldn't swot a fly with a rolled-up newspaper.'

'And your father's other brother — Maurice, with the Trebyan pottery at St Hilary — was there any friction there?'

Gerald ran his fingers through his dark hair. 'Christ! You make us sound like the Mafia or something. We're an ordinary family with the usual family squabbles.'

'But you haven't answered my question.'

'Well, there's a spot of bother at the moment. Father owns the pottery, a bit of scrubland around it and a couple of small fields. All that's left of the Glynn acres.' Gerald grinned. 'The Glynns were farmers once upon a time. Actually, the family lived at Trebyan up to a few months before I was born, then they moved next door to be near the shop.'

'So what's the trouble about?'

'Just that father wants — wanted to build houses on the scrub and on one of the fields. He was after outline planning and thought he was going to get it. Maurice is raising hell — spoliation of the countryside, damage to the rural environment, forcible eviction of rabbits — you name it.' He looked at Wycliffe with a sheepish smile. 'Maurice and young David are "Greens" and into organic vegetables, goats' milk, and yoghurt.' He became serious. 'You can't see people like that . . .' He nodded towards the adjoining office.

In his own way Gerald was more skilful at whitewashing the family than his Aunt Sara.

'Well, thank you, Mr Glynn, that's all for the moment but I may have more questions for you later.'

When Gerald had gone Wycliffe joined Fox in Matthew's office.

'You were asking about the yard door, sir; it was bolted when the local police arrived this morning.'

'By the way, any prints on the whisky glasses?'

'The deceased's on one, the other has been wiped clean.'

Wycliffe stood by the window, looking across the yard to the back of the house. He could see the back door and what was, presumably, the kitchen window. Sara said that she was standing at that window when she noticed the light in the office. At six in the morning it would be daylight, and with the curtains drawn in the office . . .

Wycliffe left the office and walked the length of the dimly lit shop. The window blinds were down and he had a feeling that he was behind the scenes in a theatre. The bay to his left was labelled 'Fiction A–H', and to his right was the cash desk looking much the same as it must have done on the day the shop was first opened.

He could just read the faded inscription painted above the window: Glynn's Circulating Library. Established 1886.

(When all the women were reading Mrs Henry Wood, and Marie Corelli was about to burst upon a waiting world.) Four generations of Glynns, and the fourth of the dynasty had got himself murdered in his own office; no heat-of-the-moment crime either, but a carefully planned murder executed in cold blood out of hatred, or fear, or obsessive greed.

The business of the yard door was puzzling; it was bolted at 11.15 and mysteriously unbolted later so that an unidentified woman was able to enter at about 11.30, but bolted again when the police arrived some time after six in the morning. Then there was the cat . . . and Sara . . .

'Second-hand and Rare Books.' Wycliffe went upstairs to look. As always he was nosing out the territory like a dog in a new home; no objective in view. The upper floor was divided into two by a wooden screen with hammered-glass panels and a door bearing a notice: 'For access to the rare books section please apply at the desk.'

Wycliffe browsed among the second-hands. Along with scores of authors of whom he had never heard he found forgotten friends: Hugh Walpole, John Galsworthy, and the redoubtable Mazo de la Roche, captivator of millions who would now be devotees of TV soap . . . He must have been more sentimental and less cynical then. But this was no trip down memory lane and there was nothing to see but books. He was on the point of returning downstairs when he noticed that the door to the rare book section was not quite closed. Out of curiosity he pushed it open. The space devoted to rare books was very much smaller than to the second-hand. A few bookcases with glazed doors were arranged around the walls leaving a central space for a table and chairs. The floor was carpeted and the impression was one of a small library in a rather run-down country house.

If he had not actually gone into the room he would not have seen Gina; she was standing against one of the bookcases hidden from him by the open door.

'Mrs Morse? . . . Superintendent Wycliffe.'

'I know.' The door of the bookcase was open but there were no other signs of how she had been engaged. For some reason though she looked guilty. 'I had to be occupied, it's so demoralizing just waiting around. It's my job to keep a check on the stock and it seemed a good chance to get something done . . .' She was flustered.

Gina was an attractive young woman, on the plump side, oval face, dark hair and eyes, a pale skin, and freckles. At the age of seven he had fallen in love with a schoolteacher like her.

'So this is the rare books section.' To say something.

'That's what we call it but most of the books are not all that rare. We go in mainly for first editions of the classics but we do have some rather nice botanical books, floras mostly, sought after for their plates . . . We make a thing of local-interest books . . .'

She was over-anxious, talking too much.

'Somebody will be asking you questions more formally but perhaps you could tell me if you went out at all last evening?'

She seemed surprised, perhaps relieved by the question. 'No, I was in all the evening.'

'Do you know about your sister?'

'Christine went to a play at St John's Hall; she came in at about half-past ten.'

'And your aunt tells me that she spent the whole evening in her room. I ask because a witness claims to have seen a woman entering your yard by the yard door at about 11.30.'

She shook her head. 'There must be some mistake. Apart from anything else that door was bolted then, my brother couldn't get in.'

'Is it possible that your father had a woman visitor? I mean, is it possible that he had some emotional involvement outside the family?'

Gina looked blank then understanding dawned. 'You mean a woman!' She laughed shortly. 'Father had more than enough of women in the house and the business.'

Wycliffe said: 'Do you remember your mother, Mrs Morse?'

'Of course I remember her; I was eight when she left.'

'And you've never seen or heard of her since?'

48

'No.'

'Surely your mother's absence must have given rise to a great deal of discussion and speculation in the family — at the time, and afterwards.'

'If so, it was a case of "not in front of the children".'

'But since you've been grown up?'

She frowned. 'It's hard to explain. There is very little discussion about anything in our family — the excuse was that one mustn't upset granny, but I think it's a Glynn thing; cut discussion to a minimum, especially of unpleasant things, and perhaps they'll go away.'

Wycliffe stood, irresolute, wondering how best to turn this chance encounter to advantage. 'Your grandmother died four months ago; has her death had much effect on family relationships?'

It was clear that she saw the drift of his question but her answer was simple: 'Granny seemed to exercise a sort of spell over her sons, her husband too, I think. I suppose the only obvious change since her death is that we no longer have our Wednesday sessions.'

'What were they?'

She smiled. 'Old fashioned shops like ours still have half-day closing. We close on Wednesday afternoons and every Wednesday Maurice and Alfred would come here for a sort of high tea, presided over by granny.'

'Even though the brothers didn't get on together.'

'Oh, granny wasn't supposed to know about that. If she did, it was never admitted.'

Wycliffe was apologetic. 'I hope these questions won't seem offensive but we need to know as much as possible about the family. How do you remember your mother? As affectionate — loving — or was your relationship with her, say, less intimate?'

The question disturbed her and she took time to answer. 'I suppose you need to know these things . . . My mother wasn't demonstrative.' She hesitated. 'I never remember being hugged. On the other hand she was never hard on us and never unsympathetic; she looked after us, made sure we were properly fed and clothed, that we went to bed at a reasonable time — all that sort of thing.' Another reflective pause. 'No one could say she wasn't a good mother.'

'Looking back, does it surprise you that she left when she did?'

'Yes, it does.' With emphasis.

'You were aware of no special crisis? No rows?'

'No, none.' She looked at him in frank enquiry. 'Does that tell you what you want to know?'

'Yes, it does, and I'm grateful, but I have one more question: Was your Aunt Sara able, in some degree, to fill your mother's place?'

She thought for some time before saying: '"In some degree" puts it quite well.'

'Were you harshly treated?'

'No.' She hesitated again. 'Perhaps the impression I'm giving isn't quite fair to Sara; after all, she didn't ask for the job.'

Wycliffe walked downstairs into the gloomy shop. A family affair. All of them at least as concerned to limit the damage as to assist the inquiry. But who could blame them? He was beginning to get to know them as individuals and to glimpse their relationships but he could never be more than the outsider looking in. He was becoming increasingly conscious of the existence of something at the core — in fact, a suspicion, a threat, which must at all costs be shielded from his probes.

It was after one. Self-absorbed and brooding, he crossed the street, oblivious of the watchers, and entered the pub opposite. He elbowed his way to the bar and ordered a lager and a ham sandwich. If he was the cynosure of all eyes he didn't notice and in his present mood he wouldn't have been troubled if he had.

Although the little hut at Trebyan was only a couple of hundred yards from the house and the pottery it was over the slope of the hill and hemmed in by gorse and hawthorn: a single large room with a verandah, built of lap boarding, raised on a brick base and set in the side of the hill. From the verandah the only sign of human habitation was the tower of St Hilary church rising out of the trees half a mile away.

Christine reached the hut from the road by a steep track through the scrub and so avoided the house. David was waiting.

'Chris!' He took her in his arms and hugged her, breathless. 'I was afraid they wouldn't let you come.'

A kiss, and she moved away. 'I didn't ask; I told Gina where I was going but I'd better not stay too long.'

They stood side by side, arms resting on the verandah rail. Although it was overcast with rain threatening, opportunist bumble bees were making the most of the gorse flowers.

David said: 'You don't have to say it, Chris; I know . . . It's worrying me too.' He put his hand to his head. 'God! I never manage to say anything properly! I meant what's worrying you as well as the awful thing that happened to your father . . .'

At twenty he had not quite grown out of the gangling stage either in the control of his long limbs or in the expression of his most deeply felt thoughts and emotions.

'If only dad hadn't lost his temper with Uncle Matt like that nobody would even think of it . . .'

Christine put her hand on his arm. 'Dave! As far as we know nobody has, but we mustn't be afraid to talk about what worries us. We're more likely to see how silly it is. Nobody who knew Uncle Maurice could possibly believe that he could do such a thing. The two of them had a row about building houses here. All right! Perhaps they would have gone to court about it, but that doesn't mean that either of them . . .'

David said: 'I keep telling myself that but it doesn't stop me worrying.'

They remained standing close, gazing out over the valley. Finally, speaking in a low voice, the boy said: 'There's something you don't know: dad told me this morning that he was in bed when I got home last night.'

'Well, he often is, isn't he?'

51

'Not last night; I heard him come in a long time after I went to bed. I don't know what time it was but it must have been late.'

'Did he have the Land Rover?'

'No, I would have heard that.'

'So he was walking.'

'There's an old bike he sometimes uses.'

'You haven't asked him about it?'

He turned towards her. 'How could I?'

'No, sorry! . . . Where is he now?'

'I left him in the house; I said I was going to see to the goats.'

It was very quiet, not a sound anywhere; the cloud cover was beginning to thin and there was watery sunshine.

'He told the police he was already in bed when I got home.'

'They've been here?'

'A detective and a uniformed bobby just after you rang. They didn't stay long and they were very polite. Dad told them he went for a drink to the pub at Goldsithney, that he left at about nine and came straight home.'

In a voice that made it sound like an article of faith, Christine said: 'We both know that your father didn't kill mine so why he was late and why he didn't tell the police about it doesn't matter.'

'I love you, Chris.'

She faced him. 'You only know what your father told you.'

He took her in his arms but she separated from him. 'Not now, love; I must get back. But Dave . . .'

He turned to her, questioning.

'Remember, whatever happens we are still us.'

When Wycliffe returned to the bookshop Dr Franks's Porsche had joined the line of vehicles down one side of the street and it was raining. Franks had just arrived with his secretary and was still in the shop.

'Oh, there you are, Charles! Have you had lunch?'

'Of a sort.'

'Lucky you! Liz, here, bought me a ham sandwich on the way down: ghastly! You've met Liz, of course.'

'No.'

'*Really?*'

The pathologist's secretaries followed one another in bewildering succession. Usually Franks was elegantly dressed in fine worsted with a silk shirt; today he wore a denim overall. 'Liz and I were going sailing, damnit! First time out for the season.'

He was walking in and out of the bays, studying the bookshelves as though that was what he had come for. 'This is a good bookshop, Charles.' He spoke as a connoisseur might speak of a cheese or a wine. 'When I was a boy my parents had a bookshop like this in Plymouth. They had second-hand books upstairs too. I used to spend Saturday mornings up there reading Havelock Ellis and Marie Stopes until the old man tumbled to it. Father was an old-time Methodist; sex and the devil were one. Perhaps he was right.

'Well, where is the *corpus delicti*, old chap?'

The ritual began. Franks made his preliminary examination of the body, dictating brief comments to his secretary. The body was moved into fresh positions with Fox recording the whole process on film.

'Rigor is almost complete. Taking one thing with another: body temperature, ambient temperature, the fact that Saturn is in the ascendant and it's Sunday, I'd say he's been dead up to eighteen hours, probably not less than fourteen, that puts it between nine and one last night. Does that square with anything you know?'

'It would have a job not to.'

Wycliffe was always irritated by Franks, by his flamboyant and casual approach to death. He went on: 'I would like the contents of his pockets now; his clothes will go to Forensic.'

'You don't need me to tell you that he was stunned first, then strangled.'

'The weapon used for the blow?'

Franks peeled off his surgical gloves. 'I don't know. Perhaps a piece of metal piping with a bit of a ragged edge.'

'How about this?' Wycliffe pointed to exhibit 'A'.

Franks grinned. 'Looks all right to me. It seems to have struck edge-on as though the blow nearly missed. That caused more bleeding than our friend probably bargained for. I expect he/she wanted to avoid being spattered.'

'And did he/she succeed?'

'Perhaps. The blood would trickle, not come in spurts.'

'What about the ligature? Anything enlightening about that?'

'Not really. Plaited flex certainly but it probably had a large knot or something to increase pressure in the region of the larynx.'

'So we are looking for someone who knew his business.'

'Someone who came fully prepared anyway.'

The body was moved once more to make the pockets accessible and Fox searched them — there were only those in his trousers; he was wearing a cardigan in place of a jacket. The contents were predictable: a leather key-fold, a couple of pounds in coin, and a handkerchief. No safe key; it would have been too large for the key-fold.

Franks said: 'Well, I'm off, Charles. Shift him when you like but the sooner you get him over to me the better. They tell me there's still a chance of a decent lunch at the hotel on the prom.'

Wycliffe saw Franks and his secretary off at the shop door. Misty rain or Sunday lunch, or sheer boredom had dispersed the spectators and Lady Street was deserted.

Chapter Four

Sunday (continued)

The family had gathered in the kitchen for a late lunch made up of left-overs. There was no appliance in the kitchen less than thirty years old; the walls were painted cream with a green dado and the red-tiled floor was scrubbed every Friday by the cleaning woman. The wall clock had 'Glynn Books' lettered on its face and had been transferred to the kitchen from the shop in some major upheaval of the past. They had eaten what there was, sitting or standing around; only Sara sat at the table.

Gina said: 'I'll make some coffee — or tea, if anybody wants it.'

Nobody spoke and she went on: 'Tea or coffee, Gerald?'

Her brother was standing by the window, looking across the yard to the single-storey extension which housed his father's office. He turned to her. 'What? . . . All right, if you like. I'll have coffee.'

'Barry?'

Gina's husband was perched on a stool by the refrigerator. To his straw-coloured hair and blue eyes he added an obvious desire to please, at least to be agreeable, attributes which were rare amongst the Glynns. In zoological terms Barry was a commensal — a tolerated intruder from another species.

He seemed startled by his wife speaking his name. 'Yes — sorry, what is it?'

'Do you want coffee or tea?' Gina enunciated the words as though speaking to a backward child.

'Yes, yes please; I'll have coffee if you're making some.'

55

Gina filled the kettle and laid out cups and saucers. In the brooding silences the ticking of the clock seemed to become louder. They were trapped in each other's company, each one wanting to break away, to do anything rather than stay there together, but none of them would risk being thought unfeeling, or odd. It was the same with talk: what is an acceptable subject of conversation when one of the family has been murdered and the police are in the house?

Only Sara seemed composed and judicial; looking directly at Gerald she said: 'The police have only just started their questioning; I think we should be very careful about what we say to them. It will be all too easy to raise in their minds questions which have nothing to do with your father's death.'

And when they had drunk their coffee it was Sara who broke the spell. She got up from her chair. 'Well, I've got things to do.'

As she was leaving, Gerald said: 'Shouldn't you tell me what it is I'm supposed to keep quiet about?'

Sara looked at her nephew but said nothing.

When the door had closed behind her Gerald waited, his eye on the door, as though to make sure that she was not coming back. Gina said: 'Why be so bloody-minded, Gerald?'

Gerald countered with a question of his own: 'Has the Big Chief grilled you yet?'

'I've spoken to him.'

'And?'

'He asked me what I was doing last night, and then one or two questions about mother.'

'About mother? What about her?'

'He wanted to know if, looking back, I was surprised that she'd left. I said that I was.'

Gerald said: 'My God! He intends to stir with a big spoon!' And immediately changed the subject. 'When I got home last night and found the yard door bolted I thought the old man had deliberately locked me out but the police reckon that whoever killed father was with him then — while I was banging on the door, trying to get in.'

Gina was incredulous. 'You're saying they think the man . . . the man who killed father locked himself in?'

'Why not? He wouldn't want to be disturbed and all he had to do to get out was draw the bloody bolt.'

'You think that's what happened?'

'I've no idea but I'm beginning to wonder if the cops don't have another idea. If the door was still bolted when they arrived this morning —'

'Was it?'

'I don't know, but if it was I think they're going to get round to some really nasty questions.'

Barry had been sitting, hunched up on his stool, his heels caught in the crossbar, now he became agitated. 'You're not saying they might think it was one of us? They couldn't! It's too fantastic!'

Gerald was patronizing. 'You'll be surprised what nasty minds some of these coppers have, Barry. They're not all like your PC Palmer, singing Schubert to well-heeled geriatrics in your Sunday concerts.'

Gina, in a bored voice, said: 'You really are a tailor-made bastard, Gerald.'

Gerald went on as though she had not spoken. 'One other thing they'll want to know is the real reason why Sara was in father's office at just after six this morning.'

Christine had been telling herself: 'This isn't something I've read in the newspapers, this is happening to us! My father has been murdered and my uncle . . . Yet we sit here drinking coffee and . . . and talking as if . . .' She said aloud, with an edge to her voice: 'What are you saying, Gerald? Aunt Sara wasn't feeling well; she came downstairs and saw a light in father's office . . .'

Gerald was gentle with her. 'It was daylight at six, Chris, and the curtains were drawn in father's office — like now. See for yourself: could you tell from here if there was a light on?'

After Franks had left, Wycliffe went to pay a courtesy call at the local station. The skies were clearing. The weather, fickle over this western peninsula, makes mock of the forecasters.

As he walked up Lady Street the sun broke through and he was able to take his first leisurely look at the pleasing medley of styles, periods, and usage. The pavements were narrow, granite slabs set at ankle-wrenching angles, so that in the Sabbath quiet it was pleasanter to walk in the road.

'M. Doble. Wine Merchant' — presumably the other chess player, now in hospital. A freshly painted shop front with shining glass and a window full of bottles. The windows over the shop were discreetly curtained so it was likely that whatever Dobles there might be lived over the shop.

At the nick he found a reception committee from the press. Even reporters are sluggish on Sundays.

'I'll arrange a press briefing as soon as I have a base and something to say; meanwhile, all I can tell you is that early this morning Matthew Glynn, the bookseller, was found dead in his office in circumstances suggesting foul play.'

'How did he die?'

'I haven't had the pathologist's report but the indications are that he was strangled after being stunned by a blow to the head.'

A wizened little man Wycliffe had known of old, said: 'Somebody didn't like him. Are you expecting to make an arrest shortly?'

'No.'

'What was the motive?'

'I've no idea, and that is the truth.'

'Anything taken?'

'Not as far as I know.'

'A break-in?'

'There were no signs of a forced entry.'

When they were satisfied that there was no more to be got they let him go.

He found Kersey, sitting at the desk in an upstair, borrowed office surrounded by house-to-house reports prepared on the premises. Kersey said: 'They're doing all they can but there's really no way they can fit us in here for any length of time. Shaw is after an available property which Trice suggested. It's just across the road from the bookshop, down a little alley; about eight hundred square feet in three rooms, up one flight of stairs.'

'You've seen it?'

'I think it should suit.'

'Good enough.'

DS Shaw who, amongst other things, acted as the squad's quartermaster, would see to the hiring, and fitting out of the rooms with equipment from central stores.

'Anything in the reports?'

In a symbolic gesture of renunciation Kersey pushed his cigarette pack farther away. 'As usual, ninety per cent waste paper, but there is something on Sara. A witness claims to have seen her in Alexandra Road last night at about 11.15.'

'Reliable?'

'Our chap thought so.'

'And that ties in with what Dippy Martin had to say about a woman entering by the Glynns' back door at around 11.30.'

In movements which could have been those of a somnambulist Kersey had retrieved his cigarettes and was placing one between his lips while feeling in his pockets for a lighter. 'You want me to follow this up?'

Wycliffe said: 'I'll think about it; we need to be careful with Sara. Anything else in the reports?'

'Only gossip. It's common talk that Alfred is around the twist and that he's got worse recently, since his mother died. They say he's been stopped from dispensing NHS prescriptions.'

Kersey stroked his rubbery nose between finger and thumb, a sure sign of cerebration. 'How do you see it, sir? A family thing or an outsider?'

Wycliffe was dismissive. 'How can anybody see it? Franks says Glynn died between nine and one, he might as well have said last night sometime. It's open to the whole family plus any outsider with a sufficient grudge against Glynn.

'The only indication we have is that somebody seems to have drawn the bolt on the yard door between Gerald failing to get in at 11.15, and the mystery woman succeeding at 11.30. It's tempting to think that the killer made his getaway during that fifteen minutes.'

'Or that somebody in the house wanted to give that impression.'

'Guessing games!'

'Now it looks as though the mystery woman could have been Sara.'

Wycliffe sighed. 'It's all speculative. I doubt if we shall get far by concentrating on opportunity; it's motive that matters in this case.'

'The brothers weren't exactly fraternal.'

'No, but I've yet to come across anything that looks like a motive for murder. Anyway, I'm off to talk to this character Swayne. You see what you can do with Alfred — better still, let Lucy Lane try; the feminine touch.'

Kersey called after him: 'Shaw has fixed us up at the hotel on the prom — is that all right?'

'Sounds luxurious. I wonder if our paymasters will stand for it.'

'They're still on out-of-season rates.'

Next door to the Glynn shop there was a narrow frontage like a slice cut from a larger premises: two storeys, one room width, with an attic. The shop window was tiny and covered by a metal grille. In it coins and medals were set out on faded velvet pads and, at the back, there were cards of stamps displayed under amber polythene to protect them from the light. A discoloured printed card read: 'Collections Valued and Purchased'.

Ronnie Swayne: probably the last person to see Glynn alive apart from his killer.

Watched by the group of people opposite, Wycliffe pressed the doorbell and waited. After an interval he heard someone coming downstairs, bolts were drawn and the door was opened by a little man with freckles and vestiges of red hair.

'Mr Swayne?'

'You're from the police.' It was a statement.

'Chief Superintendent Wycliffe.'

'I'm glad you've come.'

60

The door did not lead into the shop as Wycliffe had expected but into a minute hall with the shop door on the right, and stairs leading up. Swayne secured the door and led the way upstairs to a sizeable but cluttered room at the front of the house, overlooking the street.

Swayne wore rust-coloured trousers and a matching pull-over, his movements were erratic, rapid yet precise, so that Wycliffe was reminded of a little red monkey.

'Please sit down . . . Drink? . . . No? Smoke if you want to . . . I'm glad you've come, I was thinking of getting in touch. I had one of your chaps here this morning asking questions but I wanted to talk to someone in authority.'

On a desk by the window a tray of stamps was in process of being sorted; there were bookshelves, a cabinet of shallow drawers presumably for coins, a safe, a filing cabinet, journals and catalogues were piled on the floor and, incongruously, a pier table and a French commode stood against one wall looking uncomfortable. The room was untidy, dusty, and much used.

Wycliffe put on his cud-chewing look and settled comfortably in his chair. 'It seems likely that you were the last person to see Glynn alive, apart from his murderer, but at the moment I am more interested in what you can tell me about him — the sort of man he was — and about his friends and his enemies as far as you can. You've known him a long time?'

'Pretty well all my life. When I was young my father kept an antiques shop where the restaurant is now, so we weren't far from the bookshop; the two families were on friendly terms and I was at grammar school with the Glynn boys. Matt and I were the same age within a month but Alfred was two or three years older and Maurice quite a bit younger. But the Glynns didn't actually come to live next to their shop until about the time Matthew got married. Before that they lived out at Trebyan — where Maurice's pottery is now.'

'Can you suggest any reason why anyone might have wanted to kill Matthew?'

Swayne was emphatic. 'None! Matt wasn't the sort of man to antagonize people. I know he made the sparks fly sometimes in council committees but most of that was good humoured.'

Wycliffe's manner was easy, conversational. 'I've heard that he wasn't on speaking terms with Alfred and that the feud — whatever it was — goes back many years . . .'

A quick look from the sharp little eyes. 'You don't imagine that Alfred —'

Wycliffe cut him short. 'I don't imagine anything, Mr Swayne; I'm trying to find out as much as possible about the people concerned and I have to start somewhere.'

'Yes, of course.' Swayne took a small cigar from a box near his chair. 'You don't mind? . . . You won't join me?' He went through the ritual of lighting the cigar and took a first luxurious puff before continuing: 'It's not easy to put this sort of thing in proper perspective.' A brief laugh. 'Family feuds are hell; they don't have much logic.'

Wycliffe said nothing and his expression remained bland, almost sleepy.

'Well, Matt and Alfred had very different temperaments. Alfred, as the elder, was expected to follow father in the business but he jibbed; he wanted to be a doctor. To cut a long story short, he couldn't make the grade so he ended up as a pharmacist in the business his father bought for him as a going concern. I'm pretty sure, in the way these things work, that Alfred felt he had made the wrong choice and, illogically, held it against Matthew. But that was only the start.'

The door of the room opened a little way and a large tabby cat insinuated itself through the gap. It paused, assessing the situation, green-eyed, then it leapt on to the arm of Swayne's chair and a moment or two later it had settled, tail and paws tucked in, tidily disposed for sleep.

Unnecessarily, Wycliffe said: 'Your cat?'

Swayne stroked the creature. 'Clarence — my family, and a lot less trouble than some other families I could mention.

'Anyway, getting back to the Glynns . . . Shortly after taking over the shop Alfred fell in love with the sort of girl men have fantasies about, and she seemed to respond. Nobody knew much about her, she'd turned up in the town as a sort of companion-housekeeper to an old lady who had a house in Morrab Close, a Mrs Armitage — a widow. I think she was a relative. Anyway, Alfred couldn't believe his luck; he'd never really made it with girls and here he was hitting the jackpot. The old lady died and within weeks they'd decided to get married; they started furnishing the rooms over the shop and all was set for a wedding.'

Swayne paused, watching the smoke curl upwards from his little cigar. 'Well there was a wedding all right, but it was Matthew who married the girl.'

Wycliffe was roused. 'You mean you've been talking about — what was she called? — Inez — the mother of Matthew's children?'

'Exactly, and it didn't improve matters from Alfred's point of view when he discovered that she was already a couple of months pregnant by Matthew when she married him.'

'It must have caused a scandal.'

'It didn't actually. The Glynns have always played their cards close to their chests and, like Clarence here, they have the knack of fading into the background when it suits them. There was a certain amount of gossip but it soon died down.'

Wycliffe was impressed. 'And then, eleven years later, she walked out on Matthew and her three children.'

Swayne gave a short laugh. 'That was Inez — that was!' After a pause he went on: 'I think you'll agree that Alfred had good reason to feel aggrieved. From the time of the marriage he cut himself off entirely from his brother, but it wasn't only from Matthew: he became more and more of a recluse until now he hardly sees anyone but the people he meets in the course of his business — and they're getting fewer by the month. Until his mother died he used to pay a routine Wednesday visit but, of course, that's stopped now.'

'Do you have any contact with him?'

Swayne smiled. 'One of the privileged few. I felt sorry for Alfred at the time — I still do. I look in occasionally for a drink and a chat though he's getting more and more difficult to talk to. As a matter of fact, Matthew asked me to keep an eye on him — I think he felt guilty.'

When Swayne stopped speaking small sounds reached them from the street: a woman's heels tapping on the paving stones, a snatch of conversation from the people opposite . . . Swayne waited for some comment on his revelations, a word of commendation, even thanks, but when Wycliffe spoke it was on a quite different subject.

'What happened last night?'

'You mean, what happened here?'

Wycliffe said nothing. There were advantages in failing to define your terms. Precise questions encourage precise answers while vague ones often elicit more information.

Swayne said: 'Matt arrived about half-seven and we played chess — just the one game and it was a rout. Matt was off his game. We chatted a bit, had a drink or two, and he left at half-past nine — said he had work to do in his office.'

'The two of you were alone?'

'Yes, Mike Doble usually joins us but he's in hospital at the moment for a heart operation.'

'Would you say that Glynn was much as usual?'

A pause to consider. 'No, he was preoccupied; worried about the business. He's had problems lately: they need working capital and Matt has a dread of, as he put it, "getting into the hands of the bank". I don't think it was anything very serious.'

Wycliffe stood up. 'Well, thank you for your help, Mr Swayne. I expect I shall be calling on you again.'

Swayne escorted him downstairs and, at his own request, Wycliffe left by way of the backyard.

'Is this what Glynn did last night?'

'Yes, he always comes and goes this way.'

Some of the backs were dilapidated but the two premises belonging to the Glynns stood out in good repair: the wall had been recently pointed and colour-washed and the door freshly painted.

The door was bolted but Wycliffe banged on it and was admitted by a uniformed policeman.

He could not make up his mind about Swayne. The little man had appeared shocked at the very idea that Alfred might be suspected of killing his brother yet he had gone on, with a certain relish, to provide a convincing motive — if a motive which has lain dormant for thirty years is still convincing. Festering hatred, nurtured and cultivated like a precious plant for half a lifetime, is good stuff for the novelist, but does it happen?

He stood in the middle of the yard. To his right was the single-storey extension which housed Glynn's office with its own exit to the yard. The killer could have reached the office from the lane, or by crossing the yard from the house, or by coming through the shop from the house. The yard door was bolted at 11.15 but a woman — Sara? — was seen to enter by it at around 11.30. Presumably she bolted the door after her for that was how the police had found it in the morning.

There were alternative scenarios: the killer, an outsider, was still with his victim when Gerald tried to get in but, by the time the woman arrived, he had left. Dippy Martin had not seen anyone but he had spent some time at the top of the lane. Alternatively, the killer was someone from the house who had secured the door to ensure privacy, but opened it again after his crime to confirm the impression that an outsider was involved. There were other possibilities but for the moment these seemed the most plausible. Of course it was conceivable that the assailant had climbed the yard wall but, without a ladder of some sort, this would have been an acrobatic feat.

Wycliffe felt like a crossword addict who has some of the clues, a few of the answers but no grid on which to relate them.

The back door of the house opened and a girl came out into the yard. Christine, he supposed, the younger sister. She was shaking a tablecloth when she looked up and saw him. Her expression froze; a vague gesture and she turned to disappear indoors.

Sometimes the strangeness of his job came home to him. What had he to do with that girl? Why should she be troubled by the mere sight of him? A few hours ago he had not known that she existed, now he was a licensed voyeur, authorized to meddle in her most intimate concerns.

In the office Fox and his team had completed their work including an inventory. 'Except the safe, sir.' Fox had a grievance, his manner was indignant. 'I found the key eventually, it was in Glynn's bedroom — in a little bureau drawer with other keys. I asked to have one of the family present when I opened the safe but Gerald objects to it being opened at all without their solicitor being present. That would mean putting it off until tomorrow.'

'Well?'

'I told him I would ask you.'

'It sounds reasonable, tell him to arrange for his solicitor to be here in the morning.'

'But he's being deliberately obstructive.'

'Perhaps, but that's life, Fox. Put a seal on the safe and we'll see what's inside in the morning. By the way, have you ever taken a cat's paw-prints?'

Fox was wary. 'I can't say I have — a dog's, sir, but never a cat's.'

'Have a try with Swayne's cat next door; he might have made the bloody marks on the carpet. His name is Clarence, by the way. Be nice to him — and to Swayne — and find out, if you can, what time Clarence came in last night.'

Fox was disapproving. 'I take it you are serious, sir?'

'As a judge.'

It was late afternoon. That morning Wycliffe had heard of the Glynn family for the first time and in the few hours since he had learned something about them; about Gerald, Gina and Barry, about Christine and Aunt Sara, and about the uncles, Alfred and Maurice. But he was still a very long way from knowing enough to judge the value of what each of them had chosen, or would choose to tell him, and what they would, for differing reasons, see fit to suppress.

Above all he knew little more about Matthew Glynn than might reasonably appear in his obituary, but he needed to know the man well enough to see him going about his daily life against the background of his home and shop and in the context of his family, friends, and acquaintances.

'Glynn's bedroom — which room is it?'

66

'Opposite the top of the stairs, sir.'

'And the bureau — is it locked?'

'Yes, but the key was among those in Glynn's pocket. I've got them here.' Fox handed over the key-fold.

Wycliffe went through the shop and entered the house by the communicating door. It opened into a passage which ran the length of the house. Voices came from somewhere at the back — probably the kitchen: families seem to favour the kitchen as an assembly point in times of crisis. He had intended to visit Matthew's bedroom alone but changed his mind and went to the kitchen. He knocked and opened the door.

They were standing around in frozen postures like a group caught when the music stops in a game of Statues.

'Miss Glynn — Miss Sara Glynn?'

Sara wasn't in the kitchen but a voice behind him said: 'You wanted me, Superintendent?' He had not heard her approach.

'I shall be grateful if you will show me your brother's room.'

He followed Sara up the stairs and into Matthew's bedroom. The heavy wardrobe, the dressing-table with triple mirrors, the tallboy — all in walnut — and the matching double bed with its honeycomb quilt, belonged to the era of Matthew's father or even his grandfather.

Above the mantelpiece, in a place of honour, was an enlarged photograph of a middle-aged woman with the hairstyle and in the dress of the Forties; it was inscribed, boldly: 'To Matt, from Mother'.

Wycliffe looked at the massive double bed. 'Did your brother sleep in this room when your father was alive?'

'No, he moved in here only recently — after mother died.' A curve of the lips. 'Of course it was the bedroom belonging to the head of the house but he couldn't have turned mother out.' The irony was bitter.

'I see. I'm sorry to inflict this on you, Miss Glynn, but I want to look at the contents of the bureau amongst other things and it is better that a member of the family should be present. It's also a chance to have another word with you.'

His manner was pleasant but she was unresponsive; she stood, motionless in the middle of the room, as though waiting patiently for her services to be called upon.

The bureau which was against the window wall and the chair beside it did not match the rest of the furniture. Wycliffe unlocked and lowered the flap. Everything was in meticulous order: envelopes and headed paper in pigeon holes, a section for unpaid bills, another for receipted accounts; a box for stamps. Evidently Matthew had kept his personal affairs quite separate from his shop and council business.

The bureau had a single, locked drawer and in it, amongst other things, Wycliffe found a cheque book, a paying-in book, and a sheaf of bank statements clipped together. While still leafing through the statements he turned to Sara: 'We have a witness who claims to have seen you in Alexandra Road after eleven on Saturday night, and you may know that a woman was seen going in by the back door of this house at half-past.'

Wycliffe did not look up from the statements and for some time Sara gave no sign that she had heard; then she said: 'I've been very stupid. One does something on the spur of the moment that is trivial and perhaps a little silly, then when that action is caught up in . . . in a tragic event, one feels quite foolish telling of it.'

Wycliffe had transferred his attention from statements to cheque stubs. 'So what did you do on Saturday night?'

'As I told you, I spent some time writing letters and when I'd finished I thought it would be pleasant to get some fresh air so I went out and posted them — in the box outside the main post office —'

'What time was that?'

'About a quarter past ten. It was pleasant out of doors and I went for a walk, down by the station, along the Wharf and across the promenade.'

'Surely it was raining?'

'Now and then, but I don't mind the rain.'

'You went out and came back by the yard door?'

'Yes.'

'And you saw nothing either going or returning to the house which seemed suspicious or even unusual?'

'Nothing.'

'Did you enter the house through the kitchen door or through your brother's office and the shop?'

'Why should I go through his office? I saw the light there and assumed that he was working.'

Wycliffe said nothing for a while but continued with his study of the cheque stubs. When he spoke it was to change the subject. 'Your brother seems to have had little use for credit cards.'

She seemed surprised by the new topic, perhaps relieved. At any rate she came to stand by the bureau. 'Matthew had very old-fashioned views about credit, even in running the business.'

Wycliffe held out a cheque stub folded to expose a particular counterfoil. 'A cheque in favour of Eurotravel, dated a couple of weeks ago. Was he planning a trip?'

'Yes, a holiday; he intended to go away in May — it was a regular thing. He had two holidays a year: in May he usually went abroad for a fortnight, then in October he would have another fortnight somewhere in this country.'

'Do you know where he intended going next month?'

'He tried to visit a different European country on each of his spring trips.' She smiled. 'I think it was Bulgaria's turn this year.'

'He went on these trips alone?'

'Oh, yes; I often wonder how he managed; he wasn't the sort to make friends easily but he seemed to enjoy himself. Of course they were package tours though he seems to have spent a surprising amount on this one. Matthew was so careful with his money in most things.'

A few things remained in the bureau drawer; the odds and ends that accumulate in drawers: an engagement diary for 1981 which had only a few entries; an old wallet, empty except for an out-of-date RAC membership card.

'Your brother seems to have kept nothing to remind him of his wife.'

'Does that surprise you? When it was obvious that Inez was not coming back he packed up everything connected with her and stored it in one of the attics. He did it himself. No one was allowed to go through her belongings.'

'She was still the mother of his children.'

Sara said nothing.

Wycliffe returned everything to the drawer. He was in the act of locking the bureau flap when he said: 'Miss Glynn, what made you go into your brother's office this morning when you came down, as you say, to make yourself a cup of tea?'

She was terse. 'I told you; I saw the light.'

'No.'

'I beg your pardon!'

'It was daylight at the time and the curtains in your brother's office were drawn.'

It took her a second or two to recover. 'But I'm sure I saw a light . . . If the curtains were slightly parted —'

'Were they?'

'I am trying to remember the exact circumstances; I am not accustomed to having my word questioned.'

Wycliffe stood looking at her, his face expressionless. She was trying to decide between aggression and a more conciliatory approach but Wycliffe cut her short.

'I advise you to think very carefully about what you have told me, Miss Glynn, and then to volunteer a statement.'

When Wycliffe left the Glynn house a bell in the church, almost next door, was tolling for evening service; not the usual tumbling peal but a monotonous counting out of strokes on the tenor bell, presumably in token of respect for bereaved neighbours. He had to make his way past people converging on the church and was pointed out by several.

About half the tables in the hotel dining-room were occupied but Wycliffe, with Kersey and Lucy Lane, was placed in one of the window embrasures which gave them all the privacy they could have wished.

Detective Sergeant Lucy Lane was an established member of the Serious Crimes Squad and she more than earned her keep. She was also an attractive girl. With her mass of dark hair, her so-called classical features, and a slender body, she might have been a Klimt model clad in sober woollies instead of erotic raiment.

The fact that Wycliffe often deferred to her judgement made Kersey suspicious of her intrusion into their cosy male councils.

The food was good: a thin soup followed by pork spare ribs. A white-haired waiter with a drooping moustache confided that the marinade was a speciality of the chef. They drank Chablis, nicely chilled.

Kersey said: 'Worth starving for.'

'Let's finish the bottle.'

Lucy, with her hand over her glass, said: 'No more for me.'

With the cheese Wycliffe told them of his interview with Swayne, and of Sara's revised version of her doings the previous evening.

Kersey said: 'So Matthew married Alfred's girlfriend after getting her pregnant; not exactly fraternal conduct, but as a motive for murder it's surely worn a bit thin after thirty years.'

Wycliffe turned to Lucy: 'What did you make of Alfred?'

Lucy patted her lips with her table napkin. 'I'm not sure.' That in itself was unusual. Lucy rarely prevaricated. 'I felt sorry for him. He's living alone in near squalor and he's obviously a sick man.'

'You must have got something.'

'It was difficult. His sister, Sara, had been to see him and I think she must have upset him. Of course I don't know what he's usually like. I couldn't keep him to any particular point — he kept slipping from one subject to another without seeming to realize it.'

Kersey helped himself to a little more of the Stilton. 'In other words, he's a bit gaga.'

Lucy frowned. 'I'm not so sure about that. My impression was that I was only getting a small part of his attention, that he was profoundly preoccupied and that the one thing he wanted was to be left alone.'

'Was he afraid?'

'Afraid?' She shook her head. 'Certainly not of me or of anything I might do.'

'In your opinion, would he have been physically capable of the killing?'

'I think so; after all it wasn't a job for a muscle man. I suppose you knew that he had medical training?'

'He told you that himself?'

'In one of his digressions. He either failed or didn't take his finals; I couldn't make out which.'

Kersey said: 'I find it hard to believe that anybody, even a nut, would murder after thirty years of procrastination.'

Lucy emptied her wine glass. 'Perhaps the fact that his mother had only recently died had something to do with it.'

Wycliffe nodded. 'That's a point we mustn't overlook in all this. What was his attitude to Matthew?'

'It's hard to say. His first comment was: "I haven't seen much of Matthew recently" — as though they hadn't happened to meet in the street for a week or two — not that they hadn't spoken for nearly thirty years.'

'Any particular antagonism?'

'Not obviously. His attitude was that of a well-bred man reluctant to discuss some family difference with a prying outsider. To be honest I couldn't make up my mind about him and I'd like you to see him yourself.'

Outside the hotel window people strolled past, trailed by their dogs; Penzance must have a high rating in the doggy charts. Others watched the sea from their parked cars strung out along the promenade. It was a fine evening, the sea was an unruffled expanse of silvery blue; the Mount stood out, a grey-green pyramid with its fairly-tale castle at the top catching the low sun. Everything was in sharp focus, the horizon was a clear line dividing sea and sky; more rain about.

Kersey brushed biscuit crumbs from his jacket. 'Coming back to Sara: she went to post a letter, took a little walk in the rain, heard nothing, saw nothing and said nothing about it because she felt silly — is that it, sir?'

'Just about.'

'Do you believe it?'

'I've asked her to think over her position, including her story about seeing a light in her brother's office from the kitchen this morning. I've suggested she should volunteer a fresh statement.'

Wycliffe folded his table napkin and got up from his chair. 'Whatever Sara might or might not have done, I think I'll go for a walk.'

It was predictable whenever he was away from home — the stroll before bed — and they both knew better than to offer their company. He walked to Newlyn, where the paintings and the pilchards came from in the old days, and returned along the sea-front with the streetlamps struggling against the great plain of darkness that was the sea. Eventually he went to sleep to the sound of little waves lapping against the sea-wall.

Chapter Five

Monday morning

The Incident Room premises secured by Shaw were part of a complex of old buildings near the wharf which were suffering from planning blight. If their historical interest had saved them from the pick, the swinging steel ball, and the bulldozer, their intractable lay-out had discouraged renovators who might have put them to some use. The rooms were over a former shop now used by a small-time printer, and the clacking and rumbling of his press would underscore the activities of the squad.

Already equipment and furniture were being delivered from central stores and technicians were installing a communications unit. The smallest of the three rooms had been set aside for the officer in charge; it had a desk, a couple of chairs, and a telephone which, allegedly, would soon be functional. Wycliffe looked about him and approved, especially of the walls which, in some past time, had been stencilled with designs that were mildly but cheerfully crazy so that to look at them for long made the eyes go funny. Another plus: the window of this room looked out over grey slate roofs to the harbour and Albert Pier.

'Incident Rooms I have Known': Wycliffe could have written a book about them.

At the briefing he agreed to see Alfred, while Kersey would talk to the son-in-law, Barry Morse. 'The outsider,' Wycliffe called him. 'Gossip has it that he's a good accountant, keen on music, and henpecked. I don't suppose the three are incompatible but that's all we know about him. Among other things you might get his view of the bookshop and of his father-in-law as a business man.'

Kersey grumbled: 'I don't go down well with bank managers, accountants, and others of the breed; we are *non simpatico*. Why not let Shaw do it?'

Wycliffe was brusque. 'Because Shaw has his hands full with the Incident Room and you've got the rank. When you've finished with Morse see what you can find out about Inez Glynn's disappearance; the records should be available by now.

'Incidentally, when Inez went Matthew collected all her belongings together, everything that reminded him of her, and stored them in one of the attics; nobody else was allowed to touch the stuff. I'm arranging for Fox to go through it.'

'You think there's a connection?'

'I've no idea.'

Lucy Lane was assigned to the bookshop; among other things to keep an eye on the opening of the safe. House-to-house enquiries would continue with special attention to Matthew's acquaintances in business and in his council activities.

A steep alley provided a short cut from the wharf area to Lady Street. The street looked very different from its Sunday image; the shops were open and delivery vans effectively blocked the way for all but the most resolute pedestrians. It had rained overnight but now the sun was breaking through and the scene had a certain gaiety. Seagulls swooped and planed overhead laying raucous claim to some scrap of food in the possession of one of them. It was nine by the church clock and another clock over a bank in the town hammered out the strokes.

'Alfred Glynn MPS. Chemist and Druggist.' The sign, in faded letters, was suspended over a shop window cluttered with a dusty, neglected display of sickroom adjuncts and toilet articles along with dummy boxes and bottles and tins advertising baby foods and patent medicines. There were two or three granite steps up to the front door which had a grubby 'Closed' notice hung behind its glass panel; no bell, and no other door.

Wycliffe decided to approach from the rear. He had to go through the churchyard to reach the back lane so he counted the houses to be sure of identifying Alfred's door. It was devoid of paint and dragged on its hinges. Part of the yard was taken up with a shed, the rest was a wilderness of weed with a slate path up to the back door.

He walked up the path. There was a bell-push by the door and he pressed it. A bell sounded somewhere in the house but there was no response. After two more attempts he tried the door; it was unsecured and it opened into a little hall from which stairs led upwards.

He called: 'Mr Glynn!'

Still no answer. After a short wait he climbed the stairs and at the top he called again. The only sound came from the ticking of a clock. Several doors opened off the landing and there were ladder-like stairs which presumably led to the attics. He tried the first door, it opened into the kitchen; the second led to the living-room. He called once more without result then advanced into the room. It was L-shaped and only when he reached the corner of the 'L' could he see the whole of the room. There was no one there.

It was a cheerless, comfortless room; only tattered books on makeshift shelves and an old-fashioned record player suggested any kind of relaxation; no radio, no television. There were no pictures on the walls but on the mantelpiece, amongst a random collection of odds and ends, there was a framed photograph of an elderly woman; her hair was gathered into an old-fashioned bun on the top of her head; she had a smooth, rather spoilt face and an expression of absolute serenity. The photograph was inscribed: 'To Alfred from mother, at 75.'

A single-bar electric fire stood in front of the empty grate and a wing-backed chair, threadbare and with broken springs, was drawn up in front of it. On a low table by the chair were the remnants of a spartan breakfast — a few crumbs of toast, a tub of margarine, and a mug with coffee dregs at the bottom; also a book, open but face down: Le Carré's *The Honourable Schoolboy*.

Morning light streamed through the window searching out the shabbiness and the dust, the peeling walls and cobwebbed corners. Through the window he could see over grey slate roofs across the bay to Newlyn, a mound of little houses behind its quays and boats and sheds. A shaft of sunlight caught the hill above the village turning the fields acid green.

Wycliffe returned to the landing and tried another door: the bathroom and lavatory. The Victorian stoneware 'suite' from Mr Twyford's manufactory was decorated with flowers in willow-pattern blue but paint flaked off the walls and the linoleum had worn through to the floorboards. The next room was Alfred's bedroom: an iron bedstead with a tumbled mass of greyish bedding, a chest of drawers and a non-matching wardrobe. There were more books in a nest of shelves by the bed.

For no reason he could think of the rooms reminded him of a deserted stage set when the play has ended its run and the actors have gone.

But it was the main bedroom which came as a surprise and a shock.

The room was in the front of the house and the window overlooking the narrow street was hung with net curtains and pale blue velvet drapes which were almost completely drawn. It was a moment before his eyes became accustomed to the gloom.

The room had been vandalized — viciously so; but it was equally apparent that it had been furnished and cared for at a level totally different from the other rooms. The double bed, the wardrobe, dressing-table and tallboy were mahogany, the counterpane was of moire silk and the eiderdown was covered in the same material; the carpet was a red-ground Wilton. But the polished surfaces of the furniture had been scored, even gouged; the counterpane had been cut to ribbons and the eiderdown slit open in several places. A carriage clock lay smashed on the floor besides an art-nouveau lamp; and the bedside table on which, presumably, they had both stood, had been split almost in two.

On the carpet by the tallboy were several red carnations, as fresh as they had come from the florist, and beside them, a shattered glass spill. Water from the spill had soaked the carpet. Also on the floor were three or four framed pictures which had been trampled — stamped upon, so that the frames were broken and the glass shattered to fragments. They were photographic enlargements, head-and-shoulders portraits, all of the same girl, photographed in profile; looking up and looking down, and seen from the right and from the left.

So this was Inez, the *femme fatale* of the Glynn brothers: her features were patrician: a long, slender neck, pouting, sensuous lips, a slightly aquiline nose and sloping forehead — a model for an Egyptian tomb-painting or limestone relief. This was Inez in her early twenties, before she became the mother of Matthew's children. In the mingling of the genes the children had missed their mother's sculptural beauty and been forced to settle for mere good looks.

The double bed had been made up for two and there were two pyjama cases — relics of a past time — one embroidered with the letter 'I', the other with an 'A'. But it was obvious that the room was never used; it was a museum, perhaps a shrine. So, for thirty years Alfred Glynn had preserved this room as it had been when he still believed that the silk counterpane and the eiderdown would be the covers on his marriage bed. He had not only preserved the room, he had cleaned it with meticulous care and provided fresh flowers in the little glass spill. Here was the connubial complement to Miss Havisham's wedding feast but without the cobwebs.

Now, certainly within the last twenty-four hours, the room had been vandalized.

By Alfred himself? Or by another? And where was Alfred?

He did not remember having seen a telephone. He returned to the living-room and found that what he had taken to be a cupboard door, in fact gave access by a flight of stairs to the shop. As he descended he was aware of a distinctive blend of smells recalling chemist shops of his childhood; it was compounded, among other things, of disinfectant,

78

Parma violets, and balsam. The shop was dimly lit and cluttered but he found his way to the front door which was bolted; Alfred had not left and could not return that way.

At the other end of the shop, behind a hammered-glass screen, was the dispensary and, adjoining that, a tiny office — with a telephone. He tried the number of the Incident Room, found that it was functional, and spoke to the duty officer.

'I'm at the pharmacy. I want DS Fox here with his team and a uniformed man. They should come by the back door. Is Mr Kersey or DS Lane there?'

'No, sir, but DS Shaw is.'

'Then ask him to come to the phone.'

Shaw spent most of his time on organization and records; he was rarely involved directly in enquiries but he had been a first-class man on the ground.

'Shaw speaking, sir.'

'I want you to organize enquiries as to the whereabouts of Alfred Glynn, starting at the bookshop then going on to residents in the street who might have seen him; get in touch with his brother at the pottery. No alarm as yet; it's quite possible that he's gone for one of his walks or he may be shopping or just visiting someone, but I'm concerned.'

While phoning Wycliffe opened drawers and cupboards in the Dickensian desk at which he was standing. One cupboard was stacked with old prescription books while one of the drawers held enough sealing wax to supply a pre-war dispensary with red seals on the drug packets of a generation.

He was momentarily startled by the ringing of a doorbell. He had to climb the stairs to the living-room then go down again to the back door. They had sent him a WPC who looked like a schoolgirl dressed in police uniform for a school play.

'WPC Ferrers, sir. DS Fox is on his way.'

'Do you know Alfred Glynn?'

'Yes, sir, I've lived here all my life.'

'I want you to stay here in the yard until he returns. When he does — if he does — report to DS Fox before you let him into the house, and leave the explanations to Fox.'

'What about the front of the premises, sir?'

Young she might be, stupid she was not. 'The shop door is bolted on the inside so he can't get in that way.'

Fox arrived with an assistant and Wycliffe took him to the vandalized room. 'It's obvious that this is all fresh, probably done this morning. I want to know whether it was done by Glynn himself or by an outsider. Glynn's prints must be all over the premises so there should be no problem.'

'Are we authorized to be here, sir?'

'No, but that is my responsibility. If Glynn turns up you will be warned by the WPC. Go easy on him; one way or another he is or will be very distressed.'

Wycliffe left the house feeling disorientated as he did when emerging from the darkness and isolation of a cinema into reality and the light of day. Lady Street had returned to what must have been normal for any morning at this time; the delivery vans had gone, there was sporadic traffic in the one-way street, and people had no time to stand about gawping at the bookshop though they slowed their pace in passing and tried to look in without appearing to do so. There was a notice on the door: 'Closed temporarily; all enquiries by telephone please.'

Wycliffe turned down the alley towards the Incident Room. The printer, running off posters on his flat-bed press, was going through operations not significantly different from those performed by Caxton five hundred years earlier. Police vehicles were tucked into every available space in the crooked, meandering alley and police personnel, uniformed and CID, were continually clattering up and down the stairs which led to the room above the printer's. An alien presence had established itself in the heart of the town and people who had no connection with the crime under investigation or any other would feel uneasy until they were gone.

'Paula!' Sara was brusque. 'You were in and out of this office all the time, you must have some idea of what my brother kept in his safe.'

Paula James, Matthew Glynn's youthful amanuensis (after a one-year course in office routines at the technical college) had turned up for work as usual, unaware of the events which had robbed her of her employer. She found herself in his office, the centre of a family gathering with their lawyer and a policewoman. Slightly confused, but by no means intimidated, she assumed an air of aggressive detachment.

'What was in the safe, Miss Glynn, was nothing to do with me. I only saw it open a few times but as far as I remember there were a couple of old ledgers and a stack of pocket files.'

They were all there except Christine, even Barry Morse who must have taken time off from his job, presumably to lend support to his wife and the family. The presence of the lawyer contributed to the melodrama of the situation. Grouped around the safe, against the light, almost in silhouette, they were a study for a Victorian painter, ready-made for his party piece at the RA Summer Exhibition — *The Safe*.

Gerald was impatient. 'Let's get on with it!' He turned to Lucy Lane: 'Are you going to break those seals?'

Lucy looked at the lawyer who nodded. She broke the seals, inserted a key, turned it, twisted the brass handle, and opened the heavy door. At first sight it was as Paula had said: two ledger-like volumes, quite thick, bound in worn red leather and lettered on their spines in faded gilt. These were on the shelf and the bottom of the safe was stacked with pocket files. At the top a metal drawer extended the whole width.

'Well, let's see what's in there, Gina!'

Gina looked at her brother, about to say something cutting but changed her mind. She lifted out the books; they were quarto, half-bound in leather, and heavy. She held the faded spine of one of them to the light so that she could read the lettering: 'Journal of Martin J Beale 1852–67.' The other was dated 1868–84. The books were in manuscript and the text was interspersed with lively pen-and-ink sketches.

Jordan, the lawyer — a tubby little man, very dark, with glasses which made him look owlish — said: 'Do you know anything about these books, Gina?'

'I've never seen them before.'

Sara said: 'But rare books are your department.'

Gina turned on her aunt in irritation: 'I tell you I've never seen them before and I've no idea where they came from.'

Gina had the first volume open at the initial entry and she read aloud: '"Durban, Natal, Thursday, January 1st, 1852. It occurs to me, being in this place at this time with no sign of an approaching end to the Kaffir war and all things uncertain, that it may be of interest to record the passages of everyday life if only as a source of remembrance and reflection in later years. I am twenty-six years old . . ."'

Gina turned the pages of the other volume. 'The whole journal appears to have been written in South Africa but he moved to Cape Province, and from later entries it seems he was in contact with Cecil Rhodes . . .'

The lawyer said: 'Are the books valuable?'

Gina swept the hair from her eyes in a characteristic gesture. 'I suppose they must be, as historical documents in their own right, and as material for a publisher. I should have to get other opinions but I'd guess they would fetch a good deal of money at auction. I just don't understand where father got them or why he kept them hidden like this.'

The lawyer was cautious: 'I wouldn't say they were hidden, Gina. In any case, can we get on?'

Lucy Lane interrupted, authority in her voice: 'Before we move on, others of you must have seen the safe open from time to time; it would be useful if we could establish how long the books have been there.'

Sara said: 'I can't see what possible connection these books could have with my brother's death.'

'Perhaps there is none but it is a possibility, however remote.'

There was a brief silence then Gerald spoke up: 'I've seen the safe open several times since I've been working in the business. The books have always been there as far as I can remember. Like Paula, I thought they were old ledgers and I didn't take much notice. In any case the old man wasn't the sort to let you take a close look at anything that didn't directly concern you.'

'Miss Glynn?' Suddenly they were being interrogated.

Sara made an effort to appear offhand. 'I'm not often in here. I suppose I've seen Matthew with the safe open, and I may have noticed the books, but this firm has been going for more than a century and one doesn't take much notice of such things, one has grown up with them.'

'Mr Morse?'

Barry seemed more ill at ease than the others. 'As you know I don't work in the firm but I do give a hand with the accounts from time to time —'

'You work in here on those occasions?'

'Yes, I do, but I don't think I've ever seen the safe open.' A nervous smile. 'It is almost axiomatic in businesses like this that nothing of value is ever kept in the safe.'

Lucy said: 'That, apparently, wasn't the case here.'

'No . . . No, indeed!'

The pocket files were lifted out. All of them contained agendas and minutes of council committee meetings. The metal drawer was opened and found to be empty. There remained only a cardboard box lodged behind where the journals had been.

Lucy Lane said: 'What's in the box?'

Gina lifted it out. 'It's empty.' It was rectangular and it had a lid, like a shoe box, but it was longer. The ornately printed label on one end read: 'Hatchard's Patent Stencils: This box contains all the materials and instructions necessary to become proficient in the art of stencilling.' Gina said: 'It's Victorian.'

The box was not quite empty, it contained a tiny linen bag tied with a gilt cord and with a lavender head embroidered on it.

Gerald was impatient: 'Do we have to waste time on an empty box?'

Lucy Lane said: 'People don't usually put empty boxes into a safe. One wonders what was in it. Does anybody know?'

It appeared that no one did.

Kersey was waiting for Morse when he left the safe party. 'Detective Inspector Kersey; a word, Mr Morse . . .'

Morse looked at his watch. 'I want to put in an appearance at the office before lunch.'

'I'll keep you no longer than necessary.'

The others had left. Lucy Lane looked at Kersey. 'Will you need me, sir?'

'I think we shall manage.'

Back in Matthew Glynn's office, Kersey seated himself in the swivel chair behind the desk and casually waved Morse to a client's chair on the other side. Morse hesitated then decided there was no alternative to sitting down. Kersey lit a cigarette; before uttering a word he was finding out how the accountant reacted to boorish police tactics. The answer was with dignified resignation.

'Profitable morning, Mr Morse?'

Morse was in good shape physically, slender though muscular, even athletic, but the blond hair, the almost girlish colouring, and the Rupert Brooke profile, held no appeal for Kersey who had a face like a sad clown and the physique of a youngish gorilla.

Morse took his time to answer: 'In what way might it have been profitable?'

'A will? Isn't that what families look for in safes — especially when they invite a lawyer to see fair play. Of course I could be wrong; I'm not well up in these things.'

Morse subjected him to a long unblinking stare before saying: 'There was no will in the safe and, according to the lawyer, it is unlikely that my father-in-law made one.'

'Awkward for you all.' Kersey adopted a confidential manner. 'As a matter of fact it was about your father-in-law's business affairs that I wanted to talk to you. You realize, of course, that we have to go into these things — no details at this stage; we can get them later from his bank and his lawyer; just the overall picture. It seemed best to have a friendly chat with one of the family not, perhaps, so emotionally involved — and you being an accountant . . .'

Morse was cool. 'If you ask me what you want to know I'll see if I can tell you.'

Kersey blew out a great cloud of grey smoke. 'Good! The bookshop — prosperous? Doing well?'

Morse considered. 'I can see that such questions could seem relevant to your enquiry and for that reason I'm prepared to be frank. The business is not doing well though sales are good — higher than one might expect in a town of this size and against significant competition —'

'What's wrong then?'

'Overheads are too high and too much money is tied up in slow-moving stock. On any reasonable system of accounting, the second-hand and rare book departments are losing money and are heavily in debt to the other side of the business —'

'So what —'

But Morse would not be interrupted. 'My father-in-law was well aware of all this; it has been going on for some years but he would not do what was necessary to right the situation, that is cut out the loss makers and, perhaps, substitute other lines — stationery, office equipment, videos or any other line compatible with the book trade.'

'So what did he do?'

'He realized on other assets and used the money to subsidize the business.'

'A short-term policy, surely?'

A thin smile. 'My father-in-law was giving new meaning to the phrase "keeping a shop".'

'Does all this account for the proposed development at the pottery?'

'I suppose so.'

'A last resort?'

Morse hesitated. 'I had thought so but recently he hinted at another asset he hoped to dispose of that would bring in quite a lot of money. He did not say what it was but it may be that we found it in the safe this morning. Your sergeant will tell you about that.' Morse looked at his watch and stood up. 'Now, if you will excuse me, I really should —'

'Just one more question. Do other members of the family agree with your diagnosis and your proposed remedy?'

85

'Gerald does — decisively; my wife too, but she is swayed by loyalty to her father.'

'And Sara?'

'Sara has never concerned herself with the business.'

Kersey watched him go, an appreciative grin on his face. Full marks for presentation and content. Barry was by no means negligible.

Wycliffe was back in the Incident Room. 'Any news of Alfred Glynn?'

The duty officer was DC Holman, a local man, young enough to be ambitious and anxious to make the most of this chance to work with the crime squad.

'They knew nothing at the bookshop, sir; his sister, Sara, seemed very upset; she wouldn't believe that he wasn't at home. I think she's gone down there. Anyway, there's been a report from a chambermaid at the hotel; she says she saw Alfred just before eight this morning, on his way up the street. According to her he looked ill; she spoke to him but he didn't seem to see her.'

In the little office set aside for him, Wycliffe brooded over the accumulating mound of paper, the expanding case file, and among the rest a preliminary report from Franks on the autopsy. It told him nothing new. Matthew Glynn had become a subject: 'Caucasian male, aged fifty-two . . . No observable lesions other than those arising from the assault . . . Death due to anoxia resulting from strangulation . . .'

And there was a memo from Fox: 'Re cat, property of Ronald Swayne of 22a, Lady Street. Casts of the paw-prints of this creature were found to correspond with blooded prints at the scene of crime. Questioned, Swayne stated that the animal had been let out at approximately 9.30 on Saturday evening and was crying to be let in at a little before midnight. According to Swayne, it is the creature's habit to be out for no more than half an hour at night.'

Fox on the ethology of *Felis catus*. Wycliffe suspected that the encounter between Fox and Clarence had not been a meeting of kindred souls. Interesting all the same. Somebody must have let the cat out of Glynn's office shortly before midnight and, from Dippy Martin's evidence, the likelihood was that the somebody was a woman.

Wycliffe went to the window and stood looking out over the roof tops to the harbour and Albert Pier. The sun was shining but there was a bank of cloud out to sea; no discernible movement anywhere. Three men stood motionless on the distant pier, part of a great stillness with no other living thing in sight.

Since childhood Wycliffe had experienced episodes when he seemed to see the world about him through fresh eyes, as though, without warning, he had become an intruder in some foreign place, and he would be overcome by the strangeness of it all. There was nothing analytical in the experience, only a sense of wonder that things should be as he saw them and, in particular, that he should be involved.

Now somebody had strangled a 52-year-old man called Matthew Glynn and he was expected to identify and apprehend the killer. Men and women were busy under his supervision investigating and reporting on the lives of people who might or might not have been concerned in the death of this man. But at this moment it was as though he were watching a play . . .

Those three men on the pier, did they too, sometimes ask themselves. . . ?

There was a tap at the door and Lucy Lane came in. 'Am I disturbing you, sir?'

He motioned her to a chair and sat down himself.

Was she looking at him oddly? Perhaps to keep herself in countenance she opened her notebook although he knew that she would not refer to it.

'A couple of things, sir; I'm not sure whether either of them is relevant. First, Matthew's secretary, the girl who works in the office next door, turned up for work as usual this morning: she lives a few miles out and she knew nothing of what had happened.'

'You got something from her?'

'I had a word with her after the safe business was over. She

87

seems a bit spiteful and not very bright but what she had to say was factual.'

Lucy Lane was a daughter of the Manse, her father was a very orthodox Methodist parson and Lucy herself was emphatically committed to the side of the angels, often to those with a partiality for flaming swords. Any smoothy who saw her as a soft touch was in for a shock.

She frowned and pushed her notebook aside. 'According to her, about a week ago, in his office, Matthew had a row with his brother —'

'With Alfred?'

'With Maurice. There were customers in the shop and even they could hear it.'

'We know about that; it seems to have been almost common gossip. Did the girl know what it was about?'

'She knew that it was connected with Matthew wanting to build houses on land adjoining Maurice's pottery. It was the day after the council had agreed to a site meeting to discuss the scheme.'

'Anyway I'll be seeing Maurice this afternoon.' Wycliffe was returning to earth. 'Now, what about the safe opening? Who was there?'

'All of them with the exception of Christine.'

Lucy Lane told him about the journal.

'Where are the books now?'

'Back in the safe and I've got the key for the moment. What do you want me to do?'

'Do you have any ideas about them?'

'Not really. Gina thought they must be valuable and she's probably right; but she's puzzled as to why her father kept them shut away and never mentioned them.'

'You think they are involved in some under-the-counter deal?'

'It looks that way.'

'Anything else in the safe?'

'Nothing of interest. The lawyer was hoping to find a will but it begins to look as though Matthew died intestate.'

'That must have caused a flutter.'

'It did.' She was still preoccupied.

'Something else on your mind?'

'A small thing, sir. I said there was nothing else in the safe but behind the books there was a cardboard box — rectangular, like a shoe box, but longer.'

'What was in it?'

'Nothing; at least only a lavender sachet.'

'So?'

'You don't put an empty box in a safe; there must have been something in it when it was put there and the lavender sachet makes me think it must have been something of sentimental value.'

'That sounds reasonable.'

She grinned. 'It sounds stupid, but I can't help associating the box with the journal —'

They were interrupted by the arrival of Kersey. He came in looking sour as he usually did when he found Wycliffe conferring with Lucy Lane. 'They told me you were here, sir . . . If I'm not interrupting . . .'

He hooked one of the bentwood chairs into position with his foot and sat on it astride, arms resting on the back.

Wycliffe said: 'You've heard that Alfred seems to have taken himself off?'

'After wrecking the place — yes.'

'As to who did the wrecking, we have to wait to hear from Fox, but I've got a search organized for Alfred. Anyway, did you talk to Morse?'

Kersey felt in his pockets for his cigarettes. 'Yes, he isn't a bad bloke actually; almost human. He says the bookshop is in trouble.'

'Financially?'

'It seems that Matthew was running the thing on too big a scale for the size of the town — too much stock of the wrong sort and overheads too high.' Kersey lit a cigarette and with a wry grin enquired: 'Am I being antisocial?' He was thawing.

'Yes, but we'll live with it. What more did you get?'

'Matthew has been realizing on other assets to keep the

business afloat. Morse said it lent a new meaning to the phrase "keeping a shop".'

'And the next step was to build houses around his brother's pottery.'

Kersey nodded. 'So it seems.'

Lucy Lane said: 'I wonder he didn't cash in on the journal.'

Which involved an explanation to Kersey.

At the end of it Kersey said: 'That figures. Morse seemed to think you'd found something in the safe which Matthew regarded as a negotiable asset.'

Wycliffe was impatient. 'This is all very well but I don't see in any of it a motive for murder. I know that many killings are done for next to nothing but we are not dealing with street muggers or footloose louts, we are dealing with the middle-aged and the middle-class — people who know which side their bread is buttered and value their reputations almost more than their deeds and their share certificates. In my experience fear is the most powerful drive to violence among such people and why should any of them in this case be afraid?'

Chapter Six

Monday afternoon

Wycliffe was on his way to St Hilary, to the Trebyan pottery, and Maurice Glynn. There had been no further news of Alfred since he was seen by one of the hotel staff in Lady Street at eight that morning. Fox had completed his examination of the vandalized room and his report was conclusive: no prints, fresh or otherwise, of anyone other than Alfred himself. What was more, Fox was satisfied that the presence of Alfred's fresh prints on the damaged articles was convincing evidence that it was he who had carried out the destruction.

It was very strange.

St Hilary Churchtown is a small cluster of old, grey-green houses built around the church at a kink in a tree-lined lane. Wycliffe thought that time had passed the place by, that history must have piled day upon day, year upon year, in peace and quietude. He was wrong. In 1932 it had captured international headlines when the church was attacked by a mob of evangelical bigots who went to work with sledge-hammers, wrecking altars and destroying ornaments of which they disapproved; perhaps the last violent twitch of the Puritan tail on English soil.

Wycliffe was alone and he had to get out of the car to rouse a sleeping dog in the roadway. A woman was coming towards him, grey-haired, plump and freckled; Wycliffe asked her how to get to Trebyan.

'You just keep on for half a mile or so and 'tis up on your left. Are you police? . . . I wondered.' She put a freckled, multi-ringed hand on the car door, effectively barring him

91

from getting back in. ''Tis a sad thing about poor Matthew and no mistake! But they brothers never had much luck.'

She broke off to acknowledge an old man trudging by: 'Good day to you, Mr Ivey! Nice afternoon for a bit of a walk but don't you go overdoing it.' She followed the old man with her eyes. 'He's gone downhill, lately, poor old chap, but we all got to come to it.

'Anyway, I was saying about the Glynns: Maurice lost his wife when she was no more 'n a girl; Matthew's missus walked out an' left him with three children. Then there's Alfred — I mean, he never had what you'd call a proper life . . .'

She ran on, her voice as smooth and rich as cream.

Wycliffe said: 'You obviously know the family.'

'My dear life, I should do! They three boys — and Sara — was all brought up at Trebyan and they was all at the village school. 'Course they went on to grammar school as 'twas in they days. But they was living at Trebyan up to when Matthew got married; then their father took that house in P'nzance next to the shop. After they went, Trebyan was let for a year or two till Maurice got hisself married to some up-country girl. Pretty li'l thing she was, but delicate; you could see she wouldn' be long for this world — and they started that pottery thing . . .'

She seemed content to gossip indefinitely but Wycliffe showed no sign of impatience.

'O'course tis none o' my business but you won't find Maurice if it's him you want to see; he went off in his li'l truck when we was sitting down to our dinners. But Alfred must be still there.'

'Alfred is at Trebyan?'

It was plain that this was the pearl in her oyster.

'Since this morning. I seen him go past about nine an' I hardly knew him! I heard he was changed but my dear life, he's an old man!'

'He was on foot?'

'When I saw him, but he must've come on the bus — it d' stop at the turn an' 'twas about the time. Anyway he never walked from P'nzance, not like he was. I'll swear t' that.'

'Well, thank you, Mrs . . .'

She removed her hand from the car door; the climax had been achieved. 'Pascoe — Emily Pascoe. You're welcome.'

Wycliffe got back into his car. Odd about Alfred. They had enquired if he was at the pottery and been told that he was not.

Trebyan was a house and a group of former farm buildings on rising ground, adjacent to an area of gorse and hawthorn scrub, both in flower.

There was a farm gate painted white, standing open, and a sign: 'Trebyan Pottery: Visitors Welcome'.

Wycliffe hoped that he would be.

He drove up a gravelled track past a couple of tethered goats browsing in the hedges. The house was four-square, with a grey-slated hipped roof, overhanging eaves, and a chimney at each end — the archetypal house which children draw. Hanging by the front door was a brass bell with a cord attached to its clapper and a little notice: 'Please ring'. Wycliffe rang with timidity; even so the silence he had scarcely noticed until now was brutally shattered. But no one came.

He was in what was once the farmyard, now largely grown over; hens pecked amongst the weedy cobbles. To the right there were farm buildings which had been refurbished and through the open door of one of them he could glimpse open shelving displaying rows of pots. Over that door there was a notice: 'Retail Shop'. To his left the gorse and hawthorn sprawled over the hillside against a backdrop of little Cornish fields disposed in their unique version of three-dimensional geometry.

He was reminded of his childhood and of his father's farm; they too had kept a couple of goats.

He walked over to the shop but it was unattended. He tried other doors: one opened into a former barn, now a workshop. There were two power-driven pottery wheels, plastic bins for clay and slip, and an electric kiln at one end. A glass bull's eye on a switch-panel by the kiln glowed red; the kiln was being fired.

On shelves around the walls there were pots, vases, jugs, pitchers and plaques of all sorts and sizes, leather-hard or biscuit-fired. But the place was deserted.

He was getting that *Mary Celeste* feeling.

He found a clay store and a packing shed where, along with a mound of straw and some stout boxes, there were a couple of bicycles. He came at last to a small, lean-to workshop where a girl, seated at a bench with her back to him, was decorating a pot placed on a turntable. On her left a group of similar pots awaited attention; others, to her right, had already received the treatment, a vaguely Oriental squiggle to set buyers thinking of Leach and Hamada.

The girl must have heard him but she gave no sign.

He said: 'Christine, isn't it? I didn't expect to find you here.'

It was still a moment or two before she completed her work on the pot and turned round. 'I come here in my spare time.'

'You must have heard the bell.'

She said nothing.

'Where is Mr Glynn?'

'He's gone into Penzance to see the family.'

'When are you expecting him back?'

She glanced at her watch. 'Any time now.'

'So you are here on your own?'

'David is over in the field, hoeing potatoes.'

Her manner was unresponsive, even sullen.

'Can you leave what you are doing for a while?'

'I suppose so.' She cleaned the brush she was using then washed her hands at the sink. She wore bib-and-brace overalls which left her arms bare; the mass of her dark hair accentuated her pallor and she looked drawn, weary, and vulnerable.

'How long have you been here?'

Her responses were slow as though it required an effort to reply. 'I came over this morning just after ten.'

'Have you seen your uncle Alfred?'

'No, they phoned to know if he was here.'

94

'You are quite sure that your uncle Alfred has not been here today?'

She frowned. 'I haven't seen him.'

'How did you get here?'

'Bicycle.'

'Your uncle Maurice has been gone a couple of hours?'

'About that.'

'You saw him go?'

'Yes.'

'Was he alone?'

'Yes.'

'Was he carrying anything — in the truck, I mean?'

'No.'

'I'll be back in a moment.'

He went to his car and spoke to the Incident Room on the telephone. 'Regarding Alfred Glynn, I want you to get together a small team, with a dog handler, to await instructions. Also to arrange a check on the buses which serve St Hilary. Was Alfred Glynn on a bus which arrived here at around nine this morning? . . . I shall be in touch again shortly.'

Christine was standing where he had left her. 'You didn't stay for the safe opening this morning, then?'

'It was nothing to do with me.'

He wanted her to talk but he wasn't being very successful, her answers were as near monosyllabic as she could make them. Well, if that was how she wanted it . . . 'At what time did you get home on Saturday evening?'

'At half-past ten.'

'You had been to a play with David?'

'Yes.'

'How did he get home?'

'Bicycle.'

When a car engine sounded in the distance she said with evident relief: 'That will be uncle, I expect.'

They moved outside and saw a Land Rover pick-up emerge from the trees. It turned in at the gate and came chuntering up the track to pull up beside them. A middle-aged man, loose-limbed and lean, got out of the driving seat and slammed the door. He wore a washed-out denim jacket, jeans, and trainers; his dark hair was beginning to grey.

'Police?'

'Chief Superintendent Wycliffe.'

Glynn nodded. 'I've been to see the family; I've kept away until now . . . Of course we've been in touch by phone but I wanted to see how things were . . . Come up to the house.'

'A moment, Mr Glynn! Have you seen your brother, Alfred, this morning?'

'No, I haven't, we're worried about him; but you know that.'

'Your brother was seen passing through the village, apparently on his way here, at nine this morning.'

Maurice stood still, looking at Wycliffe, incredulous. 'But I was here all the morning. You haven't seen him, have you, Chris?'

'I've told him.'

Maurice seemed genuinely perplexed. 'I don't understand it, he hasn't been here in ten years! Where's David?'

Christine said: 'Up in the garden field.'

Maurice turned back to Wycliffe. 'I don't understand it . . .'

Wycliffe said: 'When did you last see your brother, Mr Glynn?'

'Alfred?' He ran a hand through his wiry hair. 'I don't know; I drop in now and then when I'm in town — a fortnight? three weeks, perhaps.'

'And your other brother, Matthew?'

'Matt and I had a bust-up in his office a week or so ago. I dare say you've heard about it.'

'And that was the last time you saw him?'

'It was. There was no more we could say to each other except through the damned lawyers.' He broke off and seemed to hesitate.

'Something on your mind?'

He was reluctant but it came in the end: 'I've been thinking; if Alfie really was coming here it's possible he would have taken the short cut like we did when we were boys. There's a footpath from the road up through the scrub that cuts off two sides of a triangle . . .'

Wycliffe said: 'We'd better find out.'

He moved off and looked to Maurice to follow.

'You want me to come with you?' He was oddly tense.

'Please.'

'I don't even know if it's passable — the gorse . . .'

'We shall soon see.'

The two men set off down a narrow path which traversed the slope diagonally. The path was in good shape but occasionally they had to push aside thrusting shoots. Then they came upon a clearing where there was a hut, made of lap-boarding with a verandah, and built up on bricks.

Maurice was going to continue along the path but Wycliffe stopped him. 'What is this place?'

'Originally my grandmother had it built as a sort of studio . . . We children used to camp out here in the summer . . .' He stood, looking up at the little building, feeling constrained to say more. 'This is the first time I've been down here since God knows when. It's worn well; David must be looking after it with a coat of stop-rot now and then.' He was uneasy, talking to cover his nervousness.

Wycliffe went up the steps to the verandah and peered through the window, but because of reflections it was not easy to see inside. The hut appeared to consist of one large room; there was a sink at one end and an oil stove; a lamp was suspended on gimbals from the roof. He could see a table and chairs and what seemed to be the end of a large settee.

Maurice remained standing in the clearing as though anxious to get on but Wycliffe went along the verandah to the door.

'It will be locked,' Maurice said. 'I think David will have the key; he'll show it you if you want to see it.'

But the door was not locked and Wycliffe went in.

The settee he had seen from the window was against one wall and Alfred Glynn was lying on the floor in front of it, his body oddly contorted.

Wycliffe had never seen Alfred before but he was in no doubt, the Glynn features and physique were unmistakable. He knelt down in the constricted space. Even in the dim light he could see that the face was cyanosed, deeply discoloured, and there were reddish spots or petechiae in the region of the eyes.

Alfred Glynn was dead.

Maurice was now standing outside the door with his back to the room; one hand rested on the verandah rail and without turning round he said: 'Is he dead?'

'I'm afraid so.'

In a muffled voice Maurice asked: 'How did it happen?'

'I don't know.' Then: 'If you would just confirm that it is your brother . . .'

Maurice came a little way into the room, looked down at the body and moved away again. A whispered 'Yes,' and he was back on the verandah, supporting himself on the rail, and bending over as though at any moment he might vomit.

Wycliffe was angry with himself. He had come alone deliberately in the hope that he might get farther with Maurice Glynn by keeping the interview in a low key. Now he had fallen into a trap which the greenest copper would have avoided. He was out of radio contact and faced with the alternatives of returning to the car with Glynn, leaving the body, or sending Glynn alone to telephone.

He joined Maurice outside. 'I want you to go back to the house and telephone the Incident Room. Tell the officer what has happened and that I'm here. The first priority is a doctor but the officer will know what to do. I'll write the number down.' He did so and handed the slip of paper to Maurice.

Maurice took it without a word and, after a moment, shambled off up the path by which they had come.

There would be broad grins in the Incident Room. 'The Old Man trod in it this time!'

Wycliffe turned back to the dead man. He looked at his watch. 'At approximately 15.25, in company with Maurice Glynn, I discovered the body of the deceased lying in a contorted position . . .' It was unusual for a chief super to have to give evidence of the discovery of a body.

Despite the mildness of the day Alfred was wearing a black overcoat over a dark suit which included a waistcoat and there was a homburg hat on the settee. All were so shabby they might have been worn by a dressy tramp. There had been a struggle, buttons had been ripped from the waistcoat, which was open, and a silver pocket watch dangled from its silver chain. Alfred's shirt was torn from the collar down the front exposing his thin, bony chest covered with long grey hairs.

Wycliffe looked for signs of strangulation but found none.

Alfred had struggled, not with an assailant, but gasping and fighting for air. The experts would say that he had died from suboxia — oxygen deficiency brought about in this case, Wycliffe believed, by a virulent poison. The body was still warm and there were no signs of rigor.

There was a strong smell of brandy and, for the first time, Wycliffe noticed a silvery metal hip-flask lying on the floor, almost under the settee. The stopper was missing and the brandy had trickled out to soak into the sisal matting which covered the floor.

There was nothing he could do but wait, the little hut had been the scene of a violent death and the medical and technical people must have their turn first. All he could do for the moment was to stand in the doorway and look about him.

The hut had been cared for inside as well as out and it was being used. Over the sink at the other end there was a shelf with cups, saucers, and plates; a saucepan hung on a hook and there was a kettle on the oil stove. Close to the door where he stood there was another shelf, this time of books: bird books and others on the identification and habits of small mammals.

Wycliffe went out on the verandah and stood, his arms resting on the rail. Had Alfred committed suicide? That was how it looked. But why come out here to die? Unless there was a strong sentimental attachment to the place. That was possible; after all, the brothers had spent their childhood and youth at Trebyan; perhaps for Alfred the only time of happiness he had known.

But Alfred was a pharmacist; would he have chosen such a

terrible death when a narcotic drug would have ensured a tranquil wait for the ferryman and a smooth crossing?

It was quiet, so quiet that Wycliffe listened to the silence and wondered. Occasionally he heard the distant sound of traffic on the main road; now and then a dog barked somewhere in the village. There was a movement in the undergrowth and a rabbit bobbed out into the clearing, settling to feed within a few feet of where he stood.

Had Alfred Glynn murdered his brother then killed himself in this frightful manner by way of expiation? It was as irrational as it was melodramatic, but so was the darkened room where for nearly thirty years Alfred had striven to keep alive the great illusion of his youth.

It occurred to Wycliffe with a sense of surprise that of the three brothers he had spoken only to one; he had never seen either Matthew or Alfred in life, yet he needed to know them. Physically the brothers had much in common but in personality it seemed they were very different. Matthew was the man of affairs — busy, and apparently untroubled by self-doubt. Alfred had become almost a recluse, a man haunted by his dream. And Maurice. . . ?

Wycliffe looked at his watch and wondered whether Glynn had done what was necessary. The mere fact of Alfred's death, whoever took the call, would be enough for the team to be sent and the police surgeon informed. But that was assuming that the call had been made.

At ten minutes to four he heard a car in the village and a minute or two later it was travelling along the road. Soon it was followed by another. His troops were arriving.

Now the dead man was a centre of attention for the experts. Fox, with his assistants, was searching the whole area and no rabbit would have ventured to show its whiskers.

Lucy Lane was there. 'Mr Kersey is out on enquiries, sir. DC Curnow has stayed at the house to keep an eye on Glynn.'

A good job somebody followed proper procedures.

Dr Rees, the police surgeon, was kneeling beside the body. Rees had spent almost all his professional life in the area and was part of it, ready to applaud its strengths and condone its weaknesses.

'The two brothers inside a couple of days . . . Poor old Alfie! Couldn't take it, I suppose — Matthew on top of everything else. I know there wasn't much love lost between them but, as they say, blood is thicker than water; even doctors know that.'

'You said "on top of everything else"?'

Rees sat back on his haunches. 'Well, our lot — the medical practitioners — have been on his tail for years,' Rees grinned up at Wycliffe. 'A demarcation dispute, you could call it. Alfie was fond of doing our job for us. Then, recently, he went queer — queerer, I should say — and he was stopped from dispensing NHS prescriptions. Quite right, of course, but hard on the old boy.'

Rees went on: 'Looks as though he laced his brandy. You'd have thought he'd have had more sense.'

'More sense?'

'Than to go for strychnine — that's what it looks like to me, and you can see that he had a rough passage out. Conscious to the last probably. Of course with a heart like his it wouldn't have taken long, but why pick on strychnine when he had a fair selection of the British Pharmacopoeia in his dispensary to choose from? But there's no knowing what an intending suicide will do.'

'Was he a patient of yours?'

Rees was testing the limbs for flexion. 'He wasn't anybody's patient as far as I know. He said he wasn't when he came to see me a couple of years back. Just that one visit. He wanted my opinion of his heart. I examined him and suggested referral to a cardiologist but this he absolutely refused. I told him that in my opinion he was suffering from valvular disease and that there was probably considerable dilation. He said that was what he thought himself. End of story.'

'Can you tell me anything about time of death?'

Rees got to his feet. 'According to the books strychnine raises the body temperature and so delays cooling. Anyway, rigor is in the very early stages. At a guess I'd say he's probably been dead five or six hours but don't hold me to that. Is Franks going to be in on this?'

'Yes.'

'There you are then.'

'In the circumstances we have to cover ourselves.'

Rees sighed. 'Isn't that what we all try to do? . . . You've got a visitor.'

Wycliffe turned to look. A young man was standing in the path beyond the clearing just outside the area colonized by the police, tall and slim, dressed in jeans and a denim shirt — no mistaking who he was.

Wycliffe left the hut and walked up to him. 'David Glynn?'

The boy nodded.

'Shall we walk a little way?'

A word to Lucy, and Wycliffe walked off up the path with the boy. They stopped just short of where the path ended in the yard.

'Where were you this morning between, say, nine and midday?'

'I was in the house until Chris arrived around ten, then I went to work in the little field behind the house where we grow our vegetables; I was there until nearly one. After a snack lunch I went back there.'

'So you were some distance from the hut.'

'Quite a way — yes.'

The boy had inherited his father's mannerisms as well as his features and physique; a certain hesitancy, and a tendency to look away from the person to whom he was speaking.

'You heard nothing — no cries of distress or anything of that sort?'

'No . . . You think Uncle Alfred suffered a lot?'

'I'm afraid so, but it probably didn't last long and he may not have cried out. Did you have much contact with your uncle?'

'Not much . . . It wasn't very pleasant going there and you tended to put it off . . .'

'And he didn't come here?'

'I've never known him come here until today.'

Wycliffe was looking back down the slope, over the gorse towards the trees and beyond, to another clump of trees where the slender grey spire of the church rose above them. 'Is this where your Uncle Matthew wanted to build houses?'

'Here and in the adjoining field.'

'And your father objected?'

'Yes. Father feels very strongly about this bit of so-called "waste" ground; so do I.'

'Apparently you keep the path clear and look after the little hut; does your father come here much?'

'Never, as far as I know. All the same, for him it's one of those special places.' The boy's dark eyes were on Wycliffe, doubtful if he would understand. 'I think it's to do with when he was young.'

'You spend time at the hut yourself?'

'Yes.'

'And not always alone.'

The boy turned away.

Wycliffe said: 'Let's walk on up to the house. You left Chris at about 10.30 on Saturday night and cycled home?'

'Yes.'

'At what time did you get home?'

'About eleven.'

'Was your father at home then?'

'Yes.'

'Did my brother kill himself?'

'I'm not able to answer that, Mr Glynn. It seems that he died after drinking brandy which had been laced with strychnine and we have to try to discover how the poison got into the brandy.'

'So it's possible that he was murdered?' It was as though the question had been forced from him.

'It is possible but so far there is nothing in the way of evidence to support the idea.'

Maurice had been greatly shaken; he was pale and he had difficulty in controlling his voice. He shifted heavily in his chair. 'If somebody killed him they must have had a motive,

103

but what? Yet why should he kill himself? And in that horrible way?'

Wycliffe did not answer and after a pause Maurice went on: 'What will happen now?'

'We shall treat this as a suspicious death; there will be an autopsy and, of course, an investigation to discover the source of the poison and how it got into the brandy.'

They were in what had been the dining-room of the house. An extended dining-table was littered with papers held down by little pottery artefacts from ashtrays to small pitchers and there was a portable typewriter at one end. Dining chairs were scattered about the room; there was a battered filing cabinet with a bulging, open drawer next to a massive sideboard with a marble top. The carpet was threadbare and innocent of pattern, paper was peeling from the walls but there were pictures in gilded frames.

On the mantelpiece, at one end, was the inevitable framed inscribed photograph of mother; at the other end, a head and shoulders portrait of a young woman which caught Wycliffe's attention.

Maurice noticed his interest. 'Celia — my wife.'

'She was very beautiful.'

It was true, but Wycliffe remembered Emily Pascoe's words: '. . . delicate; you could see she wouldn't be long for this world.' The girl in the photograph had a fair fragility, altogether too vulnerable.

'She died when David was four.'

Maurice was clearly moved. He fumbled in his jacket pocket and came out with a tobacco pouch and a pipe and offered the pouch to Wycliffe. His hand trembled. 'Smoke?'

Wycliffe refused.

'Just as well; I grow my own. Do you mind if I do? It annoys some people — David is one of them.'

Maurice concentrated on filling his pipe, very slowly and deliberately; he put the stem between his teeth, and struck a match — a soothing ritual. He was making a tremendous effort to appear calm, if possible to be calm.

He was the last of the brothers; whether or not he had any

part in their deaths he could be the key to a clearer understanding of the two who had died. For that reason if for no other it was essential to draw him out rather than subject him to interrogation. Wycliffe sat in an old armchair which had been moulded to comfort through use; his manner relaxed and conversational.

'You had differences with your brother, Matthew, over possible developments here, I believe?'

'Matthew wanted to build houses. In my view he had no right.'

Wycliffe asked no question and, after a pause, Maurice continued: 'You see, under my father's will Matthew got the bookshop on condition that he provided for Sara; Alfred had his pharmacy; and this place, where I had already started the pottery, should have been mine. But father had no faith in my ability to make a go of anything.'

A brief pause, perhaps a nervous smile, then: 'I've got to admit that there was evidence to support his point of view. I'd made some mistakes and as far as he was concerned the pottery could have been another. Anyway, he left what should have been my share to Matthew on condition that I was able to lease it back at a nominal rental. The point was, he'd made sure I couldn't sell it and blow the proceeds on some other scheme.

'Matthew became my keeper.'

Maurice was speaking more slowly; sometimes his lips seemed to tremble but his manner was once more tentative and self-deprecating.

Wycliffe asked: 'Did you resent the arrangement?'

Maurice clasped his hands together and seemed to study them. 'I don't think so. It gave me a sense of security — security against myself. I couldn't up sticks and away, which I might have done otherwise — regretting it afterwards. But the point was that he was holding this place in trust, on my behalf.'

'You thought it unreasonable that he should exploit the property to his advantage — is that it?'

'That was part of it, but I had another and more important reason for opposing him.'

'And that was?'

'I think it's time we stopped poisoning half the land and concreting in the rest.'

'Where exactly was it proposed these houses should be built?'

'On the scrubland and one of our two fields.'

He got up from his chair, fetched a rolled-up plan from the top of the sideboard and spread it over the litter on the table.

'Here.' He pointed with his pipe stem.

Wycliffe joined him at the table. The plan showed the outlines of a dozen houses and a service road superimposed on a large-scale map. Wycliffe spotted the little hut and saw that it would be obliterated by one of the proposed houses.

'I gather that your brother may not have made a will; so what happens now?'

'Whether he made a will or not doesn't affect me. Under my father's will, in the event of Matthew's death, the property passes to me anyway.' They returned to their seats; Maurice puffed at his pipe and seemed more relaxed.

'If your brother had lived and been granted outline planning permission for his houses, what would you have done?'

Maurice did not hesitate. 'I would have gone to law on the terms of my father's will.'

Wycliffe changed the subject. 'You've lived here alone with your son since your wife died?'

Maurice looked around at the shabby and slightly absurd incongruities of the room. 'It's pretty obvious, isn't it? I couldn't afford a housekeeper. In any case if I had any spare money it would go on clerical assistance. Paperwork is our bugbear; we can manage the housekeeping between us. David does a masterly stew and I'm not bad with a salad.' His confidence was returning.

'It must have been hard when David was young.'

Glynn held his pipe away from his mouth. 'I had to take him on more or less from the first. By the time he was two Celia was spending a lot of time in hospitals, poor girl. But people were very good; a friend from the farm came in to help out when I was in a real mess.' He smiled a wan smile. 'And Sara would take David for days at a time when I was busy in the pottery . . . She's been good to me.' He broke off. 'There's David now, with Chris.'

Wycliffe looked out of the window. The young couple were walking up the drive, arms about each other.

Maurice's eyes were dreamy. 'They're like babes in the wood, but they'll be all right. David's got more sense than I ever had and Chris is a good girl. She could make her living as a potter if she wanted to; she's a natural.'

'Does she want to?'

'That's what she says but I don't try to influence her either way.'

There was a longish pause and this time it was Wycliffe who spoke first. 'Do you recall the day your sister-in-law disappeared, Mr Glynn?'

Maurice seemed startled. 'My sister-in-law? Disappearance is hardly the word. She simply left her home and family —'

'That was seventeen years ago and she hasn't as far as I know been seen or heard of since; surely that adds up to a disappearance? Anyway, were you surprised when she went?'

He hesitated. 'Of course I was surprised. You don't expect a woman with a young family to simply walk out.'

'Can you recollect how your brother reacted?'

'You mean Matthew? Matthew was stunned; he couldn't believe she'd gone. He telephoned me late that evening — when they began to worry about her — asking if she'd been here. She and my wife, Celia, got on fairly well and Inez would sometimes drop in unexpectedly and stay rather long — but never overnight.'

'But you hadn't seen her on that occasion?'

'No, I had not.'

'And your other brother — Alfred — what about him?'

Maurice shifted heavily in his chair, making the joints creak. 'Alfred was bitter; you must know that story by now.'

Wycliffe allowed the silence of the place to resume possession. Such silences must have held sway for most of the day in this household of father and son. When Maurice was beginning to get restless Wycliffe said: 'Have you ever been over Alfred's rooms above the shop?'

'His rooms? Not all of them. I've been in the living-room — and the kitchen, perhaps. Why?'

'Until very recently the bedroom he intended for Inez and himself was fully furnished, the bed made, pyjamas laid out, fresh flowers and a ticking clock on the bedside table. There were framed photographs of Inez on the walls . . . But it was obvious that the room was never used.'

Maurice was watching him, his expression incredulous. He asked in a tight voice: 'What do you mean by "Until very recently"?'

'Early this morning or perhaps during the night the room was vandalized; everything in it was either damaged or destroyed.'

Maurice's fists were clenched, his features contorted; he got up from his chair and went to the window to stand with his back to the room.

Without turning round he said in a harsh voice: 'If you want to know about Inez, Mr Wycliffe, you must ask Sara, the two of them lived in the same house for nearly twelve years. I don't want to talk about her.'

As Wycliffe left the house he looked back and saw the gaunt figure still at the window. He walked down the path to the little hut. Alfred's body had been removed to the mortuary; Fox and Lucy Lane were still there.

Fox said: 'We've covered the ground, sir. Deceased's footprints occur in several places along the path between here and the road — wherever the ground is soft enough. I can find no evidence that anyone accompanied him or that anyone met him here.'

'Fingerprints?'

'Plenty in the hut but none of them fresh except two or three belonging to the deceased. Other than that, the hip-flask carries the prints of the fingers and thumb of his left hand, and the stopper, of the thumb and forefinger of his right.'

'And the other prints in the hut — the old ones?'

'Two people; one male, one female. Well, sir, I've got photographs of the body, of the interior and surroundings of the hut and I'm wondering —'

Wycliffe said: 'It's enough to be going on with. Even if we have another homicide on our hands this is not the scene of the crime. Just lock the place and take the key.'

Chapter Seven

Monday afternoon (continued)

Troglodytes in Records had finally unearthed the seventeen-year-old Inez Glynn file. Feet on the table and chair tilted, Kersey settled down to browse. He turned to the last report made by the investigating officer before the file was consigned to Records.

This investigation, extending over three months, has failed to provide any clue to the present whereabouts of the subject or to suggest any immediate reason why she left her home and family . . .

On the other hand there is no evidence to support the idea of foul play . . . In the past three years subject has been associated with at least two men other than her husband in circumstances giving rise to a strong presumption that the relationships were of a sexual nature . . .

Although she appears to have taken with her no significant quantity of clothing nor any substantial sum of money it seems certain that she was carrying her passport . . .

For reasons set out in earlier reports and in statements (IG 16–19), concerning her car, abandoned in Exeter station car-park, it is possible, even likely that she met someone there by arrangement . . .

'Having in mind all the circumstances I suggest that active enquiries in this case be suspended until fresh information is forthcoming.

(Signed)

G. M. Marks Detective Inspector.

Active enquiries were suspended and the file crept farther and farther down the heap until two years after Inez Glynn's disappearance, it had drifted down to archives.

Marks and Kersey had had contact in the distant past. Marks must have retired long since but he might still be around and, on the principle that half an hour's chat over a beer is worth a whole file of police gobbledegook, Kersey decided to enquire and found that Marks was still extant, sharing a bungalow with his sister and her husband in Newlyn. He telephoned.

Marks said: 'I'll meet you in the pub in half an hour — The Royal Duke — you know it?'

'No.'

'You'll find it.'

The Royal Duke was a fishermen's pub with an afternoon trade from men who had brought their catch in during the small hours of the morning. The harbour was crowded with boats berthed two and three abreast but the market sheds were empty, sluiced down so that not even a smell of fish remained. Kersey arrived on time and found Marks already seated at a table by the window with a pint in front of him.

'There's a bitter waiting for you.' He signalled the barman; Kersey collected his pint and sat down.

Marks said: 'So they made you up to DI.'

'Not before time.'

Marks had grown greyer, more hairy, more stringy in the years since their last meeting but he was the same man, shrewd, cynical, and a cop to the bone.

'Serious Crimes Squad: you chaps are like Canute these days, trying to hold back the tide.'

Kersey, who preferred to do his own job-knocking, was curt: 'Perhaps, but I haven't got my feet wet yet.'

Marks sipped his beer. 'So you want to hear about Inez.'

'What sort of woman was she?'

'The sort some men will sit up and beg for while others run; it wasn't only looks, she had style.' Marks broke off to acknowledge a greeting from a newcomer who went to the bar. 'Why she picked on the Glynns, God only knows. She

111

was thirty-six when she cleared out and she'd had three kids, but she still made younger women look and feel like there was no contest.'

'You say she cleared out; I suppose you looked at the possibility that she went — wherever she did go — not of her own free will?'

Marks showed his spines. 'Look here, boy, I wasn't wet behind the ears then and I'm not now! Anyway you can have it as I got it. Inez was friendly with a woman living in Hayle and she used to visit pretty often, usually on Sundays; occasionally she would stay overnight. Anyway, that's what she told her husband.

'Matthew knew it was sometimes genuine, sometimes an alibi.' Marks made a dismissive gesture. 'Didn't bother him; he'd reached that point. As long as she kept the action out of town.'

Marks took a gulp of beer and wiped his moustache. 'Anyway, this Sunday evening she didn't turn up and the woman in Hayle hadn't seen her — hadn't expected her. The last the family ever saw of Inez was when she set off in her little red Mini Sunday morning with twenty quid in her purse and her passport.'

'Was that the last report of anybody seeing her?'

'Almost. A woman friend saw her driving out of town a few minutes later; after that she just vanished into thin air. Your shout, I think.'

Kersey went to the bar and had to wait while a group of fishermen jointly related to the landlord a story of putting into an Irish port for shelter and being suspected by the Garda of gunrunning for the IRA.

He was attended to at last and returned to his table with the drinks. The pub was filling and the smoke haze thickened as spirits rose.

Marks said: 'Good prices for this morning's landings.' He sipped his beer and resumed where he had left off. 'Matthew notified us Monday morning and her car was reported in Exeter station car-park on Thursday — been there since Monday morning at least. The attendant reported it when news of our interest in red Minis filtered through.'

Kersey said: 'So somebody drove the Mini to Exeter — could it have been anybody other than Inez?'

Marks was po-faced. 'Could've been, but nothing to suggest that it was: her prints were all over the car and nobody else's.'

Kersey said: 'Easy enough to fix for anybody with reason to.'

'I'm not denying it, but you've got to see it from our point of view at the time. Nobody seemed all that surprised at her pushing off.'

'Did she have any relatives? I mean, did you come across any?'

'Her mother — a widow and remarried, living somewhere in Kent — and a sister, married, with four children, in Nottingham. Neither of them wanted to know about Inez.'

Marks was watching a young fisherman in the act of draining a pint tankard without swallowing. 'I could do that once . . . No there was nobody overcome with anxiety it seemed to me, not even her husband.'

'Leaving aside what you thought at the time, and looking back, could he have driven the car to Exeter after disposing of his wife?'

Marks took his time. 'That raises a question. She left home that Sunday morning all right — no doubt about that. How would he pick her up again? By appointment?'

'He could have known where she was going.'

'Even if he did it seems a bit far-fetched to think he could do anything about it. But, allowing that he could, he might just about have been able to drive the car to Exeter Sunday night. It's a hundred and twenty miles — say up to three hours in that little crate — and he could make the night train down, arriving home in the early morning and, with luck, not being recognized by anybody on the trip or at the station, and not disturbing the family.'

Meditative, Marks drew his finger around the rim of his glass. 'It's not on, boy!'

'Is that all you've got to tell me?'

'There was one thing that struck me as a bit odd when I had a chance to look back on it. I had a phone call from a chap called Armitage — Colonel Armitage — asking about her. He was the son of the old lady Inez was companion to before she married Glynn. The colonel said Inez was a distant relative and he wanted to know if there was anything odd about her disappearance. I couldn't quite make out what he was after. Anyway I gave him the gist of what had happened and he asked me if I would let him know if we found her.'

'Where did this colonel live?'

'Somewhere in London then; it's probably in the files but it's unlikely he's there now. I've got an idea they're a Cornish family and that's why the old lady was here in the first place.'

Kersey said: 'So on the basis of what you've told me you concluded that Inez was off to join her boyfriend in Exeter — is that it?'

'No, it bloody well isn't, not altogether. All this happened in early spring — the third week in March, I think — and for several weeks of the previous summer Inez had been carrying on with a man staying at one of the St Ives hotels. In the course of our investigation it turned out that this character had been lying low, wanted by Bristol CID on fraud charges.' Marks drained his glass. 'He wasn't seen again either. Are you having another?'

'No thanks. I've had my ration.'

Marks looked at him with a speculative eye. 'Let's see, you got married or something didn't you?'

'I got married.'

'Still with it?'

'Yes.'

'Any kids?'

'Two girls at university.'

Marks nodded. 'Wish I had. I'm living with my sister; she's got a boy and a girl but it's not the same.'

'About this guy in the St Ives hotel — was there any evidence to suggest that he and Inez kept in touch?'

'Not directly but we did find out that Inez had been getting letters with Spanish stamps.'

'And Spain was a cosy hideaway for our export villains; *ergo*, her boyfriend was waiting for her to join him on the Costa del Crook.'

Marks was nettled. 'You can laugh, boy, but this was seventeen years ago. We weren't still in the push-bike and whistle era down here but neither did we have whiz kids from the crime squad on our doorstep to tell us what to do and how to do it. It was a different ball-game in those days and you bloody well know it.'

When Wycliffe returned to the Incident Room the printer, like all the other business people in the town, had closed his shop and gone home, but two reporters were keeping vigil.

'Suicide, Mr Wycliffe?'

'I don't know.'

'He was poisoned?'

'Yes, the signs are that he died as a result of poisoning but this has to be confirmed.'

'Will your investigation into the murder of Matthew Glynn continue or do you regard the case as closed?'

'The investigation will certainly continue.'

'Is it true that there was a long-standing feud between the two brothers?'

'The word feud suggests a degree of acrimony for which I've found no evidence.'

Policemen are becoming as adept at verbal evasion as politicians, far outstripping bishops and trade union leaders.

Potter, the squad's fat man, was duty officer. 'There are several memos and reports on your desk, sir.'

'Is there any coffee going?'

'I'll bring it up, sir.'

Wycliffe skimmed through the accumulated paper on his table, pushed it aside, got up, and walked to the window where he stood, looking out.

The sun was low in the sky somewhere away to his right, and the castle on the Mount was bathed in magical golden light. On the south coast of the county, when the weather is sunny and calm, the hour before dusk induces a mood of solemnity. In the offices of the church it is the turn of Vespers. Wycliffe was always reminded of the hymn which sang of 'saints casting down their golden crowns around the glassy sea'. The image depressed him; if that was heaven it was best left to the cherubim and seraphim who might be turned on by that sort of thing.

Potter came in and concluded that his chief was absorbed in profound cerebration; he put the coffee on the table and crept out . . .

Kersey arrived. 'I gather I missed the excitement.'

Wycliffe turned away from the window with a sigh.

Kersey asked: 'Are we still looking for the killer of Matthew Glynn?'

'You're no better than the reporters! I'd like to be a hundred per cent sure that Alfred killed himself.'

'There's a doubt?'

'There's bound to be. Would you choose strychnine as a way out? And would you go for a bus ride followed by a longish walk to take the fatal dose in a little hut in the middle of nowhere?'

'From what we hear Alfred wasn't exactly rational.'

'Perhaps not, and he may have had sentimental reasons for going to the little hut, but I want to be sure. Anyway, I gather you've been delving into prehistory — Marks, wasn't it? I remember him vaguely. What did you make of it?'

Kersey lit a cigarette. 'I don't think they had enough hard evidence to conclude that Inez ran off with or to another man. Or, in fact, that she ran off at all.'

'Her car?'

'Anybody could have driven it to Exeter and dumped it at the station without leaving traces that would be discovered by anything short of a pukka forensic examination.'

'Are you suggesting that she was murdered and that the car business was a cover-up?'

'I'm saying that there was no real evidence against that as a possibility. I'm not carping about the way Marks handled the case; an adult woman went missing in circumstances which seemed to offer a plausible explanation. To me, the fact that she hasn't been heard of again in seventeen years puts a different complexion on it. She would be fifty-three or four now and I find it difficult to believe that any woman who has had three children wouldn't show some curiosity about what happened to them once the glamour of life had worn a bit thin.'

Wycliffe was silent for a while, engaged in such crucial activities as straightening his telephone flex, boxing up the heap of papers on his desk into a tidy pile, and scratching his chin. Kersey blew smoke rings and watched them with approval.

Finally Wycliffe said: 'There must be people still living in this town who knew her well. It should be possible to find out more about the woman from sources less prejudiced than the family.'

'The whole thing could turn out to be a mare's nest.'

'Very likely, but anything you do find out could throw light on the family. See what you can do in a couple of days.'

'A free hand?'

'A free hand. Anything else?'

'Just another thing which could be something or nothing. While Marks's inquiry into Inez's disappearance was going on he had a call from a Colonel Armitage, son of the old lady Inez lived with before she married.'

'Saying what?'

'Nothing much, really just asking to be told if they found her.'

'It could be worth contacting this colonel. If he's still around it shouldn't be difficult. As a last resort MOD might tell us if we filled in the right forms. See what you can do. If you locate him we'll send someone to interview him.'

Kersey left, and was back in less than ten minutes. 'I found our colonel in the phone book; I remembered old Marks saying he thought they might be a Cornish family. Anyway he's living at Helford, near Falmouth: Colonel Anthony Armitage CBE, DSO, Ponsyn Cottage.'

'He might not be our man.'

'He is; I phoned. A woman answered and she agreed that his mother had lived in Penzance. He's out at the moment but he'll be in later and he'll phone either tonight or in the morning.'

Wycliffe passed an uneasy night. Names and faces, phrases and vivid little pictures presented themselves to his mind in a constant succession of changing patterns like the images in a kaleidoscope. Sara, the worthy virgin, self-absorbed but acute: '. . . my sister-in-law was a very remarkable woman.' Gerald, pretending to a *savoir faire* he did not possess: 'I suppose somebody could have been in there doing the old man while I was trying to get in . . .' Young David Glynn: '. . . for dad it is one of those special places.' The scared look on the girl's face when she caught sight of Wycliffe in the yard. Maurice Glynn: 'Matthew was my keeper.' The manuscript books with their red bindings which he had not actually seen. Sara again: 'No, there was no crisis . . .' The darkened room with the double bed and the fresh, red carnations at the bedside, viciously destroyed. Swayne: 'Well, there was a wedding all right but it was Matthew who married the girl.' Alfred's contorted body lying in the little hut. Barry Morse quoted by Kersey: 'It lends new meaning to the phrase "keeping a shop".' And Lucy Lane: 'I wonder he didn't cash in on the journals.'

Did all the pieces belong to one puzzle? Only experience saved him from despairing at this rag-bag of memories.

At a quarter to four by the little travelling clock at his bedside he got out of bed and went to the window. He had sensed a change in the air, a salty dampness. At the open casement a gentle breeze blew a mist of fine rain into his face. Although there was no moon to be seen it was far from totally dark; the sea was dimly luminescent while shapes and shadows defined the land. An intermittent glow in the south-east marked the sweep of the Lizard Light while nearer to hand the harbour lights and the street lamps contributed patches of misty radiance. He closed the casement and went back to bed and to sleep.

Next morning the whole town and bay were shrouded in

mist which condensed on every cold surface. The Mount was a shadow in the air and the iron railings along the promenade dripped globules of moisture. Wycliffe walked to work with a salty taste on his lips and arrived at the Incident Room as the little printer was opening up.

At a quarter to nine he was joined in his office by Kersey. 'Good morning, sir.' Very formal and polite. Kersey liked to discharge his obligations to the hierarchy early in the day; after that he felt free to speak his mind man-to-man.

He pulled up a chair and sat down. 'I was going through the reports, trying to size up Matthew Glynn — what made him tick. On the face of it his life centred around business of one sort or another, his own and the council's. He had plenty of acquaintances but just a couple of friends — Swayne, the stamp man, and Doble, the wine merchant. Apart from the weekly chess session he seems to have had no hobby, no what you might call recreation.' Kersey's rubbery features creased in a ferocious grin. 'I mean, a double bed made up for one. After all he was only fifty-two and I'm forty-eight.'

Wycliffe said: 'He took two holidays a year: a spring fortnight abroad and an autumn fortnight in this country.'

'Alone?'

'Apparently.'

'Well, it helps to fill in the picture but I haven't finished yet. He had a car — a Volvo 244, five years old with only twelve thousand miles on the clock. According to the family he rarely used it except on Sundays when he spent the afternoon and evening with an old chap who used to work for the firm and now lives in sheltered accommodation at Carbis Bay. He would leave home immediately after lunch and come back between ten and eleven at night.'

Wycliffe was unresponsive; his look said: 'Are we getting there?'

'The point is, I rang the accommodation warden just to check; Matthew did visit the old boy every Sunday but he never spent more than half an hour with him. He would hand over the old man's baccy for the week and a few sweeties then, after a bit of chat, he was away.'

Kersey looked at Wycliffe, expecting some question or comment and when none came he went on: 'So where did he spend his time after lunch each Sunday?'

'I don't know but you're going to tell me.'

'I'm not, but I'm sending Curnow to Carbis Bay to talk to the old man. It's possible he might know something.'

Wycliffe remembered the seemingly expensive package tour to Bulgaria, booked with — was it Eurotravel? He reached for the telephone. 'Get me the Penzance office of Eurotravel please.' He replaced the phone and explained to Kersey. 'This may save Curnow a trip.'

The phone rang: Eurotravel had no local office; the nearest was Truro. That in itself might mean something. 'Get me the manager of the Truro office.'

A minute or two later he was speaking to a suave gentleman anxious to steer a safe course between Scylla and Charybdis. 'We do have to observe client confidentiality . . .'

'But your client is dead — murdered.'

'Yes, but a second person may be involved —'

'And that person could be a key witness in our investigation; but if you insist on a Court Order . . .'

'No! no, of course we wouldn't want to do that. If you will hold for a moment . . .'

It came at last: 'Mr Glynn's travelling companion was to be a Mrs Florence Tremayne of Nansallas Cottage, New Mill.'

'Was Mr Glynn a regular customer of yours?'

'Every year as regular as clockwork — ever since I've been here, and that's eight years.'

'With the same companion?'

'Always.'

Wycliffe replaced the phone. 'There we are then.'

'They must have been very discreet. Are you going to telephone her?'

'No, I'll pay a call this afternoon.'

Kersey left and the telephone rang again. 'Wycliffe.'

It was Franks, the pathologist. 'Well, Charles, I've taken a good look at your latest victim. Of course I've sent specimens to Forensic but you can take it from me that he died of strychnine poisoning; a fairly hefty dose but he'd been living on borrowed time anyway. The Old Reaper would have caught up with him in weeks, probably, months at most. Talk about dilation!'

There were times when he felt cut off by some imponderable barrier; the usual sights and sounds reached him but they seemed to do so through a screen of interference, like a badly tuned radio. He could sympathize with the computer that puts up its little sign, 'Memory full'.

It was ten o'clock; he went into the outer room and muttered to the duty officer: 'I shall be at the pharmacy.'

Fox was already there with a pharmacologist from the county hospital who was looking at Alfred's stock of drugs with a view to discovering a possible source of the poison.

He left the Incident Room and walked up the steep alley to Lady Street, into the usual morning clutter of delivery vans and pedestrians. Alfred's shop looked as though it had been closed and deserted for months; it was hard to believe that it was only three days since a few people, at least, had been entering through the rickety door with its small glass panes to buy patent medicines or seek advice. Somebody had put a notice inside the glass, 'Closed indefinitely'.

Wycliffe went round the back, rang the doorbell and was admitted by one of Fox's assistants. 'The sergeant is in the shop, sir. Shall I fetch him?'

'No.'

He climbed the stairs, went through the living-room where nothing seemed to have changed, and down to the shop. Fox met him at the bottom of the stairs. Through the glass partition they could see the pharmacologist busy in the dispensary.

Fox said: 'He was like a hungry dog let loose in a butcher's shop; not knowing where to start. He says he's never seen anything like it; he reckons some of the stuff must have been here since before the first world war. "A profile of pharmaceutical dispensing over eighty years" — that's what he called it. Odd, the things people get worked up about.'

'I'll have a word. What's his name?'

'Edmunds, sir — Dr Edmunds.'

Edmunds was thirtyish, bearded, slim, and earnest; one of the modern breed of technical scientists who believe that the ultimate secret of life, the universe and all that, must be reducible to the predictable antics of their molecules and atoms and the infuriatingly ambiguous particles which seem to compose them.

He waited for no introduction but launched into his current theme: 'It's amazing! Most of this stuff must have been here long before Glynn took over the business; it's a museum of pharmaceutical archaeology —'

'About the strychnine —'

'Yes, of course. Well, at one time — into the Sixties, actually — strychnine was used as a heart stimulant and in so-called "tonic" medicines. In fact, it has no medical value whatever and it is an extremely dangerous drug to have lying around. It is one of the alkaloids derived from certain plant tissues but synthesized in the Fifties —'

'And there is strychnine amongst this lot?'

'Oh, yes: two sources actually; a dry extract of *nux vomica* — that is to say of the ground-up seeds of the plant; this contains about five per cent strychnine; and a preparation known as *liquor strychnine hydrochloride* which contains about one per cent of the hydrochloride.'

Fox spoke up. 'I examined the two bottles for prints and found nothing identifiable on the hydrochloride, but on the *nux vomica* bottle there were fresh prints of the deceased's left hand and on the stopper good prints of the forefinger and thumb of his right hand. Also the stopper came out easily while most of the others were stuck.'

Edmunds went on in his lecture-room style as though Fox had not interrupted: 'Either form of the poison could have been administered in brandy but brandy would not by any means completely mask the bitter taste.' He added, generously: 'You may know that it was the bitter taste which made it unpopular with poisoners of the past even when it was fairly freely available.'

So Alfred had laced his own brandy and taken it to the little hut which had youthful associations, there to kill himself in a

122

manner that was almost ceremonial. Did it really matter from which bottle the stuff had come? But the courts like to know these things; it creates a comfortable illusion of precision and that's what justice is about. You can't put emotions in a bottle labelled 'Exhibit B'.

As Wycliffe was about to leave, the telephone rang in the little office next to the dispensary. Fox answered it and signalled through the glass partition.

'DS Lane, sir.'

Lucy sounded mildly excited. 'Sara is here, sir. She says she wants to make a statement.'

'So what's to stop her?'

'She will only make it to you.'

'What's she like — uptight?'

'That about describes it, not exactly agitated, but disturbed.'

'All right; I'll be there shortly. Put her in my office with a WPC if you can find one.' He turned back to Fox. 'When you've finished here you've got Matthew Glynn's attic where all Inez's stuff is stored.'

Wycliffe got Fox to let him out by the shop door. Despite the misty rain the street was busy; the pubs had chalk-boards outside advertising their lunchtime menus; two of the shops had scaffolding against them, getting a face-lift before the start of the season. He turned down the alley which led to the Incident Room. The printer had become sufficiently reconciled to their presence to give him a friendly wave.

Lucy Lane was waiting for him.

'I want you in on this. I'll talk to her; I'd rather you didn't butt in at this stage — and nothing for the record. Afterwards you can take her statement.'

Sara was sitting on one of the bentwood chairs by the desk in the bare little office; a WPC, her black-stockinged legs tucked under her chair, sat by the door. She stood up as Wycliffe came in followed by Lucy Lane.

'You can go. Tell them I don't want to be disturbed.'

Sara wore a thin mackintosh over a blouse and skirt; her handbag was on the floor at her side and a furled umbrella rested against the desk. She looked very pale and drawn, almost haggard.

Lucy Lane took the seat by the door; Wycliffe settled behind his desk. 'You wished to see me, Miss Glynn?'

His manner was formal.

'You suggested that I should make a fresh statement.'

'Perhaps you will tell me what it is you have to say?'

Sara was holding a pair of suede gloves crushed in one hand. 'What I told you about Saturday night — going out to post letters and afterwards going for a walk — was perfectly true.' She looked across the desk at Wycliffe as though for encouragement, but none came; his expression remained bland; she could not even be sure that he was looking at her or whether his gaze was focused on the window behind her.

'But I did not tell you —' She broke off, distressed. '— I did not tell you that, on the way back, as I came round the church into the lane, I saw Alfred coming out of our back door . . . He came down the lane towards me like a man sleep-walking. I spoke to him but he walked past me as though I wasn't there . . . I watched him go in by his own back door and I hurried on home. I couldn't imagine what had happened . . . I mean, I don't think Alfred had been in the house or the bookshop except for mother's Wednesday teas since we moved from Trebyan nearly thirty years ago.'

Sara stopped speaking and the silence was broken only by the thudding of the printing press below. She was kneading the gloves in her lap, gripping them so tightly that her knuckles showed white. Lucy Lane, on the point of speaking, changed her mind. Wycliffe gave no sign, and Sara was left with no option but to continue.

'I was afraid something had happened but I never imagined anything so . . . so awful. I saw the light in Matthew's office and I went —'

'Did you bolt the yard door behind you?'

'Yes, I did.'

'Why?'

She looked vague, troubled. 'I don't know; I was frightened, it seemed the thing to do . . .'

'Go on.'

124

She looked down at her lap. 'I went to the door of Matthew's office and opened it . . .'

'Did you go in?'

'There was no need. I could see him . . .'

'Did you see the cat?'

'The cat? Yes, it slipped past me as I opened the door.'

'All right; go on.'

'Well, I shut the door, crossed the yard, and let myself in through the kitchen. There was no one about . . . I went upstairs to my room.' She took a handkerchief from her sleeve and put it to her eyes, shaking her head. 'I couldn't face any more . . . I couldn't! . . . And I had to decide what I should say . . . It was a terrible night!'

'And in the morning?'

She raised her eyes. 'As soon as it was light I went downstairs . . . I pretended to find Matthew and I roused the family . . .'

It was as though Wycliffe was giving her only part of his attention; he seemed to have become absorbed in his own thoughts and when Sara stopped speaking there was an interval long enough for Lucy Lane to look at him with concern. When he spoke it was abruptly and with a complete change of subject: 'It seems that the little hut at Trebyan meant a lot to your brothers.'

'The hut?' She was surprised, startled by the abrupt change. She said: 'Yes, I suppose it did, when they were young.'

'Did you spend much time there?'

'No, it was the boys' place. They used to camp out there in the summer holidays.'

Wycliffe could not imagine Sara camping out anywhere or at any stage of her life.

'And as they got older? They must have been in their twenties when the family moved from Trebyan.'

Sara carefully separated her gloves which she had rolled up into a ball. Without looking up she said: 'I don't know what you are getting at, Mr Wycliffe; all this was a long time ago.'

'Did they meet their girlfriends in the hut?'

'I've no idea.' Very prim.

125

'Did they bring their friends home — to the house?'

'No; my father was not —' She broke off.

'You were going to say?'

'Nothing. I can see no point in these questions. I have told you what happened on Saturday night and I am willing to answer questions about it.'

Wycliffe looked at her, his grey eyes brooding and expressionless. Sara puzzled him; he had underestimated her. He said: 'When your brother Maurice's wife was ill and David was an infant I understand you looked after him from time to time.'

'I did what I could.'

'Just one more question, Miss Glynn: when your brother Alfred visited his mother while Inez was still with you, did they have any contact?'

A vigorous shake of the head. 'No. Alfred would never acknowledge that she existed.'

Alone, he went to stand by the window, looking out. Standing at windows was his favourite situation for brooding, self-examination, consoling or condemning himself . . . wondering what to do next.

It was still misty but the sun was gathering strength and the mist had acquired a pearly hue promising better things.

Sara's story made sense; it made sense in the context of Alfred's bizarre existence. Matthew Glynn had been strangled by his brother Alfred because . . . Alfred Glynn had killed himself because . . . And Sara's story explained her own ambivalent behaviour . . . Tidy. Convincing. He had no doubt that the case could be wound up on the strength of it. No trial; you can't try a dead man. The facts were accounted for and Sara's evidence at the inquest would clinch it . . .

But there were other facts: Inez Glynn had disappeared: but that was seventeen years ago. Maurice Glynn had quarrelled with his brother: obviously a coincidence. There was the unexplained presence of a nineteenth-century journal in Matthew's safe: nothing to do with the case. And there was the little hut . . . He didn't know himself what he meant by that . . . Wycliffian dialectic.

He sighed. All the same he was going to take another look.

Chapter Eight

Tuesday morning

The telephone rang and he went back to his desk. A wary duty officer said: 'A Colonel Armitage is here asking to see you, sir.'

Wycliffe went through to the little room which had been set aside for callers. 'Colonel Armitage? . . . Wycliffe. Good of you to come.'

Armitage was by no means the popular image of a colonel, irascible and autocratic; he was thin, elderly, and mild-mannered; he looked more like an old-style academic who had acquired his pale-parchment skin through years of desiccation in college libraries; but his eyes were full of vitality.

'My housekeeper drove me in — I'm not safe on the roads any more.' With his long, scrawny neck and high-pitched voice, he suggested to Wycliffe an aristocratic parrot. 'Now I spend all the time I can on the water — more room.' A friendly grin exposing yellowed but home-grown teeth.

Wycliffe led him into his office and entered upon the preamble: 'In a murder case we have to follow every possible lead. We are in touch with you because your name cropped up in reports concerning the disappearance of the murdered man's wife. That, of course, was seventeen years ago. I understand that Inez Glynn, prior to her marriage, was your mother's housekeeper-companion.'

The colonel nodded. 'Quite so. Inez was with mother until she died. It was shortly afterwards that she married the bookseller.'

'And twelve years on, when Inez disappeared, you still expressed an interest.'

'Yes, I did.' Armitage marshalled his ideas. 'In the first place, Inez was a distant relative — some sort of cousin — but I must confess to another more direct motive. When my mother died I was a military attaché at one of our embassies in eastern Europe. It was at the time of the Bulganin-Khruschev circus and my leave was very short — not long enough to clear up my mother's affairs as I wished to do.

'Subsequently I was disappointed to find that some of our family papers were missing. I approached Inez, then Mrs Matthew Glynn, and she told me that she knew nothing of them. Of course I was not in a position to contradict her.'

'But you did not believe in her ignorance.'

Armitage spread his thin hands. 'That is putting it rather more strongly than I would have done. Years later, when I heard that Inez had left her husband and that the police were investigating her disappearance, I was tempted to carry the matter a little further. However, it soon became obvious that Inez was not to be found, and everything I learned about Matthew Glynn convinced me that he was an honest man.' The colonel shrugged. 'In the circumstances there was no more to be done and I put the matter out of my mind until your officer telephoned my housekeeper yesterday.'

Wycliffe said: 'Will you tell me the nature of the missing papers?'

Armitage seemed almost as interested in the coloured stencilled designs which decorated the peeling walls as in the subject being discussed. He recovered his manners in polite confusion. 'Of course! They concerned my mother's paternal grandfather who had spent a great many years in southern Africa — Natal and Cape Colony. They comprised his journal — a fairly detailed and animated account of his life during nearly forty years up to about 1890 — and his letter books, with copies of his correspondence. In his later years, he was closely associated with Cecil Rhodes so these records might have some historical as well as family interest.'

'And considerable monetary value?'

'I suppose so — yes.'

'Was your great grandfather Martin J. Beale?'

Armitage looked at him in astonishment. 'Yes, indeed.'

'Then his journal is in Glynn's safe under seal at the moment.'

'You amaze me! I had no idea that my coming here would lead to anything of the sort.'

'The letter books you mention are not there.'

'No matter! I'm delighted to recover . . . I suppose I shall be able to recover the journal?'

'I've no doubt of that but you will have to deal with the family or with their solicitor. Was there anything else that you expected to find amongst your mother's papers that you did not?'

The colonel frowned. 'Yes, there was a collection of letters written by Martin Beale to his mother; they were of purely family interest, kept by her out of sentiment I suppose. After all, South Africa was a long way off in those days and home leave must have been a great rarity.'

They parted company, pleased with themselves and with each other.

It was past two when Wycliffe and Kersey made it to a pub for lunch; a pub not far from the bookshop. They had a table by the window in an upstair room decorated with a random collection of memorabilia from a colourful maritime past. Outside the window, on a flat roof, seagulls strutted up and down eyeing inaccessible snacks like Dickensian children pressing their noses against pastry-shop windows.

Wycliffe brought Kersey up to date but seemed reluctant to enter into any sort of discussion. Kersey watched the gulls and tried various gambits to draw him out, succeeding at last: 'I suppose Sara's story is credible and you can't altogether blame her for not coming out with it sooner.'

'No.'

'Unless she killed Matthew and Alfred's death gave her a heaven-sent scapegoat.'

Wycliffe made a gesture of rejection. 'I don't think Sara

was Matthew's killer. Look at the facts: she was seen in Alexandra Road at 11.15, the very time at which Gerald found the yard door barred against him. Fifteen minutes later, a woman, who could only have been Sara, found the door unbarred. It seems to me highly likely that the killer had locked himself in and that he got away during that fifteen minutes.'

'And that Sara met him?'

'That's another matter but it's quite possible.'

'So where does that leave us? What's the next move?'

'My next move is to talk to Matthew's woman friend — Florence Tremayne — isn't that her name? Your job is to get what you can on Inez.'

Kersey sprinkled sugar on his apple pie. 'Yes, I've got a lead there. There's an old lady living next door to what used to be the Armitage house; she was there when Mrs Armitage was alive and Inez was her companion.'

'Could she tell you anything?'

'Not much, but it seems that her daughter and Inez were close, and remained friendly after both of them married. I gather the old lady didn't approve. Anyway, the daughter now has grown-up children and is living in Launceston. I thought of going over there this afternoon.'

'Good! There's one other thing: can you recall Maurice's account of how he spent Saturday evening?'

'I can check the report but I think he was in the pub at Goldsithney until nineish then he went home.'

'Driving the Land Rover?'

'No, he had a push-bike. Why?'

'I wondered.'

A little later Kersey tried again: 'At least we know how Matthew got hold of the Beale journal and why he kept it under wraps. From what Morse said it looks as though he was trying to flog it in some under-the-counter deal, but I don't see how it helps us.'

'No.'

'You're not having any dessert? This pie is good.'

'Only coffee.'

*

'New Mill — do you know where it is?'

Lucy Lane was driving Wycliffe's car. 'I've got a cousin who farms not far from the village and I used to stay there in the holidays when I was a girl.'

Lucy's relatives seemed to be uniformly and conveniently distributed throughout the south-western peninsula.

'But you don't happen to know the lady we are going to see?'

'I'm afraid not, sir.'

Lucy Lane had been working in his team for three years but he felt that he knew her only a little better than he had done after her first month. She was a workaholic, highly intelligent, and singularly free from hang-ups, but there was a barrier. Sometimes he thought it was of his own making: he was unaccustomed to working closely with women and this one was still young and attractive which made him self-conscious.

The road was narrow, no more than a lane, prone to cows and farm tractors, but Lucy drove with a relaxed confidence which he envied. He had never achieved a rapport with the automobile and avoided the driving seat when he could.

New Mill consists of a straggle of houses following the course of the lane and a stream. Like much of Penwith it has a powerful ethos which refuses to be submerged by the modern world; the countryside is littered with artefacts spanning the centuries, from megalithic chamber tombs to nineteenth-century mine workings, and only the moron can escape a sense of continuity with and obligation to the past. If Glynn had wanted a cover for visits to his woman friend, his charitable trips to St Ives served him well; New Mill involved only a detour of a mile or so from the direct route.

'It's some distance beyond the village, by the stream.' Lucy had this from a man weeding his garden.

In fact the stream ran through Florence Tremayne's garden which was a wild garden with trees and an abundance of daffodils. The cottage itself was severe, a slate-roofed little building in the Cornish tradition, but its walls were covered with creepers now coming into leaf.

A neatly written notice on the door read: 'Knock and if there's no answer come round the back.'

There was an answer.

'Mrs Tremayne? . . . Chief Superintendent Wycliffe; this is Detective Sergeant Lane . . .'

She did not look like a predatory widow and she was no superannuated dolly-bird either; she must have been fifty, she was on the plump side, clear skinned, with a frank, open face. She wore trousers and a smock.

'I was expecting somebody, I suppose. You'd better come in.'

They were shown into a room which ran the whole depth of the cottage, bright and chintzy, the indoor equivalent of a herbaceous border. There were daffodils in vases and framed flower-paintings on the walls.

'You didn't think to get in touch with us, Mrs Tremayne?'

She was sitting on a gaily upholstered settee while Wycliffe and Lucy Lane had the two matching armchairs. 'Yes, I thought about it but I decided that the family had enough to put up with without learning about me. It isn't as though I could tell you anything that would help to explain what happened to Matt.'

Her manner was restrained; sad but not grief-stricken. Wycliffe felt sure that in normal circumstances she was a cheerful woman, more ready to laugh than cry. 'I should explain that Matt and I were not lovers in the accepted sense; we were friends — good friends, we'd known each other from childhood so we had a lot in common. I was born and brought up in St Hilary Parish; my maiden name was Scoble and father farmed Little Carn. Most of the older people in the parish remember me as Florrie Scoble.'

The sun was shining through the little window making patterns of light and shadow on the carpet and causing the polished woodwork to glow.

'You've been in contact with Matthew Glynn all through?'

'Oh, no! When Matt married Inez I was left high and dry. A year later I met a sales rep for an agricultural firm and married him. You could say it was on the rebound but I had no reason

132

to regret it. We moved to Somerset and I saw nothing of Matt for — I don't know — it must've been sixteen years I suppose. My husband was killed in a road accident in '71 and I couldn't bear to live on alone up there so I bought this place — returning to the scenes of my youth, or very nearly.'

She had a mop of unruly brown hair, streaked with grey, and she swept it back from her face with an impatient movement that was wholly girlish.

Wycliffe said: 'You implied that you and Matthew were planning to marry when he married Inez — is that so?'

'Oh, yes; at least that was my impression.' A helpless gesture. 'And Inez was supposed to be marrying Alfred.'

'Was it a complete surprise to you when Matthew and Inez agreed to marry?'

For the first time she hesitated. 'Oh, dear! This is really probing the old wound. I had no idea it could still hurt. I knew that Inez had had her turn in the little hut but I didn't know until afterwards that she was pregnant. Yes, when Matt told me he was going to marry her it was a surprise — a shock.' She looked at him, questioning. 'I suppose you know about the little hut?'

'It's still there.'

She looked down at her hands. 'I know. It sounds quite absurd but the other day I walked up the footpath from the road just to see if it was. A boy came out and looked at me, a bit suspicious, and I felt a fool, but that boy took me back thirty years. He could have been any one of the brothers. Of course, it was Maurice's boy.

'Anyway, the hut looked just the same; things wear better than people, don't they?'

'You have memories of the little hut?'

She coloured and laughed. 'When I remember it first it was a playroom for the Glynn children and any others they cared to let in; a sort of clubhouse. Later, as the boys became teenagers and young men, it became a place for them to meet their girlfriends.

'Perhaps it's difficult to believe now, but the Glynn boys could take their pick of girls. Of course Matt was regarded as

133

the prize and I suppose I was flattered when he became serious with me — or seemed to.'

Wycliffe said: 'And you met Matthew again when you came back here to live?'

'Within a year or so; a chance meeting.'

'And that started the Sunday visits and the biannual holidays?'

A short laugh. 'So you know our secrets. I suppose you must, since you're here. Anyway, that was all he wanted of me though he offered marriage. He didn't really want a deeper involvement.'

'And you?'

'Oh, I would have turned him down anyway. Meeting Matthew again after sixteen years of marriage and hearing about the rest of the family — it made me realize there was something about the Glynns . . .'

'What kind of thing?'

She was picking at a loose cotton in the hem of her smock. 'I can't quite explain it. When I think back it seems to me they were all three of them looking for a groove to settle in — tramlines that would take them somewhere without them having to think where they were going.' She laughed at her own image. 'They might have to work — the Glynns aren't lazy — but they want to make their decisions once and for all.' She looked up, questioning, wondering if she had made sense.

Wycliffe watched her, dreamy-eyed; it was impossible to say whether he was interested or not, even whether he was really listening. Lucy Lane wondered, not for the first time, what it was about him that encouraged people to talk; sometimes it was almost as though he wasn't there.

Florrie Tremayne went on regardless: 'And poor old Alfred with his shop; he'd wanted to be a doctor, a GP, plodding along in some backwater for forty years, supported by a sufficient number of loyal patients who hung on his words and swallowed his medicines with no fuss. Instead, he had to settle for a chemist's shop, and though he still tried to behave like a doctor, it didn't work. To make a living he had to sell things over the counter — like his brother.'

Lucy Lane said: 'But apart from that there was a sort of tragedy in his life — at least he saw it as one.'

Florrie looked at the girl. 'You really think so? You may be right but some people seem to dramatize a commonplace misfortune and turn it into a cult. They live on it. I may be hard, but it looks to me like an excuse for not facing the real world — perhaps a welcome excuse.'

'What about Maurice? Has he found his groove?' It was Wycliffe, giving the first indication that he had followed her argument, and she became flustered. It was almost as though he was consulting her.

She said: 'Oh, I think so — he was upset enough at the idea of Matt building houses next to his pottery, wasn't he?'

'Upset enough to kill?' The question came quietly, almost casually, but if Florrie had been flustered before, now she was shocked. 'The idea had never entered my head! I know it's not your fault, but you come here and we chat about the family, I say too much and, suddenly, we're talking about murder!'

'But that's what I'm here for, to talk about murder.'

'Yes, but my tongue runs away with me and I find it difficult to realize that Matt is dead.'

Wycliffe sat, unruffled in his chair, while Florrie calmed herself by going to make tea.

Soon she was back again and they were drinking tea and eating saffron cake.

'About the little hut — did Alfred and Maurice meet their girlfriends there?'

'Yes, but I don't think Alfred was much competition.' She looked down at her hands. 'I'm making it sound as though the little hut was some sort of brothel, but it wasn't like that at all. I mean, we were young; there happened to be more girls in the neighbourhood than boys, and we experimented — there was nothing vicious about it. Going back to Alfred, it was solemnly agreed that every couple who spent time in the hut would carve their initials somewhere. Of course it became quite a game searching for pairs of initials but I don't remember finding Alfred's once.'

She cast a speculative eye on Lucy Lane. 'Sometimes I get the impression that modern young people think they discovered sex.'

'Did Sara come in on any of this?'

'Oh, no! Sara used to spy on the boys but if she ever had anything going for her I didn't know about it.'

Lucy Lane said: 'They all seemed fond of their mother.'

Florrie smiled. 'She was always a bit of a mystery to me; her sons worshipped her — I'm not so sure about Sara. If there was anything unpleasant the first thing in the boys' minds was "not to worry mother". I've no idea how she managed it. Anyhow she lived to be nearly ninety and I'm not surprised.'

They left at last. In the car Lucy Lane said: 'A very interesting woman.'

Wycliffe agreed. 'A realist, and they're rare birds, God knows.'

When they arrived back at the Incident Room the little printer was locking up for the night.

'Good evening, Mr Wycliffe. Nice evening.'

They were becoming neighbours.

Dixon, one of the longest serving of Wycliffe's DCs and one who had never sought or wanted promotion, was duty officer. 'The chief's been on the line, sir; he wants you to ring him.'

Dixon had been in the business long enough to convey by a subtle nuance of tone that the Chief Constable was not in an amiable mood.

'Right. Get him on the line; I'll be in my room.'

His telephone rang almost at once; he was through to the chief's personal assistant, a grey-haired lady of vast experience who monitored and sometimes modulated communication (other than face to face) between the chief and the outside world — including his policemen.

'The chief's been asking for you for some time, Mr Wycliffe.' Her tone was a caution.

'I've been out.'

Bertram Oldroyd's voice came over the line. 'Charles! Where the hell have you been? Never mind, you'll only tell me and I don't want to know. The press, the TV and the radio would like to know what's going on and, incidentally, so would I. Kersey doesn't know, or he does and isn't saying.'

Wycliffe was wooden. 'What exactly is it that is not known, sir? We've had a homicide and a suicide and your office has been kept informed about both.'

Oldroyd laughed. 'All right, Charles, come off it! You know damn well the questions that are being asked — the questions I'm asking: Is this case winding up or isn't it? The facts seem to point to Matthew Glynn having been murdered by his brother, Alfred, as the climax of a long feud aggravated by Alfred's mental instability. Alfred commits suicide which, in the circumstances, might well be construed as an admission of guilt. You've no reason to doubt the suicide?'

'None.'

'Good! Then what are we waiting for?'

Wycliffe said: 'There is another piece of evidence which hasn't reached you yet. The dead man's sister, Sara Glynn, has made a fresh statement in which she claims to have seen her brother, Alfred, leaving the scene shortly after the time at which Matthew must have died.'

Oldroyd drew in his breath. 'So that's it! Surely it's over bar the paperwork.'

Wycliffe said: 'I'm not satisfied, sir.'

'What more do you want?'

'To be convinced.'

There was a lull. Wycliffe could sense Oldroyd's mind ticking over. 'All right, Charles. I've got too much respect for you to argue but I hope you'll remember that you're tying up men and equipment down there.'

'I'll remember.'

'How long do you reckon you'll need?'

'As long as it takes, sir.'

'It's a good job I know you, Charles! Have it your way. I'll get Miller to draft a statement for the media and tell him to clear it with you before release.'

'Thanks, I appreciate that.'

That evening Wycliffe's after-dinner walk took him once more to Newlyn, but it was a fine evening and still light so he continued along the coast road, past the stone quarries, to Mousehole. (Nothing to do with mice or holes but probably a corruption of the Cornish Moweshayl, young women's river — perhaps where they did their washing.) He trudged the maze of little streets, sometimes on the edge of the sea, sometimes, and unpredictably, separated from it by a row of cottages. There was a quay, said to have been started by the Phoenicians; and everywhere, on sea and land alike, there were boats. Just another Cornish village in transition from fish to tourists.

He found Merlyn Rock where, in the summer of 1595, the Spaniards landed and burned the village along with Newlyn and Penzance; then in the gathering dusk he made his way up the hill out of the village to Paul and the church of St Pol de Leon (not he of Tarsus but a Celtic gentleman), also burned by the Spaniards and rebuilt afterwards.

And all the time in the subterranean passages of his mind he was trying to come to terms with his own obstinacy. Why would Sara say that she had seen Alfred leaving his brother's yard at about the time of the crime if she had not? True, Alfred was not now in a position to contradict her, but why should she lie? To protect herself? To protect someone else? Either was possible but why did he disbelieve her? It came to him that what really troubled him was motive, or rather the lack of what he considered to be a convincing motive for the killing.

He reminded himself again that he was dealing with pre-meditated murder and the Glynns were not the sort to resort deliberately to force except in dire circumstances. They were respectable; they and their like inherit and sustain their respectability as the aristocracy guard the family silver — an ultimate resource.

He had taken a longer walk than he intended and by the time he returned to the coast road at Newlyn it was quite dark.

Chapter Nine

Wednesday morning

It was not yet May but it was a May morning; the sun was shining and there was that certain sparkle in the air; air which, despite all that has been done to it, Wycliffe still found good to breathe. And, according to the radio, doves were cooing in the Kremlin. He felt mildly exhilarated, which troubled him a little because he couldn't think why.

It was high tide and on the wharf the swing-bridge was open to allow a toy ship to enter the toy-town dry-dock. He stood and watched for a while but everything connected with seamanship is so majestically slow that he began to feel guilty of time wasting while the little vessel was still being manoeuvred through the gap.

He climbed the steep slope to the Incident Room, forcing his pace, and arrived just a little out of breath. The printer had not yet opened.

Upstairs, Dixon, the duty officer, nodded towards the waiting-room. 'A young lady to see you, sir — Christine Glynn.'

She was sitting on one of the bentwood chairs, knees together, her hands wedged between them. She wore jeans and a zip-up denim top.

'You wanted to see me, Christine?'

Without a word she followed him into his office. He placed a chair for her and she sat down, pale and anxious.

'It's about when they opened father's safe.'

'You told me you weren't there.'

'I wasn't; it was only when I was talking about it to Gina that I thought I ought to come here and tell you.'

She was holding herself so stiff that from time to time she trembled. He tried to help her: 'They didn't find much; only a couple of volumes of somebody's journal —'

'Yes, I know. And a box — an empty cardboard box.'

'You know something about these things?'

'Only that I've seen them before.'

'In the safe?'

'No.'

'Tell me about it.'

She frowned, making an effort to compose herself. 'It was about a month ago; one afternoon I sort of burst into father's office to ask him something. Paula said there was nobody with him but there was: Ronnie Swayne was there. Ronnie must have come in through the yard door without her knowing . . . Father hated to be disturbed when he had anybody with him and I could see he was annoyed so I made myself scarce; I mean I didn't stay to say what I wanted.'

'But you saw something?'

'Yes. The safe was open, and the two books were on father's desk with the cardboard box, and he was just taking the lid off the box as I came in.'

'Was it empty?'

'No, it was full of papers.'

'Papers lying on top of one another — just stuffed in?'

'No; they were sort of folded and put in next to each other, on edge.'

'Like cards in a card index?'

She looked pleased. 'Yes, just like that but they seemed too thick for cards and uneven — like folded papers. I can't say for sure; I mean, I was only there for a second or two . . .'

'Did your father say anything to you or to Swayne while you were there?'

'Not to me; I didn't stay long enough.'

'To Swayne?'

'He was saying something as I came in — something about a buyer . . .'

'Having a buyer . . . finding a buyer . . . looking for a buyer. . . ?'

140

She shook her head. 'I'm sorry, I can't remember.'

He wondered why she was so tense. 'Why have you come to tell me about this, Christine?'

'I thought you would want to know; I mean, there were things in the box that aren't there now.'

She reminded him very much of his own daughter as she had been not so long ago; on the verge of womanhood, nervous and unsure but determined not to be put down or patronized.

'You think Swayne may have the things that were in the box?'

She drew back at this. 'I don't know. Gina said that your . . . your detective seemed to think the box mattered. Perhaps I shouldn't have come.'

He was reassuring. 'You were quite right to come and what you've told me may be important. I just want to be sure that you've told me all you know.'

He sat watching the girl, wondering if there was any way of getting behind the mask. She faced him, her dark eyes anxious.

'Do you believe that your Uncle Alfred killed your father?'

'Of course I believe it! Aunt Sara saw him — she told you!' Her response was so vigorous as to be almost violent.

He gave up. 'Are you going out to the pottery today?'

'I'm on my way; I've got my bike outside.'

He thanked her for coming and saw her off the premises, but he was left wondering at her distress which seemed to arise more from fear than from grief. But that did not prevent him seeing the possible significance of what she had told him.

Back in his office he put through a call to the colonel. After the obligatory preamble on the weather he got down to business. 'When you were here you mentioned a collection of letters written by Martin Beale to his mother which came into your mother's possession later. How were they kept?'

'Kept?' The colonel echoed the word in his high-pitched voice. 'In a shoe box or something of the sort. Don't tell me you've found them?'

'No, but we may have news of them. Were the letters loose or still in their envelopes?'

Hesitation. 'I'm afraid I can't tell you that. My mother kept the box in a cupboard in her sitting-room along with all manner of other things which had been handed down through her side of the family. I remember her pointing it out to me saying what was in it when we were really looking for something else.' The colonel pondered. 'No, I don't think I ever looked inside. I suppose one gets more interested in that sort of thing as one grows older.'

Wycliffe thanked him and promised to keep him informed.

Swayne; perhaps he should have paid more attention to Swayne.

Lady Street was busy: there were even a few visitors about, weaving between the parked vans and lorries. It's extraordinary the way they materialize like flies out of thin air when the sun shines. The grill had been removed from the window of the stamp shop and the outer door stood open. Wycliffe stepped down into the little hall and pushed open the door of the shop itself. There was a chest-high counter and the space on the customers' side offered room for no more than two people. Swayne, wearing his half-glasses, was seated on a high stool behind the counter, sorting stamps, dividing the contents of a large heap into several smaller piles. Clarence sprawled on the counter as only a cat can, performing an intimate and meticulous toilet.

Swayne looked over his glasses. 'Good morning, Mr Wycliffe. Do you want to come through?'

'No, this shouldn't take long.'

Swayne went on: 'I suppose it's about Alfred. A shocking business! One feels guilty about not having understood better what was going on. I'm assuming that it was suicide following . . .'

'Following what, Mr Swayne?' Wycliffe was innocent.

'Well, one shouldn't jump to conclusions but I can't help linking Alfred's death with Matt's. I knew, of course — we all did — the bitterness which Alfred felt against his brother . . . But after nearly thirty years!'

Swayne's fingers continued busily, sorting his stamps into

142

colourful little heaps; he seemed to manage with the minimum of attention.

Wycliffe said: 'It's not about Alfred that I'm here but another matter altogether. Among the contents of Matthew's safe there were two manuscript volumes, the journal of a certain Martin Beale who lived and worked in Natal and Cape Province during the second half of the last century.'

Swayne made no comment.

'I understand that Matthew showed you those books.'

'Yes, he did.'

'Do you know where he got them or why he kept them from his family?'

Swayne looked at Wycliffe over his glasses. 'No, I don't know, Mr Wycliffe. Surely you're not suggesting that they had anything to do with his death?'

'You didn't know that he acquired them through his wife who must have got them while she was housekeeper-companion to Mrs Armitage?'

Swayne's fingers ceased sorting his stamps and he gave Wycliffe his full attention. 'No, I didn't know that.'

'In what circumstances were they shown to you?'

'Simply as a matter of interest. We happened to be talking about the diary habit which, nowadays, seems to be largely confined to politicians.'

'Did he ask you to find a buyer for them?'

The little green eyes widened. 'Mr Wycliffe, Matthew was a dealer in rare books and something of an authority, why would he consult me?'

Wycliffe was standing with one arm resting on the counter, gazing at the freckled man whose sparse red hair was combed in streaks across his skull. For an appreciable time no one spoke and Swayne began to be uneasy. The cat had stopped cleaning itself and had curled up asleep in a little pool of sunshine.

Somebody stepped down from the street and peered through the glass door but seeing Wycliffe went away again.

Wycliffe said: 'What about the letters?'

'The letters?'

'In the cardboard box; they were in the safe with the journal. Were you more interested in them? You see, they are no longer there.'

Swayne fiddled with his little heaps of stamps. 'Journals, letters — they were both Glynn's cup of tea, not mine.'

'But letters come in envelopes and envelopes have stamps on them. My mother always kept letters in their envelopes and a lot of other people must have done the same or the stamp business generally would have been the poorer.'

'I'm at sea, Mr Wycliffe.'

'Then let me be more explicit. Inez had no right to either the journal or the box of letters which passed into Matthew Glynn's possession and were shown to you. Mrs Armitage's heir is already asserting his rights in the matter but that is not my concern. My interest is in the murder of Matthew Glynn.'

Swayne was incredulous. 'But surely you know who killed Matthew?'

'No, I do not know! We have one possibility but the case is still under investigation and I am looking for possible motives. I don't know the value attaching to the stamps on those envelopes but if they are or have been in your possession you would be well advised to make a full statement of your involvement. If I can't get the information I want any other way I shall ask the fraud squad to make enquiries. At the same time you will be required to attend at the police station for a formal interview.'

Swayne made an angry movement. 'This is harassment!'

Wycliffe straightened up. 'Of course if you wish to make a voluntary statement you can come along to my Incident Room at some time to suit yourself. One of the officers there will assist you.' He left without giving the little man a chance to reply.

Out in the street he stood for a while, obstructing the pavement. Swayne was a dealer, it was doubtful whether he was making more than a bare living out of his stamps and coins. If there was a chance of real money he might be tempted . . . Assuming the cardboard box was full of letters and that each one carried a stamp — used stamps of Natal and

Cape Province between the years say, 1850 and 1890 — would they be worth much? Wycliffe had no idea but surely not enough to provide a motive for murder. All the same, he was in no doubt that Matthew Glynn had handed over the contents of the cardboard box to Swayne with a view to some sort of deal.

Give Swayne time to brood.

Without conscious intent he walked the few steps to the bookshop. The blinds were still down and there was a closed notice on the door, but there was no longer a uniformed man outside. He rang the bell of the house door and it was answered by a grey-haired little woman in an overall; a Mrs Mop. He had no need to introduce himself.

Brushing back her hair with the back of a damp hand she said: 'Your lot are up in the attics, Miss Sara is out and they're in the shop.'

He went down the passage and through the communicating door into the shop. At the back he found Gerald and Paula, the girl assistant, unpacking parcels of books.

Gerald straightened up. 'I was hoping you might put in an appearance. I know it sounds unfeeling but to be blunt we can't go on much longer without any money coming in. The coroner has issued a disposal certificate and we've provisionally arranged the funeral for Saturday — service at the church and burial in the town cemetery beside granny.' He looked at Wycliffe, oddly tentative. 'Will the police raise any objection to that?'

'Why should we?'

'And we could open for business on Monday?'

'It's up to you.'

The sound of a typewriter rattling away came from the little office and Gerald said: 'Gina — catching up on the correspondence. She'd rather do it herself than dictate to Paula.'

Gerald was uneasy, apologizing for the contending demands of the living and the dead, but Wycliffe was too preoccupied to be reassuring. 'I'm going up to the attics.'

He climbed the stairs, paused for a moment to look out of the landing window at the bay in sunshine, then continued on up. There were three attics and through the open door of one he could see Fox sorting the contents of a huge cabin-trunk while his assistant was foraging in a cupboard beside the chimney breast. The room had the steeply sloping ceiling and dormer window typical of attics.

There were heaps of clothing on the floor, roughly sorted and laid out on newspaper. Fox, house-trained and with a card-index mind, was shocked by the manner in which Inez's belongings had been stored.

'I gather Matthew Glynn put all this away himself. I've never seen such a jumble! There's a lot of very good stuff here but he seems to have gathered it up in armfuls and just bundled it in anywhere. When Leach opened that cupboard it just tumbled out on the floor.'

He stooped to retrieve an ear-ring which had dropped out of a blouse he was holding. 'Odd items of jewellery fall out of anything you happen to pick up; photographs are mixed up with underclothes . . . Handbags over here, Leach!' He reached out to take a pig-skin handbag from his assistant. 'That's the fifth, so far — one to go with each outfit I suppose . . . That fur on the floor is mink . . . One thing's certain: he didn't keep her short . . .'

Wycliffe brooded; he felt restless and frustrated, unable to make up his mind where he should be or what he should be doing. And this attic depressed him; these expensive arte-facts, stuffed away and unregarded, seemed to underline the futility of a certain kind of living . . . He tried to imagine Matthew's state of mind when he gathered up his wife's things and stashed them away. Glynn was not by nature careless or casual; he must have been under strong emotion. Grief? Anger? Remorse? . . .

'Look out particularly for any photographs or letters.'

'There's an album with snapshots, sir, mainly of the children — "Gerry at five years", "Gina at four months" — that sort of thing.'

Wycliffe was leaving when Leach lifted a bundle of clothing from the bottom shelf of his cupboard. 'There's a brief-case under this lot!'

He stooped and held up a fairly modern brief-case of the

sort office workers are said to carry their sandwiches in. Fox took it from him. 'It's locked.'

Wycliffe waited while Fox demonstrated his skill as a pick-lock. The case was all but empty — just a few letters, still in their envelopes.

'Three of them seem to be anonymous, sir,' Fox said. 'Addressed in block capitals to Matthew Glynn.'

Wycliffe took the three to a small table by the window. The envelopes had been slit open. All three had been posted in the Penzance district and the post-mark dates were: February 1st, February 22nd, and March 21st, all in 1971. The last date was significant; it was the Monday following the Sunday on which Inez left home for the last time. Wycliffe read the notes in date order; each consisted of one or two lines of block capitals, written with a ball point.

The first read: 'You know what's going on with your wife. What sort of man are you?' The second: 'Most Sunday afternoons her car is in Badgers' Wood. You can see for yourself.' And the third: 'Her car was there on Sunday.'

The other letters in the brief-case were a mixed bag and dated some time later. One was from an astrologer saying that he would find Matthew's wife for a fee; another proposed membership of a society for bereaved or deserted spouses; a third offered the services of 'a well-known and respected private inquiry agent, formerly associated with Scotland Yard.'

'I suppose neither of you have heard of Badgers' Wood?'

Neither of them had.

Outside the door he all but ran into Sara. Had she been eavesdropping? If so she had learned very little. He was astonished by the change in her since the previous day; then she had looked tired, now she looked grey and ill. Evidently the making of a formal statement had not relieved her mind.

'I heard you were up here going through what Inez left. Why? Surely you can leave us alone now?' Her manner was pleading rather than aggressive.

'I have to do my work, Miss Glynn.' Smug; but what else could he say?

'What work? You know who killed Matthew — and why. What more do you want, for God's sake?'

He could not be touched by this woman though he was well aware that she was deeply distressed. 'I'm sorry.'

She let him go without further protest.

His mind was in turmoil. He wanted to get away somewhere and think in peace, but experience had taught him that it would have achieved nothing because he was incapable of sustained logical thought. The best he could hope for was to give his thoughts free rein, to recapture phrases, images, notions, and play with them, allowing them to make patterns in his mind. While reading the anonymous notes the glimmering of an idea had come to him but he could not sharpen the focus. It was like trying to recall a dream.

Without being aware of getting there he found himself outside the printer's shop. Upstairs, Curnow was duty officer.

'I want a driver and the key to the little hut at Trebyan.'

He got one of the local uniformed men.

'Trebyan — beyond St Hilary Churchtown.'

'I know it, sir.'

'You know the area well?'

'I ought to, I was born and bred in Penzance; PC Hawken, sir.'

Late thirties, ought to have made sergeant by now but probably didn't want to. Who could blame him?

'Have you ever heard of Badgers' Wood?'

'No, sir. There's Badgers' Cross —'

'I know Badgers' Cross.'

They turned off the main road. 'Take the lane to Churchtown.'

'There's no need, sir, this road will —'

'Do it.'

If PC Hawken had heard of Wycliffe's reputation for amiability he was being disillusioned.

'Stop here.'

There was no dog in the road but they were among the little cluster of grey and brown stone houses near the church where Wycliffe had had his memorable conversation with Emily Pascoe.

He went to her house and knocked on the green door. It was answered by Emily herself, an oven cloth in her hand.

'Oh, it's you! Come in, do!'

He was shown into an over-furnished little sitting-room from which the light was almost excluded by two sets of curtains. A rich warm smell of baking came from the kitchen.

'I just this minute took my cakes out of the oven. I always bake of a Wednesday, just like my mother used to — two saffron cakes and a tray of buns — they last us nicely through the week.' She made a gesture of vigorous distaste. 'I can't abide they ol' shop cakes.'

She guided him to an armchair and sat herself on the edge of a Victorian sofa. 'What a terrible thing about poor Alfie! You could've knocked me down with a feather when they tol' me.' She studied her plump, ringed fingers. 'I come over quite queer. To think that was what the poor fella was going to do when I saw 'n pass my door Monday morning!'

'Yes, it was a terrible thing. I came this morning because I think you may be able to help me from your knowledge of the family and of the area. First, do you know a place called Badgers' Wood?'

She frowned. 'Badgers' Wood? . . . No, I never heard that name round here an' I've lived here all my life . . . Badgers' Wood — no, I can't help you there, my dear. 'Course, there's badgers up in the banks but I never heard that name —' She broke off. 'You was saying about the family . . .'

'Yes. I wanted to ask you about Maurice's wife — you mentioned her when —'

'Yes, she come from somewhere up-country. Poor li'l thing, she didn' last long. Depression. In an' out of hospital she was.' She gave Wycliffe a sidelong look. 'They call it hospital now — what we used to call the asylum. She never got over having young David — sad! But like I said before, they Glynns never had much luck.

'In the end she couldn' stand it no longer.'

'Are you saying that she killed herself?'

Emily pouted her lips. 'Overdose. Funny! Not one of they brothers got and kept a wife.'

Through a narrow gap in the curtains Wycliffe could see across the road to the churchyard with its sycamores and the little grey tower of the church pointing its slender steeple into blue sky. Not a movement, not a sound anywhere.

'Did Maurice have any help in the house when his wife was in hospital?'

'Molly Pearce. She was good as gold; I don't know what he would've done without her!'

'An elderly woman?'

'Elderly? Nothing of the kind — thirtyish I s'pose she must've bin then.' A knowing smile. 'I reckon she had her eye on Maurice when his wife died.'

'I'd like to talk to her; does she still live around here?'

'Where she always lived; she never married.'

'Where is that?'

'With her people — they farm Roskear; it's on the top road just above Trebyan. The Glynns and the Pearces are neighbours.'

Wycliffe came out into the sunshine, blinking; Emily saw him off like an old friend. She would probably gossip; so much the better.

PC Hawken was waiting in the car.

Wycliffe made up his mind: 'I shall be at Trebyan for a while.'

'Then I'll drop you off there, sir.'

'No, I prefer to walk. Are you interested in churches?'

'I can take them or leave them, sir.'

'Never been in this one?'

'No, sir.'

'Try it. Pity there's no pub.'

After twenty years in the force Hawken thought that he knew all there was to be known about the eccentricities of senior officers but he was wrong.

Wycliffe set out along the road which was no more than a lane following the course of a shallow valley. There were fields on either side with occasional stands of pine trees scattered unpredictably over the landscape. In the hedges bluebells, red campions and white ramsons made patriotic splashes of colour.

Not a single vehicle.

Molly Pearce, the helpful spinster with her eye on Maurice; she fitted so exactly that Wycliffe could scarcely believe his luck. He was beginning to find pieces which seemed to go together with the hint of a pattern . . .

Strolling rather than walking he reached the point where the footpath to Trebyan left the road; it was by no means obvious unless one was looking for it: a ditch, a screen of willows, and a stile all but covered with ivy. Once over the stile he was soon amongst the hawthorn and gorse and on the track which led to the little hut; he was doing as Alfred must have done two days earlier.

It was a strange place and it gave him strange ideas; he was oddly aware of those who had played, and loved and quarrelled there. Had they done so with more than ordinary intensity so that they had left behind something of themselves — a persistent aura? He told himself that this was nonsense; he was allowing his knowledge to influence his perceptions.

Yet Alfred had chosen it as a place to die and David had said of his father: '. . . for him it is one of those special places.'

He reached the hut and climbed the two or three steps to the verandah. The silence was absolute; the sun shone and the air was still. Then he noticed that there was a key already in the lock. He opened the door but the dimness inside was such that for a moment he could see little; then, as his eyes accommodated, he saw Maurice standing, pressed against the far wall as though he wanted to vanish through it. The hut seemed to be as he had last seen it except that the settee had been pulled out from the wall to the centre of the room.

In a voice that sounded husky and uncertain, Maurice said: 'I came down to look around.'

'So you found another key.'

151

Chapter Ten

Wycliffe sat on the settee in the middle of the room; Maurice was perched on the stool, hands and knees tight together as though, absurdly, he would make himself as small as possible.

'I suppose you know that your sister made a fresh statement yesterday?'

'She told me — on the telephone.'

'According to her statement she saw Alfred leaving the Lady Street premises by the back door at about half-past eleven on Saturday night.'

'I know.'

Their attitudes were not those of two men meeting for only the second time; it was rather as if they shared certain knowledge and could make a number of assumptions which need not be stated. For all that, the atmosphere was tense.

'You believed what Sara told you?'

'Why would she lie?'

'In two previous interviews she made contradictory assertions.'

'That was before Alfred committed suicide. You could hardly expect her to deliberately incriminate him.' Maurice produced his pipe from the pocket of his denim jacket and held it up in an unsteady hand. 'Do you mind?'

'Carry on. What Sara did would be equally explicable if she saw it as safe to accuse Alfred when he was no longer in a position to defend himself.'

Maurice was making a tremendous effort to appear calm but there was tension in his every movement. In the act of

152

filling his pipe he was hampered by trembling hands which he tried in vain to steady by pressing them against his thighs.

'I don't understand. Why should she say she saw Alfred if she didn't see him?'

'To protect someone else? Herself, perhaps?'

'You think that Sara killed Matthew?' His manner was incredulous.

'What do you think?'

He put the stem of his pipe in his mouth, gripped it hard, and spoke through his teeth. 'I believe Sara — implicitly.'

Wycliffe seemed to relax. For some time they sat in silence and Maurice went through the ritual of lighting his pipe and persuading it to draw. The sun shone directly through the little window panes creating a broad path of light which divided the hut into two and cast strong shadows on the opposite wall.

Pinned to that wall there was a 1:25,000 Ordnance map of the immediate area. Wycliffe got up from the settee to examine it. The map was annotated in pencil with sightings of birds and other animals. After an interval he said: 'I don't see Badgers' Wood marked on this map.'

For a long moment there was no response then Maurice said: 'Badgers' Wood?'

'Never mind; perhaps Florrie Tremayne will remember.'

Maurice forced a laugh. 'It was a name we invented as kids. God knows where you got it from. Have you been talking to Florrie? We used to play the sort of games kids did then: Robin Hood, cowboys and Indians, war games . . .' he was talking to stave off the next question. 'We were lucky, we had this hut and the free run of the country around as long as we didn't tread on the crops or forget to shut gates. Like kids do, we had our own names for bits of the countryside —'

'And Badgers' Wood?'

Maurice got up from his chair and came over to the map. With the stem of his pipe he pointed to a small area of green behind Trebyan, close to another country road which eventually converged with the one running past Trebyan. 'That was the place we called Badgers' Wood; it's a little cluster of pines; I doubt if anybody ever saw any badgers there.'

153

Within a short distance of the wood the map showed a group of buildings labelled Roskear.

'Did Molly Pearce join in these games?'

Another interval before Maurice said in a tired voice: 'Molly Pearce? It's a long time ago but I expect so; most of the kids about here did.'

'And later, after you were married, she came to look after you and David when your wife was in hospital?'

Maurice turned to face him, his expression both puzzled and concerned. He said: 'Yes, she did. Molly was very good, but what — ?'

'I understand that your wife died of an overdose, Mr Glynn?'

'Yes . . . She was receiving treatment for depression, in and out of hospital.'

'She wasn't in hospital at the time of her death?'

'No, she was at home.'

'That was some time after your sister-in-law, Inez, disappeared?'

'Inez went away in March and Celia died in January of the following year — 1972. I really can't understand why you are asking me all this!'

Wycliffe was cool. 'Don't disturb yourself, I am trying to get some perspective on the events. Was there an inquest on your wife?'

'Yes; and the verdict was suicide while the balance of her mind was disturbed.'

'Of what drug did she take an overdose?'

'Phenobarbitone.'

'Prescribed for depression?'

Maurice's reply was barely audible. 'No, it was prescribed for me; I was suffering from stress — it was a difficult time.'

Wycliffe nodded. He seemed to have lost interest in the questioning and he was looking around the hut with apparently casual interest. Abruptly, he said: 'Why did you shift the settee, Mr Glynn?'

'I dropped something down the back.'

'I was under the impression that we held the only key. I

154

would prefer that you do not make use of the hut until our enquiries are complete.'

'But I don't understand —'

'You object?'

'No, I don't object.'

'Then perhaps you will let me keep both keys for the time being. I don't want to go to the length of putting seals on the door and making the whole thing much more official.'

It was odd. Wycliffe's words were reasonable enough and he did not raise his voice or give them any particular emphasis, yet there was an element of menace.

He got up from the settee and stood by the open door for a dazed Maurice to pass through. Outside, he locked the door and pocketed the key. 'I shall be coming again; in the meantime I may send someone to take a closer look at things in the hut.'

He glanced at his watch; it was half-past one.

Striving to sound normal, Maurice said: 'David will be wondering where I am.'

As he came down the verandah steps Wycliffe spotted David hurrying away up the path towards the house. Had the boy been listening? What did it matter? Wycliffe went down the slope towards the road.

He felt like the fly-fisherman who makes his cast, draws his lure through the water, hooks his fish, then 'plays' it until the poor creature surrenders. Wycliffe was far from that stage but he had no stomach for the role; inflicting suffering of any kind, especially on the innocent, was repugnant to him. But if you are a policeman, a politician, a business man, a trade unionist or even a human being, you have to believe that in some degree the end justifies the means.

Hawken was waiting for him in the car. 'I had a look in the church, sir.'

'Well?'

'I liked the pictures, especially the ones painted by the little girl.'

'Are you expected home for lunch?'

'No, sir; it's canteen grub for me today.'

'Then let's find a pub where we can get something to eat.'

*

Wycliffe arrived back at the Incident Room shortly before three. Fox, the scenes-of-crime officer, was there.

'In the morning I want you and a couple of DCs at Trebyan.'

'What will we be doing there, sir?'

'I'll brief you in the morning.'

'We could make a start now, sir; there are several hours of daylight left.'

'In the morning.'

He was standing in the main room, brooding. There were only two DCs and Lucy tapping away at their word processors. The inquiry had started on a small scale, now it was dying for want of what it fed upon. Statements had been checked and rechecked; everybody in the neighbourhood had been questioned at least once; and most of this was to protect one's rear. A sufficient bulk of paper in the form of reports or computer print-outs is the only material evidence that stones have been turned, avenues explored, and the fine-toothed comb diligently employed.

But from the start Wycliffe had been convinced that this crime would prove to concern a small group of people who were closely, even intimately connected. Nowadays so many major crimes are wide open and impersonal: A kills, or rapes, or mugs B, but X, Y, or Z would have done just as well. The only hope of catching A is to field a large team, accumulate vast quantities of data, and make full use of the almost infinite collating resources of the computer. But in this case, what would he do with a large team? And what use was the computer except as a substitute for the old carousel — a convenient memory jogger?

He muttered to himself: 'By now Sara will have heard all about it.'

Lucy Lane looked up from her machine. 'Sir?'

'Nothing.'

A familiar voice at the duty officer's desk made him look in that direction. 'Take Mr Swayne to my office.'

He said to Lucy Lane: 'I want you in on this.'

Swayne was nervous, like a mouse who is doubtful about

what goes with the cheese. He was seated in the client's chair with a small suitcase on his lap. His little red fingers beat a silent tattoo. Wycliffe sat opposite him and Lucy Lane took a chair by the door. Swayne opened his case and took out a package and a stout envelope. He pointed to the package. 'The letters, still in their envelopes, as they were in the cardboard box you spoke of. There are a hundred and fifty of them, all from Beale to his mother, and they date between 1850 and 1890. The stamps on them are of interest and have some value but they won't make anybody's fortune.'

'What about the envelope?'

Swayne touched the envelope almost with reverence. 'That is a different matter. You see, Beale, in a letter to his mother in the very early Sixties, said that he had heard of the new hobby of collecting stamps and that he would send home some from time to time which she could give to his nephews in case they were interested.' Swayne could not keep the enthusiasm out of his voice.

'From then on he included with almost every letter a number of stamps, the great majority in mint condition, many with rare overprintings and surcharges, some — by chance — with printing or design faults, retouches, et cetera . . . Well, for some reason, his mother did not pass on the stamps to his nephews, she left them in the envelopes in which they had come.'

'And you were supposed to sell them on Glynn's behalf through one of the auction houses?'

The bubble of Swayne's enthusiasm was pricked. 'Well, not exactly —'

'No! Because of their questionable provenance it had to be an under-the-counter deal. But are you sure that you intended to sell them at all? Who knew that you had them other than Glynn himself? And Glynn is dead.'

'Mr Wycliffe! I am —'

'I know — I know! You are a reputable dealer, but you were willing to undertake this dubious bit of business for a friend. Unfortunately your friend was murdered, and it has taken you three days and some pressure to admit to possession of the letters and the stamps.'

'I would have approached the family —'

Wycliffe made a dismissive gesture; he sounded bored. 'Yes, of course! At a more appropriate time — after the funeral, when they have had time to settle down — this year, next year, sometime, never . . . Put it in your statement, Mr Swayne. I presume that you came here to make one? Detective Sergeant Lane will take you into the next room and arrange it.'

Swayne's apprehensive green eyes looked at him over the half-glasses, 'But what happens then?'

'I've no idea.'

'At least you are satisfied now that I had nothing to do with what happened to poor Matt?'

Wycliffe shrugged. 'I don't think you are a murderer, Mr Swayne; perhaps you are not a rogue, but I think you contemplated becoming one.'

Pressure was building; Swayne had already yielded up his morsel of the truth. To be effective, applying psychological pressure must be a gradual process, a slow build-up so that the subjects have time to think, to reflect, and convince themselves that they are grist for the mills of God.

In the absence of material evidence it may be the only way, but to use it requires a thorough knowledge of the subjects, their backgrounds, their strengths, their loyalties, their weaknesses and their fears. Especially their fears . . .

'In my experience fear is the most powerful drive to violence among such people, but why should any of them in this case be afraid?'

His own words, and he silently endorsed them now. The position was unchanged, the questions remained: Who was afraid, and of what? Perhaps, of the two, 'of what?' was the more important now.

Nit-picking by telephone from headquarters occupied him for the better part of an hour: the police lawyer worrying away at the fine detail of a case in preparation for the DPP; Wycliffe's personal assistant, the unflappable and impregnable Diane, on queries from Accounts about DCs' overtime

158

and expenses; his deputy, John Scales, about reports for a forthcoming promotions board and a possible date for a crime prevention seminar.

They were ganging up on him, and by the time it was over he had mentally lost touch with the Glynns and their bookshop, with Trebyan, the pottery and the little hut. He wanted to get back; he collected his car from outside the Incident Room and with a sense of release, he drove up Lady Street and down Market Jew — the main shopping street. (No connection with the chosen people, the name comes from the Cornish: Marghas Yow, Thursday Market.)

He intended to approach Trebyan by a different route, by the top road which would take him past Badgers' Wood, and Roskear where Molly Pearce lived with her family. On the Ordnance map he had noticed a footpath leading from the top road, through Badgers' Wood and the fields above Trebyan, down through the scrub to the lower road.

Five minutes after leaving the A394 he thought he was lost but St Michael, patron saint of coppers, had an eye on him. A few minutes more and he came upon a little cottage by a clump of pines and, a few yards farther on, a house with a cluster of farm buildings, and a gate labelled Roskear Farm.

It was not possible to turn the car in the narrow lane so he reversed back to the pines and the cottage. Badgers' Wood? The pines were not fenced off from the road; there was a way in, a beaten track through the trees wide enough for a vehicle, but Wycliffe left his car and walked.

He did not like pine woods, they reminded him of Jack London's Klondyke: frozen snow, howling wolves, and frostbite. Pines, he thought, needed the redeeming Mediterranean sun; here the late-afternoon April sunshine filtered through the branches but without warmth.

The track led to a small clearing. 'Most Sunday afternoons her car is in Badgers' Wood.' This, according to Matthew Glynn's anonymous correspondent. There would have been plenty of room for the little red Mini, hidden from the road.

A narrower version of the track continued on the other side of the clearing and he followed it to the far edge of the wood

159

where he was faced by a hedge and a stile. Standing on top of the stile he could see across a couple of fields to Trebyan, the house and the buildings around the yard. Presumably it was by this route that Inez kept her trysts; hiding her car, trekking across muddy fields . . . What possessed a mature woman with a family and a secure home to indulge in these adolescent games? It was very odd, and he was intrigued.

The first field was in grass, with cows grazing; the second, which seemed smaller, looked like a market garden, almost certainly part of the Trebyan domain.

Wycliffe set out across the fields. There was no discernible path but at the other end of the first field there was another stile. Like so many field paths this one had fallen into disuse. The second stile took him into a very small field laid out like a garden, with areas set aside for potatoes, cabbages, root vegetables, and beans . . . Here there were grassy paths between the beds.

The stile at the end of this field led, not to the house and yard, but into the scrub of gorse and hawthorn. From the top of the stile he could see the roof of the little hut but the path beyond the stile was so overgrown as to be impassable. Obviously it had once served as a short cut for people living along the top road on their way to St Hilary church or to the school. For Inez it was her way to the little hut.

From where he stood he could look down into the backyard of Trebyan. A man came out from the house carrying a large wicker basket and went to a shed in the yard. It was Maurice. A minute or two later he returned with the basket full of small logs. Wycliffe willed him to look up and just as he was about to re-enter the house he turned, and did so. The distance was too great for Wycliffe to see his expression but the hesitation was obvious. Finally, with a nervous wave, he went inside and shut the door behind him. Wycliffe, satisfied, returned to the road.

He walked along to Roskear. The farmhouse was trim and colourful — pale pink walls and white paintwork — and it stood in its own garden, quite separate from the farmyard. In the yard twenty-five or thirty black-and-white Friesians were penned for milking and Wycliffe could hear the whirr of the machine. He rang the doorbell and it was answered by a middle-aged woman, tall and very fair.

'Miss Pearce? Miss Molly Pearce? . . . Chief Superintendent Wycliffe.' He produced his warrant card.

She was an attractive woman: an oval face with good features, a mass of fair hair, and dark eyes with long lashes, but he was most impressed by the serenity of her expression.

'If I could come inside . . .'

He was shown into the parlour, a large comfortable room, obviously much used, by no means dirty but not over-zealously cleaned. There was a piano, a television, a rack overflowing with farming papers and magazines, and a set of well-worn leather-upholstered armchairs. There were three or four coloured prints on the walls, but framed photographs of farming occasions predominated.

She removed newspapers from a chair. 'Do sit down.' The only words she had actually spoken so far.

'I'm sure you will have heard about the murder of Matthew Glynn and the death of his brother, Alfred.'

'Yes.'

'I understand that you have known the Glynn family all your life.'

She did not bother to answer that.

A black-and-white border collie padded into the room, sniffed around Wycliffe then settled on the hearthrug with an eye on him still.

'Mr Glynn told me that when his wife became ill after the birth of their son you helped him a great deal in looking after the house and the baby.'

He was finding it hard going. She sat opposite him, calmly attentive, her blue eyes unwavering in their gaze. 'His sister, Sara, and I helped out where we could.'

'We have reason to think that the events of the past week are linked to what happened at and around that time . . .'

He was being forced to ask direct questions which he had wanted to avoid.

'I suppose you knew Inez Glynn?'

'Yes, I knew her.'

'Was she a regular visitor at Trebyan?'

'She was quite friendly with Celia — Maurice's wife.'

'Have you ever heard of Badgers' Wood, Miss Pearce?'

The first tremor of disquiet; she hesitated. At that moment there were heavy footsteps in the passage and the door was pushed open. A big man stood in the doorway; brown jerkin and trousers, sandy hair, an amiable teddy-bear of a man. 'Oh, there you are, Moll! I didn't know . . . Sorry! Dad's fussing because he can't find the milk book.'

'It's on the desk in the office. I saw it there ten minutes ago.'

'Oh, good! Sorry, but you know what he's getting like . . .'

The door closed again and Wycliffe said, softly: 'Badgers' Wood . . .'

She had recovered her poise. 'It comes from when we were children; the name we local kids gave to the little pine wood along the road.'

'From where there was a footpath to Trebyan and the little hut.'

She assented by a slight movement of her head. Even now she had sufficient restraint neither to comment nor ask questions.

Wycliffe went on: 'We have anonymous notes written to Matthew Glynn just before Inez disappeared telling him of her car being parked in Badgers' Wood on Sundays. I understand that at that time Maurice's wife was in hospital.'

'What has this to do with me?'

'As you were helping out at Trebyan at that time and you would, presumably, have used the footpath to get to and from the place, it seems likely you would know something about it.'

She seemed to come to some decision. 'Mr Wycliffe, you are asking me to recall things that happened many years ago. All I can say is that I never saw Inez in Maurice Glynn's house when his wife was not there. I imagine that Maurice will have a clearer recollection of what happened at that time.'

Wycliffe had to settle for that. He drove back through the lanes, thinking not of Maurice nor of Molly Pearce, but of Inez. From an unpromising springboard, housekeeper-companion to an old lady, she had laid siege to Alfred Glynn, a young man at the start of his career as a pharmacist with his own business. While their conjugal bed was still in the making she had become pregnant by Alfred's brother, Matthew. By the time her child was born she was the wife of the bookseller, while Alfred was left to turn his misfortune into a tragedy and begin constructing the fantasy which had apparently sustained him until the last few days.

It seemed that eleven years of marriage and three children had done nothing to abate Inez's taste for variety. In addition to certain nebulous exogamous relationships it now appeared that she had rounded off her Penzance period in the little hut, in Maurice's arms if not his bed; Maurice, the third and youngest of the Glynns. And this, according to the anonymous letters, was known to her husband.

So, the sixty-four dollar question: Had Inez gone off to explore new territory or had her career been brought to a dramatic end on that last Sunday?

In a letter posted the day after her disappearance Matthew's anonymous correspondent had said: 'Her car was there on Sunday.'

Wycliffe was back on the A394 and heading for the town. Time to forget about Inez; perhaps time to remind himself that all this had happened seventeen years ago; that it was only days since Matthew Glynn's murder, two days since Alfred's suicide. Was he chasing shadows?

But it was only four months since the three brothers had lost their mother; the final severance of the silver cord.

Plenty of questions but few answers and no obvious way of getting more.

He found Kersey in the hotel bar and they went into the dining-room together.

When they had ordered, Kersey said: 'Angela Bickers: fifty-two or three, good-looking woman, on the plump side, a sense of humour, and contented.' A wry grin. 'Not many of them about.'

'She doesn't sound like a friend of Inez.'

'She was though. At the time Inez went missing Angela and

163

her husband were living in Hayle; her husband was a rep for something or other and away a lot so the two women used to see a good deal of each other. Attraction of opposites according to Angela. She talked a lot, but the gist of it was that though Inez was fed to the back teeth with Matthew and Sara, she had no intention of leaving her children.'

'A pity she didn't say that to the police when Inez went missing.'

'She wanted to but her husband insisted she should keep out of it. He didn't like her associating with Inez anyway — a woman who slept around. Thought it might be catching, I expect.'

'So she admitted that Inez slept around?'

'Oh, she made no secret of the fact.'

'Did she know that Inez was having an affair with Maurice?'

'She not only knew, she acted as go-between. I fancy she got her kicks that way. At that time Celia, Maurice's wife, was in and out of hospital for treatment; she'd be in for a few days then, perhaps, home for the weekend, depending on how she was.

'Maurice and Inez had their trysts on Sundays when Inez was supposed to be visiting her girl friend. If Celia was coming home that weekend Maurice would let Angela know and she would pass the message on: "Afraid I shan't be in Sunday — see you next week."'

Kersey was tucking in to roast lamb while Wycliffe toyed with a prawn salad, his appetite still jaded by his lunchtime pasty. The dining-room was fuller than they had seen it so far; in addition to the usual sprinkling of up-market reps and business men, there were two or three family groups and an obvious honeymoon couple, like the cuckoo and the primrose, harbingers of summer.

Wycliffe asked: 'Did she ever leave a message with another member of the family?'

Kersey grinned. 'I asked her that. She did. Why shouldn't she? The message would sound innocent enough.'

'With Matthew?'

'Sometimes — yes.'

The two men ate in silence for a while then Kersey said: 'What's the programme for tomorrow?'

'I've arranged for Fox and his team to be at Trebyan. We'll go to work on the hut.'

'Expecting?'

'I'll tell you if we find it.' Wycliffe finished his salad, sipped his wine and patted his lips. 'Now, these people who've been checking on how Maurice spent Saturday evening — any joy?'

'Not so far; not a whisper. You're pretty sure he's our man, sir?'

'I'm by no means sure that Maurice killed his brother; even if I was, we haven't enough evidence to arrest a cat.'

When they reached the coffee stage Kersey said: 'Going for your walk, sir?'

'No, I'm going to talk to Sara.'

He walked along the promenade in the darkness; there was a fresh breeze off the sea, the lights of Marazion twinkled through a sea mist and there was salt on his lips. Although it was by no means rough he was more than ordinarily aware of the vast expanse of dark water and of the seemingly fragile margins of the land so that it appeared almost a miracle that the land was not overwhelmed.

By contrast the narrow confines of Lady Street were cloistered and secure. He walked up past Alfred's pharmacy. After only four days the street had become home ground. There were lights in the rooms above many of the shops and the shops were interspersed with ordinary houses. Wycliffe liked that; he felt instinctively that something went wrong when the planners started thinking in terms of 'zones', a damning word anyway when associated with human activities.

Arrived at the Glynn house, he rang the doorbell and it was answered by Gina.

'Aunt Sara? She's up in her room; I'll tell her you're here.'

'No, I'll go up.' It was a spur-of-the-moment decision.

She looked at him in surprise but said nothing.

'Which room?'

'Turn right at the top of the stairs and it's the second door.'

He tapped on the door and a voice called: 'Come in!'

She was sitting in an armchair by a gas fire, she wore heavily rimmed reading glasses and she had a book in her hands; a table lamp by her chair cast a circle of light which left most of the room in darkness.

She looked up at him in total astonishment. 'By what right —'

'I wanted a private word with you.' His manner was placatory.

Sara was disposed to aggression but caution prevailed. She was angry but she was also scared. 'Very well, now you are here you had better sit down.'

She got up and switched on the main light so that the room came to life. To his surprise it was attractive, well furnished, and functional; the in-college room of a well-heeled spinster don: a couple of armchairs and a couch, upholstered in Liberty fabric; curtains out of the same stable; a large carpet square of Persian design, perhaps of Persian origin; a business-like mahogany desk and bookshelves. On the walls there were five or six modern woodcuts of an enigmatic genre. No photograph of mother.

He did not sit down but stood looking at her books: a wide selection of modern fiction, a shelf or two of the classics, another of poetry, and a substantial collection of books on Cornwall including a number of language texts in a section to themselves.

'You read Cornish, Miss Glynn?'

'With difficulty and a dictionary.' Snappish. She was predictably unforthcoming and impatient. 'What exactly do you want with me, Mr Wycliffe? Last Saturday I had three brothers, Matthew, Alfred and Maurice. That night Alfred, sadly disturbed in his mind, attacked and killed Matthew. Two days later, in a fit of remorse, he committed suicide in a manner that is too terrible to think of.' She paused and looked him in the eyes: 'Surely we deserve some sympathy and understanding even from the police. Now that you know what happened, why do you continue to harass us?'

He was conciliatory. 'I do understand, Miss Glynn, but in a police inquiry it is not sufficient to be able to say: "Here is the culprit." One has to present the background and the reasoning which makes that conclusion not only credible, but compelling.' He broke off to settle himself in one of the armchairs, then waffled comfortably on: 'You tell me that the motive for your brother's murder is to be found in events which happened a long time ago: I have to be clear what those events were, who was involved, and the nature of their involvement. I must also look at other possibilities.'

Sara's manner was still suspicious and inclined to aggression but she was mollified. 'So?'

'So, how can I get such information except from the people most intimately concerned? Any other source is likely to be no better than gossip. I hope you understand that, Miss Glynn?'

'And if I do; what do you want to ask me?'

'I would rather that we avoided specific questions; it would be more helpful if you were prepared to talk freely about your family and about the events which might have led to these tragedies at this time.'

It was a smoke-screen of words but it made a kind of sense and might encourage her to drop her guard.

With exaggerated patience she said: 'Very well; what do you want to talk about?'

He said nothing for a while. A carriage clock on the mantelpiece ticked audibly through the silence. It was ten minutes past nine. When he spoke his words came as an anticlimax: 'You can't have found life easy during those years when you shared this house with your sister-in-law.'

A quick look to judge his motive for the remark, but there was little to be learned from his expression of bland interest. In the end she said: 'I have never found life particularly easy, Mr Wycliffe, but I have always been able to cope.' She added after a pause: 'I would certainly never have allowed my brother or his wife to drive me from my home.'

Wycliffe said nothing. If an expected response is withheld and the silence is allowed to lengthen, the chances are that the other party will feel compelled to bridge the gap. It worked with Sara: 'If I accepted the traditional role of an unmarried

167

Glynn woman it was because I chose to. As far as Matthew was concerned he couldn't do without me either before or after his wife left him — and he knew it.'

In a significant glance Wycliffe took in the room, which compared very favourably with anything he had seen in the rest of the house. 'So that you were able to stay on your own terms.'

She said nothing and the ball was back in Wycliffe's court.

'Both of your brothers seemed to have had grievances against Matthew. Was he a very difficult man?'

She considered how far she might go on this and decided to plunge. 'Matthew was spoiled by father; he was the only one of the sons who fitted father's idea of what a son should be, and want, and do.' She broke off, having become more animated than he had yet seen her and, perhaps for the first time, her words seemed to come from the heart: 'Maurice was abominably treated in my father's will, and Matthew exploited the situation.' She broke off with an irritable movement. 'But you know that already.'

In a low voice Wycliffe said: 'And Alfred? What about Alfred?'

She stopped to think before saying: 'Well, you know what happened to Alfred, that is what this is all about.'

'And what was your father's attitude when Matthew took Inez from his brother? Or were you too young to understand much about it?'

'Of course I understood what was happening! I was eighteen! Father's attitude was indulgent towards Matthew and contemptuous of Alfred. I remember him saying to mother: "Alfred will never run a successful business or keep a woman."'

The silence in the room was complete so that a casual exchange between two passers-by in the street reached them with startling clarity. Sara had spoken with an uncharacteristic lack of restraint, even with excitement, and Wycliffe wondered whether he could lead her farther along the same path.

Very quietly, he said: 'And what was your mother's attitude to her three sons?'

Sara shifted in her chair, rearranging her skirt in a way that had become familiar to him when she was playing for time. He expected that she would evade the question or offer a conventional response; instead she was devastatingly objective.

'It is not the sort of thing one should say about a recently dead parent but my mother flirted with her sons.' Sara's hands were clasped tightly in her lap and she was looking down at them. 'Mother distributed her favours in such a way as deliberately to create jealousies, then she would chide them, playing with them like a . . . like a . . .' Her voice faltered and she broke off. She looked up and Wycliffe was astonished to see her eyes glistening with tears.

'Just one or two more questions, Miss Glynn. Do you remember clearly the Sunday morning your sister-in-law left home for the last time?'

'I remember it very well.'

'Was your brother Matthew at home when his wife left?'

'No, at that time Matt took long walks of a Sunday; he would go off in the morning and come back in the afternoon having had a snack lunch in one of the pubs on his route.'

'Was young David with you that weekend?'

She looked at him in surprise. 'So you know about that. We always had him here when his mother was coming home. It was one of the strange features of her illness that she couldn't bear to see her child.'

'Did he stay long?'

'Several days — it gave Maurice a chance to catch up on his work at the pottery.'

Wycliffe walked back to his hotel hardly aware of his route. For once he walked beside the sea at night without being impressed or even aware. He was thinking of Sara. She had given him more than he had expected, more than he had hoped, but she remained an enigmatic figure at the very core of his case. He had made a decision based more on an intuitive feel for the way people behave than on evidence, and he was staking his credibility on that decision.

Chapter Eleven

Thursday morning

Wycliffe was awakened by Kersey tapping on his bedroom door. Kersey in his dressing-gown stood by the bed, just visible in the thin, pale light which found its way through the window curtains.

'The duty officer chickened out from disturbing you and asked for me instead. The hut at Trebyan is on fire; the brigade is attending but it's unlikely they can do much. The fire was reported by a patrol car crew and, knowing our interest, the duty officer thought he ought to tell somebody.'

Wycliffe had been engaged in a frantic search for his parked car in a Kafkaesque town where streets, with no names, were all alike and the inhabitants appeared to be both deaf and dumb. For some moments at least reality was a relief from the dream.

He looked at his travelling clock; it was 5.37.

'I suppose we'd better get out there.'

'I don't see there's much we can do until they get the fire out.'

'We can try to find out who set it alight.'

'Surely that's obvious, it can only have been Maurice.'

Wycliffe was getting out of bed. 'Would he be such a fool?'

They scrounged coffee and rolls through the night porter and by soon after six they were on their way in Wycliffe's car with Kersey driving.

As they drove along the waterfront the great peninsula which reaches to the Lizard was as if it had never been; even the Mount was no more than a shadow. Sea and sky and land were merged in a moist grey continuum and though it was not actually raining the screen wipers were in constant use. April had once more changed her mood.

They turned off the main road out of the town towards St Hilary. Kersey said: 'You don't seem very upset, sir.'

'At least it gives me an excuse for doing what I intended to do anyway.'

The fire tender and a police patrol car were parked close to the stile where the footpath through the scrub left the road. They were pumping water from a nearby stream and a hose snaked over the stile and up through the undergrowth. The fire was almost out but smoke and steam rose like the Israelite's pillar of cloud in the moist, still air and everywhere there was the acrid smell of charred wood.

The fire officer said: 'It went up like tinder; we might as well not have come for all the good we could do.'

'Deliberate, presumably?'

'It certainly looks that way but we shall know better when we've had a chance to examine the debris. I gather you've got an interest here apart from possible arson?'

'You could say that.'

Wycliffe and Kersey crossed the stile and followed the path up through the gorse to the site of the little hut. There were two uniformed men from the local nick and a couple of firemen. In the capricious way of fires, much of the back wall of the hut and the frame of one end still stood; the roof had vanished and the floor had collapsed into the cavity below it; the verandah steps were intact and the planks of the verandah itself, though heavily charred, were still in place. In the cavity below where the floor had been Wycliffe could see the carbonized framework of the settee lying at a drunken angle.

One of the uniformed men said: 'PC Evans, sir. We observed the fire from the road at 04.50 and, after investigation, alerted the brigade. The place was well alight and unapproachable; there seemed a risk that the fire might extend to the scrub.'

'All right; you couldn't do anything, you reported on your

171

radio and asked for assistance. Did anyone turn up from the house?'

'Not at once, sir. The brigade arrived at 05.10; Glynn and his son showed up a little later. Glynn said he happened to wake and saw the glow through his window.'

'What was his attitude?'

Evans hesitated. 'Well, puzzled is the best word I can think of. He really didn't seem to know what to make of it.'

'Where are they now?'

'I insisted that they go back to the house, sir.'

'All right; you can get back now and put in your report.' Wycliffe turned to Kersey: 'Get Fox over here; he was expecting to come anyway after the briefing. You'd better stay. As soon as it's at all practicable I want the debris cleared from the cavity under the hut floor.'

'Shouldn't we get forensic in on it?'

'To hell with forensic! Fox is quite capable of handling this. I'm going up to the house and I shall be there if you want me.'

The front door stood open to the slate-flagged passage. He looked in the one-time dining-room but it was empty. Through the open front door a damp chill seemed to have invaded and taken possession of the whole house. Wycliffe heard voices somewhere at the back and he went down the passage, past the stairs. The voices came from the kitchen. Through the half-open door he could see a sink and draining-board with a wooden plate-rack over.

A woman's voice was saying: 'I told him nothing, Maurice, but if I'm asked direct questions I don't intend to lie.' She broke off. 'What's the matter with you, for God's sake? You're shivering! Let me make you a cup of coffee or something . . . Where's David?'

'I don't know; he was here not long before you came.'

Wycliffe tapped on the door and pushed it open. Molly Pearce was in the act of running water into an electric kettle while Maurice stood, hands thrust deep into his trouser pockets, looking utterly dejected.

Molly was the first to recover her poise: 'I came down to see if I could be of any use.'

Wycliffe said: 'I'm quite sure you will be, Miss Pearce.'

Maurice had momentary difficulty in finding his voice. 'I don't know what to say about this fire, Mr Wycliffe.'

'It will be time enough to talk about that when we have completed our investigation. Now there are other more important things.' His manner was brusque, but not unfriendly.

Maurice looked uneasily at Molly Pearce. 'Perhaps we should go into the other room. Molly won't want —'

'We can talk well enough here and I would rather Miss Pearce stayed.' Wycliffe turned to the woman: 'Go on with the coffee if you want to; I'm sure Mr Glynn can do with it.'

The kitchen could not have changed significantly since the Glynn family shifted *en bloc* into town nearly thirty years earlier. And it was still essentially a farmhouse kitchen as it been for long before that. The floor was of stone slabs covered with matting; the massive farmhouse table was still there though the top was covered with heat-resisting plastic. The walls were painted a dreary green and ranged against them were an electric cooker, a refrigerator, and a washing-machine. The Glynns moved with reluctance into the modern world.

Wycliffe was in no hurry; he ambled about the room with apparent aimlessness and Maurice watched him as a cat watches the restless peregrinations of a strange dog. Molly Pearce went on preparing the coffee but she hardly took her eyes off him.

Then, at a certain point, Wycliffe said: 'Why don't you sit down, Mr Glynn? After all, it's your house.'

He spoke casually but Maurice pulled up a kitchen stool, sat on it, and seemed to relax.

Good policemen are actors, they acquire a persona which is both authoritarian and inquisitorial without, by nature, being either. Over the years Wycliffe had developed a technique of interview which blended the man with the persona and seemed to achieve results.

173

Molly put three mugs on the table. 'Milk for you, Mr Wycliffe?'

'No thanks.'

Maurice sat on his stool, his long legs twined around its legs. He was unshaven, his eyes seemed sunken and dark in contrast with his pallid skin.

'I want to ask you both one or two questions about things that happened a long time ago, but before I start I'll tell you what I know already so that we have no misunderstanding.'

He turned to face Maurice Glynn and his manner was conversational: 'I know that at the time of your wife's illness you were having an affair with your sister-in-law, Inez. You met when you could on Sundays in the little hut; one of her woman friends acted as a go-between, passing messages, in particular letting Inez know whether your wife would be spending the weekend at home or in hospital. Either out of caution or from a sense of propriety the two of you did not meet if your wife was at home.'

Maurice said: 'I really can't see what that has to do with what has happened recently.'

There was an old wall clock over the mantelpiece which struck the hour on a coiled wire and it chose this moment to dole out eight tinny strokes. Wycliffe waited until it was over then went on as though Maurice had not spoken.

'You may not know it, but Matthew was kept informed of these meetings through a number of anonymous letters.' He paused, looking first at Maurice, then at Molly Pearce.

Molly returned his gaze in silence, apparently unperturbed. Maurice seemed about to speak but changed his mind.

'Now for my questions: Sunday 20th March 1971 — a long time ago, but I'm sure you both remember it; it was the day Inez was seen by her family for the last time. Was your wife at home or in hospital on that day, Mr Glynn?'

'She was at home.' Maurice was holding his coffee mug half-way to his lips but he did not drink.

'Had you sent the usual message through your go-between, warning Inez not to come?'

Maurice hesitated for some time before saying: 'Yes.'

Wycliffe seemed in no hurry; there were long intervals between question and answer accentuated by the silence; it was as though time itself had become sluggish.

'So why did she come?'

'She didn't come.'

'You didn't see Inez that Sunday?'

'No, I did not see her.'

Wycliffe turned to Molly Pearce. 'And yet Matthew received an anonymous note saying that Inez's car was in Badgers' Wood on that day.'

Again Molly said nothing but this time Wycliffe persisted: 'Miss Pearce, I'm going to ask you an important question and I would like an answer: Did you see Inez's Mini parked in the pine wood that Sunday?'

She looked at Maurice before saying: 'Yes, I did.'

'Mr Glynn?'

Maurice put down his mug and spoke in a low voice. 'If Inez came that day I didn't see her. We had an arrangement in case of any slip-up: she would wait for me in the hut and if I didn't come she would go again.'

'When did your wife return to hospital?'

'On Sunday evening; a weekend at home meant that I fetched her on Friday and took her back on Sunday evening.'

'I see.' Wycliffe stood up. 'Well, that is all for the present. Later you may be asked to make statements about what precisely happened during that weekend.'

They had assumed that his questions were only beginning and he was at the door before either of them realized that it was over. Maurice followed him down the passage. On the doorstep he said: 'I don't understand what's happening, Mr Wycliffe.'

Wycliffe said nothing and walked on down the drive.

Through the open door of the workshop he could see Chris and David in close embrace. Although the boy was a head taller she was patting his shoulder as one consoles a child.

Wycliffe muttered to himself: 'Babes in the Wood is about it!'

*

175

It was afternoon and the debris of the hut had cooled off sufficiently to be handled. Fox and his two assistants began the work of clearing the brick-walled cavity below where the floor of the hut had been. Each partially carbonized beam or strut or plank was lifted out and laid on the grass of the clearing. Those contents of the hut which had survived the fire were similarly treated: the paraffin stove, badly buckled, with every scrap of paint burned off; the framework of the settee, which fell to pieces as soon as an attempt was made to shift it; a chair, badly charred, but intact; a metal cupboard; a galvanized bucket; a stool . . .

When they had cleared the larger items, there remained, apart from a mass of burnt paper, half-consumed books, and charred fabric, a multitude of smaller things, from items of cutlery and cups and saucers to a much damaged pair of binoculars and a radio. Fox gave as much attention to each find as an archaeologist devotes to his artefacts. At intervals he stopped the work to record progress on film. When most of the debris had been cleared they had reached the more or less level surface of an earth floor.

Wycliffe and Kersey, resplendent in yellow oilskins, stood by. The mist had not lifted, the grass was sodden, and globules of moisture glistened on every spine of gorse. A female blackbird went on with the serious business of provisioning her brood somewhere close at hand, ignoring the disturbance.

Kersey said: 'No sign of how the fire was started.'

Wycliffe was morose. 'Somebody broke in, splashed paraffin over the place and set it alight or, perhaps, he set up a delayed-action incendiary device with a bucket of paraffin and a lighted candle floated on top. I don't know and I don't damn well care how it started or which idiot started it!'

Kersey said: 'Sorry I spoke.'

Now Fox and his helpers were retrieving quite small objects from the floor of the cavity; scratching around in the soil which was calcined in parts, untouched by the heat in others. They turned up some coins, an old fountain-pen, glass bottles and jars, nails, screws . . . Fox garnered them all into his harvest.

Finally he looked up at Wycliffe: 'I think that's it, sir.'

Wycliffe said: 'The soil level is a good deal higher in the cavity than the ground outside — try a probe.'

Fox looked stubborn. 'You wouldn't expect a concrete base in a building of this sort, sir.'

'I'm not looking for a concrete base.'

Fox pressed a stick down into the soil and it sank easily. He tried in a number of places with the same result.

'Try nearer the front of the hut.'

At the second try the probe met resistance at a depth of about a foot and successive probes met similar resistance in a line close to and parallel with the front of the hut.

Wycliffe said: 'This is where you start digging.'

There was no problem; within the boundaries of the brick foundations the ground was soft and unconsolidated. Fox and one of his assistants worked with care and within a very short time they had uncovered parts of what seemed to be a roll of black polythene. A few minutes more and it was clear that what they had found was something that had been rolled in polythene and made up into a rough parcel, the shape and size of which resembled a human mummy.

'Photographs, Fox.'

Kersey said: 'So you've found what you were looking for, sir, a gilt-edged motive all neatly wrapped up.'

Wycliffe was too preoccupied to take the bait. 'Get hold of Dr Rees and ask him to come here; then locate Franks and try to have a word with him. Explain to Rees and to him what's going on.'

'Am I supposed to know?'

Wycliffe snapped: 'Don't be childish! By the way, Rees had better come prepared — and we shall need the van.'

Dr Rees looked down into the pit. 'What have you got there, for God's sake?'

'That's what I want you to tell me.'

With the aid of plastic slings they hoisted the bundle out of the pit and on to a sheet spread on the ground. It had been tied about in several places with nylon cord which, like the polythene, showed little sign of deterioration.

Wycliffe said: 'Expose just enough for us to be sure of what we've got.'

Wearing surgical gloves and a mask Rees slit a nylon cord at what appeared to be the head end. The polythene had been doubled over at the ends and had to be folded back and spread out.

Rees said: 'How long is it?'

'Seventeen years if I'm right.'

'So we can expect anything. Interesting to see what effect bundling up a corpse in polythene may have — whether mummification or the formation of adipocere takes over.'

He parted the edges of the polythene and spread it abroad revealing a human head. The most striking feature was the rich black hair which seemed to have changed little from its condition in life. The face was repulsive, mainly because the eye sockets appeared to be empty and something had happened to the end of the nose and the lips, exposing the teeth. Even so Wycliffe believed that anyone who had known that face in life would recognize it now.

'Cover her up.'

Rees said: 'Inez.'

'You knew her?'

'As a patient.'

Wycliffe turned to the men with a stretcher. 'Take her away.'

When they were gone Kersey said: 'You want me to bring him in?'

'Maurice?'

'Who else?'

'When we bring him in I want to be in a position to hold him.'

'But we could charge him, for God's sake!'

Wycliffe's manner relaxed. 'We are getting at cross-purposes, Doug. You assume that Maurice killed his brother Matthew because Matthew intended to build houses on this site, a scheme which would have been sure to uncover what we have just found.'

'Yes; evidence of his earlier crime. And you don't agree with that?'

'The point is that unless Sara changes her testimony it would be futile to charge Maurice with the murder of his brother; we could never make it stick.'

'Perhaps not but there's enough circumstantial evidence to charge him with the murder of his brother's wife.'

Wycliffe hesitated. 'Bring him in for questioning in connection with the discovery of Inez Glynn's body. We can probably find a holding charge there if we need it. Agreed?'

Kersey was mollified. 'You're the boss.'

Wycliffe said: 'I'll join you at the nick as soon as I can.'

The white light shone down on the outstretched form which was clothed as a woman: a blue, woollen jumper and a quality tweed skirt. Pinned to the jumper at the breast was a silver brooch in the shape of a butterfly.

Something unspeakable had happened to the legs, and the shoes — walking shoes for the discerning countrywoman — were splayed at an angle unattainable in life. The neck, impossibly shrivelled, was hung about with a double string of white coral beads. Then there was the face, the head, and the hair . . .

Wycliffe said: 'Thank God you no longer use formalin.'

Franks contemplated his subject. 'She'll go into the textbooks. In view of the type of soil, preservation is quite remarkable. I've tidied her up as much as I can; who's going to identify her?'

'The sister-in-law, Sara Glynn — she's on her way with Lucy Lane.'

'Good! Then I'll be able to get on.'

Franks and his assistant covered the body with a sheet and they all moved into the anteroom where an attendant sat at a desk.

Wycliffe said: 'The clothes will go to forensic though I don't imagine they will tell us much. Any ideas yet about how she died?'

'Off the record: she was hit on the head, then throttled. Your killer seems to have a one-track mind.'

They waited, but not for long: the wall clock in the dismal little room showed ten minutes to six when Sara came in followed by Lucy Lane. She was desperately pale but she had herself well under control. She glanced about the room, acknowledged Wycliffe, hesitated, then in a low voice she said: 'I must talk to you. May I come to the Incident Room this evening?'

'It will have to be late, I'm unlikely to be there before nine.'

'I'll come at nine and wait.' She turned to the white-coated Franks; Lucy Lane followed them into the next room. They were gone very briefly. When Sara returned she looked shaken. Lucy piloted her to the desk. The attendant murmured: 'Do you positively identify the body you have just seen as that of your sister-in-law, Inez Glynn?'

'Yes.'

'Then perhaps you will sign here.'

Sara signed.

Wycliffe was back in his little office, initialling reports. The church clock chimed and struck seven. The mist which had persisted through the day was denser than ever and the view from his window was limited to the neighbouring slate roofs gleaming with moisture. Now and then he could hear the bleat of a distant foghorn. There was a tap at the door and Lucy Lane came in.

'Molly Pearce is here, sir.'

'Ask her to come in.'

Molly wore a thin woollen frock, apple green, with a matching cardigan. She looked composed. Wycliffe placed a chair.

'I've asked you to come here because the situation has changed since this morning. You know that, I suppose?'

'Yes.'

'The body found under the burned-out hut was Inez Glynn's and the pathologist says that she was murdered. You are here voluntarily and you are free to go whenever you wish. On the other hand I think you can help us by answering one or two questions.'

'I understand.'

'It was you who wrote those anonymous notes to Matthew Glynn telling him of his wife's infidelity?'

'Yes.' She looked away. 'I could say that I did it out of sympathy for Celia — Maurice's wife. I wish that were true.'

'Your conduct only concerns me in so far as it may help to explain what happened on the day Inez Glynn disappeared. You told me this morning that you saw Inez's car in the pine wood that Sunday. At what time did you see it?'

'I saw it first at about eleven in the morning and again late in the afternoon. I was puzzled to find it there on a day when Celia was supposed to be home.'

'Did you call at Trebyan during that time?'

She flushed. 'Actually I was there twice, once in the morning and again at about five. The second time it was to give her some eggs to take back with her — we had hens in those days. They were just leaving when I arrived — Maurice was taking her back to the hospital.'

She added after a pause: 'There was nothing unusual about me calling to see Celia; we got on well before she was ill and whenever she was home I would look in at least once. It seemed to cheer her up.'

'As far as you could tell, was everything as usual with Maurice and between Maurice and his wife?'

'Yes; actually Celia seemed a lot better than the last time I'd seen her. She even asked about David which was quite new; usually just to mention the boy's name was enough to upset her. That was why he always went to stay with his Aunt Sara when his mother was home.'

It was almost eight when Wycliffe arrived at the police station to join Kersey.

'He's in the interview room; he's been offered a meal but settled for coffee.'

Maurice Glynn was seated at a bare table in a little room with a high window. There was a tape recorder on a shelf near the empty chair on the other side of the table. A uniformed man stood just inside the door and a framed notice on one wall advised the subject of his legal rights. Maurice wore the jeans and denim jacket in which Wycliffe had always seen him. He looked ineffably weary.

Kersey took his seat; Wycliffe remained standing. Kersey switched on the tape recorder and, very brisk, recited the formalities, ending with the caution: 'You do not have to say anything but what you do say may be taken down and used in evidence. This interview begins at 20.08 hours.

'You recall Sunday 20th March 1971?'

'Yes.'

'Your wife was home from hospital for the weekend and your infant son was staying with his aunt in Penzance; is that correct?'

'Yes.'

'You were not expecting a visit from your sister-in-law, Inez?'

'No.'

'Why not?'

'Because I had sent a message to say my wife would be home.'

'Did you know that throughout the day her car was parked in the pine wood adjoining Roskear Farm?'

'I did not know it at the time.'

'When did you discover that it was in fact parked there?'

The first moment of hesitation, then: 'Molly — Miss Pearce — mentioned it to me on the quiet.'

Wycliffe intervened. 'Molly Pearce visited you twice on that day; on which visit did she mention the car?'

'The second; she came just as I was about to drive my wife back to the hospital.'

'What did you do?'

'I did nothing then. I was very puzzled and worried. When I returned from taking my wife back I went to the pine wood to see for myself, and Inez's car was still there. I couldn't understand it.'

Maurice had started calmly; now he was becoming agitated; he began to move uneasily in his chair and he kept clasping and unclasping his hands which were resting on the table in front of him.

'Once more: what did you do?'

'It was getting dark by this time but I decided to look in the hut to see if she had left any message. I just couldn't think of any explanation . . .'

'Go on.'

'I went down to the hut; the door was shut and everything seemed normal. I opened the door . . . And then I saw her. She was lying on the settee; her skirt was pulled up and her knickers were around her ankles; it looked as though she had been raped . . . And then I saw her face . . . There was a wire twisted around her neck . . . She was dead.'

He looked so pale that Wycliffe thought he might faint. 'Would you like a glass of water?'

Maurice shook his head. 'I didn't kill her! I didn't! My God, why should I ever want to? She was keeping me sane; I mean, with my wife in hospital and the child, and the pottery . . .'

He was trembling.

'So what did you do?'

'I don't know what I did. I couldn't think. Then I realized that I must phone the police . . . I went back to the house and I had the telephone in my hand when I suddenly saw the position I was in; a man having an affair with his brother's wife while his own wife was mentally ill . . . The woman strangled on the settee where . . .' His voice failed him and it was a moment or two before he could go on. He made a vague gesture. 'It seemed impossible that I would be believed . . . I mean, how could it have been anybody else?' He looked from Kersey to Wycliffe, a wild look. 'I reached such a point that I half believed I'd done it!'

There was a long pause then he went on more quietly: 'It would have killed my wife . . .' He put his hands over his eyes. 'I've lived for seventeen years with the nightmare which started then . . .'

'What did you do?'

'I realized that I must get rid of the body — hide it. There were loose floorboards in the hut. I got some of the black polythene we use for warming the soil for early crops and I wrapped her in it and tied it around her as tightly as I could, then I removed the boards and lowered her body into the space under the floor.'

'When did you do this?'

'I don't know; I'd lost count of time but it must have been early in the night. I know I had the lamps lit in the hut.'

'Go on.'

'I had to get rid of the car. I thought of driving it into a quarry or over a cliff . . . But I knew it would be found. Then I thought of making it look as though she'd gone away — I decided to drive the car to some place where she might have arranged to meet somebody, and Exeter seemed the sort of place . . . I was desperate . . .'

'Did you take any precautions to avoid leaving traces in the car?'

'I wore gloves.'

'How did you get back?'

'I parked the car in the station car-park and caught the early-morning train. I didn't go all the way to Penzance where they know me at the station, I got off at St Erth and walked, it's only four miles . . .'

Wycliffe said: 'When the body was found it was buried in the earth.'

He nodded. 'Over the next few days — weeks, I don't know! — I dug a trench and laid her in it, then I heaped on soil that I wheeled down in a barrow and I levelled it off. After that I nailed the floorboards down . . .'

He leaned back in his chair and looked at them with a curiously blank stare. 'Nothing happened . . . Nothing happened! Nobody asked me a single question!' His voice was rising hysterically; once more he covered his face with his hands and this time he burst into tears.

Kersey's calm voice dictated to the tape: 'This interview interrupted at 20.31 hours.'

Wycliffe left Kersey at the police station and walked back to the town centre. It was almost dark and the town was quiet. His mind was in turmoil. Almost thirty years ago Alfred Glynn had planned to marry Inez and started a chain of events which twelve years later had led to murder and, seventeen years after that, to a second murder and a suicide. Perhaps the strangest aspect of the affair was that during those twenty-nine years the family had been able to present a public image of normal, perhaps above average respectability.

With something approaching desperation Wycliffe was trying to see the events in perspective, to relate them one to another and to imagine the repressed tensions and the accumulating bitterness which had finally surfaced. But what troubled him most was the thought that he was being pushed beyond his role as an investigating officer into decisions which were either moral or judicial or both.

He turned down into Lady Street and was greeted by a southerly breeze which stirred the moisture-laden air and promised a clearer night. He passed a restaurant where the tables were visible from the street and was reminded that he had not eaten, but he was in no mood for food. At the Incident Room the duty officer said: 'Sara Glynn is here, sir; she says you are expecting her.'

Sara was in the smallest of the three rooms, seated on a hard kitchen chair, her legs tucked in, her handbag and gloves in her lap. She wore a dark green raincoat.

'I'm sorry if I've kept you waiting.'

'It doesn't matter.'

He took her into his office and settled her in a chair by his desk.

'You have something to tell me?'

It was clear that she was having difficulty in choosing her words though he had no doubt that she had rehearsed the occasion. Finally she spoke: 'There is something I want to make clear — something which, if it is not understood between us, could create unnecessary difficulty and suffering.'

He waited.

'I want you to understand that I did see Alfred leaving by the yard door when I returned from my walk last Saturday evening.' She spoke slowly, emphasizing every word. 'He was distraught — so far gone that I doubt if he even saw me though I tried to speak to him.' She paused for a moment or two as though to lend further weight to her words. 'I suspect that you

185

do not believe me — that is up to you, but it is the evidence I shall give wherever and whenever I am required to testify.'

'In other words you stand by your statement.'

'I do, and I shall.'

'Perhaps you had some additional reason for coming here?' He was polite but distant.

'There was something else. I would like you to know that my brother, Matthew, was not a man to turn the other cheek. It was a very great surprise to me that he seemed to accept his wife's infidelity; a very great surprise.'

It was as though she was teaching a lesson to a child, speaking slowly and distinctly, and offering one simple idea at a time.

'When did you last speak to your brother Maurice?'

'I was with him this afternoon when the police came to take him away.'

The pride in her voice was unmistakable.

She got up from her chair, gathering together her handbag and gloves. 'That is what I came to say, Mr Wycliffe.'

Wycliffe saw her off the premises and watched her as she walked up the steep alley and disappeared into the darkness. A remarkable woman.

Chapter Twelve

Friday morning

Wycliffe had spent an hour at divisional headquarters for a media briefing and he was depressed; the reporters believed that he was holding out on them whereas he only wished that he had something to hold out about.

'The body has been identified as that of Mrs Inez Glynn who went missing from her home on March 20th 1971.'

'And she'd been there ever since?'

'That seems likely.'

'How was she killed?'

'The indications are that she had been strangled.'

'So you are now looking for the killer of Matthew Glynn and his wife?'

'We are investigating two homicides.'

'Two killers or one?'

'That remains to be seen.'

'Maurice Glynn is still in custody?'

'Mr Glynn is providing us with information which may be useful to our inquiry.'

'Are you expecting to bring charges in the near future?'

'We haven't made an arrest yet.'

That was the substance but the questions and the answers were repeated in various disguises *ad nauseam*.

A tap at the door and Kersey came in carrying a tape recorder and looking dynamic. 'Good morning, sir! Maurice's statement — second instalment.' He put the little machine on the table and ran the tape to the position of his choice. 'Listen to this!'

Kersey's voice on the tape: 'Who did you think had killed her? You must have thought about it.'

A longish pause, then Maurice, speaking in a low voice: 'Oh, yes, I thought about it . . . It seems I thought about nothing else for God knows how long . . . I couldn't sleep, I was on tranquillizers . . .'

'You haven't answered the question.'

'No; I haven't answered the question. Sometimes I thought it must have been Matthew; sometimes Alfred . . . sometimes that it could only have been some pervert, a stranger . . . Then I remembered that Inez shouldn't have been there if our arrangements had worked . . .'

'And?'

'I wondered if she'd arranged to meet somebody else there; it wouldn't have surprised me. More than half her kicks came from taking pointless risks.'

'But she left her car in the wood — the chances were you would find out.'

The tape ran in silence for several seconds then Maurice said in a voice that sounded desperately weary: 'You think that would have bothered her?'

'So in seventeen years you reached no conclusion?'

'Does that surprise you?' He sounded frustrated; perhaps by his questioner's lack of understanding. 'I didn't even want to. Mainly I wanted to forget, and in recent years I've come damn near succeeding.'

The telephone cut across the growing tension. Wycliffe picked up the instrument, snapped: 'No calls!' and slammed it down.

Kersey's tape voice was saying: 'What started it up again?'

'Isn't it obvious? Matthew's houses started it up again.' There was a tremor in the voice on the tape. 'To me it seemed like Nemesis . . .'

Another long pause which Kersey did not interrupt, then Maurice went on: 'It was only when I went to see Matthew, when we had that row, that I realized it was all a trap.'

'A trap?'

'Don't you see? He knew what he was doing to me and after

mother's death there was nothing to stop him . . . He must have gloated over it for years . . . He didn't have to build the houses, only threaten . . . If I was scared of being accused when it happened, where would I be now?' The sentence ended in a dry sob.

'Did you or he refer to his wife's death?'

'Not a word! I didn't dare and he didn't need to. I can't describe his attitude — challenging and at the same time, contemptuous. My God, I understood!'

The tape was silent for so long that Wycliffe thought it was over then Kersey's voice came, softly insinuating: 'So you killed him.'

There was a quick intake of breath then, speaking through his teeth, with hysterical emphasis: 'I did not kill him! He deserved to die, but I did not kill him!'

Kersey switched off the tape and they were silent for a while; then Wycliffe said: 'And Sara will back him up to the last ditch.' He lifted his arms and let them fall to his sides in a gesture of helplessness. 'Now we are in the trap.'

Wycliffe spent the next half-hour on the telephone to Bertram Oldroyd, the Chief Constable.

Oldroyd summed up: 'So in your view, Charles, there are no grounds for believing that Maurice Glynn was responsible for the woman's death?'

'None. Apart from the absence of any apparent motive he doesn't seem to have had the opportunity either; it wasn't until late evening on that Sunday that he knew she was there. Fox is carrying on at the scene but I don't expect much; I haven't had Franks's final report but he isn't hopeful of being able to tell us anything beyond the cause of death.

'The long and short of it is that even if we believed him guilty as hell we wouldn't stand a chance of a conviction.'

'And Matthew? Have you changed your mind about accepting the sister's evidence?'

Wycliffe was dour: 'Whether or not I've changed my mind about believing it I don't have any choice about accepting it.'

'So we are left with framing charges against Maurice:

189

concealing a death and the unlawful disposal of a corpse. From then on it's up to the coroner. If his verdict names names that's up to him. You agree?'

'I have to.'

'Good! I want you back, Charles. We shan't come out of this with much kudos but at least the lawyers won't make their fortunes.'

The professional view.

Wycliffe believed the criminal law should aim at damage limitation rather than at some abstraction called justice. With a profound sense of irony he now asked himself whether Sara had carried his argument to its logical conclusion. God knows enough people were going to suffer, in particular the innocent, and who would benefit from Maurice Glynn spending fifteen years in a squalid jail?

But such relativism troubled his conscience which was still the property of his Methodist upbringing. He was also troubled professionally, because he had failed.

He sent for Lucy Lane and made her listen to the tapes of Maurice's interviews, then he told her of his conversation with the chief constable.

'This is a damnable case, Lucy. I want you to talk to the family; explain the meaning of the charges against Maurice; the significance of the adjourned inquests on Matthew and on Alfred; and of the inquest which will now be held on Inez. They must understand too that although no charges can be brought against the dead there is nothing to stop the coroner naming them in his verdicts. I doubt if he will but they should be prepared. You understand?'

Lucy Lane knew her Wycliffe. 'I think so, sir. You want me to put them out of their misery as far as the facts allow without fouling any of the legal trip-wires.'

Wycliffe's smile was thin. 'You should have been a lawyer, Lucy.'

Wycliffe drove himself to Trebyan that afternoon; he went alone because it was a private thing. For the first time that day

190

he noticed that the sun was shining. The white gate was open and he swept up the drive past the tethered goats and into the same stillness he had known on his first visit, but this time he could not bring himself to shatter it by ringing the brass bell. The front door was open to the stone-flagged hall but he did not go in.

He found them in the workshop unloading the kiln, and stood in the doorway as they dismantled the edifice of biscuit-fired pots and pitchers, bowls and beakers, transferring them to wooden shelves. When they saw him they stopped as though transfixed.

'I want to talk to you.'

They seemed to move with unnatural slowness. It was Christine who said: 'Do you want to go into the house?'

'That would be best.'

In the former dining-room it was Christine who offered Wycliffe a chair, then she and the boy sat side by side on the sofa. David spoke first but Wycliffe felt sure he had been prompted.

'My father didn't set fire to the hut, I did.'

Wycliffe was dismissive. 'An idiotic thing to do. You thought you were protecting your father against something with no idea what. In fact we found what we expected to find so what you did is no concern of mine; it's between you and your father.'

Christine reached out her hand and placed it on the boy's knee. David's face had been pale, now it was flushed.

Wycliffe went on: 'Miss Lane must have explained the situation to you. All I can say is that your father is being released on police bail this afternoon.'

They sat motionless, afraid to ask questions; afraid almost to breathe. In the end it was Christine who spoke. 'What sort of sentence is Uncle Maurice likely to get?'

'I can't predict what the court will do but whatever the sentence a large part of it — perhaps all of it — is likely to be suspended.'

Christine went on in a voice that was barely recognizable: 'And about my father?'

'The police accept your aunt's statement. No action can be taken against a dead man so, after the inquest, the case will be closed.'

Christine's fingers tightened over the boy's knee and he placed his hand over hers.

Wycliffe said: 'This is a terrible time for you both; you must make up your minds to see it through.'

Christine nodded. 'We shall go on as before — as nearly as they will let us.'

Gina, Gerald and Barry were in the kitchen, seated around the table, picking away at cold food.

Gina said: 'God, I wish tomorrow was over!'

Her husband tried to be consoling. 'It will be a purely family thing; nobody has been asked to come; we haven't even made an announcement.'

Gerald spoke with his mouth full. 'The press will be there; you won't keep them out.'

Gina stood up. 'I'll make the coffee.'

Sara was in her bedroom, standing in front of her wardrobe mirror. She wore a charcoal-grey coat with a fur collar which she had discarded four or five years ago. She turned this way and that in a critical inspection of her image in the glass.

'It still fits . . . I suppose it will do.'